My Lives with

Lucifer, Satan,

Hitler and Jesus

A novel

# My Lives with Lucifer, Satan, Hitler and Jesus

Kim Michaels
More to Life

My Lives with Lucifer, Satan, Hitler and Jesus

MORE TO LIFE PUBLISHING

www.morepublish.com

For foreign and translation rights,

contact: info@ morepublish.com

ISBN: 978-87-93297-44-9

# Content

Wise is the person who, before rejecting a new idea,
considers whether it might explain something
that existing ideas cannot explain.

Every human being is having an entirely subjective
experience. All struggles between people
is the result of some people presenting their subjective
experiences as universal and
seeking to force them upon others.


The struggle between individuals and groups of people
is caused by the desire to make a subjective experience
universal through the use of deceit or force.

# PART 1:
# MY EXISTENCE
# BEFORE COMING
# TO EARTH

# 1

People can be divided into two categories: those who have considered the question "Why am I here?" and those who have not considered this and related questions. Because the physical matter that makes up earth is so much denser than on the vast majority of inhabited planets, it is easy to ignore certain questions here. However, due to the density of matter, one cannot ignore these questions forever. Dense matter defines a limited lifespan for the bodies we are using as vehicles for interacting with this planetary energy matrix. So there will come a point where one has a VRA (Very Rude Awakening) and realizes that one's current body will die within the foreseeable future. This does make certain questions spring to the forefront of one's mind. One can postpone these questions for a while, but they are *inescapable* questions—*eventually*.

Among those who have considered these questions, one can again create a division between those who *have not* found answers and those who *have*. I have found answers to the question of why I – personally – am on this planet, which belongs to the lowest category of inhabited planets in our universe. My purpose for writing is to give the full explanation of why I am here. And by describing key aspects of my long journey on this and a few other planets, I will indeed give a *full* and *complete* explanation.

I want to make it clear that I will give an explanation of why *I* – personally – am here. It will be an *individual, subjective* explanation. I am saying this because the central problem on dense-matter planets like earth is that most inhabitants of such planets (of which there is a relatively small number left in our universe) have not understood the central dynamic on these planets.

The basic dynamic on dense-matter planets is that every single inhabitant is having an individual – a *subjective* – experience. On a dense-matter planet, it is categorically impossible to have anything but a subjective experience. In fact, the very purpose of a dense-matter planet is to give people an entirely subjective experience. We will have this type of experience until we have had enough of it and can rise to a less dense planet to continue our individual evolution. At the same time, due to the density of matter, most inhabitants of dense-matter planets do not understand why they are on such a planet. We are here because we have not yet overcome the desire for wanting to make our *subjective* experience *universal*.

Look at planet earth. You see innumerable conflicts and problems. On a superficial level, they may seem to have many different causes. When you look behind surface appearances, you see that the struggle between individuals and groups of people has only one cause. Most people have some need to make their *subjective* experience *universal*. We can't just experience and let experience. We have to try to get other people to accept *our* subjective experience and validate it as being universal and superior to *their own* subjective experience.

\*\*\*

For a relatively small minority of people this need has reached epic proportions and become obsessive-compulsive. They are not having a need; the need is having them. These people have attempted to invent any number of explanations that give some kind of infallible and irrefutable authority to their subjective experience. They desperately want to provide a universal and authoritative explanation for why their subjective experience is not subjective but universal, why it is not relative but absolute, why it is not temporary but has some long-lasting, even eternal, significance.

As the primary tool for doing this, they invent various belief systems and claim that the ideas that make up the system have some unquestionable authority. Religions claim their ideas are given by some infallible god, a god who is always somewhere else so that you cannot verify their claims but must accept it because they say so. Political ideologies claim a political or historical necessity, meaning that one day society *will* conform to their claim although there is no proof. And the religious-political system called scientific materialism claims that science has validated its ideas or that they are based on laws of nature.

Whatever the system, the basic dynamic is the same. Some people are using the system in order to say to the rest of the population that they should be having a certain kind of life experience on this planet. There is only one struggle on earth, and it is caused by several minority groups wanting to control the life experience of the majority. Power struggles are never about physical resources, land or power. They are always about controlling what goes on inside people's minds. The physical conditions are only a means to the end of controlling your life experience. This is done because those who control your life experience can control what you do with your life energy. And energy is far more important than money or power because energy *is* money, power—and everything else.

On a dense-matter planet there is absolutely no universal experience and there is not meant to be. You are meant to have a subjective experience until you realize that you are having a subjective experience and consciously decide that you want to step up to the next level of experiences possible in our very vast and complex world (I am not saying "universe" because our total world is far more than the material universe). It is precisely the density of matter that allows you to have a subjective experience because on a dense-matter planet, you cannot directly perceive that there is something beyond matter. You can believe that your subjective experience is universal because you cannot directly perceive how subjective is your sense of universality.

The essential problem on earth is that certain people have managed to export their subjective experiences to others by creating a system that – while still springing entirely from a subjective experience – has been given an appearance of universality by a large number of people accepting it and allowing it to shape their subjective experiences. The originators of such systems all believe that if only they can get *all* people on earth to accept their system, then it will indeed gain some universal validity and authority. They believe this will give them what they ultimately crave, namely total control over the universe—as they see it.

These people were not among the original inhabitants of this planet, but they have been here for a long time (a lot longer than I have). In every epoch they have formed various power elite groups, which is why I call them PCBs (Power and Control Brokers). By the way, I am not advancing a conspiracy theory because the PCBs are inherently divided and are often opposing each other in two or more groups seeking ultimate control. Thus, they cannot truly conspire. Most of the conflicts seen throughout history (which goes back far further than currently accepted) have their causes in this rivalry. One group of PCBs form an established elite and they are being fought by another group that forms an aspiring elite. Members of the established elite have turned the population into their slaves. Members of the aspiring elite claim they will free the population from this slavery, but their real aim is to make the population the slaves of themselves.

As I will describe, I have been around such people for a very long time, and by observing them create some of the most bizarre events of history, I have realized that their quest is futile from the outset. I have also seen that once you create or accept one of these universalist systems, you become the victim of the most common syndrome on this planet, namely CIA (Crippled Imaginary Ability).

This inevitably puts you into a constant struggle with a self-defined enemy, causing you to look at other human beings through a particular filter that gives you USA (Unsubstantiated Social Anxiety). You can no longer accept that you are on a planet where free will is the basic law. You cannot allow other people to express their free will, you simply have to try to force the free will of others. For some people this leads them into the next level of paranoia where they want to actively suppress the freedom of others, therefore suffering from USSR (Uncontrollable Social Suppression Response). This happens because all PCBs suffer from PRC (Pathologically Restricted Cognition) and therefore cannot see any connection between themselves and other people. They have fallen victim to one of the most common illusions on this planet, namely that you can harm other people without harming yourself.

\*\*\*

The reason I am starting out by making such a big deal of these PCBs is twofold. First of all, my personal story (on earth) is very closely linked to these beings. It is not too much to say that they are a big part of why I am on this planet and why I am *still* on this planet, as is the case for most of us. Neither is it too much to say that it was only in figuring out how to personally deal with PCBs that I realized why I am here and what it will take for me to get out of here. So they are an inescapable part of my personal story.

Another reason for talking about PCBs from the outset is that they have severely limited my ability to tell my story. In order to tell the story of how I came to be on this planet, and how I eventually gained awareness of who I am and why I am here, I have to give you many concepts that will be completely alien to – and most likely in opposition to – your current view of life. This view is very heavily influenced by the PCBs and the WCs (Weapons of Control) they have created.

In telling my personal story, I will have to go very far beyond what you have been brought up to believe about life. I will have to violate your PIN (Programmed Illusion of Normality) so severely that most people are likely to reject what I am saying. The brutal fact is that 99 percent of human beings have been so brainwashed by the PCBs that they will reject the realizations that could set them free from the WCs. Your brainwashing may be so complete that you will protest and claim that you have not been brainwashed but that your system tells you the truth about life. You will resist having a VRA by attacking what could liberate you.

Again, because I have been on this planet for such a long time and seen the outplaying of the PCBs through several historical epochs, I have developed complete respect for free will. If you want to believe that you have not been brainwashed, I am happy to leave you in that state of mind (anyway, I can say nothing that you will accept). I know that you have not yet had enough of this experience and that the inescapable wheel of time will eventually bring you to a point where you will want something higher. This may happen long after I am gone from this planet, and thus it is not my responsibility. In fact, I now know that I will not get off this planet until I fully accept that other beings are not my responsibility. I am not here to change others (especially not the PCBs) but only and exclusively to change myself. Nor am I here to change anything on this planet.

I know some will refer to a common definition of brainwashing and say that according to current psychological doctrine, brainwashing is only possible when people are kept in an isolated location and have no contact with anyone outside their prison. Therefore, they have no objective frame of reference to evaluate what they are being told by their programmers. A common example is American soldiers brainwashed during the Korean war. So my questions are: "When was the last time you took a trip away from this planet? When was the last time you left your physical body? Have you had much contact with supra-terrestrial beings lately?"

Yes, you are indeed confined to a very limited environment, and you have no frame of reference from outside this planetary unit. So how can you avoid accepting some of the heavy programming from a small elite of PCBs who are desperate to make you accept that instead of having *your* subjective experience, you should be having the subjective experience they have designed for you and worship them as the universal and unquestionable authorities of earth?

I know Abraham Lincoln is famous for saying that while you can fool some of the people all of the time and all of the people some of the time, you can't fool all of the people all of the time. In a way he was right, but I think he had little conception of the real time scale. I can personally witness that it is indeed possible to fool all of the people for at least a couple of million years, and I doubt that is what good old Abe had in mind.

\*\*\*

So let me just end what turned out to be a strange introductory chapter by saying that I am quite aware what the PCBs will say to my writing. First of all, they will try to ignore it and hope that most people will do the same. Here, they will be helped by the PIN they have created because what I will say will go far beyond the doctrines of their WCs.

If enough people refuse to be limited by the PIN and begin to pay attention to what I am writing, the PCBs will say: "By what authority do you speak?" They will want me to prove my authority and prove the validity of the ideas I am presenting. Do you see the irony here?

I am going to tell you a story that goes very far beyond the PIN created by the PCBs through their WCs. Yet they will be saying that unless I can prove my authority and my ideas *according to the standard defined by their PIN*, I have no authority and validity. This is the very central dynamic that prevents people on dense-matter planets from waking up and freeing themselves from the PCBs. It is what often creates a self-reinforcing downward spiral on such planets that leads to very destructive physical conditions. This has happened several times in now forgotten epochs of this planet. It has erased several civilizations that had achieved a far higher state of technological sophistication than ours (without the raised consciousness that allows people to use technology in a way that does not destroy themselves—in which they are much like *our* civilization).

My answer is that I claim no authority and I will present no proof or even argument for my ideas. I have come to know the ideas I am going to tell you through a very long process of seeking answers from a higher source than the PCBs. For those who have not gone through their own personal process of discovery, my ideas will seem like fantasy, heresy or nonsense (or all of the above) and that is exactly how it should be. People will not free themselves from the PCBs until they are ready to question the PIN, and for those who haven't started this process, my ideas will seem too far-fetched. I have learned through hard lessons that there is nothing I can do about it—and I have accepted that I don't have to. For those who have gone through the same process I have gone through, my ideas will be validated because they resonate with what they already know from within. Nothing, of course, scares the PCBs more than people who realize they can know from within and do not need an external authority. The other thing the PCBs will say is that I am doing exactly what I accuse them of doing, namely taking my subjective experience and seeking to make it universal by getting you to accept it. This is precisely the kind of "sophisticated" counterargument they use to neutralize those who have begun to question their WCs. It springs from their DDT (Deliberately Deceptive Thinking), and they have a very long experience in using it against others and each other. It is true that on their fruits you can know them, but this includes more than actions and you can quickly learn to identify them by their thinking.

In reality, I am not writing this because I want you to accept it. I am writing it because doing so is part of my own personal process of qualifying for my final exit from this planet. I need to write this in order to clarify things in my own mind and in order to see if I'm still attached to changing anybody or anything on this planetary unit. (I was tempted to say "screwed-up planet," but that would have been a value judgment, which is one of the tell-tale signs of an attachment.)

Frankly, my dear, I don't give a damn how you or the PCBs react to this book. I realize that writing it is an entirely subjective process. You reading it will also be an entirely subjective process. However, here is the reality of the situation.

The PCBs believe that if they can make their subjective experience universal (by making all people on this planet accept it), then the authorities in the realm above earth must accept the PCBs and let them in. In reality, the only way to get out of this planet is to raise your subjective experience to the point where you are no longer identified with it. You see that it is subjective and instead of trying to make it universal, you accept that it will always be and can *only* be subjective. You then realize that you are more than the subjective experience.

It took me almost two million (I said 2,000,000) years on this planet to come to this realization. You have to follow your own process of reaching this realization. However, I had teachers along the way who helped me. We do need to have a certain amount of experiences on this planet before we are ready to see the dynamic I have described. But we do not need to have every possible experience because we can indeed learn from the experiences of others. As I have been helped by others, perhaps my story can help you; not by you blindly believing it but by it triggering an inner experience in you.

*** 

In its essence, life on this planet is a progressive process where we start at a lower level of self-awareness and gradually (sometimes agonizingly gradually) rise to a higher level of self-awareness. Each step on this journey is triggered by an experience of awakening from a lower sense of identity. We realize: "Oh, I am not this limited self; I am more than this self." This is a VHA (Very Happy Awakening).

This experience can be triggered in two ways. One is that we have an actual physical experience that then triggers the shift in the mind. However, the only way any of us can make it within a reasonable time-frame (and two million years is actually quite reasonable, given the complexity of the task) is that we also have shifting experiences that are triggered without the physical experience (which always takes time, sometimes an incredible amount of time and repetition). In other words, we have an experience that is produced in the mind itself (without the need for a physical experience) because of inspiration from outside the mind. (This is what really scares the PCBs.)

One way to have this inner shifting experience (an experience vehemently denied by the PCBs and all of their WCs) is to be inspired by the experiences and insights of others. So perhaps my writing this story can trigger a shift in others. And perhaps me saying this demonstrates that I have not yet fully overcome my desire to change something on this planet, the very desire that brought me here in the first place.

So I am not (consciously) writing this in the hope of convincing anyone of anything. I am writing because I have realized and accepted that I have a right to be in embodiment on earth. I have a right to be who I am, meaning I have a right to go beyond the standard for what it means to be a human being according to the PCBs and their PIN. I have a right to express myself. I have a right to tell my story.

# 2

I know well that some people will interpret the ideas in this book to have some universal validity, perhaps even authority. I am not saying they do and I am not saying they don't. I am only saying that any validity or authority *you* give to this book is entirely a product of your personal experience. I refuse to try to export *my* personal experience to *you*.

That being said, a personal experience can be subjective or it can be individual. We all have an outer mind or personality and when we look at the world through it, our experience is entirely subjective. Yet we also have the ability to go beyond the outer personality and have an experience that is not subjective but still individual. This requires you to accept only what is validated from deep within yourself, by making contact with the part of you that came from beyond the level of subjective experience and can return there when you resolve the enigma that brought you here. We might compare this to you standing in a certain location and looking out over the landscape. When you are wearing colored glasses and don't know it, your experience is subjective. When you take off the glasses, your experience is no longer subjective but still individual because you are looking at the landscape from a localized vantage point. It can be no other way as long as you are in a physical body on a dense-matter planet.

Now, you see, in the preceding paragraph I have already hit against and violated the "thought ceilings" defined by several of the popular WCs on this planet. What do the most popular WCs say about you? They say you are an inherently limited being, that you are a product of factors entirely beyond your control, either a remote god in heaven, random changes or invariable laws of nature. The fact is that none of us are inherently limited beings. We do start out with a very localized sense of self, but we have the potential to expand our sense of self and there is no inherent limitation to how far we can take this process. No force outside ourselves can actually limit the expansion of self-awareness.

On planet earth, the PCBs have managed to make most people believe that there are such limits. They have used either a religion, a political ideology or materialism to define you as a limited being. They do this, as I said, because of their obsessive-compulsive need to control us, which is a product of their USA, including the completely flawed belief that they can make their subjective experience have universal validity and authority.

So we have a peculiar situation on earth. In reality, no force outside yourself can limit the expansion of your self-awareness. Yet most people believe their self-expansion is limited, and this actually has some temporary "reality." The PCBs are an external force and they have managed to make most of us believe that our self-expression is limited. And as long as you *believe* you are limited, you *are* indeed limited. Or rather, you will behave as if you are limited, and this means you can be controlled.

Do you see the central irony of earth and other dense-matter planets? Because matter is so dense, it seems that we have a very limited ability to change matter. This reinforces the illusion that we are powerless beings. As long as we believe we are limited, we will more readily submit to the control of the PCBs. Meaning, that as long as we believe we should allow them to control us, they *are* indeed controlling us. Yet their control is based on upholding the illusion from which it springs. And that is why they will take all possible measures to silence those who challenge the central illusion that allows them to continue to believe they are in control. As I will explain later, I have seen how far they will go. The PCBs do indeed have an obsessive-compulsive need to feel they are in control, and this need is completely controlling them. You cannot seek to control others without being controlled yourself.

Anyway, I am digressing. What I really wanted to do was to start this chapter with the words: "A long, long time ago in a realm far beyond the material universe."

Again, we hit the thought ceiling defined by the WCs. Some of them say there is nothing beyond the material universe. Others say there is some remote heaven world, but it is inhabited only by perfect beings and since you are inherently flawed, you did not come from there.

These are all lies aimed at controlling you. The PCBs believe that if you awaken to who you really are, this is the ultimate threat to their reign on earth (and for once, they are right). So they have done everything they can think of with their CIA to make you believe some fiction about who you are, where you came from and what you can do on this planet. Now, let me tell you what I have discovered about who we really are.

***

You are not a product of the material universe. You did not origi-nate in this universe. You came from a different realm and you originally entered this universe in a state of self-awareness that was very different from what you have now. Over a very long period of time, which includes taking on many different physical bodies on this and other planets, you have built your current sense of identity, your current sense of self. You have built this self in reaction to the, most likely very violent and hurtful, experiences you have had in this universe and specifically on this planet. You will get out of this limited realm only by allowing this reactionary self to die gradually while returning to your original sense of identity, your original innocence. Here, of course, is another problem because what I have just said goes against all of the WCs on earth.

The earth is a dense-matter planet. Out of the literally billions of plan-ets in the material universe with self-aware life-forms, there is only a very small fraction that have matter as dense as earth. Most of the self-aware beings who are part of our universe have now evolved to such a level of self-awareness that they live on planets where matter is far less dense and therefore more pliable, more responsive to the mind.

The function of a dense-matter planet is to serve as a sort of last-ditch attempt to help the beings who have not yet been willing to accept the fundamental realization of the material universe, namely that matter is sub-servient to mind. Yes, contrary to what all WCs on earth tell you, matter takes on form because it is acted upon by self-aware minds (included, but not limited to, ours). When you accept this, you can begin taking embodi-ment on planets with a lower density, and this makes it easier for you to develop your ability to consciously shape matter by using all four levels of your mind. Of course, most of us started our journey on planets with a lower density of matter.

Over the cause of the incredibly long time span that our material uni-verse has existed and has been the home of self-aware beings, the vast majority of its inhabitants have accepted this fact. A very small percentage have not been willing to do this, and there can be only one reason. These beings are not willing to accept that they themselves have created the phys-ical circumstances they encounter in the material universe. They have not been willing to take responsibility for themselves and their situation. In order to give them another opportunity, they have then been moved to dense-matter planets.

I know this can seem contradictory. I mean, on a planet with the mat-ter density of earth it is easy to believe that our minds do not have power to shape matter and that our circumstances are created by forces entirely beyond our control, be it some god in the sky, some other group of people or some laws of nature. So it would seem that the density of matter only serves to reinforce the illusion that we have not created our circumstances.

I understand this can seem like a paradox. Why place beings who suffer from an illusion in an environment that reinforces the illusion? The reason is simple. The beings who have come to earth have not been willing to respond to the inspiration from others. They need to have a physical experience before their minds can shift, and it needs to be an extreme experience. This is what they get on earth. Because matter is so dense, it is possible to create some very severe physical circumstances that create incredible amounts of suffering. You just need to cast a quick glance at the history books to see what I mean. Or perhaps you have actually experienced what I mean. The rather disturbing fact is that the vast majority of the people currently embodying on earth are not open to learning the easy way, so they have (unconsciously, of course) enrolled themselves in the SHK (School of Hard Knocks).

Now, I know this sounds paradoxical, but when it comes to the mindset that dominates earth, paradox is built into its very foundation (as I will explain later). So the reality is that when beings will not listen to others, they can change only by seeing the outpicturing of their mindset to such an extreme degree that they finally have a VRA and begin to question the basic mindset of their planetary unit. In past ages, the willingness to question the PIN was limited, but in this age, millions and millions of people have reached the level of their personal development where they are ready to question what kind of planet they are on and why there is so much suffering. They are ready to have a series of VHAs.

Okay, I got lost in giving you some basic explanation so let me get back to what I was trying to say. Earth has a certain number of beings who were created to start their evolution from this planet when it was in a purer state. However, it also has a very large number of beings (now the majority) who came from other planets. Some are here because they failed the initiation of accepting responsibility for the creative abilities of their minds. Others came here on various types of self-defined rescue missions to try to affect a positive change on this dense-matter and low-consciousness planet (they failed another initiation, which I will describe later). The PCBs are here for another reason that I will also explain later.

My point was that because we have come from so many different backgrounds, it is very difficult to say anything general about what brought us here and what previous experiences we have had. This is one reason it is so difficult for people to communicate and feel basic kinship. Another is the engineered conflicts created by the PCBs. So again, I can only tell the story of my personal background, and it will say *something* but probably not *everything* about yours.

***

Okay, so you have probably noticed I have a tendency to digress, but that's partly because there is such a huge gap between the PIN on this planet and the basic ingredients of the story I will tell you. I am constantly finding that in trying to explain what I consider self-evident, I have to give more information for those who have not walked the same path I have walked. I started to say that I had my origin: "A long, long time ago in a realm far beyond the material universe." Even this, of course, goes beyond the PIN, so let me give you a bit more background.

Science on this planet has finally reached a level that most other planets reached at least a half billion years ago (and which, in fairness, was reached on earth in several past epochs that are now largely forgotten and denied by all WCs). That level is where science has conclusively proven that we live in a universe where everything is made from energy. This is significant because matter, as people on earth conceive of it, does not respond to mind, as people conceive of mind. Once people realize that matter is made from energy, they see that thoughts are also a form of energy. Because all energy is made up of waves and because waves can interact, thought energy can indeed influence other forms of energy. Once you realize that what your senses tell you is solid matter is truly made from vibrating energy, you can fairly quickly make a shift and accept that mind can influence matter—or at least the basic energy out of which matter is made.

I say you can "fairly quickly" make this shift because Einstein proved that matter is energy in 1905 and the vast majority of people, including scientists and philosophers, have not even begun to accept what this truly means. This is partly because the PCBs have used their WCs to deny the philosophical implications, but also because so many people still don't want to take responsibility for the creative powers of their minds. This is now changing rapidly with more and more people opening their minds to a new way of looking at reality.

The PCBs deny the power of our minds today because it is by getting us to deny the power of our minds that they managed to get control over us in the first place. Only by keeping us in this state of denial, can they maintain their control over us. Only by maintaining control over us, can they continue to exist, as I will explain later.

Because everything is energy and because energy is vibration, the material universe is not a closed, isolated unit. We know there are sounds our ears cannot hear and forms of light our eyes cannot see. The reason is that our total world is made of vibrations. Earth is made of energy that vibrates at some of the slowest frequencies in our world. That is why it is so hard (but by no means impossible) for us to have a direct experience of a realm beyond what our senses can detect. It is also why it is so easy to deny that such realms exist, and the PCBs have taken full advantage of this. Basically all WCs on the planet are aimed at preventing you from having a direct experience of a realm beyond the material universe (this includes most religions).

The material universe at large vibrates at higher frequencies than earth, and many inhabited planets are at much higher frequencies. Beyond the material realm are other levels of vibration. We can roughly compare this to the tonal scale where sounds can be divided into octaves. At the lowest frequencies we find the lowest sounds and in higher octaves we find higher sounds.

As we go beyond the material octave, we enter a level of vibration I will call the emotional octave. It is here our emotions are shaped. Beyond this is the mental octave where our thoughts originate. At the highest level of our world is the identity realm, which is where our deepest sense of identity is defined. Beyond the identity realm we find realms that are in a higher category because they have achieved permanence. The four octaves of our world are still temporary, meaning they have not (by the inhabitants, meaning us) been raised to a high enough level to attain permanence. When a world is created, it is given a certain base level of vibration, and it is up to the self-aware beings who inhabit the world to raise that vibration to the point where their world attains permanence. There are several levels of the higher realm that have achieved permanence, but I will not go into that for now.

# 3

I personally had my origin in the lowest level of the higher realm, the level or sphere that became permanent just before our world was created as the next link in the creative chain. I had two "parents" who created the core of my being, namely what we can call my higher self, spiritual self or (as a more technical term) I AM Presence. It is difficult to describe this with the limited words currently used on this planet (due to the manipulation of the word by the PCBs), but as a crude explanation, we can say that my I AM Presence is a unique, individual being that contains the original blueprint for my individuality. You, of course, have your own I AM Presence.

My I AM Presence can be described as a self-aware being, but it is created with a localized sense of self-awareness. It is, as everything in the created world, created in order to grow. How does my I AM Presence expand its self-awareness? By sending me into the non-permanent world. I am an extension of my I AM Presence and I am, so to speak, its ticket to immortality. It is through my experiences and exploits in the non-permanent world that my I AM Presence expands its self-awareness. As I pass the final exam of the non-permanent schoolroom, my I AM Presence attains immortality, as do I by reuniting with my Presence.

You might ask why the I AM Presence doesn't descend by itself. One reason is that the Presence stays in the higher realm where it cannot be damaged or destroyed by anything that happens in the non-permanent world. Another reason is that the I AM Presence is so complex that it could not fit into the bodies possible in a non-permanent world. A third reason is that in order for my Presence and I to have a complete experience of my sojourn in the non-permanent world, the Presence needs to stay in the higher realm in order to experience my experiences from that viewpoint. My Presence experiences everything I experience, but it does so from the outside, without being directly affected by it. This allows the Presence to use any experience, regardless of how I experience it, to form a positive life lesson. The astonishing importance of this will become clear later.

The inhabitants of a non-permanent world have not yet reached a level of consciousness where they have completely transcended subjectivity. By this I mean that most of them still see themselves as separate beings and therefore do not experience that all life is one. On a dense-matter planet like earth, this means people do not see that what they do to others, they are also doing to themselves. They think they can get away with doing things to others without affecting themselves. You can clearly see that this illusion is still very persuasive on earth (and only partly due to the density of matter, more due to the density of consciousness).

The short way to characterize a dense-matter planet is to refer to the old bumpersticker: "Shit happens." Which could be rewritten as: "The PCBs make shit happen." If the I AM Presence descended into a non-permanent world, it might be damaged or even destroyed. Given the effort required to create an I AM Presence, with an individuality that is different from the trillions and trillions of other individual beings in our total world, no sane being would risk this. So my I AM Presence sent *me* into the non-permanent world.

So who am I, then? I am nothing—I am no thing. You cannot define me with the limited words currently in use on earth. We can approach an explanation by saying that I am pure awareness. My I AM Presence has individuality, I do not. I have no personality, no individuality. I have self-awareness but not self-awareness as being a specific self. I know this sounds paradoxical, and it has taken me several millions years of earth time to resolve this enigma. I know it also sounds very disturbing because we are so desperate to retain our individuality. The brutal fact is that in order to discover our *immortal* identity, we have to be willing to let our *mortal* individuality die daily.

But what individuality is that? I just said that the individuality of the I AM Presence cannot die. Well, the self that I am can descend into the non-permanent world, but it too cannot die. I am no thing because I am not defined by anything in this world, which means I cannot be changed or destroyed by anything in this world. It also means that I cannot do anything in this world. I can witness what is happening in this world, but I cannot experience it from the inside and I cannot act.

In order to be able to experience this world from the inside and in order to be able to do anything here, I had to create a vehicle. This vehicle had to be made up of the four levels of energy frequencies that make up this world. Before I descended into this world (a very long time ago with earth time), I had to create a vehicle consisting of an identity "body" (defining how I saw myself in relation to this world), a mental body (defining my thoughts in relation to how this world works and what I can do here), an emotional body (defining my emotions relating to this world) and a physical body that allows me to do something in the physical octave on an inhabited planet. It was in this soul vehicle that my worldly individuality was defined. The original identity has, naturally, been changed and shaped by everything I have experienced in the non-permanent world and especially by the incredibly violent and destructive experiences I have had on earth.

***

I created these four lower bodies in a protected level of the identity octave under the supervision of experienced guides. When my guides and I decided my vehicle was ready, I descended for the first time into physical embodiment on a planet. This planet was not earth, but another planet with a much higher level of collective consciousness and much lower density of matter than what we currently see on earth. The significance of this was that my first planet had none of the violent and destructive manifestations so common on earth. This may require some explanation.

Our total world forms a kind of chain in which each link is created by the link that came before it. One link in the chain, one sphere, starts out as a non-permanent world and then, through the conscious co-creation of the beings inhabiting it, attains permanence. Our non-permanent world was created by self-aware beings in the realm that had attained permanence right before ours. Our world is actually the seventh link or sphere in our total world. This means there have been six worlds that attained permanence before ours.

The self-aware beings who created our world had started in the sixth sphere and had developed their creative abilities to the point where they could raise their world to attain permanence. Some of them then chose to create the next sphere, namely the one in which we live. After having created the four levels of the material world (out of their own substance), they then created (out of their own beings) beings with self-awareness and sent them (us) into the four levels of the new world. We are meant to develop our creative abilities (as our spiritual parents did) until we can collectively raise our world to permanence.

You might ask why a world is not simply created in a state of permanence? The reason is that the purpose of creating worlds is to give self-aware beings an opportunity to start with a very localized sense of self and gradually expand it to the ultimate level of self-awareness (which is so far beyond ours that I am not even able to describe it). In order for us to go through this process, we must have completely free will. This means we must have complete freedom to create any condition we like and then experience our own creation.

Given that we start out with a very localized sense of self, it should be easy to see the potential danger. A world is an interconnected whole. Contrary to what the PCBs want us to believe, earth is not a separate unit floating around in space. We are connected at a deeper level than matter to the entire material universe with all of its four levels (science has actually proven non-locality, but the PCBs have not allowed it to affect the PIN). All life is one, and thus what one individual, self-aware being does affects the whole. The purpose of the process of growth is that you gradually expand your awareness until you also realize that you are not a separate being but part of a totality.

You start out with such a localized sense of self that it is almost inevitable that you will use your creative abilities in ways that do not consider the whole. You will not start out by deliberately hurting others, but you can very easily do so without knowing it. If you were created in a permanent world, everything you did would become permanent. Thus, you are created in a non-permanent world where you can easily uncreate what you have created. The idea is that it is inevitable that you start out with such a localized state of awareness that you will create things you later want to change.

We might say that in order to freely and voluntarily join the permanent world, we have to have used our free will in all ways possible, including by acting as separate beings who can do whatever we want regardless of the consequences for the whole. Only when we have had enough of this experience, can we join the permanent world in which we would never choose to damage the whole or other beings. There simply is no other way for free will to work itself out.

***

When you first come into embodiment in a non-permanent world, you start by creating something based on your current awareness. As you experience the results in all four levels, you expand your awareness. This allows you to create something more advanced, something that is *more*, meaning that it comes from a higher level of awareness. In this way, you gradually expand your awareness through direct experience. As you complete this process and reach the ultimate level of self-awareness, you have had a direct experience of all levels of the creative process, meaning you have a deep appreciation for the complexity of creating a sustainable world. Why this is important I will leave for later, as it is too far beyond the PIN.

Even though we all start out with a localized sense of self, we do not start our creative process in a vacuum. The beings who created us have created a world for us that is sustainable. They first created the galaxies, solar systems and inhabitable planets you see at the physical level (which naturally required them to first create the corresponding structures in the three higher octaves). Then, they created our I AM Presences and gave them the choice of whether they would send extensions of themselves into the new world. Our Presences could also choose which of the four levels and to which specific planet they would send an extension.

The original planets to which we descended had a vague resemblance to the idea of a lost paradise that you find in so many cultures and religions on earth. They were created with a lower density of matter than what you find on earth. The significance of this is that while we did have physical bodies, we did not have to perform physical work in order to sustain them. On a planet with a lower density of matter, even a newly created being can bring forth what is needed for the sustenance of its physical body by using the powers of its mind. We do not have to work at the sweat of our brow in order to sustain our bodies. Our bodies are vehicles for exploring the planet; they are not tyrants that eat up all of our energy and attention for their sustenance. All planets started out this way, including earth. I will later tell the story of how earth came to have a higher density of matter and the incredibly self-centered manifestations we see today.

These original planets were by no means finished creations. The beings who create a planet do so specifically in order to give those of us who will later embody on this planet the opportunity to exercise our creative powers. Because matter is not so dense, we can easily mold the original conditions, and we have two options. One is that we build upon the foundation set by the creators of a planet. We, so to speak, multiply the talents we have been given and create an upward spiral. The other option is that we tear down this foundation, as we have collectively done on earth.

The inhabitants of a growing planet will collectively create an even more beautiful planet than what they were given. They can do this according to their individual creativity as it is combined. This happens when beings have no intent to control each other. This does not mean they are perfect because they are still relatively inexperienced. Yet if most beings on a planet are willing to learn, they can create an upward spiral that raises the basic vibration of the matter out of which the planet is made. The inhabitants can create incredible beauty that is impossible to imagine for people who have inhabited on earth over many lifetimes.

# 4

The planet upon which I first descended was a newly created planet. I was in the first wave of beings taking embodiment on it. Compared to earth, it had incredible natural beauty. The crude language used today on earth simply cannot be used to describe the beauty of my first planet. If you have seen the movie *Avatar,* you may have some idea of how a more beautiful planet can be, but my first planet was way beyond what the creators of *Avatar* could imagine with their CIA.

I first took embodiment in a valley nested between high mountains. They were not like earth mountains because they were not created through a physical, geological process. They were creations of the minds of the beings who created the planet. These beings formed a blueprint in their minds and used the creative powers of their minds to lower it through the identity, mental and emotional realms until the planet appeared in the physical spectrum of vibrations (vibrations that were much higher than those of earth today).

The mountains around my first living place were exquisitely beautiful, with gently rounded forms, yet taller than any mountains on earth. The matter out of which they were made was partly transparent, and from a distance the mountains would seem ethereal rather than solid. In the early morning and right before sunset, you could see the rays of my planet's sun shining through the upper edges of the mountains. Even at night, they gave off a gentle glow from within the rock so my planet was never entirely dark. Even in the middle of the night, you could always move around without artificial light.

I would like to call this type of planet for a "natural" planet because what you see on earth is not natural at all. So on a natural planet, matter is not completely solid. It is always a bit translucent and emits a glow of light. This reminds you that you do not live in a separate world; you live in a world that is part of a larger continuum of energy vibrations. You can directly perceive that even the densest form of matter is made from vibrating energy.

Once you gain your bearings on a natural planet, you know that matter does not exist on its own. Matter is created by a stream of energy that comes through the emotional, mental and identity octaves, but beyond that comes from the permanent realm. You know that this stream of energy is real because you can directly observe it in your own mind, being consciously aware of all four levels and how energy flows through them.

Likewise, the living creatures on my first planet were of indescribable beauty. On a newly created planet, there are no animal life forms, but there are usually some forms of plant life. The inhabitants can create animal life forms and they can create new plant species. On my first planet, the plants had amazing shapes because they were not limited by the very restrictive (so-called) laws of nature you find on earth. With a lower gravity, plants could grow larger and especially the flowers were incredibly large with translucent petals that created indescribable patterns when the sunlight would shine through them.

The body I had on this planet had a vague resemblance to human bodies, but it was larger and far more beautiful. I could physically observe that my body did not live by its own power or the power of the physical octave. Many people on earth are aware that our physical bodies have an aura or energy field around them, which is actually the three higher bodies (identity, mental, emotional). Some people have the ability to see these auras, including myself, and science will soon validate this through the use of special digital cameras. On my first planet, I could not only see my aura around my physical body, I could also see the energy centers in my aura, called chakras on earth.

In the center of my chest, in the heart chakra, I could see a non-physical "flame" with three plumes, one corresponding to each of the higher bodies, blue to the identity body, yellow to the mental body and pink to the emotional body. I could feel the stream of energy flowing through my four lower bodies and I was therefore consciously aware that everything I created was created by using the energies that came from a higher realm and were then lowered in vibration through my four lower bodies until they took on a physical manifestation. I also knew that this stream of energy sustained the life of my physical body (as is even the case on earth).

On earth we are so used to having to do everything with the limited powers of the physical body or with the still very limited powers of technology. The only parallel we have on earth is that you are using a computer program to create a form that can be almost anything you can imagine. Thus, your imagination is the only limitation. On my first planet, I could create anything I could imagine, but not as an image on a computer. I created it as an image in my identity body, made it more concrete in my mental body, gave it momentum in my emotional body and then lowered it into the physical spectrum as a complete form.

Of course, this is still the way we all create on earth. It is just that because most people are not aware of their three higher bodies, they have no conscious awareness of or mastery over what and how they create. Another factor is that due to the density of matter, it takes longer to bring a form into physical manifestation, meaning we are not aware that we have (collectively) created current physical conditions on earth. What we are reaping today, was something we sowed a long time ago.

***

In the beginning I was, of course, not very good at creating, but I received plenty of help. I lived in a small community with many other new beings, and we had the constant guidance of some of the beings from the higher realm. These beings had not taken on bodies that were quite as dense as ours. But they had taken on bodies that we could perceive with the senses of the physical body.

We had the kind of community that many people dream of having on earth but that is so rarely achieved. We never had an argument and you truly never heard a discouraging word, as the old song goes. We started by engaging in various building projects under the supervision of our guides. We created structures for ourselves to live in and then we created structures for communal activities.

It was an amazingly wonderful experience to be part of such a harmonious community and to see how we all grew in awareness and creative ability by creating these structures together. None of us had the creative power yet to create, for example, a house on our own. But by combining the power of our minds, we could indeed create such structures.

Our physical bodies did not age, partly due to the low density of matter on the planet, but mostly because our minds had no dualistic beliefs and thus did not qualify energy below a certain vibration. Each planet has a ground level of vibration. Any energy that vibrates above that level will not break down the structures on the planet. So if you do not use your mind to lower energy below the ground level, your body never ages. You can, of course, shape it over time and make it as you would like it, but you basically uphold the same physical body for as long as you desire to be on that planet. Thus, reincarnation was not necessary. It only becomes so when the majority of the inhabitants of a planet go into the dualistic mindset and densify matter by generating a lot of energy that is below the ground level of the planet.

As you continued life on my first planet, you would gradually grow in creative ability. This means primarily two things. One is that you expanded your ability to envision structures and forms. The other is that you expanded your power to bring structures into the physical octave. Even on a natural planet, the increasing density of the four levels of matter require a certain creative power or momentum in order to bring a form into the physical and lowest octave.

In the beginning, I was entirely focused on myself and expanding my creative abilities. From the start, I was working with others, and gradually I began to focus on expanding my ability to work with others in harmony. After a long time, I realized that working in harmony is one thing, but there is a higher level, namely oneness with another being. As part of this process, I found my first partner and we lived together in a greater union with each other than we did with the other beings in our community. However, this was very different from planet earth and the relationships you see here.

Although our bodies had what you could call a female and male polarity, we did not have physical sexual organs. The main reason being that there was no need for procreation in the physical octave. You might say this sounds boring because we could not have sex. And I understand that for many people sex gives them a brief moment of contact with a realm beyond their normal state of consciousness. However, on my first planet, we practiced a kind of non-sexual union with all four bodies that was infinitely more pleasurable and enjoyable than sex on earth. I am not trying to knock sex. Compared to many other earthly activities, it can be quite transcendental, but compared to the activities on my first planet, it pales completely. The difference is simply indescribable because this planet gives no frame of reference for locking in to what I have come to remember.

\*\*\*

My first partner and I lived together for many years in complete harmony, supporting each others growth. We eventually came to the mutual consent that we were no longer experiencing maximum growth. We separated on positive terms. My partner went on to find another partner, but

I decided to move to one of the cities that had now been developed on my first planet. I moved to the cultural capital of my planet, and here I engaged in communal activities, primarily with the theatre and performing arts.

The theatre performances we created had the purpose of helping people grow by becoming more aware of their three non-physical bodies and how to use their creative abilities. We were also seeking to help people avoid developing conflicts by learning how to deal with the emotions that came up because people lived together. There were no villains in our performances, as is so common on earth. The reason being that there were no villains on the planet. The collective consciousness stayed above the level where it was possible to deliberately harm others while thinking this would not harm yourself. We could say that no one was unaware enough to harm another and believe this would not affect themselves.

We had quite elaborate special effects, even more advanced than what you see in movies made with computer technology. Only, our special effects were not produced by technological devices but by the power of the combined minds of the performers and other personnel. It was an extremely fulfilling experience to be part of a team of people who dedicated their full attention to creating these incredible performances. It was a joy beyond anything this planet has to offer. I also found a new partner at this stage and we shared our journey for a very long time.

After working with the theatre and other forms of culture for a long time, I eventually moved into government. I started with a modest position in local government. Over a long time span I worked my way up to a position as member of the planetary council. When you consider how government, even in democratic countries, works on earth, you can hardly imagine what it was like to work in government on a planet that had no selfishness. It was a complete joy and we saw ourselves as mere facilitators, never thinking we had personal power to do anything or that we were more important than other people. We were always serving, and we facilitated the relationship between the broad population and the councillors of our planet, meaning those in the higher realm. This is the primary spiritual activity found on a natural planet, and one can go into it after serving for a time in government. I did this also and found it very fulfilling to interact with the spiritual beings guiding my first planet.

I lived on my first planet for a very long time, always maintaining my physical body in a completely healthy and youthful state. Disease or ageing were not concepts that we even had in our minds. It is difficult to say exactly how long I was on my first planet in earth years because time was so different. As you know, time is different on the moon, with a day lasting 14 earth days, so you know time depends on gravity. However, the strength of the force of gravity depends on the density of the matter of a planet, and that depends on the collective consciousness of the inhabitants. If I were to make some kind of comparison, I lived for about one million earth years in the same body on my first planet.

After that time span, I had raised my consciousness to such a level that I had little to learn on that planet. During this process, I had become more and more conscious of my counsellors from the higher realm (whom we called "ascended masters"), and I had developed a closer relationship with them. Through their help, I was allowed to investigate other planets that matched my level of development, and I eventually chose one that was quite different from my first planet.

I now went through the process of dissolving the four lower bodies that I had created in order to embody on my first planet. I then created four new bodies adapted to my second planet. This was an amazing process because I was now much more conscious than I had been the first time.

I lived on my second planet for even longer than my first. Again, this was a planet with no conflicts, violence or disharmony. I eventually moved on to my third and fourth planets, before I was ready to consider embodying on a planet like earth (in the beginning no such planet even existed). I will next talk about the process that led me to this stage.

# 5

When you are a new being, you go through a very long stage where you are focused on yourself and your own growth. However, this is nothing like the self-centeredness or narcissism you see on earth. On a natural planet, you know there is a realm beyond the material world and you know you are connected to it. Although you see yourself as an individual being, you can never believe you are a *separate* or *isolated* being. You always know you are part of something greater than yourself, including a realm beyond the material and the other beings in your local community. You are not trying to hold on to a particular sense of self; you are constantly seeking to expand your circle of awareness.

In the beginning, your sense of self, your self-awareness, is completely localized. As a crude illustration, we can say that your self-awareness is like a single point. It is as if you are standing in the darkness with a small light above you that is casting light on your body and the area immediately around it. You simply can't see anything beyond that small circle. As you have experiences on your first planet, you gradually expand your circle of awareness and this means your self grows to encompass an awareness of more and more. This first involves your local community. It then will involve one or more partners. It eventually will involve taking on the role of some kind of leader in your local community, then a wider community and eventually maybe the planetary council found on all natural planets (on earth people are too divided to develop a true planetary council).

Yet even though you are clearly expanding your self-awareness, it is still normal that you do this for the purpose of developing yourself as an individual. You have a clear goal in the sense that you know that the goal of life is to expand your self-awareness to a higher level. As you become more aware, you realize that it is possible to expand your self-awareness to the point where you graduate from your first planet and can move on. This means you have now learned everything there is to learn and mastered the energies of the planet to a high degree. You can then move on to another planet in order to get a different experience and also expand your mastery there. This can go on for a long time before you become aware of the next level.

***

A new, non-permanent world has a very long time to grow and evolve and there are billions of planets in the material universe and many other places to grow in the three higher octaves. So you can literally continue this process of self-development for a very long time. This means you can achieve an amazing mastery in using the energies of this non-permanent sphere. You can become very powerful in formulating a vision and making it a physical manifestation.

In doing this, you develop the sophistication of all four of your bodies, but you especially develop the power to fashion energy into physical forms. You can therefore become very powerful in creating compared to others who are not as far along. This is not the same as what is currently seen as powerful people on earth where the PCBs have perverted the concept of power from being creative to being controlling.

Some beings will eventually grow to become far more powerful than others. This is, of course, ultimately a product of the fact that all beings have a will that is completely free. I have said that none of us are inherently limited and it is not so that the design of individual beings predisposes some to become more powerful. It is all a matter of what a being does with its free will and the energy it receives. It is truly a matter of where you choose to focus your attention.

The law is very simple. As you sow, so shall you reap. I know this saying has been made sort of ominous by the fear-based religions created on earth by the PCBs (and yes, all religions on earth are WCs). They want us to believe that this saying means that if you do something bad, you will be punished. In reality, it simply means that all of the energies you project out, will be returned to you multiplied. You can put one grain of wheat in the ground, and you receive 20 grains in return. As a new being, you receive a certain flow of creative energy from your I AM Presence. As you use this to expand your sense of self, as you multiply the talents given, the stream will be expanded. You will now have more creative energy and thus you have more power to create. This expansion can go on for a very long time, but there is a limit.

There are stages in the ideal growth of an individual. First, we have a stage where one is focused on developing all four lower bodies. Then one becomes focused on working with others in a local community. Then one may have one or several partners. Then one goes on to serve society in a wider capacity, for example through arts or through building, invention etcetera. Then one goes into some form of government and finally one can go into the spiritual activities found on a natural planet (which are very different from religions on earth).

The thread that runs through it all is that one develops the sense of self, expands the circle of awareness. Yet where is it all leading? Well, I have talked about six previous realms or spheres that all became permanent whereas our world is impermanent. How does a sphere become permanent? It does so when the vast majority of its inhabitants have grown beyond the level of being focused on themselves by resolving the enigma that we are individual beings but still part of one, interconnected whole. We have individual minds but are still part of one mind. If this sounds nonsensical to you, it is no surprise. You are (still) on earth because you have not yet resolved this enigma. This is not meant as a criticism, as the PCBs have made it extremely difficult to solve this enigma on earth.

My point is that it is quite possible to expand your self and increase the sophistication of your soul vehicle without truly understanding the purpose of it all. This will require a very subtle explanation because the PCBs have never even begun to understand this, and as a result all of the WCs they have created on earth will deny what I will explain next.

The basic illusion of all PCBs is that they can reach such a level of sophistication and perfection that their outer vehicles (their four bodies) can attain permanence. They also believe that this will eventually give them control over the entire universe, as they see it with their PRC.

The basic reality is that a self-aware being is meant to go through three phases. First, you have the phase where you are focused on building your self, the self you have created in this world. Then, you begin to realize that nothing in this world is permanent and therefore it really has no importance in itself. This world is only a vehicle for the development of the beings who live in it. This world can become permanent, but this does not mean that any of the structures created in it will attain permanence. The world attains permanence by being raised to a level of vibration that is so much higher that none of the structures in the world can be sustained. All will be made new. This includes the most elaborate cities created on the most developed planets, it includes the planets themselves and all solar systems and galaxies.

Most importantly, it includes the outer selves created by the self-aware beings in our world. Yes, first we labor for a very long time in order to create a sophisticated outer self, and then we – ideally – begin to understand that this self was just a temporary vehicle. It facilitated our growth in self-awareness, but it is not meant to or capable of ascending with us to the level of permanence. You can indeed attain immortality by ascending to the higher realm, but you cannot do so by taking your outer self with you. Only the being that descended from the higher realm, can ascend back to the higher realm. The real growth in self-awareness happens in your I AM Presence.

\*\*\*

The crucial dividing line is whether a being gets this or not. If a being gets it, it will gradually begin to dismantle its outer self and raise its sense of self beyond it. It will also begin to focus on helping others raise their awareness instead of creating sustainable structures in this world. If a being does *not* get this, it will think it has to continue to expand its outer self until it achieves the ultimate state of perfection (according to its own perception, which it thinks is universal instead of subjective). It thinks this will give it entry into immortality. It may also think it can create structures in this world that are so sophisticated they can attain permanence.

As you, meaning the self that is pure awareness, experienced the non-permanent world through your four lower bodies, your I AM Presence had an entirely different experience. Your experience is colored by the contents of your four lower bodies, which may be heavily affected by your environment (that is why your experience can only be subjective, never universal). For example, on a dense-matter planet like earth many people have a soul vehicle that experiences a lot of suffering and a sense of being powerless. Yet while this is happening, their I AM Presences have an entirely constructive experience and learn timeless life lessons. It is these lessons that will form part of your immortal identity; *not* the experiences you have through the soul vehicle.

In order to permanently ascend and become an immortal being, you can take nothing with you from your experience in the non-permanent world. You have to systematically dismantle your soul vehicle. This includes looking at all of the choices you made while having a limited self-awareness and then replacing them with the self-awareness of a being who is one with the All. It also includes raising the vibration of all energies qualified with a lower vibration than the base energy on the planets on which you have lived. You have to raise all fear-based energies to the level of love. Once you have done this, the self that descended can ascend back and reunite with the I AM Presence out of which it came. You become one with your I AM Presence or you give up the illusion of being out of or away from the Presence. You become the Presence once again. I realize this is difficult to explain with earth words, but the experience is simple. You have to give up everything you thought you were in this world.

# 6

Our non-permanent world has existed for a very long time. In that time span the vast majority of beings have come to see what the process of growth is all about. There are billions of planets that are ascending in vibration because the inhabitants are on the path of dismantling their outer selves and qualifying for the process of ascending to immortality. Incidentally, on any of these planets, your current physical body simply could not exist. If your body was somehow transported there, its cells and molecules would be shaken apart by the higher vibrations in a split second.

There is no question that making the shift from being focused on raising the outer self and then beginning to dismantle that self is a very subtle challenge. Most beings go through an in-between state. They have gone into the phase of selflessly serving some greater cause or their community, but they have not fully grasped that the outer self through which they do this must die. That is why so many people on earth are open to a religion that promises a form of salvation without consciously dismantling the outer self. The PCBs create this illusion by promising that an external savior will take you to a higher realm, rather than you having to do it by fundamentally changing your sense of self. The PCBs don't want to change their sense of self. They don't want to give up the separate self they have crafted over a very long time. They want to think this self can one day enter a higher realm and become immortal.

Back to my own story. On my fourth planet, I did reach the point of beginning to selflessly serve something greater, but I had not even begun to understand the need to let the outer self die. I thought it was my role to make this outer self perfect, meaning it would become completely selfless. In reality, it is an illusion that the outer self can become selfless or objective, but I did not understand this. My councillors tried to explain this to me, but I could not grasp it and paid little attention to their advice.

This has something to do with the fact that I had been a very eager student and very willing to make an effort to develop my creative powers. I had attained a very big momentum on imagining forms and making them a physical reality. I had been in leading positions for a very long time, and I had come to believe that I really was a powerful creative being and that I had great wisdom and understanding of how the world works. And I was not wrong; I *did* have power and insight in how the material world works, but I did not grasp the non-material reality. My attention had been focused *horizontally*, not *vertically*.

The result was that I came to a point where I became less willing to listen to advice. In retrospect, I can see that my councillors knew exactly what was happening to me. They had seen it before, and some of them had even gone through the same phase. Yet they also knew that for any student, there is a limit to what that student can learn by being told. There can come a point where the student thinks it knows so much that it cannot learn from a teacher. It can learn only by pursuing a certain cause of action and then eventually realizing that it does not work because it is based on a flawed vision. Only then, will the student again have an open mind to the teacher.

***

During this phase, I began to consider one of the most difficult questions that beings have to deal with as they develop self-awareness to my level. On the planets upon which I had so far embodied, no being had ever misused its free will to deliberately harm others. All had, as did I, stayed in the level of innocence where you always qualify energies with love and never with fear.

Yet there comes a point where a being has to deal with the fact that free will is completely free. There is no higher authority that limits your free will. You can literally do anything you can imagine doing because you are allowed to have any experience you desire to have. Growth happens only when you imagine an experience, then make it a physical circumstance so you experience it through the physical body and the other bodies. After having experienced this for some time, perhaps a long time, you finally come to the point where you have had enough of that experience and want more, want a higher experience.

It is possible that instead of always seeking to expand your sense of self, you can decide that you want to maintain a certain sense of self over time. You can also decide that you want to maintain a certain physical circumstance over time. This means that instead of flowing with the upward movement of the entire sphere, you will have to deliberately go against the upward flow created by all of the other trillions and trillions of beings in our world.

Flowing with the current in a river is easy, swimming against the current requires a greater effort and it quickly becomes a struggle. You are indeed allowed to use your free will to go against the upward current created by all other beings with free will. Yet you cannot expect that they should all stop growing because you do so. This means that if you make the choice to go against the creative flow, your life will become a struggle. It is like you are still in the river, but you are trying to keep the same position instead of letting the current carry you along.

Because this requires a struggle, it is possible that you can come to a point where you are no longer content to try to maintain your own position. You also want to maintain a physical condition that involves other beings. You are not only trying to keep yourself in position by resisting the current, you are actually trying to stop the current.

Again, the Law of Free Will is the basic law in a non-permanent sphere so it allows you to have even this experience. Yet how can you have it? You obviously cannot stop the forward movement of an entire sphere, but you are allowed to have the experience of stopping the creative current in a local environment. If a majority of the people on a planet decide to stop the flow and maintain a certain experience, then that planet is allowed to lag behind the movement of the rest of the sphere.

\*\*\*

Yet there is a twist. Scientists on earth have discovered what is called the second law of thermodynamics. It officially says that in a closed system, disorder (entropy) will increase until all structures are broken down and the system is at its lowest possible energy state. It's a good discovery, but unfortunately materialistic science has made a mess of interpreting it, as they do with everything else. The real meaning is that any closed system will inevitably self-destruct because it will create a resistance that will increase until no power within the system can overcome the resistance and the system breaks down.

In reality, there are no closed systems. Everything in our total world was created from the same source, the same mind, and it is interconnected in consciousness. So everything affects everything else, everything pulls on everything else. Yet because of free will, it is allowed that a group of beings in an unascended sphere can temporarily set themselves outside the upward movement created by all of the other self-aware beings in our world. In order to do this, they have to take whatever creative momentum they have and use it to create a force that works against the current of life, the River of Life. This is no longer *co*-creation but *de*-creation.

Doing this will inevitably require a struggle. When you seek to maintain your self or a particular physical condition, you are effectively saying that you want to experience what it is like to struggle instead of co-creating. A struggle implies that you are a separate being and that something outside of you resists or opposes what you want to do. In order to experience a struggle, there must be something for you to struggle against. On a natural planet, there is nothing to oppose you and you cannot maintain the illusion that you are a separate being. Matter on a natural planet effortlessly takes on any form your mind projects upon it. Matter is not opposing your co-creative efforts but facilitating them.

This is actually explained in a veiled way by the story of the Garden of Eden. At first, Adam and Eve needed to exert no physical effort for their sustenance. When they left the garden, they had to work out a living at "the sweat of their brow." As with the materialists, religious people have made a mess of interpreting this (as they do with everything), and they think it should be taken literally to talk about the first two people. In reality, it symbolizes the fall in consciousness, from love to fear, that all people on earth have gone through. Of course, the story does not make this clear, and it incorrectly portrays the god in the garden as some kind of tyrant. The reason being that Genesis was highly influenced by the PCBs from the beginning, as I will explain later. In reality, everything is a result of the free-will choices we make and no higher being ever forces us. There are fear-based non-material forces that seek to force us, but I will return to that later.

Only when a planet sinks below the level of love and becomes dominated by the vibrations of fear, can the sense of struggle be de-created. The law still works, meaning that whatever energies you project out, must be returned to you multiplied. So when the inhabitants of a planet begin to struggle, they will actually send out a certain amount of fear-based energy that will be returned to them multiplied. This return has the effect of densifying the matter on their planet. Denser matter gives more resistance to the creative efforts of the inhabitants of the planet, and this is exactly what they want to experience.

In the beginning phase, this can actually give the inhabitants on a planet a certain sense of having power over other people, over nature or even over the forces of the universe. This is because they still have the creative momentum they had garnered until they stepped into fear and separation. As long as this is not used up, they will have a sense of having power and control over their destiny. Yet there will inevitably come a point where all of their love-based momentum has now been converted into fear-based energy and used to resist the current of life.

At that moment, the inhabitants could potentially turn around and start climbing back towards their starting point. Yet in many cases they do not want to consider doing so because they have now become convinced that they are right in doing what they are doing. Or they have forgotten that it was their own choice that started the process. This is partly caused by the fact that when the matter on a planet densifies, the physical bodies can no longer be maintained indefinitely. The denser the matter, the shorter the lifespan of the body, which means that all such unnatural planets need to have reincarnation. Yet because of the density of matter, people tend to forget that they have incarnated before and they become convinced they were born into the dense and limiting circumstances that they themselves helped de-create in the past.

They now easily begin to believe that they did not create their limited situation out of their own choosing and by using their own creative momentum. Instead, they often believe they are victims of some force outside themselves. They feel this is unjust, and they often struggle against it with all the power they have left, making the situation even more intense. This can go on for a long time. It can lead to incredible amounts of suffering as the inhabitants always fracture into several groups that oppose each other. It has in some cases led to the inhabitants of a planet creating such resistance (so much fear-based energy) that the planet could no longer bear the strain. This has led to cataclysmic events, what people today mistakenly call natural disasters, that have erased entire civilizations. It has even happened that a planet has been blown apart by the energies created through the warring of its inhabitants.

When I began contemplating these ideas, there was a fairly large number of planets (a greater number than today) where this had happened. I had no awareness of this on my first four planets because they had been in the creative flow. Yet as I was coming to the point where I had little more to learn from being on my fourth planet, I became aware of the possibility that beings can use their free will to go against the creative current. I also became aware that this had been done on a number of planets, and I became aware that a lot of beings had become stuck on such planets. The mechanics of what it requires to go against the creative current makes it possible, even likely, that beings will become stuck in a lesser sense of self because they believe they cannot raise themselves above it. This realization had a life-changing impact on me and set me on a course that I have later regretted many times.

***

On a natural planet, you are also wearing a physical body, but because the vibrations of the planet are so much higher (matter is so much less dense) the body is not nearly as limited as earth bodies. The body on a natural planet does not age or get sick, but the most important consequence in this context is that its senses have a far greater range than the senses of earth bodies.

On my first four planets, I had bodies that could directly sense that the matter of my planets did not exist on its own but was created by energies that streamed from a higher realm. That is why it never occurred to me that I was a separate being, living in a separate world. You simply could not have made me believe in what is today the most common illusion on earth (upheld by every WC created by the PCBs).

For example, on earth there are people who have clairvoyant or extrasensory perception and who can see auras around people's bodies. Even science is beginning to realize that such energy fields exist. Yet many people still believe the aura is produced by the body whereas the reality is that the physical body is produced by the aura. The aura is simply the three higher bodies and the physical body is created and maintained by the energy streaming through these bodies.

When I first descended to earth, I had the ability to see auras. As I sank in consciousness, I lost it, but I have now regained it. One consequence of this is that no one can lie to me. I can see in their auras what their intentions are and I can see if they are lying. When you consider how the vast majority of people on earth are lying every day or want to hide their intentions, thoughts and feelings from others, you can see why they are not ready to take responsibility for themselves. You can hide what goes on in your mind only because matter on earth is so dense, but the price you pay is that denser matter makes life a struggle, ages your body and creates diseases. The privilege of lying leads to the consequence of death.

I am getting lost in details. What I wanted to explain here is that the denser matter on earth blocks your direct, sensory experience, telling you that there are energies beyond the material spectrum. This is what makes a dense-matter planet a kind of dead-end, a catch-22, from which it is very difficult to extricate yourself, once you have bought into the illusion that you are a separate being living in a separate world.

We are experience-based beings. As beings who have not yet attained immortality, our primary goal is to expand our sense of self. We do this by interacting with our environment, which gives us an experience that is based on the senses of our physical bodies but is truly processed by our three higher bodies. It is this total experience that can shift our sense of self, our sense of identity, upwards or downwards. On a natural planet, interacting with your environment leads you to shift your sense of self upwards. On an unnatural planet, this is very difficult to do. It is far more likely that people will have a total experience of their environment that causes them to shift their sense of self downwards. They gradually come to feel powerless and insignificant. It is exactly this trend that the PCBs use in order to control us. All of their WCs are designed to get you to feel more and more powerless and to prevent you from ever climbing out of the hole you have dug for yourself.

*** 

Just look at earth. Your physical senses cannot directly show you that there are energies beyond the material spectrum of frequencies. Therefore, you have no frame of reference from beyond the material (and this is why materialism has appeal to so many people). Sure, you may believe that there is a heaven world, as described by a religion. Or you may believe such a heaven world is pure superstition, as described by the religion of materialism. But this is mere belief and not a direct experience.

Because you have no direct experience, no frame of reference, you have come to believe one of the most subtle illusions spread by the PCBs, namely that your mind does not have the power to directly influence matter. You believe this because you experience that at your present level of awareness, you cannot change your life circumstances or even move a rock by the power of your mind.

In reality, this is a complete lie. Sure, you may say that you do not have the power to influence matter with your mind, and you are right. However, you are right only because you have become a self-fulfilling prophecy. It is true that your mind cannot change matter—*at your present level of awareness*. Yet the lie is that your present level of awareness is the only level of awareness available to you. It is a much lower level of awareness than what is possible. You have descended into this lower state through your own choices. You were manipulated and deceived by the PCBs, but you still made the choices. The magic of admitting this is that you can also undo the choices you have made. Any choice you have ever made can be undone by making a more aware choice. The PCBs cannot prevent you from doing this, and this is what they really do not want you to know and accept.

Here is the basic Law of Free Will. You can create any sense of self you want, but you can *never* create a sense of self that you cannot get out of. You can get yourself *into* a very deep hole by making choices, but you can never create a hole so deep that you cannot get out of it by making more aware choices. By the way, all PCBs and their WCs will vehemently deny what I just said. Their basic lie on earth is that you can indeed make certain choices that cannot be undone by making new choices. This is how you can expose any theory or thought system and know it is created by the PCBs with the deliberate intent of controlling you.

So back to my story. When I started studying planets that had fallen below the level of fear, I realized that once they cross that threshold, the people embodying on such planets have no direct experience that there is anything beyond matter. Therefore, it becomes virtually impossible for them to regain their awareness of themselves as coming from a higher realm. The planet becomes a closed system that will inevitably have such internal resistance that it might self-destruct.

I felt deep and honest compassion for the beings who had become stuck on such planets, and I developed a sincere desire to help them. Because I did not understand fully how free will works, I thought something had gone wrong and that someone (me) needed to correct this. I developed the sense that I should do something to save them, and I soon realized there was only one way to do so. I had to embody on such a planet and demonstrate to the inhabitants that there was a higher way, a higher sense of self. I realized that giving these people a theory, such as a religion, was not enough in itself. They needed to have a direct experience that a person in a body like themselves could raise his or her consciousness beyond their level. Only then, might they accept that this was possible for themselves also.

During this process, I did, of course, talk to my councillors. I can see now that they were trying to explain something to me that I was not capable of understanding and not truly willing to consider. I can see how they finally resigned themselves to the fact that I simply had to be allowed to have the experience of descending to an unnatural planet in order to act as a savior. Today, I clearly see that I had developed a savior complex, but back then you could not have explained it to me. And that only proves how we need direct experience in order to learn our lessons and shift our sense of self.

So I was allowed to take embodiment on an unnatural planet, and I chose earth. I will now describe my first pivotal embodiment on this planet.

# PART 2:

# MY FIRST

# EMBODIMENT

# ON EARTH

# 7

I have already mentioned that on a natural planet you create a physical body. You fashion a matrix at the identity level and push it into the mental where you make it more detailed. You push it into the emotional where it also becomes more concrete and gathers momentum. Then you push it into the physical as you are pushing yourself into it. On a dense-matter planet like earth this isn't possible, due to, of course, the density of matter.

I have mentioned that earth was not created in its present state. In its original state, earth was not a dense-matter planet. For a very long time, earth served as a platform for the ascension of several waves of beings (three to be exact). Then a fourth wave descended, and they were the first to start lowering the vibration of the planet. Over a long time-span, this lowered the vibration of the planet until matter became so dense that physical bodies evolved that had sexual organs and were able to reproduce at the physical level. Manifesting a physical body had now become a mechanical, not a creative, process. From that point on, reincarnation became a necessity because it is the only way to give a being the opportunity to reclaim the energy it has misused on a dense-matter planet. As mentioned, once you lower energies below the level of the planet's original vibration, you cannot leave that planet until you have raised them again. And it is very difficult to raise (or balance) energies when you are not in physical embodiment.

My first embodiment took place around two million years ago. I cannot give you an exact figure because time changes over time, or rather, it changes with gravity as Einstein discovered. And gravity changes with the collective consciousness. Because I had no prior history on this planet and had not qualified any energy below the level of love, there was nothing that mandated that I had to take embodiment at a certain time, in a certain place or with a certain group of people. I therefore had relative freedom to choose where and when I wanted to embody, the condition being that there had to be a woman who was pregnant so that there was a body for me to descend into. Because of my savior complex and my belief that I could come here and have a positive impact on the planet, I chose to be born as the son of the leader of the biggest and most powerful civilization that existed at the time. Needless to say, this civilization is no longer in existence and this flies in the face of the current WCs in (at least) two ways. They all say that there was no sophisticated civilization on earth two million years ago and some of them also say that life on this planet started at a very primitive level and evolved from there, meaning our civilization is the most sophisticated ever to exist.

What incredible hubris! Imagining that the current civilization deserves to be called sophisticated is just such utter ignorance and arrogance that anyone knowing reality can only laugh out loud. You may, of course, say that I am the one who is arrogant, but in order to prove my case that our current civilization is primitive, I only have to say one word: "War."

The first three groups of beings that took embodiment on earth created civilizations that do deserve to be called sophisticated. Since the fourth wave of beings, several civilizations have reached a much higher level of technological development than the present civilization. Yet they have still been at a level that was so much lower than what you find on a natural planet that it is difficult to describe the difference.

\*\*\*

The civilization I was born into was much more technologically advanced than the current one. It was, as the current one, also fear-based, which means that technology was based on force. Instead of developing love-based technology that works *with* nature, force-based technology is based on the illusion that humans are separated from nature and therefore need to force nature in order to get their way.

In many ways life in my first earthly civilization was much easier and more abundant than today. Yet because the civilization was fear-based, it also had weapons that were far more powerful than what is known today (at least by the public). My first civilization was the last in a long line of fear-based civilizations, which means weapons had gradually been developed to the level where they could have a cataclysmic impact on the planet. In other words, my civilization had the power to destroy itself.

You might say that so does the current one, but that is not necessarily the case yet. Even if all current weapons were used, it would take quite a bit of luck to wipe out all human beings on the planet. But certainly, it could have a major negative impact. What I'm trying to say was that my first civilization had even more powerful weapons than we do today. It was not even the first civilization to have developed such weapons. Three previous civilizations had literally destroyed themselves and in the process created such cataclysmic planetary effects that there are no traces left of them. Actually, there are traces, but because we do not have the same level of technology, we do not know how to read the geological records. We cannot see that what we call natural rock or mineral formations are the remnants of man-made materials. And because of the PIN, we will not admit that the glass found in various places (and that can only have been created by extremely high temperatures) were created by previous civilizations waging nuclear war.

*** 

For me, coming into embodiment was quite tricky. The leader of the civilization had several wives and many children. Yet because he had a history on this planet, there were many souls who were waiting for an opportunity to balance the misqualified energy (or karma, as it is often called today) they had with him. So I had to wait several years before one of his wives had a pregnancy that was not already determined to go to someone else. This was, of course, new to me, but I realized coming into embodiment on a dense-matter planet would be a different experience so I took it in stride. Had I known *how* different it is to embody on such a planet, I would have reconsidered.

When you have never been in embodiment on a dense-matter planet, you have no experience-based frame of reference for evaluating what it will be like. The difference between a natural planet and a dense-matter planet is simply so huge that no amount of theoretical knowledge can give you an impression of what it is like. So I understood that there comes a point where the only way forward is to get the direct experience and then go from there. I had no doubt that I would be able to handle myself well. How wrong I was, and this was truly hubris and arrogance on my part!

*** 

On a dense-matter planet, you have to wait for a physical body to be available, but you do have some influence on your three higher bodies (the first time, because after that, you carry them with you from previous lives). However, even here there are restrictions, as a given physical body will have three higher bodies that you also descend into. The first time you take embodiment, you can have some influence on these bodies, but only within the framework set by the previous history of the parents and the soul group from which the body springs.

How ignorant of current science to think that our heritage is only physical and determined by our DNA. Actually, science has already discovered that DNA cannot account for all of our inherited traits. Nor can it account for the complex machinery of our physical bodies, and even less so for our minds and psyches. The reason is, of course, that we have *four* bodies that are the result of the past history of ourselves, our parents, our family and our soul group (which is more than nationality, ethnicity or race) and even humanity as a whole. Why have these discoveries not been acknowledged? Simply because the PCBs who are using scientific materialism as their WC have managed to delay the broad acceptance that a new scientific paradigm is needed. They will not rock the boat and disturb the PIN they have so carefully crafted.

From the moment my first physical body was conceived, I started working on the three higher bodies. This doesn't mean that I descended into the foetus on a permanent basis. Yet from the beginning, I had brief stints of going into the foetus and experiencing what it experienced from the womb. Again, science is wrong in assuming the foetus can experience only through its physical senses. Once you are in the physical body (even if it consists of only a few cells), your three higher bodies can perceive all of the energies around the foetus. You can, for example, perceive the energy field of your mother and your father (if he is around), your older siblings and family members. You can also perceive how your family members experience life in general, how they experience their specific situation and life in their society. You can process these experiences according to the level of awareness you carry with you.

Most people are not aware enough to make use of this, but in my first embodiment I had the awareness to take my impressions of the situation and prepare my emotional, mental and identity body to deal with it. I thought I had also prepared myself for what it meant to be stuck in the body and be born, but that was far from being the case.

\*\*\*

After eight and a half months (the gestation period was slightly shorter back then), the moment of birth had arrived. I had spent more and more time in the foetus, but in the womb I didn't experience any physical pain (because my mother was healthy). I had not really considered what it would mean to be born, instead focusing on what I would do when I could start acting with my physical body.

One does not necessarily have to descend fully into the foetus until after birth, but since I was curious to experience life on a dense-matter planet, I decided to do so. I descended fully, and I had expected a couple of days to experience life in the womb. To my surprise, the descent of my being into the physical body immediately triggered my mother's contractions and the birth process began.

I had not even considered this, but the issue was that my mother was a fairly developed women compared to the standard of that civilization, but she had a much lower level of consciousness than mine, having been in embodiment on earth for a long time. So she simply could not handle having the intensity of my energy or light in her auric field and immediately had to push me out in order to regain some kind of composure. I mean, she literally went into a state of panic as soon as she felt the fullness of my auric field, and she was screaming for the doctors to help her get this over with.

From the moment the contractions began, I started feeling something I had never experienced before, namely pain in my physical body. I know it will seem surprising, but on my first planets, I had never experienced physical pain (nor pain at the emotional, mental or identity level). Now I was experiencing this, and it was both shocking psychologically and very unpleasant physically. The pain intensified when I was (much against my will) squeezed into the birth canal.

At that moment, I began to realize something I had never considered before, namely that the physical body can influence the three higher bodies. On a natural planet, the flow of energy is always from the higher bodies to the physical. Of course, you have experiences with the physical body, but they have no direct influence on the higher bodies. A physical experience can, for example, trigger an emotion, but only if you consciously allow it to do so. In other words, there can be a flow from the physical to the higher bodies, but your conscious mind is in control of what gets through. This is not the case on a dense-matter planet, and the significance of this will become clear by what I experienced in my first embodiment.

In the birth canal, I experienced how the intense discomfort and pain of the physical body triggered feelings that I had no conscious control over. These were emotional responses programmed into my emotional body by the experiences of all of the people who had previously been born in my family line. I started feeling a sense of panic and a fear of what would come next, even a fear of how severe the pain would become.

As I was sliding out of the birth canal, I was not in any way identified with these feelings. I knew they were not actually *my* feelings because I had not chosen them. Yet even though I was not fully absorbed in them, I could not avoid them either. I could not turn them off, as they were already in my emotional body. In my previous experience, nothing got from the physical body to the higher bodies without me making a conscious choice, but here I had no choice (I had the choice to descend into the body, but once this choice was made, I did not have the choice to avoid the consequences).

I also experienced certain thoughts about what dangers might await me, and this was also a purely programmed response. On the conscious level, I was still fully confident that I could handle anything this planet could throw at me, but in my mental body and identity body I noticed powerful thoughts about what "they" might do to me and how limited of a being I really was. Again, I was merely observing these without identifying with them, but I was beginning to realize that this was also something I could not turn off.

Before I really knew what had happened, I was pushed and pulled out of the birth canal (the doctor had cold hands), and a doctor held me up by the legs and they cleared my airways with a suction hose. He then held me still, and I became aware that all of the people in the delivery room were looking at me with expectation in their auras. I was completely absorbed in processing my impressions, but finally had the thought: "What do they want from me?"

The doctor then started massaging me and they were beginning to talk with concerned voices. They could clearly see I was breathing, but apparently that wasn't enough because suddenly one of them slapped me in the butt and I again felt pain. "Why isn't he crying?" said one person and the thought came to me: "What is crying? What do they want me to do?" Then someone slapped me in the butt much harder, and to my surprise, my body reacted by letting out a very tentative cry. They all looked relieved and were about to put me down next to my mother, but by that time, the thought came to me: "Oh, this is crying? So they want me to cry? Well, let's see what this baby can do!" I then let out a cry that shocked them so much that the doctor nearly dropped me. I later heard someone say they had never heard a baby cry so loudly.

Well, they got to hear it all right, because once I found out how the body cries, I didn't stop for two full days. I mean, I cried for 48 hours straight because I simply couldn't process all of the emotions that had come up in my emotional body as a result of being born and suddenly feeling the energies in the physical octave full force.

***

Nothing could ever have prepared me for the contrast between a natural planet and earth. On a natural planet, there is no discomfort in being in a physical body. On earth, just being in the body feels intensely uncomfortable. By now, of course, I have gotten so used to it that I hardly notice, like everyone else. Yet the first time I came into embodiment, it was such an utter shock that it took me 48 hours to find some kind of equilibrium.

It wasn't just a matter of being in a physical body but even more experiencing the energies of earth through my four lower bodies. The energies on this planet were so intense compared to what I had experienced before, especially because I experienced so much fear, anger and hatred that I simply could not believe human beings could even have such feelings towards each other. I could not believe that they did not experience how toxic such emotions are to themselves. I thought that if a sane person experienced what effect it had on ones own four bodies that we send hatred towards another human being, that person would never allow itself to feel hatred. I mean, I thought no one could be so stupid that they knowingly hurt themselves (now I know the PCBs really are that stupid). I was so shocked by feeling the energies people were sending at each other that I felt completely overwhelmed, and it took me two full days to adjust to the point where I could handle being here.

Another aspect of my discomfort was that I had lost my conscious connection to my councillors and my I AM Presence. I knew, of course, that this would happen on a planet as dense as earth. I had not really worried about this because I knew that even on a dense planet, it is possible to regain this contact. After an initial period of forgetting who you are and where you came from, you can adjust to the energies and begin to restore some contact with the higher realm. I was sure I would be able to do this, but I did, of course, forget my origin. I had an inner sense that I had forgotten something very important but because I had no conscious idea what it was, it was a very unpleasant feeling of not belonging here.

During the first two days, I didn't eat, despite the fact that they offered me my mother's breasts and all kinds of artificial devices. I simply cried and spit our whatever they tried to stuff into my mouth. Needless to say, I was then separated from my mother, and since I woke up all of the other babies, I was put in a room by myself.

I cried the first day because it was so damned uncomfortable just to be in the body. On the second day I cried because my body was so damned hungry. Although they looked at me and examined me regularly, they had apparently given up trying to feed me after the first day. Finally, it dawned on me that perhaps they would feed me if I stopped crying, and that proved to be the case. No sooner had I stopped crying than I was put next to my mother and a soft nipple was pushed into my mouth. I drank pretty much the same way I had cried: "Damn the torpedoes; full speed ahead."

# 8

I can't say I had a happy childhood. But then again, I can't say I had an unhappy childhood because I had no frame of reference for what it meant to be a child on earth. I can, in retrospect, see that I definitely did not fit in.

On a natural planet, you descend into an adult body that can do anything a body can do. Having to wait 16 years before I was considered an adult was sheer agony, and I could not wait until my body had reached the level where I could start doing what I came here to do. Of course, I had no conscious awareness of what I knew before I took embodiment, but I had very strong intuitive impressions of having a purpose for being here and wanting to do something.

My mother never adjusted to the intensity of my energy field and spent as little time with me as possible. As an excuse, she tried to label me as a strange, even mentally ill, child, but anyone who got to know me disagreed with her. I must admit, I had no particular feelings for her because I had no previous history with her, and she had, quite frankly, just been a tool for me to come into embodiment. So I fully understood why she did not have strong feelings for me and I had no problem with us being separated. I was placed in a kind of communal setting with many other children, some of them my father's children with other wives and some of them the children of the leading people in my father's court.

I did relatively well there, although I never formed friendships with any of the other children. This was due to the fact that because I had never embodied on earth before, my creative faculties had not been dulled. I learned extremely quickly, and I could walk, talk and read much earlier than other children. I had some problems figuring out how the body works, so for many years I did not do as well as others in physical activities. Yet once I reached the teen-age years, I excelled in any kind of sport.

I also excelled in any kind of book learning, and this made the other children keep a certain distance to me, a combination of jealousy and fear. I, of course, did not act in any superior or arrogant manner towards others as I felt my abilities were far less than what I was used to. I thought I was doing rather poorly compared to the intuitive sense I had of what should be possible.

Of course, I did know more than most people, and I had an intuitive sense of what life *could,* and *should,* be like. So I would often ask both children and adults what they considered very strange or even threatening questions. When I came across some condition on earth that I intuitively knew did not occur on a natural planet, I would ask questions about why we were doing these kinds of things. Naturally, people were doing them because they had been brought up to do them, and the actions had become part of the PIN of the time, so people had never questioned why they were doing this. Consequently, they found it very unpleasant to deal with my questions. This didn't stop me from asking, as I was not very concerned about the feelings of other people. But it did stop them from giving me an opportunity to ask and I spent a lot of time alone.

***

One of the few people who could handle the intensity of my energy field was my father, and as I grew older, we spent more and more time together. I enjoyed being in his energy field because, although it was lower in vibration than my own, it was still the highest on the planet at the time. He enjoyed being around me, and he would often say I reminded him of something, but he couldn't remember what it was. I didn't understand it consciously at the time, but I reminded him of his own origin.

My father was also a being who had not been created to live on earth. He had volunteered to come to earth on a rescue mission as he conceived it. He had at the time been embodying on earth for so long that he had forgotten this and he had also lowered his energies considerably. Yet because he had held on to much of his integrity, his energy field was still much higher than any person around him.

The civilization had a very hierarchical society with my father as the undisputed supreme leader. Yet although he had unlimited power, he never abused it. He was what you might call a just and wise ruler, a philosopher-king. On a natural planet, he would have done very well and would have taken his civilization higher than when he started his reign. The difference being that on a natural planet, there are no PCBs in embodiment and therefore a ruler can afford to be just.

What I mean is that my father was just in the sense that he followed a code of ethics and the laws of society. This meant that although he suspected certain people of plotting against him, he did not use his power to get rid of them but felt he could not act until they had proven their intentions. And although this is honourable, it simply doesn't work when you are dealing with PCBs, and it became my father's downfall and the downfall of the entire civilization. But I am getting ahead of myself because in my first embodiment I had no awareness of PCBs and how different they are from what we might call natural beings. Let me instead describe what I experienced and how I looked at it.

*\*\*\**

Because I had no awareness of PCBs and how they work, I thought my father's actions were completely admirable. I had come from natural planets where beings never plot to harm others, and I could not imagine why anyone would want to do this. It was obvious to me that my father was the ruler, and furthermore he was clearly the person in the court most capable of ruling. I could not even imagine that anyone would think differently.

However, I did have certain abilities that people today consider psychic or clairvoyant. One of these was that I could both see and sense other people's energy fields. My father, for example, had the brightest energy field of any person I met during my childhood (apart from my own, but I could not see my own because I was inside it). Some of his councillors also had fairly bright energy fields, with one notable exception.

My father had an older brother who was one of the high-ranking officials in my father's government. With the sensory capability that most people have today, there would have been nothing special about this person. He looked like any other man, although he had a distinct physical appearance, being very tall and strong with a sharp profile. He also had a very intense demeanor with a strong gaze that most people could not endure for even a second.

With my sensory capabilities, I noticed something strange about this man from my early childhood. My father had an energy field that radiated light of a pure vibration, meaning clear colors. His older brother had an energy field that was so dark that it absorbed light much of the time while sometimes radiating light of lower vibrations, such as red, orange, black or muddled colors. I did not know at the time that this is one of the tell-tale signs of a PCB in embodiment.

Now, the civilization had a clearly patriarchal rule (the suppression of women had started millions of years earlier when the first PCBs embodied on the planet). The succession of the throne was determined by inheritance, meaning only a son of the previous ruler could inherit the throne. Yet it was not automatically the oldest son that would inherit. The civilization was conscious of its past, and we were taught how previous rulers had almost destroyed the civilization. This was because the oldest son of the ruler would automatically inherit the throne, even if he was unfit to rule.

Instead, my civilization had created a system where the ruler would take multiple wives and father many children. A council of elders would then select one of the sons as the next ruler based on how they saw his abilities to rule. This explains why my father had been selected as the ruler instead of his older brother. His brother had, from a superficial perspective, accepted this and had always acted with outer loyalty to my father. He had fulfilled his position very well and was extremely capable of organizing anything from affairs of state to large building projects. This was due to his uncanny ability to bend people with his will-power.

Let me insert a practical note here. My father's name in that embodiment was Jeshu and my uncle's name was Lucifer. I know this latter name (and some I will use later) causes a certain emotional reaction in today's world, but back then they caused no such reaction. I will use these names from now on in order to make it easier to identify these two beings. As will be clear, I have embodied with these two many times in many different situations, and they have not always been my father or uncle. Their names have not been the same either, but for practical purposes I will use the same names about these two beings.

\*\*\*

Due to his position, my uncle was often around whenever I had contact with my father. In the beginning, I didn't notice Lucifer paying attention to me, although I now know he was keeping a sharp eye on me from before I was born. As I grew older and my father started spending more time with me, I often noticed my uncle looking at me, and when he did so, his aura took on a deep, red hue, almost like molten lava. I knew this meant he was angry with me, but I could not see why as I could conceive of no reason for Lucifer's anger.

When I was 12, my uncle got my father's permission to take me hunting, which was a sport enjoyed by many of the people in the leadership of society. I thought nothing of it, although I had no particular interest in pursuing an animal and killing it with a spear. We were riding on animals similar to the horses of today and we were hunting animals that were somewhat similar to today's lions. We rode out in a big group, but as we encountered a pride of lions, we began to spread out.

Suddenly, I found myself in a canyon that turned out to be a dead end. As I turned my horse around and started riding out, I saw Lucifer come riding towards me with a very determined look on his face. As he came closer, he made no sound, but looked me directly in the eye with an intensity in his gaze that I had not seen before. He clearly wanted my attention, and as he came up next to me, he stopped his horse and grabbed the reigns of mine, holding us so our faces were close to each other.

He then looked me straight in the eye, and although I looked back, my peripheral vision perceived a dark energy radiating from his aura. It enveloped my body and for a moment I felt a physical paralysis. Then I thought: "What is he trying to do? Interesting, that he is directing this dark energy at me. What would happen if I directed my light energy back?"

I then focused on my heart chakra and directed the most intense energy of love towards Lucifer. This was something I had practised doing during my childhood because I had learned that some people were able to handle it and it would have a positive effect on them. For example, my father would sometimes call me to his chamber when he had been through a difficult experience, and in a few seconds of directing love at him, he would feel restored to his normal energy level. So I now directed this energy at Lucifer, and it took him a few seconds to realize that I was not responding as he clearly expected.

He then looked even more intense and clearly gathered all of his psychic power, directing an even more intense wave of dark energy at me. I felt kind of amused, as it was obvious he thought his dark energy could overpower my love, which I was convinced was an impossibility. So I directed an even more intense ray of love back, and it started dissolving the dark energy from my uncle. After a few seconds, I could see how the love energy was starting to penetrate his aura. He also sensed it, suddenly looking very agitated. After a few more seconds, there was a visible shift in his demeanor, as the intensity disappeared from his eyes and he suddenly looked like a normal man.

He was clearly shaken, but very quickly regained his composure, another hallmark of a PCB. In a split second, he took on a concerned look and said: "My prince, it can be dangerous to separate from the group, I suggest we join them again." He then let go of my horse, turned his own around and rode out of the canyon without looking back. I became aware of a very strange sensation, which I had never before experienced. Yet in my succeeding embodiments, I learned to know it well: The sense of euphoric relief one has after having escaped a very great danger.

***

Lucifer quickly disappeared from view and I slowly rode towards where I thought the group would be. After some time, I was in an area with dense brush when I heard a voice up ahead. I slowed down my horse and stopped behind a bush where I was hidden but could overlook a small clearing. Here I witnessed my uncle with one of this close subordinates. Lucifer was talking to the man in an extremely derogatory tone of voice while at the same time directing a very dark energy at him.

I could see how the energy enveloped not only the man's physical body but his entire aura. I could see how his aura literally contracted. I then saw a flame of the dark energy from my uncle form a kind of hook that was directed straight into the man's hearth center. I saw how the man completely submitted himself to my uncle and how the hook extracted a small cloud of light energy from the other person's energy field. The hook was then drawn back into my uncle's field, and for the first time I noticed (due to seeing it at a distance) how fragile and tattered Lucifer's aura looked. It was obvious that his attempt to overpower me had deprived him of energy, and he was now in the process of stealing it from the other person. When Lucifer's aura absorbed the light energy from the other person, it was quickly restored to its normal appearance.

As soon as my uncle felt this, he made some final remark and left the man, who immediately fell to the ground and looked almost dead, his aura being very scattered. I then directed love energy at the man, and within a few minutes, his aura was restored to normal. He got on his horse and rode after my uncle, neither of them having seen me.

I thought: "Was that what my uncle was trying to do to me?" Yet I realized he was not simply trying to steal energy from me. Upon reflection, I thought he might have been trying to either test me or to actually overpower me, as he had clearly overpowered his subordinate. I suspected he had been trying to bend me to his will for some purpose that clearly could not be good. In the coming time, I observed Lucifer whenever possible, and I realized all of his subordinates had submitted themselves unconditionally to him. For them, his word was the ultimate law. I was amazed and I thought: "Did he really think he could do that to me? Did he really think he could overpower me with fear-based energy and that love would submit to fear?"

Had I only realized how easily fear can overpower love on earth, I might have run away and avoided the most traumatic experience imaginable, an experience that it has taken me two millions years to rise above.

# 9

As I became older, my father and I developed a closer and closer relationship, and it became clear to many people that he was grooming me to take over the throne after him. Not that he could decide this on his own, but he was clearly educating me to be the best candidate, trusting the election council would do their work as they were charged with doing.

What I did not quite realize was that my uncle did not trust the election council. Or perhaps I should say that he did indeed trust them to choose the best candidate, but he had his own candidate and he wanted to make sure he got elected. This candidate was my father's first son, and I was aware that he and my uncle had a special relationship. I could also observe how my older brother's energy field submitted itself completely to Lucifer. I began to realize that my uncle had been furious that he was not selected as regent even though he was the first-born son. I saw how he lusted for power and how he was grooming my older brother to become regent so that Lucifer could control him.

However, because I was so innocent or naive, I could not quite see why my uncle was bothering to do this. Given that Lucifer was 22 years older than Jeshu, it was likely that my father would reign long after my uncle had died so what good would it do him to control the new regent when he was dead? I simply couldn't understand this, and the obvious explanation didn't occur to me, namely that Lucifer did not plan to let Jeshu live out his natural lifespan.

I attempted to talk to my father about what I observed in my uncle, but although he respected my observations when it came to other people, he felt a loyalty to his brother. My father was brought up to see the family as something sacred, and he refused to look objectively at his own brother. And I could not fault him. Lucifer had always shown an outer loyalty to Jeshu and to our civilization. He had performed every task he had been given very well and had always shown dedication to the state and to my father. I had no evidence against my uncle, only my clairvoyant observations, and I understood why my father wanted more. The only problem being that when the outer proof was given, it was too late to avoid the downfall of our civilization.

*\*\*\**

Shortly after I turned 18, a conflict developed between our nation and the second-largest civilization. We clearly saw ourselves as the largest and most sophisticated civilization, and as is usually the case, we had taken some privileges to which we felt entitled. As a reaction to this, a federation of smaller states had developed, and they had now become so powerful they were beginning to challenge some of our privileges. This came to a head when they attacked some of our ships and occupied some small islands that were thought to have a great mining potential.

My father first took a cautious approach and sent envoys to inquire as to the federation's grievances and their desires. It first seemed that a negotiated settlement would be possible, but soon other minor events escalated the tension. Taken at face value, these events were insignificant, but as triggers in the already tense situation, they had the potential to lead to an armed confrontation. My father knew our weapons and armed forces were superior to those of the federation, but it was difficult to evaluate how powerful their combined forces had become. He was therefore determined to do everything possible to avoid a war, even though many people in our civilization encouraged it. One of these was, needless to say, Lucifer who argued that war was inevitable and that we should strike first.

My father ignored these people and instead listened to the more moderate among our leaders who encouraged further negotiations. Jeshu went out of his way to bring about negotiations, including refraining from striking back when further armed provocations took place. He sent a delegation to the leader of the opposing side, and he invited their emperor (whose name was Satan, a name I will use from now on because I also encountered this being in many succeeding embodiments) to come to our capitol for negotiations, making him a very generous offer of concessions he was prepared to make.

While our delegation was traveling, further provocations took place and Satan used this as an excuse for why he would not leave his headquarters at such a critical time. Yet he did not close the door to negotiations but answered that they could only take place if Jeshu was willing to come to him. This was clearly a provocation, as the leader of the greatest party does not come to the leader of the smaller party, but my father still asked all of his advisors for input on whether he should accept the invitation, as it seemed to be the only way to avoid war. Most were against this, but the more peaceful were for it. These councillors felt, as my father did, that Satan was a basically honorable man and that he was sincere about negotiating.

I was somewhat surprised that my uncle did not play a very active role in the negotiations, but I did notice that his aura was even darker than normal. At a critical point in the negotiations, I saw my uncle exchange a look with my older brother, who rose and spoke before the council.

My brother said that he had received some information that Satan was suspicious of our intentions and feared for his safety. He said that knowing who we were, this was clearly ridiculous, since we would honor our word. Yet perhaps it was understandable that Satan would feel this way since he did not know us as we knew ourselves.

He then said that obviously, one could level the same suspicion against Satan, namely that he was plotting against my father. Yet my brother felt that there was no possibility that the other side, being clearly inferior in military strength, would actually dare to violate their word, as we would retaliate with our full strength in case of such a betrayal. He also said that everyone could see that if tensions continued to escalate, war was inevitable. He said he was ready to fight such a war, but if the elder people in the council wanted to make one more effort to avoid war, my brother could see only one possibility, namely that my father would accept the offer to visit the federation's capitol.

This suggestion won general approval, and I could see from my father's aura that he had already made up his mind. It therefore did no good that I later told him I felt very strongly that there would be a betrayal and that he should not go. My father did ask me for my reasons, but I could give no facts, only my very strong intuitive sense that this would have extremely severe consequences. Again, because I had no other evidence, my father said he could not go against the advice of so many people based on my intuition. And again, I could not blame him. I knew I would have chosen differently, but that was because I personally had the intuitive foreboding. If I had been in my father's position, I would have done what he did.

\*\*\*

It took about a week to arrange everything and prepare the huge delegation that would accompany Jeshu. The day before they would leave, my father called me to his office, and as I entered I found most of the members of the selection committee present. Jeshu explained that he had for some time realized that I would be the best candidate for replacing him. He said he respected the committee's authority and did not want to tell them whom to choose. But he did want them to know that I had certain intuitive abilities and that these had told him not to go. If something should happen to him, then obviously my intuition would have been proven correct, which would prove I had extraordinary abilities and was best able to rule. He wanted the committee to know this so they could make it part of their deliberations.

Jeshu then dismissed the councillors and we said our good-byes. I cried openly, as I could not hold back the feeling that something terrible would happen. It was therefore not the happiest of occasions.

***

Later that evening, I received word that my uncle had requested my presence in his office, which was located in a more secluded area of the palace. I was instantly suspicious, but because of his position, I had no reason to reject his invitation. As I entered his office, my older brother was also there. Lucifer now began one of the cleverest attempts at deception I have ever witnessed, even though I have witnessed many such attempts since then.

Lucifer presented a very convincing case that my father had developed a mental illness that meant he was no longer able to make rational decisions and understand the potential consequences. Lucifer said Jeshu was so in love with an ideal of his own benevolence that he ignored the realities of what was a danger to the state. He also presented much evidence for how Satan had plans to hold my father hostage and use it to gain an advantage in the negotiations. Lucifer explained that he had spies that had obtained Satan's plans. Satan intended to use my father to get what he wanted by negotiating. He would then kill my father afterwards. Therefore, my father was as good as dead if he left the palace.

Lucifer also said that if Satan did not get what he wanted in negotiations, he would still wage war. My uncle made it clear that Satan had become obsessed with power and did not simply want advantages but wanted to have absolute power on earth by relegating us to second position or destroying us.

I was so taken aback by this that I just sat there and listened to it all. Of course, I was also curious to see where it was leading. My uncle obviously found my silence encouraging and began to act as if we were already on the same side and were there to determine what was best for the state. He played very cleverly on the fact that he knew I was very concerned about my father leaving. During the whole session, I saw the anger in him, but I also saw how he was very careful not to direct any fear-based energy at me. He had clearly realized from our first encounter that he could not overpower me so now he was using all of his skills to persuade me. And quite frankly, had I not had the ability to read his aura, I would have been persuaded.

After some time, his real purpose was revealed. Lucifer said that according to a little-known paragraph in our constitution, it was possible to dethrone a regent if he had lost his ability to govern in the best interest of the state. However, this could only be done if two of his sons were willing to agree on this. My older brother had already agreed to support this move, and now he was asking for me to be the second son to support it. He said that this was only for the good of the state and also to save my father from his own good but naive intentions. He proposed that he himself would become temporary ruler until the selection committee could choose whether my older brother or I should be the new regent (my uncle was excluded from becoming regent because the current regent had sons of the appropriate age). He then turned to me and said with his most "endearing" tone of voice: "So what do you say, my boy, will you help us in securing a bright future for our civilization?"

At that moment, I felt how a powerful energetic hook was extended from his aura and attempted to penetrate mine. I took some seconds to answer, and said: "Uncle, you make a very convincing case." I paused and observed how his aura pulsated, as he apparently thought he had me convinced. I then continued: "Yes, you might have convinced me, if it wasn't for the fact that I have the ability to read your energy field and your hidden intentions. I have known since our hunt in the desert that you do not have good intentions towards my father. I think the only thing true in your presentation was that Satan has an obsessive desire for power. What you forgot to mention is that his obsession with power is second to your own. Therefore, I will never, ever support you in your quest ..."

I stopped, partly because I observed how a bright red glow started to emerge from his aura and partly because it had just occurred to me that I had made a fatal mistake. It became obvious to me that my uncle had revealed his intentions to me, and because I had rejected him, he could not afford to let me leave the room as I would clearly expose him to my father. Yet I barely had time to consider what his options might be when he did something that truly surprised me (mostly because I was arrogant enough to think he would not harm a person of my status).

With incredible speed, Lucifer pulled a gun from his garment and shot me with an energy ray. The energy paralyzed my body so I could not move. Yet I was still conscious and my physical senses were working so I was aware of everything that was going on. Lucifer looked my older brother straight in the eye and said: "Now you will see what happens to anyone who crosses me. Remember it well when you become regent!"

Lucifer then pressed a button on his desk and a hidden door opened behind him. Four men dressed in black clothes and hoods came out and carried me into a narrow passageway. They carried me down many stairs until we reached some basement I never knew existed. I was stripped naked and locked in a very small cell with no windows. It took only a half an hour before the effect of the energy gun wore off and I could move around in my cell. However, there was no human contact for what I estimated to be several days.

# 10

My cell turned out to be a sophisticated torture chamber. The floor, ceiling and walls were made of metal and could be heated up or cooled down so they became unpleasantly hot or cold. The temperature was changed constantly so it never felt comfortable.

I was exposed to constant noise of a kind very similar to the most aggressive forms of modern rock music. Our civilization had a good understanding of energy and knew that music has a profound effect on our four lower bodies and on the mass consciousness, even on matter itself. The kind of noise I was exposed to (it would not have been called music back then) was outlawed precisely because it had been proven to have negative effects. I was also exposed to various energy rays that were aimed at destabilizing my emotional body and overwhelming my mental body.

I was not overly concerned about all this, as I had developed some mastery over my bodily reactions and could keep my equilibrium. In the beginning I was outraged that anyone could dare to expose a prince to this kind of treatment. But I soon realized this would not make it easier for me to handle the situation so I put it aside and focused on dealing with my physical, emotional and mental bodies. I figured someone was trying to wear me down, and I was determined not to let that happen. So I focused within and controlled my bodies.

What I did not realize was that whoever was controlling the chamber was not trying to wear me down. They were trying to test me to see what I could handle, looking for any weak spots that could be exploited once the actual torture started. As I seemed to handle the temperature changes, noise and energy waves well, the walls of the chamber suddenly started moving closer together. I eventually had to stand up straight and for some seconds it seemed like the walls were going to crush me. They then stayed in a position where it took great effort to breathe.

After a very long time, the walls moved further apart, but I could not lie down or even sit cross-legged on the floor. I had to stand in a halfway upright position that quickly became so uncomfortable that my muscles would shake uncontrollably.

Again, I learned to adjust so that the discomfort was bearable. Apparently, the operator had seen what she wanted to see (I later learned it was a woman) so the chamber just kept me uncomfortable for what seemed like

2-3 days. It is amazing how you lose track of time when there is no natural light and you are constantly uncomfortable. In the beginning I felt hunger and thirst, but even that faded away because when you have not slept for more than 24 hours, all other bodily needs retreat into the background.

\*\*\*

Suddenly, the walls started moving apart and the door opened. Four people wearing hoods carried me out of the room while a fifth person stood by with an energy gun in case I should resist. They carried me to a fairly large chamber of a design with which I was somewhat familiar. The entire one side of the room was a quarter of a sphere, meaning the floor was flat but the walls formed a 180 degree circle and they curved into the vaulted ceiling. The walls were covered with the equivalent of a contemporary television screen although of a more sophisticated design and with higher resolution. The entire quarter sphere could be covered with pictures, giving the same effect as if you were standing in an actual room or outside. Many upper class homes had a similar installation, and it took watching television to a level where it felt very real and thus had greater impact on your four bodies.

On the other side of the room was an installation I had not seen before. It bore a vague resemblance to a cross made of metal. However, it had various contraptions that made it possible to strap your entire body in so you could not move very much. I was quickly strapped in so that I could not even turn my head, which was facing the screen. I then had a special kind of tape put on my eyelids so I could not close my eyes. I was thereby forced to watch the screen. I also had attached various sensors that measured the activity of my brain and nervous system.

The people left, and soon various images started filling the screen. In the beginning, they were fairly normal scenes of everyday life and various nature scenes. I assume this was to establish my normal reaction. Then, the images became more violent and displayed all kinds of aggressive acts, including people being killed, beaten, tortured or burned alive. I should mention that the noise was so loud that my whole body seemed to shake.

I was naturally shocked as I had never seen real-life situations or images like this before, but I did everything I could to keep my reaction neutral. The images changed constantly, and it was obviously a systematic check of my reactions to various forms of violence. After a long time with violent scenes, there followed scenes of a sexual nature. It started with naked women in provocative postures, then naked men, then sex scenes between men and women, women and women, men and men and a mix of all of the above. Then followed images of sadomasochistic sex, and I think there were more than 50 shades of grey. Finally, the images became more violent with rape, violent sex, child pornography, sex with children and even people being killed during or after the sex act.

Again, I was shocked. I had not yet been sexually active but obviously knew about sex. Yet I had never seen or imagined the kind of perversions displayed on the screen and I began feeling a deep sense of shock. I knew, of course, how movies can create an image that seems real although it is all faked, but this did seem very real. I felt shock that people could actually do this to others in order to make a movie, and I felt shock that someone would expose me to this.

After some time came a long section of images with people who were publicly humiliated and punished or ridiculed. This actually shocked me even more because I began to realize that whoever had come up with these images had a kind of destructive intent that I had never even imagined. I was sure these images and the chamber were not constructed just for me, and the thought of how many other people might have been exposed to this treatment gave me a clear impression of an intent that could not be entirely explained by wanting to control other people. It is one thing to want to break someone down in order to control them, but this seemed to go beyond and be driven by a desire to punish or even destroy the soul. I was deeply shocked by realizing that there was no way to reason or negotiate with people who had such complete insensitivity and such a non-compromising willingness to destroy.

I am not sure how long this all lasted. I had not slept for several days and my physical body was beginning to break down so I would occasionally black out. The images kept grinding on with new and more extreme scenes coming all the time. Although I had to watch, I eventually put myself in a half-way comatose state where I no doubt took in the images subconsciously but my conscious mind was engaged very little.

\*\*\*

Suddenly, the screen went black and the noise died out. A door opened and Lucifer came in along with a woman I had never seen before. She had a very distinct appearance with extremely pale skin and completely black hair. Her face had probably been beautiful, but it was covered in tattoos of a very strange design I had never seen before. She also had numerous piercings with rings all over her face and ears, many of them of a strange design. Interestingly, her facial expression was almost neutral, one might say as a scientist looking in a detached manner upon an experimental subject.

The woman removed the tape from my eyelids, and after I had blinked for a while, I was able to see normally. I first focused on the woman's aura and saw that it was much like my uncle's in that it did not radiate but absorbed light. However, she did not have the same anger as my uncle. It occurs to me that I should explain that normal people's auras radiate light of many different colors. For people like my uncle and the woman, their auras did not radiate this multicolored light but appeared black. Under some circumstances, the aura radiated a red, orange or even black light. The woman's aura had a certain pulsating glow, as if she had recently received a large inflow of energy. I did not realize at the time that it was energy she had stolen from me as I released it during my torture. My uncle spoke: "Well, my boy, we have learned a lot about you during these past six days." This was actually a lie, as my treatment had lasted only three days, and it was a deliberate attempt to confuse me.

"Of course, many things have happened in the big world out there as well. Would you like to see how your father has been getting along with the Emperor?" He didn't wait for an answer (and would have received none) but turned to the screen, which sprang to life. It displayed a big hall filled with people. On a stage stood a person dressed in black. I had seen still images of Satan and recognized him immediately. Yet on a still image, it is harder to read a person's aura because you cannot see how it pulsates. I now saw that Satan had an aura like my uncle's and the woman's, namely one that absorbed normal light while radiating an intense red light. Satan's anger seemed even more intense than my uncle's.

Satan was leading the crowd in a chant and I could see how the thousands of people were releasing energy through the chant that was immediately absorbed into Satan's aura. When he seemed to have gotten his fill of energy, he raised his hand and stopped the chant. He then walked to a curtain and pulled it down, revealing my father standing naked and tied to a cross-like contraption. I might add here that in our civilization, being shown naked in public was considered close to the ultimate form of humiliation. Satan said, or rather yelled: "Behold the person who considers himself the mightiest leader of the mightiest civilization on earth. Behold what happens to those who cross the Federation and its Emperor."

He made a sign and some scantily clad women appeared and started dancing an erotic dance before my father. He remained calm and was apparently able to control himself so that he did not have an erection. When it became clear that he could not be tempted into it, a jolt went through his body and from his aura I could see he had received a mild electric shock in several places. This did cause him to have an erection and the crowd laughed. One of the women began performing oral sex on him, but soon I could see the electric current had been turned off and his limb went limp. The woman moved aside and pointed demonstratively, causing the crowd to roar with laughter at the seeming impotence of the mighty ruler.

Then, the women literally sat down and defecated on the stage, picking the excrement up with their hands and smearing it all over my father's body and face. Satan made another sign and the camera moved out, showing a number of men standing on a platform above my father. They proceeded to urinate all over him, and they must have used some artificial device because no one can urinate for that long. Anyway, the crowd roared with laughter and applauded wildly.

***

At this point, Lucifer dimmed the screen and said: "My boy, I want you to know that I have for a long time been working with Satan. In fact, I was the one who trained him and later put him in position to rule the Federation. He is, therefore, under my control, and I can make him stop this humiliation of your father any time. All I want is for you to publicly denounce your father and recommend me as temporary ruler, as I have already asked you to do.

If you do not agree to do me this small favor, I cannot guarantee how far Satan will go, and your father may be seriously hurt, even killed. You should know also that our people do, of course, know that your father has been taken hostage. There is a huge outcry for using our mighty army to bring him back home, and although no one is appointed temporary ruler, there is widespread agreement that even the slightest provocation from the Federation will release a retaliatory strike. Of course, the footage you have seen has not yet been broadcast outside the hall in which it is being filmed, except for here, of course. But Satan will soon want to display his triumph to his people, and you know how quickly this will reach our people as well.

It really is up to you to stop this madness and restore order to our society and dignity to your family. I am sure you have realized by now that I cannot just be blown off, as you attempted to do in my office. So you will have to take a stand, whether you want to or not. Do you want your father dethroned but alive, or do you want him dead? The choice is up to you. What do you say, my boy?"

I said, as calmly as I could: "Tell me, Lucifer, what do you think you will get out of this? Are you not aware that the universe is like a mirror that returns to you what you do to others? Surely, you must know that every erg of energy we direct at others is returned to us multiplied? You may think you will gain a temporary advantage, but you must be aware that there is no way you can avoid the karmic return of your actions?"

This caused an intense volcano-like eruption of red-hot anger energy in Lucifer's energy field. He literally ground his teeth, but after a few seconds, he managed to speak with relative calm: "Beings of my special status have learned to dodge the karmic return by getting the people to agree with our decisions and thereby make themselves take on the karma. But you should be less concerned about the consequences for *me* and more concerned about the consequences for your father, your people or yourself. Surely, there must be something or someone in this world you care enough about to fear for their future."

I answered: "There is nothing on earth that I care enough about to compromise who I am, and giving in to you would indeed compromise who I am. I also know from observing your aura, and observing your actions over the years, that giving in to you would cause far more suffering for my father and the people. Surely, you must be intelligent enough to see that you have just told me how you get the people to take on karma by making them agree with you. Obviously, you are now trying to do the same to me."

At this point, my uncle looked like a person who realizes he has made a fatal mistake. For a split second, he appeared almost human, but then the volcano of anger spilled over and his eyes became almost insane. However, before he could speak, I continued: "I also can see that while you may think you have control over Satan, you are mistaken. You obviously have an agenda, and although I do not understand what it is, I am sure that to you it has some kind of rationality. You therefore expect Satan to also act rationally, but I can tell you from observing his aura that his ultimate motivation is the empowerment he feels by destruction.

His goal is to destroy our civilization, and he is fully prepared to destroy his own in the process. He thinks he will survive it and that he can manage to absorb much of the energy released when people are killed and complex structures broken down. Therefore, your apprentice will either control you or destroy you. Which is why I now see that it makes no difference whatsoever what I do or don't do. Your fate is sealed either way."

At this point, my uncle's aura looked like it was going to explode, but he again managed to gain some measure of self-control and turned to the woman in great anger: "What do I employ you for? You have never before been unable to find some attachment in a person. How do we break him? What does he react to?"

The woman answered: "My Lord, I have never seen a being like him. He has no attachments to anything on earth. We cannot tempt him, persuade him or force him. There is nothing he is so attached to that he will compromise for the sake of something outside himself. And he has not yet understood how karma works on earth so he does not see that you have put him in a situation where he will make karma no matter what he chooses because inaction is also making a choice.

I can only draw one conclusion from this, namely that he is an avatar. He came here with no karma and this is his first embodiment on earth. This explains why he has not formed any attachments and why he does not realize that we can force him to make karma even if he does not react for or against us."

My uncle turned and looked at me with a penetrating gaze. Then he said with a strange form of excitement, bordering on exuberance: "Of course, how blind I have been that I have not seen this earlier. The boy stuck out from the crowd from the moment he was born."

He turned to the woman and said: "Do you know what this means? His father, Jeshu, was also an avatar and came to earth a long time ago. It was my mentor who tempted him into a reactionary pattern that has made it possible for our brotherhood to manipulate him. My mentor used to tell me what a triumph it had been for him when he finally managed to break an avatar and draw him into a reactionary pattern. Jeshu released so much light that my mentor was drunk with it for a hundred years and could greatly increase his powers.

This changes everything. Nothing really matters anymore in the outer situation. What is the power over civilizations compared to having power over an avatar? No power compares. It is like having power over god, or at least a part of god.

I need time to figure out how to deal with this because I need to contact my mentor, and I cannot do this while I have to be concerned about outer matters."

"But my Lord," said the woman, "decisions have to be made in order to avoid a war. What will you say to the council and how will you deal with Satan?"

My uncle looked annoyed and said: "You will have to communicate with both. Tell the council not to do anything for 24 hours. Tell Satan the same. Tell him I have discovered something that will be a great advantage for both of us, but I need time to deal with it so he needs to keep the status quo for that long. I will be in my sanctuary and I do not want to be disturbed under any circumstance."

# 11

My uncle hurriedly left and the woman, who called herself Maleve, turned to me and said: "Well, my sweet avatar, it seems I have you all to myself for 24 hours. But I think we have to get you into better shape before we have some fun."

She called some guards who set me free me and carried me into a normal-looking room with a bathroom, table and bed. Maleve told me to take a shower and when I was done, there was food waiting on the table. I hurriedly ate something and then went to bed where I fell asleep almost immediately.

In my civilization we had beds that used a combination of magnets and energy rays to give us a much more efficient sleep, meaning we could sleep less than six hours and still be rested. I did sleep longer, but when I awoke, I felt reasonably rested.

I realized I had awoken because Maleve was holding a jar under my nose that contained an incredibly pungent substance. She gave me a suggestive look and said: "Well, my sweet avatar, let me take you for a little ride."

At this point I realized I was in a different room, lying on my back in a large bed. As I tried to move, I realized I was tied to the bed so I could barely move. Needless to say, I was naked.

Maleve went to the end of the bed and started taking off her clothes very slowly while making suggestive gestures and giving me looks. It soon became clear that the tattoos and piercings were not limited to her face and head but pretty much covered her body. I realized it must have the purpose of changing the energy flow through her four lower bodies, but I had no interest in exploring the topic further.

Maleve tried her best to engage me, but I refused to be tempted and avoided having an erection, even when she started touching me. I realized she must have given me some chemical in the food because my body was unusually sensitive to touch. Yet I had no problem keeping myself from being tempted by her.

"Well, isn't that interesting," she said, "it seems an avatar cannot be tempted by conventional means. Well, we will just have to take heaven by force then, won't we."

She then pulled out a device that was used instead of the injection needles used today. It could insert a chemical substance into your bloodstream without puncturing the skin and veins. She held it up to the vein on my arm and pushed the button. I could feel how a hot liquid entered my blood and started spreading. As it reached my loins, I quickly had a huge erection. Maleve then climbed on top of me an inserted my limb into her vagina. She started moving up and down with increasing speed and was soon screaming with pleasure.

I was completely unengaged at the emotional, mental and identity level, but my physical body was reacting on its own. Within a fairly short time, Maleve had one of the most violent orgasms I have ever seen, and my physical body ejaculated. I can't call it an orgasm because it was purely physical.

I thought she would stop, but my limb was still hard and she kept moving, having a whole series of orgasms. The session must have lasted well over an hour and I soon gave up counting how many orgasms she had. As it was going on, my mind was calmly observing the process, and I realized that even though I was not engaged or having any pleasure from the interaction, energy or light was still being forced out of my chakras and she was absorbing it, becoming literally drunk with it. Maleve was finally so agitated by the energy that she could not stand it anymore and jumped off. She laid down next to me, looked me in the eye and said: "Well, my dear avatar, you have just received a lesson in how the physical body can be used to force you to release light even when you do not want to. Sex is just such a close physical encounter that you cannot do it without releasing your light to the other party. Assuming you have any light to release, of course. Now you know the main reason for most of the sex in the world: Someone is trying to steal the energy of someone else.

You will soon learn that there are other ways to use the physical body to force a release of light, but I will let Lucifer take care of that part of the educational process."

Maleve then ran out of the room while laughing hysterically. I noticed her aura was pulsating very rapidly but still not giving out any light of pure colors. I could feel almost like an empty hole in my own aura and I became aware that my base chakra was spinning the opposite way of normal.

***

After a few hours, Maleve came back, gave me a new injection and repeated the process. Yet this time she could not go on as long, but had to break off after half an hour. I noticed there was a great upheaval in her aura, and she looked physically sick as she staggered out of the room.

I fell asleep and after several hours, I was awakened by four men who came in and carried me back to the room where I had the latest encounter with Lucifer. They strapped me into the device as before, and they had barely finished when Lucifer came in, looking like he was very pleased with himself.

His smug look was replaced by a scowl when he saw I looked clean and rested. He turned to the guards and commanded them to get Maleve. It took some time before she came, and she could barely walk into the room. Lucifer asked what she had to say for herself and she answered calmly: "My Lord, I have simply done what you told me to do, namely study him to learn his reactions."

To my surprise, this made Lucifer laugh and he said: "Well, you always were good with a quick answer, and I can see you have already been punished. When I said my mentor used Jeshu's light for a long time, it was because he took it in only in small portions instead of seeking to absorb too much at one time. Your aura now has the same reaction as if you are cleansing your body and too many toxins are flushed out at once. Well, stay and observe, as I have a go."

Lucifer then pushed a button and I realized the contraption I was tied to was on a platform that could rotate. It turned 180 degrees and I was suddenly facing a large room with rows of seats, arranged like an amphitheater. I was standing on a stage that was elevated above the floor. In the room were seated about 200 people, all dressed in dark robes with hoods.

Lucifer made a sign, and four hooded men carried a young girl onto the stage. She was naked and I recognized her as the daughter of one of the ministers in my father's government. She was about 15. She looked conscious and very scared, but also as if she had little power to resist.

Lucifer pushed a button and a strange-looking table emerged from the platform. It was located right in front of the contraption holding me. The four men strapped the young girl to the table so she could barely move. She was leaning forward and her legs were spread out. Lucifer then pushed another button, and I was lowered so the girl's face was very close to mine. I was looking straight into her fearful eyes, and she was whispering: "'Help me, please help me."

Without any words, Lucifer made another sign and the crowd started chanting a very strange, rhythmic chant I had never heard before. Even for me, it felt like a very unpleasant energy and the young girl became terrified. The chant when on for about ten minutes, and then a row of men started moving up towards the stage. One of them went behind the young girl, pulled up his robe and raped her. When he was done, the next man moved in and did the same. As this was happening, the chanting became louder and louder, sounding more and more ecstatic, as if all of the people in the audience were having orgasms from watching. Needless to say, the young girl was screaming right into my face, pleading for me to help her, while clearly not seeing I was in no position to do so.

After about a dozen men had raped the girl, Lucifer made another sign and the chanting and the rape stopped. Lucifer stepped up to me and spoke with a voice that was clearly affected by him taking pleasure in the spectacle: "Well, my boy, you have now seen that I, and our little brotherhood here, have no compunctions about hurting people. We can go on with this for as long as it takes, or at least until the girl here can take no more and dies. Of course, then we have other girls.

Yet *I* am not the one deciding how long this will go on. *You* are the one deciding. You have the power to stop this any time. All I want from you is that you say to me: 'Lucifer, I worship you as the supreme authority on earth and I promise to obey you forever.' Is that so much to ask in order to save the life of a young, beautiful girl?"

He paused and clearly expected me to say something. I remained silent because I had seen in his aura that he had no intention of saving the girl's life. She was a witness that had to be silenced for good. Furthermore, I could see he had a hidden intent, but I could not grasp what it was. I knew he was trying to manipulate me, but because I had no understanding of how his kind of beings were thinking, I simply could not fathom what he was hoping to gain.

I was deliberating in my mind what his purpose could possibly be, but I had no frame of reference because his mind worked in a way that was so fundamentally different from mine. The big question that flashed in my mind was: "How can he possibly believe he will gain any advantage from this?"

What I did not realize at the time was that in formulating this question, I had tied myself karmically to Lucifer. Not in the sense that I had done something to him for which I needed to compensate, but in the sense that I had formulated a desire to understand him. I also had the hope that if

I could understand him, I might be able to help him see the error of his thinking so he could liberate himself from the mental prison I perceived him to be trapped in. I could clearly see that his aura was a very unpleasant place to be and that he had no way to free himself from it. In my arrogance, I thought that if I could help him see the error of his thinking, he would want to be free from his prison. It took me one and a half million years to understand how Lucifer and beings like him think. It took me even longer to realize that I had no chance of helping them whatsoever.

***

My thoughts were interrupted when Lucifer said loudly: "Well, my boy, will you surrender to me or shall we continue?"

I looked him straight in the eye and said: "Please tell me what you think you will gain from this?"

He looked very pleased with himself, as if he felt I had gone right into his trap and said: "I simply want you to swear to serve me and do everything I say. How big of a sacrifice is that for you, compared to the ragnarok I am prepared to unleash if you do not obey? How selfish can you be in denying me this and thereby being directly responsible for the suffering of so many people? I thought you had come here to help free people from the suffering of this planet, and I am offering you a very direct way to free this young girl and our people from suffering."

I looked him straight in the eye, and the words came to me from deep within my being: "The suffering you can unleash with your present power is nothing compared to what you will unleash if I surrender to you and give you access to misuse my light in order to gain power over others."

Lucifer looked completely shocked, and I probably did too because I had no idea at the time where the words came from. They certainly did not come from my conscious mind, which was deeply confused over seeing the evil intent of Lucifer. I simply could not fathom that any being could have such complete insensitivity to others and such unrestricted willingness to cause them suffering. I could not fathom what anyone would get out of this.

Lucifer quickly gathered himself and said: "Well, let us just see how long you can keep up this arrogance to the suffering of others. And remember, that only *you* have the power to stop this."

He made a sign, and the chanting started again. So did the rape, but the young girl had gotten into her mind that I could stop the rape and she was screaming at me to make them stop. As the rape went on, she became more hysterical, starting to blame me and calling me selfish, arrogant and insensitive. And I probably *was* insensitive because I paid little attention to her.

This was in large part because at this point, I was in a state of shock. My own treatment had not really shocked me because I was not that concerned about how it would affect me. Yet watching the girl suffer so severely made me realize that Lucifer really had no sensitivity to life what-soever. I, of course, had with me the sensitivity to life that is normal on a natural planet. I did not want the girl to suffer and would gladly have done anything to save her. Yet I sensed that no matter what I did, it would not save her and it certainly would not save others in the long run.

So I was facing a dilemma, and the PCBs are experts at putting all of us in situations where it seems like no matter what we do or don't do, it will have unbearable consequences. Because I had not been on earth before that lifetime, I had not developed any close bonds with anyone so I had no personal attachment to the girl. That is why I am saying that according to a normal, human perspective, I was indeed insensitive to her. I realized she was simply a tool for Lucifer, and so was I.

This, of course, was a state of mind that was utterly alien to me. I simply could not imagine what kind of being would deliberately use another human being as a tool, even to the point of being willing to torture and kill that person in order to accomplish an end. I had never before encountered such total disrespect for the free will of others, as beings on natural planets have total respect for other people's free will. So my feelings were on overload with compassion, my mental body was paralyzed by the dilemma of what to do, but the most numbing aspect of the situation was that my identity body was unable to figure out what kind of being Lucifer was and what kind of being I was in relation to a being like Lucifer. I could see that there was no way Lucifer could be the same type of being as myself or Jeshu, but then what other kind of being is there in human bodies?

I knew who I was on a natural planet. I had lived a very protected life on earth up until that point and had not seen some of the more shady or brutal aspects of our civilization. So I had built a sense of identity as a human being on earth based on a very naive and idealized view of what this planet was like. This view had now been totally shattered, and I was struggling to find out what kind of being I really was when faced with this kind of unimagined brutality and insensitivity to life.

My mind was racing, trying to figure out what was actually going on in the situation. I clearly sensed a radical danger in surrendering myself to Lucifer and promising to obey him. Yet I was trying to figure out if I could make the promise to him and then just walk away from it when he had stopped torturing the girl. I could not at the time see why I shouldn't be able to change my mind and undo a choice I had made under duress.

Yet I also sensed that if I did so, what was to stop Lucifer from torturing other people? I knew that if I gave in once, he would know that he could force me again so how could I actually get away from him? I even considered if making the promise and later killing myself was a way to stop the torture and run away from my promise. Yet I also sensed that I would then have to reembody with Lucifer, and the situation might repeat itself.

I clearly knew there was something here I had to figure out, but I also sensed that I simply did not have the knowledge I needed in order to make the right choice in the situation. While I was thinking about this, trying to play out various scenarios in my mind, the rape went on until the young girl literally died before my eyes. I had observed that for each rape her aura had become more and more scattered, and in the end it was completely shattered into so many pieces that it apparently was not enough for her to stay in the body. I watched her soul leave the body and disappear from my view, leaving an empty shell that looked incredibly lifeless. I later learned that many people still look alive right after the body dies, but this girl's body looked as if every erg of life-giving energy had been sucked out of it.

At the same time, the men who had raped her had all absorbed some of her light and their auras were now pulsating. I was shocked to see that while some of the men had auras like Lucifer, that did not radiate light, some of them had normal auras. I could not fathom how they could get themselves to do something like this. I even noticed that while these people had received light from the girl, there was also light going out of their auras to Lucifer. I then realized that they had been overpowered by Lucifer to do this and that he could then steal their light when they violated others. It was not much of a leap to realize the same would happen to me if I surrendered to Lucifer.

***

Lucifer made a sign and four men carried the dead body out of the room while there seemed to be a changing of the guard in the audience. The men who had raped the girl left and others came in. Lucifer spoke again, and he was clearly intoxicated with all of the energy released in the session: "Well, my sweet prince, it seems I have underestimated you. I thought for sure that an avatar who comes here to save people from their suffering would take the opportunity to save one who is so obviously suffering by no fault of their own.

Yet I hope you are beginning to realize that on earth there are different rules than on other planets. On this planet, there are situations where doing nothing still causes you to make karma. Oh yes, I know you will say that I was the one who caused the young girl to be killed, but you could have stopped it and therefore you have also made karma. You may think I made the bigger portion of karma, but I can assure you it is like a drop in the ocean compared to what I have already made. And I will get away with it too, for nothing can hold me accountable on this planet.

You, on the other hand, came here thinking you could remain non-attached and avoid getting your hands dirty. You came here with the arrogant attitude that you were superior to any being on earth and that you could save people without making any karma yourself. Yet you have just made your first karma so how does it feel, my sweet avatar, to have sullied yourself as all other people on this planet? How does it feel to suddenly have become no better than a human being? How will you ever return to your lofty estate and escape the stain that all other people have?"

At this point, he laughed hysterically, and I again looked him in the eyes and said: "Lucifer, I take upon myself none of your karma. It is *your* karma and yours alone, let it all be upon your head!"

He became greatly enraged and screamed at me: "Well, then, let us up the ante and see how long you can keep up this arrogance!"

He made a sign and four men carried my mother into the room. She was naked and they strapped her to the table in the same position as the young girl. Lucifer then explained to her that I was refusing to submit to him and that it was up to my mother to try to persuade me to change my mind. He made another sign and the first man stepped behind my mother and started raping her. As the man penetrated her, she screamed and Lucifer told her that only I had the power to stop this and that she needed to make me understand this.

There now followed a very long session where my mother tried to persuade me to give in to Lucifer's demands in order to save her. She first argued that because she had given me life, I owed her this much and used other similar arguments. She then became angry and started blaming me for being selfish, egotistical, arrogant, narcissistic and every other name in the book. I tried to explain to her that Lucifer would kill her anyway, but she at first refused to believe me.

During the session, I tried to send her love energy, as I had done to many people during my youth, but it had no effect as she was too agitated to absorb it. (I had tried to do this to the girl also, but soon realized the men raping her absorbed it and that it would only prolong her suffering.) I noticed that seeing my mother being raped had a greater impact on me than seeing a young girl I did not know. I felt how more light was being forced out of my chakras, as when I had been raped by Maleve. I was wondering if this was what Lucifer had meant by saying I could not avoid making karma? It was clear to me that some of the energy was being stolen by Lucifer and he would be able to use it to increase his power over others.

Because my mother had been sexually active and had a more dense aura than the young girl, she could withstand a lot more rapes without having her aura shattered. But finally the pain became so intense that she completely lost control and screamed hysterically for what seemed like a very long time. Suddenly, she fell silent, then looked at Lucifer and yelled at him: "How could you do this to me; you promised that no harm would come to me. How could you to this to your own son, how can you do this to your own flesh and blood?"

Upon hearing this, Lucifer with great speed pulled out a small knife and slit her throat while screaming: "You keep your mouth shut, you dirty whore, you have no right to ruin my plans . . ." He then stopped, as if he realized he had said too much. My mother drew her last breath while looking into my eyes, her blood spraying all over my face, running into my mouth.

\*\*\*

Lucifer had my mother's body carried out and then turned to me: "Well, my boy, I see that we got more of a reaction from you this time. How does it feel to give your light to someone like me, knowing how I am willing to abuse it? It is still *your* light, and you are responsible for what you do with it."

I asked him: "Is it true what my mother said that you are my biological father?"

He first looked angry, but then pulled himself together, which gave me the impression of watching a snake just before is strikes: "Yes, my boy, she was right. I was instrumental in making her father offer her as a wife to your father. Jeshu accepted, not because he was particularly attracted to her but for political reasons. I made a deal with her to let me impregnate her after the wedding night. I thought that by giving your father a son with my own genetic material, I could control you through my genes. Yet that was before I realized you were an avatar. Had I known that, I would have known that your consciousness was too high to be ruled by your genes and I would not have bothered. After all, I already had your oldest brother.

Well, I see that because you have seen what I am capable of doing, knowing I am your father makes no difference to you. You still see Jeshu as your father so let us see how you respond to him."

He then made a sign, and four men carried my father into the room, strapping him to the table. At the same time, there was another changing of the guard, and the men who now entered the room had even darker auras than the ones who had raped the two women.

My father looked me straight in the eye and before anyone could react, he said: "Whatever they do to me, do not give in to Lucifer. Do not let him drag you into reacting against him. I am already dead so do not be concerned about me but stay away from making karma with Lucifer. Do this for me!"

Lucifer was obviously taken by surprise, and it took him a few seconds to react. He slapped my father across the mouth and the crowd then started another form of chant that sounded even darker than the previous one. Man after man came up to the table and raped my father who remained silent during the entire ordeal. I also remained silent and sent my father love energy, which he absorbed and used to put himself into a state where his aura was barely affected by the rape.

After a long time, there came a point where the 200 men had all raped my father, some of them more than once, and they simply could not go on. Lucifer had looked increasingly angry, as he realized his scheme was not working. He finally flew into a rage and punctured one of my father's neck arteries, causing him to bleed out very slowly in front of my eyes. His last words were: "Do not give in!"

My father and I looked into each others eyes for what seemed to be an eternity, and this formed a very strong bond between us that caused us to reembody together many, many times right up until the beginning of the modern age. As my father drew his last breath, the thought came to me: "What can Lucifer possibly do next?"

# 12

At this point, the energy in the room had shifted and become much more dark. It seemed that even though a large portion of light energy had been released, the actions performed had also generated a dark energy that was now weighing down everyone present, making their auras look almost lifeless.

Lucifer had my father's body carried out of the room. Some people came in and washed the stage off with water hoses, washing the blood off me also. The men who had raped my father left and a fresh set of people came in. They were dressed in long robes and hoods, but it was obvious from their movements and auras that they were women. They started to chant, a lighter form of chant than the previous ones, and it started to lighten the energy in the room.

Lucifer still looked half-dead, and he made a sign to Maleve. Without any words, she pulled off her robe and walked naked to the table in front of me where she bent own. Lucifer pulled up his robe and had sex with her without strapping her in. They both had an orgasm at the same time and I could see how some of the energy Maleve had stolen from me was transferred to Lucifer, empowering him to go on. He turned to me and said: "Well, my son, it seems I cannot get you to submit to me and swear me allegiance. A father should be able to expect that much from his son, but clearly you do not feel bound by anything on earth. However, you are indeed bound to your physical body, and there are amazing things we can do to the physical body in order to affect the three higher bodies."

He made another gesture, and a person came in wearing a black box. Lucifer opened it and took out an instrument that looked much like the whips known from the Middle Ages. It had a handle made of one artificial material and nine straps made of another material. At the end of each strap was a small metal ball. Lucifer pressed a button and the contraption holding me was raised so that my full body was above the stage. I was standing naked, front forward in a position similar to Leonardo's Vetruvian man.

Without any further words, Lucifer then started whipping me, and the very first blow sent a pain through my body that was worse than anything I had experienced previously. During the previous days, I had experienced quite a lot of bodily pain, but I had been able to deal with it, and I had half-way thought I would be able to handle any pain inflicted upon my physical body. The moment those nine metal balls hit my genital area, I realized I had been wrong.

I managed to avoid screaming, and I kept this up for quite some time. Lucifer had obviously expected me to scream from the first blow, and he became visibly upset when that did not happen. Yet he kept his composure and systematically whipped me so that the skin on the entire front of my body and face was ripped and bleeding. He then started to hit the same areas again, and this was an entirely new level of pain.

It is a sad fact of the physical body that even though the skin and the flesh can be destroyed, the nerves continue to function. The first time the whip hit an area, it caused excruciating pain, but the succeeding times were far worse.

Lucifer revealed his truly sadistic nature in that he did not whip me uncontrollably. He made a pause between the blows. This had the effect that the nervous system was just starting to relax when the next blow came, and this made the pain even worse. Pretty soon, there was a purely bodily reaction that expected the next blow, and I simply could not keep myself from screaming.

Lucifer kept going for what seemed like a very long time, although he also looked more and more depleted with each blow. After some time, the pain was no longer only physical but released an emotional reaction that I could not control. It started like a great sense of injustice that this was happening, but eventually changed into a white-hot anger. The anger released certain thoughts about why this was allowed to happen, and eventually even my identity body started questioning why I had come to a planet like this.

It wasn't just the physical pain that affected my higher bodies. Everything that Lucifer and Maleve had done and said previously now started having an effect on my higher bodies. They way the PCBs bring pain to your physical body is, of course, through physical means. They way they bring pain to your emotional body is to do physical acts that shock you (such as raping or killing other people in front of you) or to accuse you of being wrong. It doesn't matter what they accuse you of or whether it is true, all that matters is that they accuse you with enough force so that your emotional body will react. The way they bring pain to your mental body is to do or say something that makes you doubt anything and everything you believe in. Again, it doesn't matter whether what they say is true or not. Finally, the way to bring pain to your identity body is to tell you that you are a fundamentally flawed being, that you have no right to be here or that you have no right to express your light. The reason this works is simple. When you have some sense of the oneness of all life, as I had taken with me from the natural planets, you will be sensitive to what other beings say to you. You cannot ignore it or brush it aside. You can have a sense that it is not right that they are attacking you with such aggression and force, but you simply cannot stop yourself from wondering why they are doing this. You cannot fathom how one part of life can do this to another part of life, and it makes you curious to understand why they are doing this. It is also very difficult to avoid considering whether you have done something to make them feel so threatened by you. You could not imagine doing this to others or being so angry with others so you have to wonder if you have done anything to provoke their anger. All of this opens your three higher bodies to their influence.

I was not aware of this at the time, but on my previous planets, I had (as I said) never experienced a reverse energy flow. I had always had the energy flow from my I AM Presence into my identity body, from there to the mental, from there to the emotional and finally into the physical. On a natural planet, nothing in the physical octave had affected my three higher bodies. Now, I was experiencing energy flowing from the physical body and literally taking over my three higher bodies. This greatly reinforced the physical discomfort and it quickly became completely unbearable.

The effect was that there came a point of total pain. My physical nervous system was experiencing more pain than it could handle, but so were my three higher bodies. I had reached a state of total pain in all four of my lower bodies, and the formless self simply could not bear to be in those bodies. Without any conscious thought, my Conscious You withdrew, and I was no longer aware of what was happening.

I have later learned that Maleve was observing my aura and saw when this happened. She then signalled Lucifer who stopped whipping me. He then walked very close to me where he started talking to me with great intensity. At the same time, the women in the room started chanting words that were similar to what Lucifer was saying.

You might recall me saying that your conscious self is supposed to be in command over what you take into your four lower bodies and that nothing is allowed to enter against your choosing. Well, the exception is that if you are brought to this state of total pain, your Conscious You will withdraw, and this will give unrestricted access to your four lower bodies. We might say that even though the conscious self is not making a free choice to withdraw, it is still making a choice. Of course, no normal being would ever do this to another, but the PCBs are not normal beings. They have learned to do something that no one had predicted would be done when our four lower bodies were designed.

\*\*\*

What Lucifer and his congregation did was to program certain matrices into my four lower bodies. The purpose was simple: to destroy my four bodies (my soul) so that I could not fulfil the purpose for which I came here. Lucifer saw my light as a threat. Ideally, he would have liked to steal it by making me submit to his will, thereby being able to use my light for his purposes. Since he decided that he could not achieve this, he instead attempted to make sure that I could never again express my light on earth. He literally attempted to insert blocks or devices that would make it impossible for me to receive and express the high-frequency energy from my I AM Presence.

Lucifer and the congregation worked systematically on each of my four lower bodies, and they used a system of black magic that had not been developed by Lucifer himself. He had received it from his mentor who had again received it from *his* mentor. The system had been handed down for a very long time among the PCBs. It was already quite developed when the first PCBs came to earth. Since then, it has been used to attack and either suppress, destroy or manipulate each avatar who has come to this planet. I will later explain why this is done, but for now let me stay with the story of my first embodiment because I did not learn these things until much later.

Lucifer used numerous tricks to program my four lower bodies, including inserting certain statements in my emotional, mental and identity bodies. These were all of a derogatory nature, and there were too many to mention. The following is just a small selection in order to give you a feel for the purpose and the intent behind it.

- You were wrong in coming to earth. You have no right to be on this planet.

- Your light is not wanted here and you have no right to express it.

- Earth is ruled by free will, and we have a right to rule this planet without being disturbed by beings like you.

- God has given planet earth to us and you have no right to interfere with our free will.

- The people of earth have chosen to submit themselves to us and you have no right to save them. It is against *their* free will and *our* free will and thus it is against the law of god.

- You are such a pathetic idiot for thinking you can come here and save people. We have them completely trapped and there is nothing you can do to set them free. They are so programmed that they don't even *want* to be free from us.

- You are a no-good being and now you realize you have no power on earth.

- You are powerless to defeat us because you are not prepared to do the things we are willing to do.

- Matter is so dense on earth that your light cannot even free the people. They are far too trapped and we are in complete control of this planet.

- By coming here you have violated the Law of Free Will. By seeking to free the people, you have violated *their* free will and *our* free will. Therefore, you have already made karma by coming into embodiment.

- Coming here was a total mistake because you were blinded by the arrogance of thinking you could save people against their free will. You can never undo that mistake.

- By reacting to us, by engaging with us, you have made karma. You have been stained as we are stained, and there is no power at your disposal that can ever free you from this stain.

• There is nothing you can do to undo your mistake. Earth is so dense that you cannot undo your mistakes.

• You are trapped on earth forever, as the ignorant people are trapped forever.

• We are the rightful rulers of this planet. Our words is the law on this planet.

• We have created our own laws and by entering a physical body, you have made yourself subject to our laws.

• You have made such a fatal mistake that nothing could ever make it good again.

• You might as well accept that you are lost forever, for nothing will ever make you pure again.

• You are a completely selfish and insensitive being. You are thinking only about yourself.

• You saw people killed before your eyes and you could have stopped it but you did nothing. What kind of being would do that?

• You don't care about other human beings. You only care about yourself.

\*\*\*

You get the general idea. The PCBs have made themselves the undisputed rulers of earth and they have trapped humankind as their slaves. An avatar comes here to free the people, but the PCBs will do anything to prevent this by seeking to destroy you and program you to think you have no right to be here, to challenge the PCBs or free the people. They even want you to believe that coming here was a violation of the Law of Free Will and that you have made karma and been stained just by coming here. They want you to believe that the people do not actually want to be free.

Lucifer, Maleve and their companions continued this programming for almost 48 hours, having new people come in and do the chanting at regular intervals. They kept my conscious self out of my four lower bodies by a combination of whipping me and spraying my wounds with salt water. I was, of course, unaware of what happened so I did not realize that they had intended to continue even longer. They were interrupted because Satan lost his patience and did something Lucifer had not foreseen—as I had predicted.

# 13

Satan had his spies in our government and among the people who helped Lucifer. Lucifer had created a semi-religious cult around himself, and an elaborate initiation ritual was required in order to become a member. Yet precisely because it was a secret cult, it had been easy for Satan to place a mole inside of it. He therefore knew Lucifer had killed my father and he knew Lucifer had become obsessed with me. He also knew that our government and armed forces were somewhat paralyzed by the fact that my father was missing and that no new leader had been appointed. The strength of any dictatorship is that if the leader is decisive, a lot can get done. The weakness is that when the leader does not make decisions, *nothing* gets done.

Satan saw this as the opportunity he had been waiting for, and he launched a first strike against our armed forces with most of the weapons available to him. His aim was to take out our ability to strike back and then present us with an ultimatum, demanding that we surrender or he would expose us to "total annihilation."

Lucifer had been completely taken aback by this because he thought he had Satan under his control. This is a typical pattern among PCBs. Lucifer had been a tutor or guru for Satan, and he did this for various reasons. One was pure vanity and pride. Lucifer felt so superior to human beings that he realized they could not appreciate how sophisticated he was. Only by taking on a student and raising him or her to see his real mastery, could Lucifer feel truly appreciated. Yet because PCBs never have any real loyalty amongst each other, the student will often come to think he or she is superior to the master and will grab the first opportunity to take over the master's position.

You can see this in known history. One power elite group is the established elite and another forms the aspiring elite. When the opportunity seems right, the aspiring elite will seek to take power from the established elite. This will often lead to open conflict that can mean the destruction of the established elite, the aspiring elite or both. In the worst of circumstances, it can mean the destruction of the entire civilization or even the planet's ability to sustain life. One modern example is the conflict between the Catholic church and scientific materialists, another is the fight between capitalism and communism.

Once they stopped whipping me, it did not take long before I regained consciousness. I was still in very severe pain, but it was not the total pain and I was very much back in my four lower bodies. I had been placed in a small steel cage and the cage was situated in a corner of our command bunker. I therefore had full view of how Lucifer reacted to this. Before I came back to consciousness, Lucifer had managed to insert himself as leader and get all of our generals and most of our politicians to submit to his leadership. He had also killed three of his personal aides in his anger over Satan's betrayal.

My first memories is of a group of generals sitting at a table around Lucifer and discussing how to respond. Behind them was another of the large screens, upon which they could display images of various locations and the condition of our remaining armed forces. It became clear that although Satan's first strike had dealt a severe blow to our military, we still had plenty of capability to retaliate. Lucifer was obviously completely enraged by Satan's betrayal (as he saw it) and was arguing for a full-scale retaliation. Yet he was rational enough to ask the generals to asses our capabilities versus the remaining capabilities of the Federation.

The discussion went back and forth, and it soon became clear that there were two groups. One wanted a retaliatory strike and the other wanted to negotiate. The first group argued that we had enough capability left to win a war with the Federation, even though their forces were intact. The other group thought we could not win, but because the Federation had depleted its arsenal to launch the first strike, Satan would be willing to negotiate.

Each group was led by one general, and I noticed that each of them had a "black hole aura," like Lucifer. I have later been able to look at the energetic records and see that the general who wanted to negotiate was loyal to Satan. The general who wanted to strike back was loyal to himself and was hoping to take Lucifer's position. He thought that whether or not the strike was successful, he could use the confusion to kill Lucifer and claim the throne. This was clearly madness (given our laws), but madness does not exclude achievement, as has been proven by many PCBs throughout history.

This general argued that it was a known fact that our military was superior to that of the Federation. Therefore, in order to destroy as much of our military as possible, Satan would have had to use everything he had, meaning his arsenal was so depleted that we could actually win even though our forces had been reduced. This argument seemed to sway most of the generals, but then the general loyal to Satan spoke.

He said that he had received information from his spies that Satan had developed a doomsday weapon. This was a nuclear weapon of such power that it could create a chain-reaction that could unleash destruction on a planetary scale. Our civilization had for a long time had the capability to develop such a weapon (a more primitive form of which was actually developed by the Soviet Union). We had not done so for the simple reason that we felt we had such military capacity that we did not need it and because the consequences of using it would be too destructive to ourselves. The general argued that he was in agreement that we could probably win a war with the Federation, and if Satan felt he had his back against the wall, he would therefore use his doomsday bomb.

What followed was a heated discussion about whether the Federation really had such a weapon. This was denied by most, and some even denied that its effects were as devastating as claimed. Even in my debilitated state, I could see the conflict in the general's aura. He clearly knew that Satan had the weapon and was willing to use it. Yet he could not reveal this without giving himself away as knowing something he could have learned only from the opposing side. So he had to sit there and hold his tongue, meaning he lost the argument. After some time, Lucifer cut through the discussion and ordered a full retaliation with all the forces we had left.

*** 

It took some hours to prepare for the attack, but it was soon launched. We could follow the result somewhat on the giant screen. The attack involved our equivalent of today's hydrogen and neutron bombs and an array of sophisticated energy weapons. The effects were truly devastating and hundreds of millions of people died in a single night, most of them civilians.

The Federation had greater capabilities than our generals had anticipated, and for two days it seemed the battle was raging back and forth with no clear winner. Then it became clear that our forces were gaining the upper hand, and as soon at this was established, Lucifer took another step that exposed his true being. In areas where the Federation's army was destroyed or retreating, he ordered our forces to use their weapons in a purely punishing action against cities full of civilians. In the span of one day, over one hundred million civilians were killed in one of the biggest bloodbaths this planet has ever seen. I was amazed to see how Lucifer absorbed so much energy that his aura began to glow with a red energy that seemed to almost be a fire beyond fire, like burning plasma.

After three days, all the generals assembled in the command center, and then an image of Satan appeared on the giant screen. He and Lucifer then engaged in one of the most bizarre discussions I have witnessed in two million years. Lucifer and Satan traded insults, called each other names as two schoolboys and chided each other for their failings and mistakes. The generals were completely dumbfounded and sat there and watched with open mouths. I would have been surprised too if I had not been able to see their auras. Beyond the spoken words, there was an intense battle fought with psychic energy.

The pretext of the meeting was to negotiate an end to hostilities, but it was clear that none of the two had any intentions of negotiating. Instead, the real purpose of the meeting was that each of them believed they could overpower the other with psychic means. The arrogance that radiated from both of them was astounding, but it was overshadowed by the hostility and hatred that shot our of their auras as missiles of energy. The battle went on for a long time with none of them seeming to get a decisive advantage.

Then, it was as if Lucifer decided he had played enough, and it seemed like he threw away the veil that had been hiding some of his powers. I had never before seen such a display of psychic power because this never takes place on a natural planet. I can only say that it was even more frightening than all of the physical battles and killing I had witnessed in the days before. Lucifer suddenly seemed much bigger and his aura was filled with this intense, plasma-hot energy that he shot at Satan like a burning flame. Obviously, Satan had completely overestimated his own powers and underestimated those of Lucifer because he literally fell over and was rolling around on the floor in great agony. Mind you, the two were not in the same room and this happened over a distance of thousands of kilometers.

Over what seemed like a very long time, the stream of energy from Lucifer held Satan in a state of intense agony that rendered him incapable of doing anything. Suddenly, the energy stopped, and I could see that Lucifer's aura was almost completely depleted of red energy. However, he managed to look calm physically and literally hissed like a serpent: "Now you see who is master and who is merely student. Now you see the power that I could have taught you if you had been truly loyal, but now you will never get it."

Satan took some seconds to gather himself, then looked at Lucifer and said: "Let us see who will be master in the physical." Then he made a gesture and instantly the transmission was cut off. Lucifer would have been enraged if there was any energy left in his aura. It was clear that he had no response to this, and we all waited in silence for what seemed like an eternity and a half.

Then, we started feeling a vibration that rapidly grew more powerful until everything in the command bunker started shaking violently. All of us were aware that the question of whether the Federation had a doomsday weapon and whether Satan was willing to use it had now become academic. Within seconds, the ceiling started breaking into pieces that fell upon everyone in the command bunker. I was, of course, the only one who did not get hit because I was locked in what turned out to be a very strong steel cage.

The room was filled with dust, and all I could hear was the moaning, groaning and screams of the other people in the room. It turned out the door had been blocked and no one had escaped. Some of the generals had climbed under the table, but even that had collapsed.

At this point, I should insert an explanatory note for those who are wondering how I could see anything in an underground bunker that had just been subjected to a devastating attack. In the modern age, the electricity would have been cut off and the bunker would have been in total darkness. Yet in our civilization we had a power source that was not dependent on a central electrical grid. The bunker was equipped with lights that had an internal power generator and that is why some of them were still working.

As the dust slowly settled, I could see that all of the generals were dead or dying. I looked for Lucifer and at first could not see him. I then realized he was lying very close to me, as he had apparently run towards the cage, thinking he could lie next to it and be protected from the debris. However, he was not fast enough and a large piece of concrete had crushed both of his legs and his lower body. He was looking straight into my eyes from a distance of one meter and his look was that of a complete madman.

I was so transfixed by the sight, that I stared back for what seemed like an eternity. I was aware of an exchange of energy between us, but I had enough power to resist. Thus, we never formed the kind of bond that I had formed with Jeshu as he was dying in front of me.

After a long time, Lucifer gathered himself and spoke with great difficulty: "There you see, Avatar, what you have done. I told you that if you had supported me as the new ruler, I could have handled the situation without any war and killing. Now hundreds of millions of people have died, and it is all your responsibility.

You see how I could have controlled or destroyed Satan at will, but you created the diversion that allowed him to go behind my back. This is all your fault and may the karma of it be upon your head forever and ever. You will never again rise from this, you will never fulfil the reason for coming here. You have not brought salvation to the people, only more destruction than even I had envisioned. You will have to live with this forever—I will see to it."

At this point, he had no more strength to talk, but as he spoke, I had felt completely calm inside. Because of the havoc Lucifer had wrought in my four lower bodies, it would take me over a million and a half years to reclaim my ability to consciously channel energy from my I AM Presence, but I would still on rare occasions feel an impulse coming from that part of my being. This was such an occasion and without forethought I said: "Again, you are wrong. This is all the responsibility of yourself and Satan. You have become a victim of what you just did to me. You proved that even though I have the psychic power to resist your psychic dominance, you could use my physical body to neutralize my psychic power. Even though you had greater psychic power than Satan, he has just used physical power to neutralize it. You have become a victim of your own scheme.

I will take upon myself no responsibility for your choices, not now and not ever. You are responsible for the destruction you have wrought upon others, and it will come back to you in the end."

At this point, Lucifer died in front of me, having no strength left to talk. It took me several minutes to regain some kind of composure. I looked around the room, and suddenly a thought came to me: "I wish I had taken that class in how to pick a lock."

I was locked in a steal cage with no way to get out on my own and no one else around. It seemed I was destined to die from starvation while surrounded by rotting corpses. Not really what I had imagined before I decided to take embodiment on this planet.

\*\*\*

In the next two days, I was alone in the bunker. I wasn't really worried about dying and almost looked forward to it, as I assumed it would give me relief from the pain of my body. My wounds were still raw, but my main focus was my psychology. I had, of course, no conscious memory of what had happened while I was outside my physical body. So I didn't know anything about the programming I had been exposed to. Yet I had a sense that something very devastating had happened.

As I was in the room, I became aware of how I no longer seemed to have the command over my psyche that I was used to having. Suddenly, I would have a feeling come up that was not the result of any thought I had thought. I was used to having a flow through my four bodies from the identity, to the mental, to the emotional, to the physical. Now, it seemed like my emotional body would suddenly bring up a feeling with no conscious thought preceding it, and this gave me a very disturbing sense of not being in control of my emotions. Likewise, I would have many thoughts that did not originate with a sense of who I am at the identity level, making me feel I was not in control of my thoughts. My thoughts would often engage in mental arguments, as if two people inside my head were debating an issue. Furthermore, some of the thoughts clearly came from a sense of identity that was very different from what I had known a few days ago, a very divided and conflicted sense of identity. I had the sense that I was more than one person and that I could only watch this entire spectacle taking place in my mind and that I had little power to stop it.

I realize, of course, that many people in today's world will say: "Well, but isn't it normal to have this psychological turmoil?" And indeed, it is *normal,* but it is not *natural.* It is an artificially created situation because we have all been exposed to such trauma and programming by the PCBs that we have lost conscious control over our emotions, thoughts and sense of identity. I am not hereby saying that all people on the planet have been exposed to the same targeted attack to which I was exposed. This kind of treatment, the PCBs reserve for avatars. Yet all people on earth have been exposed to trauma by seeing what the PCBs have done on this planet. Because you cannot understand how anyone can do this, your subconscious mind has been opened to various forms of programming aimed at paralyzing you psychologically so that you are easier to control for the PCBs in embodiment (they are controlled by beings out of embodiment, as I will explain later).

# 14

You might be wondering what happened to the lady with the thousand tattoos, Maleve. I had not actually thought about it, but after two days, I heard some loud noises as someone was obviously trying to dig into the command bunker. A large piece of ceiling was overturned, and a group of men came in. After them, came Maleve and she quickly surveyed the scene. When she saw Lucifer, who was obviously dead, a pained look came into her eyes. Yet she quickly gathered herself as if she had accepted the inevitable and instantly went to Plan B. As her eyes fell on me, she got an almost happy look in her eyes and said: "Well, well, I see my pretty little avatar has survived. I am sure you and I are going to be good friends, aren't we?"

I said nothing and she continued: "Now, don't tell me you are going to be difficult. I will treat you well if you treat me well, and believe me, you will want to be with me rather than falling into the hands of Satan. His people cannot be far behind us. So if I let you out of that cage, will you come willingly, or do we have to carry you?"

I said: "I will come willingly, but you will still have to carry me. I don't think I can walk."

She smiled, and her men broke the lock and then carried me for a long time through underground tunnels. Maleve had given me something to drink, and it probably had a sedative in it because I soon lost consciousness.

When I woke up, I found myself lying in a comfortable bed in a room with no windows. Beside the bed, there was a dining table, some arm-chairs and a giant screen. There was also a bathroom. My wounds had been treated and the physical pain was now bearable, probably because of some strong painkillers.

Not long after I woke up, Maleve came in and lay down next to me. She cuddled up to me and started stroking me very gently, in the few places that weren't bandaged or bruised, while whispering calming words into my ear. I was in such a state of shock that I found myself longing for comfort, and I cuddled up to her. She seemed very pleased with this and stayed for some time, ensuring me that everything would be fine, that my troubles were over, that she would take care of everything and that she and I would become good friends. I finally fell asleep in her arms, feeling somewhat secure and at rest for the first time since Jeshu left to visit Satan.

Every day, some women accompanied by guards came in and treated my wounds. I slowly started healing, but the wound on my penis required surgery a couple of times in order to heal. I estimate my recovery to some state of normality took over two months. During that time, Maleve visited me often, even though she would sometimes stay away for several days. When I tried to talk to her about where I was and what had happened, she was evasive and said that because of my trauma, it was best that I not concern myself with practical matters. I needed to focus on healing, and then she could answer my questions. I really wasn't in a state to resist, and I accepted this.

\*\*\*

There now followed a rather long period of stability, during which Maleve and I developed a close but still very strange relationship. When I had recovered physically, I was moved to a suite of rooms that were quite luxurious. However, I was told by Maleve that I could never leave the suite because she was keeping me hidden from Satan who now had control over what was left of any form of civilized world. My suite was underground, and I was told this was necessary to protect us from nuclear radiation. I didn't have to work, and food or other necessities were brought to me by servants. This was clearly a strange set-up, but I never really questioned it, mainly because it suited me well. I was simply so psychologically wounded that I needed some stable time to try to find some way to recover.

Maleve came to me quite often, although at irregular intervals. I never really knew when she would show up and when she would have to leave. But even this suited me, as it gave me a variety of being alone and having company. My alone time I would use to try to process my psychological wounds, and my together time I would use to try to forget them.

Needles to say, Maleve and I started a sexual relationship as soon as I was physically fit to do so. I can't say I ever came to love her as I had loved my partners on natural planets and as I have loved other partners on earth since then. Yet I did come to feel a certain closeness to her and I developed a need for her company. She turned out to have some endearing qualities and was always kind and gentle with me, never again seeking to force me in any way. I can see now that this is because she had realized that force could not affect me so she was trying a different way.

Yet although Maleve was clearly using me to steal my light, she also did develop some genuine feelings for me, as she was capable of doing so with her deeply split psychology. Truly, she was a being with contradictions, but she still managed to treat me well, and it was my nature to treat anyone well. So we got along and were of some comfort to each other. Naturally, this developed a bond between us that meant we would re-embody with each other in succeeding lifetimes. And since Maleve had a strong bond with Lucifer who had a strong bond with Jeshu and Satan, the five of us would re-embody together in all kinds of circumstances over the millennia that followed.

The main focus for me during this time period was an attempt to come to grips with what had happened. Needless, to say, this was so far beyond what I had ever expected before I embodied on earth that I was in a state of shock for several years. The main problem I faced was that on natural planets I had been used to a straightforward energy flow through my four lower bodies. My lower bodies were always in alignment with my higher bodies.

Now, because of the experiences themselves and the programming inserted by Lucifer, I had limited control. I experienced such emotional trauma that it severely affected my thoughts, and I could not control my emotions with my mental body. I experienced such mental doubt and turmoil that it affected my sense of identity, and I could not control my mental body with my identity body. And my identity body was for the first time divided about who I was and why I was on this planet, even why I existed at all.

It was agonizing, and my mind would shift between having my emotions run wild and having my thoughts run wild. I simply wasn't able to stop my emotions and thoughts as I had been able to do before the traumatic events. This in itself was greatly disturbing to me. I obviously had doubts about whether I should have handled the physical situation differently, but the realization that I did not have control over my own mind hit me much harder. It made me feel powerless and worthless.

This state literally lasted for three years before I started regaining some control over my emotions and some clarification in my thoughts. After the total chaos was over, my mind became dominated by a long line of questions about the entire experience. There was an almost endless line of questions that presented themselves very aggressively to my mind. Some of them were clearly programmed into my mind by Lucifer, but I eventually learned to recognize this, although I was not consciously aware of the programming that had taken place. I intuitively knew that these questions did not come from myself, meaning from my higher mind.

I then became aware of a series of questions that *did* come from my own mind. They all centered around the same topic, namely how a being like Lucifer could do what he did and even how such a being could exist. I sensed very clearly that there was a fundamental difference between Lucifer and myself. I sensed that he felt no kinship with me at all, and this was impossible for me to understand. On a natural planet, you feel kinship with all life and thus you respect all life. You would not even dream of violating it as Lucifer had done. Even though I had forgotten how it was to live on a natural planet, I still had the inner sense of kinship with life, even with Lucifer.

Yet I had experienced so clearly that he had no sense of kinship with me or anyone else, and that is why he had absolutely no respect for the rights of other people. For him, other people were just tools to be used to accomplish his ends. It was clear that for Lucifer the end was more important than people.

I knew with absolute certainty that I could never have done to Lucifer (or anyone else, of course) what he had done to me, my father and so many other people. I also saw clearly that his actions had been rational from his own perspective, but from a greater perspective they had been destructive, even self-destructive. I could not fathom how he could be prepared to kill so many people and destroy an entire civilization in order to accomplish a certain goal. And I really could not begin to understand what Lucifer's goal might have been. I also could not fathom how he could fail to see that his actions would be destructive for himself.

This presented me with an existential dilemma that I simply had to solve. I could not live with this question unresolved, yet I also had no way of resolving it. This made my life almost unbearable, even though I gradually developed the ability to live with the dilemma. Yet this dilemma would dominate my life through thousands of succeeding embodiments, and it has dominated my life right up until the modern age. I did eventually come to resolve the dilemma and understand where beings like Lucifer and Satan came from, why they are the way they are and why they are allowed to be on earth. But this only happened relatively recently, and it was a very long and gradual process. That is why I will not give you the answer right away but tell further aspects of my story in order to prepare you for what truly is the most shocking aspect of life on earth, namely the question of the origin and continued existence of evil.

\*\*\*

After I had healed sufficiently to regain the ability to reason, I started talking to Maleve about Lucifer. She also had great difficulty processing the entire experience because she felt betrayed and used, and we ended up having many conversations about this. In the beginning, they went around in circles, but gradually I began to learn more about how Lucifer saw himself. It turned out that Maleve had been an apprentice of Lucifer, even though she had also studied under other teachers. I had the impression that Lucifer looked to her as an expert in certain matters and that he saw her as having some of what you today call clairvoyant abilities (even though on a natural planet, they are normal). Yet this happened only after Maleve had submitted to a very strict apprenticeship program under Lucifer. Maleve herself had never suspected this, but I quickly saw that the program was designed to make Maleve unquestioningly loyal to Lucifer. Only when he felt he had her absolute loyalty, did he trust her advice.

Lucifer had told Maleve that he did not come from our world or universe. He originated in a previous world that had existed before ours. In that world, he had belonged to an elite group of beings who had developed great powers to create and to lead. This had caused the god of that world to become jealous of their power and abilities, and there had been a confrontation where the god had judged Lucifer and his fellows unjustly. They had therefore been cast out of that world instead of having been given the leadership positions that they rightly deserved. It was because of this that they had ended up incarnating in our universe and eventually on planet earth.

Lucifer was extremely negative and judgmental towards what he called god, but he was quite unclear about what he actually included in the concept of god. I still had enough intuition to sense that his view of god was quite different from how the concept of god was viewed on natural planets. But since I could not talk to Lucifer directly about this, it was difficult for me to understand exactly what the differences were between a natural view of god and Lucifer's view. I would come to understand this to some degree much later when I got to know Lucifer and his way of thinking. However, it would take me over a million years to fully understand what had happened to Lucifer and just how deceitful and distorted was his version of the events.

The reality of who Lucifer was and where he came from is the full explanation for the presence of evil on this planet (and the entire universe), and it is a tale so far beyond what we have been brought up to believe that most people would refuse to seriously consider it. It is completely beyond the PIN and the WCs created by the PCBs. The reason for this is that the PCBs have done everything they could to hide their true identity and origin. They have done everything possible to make people reject the real story of who they are. And the reason is that if people on earth knew the true story, the PCBs could not get anyone to follow them. Their existence on this planet literally depends on keeping up this deception. But again, I am getting ahead of myself.

Maleve believed Lucifer's story and had never really questioned it. Yet she had been so shaken by the war and the destruction of our civilization that she no longer quite knew what to believe. She sensed that something had to be wrong with Lucifer's story, but she could not intuit what it could be. I did in no way believe Lucifer, but I did not have the intuitive ability to find knowledge of the real events so I had difficulty explaining to Maleve why I felt something was wrong with the story.

Naturally, I forgot this story in my next embodiment, but I kept rediscovering it in many later embodiments. It has different versions, but they all point in the same direction, namely that we human beings really cannot trust this god in the sky that has been created by the PCBs as their basic WC. Today, you find the PCBs' distorted view of god as the foundation for most of the major religions.

It was rather difficult for me to question Lucifer's story because he had programmed so many lies into my emotional, mental and identity bodies that were designed to make me feel negative feelings towards god or to doubt god in various ways. Most people on earth have been exposed to this artificially created conflict. A classical example is the argument that because we cannot deny that there is evil on the planet, it shows that either god is not almighty or god is not good. If god was almighty, he could have defeated or removed evil. And if god was entirely good, he would have wanted to remove evil. Therefore, god either is not capable of removing evil, and therefore not almighty, or god is not willing to remove evil, and therefore not good. The resolution to this artificial paradox (all paradoxes are artificial and created by the PCBs) is quite simple, but only when you know the story of the origin and intentions of the PCBs. By the end of this book, this paradox will literally have evaporated from your mind and you will see how artificial it was. It is clever, I will admit that, but only when you do not know the full story about the origin of what people call evil.

\*\*\*

During the following years, I gradually learned from Maleve what had happened to my civilization and the Federation as a result of the war. Our beautiful capitol had been almost completely destroyed and several hundred million people had died. However, the further one moved away from the capital, the less destruction there had been, and over 60 percent of our people had survived. About the same percentage of the people in the Federation had survived and its capital was almost untouched.

Because our armed forces and our government institutions had been largely destroyed, our civilization had surrendered to Satan who had declared himself emperor of the entire earth. He had attained absolute power and executed it through a secret police that was willing to kill anyone who seemed to be a threat. In fact, he had instituted a policy of random killings that was meant to demonstrate that no one could feel secure.

Satan had taken complete control over the media, and he had engaged in a very heavy propaganda effort to make our people abandon all loyalty to our civilization, and especially to Jeshu and myself. According to Maleve, Satan had made my father and I almost completely responsible for the destruction of our civilization, having portrayed us as having deliberately started the war because of a hidden agenda. Satan portrayed himself as the savior who had rescued our civilization from an even worse fate if our plan had succeeded. He claimed that we had planned to establish a form of dictatorial control that was beyond what he himself was exercising, and he claimed we would have sent millions of people to concentration camps. He claimed that my father would have done away with the governing council and set himself up as an all-powerful dictator who answered to no one. We also planned to insert me as his successor without going through he council.

Maleve explained that Satan had systematically hunted down all of my father's children and killed them in order to make sure no one could claim the throne. I was the only one he had not found, due to Maleve saving me. That is why he had to discredit me in case I should surface in the future. She said my father and I were so unpopular among our people that it would be dangerous for me to expose that I was still alive. I am not saying I believed this, but since I had no ambitions of trying to overthrow Satan and set myself up as leader, our arrangement suited me fine for the time being.

# 15

You might think this was the end of my first embodiment, but there was one more twist, and it was the one that really broke me. My "back-in-the-womb" experience with Maleve lasted five years. One day, with no prior warning, people in uniforms entered my room, paralyzed me with an energy gun and carried me away. I was thrown in a very small cell with no windows. I received very little food and water, and I was there with no explanation for what seemed a couple of months. I had not seen Maleve during the time and had no explanation of what had happened to her, nor any explanation of who had captured me and what their intent or purpose was.

One day, I was served a very large meal. I thought it might be the condemned man's last meal and that I would be executed the next day, so I ate it all. The next day I was taken out of the cell and brought to a public square in what was Satan's capital city. I was stripped naked and locked in a device that was a more sophisticated version of what we today know from medieval times as a pillory. In other words, I was in a very uncomfortable fixed position in a public square that was filled with people who were yelling and screaming abusive words at me, even throwing rotten fruit or small stones at me.

After a short time, a group of people entered and took positions in some chairs on a platform behind me. Behind them was a giant television screen. The pillory in which I was locked was on a platform that could rotate, and I was turned so I faced the judges and the screen. The idea was that the judges would conduct a public trial, holding me responsible for my crimes of conspiring with my father to start the conflict and war that had brought down our civilization.

The head judge began by listing the crimes for which I was accused, and it was an entirely – and I mean *entirely* – fictional account. The actions, arrogance and intent of Lucifer and Satan were hidden and everything was made to seem as the result of the scheming of Jeshu and I. At certain times, images would be displayed on the giant screen. Mostly, these were images of the consequences of the war and the suffering this had created for the people, but there were some images that showed Jeshu or myself saying things that sounded like we were plotting everything. These images were naturally faked by using our version of computer technology and trick photography, but you would have been hard pressed to detect this from the images themselves. I knew the images about me were faked because I had not experienced those situations, and I knew the images with Jeshu were faked because he would never have said some of those things. He was made to say some things that voiced deep disdain for the people, and he was actually made to say exactly the kind of things Lucifer and Satan said about the people when they were in a private setting. This is the old story of the PCBs accusing others of doing what they themselves are doing while making themselves seem as the saviors of the people.

Obviously, this trial was broadcast all over the planet, and anyone who had a screen could watch it. As the trial progressed, they also started showing responses from people. Apparently, in most cities, cameras had been set up where people could come and voice their response to the trial and to myself. Needless to say, there was not any hint of support and all of the people shown had bought the false story hook, line and sinker. This was especially true about the people who had lived in *our* civilization and who had suffered the loss of their secure and abundant way of life, many having lost all of their family members. They were understandably extremely angry, and they seemed relieved to have a scapegoat towards whom they could direct their anger. The live crowd behind me also voiced their anger continuously during the trial.

On the first day I was not really so focused on this, because it soon became apparent to me that I had a much more pressing problem. I was standing naked with my back to a large crowd and television cameras, and the large meal I had eaten the day before had made its unstoppable way through my digestive system (I had been deliberately given this meal in order to produce this reaction). I simply had to go, and I really did not want to urinate and defecate all over myself in front of a planetary audience. For several hours, I managed to hold it back, but there simply came a point where the strain became too great, and I had to let it go. If you have never (in this or a past life) had the experience of watching yourself defecate all over yourself on a giant screen and knowing it is watched by millions of people, who are loudly laughing and sneering at you, I can assure you it is quite humiliating. In fact, it is more humiliating than being publicly accused of a crime that you know you did not commit.

This is not to say that I was not affected by the trial. It was heartbreaking for me to watch the people because I knew that their suffering was very real and had been devastating to them. Regardless of the fact that they were directing their anger at me, I felt a very deep compassion for them and I deeply wished I could have helped them. Obviously, I could not and I never had an opportunity to speak during my trial.

***

The trial lasted for a week, and it took a heavy toll on me psychologically and physically (it is almost impossible to sleep in a pillory and I was locked in during the entire trial). This is one of the ways that PCBs can break those of us who come to improve life on this planet, what Maleve had called avatars. We are here because we have compassion for the people. The PCBs have no compassion for the people on earth, seeing them only as tools. The PCBs know that by causing outrageous suffering to the people, we avatars cannot avoid reacting because we cannot turn off the compassion that brought us here. And once we are in a reactionary spiral with the PCBs, they have us exactly where they want us and they can keep us from doing what we came here to do. I will later explain exactly how this works, but for now, back to the trial.

There finally came a point where the people engineering the trial could not come up with any more accusations and evidence (due to their PRC and CIA) and there was the final judgment. I was obviously declared guilty, and my punishment was that I would remain in the pillory and the people would be allowed to come up to me and voice their opinion, without being allowed to physically do anything that would endanger my life.

The pillory was again rotated so I faced the square, and from that moment on, I was standing there and facing a line of people walking by me, each person or group of people screaming their anger and accusations against me, blaming me for everything that had ever gone wrong in their lives.

In the beginning, I tried to talk back and explain the reality of the situation, but I soon realized the futility of this. In a moment of clarity, I saw that these people were in a psychological bind, a catch-22, cleverly engineered by Satan.

The people from my old civilization all had some awareness that Satan's version of events was not entirely true. Yet because of his secret (or rather, not-so-secret) police, they were afraid to voice this publicly. At the same time, they had suffered such devastating losses personally that they had a lot of pent-up anger. And when they were offered a target towards which it was safe to express that anger, they could not refuse the opportunity.

In the beginning, this literally went on 24 hours a day, but soon I became so physically weak from the lack of sleep that my captors realized my body would die if it continued. I was therefore allowed to sleep six hours every day so I only had to endure the accusations for 18 hours. This didn't mean I could leave the square. The pillory was simply lowered so that I could lie down and therefore get some kind of sleep. Of course, since I was constantly defecating on the spot, I was literally lying down in my own excrement.

This scheme continued for months, and then a new twist was added. One day, a group of workers entered and started installing a metal ring in the floor of the square not far from me. When this was done, a naked Maleve was brought in and chained to the ring. Her chain had the exact length that allowed her to move towards me without actually touching me. Next mealtime, a dish of food was brought in and given to her. She was now given instructions that she was to lean over and feed me while not touching the food herself. If she tried to eat any of the food, she would be paralyzed with an energy gun and the food would be taken away from both of us for that day.

I don't think either of us suspected the real scheme behind this bizarre set-up. But after a few days, we began to realize that Maleve was not given any food herself. She was literally ordered to feed me while starving to death herself. My choice was whether I would eat while watching her starve to death.

As another twist, Maleve and I were not allowed to talk. There was constantly a guard, and if either of us said anything, Maleve would be shot with an energy gun and would be paralyzed for half an hour. Obviously, it was possible for her to get half a sentence out before she was paralyzed, so over the next several days, she managed to give me a sketchy explanation of what had happened.

Apparently, Maleve had become a special advisor to Satan after the war. I can only surmise that she simply could not keep away from men who had absolute power. She had kept my survival secret for him, but after five years he, or his police, had figured out that she kept me hidden under her private house. She had been detained the same day I was, and Satan had decided he no longer wanted her. This was his way of executing her so that both she and I experienced maximum pain.

After some days, I decided to refuse to eat. After all, starving to death would be less painful than facing the people. This lasted a day, but when Satan was made aware of it, he ordered a person to come in with a whip. He started whipping Maleve, and I was told he would continue until I started eating.

Maleve was given liquid so as to prolong her life. It took 43 days before she was so weak that she could no longer feed me, and then it took another five days before she finally died before my eyes. As a completely irrelevant side note, when a tattoo has been made while a person is in normal health, it shrinks in a peculiar way as they lose body weight. The image becomes distorted as the skin shrinks, and in Maleve's case, it gave her body a horrific appearance. I still can see it for my inner eye. Some memories simply don't fade with age. In all of my embodiments, I have never wanted to have a tattoo.

***

My exposure to the people's wrath lasted for almost three years. It only stopped because the people eventually stopped coming. Apparently, all those who wanted to voice their anger had done so. I sensed that for some time, people were ordered to confront me, but it simply did not have the same effect.

So what effect did it have on me? Well, in the beginning, I was consumed with compassion, but when exposed to too much suffering, there comes a point where the mind has to shut down in order for you to survive psychologically (a mechanism often used by the PCBs to get human beings to kill or torture each other. People kill or torture others without consciously acknowledging what they are doing.) Yet while my emotional mind shut down, the mental and identity levels of my mind were very active in trying to find out how to deal with the situation.

During this phase, something in me literally broke. Today, we have the expression that your heart breaks, and it is at least some approximation of what I felt, although I would say that my soul broke. This was due to the fact that regardless of how I applied my intelligence and reason, I could not see a way to change the situation on earth.

You might notice here that during the entire ordeal, I had never really thought about myself. I had not felt sorry for myself and I had not been angry and had not blamed Lucifer, Satan, the people or god for what was happening to me. I was intuitively aware that I had come to earth to set people free, and the entire ordeal had made it clear to me what the people really needed to be set free from, namely the PCBs. Before I had come, I had assumed that the descent of earth was a kind of accident, now I knew it was an accident by design, perpetrated by the PCBs.

Yet with all of my faculties, I could not see how I could possibly set the people of earth free from the PCBs. I had become very acutely aware that there was no way to reason with Lucifer or Satan, especially Satan. You will notice that while Lucifer had tried to persuade me personally, Satan had never even met me personally. He had no interest in trying to persuade me to believe in anything; he simply wanted to destroy me. I could see no way to negotiate or reason with that kind of absolute destructive intent.

So how could I free the earth from people like Satan? I could not see a way because, as far as I could see at the time, the only way to defeat Satan was to do to him what he was doing to others. And I knew with absolute certainly that I could never do to him what he had done to me. It simply was not possible for me to sink to a level of consciousness where I was willing to do to him what I had seen him do to others—or so I thought at the time. And actually I was right—sort of. I also knew that I could not lie and completely make up accusations against other people, as he had done and as I had seen Lucifer do.

***

After the people stopped coming, there came a point where they stopped feeding me. My body was at that time so weakened that it took only 33 days for me to starve to death. So there I died, in a pile of my own excrement in a public square in a long-forgotten city. To say that this was not what I had expected before coming into my first embodiment on earth would be the understatement of my time on this planet.

Death was a relief for me. Yet I had made karma that ensured I would embody again on earth, and I had formed bonds and a desire to understand that ensured I would embody with Jeshu, Maleve, Lucifer and Satan.

I remember shortly before I died forming a decision in my mind. It was not an ordinary decision, but one of these decisions made with every fiber of your soul, your four lower bodies. It was not an *absolute* decision, but it was a *defining* decision. I decided that I never again wanted to personally experience anything as humiliating, devastating and unbearable. I also decided that I never wanted something like this to happen to any other being.

This decision would define me and my embodiments for the next two million years. It has literally taken me that long to free myself, my soul, from the binding constraints of that decision. You may think is was an understandable, even a reasonable decision. But that is because you do not yet understand exactly how clever the PCBs, or rather those who control them, truly are. They know exactly how the Law of Free Will works and that once you have made a defining decision, only *you* can undo it. They also know that such a decision will put you in a reactionary pattern with them, and as long as they can keep you engaged in that pattern, you will not be able to see what the decision really does to you and you will not be able to free yourself from it.

I am not hereby saying that I think the PCBs or their non-material masters are really clever. In fact, the greatest mystery is how they can use this mechanism to trap others while failing to see that they themselves are even more trapped than their victims. It took me a long time to resolve that mystery, but let me not get ahead of myself. First, we need to understand who PCBs are and why they came to dominate life on earth. Who came up with the idea to let PCBs embody here and what were they thinking? It will, however, take me some time to set the stage for explaining this.

# PART 3:

# THE DOWNWARD

# SPIRAL

# 16

After my first embodiment followed a very long period of time that I now see as a downward spiral in which I became more and more trapped in a reactionary pattern with the PCBs, especially Lucifer and Satan. I was so wounded after my first embodiment that I only wanted to live a peaceful and secluded life, but I had to embody with Lucifer and Satan in almost every embodiment. They often managed to force me away from living any kind of peaceful existence.

Obviously, Lucifer and Satan were not always rulers of civilizations who had great power over people. But as can be seen today, even in families there can be incredible cruelty and abuse. And no matter how much or how little power Lucifer and Satan had, they were always able to perpetrate incredible cruelty and abuse towards other people and each other. Their rivalry and competition led to the most bizarre actions on both of their parts, and the consequences often affected entire civilizations.

In my first many embodiments with them, I managed to remain non-aggressive. When they did something aggressive towards me or others, I did not respond with aggression. In many cases, I tried to reason with them and I always attempted to understand them. Yet it never had any effect on either of them and I made no progress towards understanding them. Well, actually I did make progress towards understanding how their minds worked. Yet the more I understood how their minds worked, the less I could understand why their minds were working that way and why they existed at all.

The effect was that I gradually started having severe, even existential, doubts about the workings of the universe and how beings like this could be allowed to exist. I became affected by the view, so common even back then, that there is a remote god in the sky who has created the universe. I simply could not understand why such a god could create beings like Lucifer and Satan. Nor could I understand why such a god would allow them to embody on earth. Neither could I understand why they were allowed to continue to embody on earth, considering the incredible amounts of suffering they perpetrated.

Over a period of almost 100,000 years, I gradually sank into a state of being a sceptic who doubted everything about the origin and workings of the universe, including the existence of a benevolent god behind it all.

Then, came an embodiment that took my downward spiral into a decisively new phase.

*** 

I was born into a civilization that was sophisticated in the same way as the Roman Empire, meaning it had the same level of weapons and the same kind of centralized structure with an almighty emperor as the leader. As an explanatory note, civilizations tend to go up and down. For example, after my first embodiment where there was such massive destruction, there followed a period with far fewer people in embodiment and where society degenerated to something close to what we today see as the iron age. Much of the technological knowledge of my first civilization was lost, as it has happened many times since humankind fell into duality. From this low point, there was a climb towards more sophisticated civilizations.

The emperor of this civilization was Lucifer and Satan was his son. Needless to say, there was an uneasy relationship between the two, but nothing came to a head until Satan reached the age of 20. Jeshu was an advisor to the emperor and I was a simple palace servant who did various jobs in the court, sometimes manually fanning the emperor when he was on his throne. In other words, I was always close to the leaders but unnoticed.

I should add here that although I had obviously lost much of the high-frequency energy, my life energy, I had taken with me to earth, I still had more left than most people. Yet I had learned to hide it so that Lucifer and Satan did not always recognize me and therefore sometimes left me alone since they did not see me as a threat. This was one of those embodiments where none of them had recognized me and therefore had not attempted to destroy me, as they had done in many other embodiments. Jeshu and I also did not recognize each other and had no special relationship in that embodiment.

Jeshu had a daughter, and from an early age, I had a very special feeling about her. It only grew stronger as I watched her grow up. Everyone else also noticed that this girl was very special, even Lucifer and Satan. Yet Jeshu was very protective of her, and none of them were able to do anything to her, even though I suspected both of them of wanting to abuse her sexually. Both Lucifer and Satan were pedophiles in many embodiments. They always needed to find some way to steal other people's life energy in order to survive, and sexual abuse of children is one of the most "efficient" ways to steal energy from others. This is the sole motive behind pedophilia, in the past as well as today. It is perpetrated by people who have spent their own life energy and therefore have to steal energy from others in order to survive.

I later learned that this girl, whom I will call Magda, was an avatar and that this was her first embodiment. It was the life energy she carried with her that I recognized. I later learned that she had been a partner of Jeshu on a natural planet, and she had decided to take embodiment on earth in order to help Jeshu out of his reactionary spiral with the PCBs. She was therefore completely innocent to the ways of the world, yet here she was, in close proximity to Lucifer and Satan, as I had been in my first embodiment.

*\*\*\**

When Satan turned 20, he perpetrated a very cunning and brutal take-over of power, in which he had Lucifer murdered. Yet instead of admitting this, he created a fictitious scenario where he blamed Jeshu and his daughter, who was now 16, for having started the plot. Obviously, this was very similar to what he had done to us in my first embodiment, and it was a pattern Satan attempted to repeat many times. As I said, all PCBs have CIA.

There came a point where there was a public trial in which Jeshu and Magda were accused of being behind this coup. I was a servant standing behind Satan, who was now in the emperor's seat. It was obvious that both Jeshu and Magda had been tortured and suffered greatly. They both refused to admit to their guilt, but Satan continued to present evidence, including witnesses who swore falsely that Jeshu and Magda were guilty.

As the trial progressed, I became more and more disturbed, although I was careful not to show this outwardly. I obviously had no recollection of my first embodiment, but I started becoming aware of a very deep and strong feeling that I could not allow this to be done to Magda. At one point this became such an overwhelming sensation that I literally lost control.

I was standing close to Satan, and next to his throne were two guards with swords. At one point, I looked into the deeply shocked eyes of Magda, and I felt all of the pain from my own first embodiment well up within me.

I then looked into Jeshu's eyes, and I saw his pain, as he knew he would not be able to protect his daughter from Satan's abuse.

Without having planned this, I suddenly grabbed the sword of one of the guards. Everyone was taken aback by this because they had not expected that an "invisible" palace servant could do such a thing. So I got the sword and ran it into Satan's stomach while yelling: "This cannot be allowed to happen!"

There was this moment where the situation seemed frozen in time. I stood there with the sword in my hand, and the blade was buried in Satan's stomach, the blood running out. He had not even had time to feel the pain, but looked at me with complete surprise and shock in his eyes. Everyone else seemed completely frozen for what was probably only a split second, but seemed like an eternity. Then Satan screamed in agony and the palace guards sprang to life, killing me instantly.

I was out of embodiment and did not experience the rest of the story. Since Satan was also out of embodiment, he could not destroy Magda, but this did happen in a later embodiment where I could do nothing about it.

***

This was a decisive change for me because there is a fundamental difference in the consequences you create for yourself when you take physical action against other people, including PCBs. Contrary to what most people want to believe, every thought, feeling and action generates an energy impulse that you are sending into the four levels of matter. The most basic law of our world is the Law of Free Will. It states that you have completely free will as to what you want to do with the energy available to you. Yet it also states that the four levels of the material universe form a kind of mirror, meaning that every energy impulse you send out is returned to you multiplied.

No one can escape this energetic return. I know this is confusing because we have all seen people who committed atrocities, and they were not struck dead by a bolt of lightning immediately afterwards. Yet because of the density of the material universe, there is a delay factor. This is actually an opportunity for us to change our consciousness before the energetic return comes back. If you do not change your consciousness, the energetic return will hit you full force. Due to the delay factor, this will often happen in a future lifetime. If you do change your consciousness, the return of they energy can be mitigated or completely neutralized before it reaches the physical octave. Contrary to what many people say about karma, the energetic return is not a punishment. It is actually a way to demonstrate to you the consequences of the choices you have made. If you did not see a consequence of the choices you made, how could you ever evaluate whether you want to change those choices?

I know this is still confusing because if Lucifer and Satan had met the full return of what they sent out, they should have been incapacitated. Yet, as Lucifer said in my first embodiment, some PCBs have learned to neutralize or postpone the return in various ways. This does not mean they will ultimately escape accountability before the law, but it does mean they can continue for a long time to dodge their returning energy. This is actually why Satan conducted this very public trial of blaming me and Jeshu for what happened to our civilization. By getting people to believe this and direct their anger at me, he got the people to take on some of the karma he had created. He will not ultimately escape this karma, but it can be delayed for quite some time.

My point is that the energetic return is completely unaffected by human opinions and by circumstances. I know there is a very subtle belief floating around in the world that god's judgment or your karma depends on the situation and your intent for doing what you did. There is a very widespread belief that killing another human being is justified under some circumstances. This belief was created by the PCBs because they want to believe, and they want the rest of us to believe, that the energetic return is affected by how they look at situations. They want to believe that god or the laws of nature is affected by their perception of the situation and how they define what is right and wrong.

Just look at history and see how often, even in modern times, people have believed that when you kill a criminal or an enemy in war, your karma or sin is not as severe as when you kill a person who has done nothing to deserve it. There is an entire myth built up that says it can be justified to kill people, and many people believe they will not make as severe karma or be punished by god for killing people who somehow deserve it.

This is all a lie perpetrated by the PCBs. Some of them believe in it themselves, but the most cunning of them do not believe it. They simply know that they can make *us* believe it. Once we do, they can get us to kill each other far more easily. Just look at today's world where the president of the greatest nation on earth claimed to be a Christian but still believed it was justified to invade Iraq in 2003. Look at how Muslim groups kill infidels while believing this will be rewarded with 70 virgins in heaven.

So the bottom line is that regardless of what people believe, karma works as unfailingly and as impartially as the law of gravity. It doesn't matter who you are and what good you have done, if you step out into thin air from a tall building, gravity will turn you into a read dot on the pavement. It doesn't matter who you are or how justified you think you are, you will always make a severe karma for physically killing another human being. The reason is that killing someone is the only completely irreversible way to take away the opportunity that an embodiment represents to the soul.

There is a fundamental difference between thinking about killing someone, feeling the desire to kill someone, and then the physical action of killing someone. You will still generate an energetic return through your thoughts and feelings, but it will not be nearly as severe as taking physical action. Your thoughts and feelings can also affect another person (contrary to what modern-day materialists claim), but the person still has a choice as to how he or she will allow your psychic energy to affect him or her.

Yet once you take a physical action that kills someone, the other person has no choice as to how to react. Well, the person has a choice as to how to let it affect his or her soul, but there is no choice as to what to do because the person is out of embodiment. Almost anything else you can do to a person leaves them with a choice (if they are still alive and conscious). Once you kill their physical body, the physical choice is taken away, and this generates a more severe energetic return because it is the most severe violation of free will. You take away the person's opportunity to react.

\*\*\*

This first act of aggression greatly accelerated my downward spiral. I had naturally felt the shock of having killed another human being. This is something that all people feel in the beginning, including PCBs. Yet the more people you kill, the less you notice this, and the PCBs have long ago reached the point where they can kill without even noticing the instinctual shock. I say "instinctual" because one of our deepest instincts is to *not* kill members of our own species, and one cannot do so without feeling a very deep sense that this is wrong. The PCBs have learned to ignore this, and many human beings have also learned this. I myself learned this in later embodiments. When I came into my next embodiment, I carried this sense of shock with me. However, instead of truly acknowledging it, I started seeking to explain it away and justify it. In doing so, I used the exact same serpentine logic used by the PCBs. In fact, in my next several embodiments I became very good a justifying why killing is necessary in order to prevent a greater calamity.

I had several embodiments in which the same pattern repeated itself. Jeshu was a ruler of a civilization. I was his brother or advisor. Lucifer or Satan were either his sons, brothers or other people close to him. I saw that Lucifer and Satan were plotting to betray Jeshu, and I argued for him to prevent this by sending them away, imprisoning them or outright killing them.

In the beginning, Jeshu resisted my attempts. This was not because he was unwilling to use violence. As a ruler in a rather primitive part of world history, he often had to use military power to defend or expand his empire. Yet he was reluctant to use violence against people close to him, especially family. He felt a loyalty to family that I had never felt—except towards him.

In several embodiments, Jeshu was indeed betrayed. Lucifer or Satan killed him and took over as leaders, always with disastrous consequences for our civilization. After several embodiments like this, Jeshu started listening to my arguments, and there came a time when he started taking actions to prevent the betrayal of Lucifer or Satan. This did in several cases prevent Jeshu from being killed, and it prevented the downfall of civilizations and the brutal killings of millions of people.

To me, this was perfectly justified. Also, in several embodiments I could see how Lucifer and Satan were about to unleash a major calamity that would kill tens of thousands or even millions of people. I therefore justified to myself why it was perfectly okay for me to kill one or both of them, which I did many times. Again, this prevented widespread death and suffering, and even today many people would say it was justified. Yet the law of energetic return pays no attention to human opinions or the subtle serpentine logic.

# 17

There now followed a long period where Jeshu and I became very good at physically resisting the plots of Lucifer and the direct assaults of Satan. We both became extremely good warriors at the personal level, and it soon came to the point where neither Lucifer nor Satan could defeat any of us in open combat. We also became very good leaders of nations and armies, and it became very difficult for Lucifer and Satan to defeat us in any way. We became very alert to the lies and plots of especially Lucifer, and there came a point where even he realized he found it difficult to defeat us.

I admit that I took a certain pride in this. I felt that no one on earth could defeat me, and it made me feel a certain sense that I was doing something to improve conditions on earth. I think Jeshu had some of the same feelings, although he was never as caught up in fighting the PCBs as I became. I started feeling that by neutralizing and defeating the PCBs, I was doing *something* to protect the people of earth from their schemes.

What neither Jeshu nor I saw was that we were not doing *anything* to remove the PCBs from earth. On the contrary, the more we fought the PCBs, the more ensconced they became on this planet. The law of energetic return really can be a hard schoolmaster.

\*\*\*

Jeshu and I were not always in the same positions. Sometimes I was the leader and sometimes Jeshu. But for a very long period of time, we were always in agreement and always supporting each other. We seemed to have an unbreakable bond that carried over from lifetime to lifetime. Yet nothing on earth is unbreakable.

I have later learned that the disembodied Dark Master (a being in the identity realm) who controlled Lucifer (and in some lifetimes both Lucifer and Satan) had a great rivalry with other dark beings. Some of these controlled Satan in some lifetimes whereas in other lifetimes he was impossible for anyone to control, being dedicated to destruction for its own sake. The Dark Master and his rivals often attempted to settle the score by using their apprentices, which is why Lucifer and Satan so often worked against each other. Yet there came a point when the Dark Master realized that Jeshu and I could no longer be fooled or defeated by Lucifer or destroyed by Satan. He then decided to take another approach and attempt to use both Lucifer and Satan to separate us.

This took a long time, but he very cleverly used a subtle difference between Jeshu and I. Jeshu had in many embodiments been a great warrior and killed many people personally (as had I). He had also been a great leader and general who had led many armies in battle and thus caused many people to be killed (as had I). Yet despite all the killing, Jeshu retained an intuitive sense that killing someone was wrong and should be the last resort. I had developed the logic that as soon as you identified a PCB (I didn't call them that back then), you killed him in order to prevent a greater calamity. Mind you, I would never kill a person I perceived as being non-aggressive towards others, as PCBs will do. Yet I would kill as soon as I detected that aggressive intent in someone. I would kill to defend others who could not defend themselves.

Jeshu sensed this was wrong, but given that he had so often experienced the disastrous actions of PCBs, he could not refute my logic. However, he started resenting my logic and distrusting my advice. The Dark Master cleverly exploited this by getting Lucifer and Satan to play upon our differences. In several embodiments, Lucifer would give Jeshu advice on how to be less violent, while Satan would precipitate such outrageous actions that I took action to kill him and neutralize his army or civilization.

Jeshu could not refute that my actions were based on logic and that they were efficient in stopping Satan and often preventing a larger calamity. Yet he was gradually persuaded by Lucifer's logic that I was too eager to kill and that I had become worse than the people I was fighting. This wasn't necessarily a lie since I had become a formidable warrior and a very efficient army leader. And I was indeed very quick to take actions when I recognized the kind of aggressive intent that was Satan's hallmark.

Over several embodiments, this created a distance between Jeshu and I, even a certain mistrust. Jeshu several times attempted to stop me from taking action against Satan. In some cases, I refused to do so and although he could not refute that I had prevented greater bloodshed, he still resented this. In some cases, I did follow his prompting or orders, and the results were often disastrous, making me resent *his* reasoning.

\*\*\*

Then came a phase where the Dark Master became even more subtle. He created a situation where I clearly saw Satan as a threat and I was ready to take action. Lucifer argued against this, and I (out of loyalty to Jeshu) followed Jeshu's call not to act. Then, instead of taking advantage of the inaction (as he had done before) the Dark Master managed to keep Satan passive. This caused Lucifer to argue that I had been wrong and that he had been right. Such situations gradually swayed Jeshu into becoming less willing to use violence. I did not blame Jeshu or resent him, but I did start feeling that he did not have what it took to be a decisive leader. He started feeling I was a loose cannon and too quick to use violence.

As I probably should have explained earlier, we most often cannot remember our past embodiments. So we do not know exactly what someone else did in a past life. Yet what happens is that a particular event, especially a dramatic event, will create certain tracks, patterns or matrices in our emotional, mental and identity bodies. These three higher bodies we carry over from lifetime to lifetime. So when we come into our next lifetime, we carry with us the patterns built in the last lifetime and all previous lifetimes. This explains why we can meet a person for the first time and feel that we know him or her. We do know that being or soul from perhaps many past lives and we have built certain patterns of interaction that we can immediately resume in this lifetime.

This mechanism meant that Jeshu and I came into a phase where we would still embody at the same time, but we would not be close to each other. We would not be in the same family and often not even in the same nation or civilization. This eventually led to situations where we embodied in civilizations that were in competition or even conflict with each other, a situation greatly exploited by the Dark Master behind Lucifer and Satan.

*** 

There came a lifetime where I was the leader of one powerful civilization and Jeshu was the leader of the other. Lucifer was a brother to Jeshu and Satan was a brother to me. Without knowing consciously what they were doing, Lucifer and Satan (taken over by their master) plotted to get Jeshu and I to go to war against each other. Through a series of lies and secretly planned aggressive actions, they finally succeeding in creating a war between our civilizations. Naturally, I was the one who attacked first while Jeshu tried to prevent the war.

This was a time when we only had iron weapons, such as spears and swords. It was also a time when the leaders would fight on the battlefield. After several smaller battles, there came a day when our armies were lined up against each other on a huge plain. This is one of the cruelest battle situations because there is no terrain that allows you to take evasive or covert actions. You are lined up in full sight of the other army, and there is nothing to do but face each other head-on. The battle started early in the morning and waved back and forth with neither side gaining a decisive advantage.

In the late afternoon, both armies had been decimated to the point where all fighting should have been stopped, but neither Jeshu nor I would give up. Regardless of the terrible weapons developed in our civilization, there is hardly anything more brutal than hand-to-hand combat with iron weapons. The cuts and punctures people get with such primitive weapons are unbelievably brutal, and the entire battlefield was strewn with dead and mangled bodies. There were places where the ground was saturated with blood, and the screaming of the wounded, for whom no one did anything, was terrifying. Yet those of us who were still in the thick of fighting could not hear the wounded over the clashes of weapons and the battle cries of soldiers.

There finally came a point where both armies had been decimated to the point that only the personal guards surrounding Jeshu and I were left. We clashed with each other, and there came a point where most of the guards were dead and Jeshu and I approached each other with swords drawn. We ran towards each other, screaming at the top of our voices, but when our swords clashed, something strange happened. Our swords locked and so did our eyes.

This was another interval where time stood still. Jeshu and I looked into each others eyes, and something stirred within both of us. We did not consciously recognize each other and our history together, but we did recognize that there was a strong bond between us, a bond that we simply could not break by killing each other.

At the exact same time, and without having said a word, we threw down our swords and shields and stepped back, still having our eyes locked. I took off my helmet, and Jeshu did the same. We then embraced and Jeshu said: "No matter what happens, I swear that I will never fight you again, my brother." I said the same thing, and we looked into each others eyes with tears running down our cheeks.

***

Our battlefield rendezvous was soon interrupted when Lucifer and Satan appeared on the scene, each with their personal guards. They had both managed to remove themselves from the action and keep their forces intact. It instantly became obvious to myself and Jeshu that neither Lucifer nor Satan were happy to see us alive. They wanted us dead so they could take over, each of them hoping to use the battle to kill the other and become the supreme leader of both civilizations.

After a few moments of hesitation, Lucifer and Satan ordered their guards to kill us. We barely had time to pick up our swords and shields before we were attacked by these 40 elite fighters. There was nothing to do but fight for our lives, and after almost an hour, we killed the last man. Both of us were completely covered in blood, some of it our own. We each had many smaller wounds, but none of them serious. We again looked into each others eyes, and there was this recognition that we had each fought bravely and magnificently. This is the sense sometimes developed between experienced warriors of a job well done. I today look at this as being very primitive, but back then we both took a certain pride in being able to defeat 20 soldiers each.

We then turned to Lucifer and Satan, and although they were both armed and protected by armor, neither of them had the courage to fight us. They both started retreating, and I quickly picked up a spear and threw it so that it hit Satan in the chest and killed him. I was looking around for another spear, when Lucifer threw down his arms and started pleading with Jeshu to spare his life. Jeshu looked at me and said: "My brother, you are so quick to kill these people. What can they do to us now?"

I walked over to him and put one hand on his shoulder: "My brother, I have learned that I simply do not have the imagination to predict what they can and will do. They always come up with something I could not imagine so it is safer to stop them while I have the opportunity."

Jeshu looked back and said: "I cannot argue with your logic, but I have been thinking over this problem for what seems like a long time."

He then made a gesture towards the battlefield: "Look around you and see how many people have been killed here today. I feel I have experienced so much killing in this life and in the past, and my soul has had all it can take. My brother, there must be a better way to deal with such people, a way that does not involve killing!"

As he looked into my eyes, I felt as if I was transported out of my body, and from a distance I saw that he was right. It was one of those intuitive, mystical experiences of knowing from within that something is true, even though your outer mind cannot argue why it is true, but may indeed be able to argue against it. I again looked at Jeshu and said: "My brother, I now see that you are right, but I have no idea what that way might be."

Jeshu answered: "I don't see the way either, but I sense it must be there. Will you go with me on a journey to find it?"

I said: "I will go with you, and let us never again work against each other."

We then took off our battle dress and walked away from the battlefield and our roles as leaders of civilizations. We walked into the unknown, not even knowing what we were looking for, but knowing there was something to find.

# 18

What Jeshu and I experienced on that battlefield was what me might call a decisive soul turn-around produced by the School of Hard Knocks. We came to a point where we had had enough of a certain aspect of how life is on earth, and we formed this soul decision to raise ourselves above the consciousness that had precipitated this aspect. In our case it was violence, warfare and killing, but it can be many other things. Let me try to explain.

There are basically four types of souls or beings who embody on earth. The first category are the original inhabitants, those who belonged to the fourth wave of beings that came to earth. They were the ones who started going lower and breaking down the earth. The second category are beings from other planets who have come here because their planet was raised to a higher level or even the level of immortality but they could or would not raise their consciousness so high. Therefore, they had to start embodying on a planet that corresponded to their level of consciousness and they ended up here. The third category are the PCBs, and I will later explain where they came from and how they came to be here. The fourth category are the beings who came here for some kind of rescue mission, what I have called avatars.

Here is where I once again have to contradict some of the WCs created by the PCBs in order to keep people trapped. There is a very subtle sense among many spiritually inclined or religious people that at least one being is in a different category than all others. For example, many Buddhists believe the Buddha came here with no karma and that he was, from the beginning, in a category far beyond other human beings. Many Christians believe that Jesus was the son of god and that he had no sin, never sinned in any past lives and was fundamentally different from other people.

This is where it gets subtle. The Buddha and Jesus were both avatars. They *were* different from the original inhabitants of the earth in the sense that they had reached a higher level of consciousness before they came to earth. Yet here is a reality that will be denied by many. Neither the Buddha nor Jesus were fundamentally different from all other beings with self-awareness and free will.

An avatar was not created to live on earth and did not have to come here because his or her original planet was raised. The avatar made a choice to come here. And there was a reason why we made that choice, namely that there was something we wanted to learn from embodying on a planet like earth. I will wait a while before I talk about what I had to learn, but the important point for now is that all beings who have ever been in embodiment on earth have had something to learn from being here. We had something we needed to learn before we could qualify ourselves for ascending to the level of immortality.

What we have to learn is individual, but the way we learn it is universal. As I said, there are innumerable planets in our world that have never descended to the level you see on earth. They have never become unnatural planets. There are innumerable beings in our world who have learned a certain lesson without having embodied on an unnatural planet. Those of us who are avatars yet who have chosen to come to earth, did so because there was a lesson we had not learned on natural planets and we needed to embody on an unnatural planet in order to learn that lesson.

Here is the crucial point. We cannot learn these lessons through a theory or by being told by someone. As I described earlier, we all have teachers or guides who seek to help us grow. Yet there can come a point where a being cannot learn any more from its teachers, and therefore it needs to learn through direct experience. That is when we might decide (for whatever reasons we have in our minds, including thinking we are doing this to save others or a planet) to embody on an unnatural planet.

Now, I know how desperately some people want to hold on to the belief that there are certain beings (or at least one) who have come to earth without sinning, making karma or making any mistakes. Buddhists will be very reluctant to admit that the Buddha had previous lifetimes in which he made as many mistakes as most other people. Christians will refuse to believe the same about Jesus and will accuse me of being of the devil (as they have probably already done for other reasons). Many New Age people will be attached to seeing their particular guru as being above and beyond other human beings.

Yet the fact is that no being has ever come to earth without having something to learn, something that could only be learned by going through what I call the immersion phase. All beings on earth go through two distinct phases. The first one is the immersion phase where we immerse ourselves in the activities and experiences this planet has to offer to the point where we identify ourselves fully as human beings, whatever that means at a particular time and place in history.

We can stay in this immersion phase for a very long time. Many among the original inhabitants of the earth are still in that phase despite having embodied here for millions upon millions of years. The PCBs who have taken embodiment have been trapped in the immersion phase for infinitely much longer (being trapped in it before they came here). Yet even an avatar will have to go through this phase in order to learn the lessons that we simply cannot learn in any other way.

The trick is to realize that from a natural perspective, there is absolutely nothing wrong about this. There is no being in a higher energetic realm that looks down upon us and judges us, as the PCBs want us to believe. They also want us to believe that such beings judge us according to a standard defined by the PCBs, or rather their "masters" in the emotional, mental or identity levels.

The Law of Free Will is *free,* meaning there is no need to judge us. We are allowed to have any experience we want for as long as we want it (within a very, very wide range). We will continue to have a certain experience until we come to the point that Jeshu and I came to on the battlefield. You feel you have had enough of a certain experience, and you form a determination to raise yourself to a higher level of experiences.

Mind you, no teacher in a higher realm can (or want to) force you to get to this point. You must reach it by immersing yourself in a certain experience until you are saturated and want more. This is the law. The law also says you will face the return of the energies you have generated while you were having a certain experience. And you need to balance or restore those energies to the level of love before you can be entirely free from the level of consciousness that caused you to be immersed in and identified with the experience (thinking you were the kind of being who did what you did and experienced what you experienced). This is the School of Hard Knocks.

The law also says that when you do reach a saturation point, you must be given some form of guidance that can help you raise yourself to a higher level, according to your willingness to apply the teaching given. This law could be stated as follows: "When the student is ready, a teacher must appear."

# PART 4:

# THE UPWARD

# CLIMB

# 19

Jeshu and I now started a period that I will call the upward climb, although it was not a smooth process. In the beginning, it was agonizingly slow with many setbacks. We perfectly outpictured the saying that for each time you take one step forward, you slide two steps backwards. In one embodiment, we managed to stay away from violence, but in the next two we went back into a reactionary pattern with Lucifer and Satan.

You might think that our time is a violent time or that it was even more violent 500 years ago. Yet the period we lived in during the first many embodiments after our turnaround was even more violent than anything seen in official history. Back then, *might* was truly *right* and the stronger would suppress or kill the weaker. This does not mean there was lawlessness or anarchy because there was always one or several strong civilizations that had the kind of dictatorial, elitist rule you saw in the Roman Empire and many other societies, even what you have seen in communist countries during the modern era. This is a society where the PCBs form a power elite that has near total control over the citizens, being ready to kill anyone who objects or resists. Yet it was always the case that such a society could not appear alone. The PCBs are trapped in duality, and when people are in a dualistic state of mind, there will always be two opposing polarities.

The effect is that you have a society where one civilization cannot have total control over the world. At least two opposing power factions exist and they cannot co-exist peacefully. Such civilizations will always be ruled by PCBs, and they will be locked in a rivalry because both sides want ultimate power. PCBs cannot live and let live, they must live and let die.

Yet despite the fact that these were violent times, even compared to today, there was always some teacher who preached non-violence and an alternative to duality. Jeshu and I managed to find such a teacher in almost every embodiment. In the beginning, we found them in the warrior tradition, such as you see outpictured today in the martial arts. The teacher did teach some form of combat, but there was also a deeper teaching about non-violence, even transcending the consciousness of violence. For some teachers, the teaching on combat was really just a way to sort out the students that had the potential to grasp the deeper teaching.

There soon emerged a pattern where Jeshu became my teacher because he would grasp the teaching of our outer teacher first and then "translate" it to me. Once he had grasped an idea, he had a unique ability to express it in ways I could understand.

***

You might be thinking: "Why does one need a teacher in order to escape the reactionary pattern with the PCBs?" The reason you are thinking this is that the PCBs have, since not long after they first came to earth, managed to largely suppress the concept that you need a teacher. There is nothing they fear more than the concept that we are trapped at a certain (limited) level of consciousness and that in order to rise above it, we need a teacher who has already raised his or her consciousness beyond the level of duality. The PCBs have done everything they *can* to eradicate this concept, and this is why many modern societies do not have the idea that there are beings in a higher realm who have ascended from earth by mastering their consciousness and raising it beyond duality. These beings, or ascended masters, can serve as our teachers, and without them, we simply cannot escape duality. As I will explain later, the PCBs have never been able to completely eradicate the belief in an otherworldly god (except for brief periods of time), yet they have indeed been able to almost completely hide the concept that we have ascended masters as our teachers or guides.

So the first line of defence by the PCBs (meaning both those in embodiment and those existing in the emotional, mental and lower identity realms) is to remove the concept that there are teachers beyond earth. In today's world, they have a second line of defence, namely intellectualism or rational thinking that makes many people unable to understand why we need a teacher. Many people think that we should be able to think our way out of any problem. So if we are today in a lower state of consciousness that causes violence, we must be able to think our way out of it by using the intellect and rational reasoning.

This is a grand illusion that has existed in many previous eras, and it has never set people free. The reason is that it was precisely the intellect and rational thinking that got us into duality in the first place. And as Albert Einstein said, we cannot solve a problem with the same state of consciousness that created the problem. The reason for this is that once you step into duality, you become a self-fulfilling prophecy. Let me use my own example.

\*\*\*

I came to earth without having ever considered that there is a state of consciousness that is fundamentally lower than the state I had encountered on natural planets. My teachers would have given me at least some understanding of this ahead of time, but I was not open to receiving it. I was convinced that people on earth were simply suffering from an illusion, and by me appealing to their better nature and rational thinking, I could awaken them from the illusion and all would be well.

I did not understand that once people step into the dualistic consciousness, they cannot get out of it by using rational thinking and intellectual analysis. The reason for this is actually very simple, but it has been my experience that it is extremely difficult to explain this to people.

When I came to earth, I was sure I could convince people to abandon violence and suffering. I assumed that they wanted to escape violence and suffering and that they would be open to being shown a way out of it—a way that seemed so simple to me before I came here. After my first embodiment, I realized that the vast majority of people on earth actually are not ready to escape violence and suffering, nor are they open to being shown the way out of it. They no longer see or accept that here is an alternative.

I came to earth with a rather naive understanding of what kind of planet this is, and therefore I was completely shocked by what I experienced in my first embodiment. The encounter with Lucifer and Satan was a total shock to me because I very clearly sensed that they wanted to create violence and perpetrate suffering upon others.

Here is the really tricky part to understand. In my mind, violence and suffering was *wrong*. It was a mistake, something that was *not* supposed to happen, something that was not supposed to be on earth (or any planet). I was assuming that earth should have been like the natural planets and that the people of earth were suffering from living on a planet like this and would welcome any chance to escape it.

In my first few embodiments, I gradually came to realize that there are two rough categories of people on earth. There are the PCBs and there are the majority of the people who blindly follow the PCBs without knowing why and without realizing the consequences of what they are doing. It was a shock for me to encounter the PCBs because I saw that they deliberately caused violence and suffering, and it took me a long time to understand why they do this. It was equally shocking to realize that the majority of people on earth do not want to be set free from being dominated by the PCBs for the simple reason that they are not ready to take responsibility for themselves and the process of raising their consciousness. They actually want to be blind followers of the blind leaders because they do not want to make their own decisions. They want someone else to make decisions for them, and the PCBs are always ready to make decisions, as long as it is other people who must bear the consequences.

When I experienced the dominant dynamic on earth, I reacted in a way that got me trapped in duality at the end of my very first embodiment. In a sense, I already had some dualistic thinking before coming here because I felt that the violence and suffering on earth was wrong and should be changed. What I did not realize was that the violence and suffering on earth is a result of the free-will choices of the inhabitants of the earth. The Law of Free Will mandates that the inhabitants of a planet must be allowed to create any kind of situation they want to experience, and they must be allowed to experience it until they have had enough and cry out for help (within wide limits).

So when I came into embodiment, I had the idea that something was wrong on this planet, and I was here to change it. When I encountered the PCBs, it was not hard to identify that the "something" that was wrong on earth was the presence of the PCBs and their relentless drive to actually create violence and suffering for the population. I therefore quickly forgot the sense of oneness with all life that I had known on my natural planets. Instead, I came to see myself as being separated from the PCBs because they did something very shocking, and I knew I could never do what they did. I therefore, in my mind, set myself up as being against the PCBs, seeing it as my role to counteract their doings and to free the people of earth from their misuse of power and deception.

*** 

As a result of this, I gradually came to that embodiment where I for the first time reacted with violence and killed Satan with a sword. I then experienced a gradual awakening by feeling the instinctive shock of having killed another human being. Yet in succeeding embodiments I used my intellect and my reasoning ability to justify why I had to kill someone, and

I then started seeing killing as the only realistic solution to the problem on earth. I felt that since it was obviously impossible to reform or awaken the PCBs, it was better for the population that they were neutralized with all means possible, including killing them.

Now, it is important to grasp that I felt absolutely convinced that it was justified to kill the PCBs, as many people today feel equally justified in killing those they see as the enemies of themselves or their "just cause." Yet this is an illusion created by using the duality consciousness. The deeper reality, the *cosmic* reality, is that all life is one because all self-aware beings are connected in consciousness. Killing one human being affects all people on earth (even all beings in the cosmos), and it also affects yourself. Take note that I am not hereby saying that killing is "wrong" in a cosmic sense because in a cosmic sense the concepts of right and wrong are meaningless. I know that will be difficult to grasp, but it may become clearer later.

Let me stay with the fact that I was convinced killing was justified. How had I convinced myself of this? By using the dualistic state of mind, which operates with a special kind of logic. I have called it serpentine logic in order to link it to the story of how the serpent convinced Eve in the garden of Eden. The serpent persuaded Eve to go against what she instinctively knew was right, as I persuaded myself to go against my instinctive experience that killing is wrong.

***

Dualistic logic is a *relative* logic, but this can be difficult to grasp because it is so subtle and the PCBs are so good at camouflaging it. Again, let me give a simplified version at this point. Dualistic logic is relative because it always operates with an absolute right and an absolute wrong. In doing so, dualistic logic creates an existential, inescapable division between two concepts. This is a *relative* division, meaning it is artificially created and that the two opposites can only be defined relative to each other. It is in contradiction to the reality of the oneness of all life, but it has the effect of hiding this reality.

On my natural planets, I had a direct experience of the oneness of all life. You could have come to me and argued all day why life can be divided into opposing polarities, but it would have had no effect on me because my direct experience of oneness was my ultimate frame of reference. Nothing you said could counteract my direct experience. Imagine that you have been brought up to believe the earth is flat. This was the case for many people 500 years ago, and they took it for granted without truly reflecting on it. Some could come up with "sophisticated" arguments for why the earth had to be flat and could not be round. These arguments seemed watertight to people 500 years ago, but they seem primitive to us today. Now imagine that you took a person from medieval times and flew her out in a spaceship so she could directly see that the earth is round. Would the arguments have any effect on her in light of her direct experience? In most cases, this direct sensory experience would cause her to doubt her intellectual reasoning.

So here is the kicker. Once you step into the dualistic state of consciousness, it is like putting on a pair of goggles, like the virtual reality goggles we have today, that distorts your vision. You no longer have the direct experience that all life is one. This means you become lost in the serpentine logic, which says that some people are wrong or different, and therefore it is justified to kill them.

This psychological mechanism explains why it is possible to get human beings to kill each other. It also explains why it is possible to get people to reason away the instinctual shock that causes us to have an inner experience that killing is wrong. You might notice that I earlier argued that from a cosmic or natural perspective, the concepts of right and wrong have no meaning. Yet I have also said that when we kill another person, we have an instinctual experience that killing is wrong. You may think this sounds contradictory, but there is a subtle explanation.

We cannot kill another human being while we are in a non-dualistic state of mind. As long as we have a direct experience that all life is one, we cannot kill. It is only after we have already gone into duality (and lost the direct experience of the oneness of all life) that we can kill. Killing will give us a shock, but we still experience it through the filter of duality, which means we experience killing as "wrong." We can potentially use this experience to go deeper and grasp why killing feels wrong and what is the deeper reality behind it (because of the oneness of all life, we are literally killing a part of ourselves). A few people have done this, and it was what Jeshu decided to do just before we experienced that run-in on the battlefield.

Yet if we do not go behind the experience, it is so easy to do what I did after first killing Satan. If something is wrong, it follows that it is in opposition to something that is right. Thus, if only you find the "right" relative argument, you can convince yourself that although killing feels wrong, there are certain circumstances where it is justified. You can then learn to ignore the instinctual shock, even to the point of no longer feeling it consciously, as you see with psychopaths. And in some of my embodiments, I *was* a psychopath, although I would not have been labelled so because my killing was "justified" by me defending the defenceless.

\*\*\*

As an example of how dualistic logic works, let me use Adolph Hitler because he is so universally recognized as being evil, meaning it should be easy to identify him as a PCB of the worst order. Once you step into relative, dualistic logic, it is possible to come up with an argument that justifies absolutely anything. Any viewpoint can be justified and any viewpoint can be doubted. As an example, look at the fact that our so-called modern society for several hundred years has been caught in a battle between mainstream Christianity and scientific materialism. Why can't we settle the debate about whether god exists, why is there no ultimate argument? Because in duality, there can be no ultimate argument that will convince everyone. You can come up with arguments for any viewpoint that will convince some people, perhaps even many people. Yet you can also come up with an argument against that same viewpoint that will convince other people. The duality consciousness is uniquely suited for creating arguments but equally unsuited for settling them.

So back to Hitler. What you do in duality is that you create a viewpoint that clearly identifies something that is right and something that is wrong. The right is right in an epic sense, meaning it has some cosmic importance that right wins over wrong. Hitler used this trick to create the myth that it had cosmic importance to purify the human race of all wrong influences. In essence, he used the violence and suffering created by the PCBs throughout the ages to argue that in order to overcome this, we had to identify the problem and eradicate it. This has happened literally thousands of times since the PCBs came to this planet, and people still fall for it.

Hitler then also personified the epic struggle by identifying the German people as the ones who were already pure and the Jews as the ones who were impure. The solution was simple: It was justifiable to kill the Jews in order to avoid a calamity of cosmic proportions.

Now, notice the subtleties of the dualistic consciousness. Hitler argued that the Jews were wrong or bad, and today most people can clearly see that this is a relative viewpoint. Jews are human beings like everyone else, meaning there is no cosmic truth that says they are worse than anyone else. By the way, there is also no cosmic truth saying the Jews are better than anyone else, and yes that does mean the Old Testament idea that the Jews are god's chosen people is not based on cosmic truth. God has no chosen people, as all life is one.

What Hitler did was to first create a relativistic viewpoint in order to label the Jews. Then, he took that relativistic viewpoint and elevated it to the status of being absolute. This is the very central trick of the PCBs. They use the relative state of consciousness to create a viewpoint, and then they use the same relative logic to argue that it is not relative but absolute and therefore has cosmic truth and significance. Simple, clever and deadly effective. It works almost every time. By the way, it was the exact same form of logic used by George W. Bush (or those pulling his strings) to argue why the United States had to get rid of Saddam Hussein.

So with this long-winded explanation, I am coming back to the point I started out with. Once we step into duality and use the relative logic to create viewpoints that we think are absolute (because we never need to question them), we are trapped. We then become a self-fulfilling prophecy and there is no way for us to escape the trap from inside the trap. We have no frame of reference from outside our relative viewpoint so we can't see that it is relative. The absolutely only way out is that we make contact with beings who are not trapped in duality and then allow them to gradually raise us beyond the illusion that traps 99,99 percent of the people on this planet.

You cannot use the intellect or reason to escape duality. If you don't believe me, just read how Western philosophers have been arguing about the same points for 2,500 years without coming closer to a final argument. The reason is that in duality there can be no final argument. The philosophers have not been willing to question why they have not found a final argument and what this says about the mind itself. They have not been willing to look in the mirror.

The only way to resolve the dualistic arguments is to transcend them by raising our consciousness to the point where we see the oneness of all life. We *must* reach beyond duality in order to again have that direct, inner mystical experience of the oneness of all life. Only this experience can serve as a frame of reference for guiding us through the maze of duality and helping us cut the Gordian Knot of the serpentine absolutist appearing, but truly relativistic logic.

# 20

For a very long time, Jeshu and I found various teachers, as there have been, in every time period and in every civilization, some people who had a level of consciousness that was slightly above the collective consciousness of their time and place. And this was the entire problem. The teachers we were able to find were the ones that were above *our* level of consciousness, but not too far beyond. Why is this so? Because if a teacher is too far beyond your level of consciousness, you cannot recognize him or her.

As I have said, we all have teachers who are not living in the four levels of our universe and who are therefore beyond duality. Yet once you sink into duality, you lose direct contact with these ascended masters and therefore you lose the perspective that only they can give us. A teacher in embodiment will always be looking at life from inside the body and the mind, from inside the material universe. There is a fundamental limit to what one can see from this vantage point. Our ascended teachers do not have this restriction and can tell us the reality of how the universe functions. The problem is not the teacher's ability to *formulate* the teaching but our ability to *receive* the teaching. Let me give you one of the most stunning examples of this from earth's history, an example that Jeshu and I were fortunate enough to experience first-hand.

I want to mention first that Jeshu and I had indeed gone through a decisive turn-around. We had made one of the fundamental decisions that needs to be made in order to free oneself from the entanglement with the PCBs and the consciousness they represent. That decision is very simply that we don't respond with violence when we are exposed to violence, that we turn the other cheek, as Jeshu would later express it. Yet our upward climb was not a steady progression.

We had many embodiments where we were severely tested by being close to Lucifer and Satan and being exposed to all kinds of aggressiveness and humiliation from them. We had to demonstrate many times that we were willing to respond with non-violence to anything they did to us. And we did very gradually dig ourselves out of the hole and bring ourselves to a point where we started embodying with Lucifer and Satan more rarely. There was a phase where we would embody with them, but when we responded with non-violence, we would be able to move away from them and find a teacher that could help us take the next step up the stairway of consciousness.

You may wonder why you have never heard about the stairway of consciousness or the potential we all have for consciously and deliberately raising our level of consciousness. The reason is that the PCBs have done everything they could think of to hide the existence of a systematic path that leads to higher states of consciousness that are beyond duality. They did this because they do not want people in general to understand the existence of and the mechanics of this path, which would allow people to free themselves from the reactionary patterns with the PCBs. Of course, I have already mentioned that the PCBs want to keep people in these patterns because it causes people to qualify energy with fear and this fear-based energy is the foundation for the PCBs maintaining their existence. They are trapped in duality and can only control us by keeping us trapped in duality. They know how to trap *us* in duality, but they do not know how to free *themselves* from duality.

So very slowly and very gradually, over hundreds of thousands of years, Jeshu and I raised our level of consciousness so we did not have to always embody with Lucifer and Satan. This, however, had an interesting effect. Although Jeshu and I had lowered our level of consciousness by going into a reactionary pattern with them, we had never lowered our level to the level of Lucifer and Satan.

I might mention here that there are 144 levels of consciousness possible on this planet. If you go below the zero level, you are no longer allowed to embody here. If you go beyond the 144th level, you will ascend to the level of immortality and become an ascended master. We can therefore see these levels as a ladder or stairway that one can ascend and descend according to ones free-will choices.

Now, when I say free-will choices, this needs to be explained. You might say that in my first embodiment, I did not freely choose to be exposed to the aggressive acts from Lucifer and Satan. Yet I had freely chosen to embody on earth, and I had freely chosen not to fully educate myself as to how this planet functions. Naturally, what Lucifer and Satan did to me violated my free will and the Law of Free Will. Yet the reality is that on a planet like earth, this is what one must expect.

Therefore, given the special (temporary) state on this planet, it was allowed by the Law of Free Will that I be exposed to these actions. The reason is that I still had the free will to choose how I would respond to these actions. Yes, I know some will say that this was not much of a choice, but take note that planet earth is not a natural planet and therefore one cannot expect that things work as they do on a natural planet.

By the way, this is a mechanism that often trips up many sincere spiritually interested people. Millions of people have chosen to come into embodiment on earth in order to help bring this planet forward. Many of them have not been in embodiment as long as I have, and one can for a long time retain an inner, intuitive sense of how things are on a natural planet. When one comes into embodiment on earth, one forgets the specifics of how one lived on a natural planet, but one retains some of the sense of how things were, meaning one has an expectation of how things should be on earth. This inevitably leads to disappointment and shock, which is mercilessly exploited by the PCBs to get us to go into a reactionary pattern with them. Okay, I got side-tracked again.

***

My point was that life on earth can be seen as a process where one goes up and down on the staircase of the 144 levels of consciousness. When you first come here, you are at a certain level, depending on your past history. Your option then is to use your experiences on this planet to go up or down. I have said that most of us need to go down for a while, and it is what I have called the immersion phase. We end up fully identifying ourselves as human beings, as this is defined by the collective consciousness of the planet. Then, most of us come to a turnaround point where we feel we simply will not go any lower, and from there we start climbing back up. You can look at every person you know, and they will be at a certain level of consciousness. You can look at public persons and they will be at a certain level of consciousness. You can learn to sense this intuitively, and you can learn to sense whether people are going up or down in consciousness.

There are two distinct dividing lines on the staircase of consciousness, namely at the 48th level and the 96th level. The original inhabitants of the earth came into embodiment at the 48th level (although the scale was different back then). They were then offered a path where non-dualistic teachers in embodiment would take them through seven levels of initiations until they reached the 96th level. This is the level where we can begin to discern between duality and non-duality through a direct inner experience, meaning we become more self-sufficient and need to become independent of outer teachers on earth. We can then make inner contact with our ascended teachers and rise to the 144th level after which we can ascend to the level of immortality.

This systematic path of growth has been in existence in similar forms on all planets with self-aware life. The first three life-waves on earth followed this path and did not go below the 48th level (or only went slightly below and quickly rose again). The fourth wave was different in the sense that some followed their teachers while a substantial number started going below the 48th level. The 48th level is sort of the neutral level, in the sense that at this level you are entirely focused on yourself, but not in a way that would be called egotistical or selfish with today's standard. You are focused on yourself, but you are not deliberately harming other people.

When you follow the upward path, you are still focused on your own growth and on attaining the mastery of your co-creative abilities, meaning you strive to attain the mastery of mind over matter that is our true potential. When you reach the 96th level, you have a decisive choice to make. You can choose to stop focusing on yourself and instead seek to help other people, whereby you start climbing towards the 144th level where you become completely selfless because you realize that all life is one. Thus, the only way to truly do something for yourself is to do something for others.

The other option is that you want to continue to use your abilities and attainment for your own sake, which actually means you can easily fall below the 48th level. In a way, your attainment is reversed because you do not lose the ability to influence matter, but you turn it into a skill used only for your own gratification. This is what you see with PCBs. Lucifer had a rather stunning ability to influence matter with his mind, and it came from the fact that he had once (in a previous world, as I will explain later) attained a high level of mastery and then inverted it by choosing to focus on himself instead of seeking to raise the whole.

So what happened in the distant past was that the fourth wave of lifestreams to embody on earth started going further and further below the 48th level of consciousness. Now, it is one thing that an individual goes below the 48th level, but the decisive matter is the collective consciousness of an entire planet. For some time, the 4th wave had kept the collective consciousness on or above the 48th level, but they eventually took it below.

Once that happens, the inhabitants of a planet can no longer maintain a direct connection to the teachers who are beyond duality. They now

become confined to having only teachers in embodiment, and those teachers cannot be too far above the level of the collective consciousness or
people will not recognize them. That is why this planet fell below what
we might call natural spirituality, the kind of spiritual guidance found on
natural planets. Instead, earth got the kind of spirituality we see now in the
form of dogmatic religions. Common for these religions is that they give
you articles of faith or dogmas that you are supposed to believe. Natural
spirituality seeks to give you direct, intuitive, mystical experiences that take
you beyond belief.

The dramatic change came when the collective consciousness of earth
sank below the 36th level. This was when it was decided to allow PCBs
to start embodying here. Now, the first PCBs that came here were not in
the category of Lucifer and Satan. They were not nearly as aggressive and
willing to use violence. Yet they still were willing to set themselves up as
leaders because they felt they were superior to human beings. They did
this primarily through the kind of dogmatic religions we still see today,
although their exact form was different. These PCBs introduced the idea
that some beings are higher, better or more important than others, meaning they gave birth to the elitist mindset that is the most severe form of
denial of the oneness of all life.

Over a long period of time, this caused the lowering of the collective
consciousness even more, and gradually more and more aggressive PCBs
were allowed to embody here. Finally, there came a point where the collective consciousness was so low that PCBs in the category of Lucifer and
Satan could embody here, and this is when warfare was introduced to this
planet. Before that, systematic, large-scale warfare had been unknown here
although some weapons had existed, mostly developed for hunting. I will
later explain why these beings were allowed to embody here, but it is a
complicated issue that requires me to set a better foundation.

\*\*\*

Where I am going with this is that there is a cosmic council of non-
dualistic masters who are constantly evaluating the state of the collective
consciousness and what can be done to raise it. So I now want to jump
back to the time when Jeshu and I had started freeing ourselves from Lucifer and Satan. I said that this had an interesting effect, and here is how this

worked. While Jeshu and I had embodied in close proximity with Lucifer and Satan, we had to some degree held back their aggressiveness. We had either done this physically by opposing or even killing them or we had done so psychologically through the influence on them that we gradually developed. What this had created was a situation where the population of earth had (over many lifetimes) experienced two kinds of leadership. Jeshu and I (usually Jeshu as the main leader) had represented leaders who were clearly ready to use violence and were good warriors but who also had a certain integrity and fairness. Lucifer and Satan represented leaders who had no integrity and fairness and who suppressed the people violently and ruthlessly.

Now, you might think that the choice between the two forms of leadership was a no-brainer, and indeed it is, meaning that the population of the time really weren't using their brains, or rather their intuitive faculties. As Jeshu and I withdrew from leadership in order to raise ourselves beyond duality, we left a vacuum that was filled by Lucifer, Satan and other PCBs. This quickly made it clear that the majority of the people on earth preferred the kind of dictatorial and abusive form of leadership represented by the PCBs. People actually wanted to follow the PCBs. You might think this was crazy, but look at the world today. Look how the population of Russia and China repeatedly attract abusive leaders. Look how democratic countries repeatedly elect politicians with no personal integrity and no vision. In the "oldest democracy of the world," the so-called *United* States, things have gone so low that a person with personal integrity and vision cannot even be nominated as a presidential candidate.

Why do human beings tend to follow the PCBs? Because the PCBs offer people something they want more than freedom, democracy and a society based on integrity and vision. The PCBs promise people that they will deliver an ideal world (or at least a better world) and the people don't need to wake up and make conscious decisions. They can stay asleep and live their lives, and one day "PUFF" the world will have changed.

Back in that distant time, it became clear that the original hope of allowing PCBs to embody here had not been fulfilled. Instead of having had enough of this abusive leadership, people continued to follow the PCBs blindly and actually preferred them as leaders. People would rather continue to believe in empty promises than take responsibility for their own growth and the state of the planet. They wanted to stay in the spiritual coma they had been in for a very long time.

Unbeknownst to Jeshu and I, the cosmic council overseeing the earth were deliberating whether the earth was a sustainable planet. It was decided that the earth had gone into such a downward spiral that it really had no purpose in terms of serving as a platform for growth. It was considered whether the earth should be allowed to go into the last phases of self-destruction that would allow the planet to literally collapse and seize to exist (as has happened to a relatively small number of planets).

Of course, this is not as ominous as it might sound. Lifestreams who were in an upward spiral could embody on other planets. And there is always a possibility that seeing their planet disintegrate can awaken lifestreams so they can begin an upward spiral elsewhere. Our non-dualistic teachers have no particular attachment to a planet, although they have naturally invested a huge amount of their own energy and attention in creating it. They would prefer to have it fulfil its original purpose, but if that no longer seems possible, they will allow it to self-destruct as a final learning opportunity for the inhabitants. So there literally came a point where the continued existence of the earth was at a tipping point that could have gone either way. Then, a rather momentous occurence occured.

# PART 5:

# THE VENUSIAN

# MYSTERY SCHOOL

# 21

With today's primitive religion, primitive science and primitive sensory perception, we are not aware that there is self-aware life on the other planets in our solar system. There is life on all planets, although not in the same frequency spectrum as that of our physical bodies, which is why we cannot perceive this life and why we see the other planets as unsuited for life. They are indeed unsuited for the kind of physical life we have on this planet, but there is a large array of frequency spectra in which life can exist.

Venus has a higher level of collective consciousness than earth and the inhabitants are far above the level that corresponds to the 48th level on earth. At the time that the cosmic council for earth was deliberating the future of this planet, one of the ascended masters working with Venus stepped forward and offered to make a last-ditch attempt to turn this planet around and get it into an upward spiral. His name is Sanat Kumara, and he was just finishing a cycle of working with the inhabitants of Venus and getting them to raise their planet into a positive spiral.

After some deliberations, it was determined that Sanat Kumara would set up a retreat in the identity realm on earth. From there he would attempt to teach human beings in embodiment a higher path beyond duality. It was also determined that in order for this to be successful, he would need the help of a large number of lifestreams from Venus who would take physical embodiment on earth. This would raise the collective consciousness of earth significantly and it was the hope that some of the people embodying on earth would be able to make use of this to intuitively attune to Sanat Kumara and his retreat. The result was that 144,000 lifestreams from Venus took embodiment on earth, which was quite a sacrifice, given their higher level of consciousness.

Jeshu and I had taken embodiment on earth as avatars, but we had not had the experience of raising a planet to the level beyond duality. The 144,000 from Venus had indeed had the experience of the long and agonizingly slow process of raising Venus beyond duality, and it was therefore (given that they had not yet ascended) quite a contrast, a sacrifice and a risk for them to once again embody on a dualistic planet, especially one as dense as earth. I realize most people have no sense of co-measurement for how big of a sacrifice this was for the venutians, and most people will just shrug their shoulders, but anyway, it has been said.

Those who came from Venus had to take embodiment as anyone else, meaning they would lose the conscious memory of who they were and where they came from. They would then have to use their intuitive faculties to tune in to Sanat Kumara, which was naturally easier for them than for those of us who had been on this planet for a long time and did not know him. After some time, many of them gradually awakened and they started finding each other and developing a new civilization in what is now the area of the Gobi desert. Back then, it was also a wasteland where no one lived so they had the opportunity to build a new civilization without too much interference from anybody. The physical area was close to the location of Sanat Kumara's retreat in the identity realm. Many ascended masters have such retreats and they use them for various purposes. Some of them serve as schoolrooms where we can travel at night in our identity bodies in order to receive instructions that we may not remember clearly but can still use in our waking consciousness.

The civilization built by the venutians was very different from any other seen on earth at the time in that it was dedicated entirely to spiritual growth. It was not what we would call a religious society based on today's dogmatic religions. It was centered around the individual, mystical path that was aimed at developing the intuitive faculties of people without making them co-dependent on an outer guru, teaching or institution.

All of the inhabitants of this society worked together on the common goal of building their society. Most of the people served to provide the economical foundation through farming, mining, building industries and so forth. Yet in their spare time, they would all volunteer to help build the central city, which was centered around a temple complex where people could practice the mystical path. All inhabitants saw it as their goal to support their society and also walk the path themselves.

After they had established this unique society, Jeshu and I started picking up whispers about it, and in one embodiment we found our way there. It was a very special experience for us when we walked into what was the central temple complex of the city. The architecture was so different from anything seen on earth at the time, and the closest we can come today is some of the Greek temples, although the Gobi civilization was a much more refined architecture with an airy or ethereal appearance. The buildings seemed to float effortlessly and barely touch the ground.

Yet beyond the outer appearances, what was most special what the energetic vibration in the temple complex. The modern materialistic mindset scoffs at this (the PCBs scoff at anything they do not understand or are not willing to acknowledge), even though for a century we have known through science that everything is energy. Many people can intuitively sense the difference in the energy level of various places, some being dark and some having a lighter energy.

The venutians had created a temple complex where the design of the buildings and their placement was dedicated to creating a specific energetic matrix or forcefield. Yet what really raised the vibration was a combination of the permanent staff at the temple complex who performed daily exercises and the fact that every Sunday people from all over came to the temple to perform these exercises in a group. The exercises they did had the purpose of invoking high-frequency energy from the higher identity realm and the realm beyond the identity level. This was done primarily through the spoken word in a way that is somewhat similar to chanting. Similar exercises have actually been released in today's world by the ascended masters.

When Jeshu and I first entered the temple complex, we clearly felt the difference in the energy level between the city and the surrounding world. The contrast was so noticeable that only the most dense people would have failed to feel it. We felt as if some of our burdens fell away as we walked closer to the temple complex. We were not allowed to enter the inner temples until we had been initiated, but even being in the central square where tens of thousands of people would meet and do their invocations was a special experience.

Jeshu and I applied to become apprentices in the school of initiation that was offered, and after some trials, we were accepted. It was like a homecoming for me to find myself in this initiatic school because it awakened in me a sense of how life was on a natural planet, something I had forgotten for so many lifetimes. Jeshu and I responded very well to the path of initiation that was presented to us, and we quickly made progress.

We were, of course, not the only students. Many were the venutians who had found their way as close to home as they could come, but there was also a substantial number of lifestreams that had embodied on earth for a long time, some of them avatars like ourselves. Among them we met several that we would embody with in later times, some of them coming to have a great impact on world history (as would Jeshu). I want to mention in particular Maitreya and Gautama. They were further along than both of us on the path of overcoming duality, and they would later help us in crucial ways. We would meet Gautama in a later embodiment and he would have a great impact on the growth of both of us.

# 22

What the venutians had created was something we might call a Mystery School where the entire purpose was to initiate people in the inner path towards a higher state of consciousness. As I explained in the beginning, this path is the normal way of life on a natural planet, but on such planets it is not seen as the "mystical" path because there is nothing mysterious about it. It is freely and openly taught to all. It is only because the path towards self-knowledge has been systematically eradicated on earth by the PCBs that it seems mysterious or unknown here.

Obviously, in today's world the materialists will reject any thought of a mystical path because they reject anything that points to a reality beyond the material. Yet even the majority of religions reject such a path and instead promise people that by following the outer rules and dogmas of the religion, they will be saved by some external force. The reality is, of course, that everything in your life depends on your state of consciousness. You are ultimately responsible for what you do with your mind or what you allow others (meaning the PCBs) to do with your mind. The doorway to the spiritual realm can be freely entered by all who have raised their consciousness beyond duality, and it will remain hermetically sealed to all who still have dualistic elements in their minds.

The venutians were quite aware of what it takes to raise people beyond duality as they had walked the path themselves on their own planet. They had therefore created a very rigorous program, and Jeshu and I enrolled ourselves in the neophyte or beginner's course with great eagerness. The beginner's course was basically a cleansing of our four lower bodies, the four levels of our minds (including the physical mind), plus the physical body.

We were on a very strict diet consisting of vegetables and special herbs that helped cleanse our bodies from toxins and parasites. We would do physical exercises that are similar to today's yoga for the simple reason that today's yoga is based on the Venusian techniques (with a smaller or greater degree of purity preserved). We did physical work in terms of helping to build the temple complex or working in the extensive gardens. We walked on the dew in the morning and took hot baths interspersed with cold ones.

First of all, we performed special exercises where we spoke aloud certain verses that rhymed. The venutians called them "decrees" and they had the purposes of invoking specific types of high-frequency energy and directing it at issues in our four lower bodies. In the beginning, we did these decrees in groups without having personal instructions. We received general instructions about the four lower bodies and were then left to ourselves as to how we applied them.

We would get up early in the morning and start with walking on the dew, then hot and cold baths, then some yoga exercises and then a light breakfast. After breakfast, we would go to a hall with several hundred other people and do the decrees for several hours until lunch. In the beginning, our vocal cords could hardly handle this, but we quickly got used to it. The decrees were given very quickly, and it took us some time to be able to follow the speed, but then it became effortless. After four hours of decreeing at high speed, you would feel a natural high and you felt a definite clearing of your consciousness. Then we had a light lunch, did some more yoga, and then we decreed again for the afternoon (or worked on certain days). Then dinner, yoga and again four hours of decrees in the evening.

It was an amazing program, and over a matter of weeks you could feel a shift in your consciousness towards more clarity. It was not an easy program, but Jeshu and I had no problem mustering the necessary self-discipline. It wasn't that the program was comfortable because it had the same effect as if you do a physical cleansing, namely that all kinds of psychological issues were brought up, and we had to deal with them.

As I mentioned before, in my first embodiment I had the ability to see people's energy fields. In our auras there are seven energy centers, and today they are known as "chakras." Each chakra corresponds to a specific type of high-frequency energy, what the venutians called a "spiritual ray." Their program was designed to clear all of the seven chakras in a systematic manner. First, we had a period where we took one chakra at a time and focused on it for a month. We were given teachings about the chakra and the type of energies that correspond to it. We were also taught the creative potential of a given chakra. Anything we do is, as I have explained, done with energy that streams from our I AM Presences through the four lower bodies. Yet this energy enters through and is expressed through the chakras.

When we go into duality, we are still using our chakras to do things, but now we are using perversions of the creative potential, justified by certain dualistic lies. This creates certain psychological mechanisms or reactionary patterns, and what the venutians had us do was to flush out some of these so they came to our conscious minds. We would then have to deal with them based on the general instructions we received. For the first seven months, we received no personalized guidance. It was a trial by fire, and those who were not willing to face their own psychological demons would simply drop out. This may seem harsh, and it was, but the venutians had a specific purpose for their program, and they knew some were willing to give their all to it. Those who were not willing to give their all were offered a milder program and could become members of the larger community that supported the Mystery School. Yet those who were willing to endure the first seven months were then ready to receive more personalized instructions.

*** 

Jeshu and I had many discussions (in the short amount of spare time we had together) about what came up in our psychology. We both so clearly sensed that being in this Mystery School was an opportunity we had longed for during many previous lifetimes. We knew this was a unique privilege and we were determined to make the most of it by looking at everything in ourselves. Yet this didn't make it any easier to deal with the very intense emotions that were forced to the surface by us invoking so much high-frequency light. There were times when we felt like our four lower bodies were shaking uncontrollably and we almost couldn't focus on practical tasks, like eating.

Both of us had to deal with emotions related to violence and fighting, especially fear and anger. I had a period where I felt such debilitating fear that I was literally afraid to get out of bed, but wanted to hide under the blanket. Jeshu stayed with me and talked me through it, but it took two days before I was able to face the world. These fears went back to some of the violent torture I had been exposed to by Lucifer and Satan in my first embodiments, but they were buried so deep that I had no way of knowing where they came from, making it much harder to deal with.

Jeshu had a period where he became obsessed with such an intense anger that he could not be around other people. I remember seeing him coming towards me with an expression of such anger that I had never seen in him before. He walked right by me, seemingly without seeing me, and I followed him as he walked into the hills near the temple complex. I stayed at a distance to make sure he would not do damage to himself and watched him walk around in circles for hours while shouting at himself, the trees and the heavens.

After several hours, he seemed a bit calmer, and I walked over to him and said casually: "So my brother, why are you carrying that pile of shit around on your shoulders?" He first looked at me like he was going to explode in anger, then he exploded in laughter and we both laughed for several minutes, tears streaming out of our eyes. Then we had a long conversation about why we both felt such anger, and we ended up realizing we were angry at ourselves for something we had done in the past, something that was sealed from our conscious memories.

Jeshu finally said: "I am so angry with myself for having done so many things that I knew were not right, but I can't see why I did them."

I answered: "I know how you feel. I know I have also done many things that I knew were not right, but I also know I had some reasoning for doing them. Yet because I can't see my reasoning I can't do anything about it. We have to break this deadlock." Of course, the venutians knew what we were going through and had already created techniques for helping us.

\*\*\*

After the seven-month crash course, we entered a new phase. We were now evaluated by our instructors, and it was a very simple form of evaluation. Some of the instructors could see auras so they could simply see which of our chakras were the most in need of clearance. We were then put in groups based on this, and we now received personalized instructions and did both individual and group exercises. We still did some of the decrees together with the entire group of "survivors," and on Sundays we had special services together with the entire community in the main temple square.

Jeshu and I were first put in a group that dealt with anger. This is a primary perversion of the so-called power chakra. It is "located" in the higher bodies in a position that corresponds to the physical throat, therefore also called the throat chakra. It relates to the first spiritual ray of will and power and regulates how we express our will and our creative power. It is the chakra that is the beginning of the creative process because before you can create anything, you must have the will to create and you must concentrate and direct psychic power towards manifesting your creation.

When you look at world history, you can see that all of the so-called powerful people known to current history (and many more not currently known) had very powerful throat chakras. What you see today is also that 99 percent of the powerful people became powerful because over many lifetimes they had perverted their throat chakras. Naturally, Jeshu and I had done this also in order to fight Lucifer and Satan.

The perversion of power is force, meaning that instead of expressing natural power based on the knowing that all life is one, you express force based on the sense that you are a separate being who has to accomplish a goal for itself or for the world, a goal that is opposed by others. The conscious excuse we have for perverting the expression of willpower is that we have to accomplish a goal that is so important that it necessitates and justifies the use of force in order to overcome those who oppose the goal.

Yet the deeper reality is that we can never fully believe that force is justified. We often do not know why this is so, but we have an instinctual or intuitive knowing that forcing others is not natural. How do we go beyond this? By perverting our natural creative energy into anger that then accumulates in our auras, especially in the throat chakra. When the accumulation becomes intense enough, the anger blinds us to our intuitive knowing, and we can now consciously feel justified in using force. Yet for each time we do so, we have to create more anger, and this becomes a self-reinforcing spiral (an emotional and mental addiction) that can be very difficult to break.

Our instructors helped Jeshu and I work on this problem, but it was not something that could be done in five minutes, as so many New Age gurus claim today. We literally worked on the throat chakra for an entire year before moving on to the next chakra. It therefore took us 10 years to work through all seven chakras, which meant we could graduate from the neophyte program and enter the intermediate program.

\*\*\*

It was good that we had come to the Mystery School at a young age because it took us another 10 years before we could enter the advanced program. In this program we had even more personalized instructions, and some of the experienced instructors started using a technique to take us into consciously experiencing past lives. They did this by using techniques somewhat similar to what is today known as hypnotherapy and EMDR, but it was supported by the invocation of light through decrees and other exercises that combined decrees with positive affirmations (the venutians called them invocations). This invocation of light was crucial in making it easier and more efficient to deal with past life traumas.

The instructors had realized that Jeshu and I had many past lives together and that we needed to resolve many things together. They worked with us individually but also with the two of us together, and we had many discussions where we processed what we had seen about our past lives. The interesting thing about accessing a past life is that it has two components, a universal and a subjective.

I have said that everything is energy and that there are many forms of energy that we cannot detect with our senses or with today's rather primitive technology (scientists can actually detect many non-material forms of energy but because of the materialistic blinders, scientists have not interpreted their findings in a non-material context). One effect of this is that there is a certain vibrational spectrum that acts as a sophisticated recording device. Everything that has ever happened on earth is recorded in what the venutians called Akasha or the Akashic Records.

What our instructors did was to take us into a deep meditative state (not truly a hypnotic state) and then help us access the recording of a specific situation in a past life. Yet this Akashic recording is like watching a movie of the events. You see what actually happened and what you did, but you do not see your own feelings or thoughts about the situation. So the Akashic recording is the universal element. The subjective element is that watching this recording will bring up the psychological wounds, traumas and reactionary patterns that you are still carrying in your four lower bodies. It is then up to you to process these—with the help of the instructors, of course.

The program we followed was that we would be taken into deep meditation and guided to access a past life. In the beginning, it was impossible to predict which life would come up so it was simply a matter of starting somewhere. We would then be guided to become more conscious of the feelings involved, the feelings that came up when we thought about that lifetime. We would use decrees and invocations to invoke light that would transform the feeling energy. Feelings are simply a form of energy and any fear-based feeling has a vibration beneath a certain level. As scientists know from simple wave interactions, when two waves meet, they can create an interference pattern that creates a new wave.

If you have a certain pocket of feeling energy stored in your emotional body, you can invoke energy of a higher vibration and direct it into the pocket of lower vibrations. When the waves of higher and lower frequencies meet each other, they create an interference pattern that raises the vibration of the lower waves. When you repeat this process long enough, you can transform the pocket of fear-based energy. This has a two-prong effect. Firstly, it removes the intensity and the often debilitating and paralyzing effect of these emotions. Secondly, it now opens up for a conscious view of the thoughts behind the feelings. If you do not invoke energy to transform the feeling energy, you can go around in these emotional circles for a long time, as proven by modern psychotherapy.

As I have explained, the natural flow of energy is from your I AM Presence into the identity body, then into the mental and then into the emotional. On a natural planet, you are conscious of the entire process, but on a dense planet like earth most people are not conscious of very much of what goes before their feelings. They therefore get stuck in paralyzing emotions and cannot get beyond them, often for a lifetime or many lifetimes. Once you invoke light to raise the vibration of the fear-based emotions, you can move forward in seeing the thoughts behind them. Once you see the thought patterns that gave rise to the feelings, you can begin to reason with these fear-based beliefs and replace them with love-based knowledge. Again, you can invoke high-frequency energy to deal with the mental energy.

Consider how many people in today's world are stuck at the mental level, endlessly analyzing thoughts without realizing that they come from a higher level. Once you free yourself from the dead end of mental analysis, you can see the pattern in the identity level that gave rise to the thoughts. This leads you to the decision you made when the reactionary pattern was created, and then you can consciously change that decision. When you resolve the pattern in the identity level, you are free of a certain behavioral pattern.

What I am telling you here could revolutionize modern psychology and could help billions of people (in fact all people on earth) overcome some of the extreme traumas they have received during their many past lifetimes on this very difficult and dense planet. I am not saying that all people have been subjected to the kind of direct, personal attack I have described in my first embodiment. However, all people have experienced wars and other atrocities so we all have deep traumas from past lives. Until psychologists recognize that the deep problems they encounter were not created in the current lifetime, they will not be able to truly help their patients. Of course, the PCBs and their puppet masters do not want this to happen, which is why they have done everything they could think of to lock modern psychology firmly in the blind alley of materialism. Yet more and more people are beginning to realize from personal experience that materialistic psychology simply isn't helping people so there is a potential for change. Yet it will obviously require that a sufficient number of people confront the PIN that currently rules the field of psychology.

Anyway, the venutians had created a very efficient program, and Jeshu and I applied ourselves to it with everything we had. It took many years of going into past lives before we started getting back to our original traumas. For a long time, we had very short glimpses of our first embodiments, but it took an agonizingly long period of time before we came to a more full understanding of what had happened to us when we first came to this planet and encountered beings like Lucifer and Satan.

***

Jeshu and I started working with some of our instructors on systematically uncovering our entire history on this planet. In many cases, one of us would get glimpses of a certain embodiment and then the other would get more details. Gradually we would peace together a time line going back to both mine and Jeshu's first embodiments. We uncovered that Jeshu had been wounded as badly as I had in his first embodiment, and for him it was also Lucifer and Satan that had been the physical instruments for his earth birth trauma. This naturally gave rise to a lot of questions about who (or rather, what kind of beings) Lucifer and Satan were, why they were doing what they were doing and why this was allowed.

The venutians made it obvious for us that we are not alone here on earth. There are numerous other beings in our world, both in the physical octave, in the other three octaves and in the higher realm, the realm of immortality or the ascended realm. They also made obvious what we already knew intuitively, namely that there is a plan and a purpose for life. There is a movement towards raising all life to a higher state. There are beings, namely the ascended masters, who are directly working with earth in order to help us raise our consciousness.

Yet even though this was obvious to both of us, it only made our confusion worse, as we could not understand why these benevolent beings would allow Lucifer and Satan to have free reign on earth. And we still could not understand how such beings could even exist. We had many discussions about this and could not make out where such beings came from. We sensed they could not have been created by a non-dualistic source, but then what was their origin? It turned out the venutians had profound answers to these questions, but we had to reach a certain level of consciousness before we were ready to receive them.

# 23

The venutians had a very clear goal with their Mystery School, and since our modern world has lost all conception of what the venutians knew, I would like to try to explain it. If you look at modern media coverage, what do you see? In every case, the journalists have no opinions but refer to experts. What's the underlying message? If even the journalists don't dare to have opinions but always refer to experts, what should *you* do? What do you see in the dominant religions today? They also have experts who are the only ones who can interpret the scripture from the past. Again, the message is that *you* can know nothing and that you should rely on the authorities. What do you see in the scientific field? Again, only the experts can conduct experiments and interpret the results. The pattern is obvious. *You*, the "ordinary" person cannot know anything on your own. You should not think you can know anything or have opinions about anything. You should in all aspects of life rely on experts. And who are the experts? Well, they are not all PCBs but rest assured that in every field, there are PCBs pulling the strings.

The message is clear, namely that ordinary human beings can know nothing and that only the PCBs can tell us anything worth knowing. It has been this way ever since the first PCBs started embodying on earth. The venutians understood this fully, and their Mystery School was designed to counteract it. What have the PCBs used as their tool to control us? They have used the main feature of the duality consciousness, namely that there is no ultimate argument. The PCBs use this to make you doubt that you can really know anything. They can present arguments for and against any issue so that people get so confused that they don't know what to believe.

Then, the PCBs use the very same relativistic consciousness to define one relative argument as being absolute, and they get some people to believe in this. Because the claim to absolutism is based on the relative consciousness, it always has a counterclaim, meaning there will always be opposite claims to ultimate authority, such as capitalism and communism or scientific materialism and dogmatic religion. This only works in favour of the PCB's ultimate cause, although the lower-ranking PCBs fail to see this and truly believe they are working for a worthy cause by fighting for a relative system. What is the overall cause of the PCBs (and the puppet masters in higher octaves)? It is to dis-empower all people on earth by making us think we can know nothing from within but always need an external authority to tell us what is true, right or absolute.

The venutians knew that we all have a potential to go within and establish a direct contact with a source of knowledge that is beyond duality. We can do this through something that is built into our minds. I have said a long time ago that we are extensions of our I AM Presences who reside in a higher realm. What descends is a Conscious You, which really is only awareness with none of the individuality defined in the four lower bodies. I have also said that our evolution on earth has two phases, namely immersion and awakening. As long as you are in the immersion phase, you will have forgotten who you are. You will be fully identified with your four lower bodies and will not be open to the fact that you are a Conscious You who is only using the soul vehicle to experience the world.

When you begin to awaken, you become open to the possibility that there is a part of you that can step outside of your four lower bodies and therefore gain a fundamentally different perspective on life. I said in the beginning that we are all having a subjective experience and that we can never have anything else. I also said that all problems on earth come from the fact that some people are trying to make their subjective experience universal by projecting it upon others. When you begin to awaken from identification with your four lower bodies, you can have glimpses of a state of consciousness that is beyond what you have when you see the world through the perception filter of those four lower bodies. As long as you are identified with your soul vehicle, it is like you are wearing four pairs of colored glasses that all distort your vision. When the Conscious You steps outside this perception filter, you can have a very different experience of life. You can begin to see that your four lower bodies are not providing you with the *only* possible way to look at life. They are simply *one* way of looking at life.

I am not here talking about whether what you see is right or wrong, accurate or inaccurate. The reality is that you need your four lower bodies in order to interact with the physical realm. And you need to interact with the physical realm in order to grow in self-awareness. So until you ascend, you need your four lower bodies. Yet when you stop being fully identified with them, you can begin to see that you can actually purify your four lower bodies of artificial elements, and this means you will gain a more constructive perception of life. This has three effects.

The first one is that when you are no longer identified with your feelings, your beliefs or your sense of identity, you can begin to see that your four lower bodies are like containers or repositories. During your long journey on this planet, various elements have been deposited there from the outside, and they form the filter through which you perceive the world. Once you no longer identify with these elements, you can take a critical look at them and evaluate whether they actually serve you or not. You will then begin to see that many of these elements are deliberately put there (programmed in there) by the PCBs for the sole purpose of dis-empowering you so that you can be controlled by forces in this world, forces that are dualistic and do not have your best interest at heart. When you engage in a systematic process of purifying your four lower bodies from the artificial elements, you can avoid being pulled into self-destructive patterns and avoid seeing the world through a distorted perception.

*** 

The other thing that will happen is that you will start having more frequent experiences of a state of consciousness that is beyond duality, beyond your normal perception filter. You can begin to see the world in a more neutral way and you can also begin to see beyond your own four lower bodies. Again, consider the four lower bodies as four pairs of glasses that distort everything you see. As long as you do not have a frame of reference, you will think this is the only way to look at the world. Once you start having a direct experience that there is a different way to perceive the world, you can raise your vision so you begin to see things that you simply could not see before. A very simple analogy is that you are walking up the spiral staircase inside a lighthouse with windows along the staircase. The lighthouse is surrounded by trees so for the first many steps, you cannot see anything but the trees. Then you come to a point on the staircase where you can begin to see above the treetops, and now you see a much broader perspective.

The third effect is that once you begin to see beyond your own four lower bodies, you can begin to make contact with your spiritual teachers in a higher realm, namely your own I AM Presence and the ascended masters. This is what will give you the ultimate frame of reference for escaping the maze of dualistic lies. What you get through these direct inner experiences is not a relative, intellectual, analytical argument. You get a direct experience of a higher reality, and once you lock in to this, you can never again be fully fooled by the serpentine logic of the PCBs. You will then be able to receive certain information directly from within. In the beginning, this ability may be somewhat sketchy, and it often means that you will get an inner confirmation that a certain outer teaching is valid.

For example, why are you still reading this book? What I have presented up until this point goes so far beyond the PIN of any society on earth that you have been programmed to reject it with the outer mind. If you had been completely identified with your outer mind, you would indeed have rejected this book long ago. So why are you still reading? Because there is something within you that gives you a confirmation that something in this book is valid. There may be some of the things I have said that your outer mind cannot accept. There may be many things that conflict with the contents of your four lower bodies. Yet because you are not fully identified with those contents, you have an inner knowing that something in this book is valid and is important for you. It is this inner knowing that is the very foundation for the mystical path taught by the venutians.

It is also this inner knowing that is the greatest fear of the PCBs because they know that as you continue to activate your inner knowing, they will eventually become unable to control you. And there is only one thing they fear more than an individual who is uncontrollable, and that is *many* individuals who are uncontrollable and in embodiment at the same time.

So my point is that the Mystery School of the venutians had one clear goal. First, to purify our four lower bodies of fear-based energies and the lies programmed in there by the PCBs (A trauma is more than emotional wounds. It is basically a belief about your own limitations or the belief that there is something wrong with you, and this is always programmed into you by the PCBs.). Then, to strengthen our ability to go outside your four lower bodies and have direct experiences of a higher reality. This would eventually lead us to have direct, inner, personal contact with the ascended masters, and it was by attaining this that Jeshu and I finally started getting answers to our questions.

\*\*\*

Before we reached that level, we spent another five years clearing out the destructive beliefs that Lucifer and Satan had programmed into our four lower bodies. For this work, we formed a team with Maitreya and Gautama. They were also avatars but had come to earth a long time before Jeshu and I. They had also encountered the PCBs, although not Lucifer and Satan. They too had been programmed and they were further along than us in de-programming themselves. Because they sensed how sincere we were, we formed a team and worked together on uncovering our programming.

Because we had done so much preparatory work, this was not all that difficult. We would take turns putting each other through a regression where we could uncover a particular illusion. However, after that, we would then have to unravel how it had affected all of our four lower bodies. The thing is that when a lie is programmed into your identity body, your mental body cannot override what is in the higher body. Therefore, your mental body will believe it uncritically and will look for mental arguments to defend the belief. This will then filter down to the emotional body, which uncritically accepts what comes from the mental body. This gives rise to feelings, and if your conscious mind does not question these, you will act out on the pattern without really understanding why you are doing it.

So we had to go into the identity body and see the belief and then see why it was not real. We would then have to uncover the mental arguments and counteract them. Although we had done a lot of work to clear our emotional bodies, we would often have to also clear the feeling body from both energies and the belief that certain feelings were necessary or justified and that it was justified to act on them.

Maitreya and Gautama became invaluable to Jeshu and I. Maitreya became a tutor or guru for Jeshu and I formed a bond with Gautama. Jeshu would retain his bond after Maitreya ascended, and Maitreya helped Jeshu in hid most crucial embodiment. But I am getting ahead of myself.

*** 

There came a point where Jeshu and I had been in the Venusian Mystery School for 33 years. We had worked very hard and had never tried to avoid looking at anything in our own psyches. We had early on realized that the path taught was entirely about dealing with your own four lower bodies, as that is the only element over which we have the potential to take complete control. You cannot control what happens in the world and you cannot fully control other people. Trying to control the world is futile and trying to control other people is possible but will only keep yourself trapped in the dualistic state of consciousness. We realized this early on and applied ourselves fully.

In doing so, we overcame what is for most people in embodiment today the greatest obstacle to their progress. Because society gives us no understanding of the fact that there is a path to a higher state of consciousness or what it entails, most people are trapped in a state of mind where they are programmed by the PCBs to project that the problem is "out there." Just look at how many people think that the only way to improve their lives (to be happy or avoid suffering) is to try to control your outer circumstances and other people. As long as you do this, you cannot even discover the only true path to freedom, which is to take control over what happens *inside* your mind instead of seeking to control everything *outside* your mind. Until you give up this programmed response, you cannot truly discover the only path to freedom because you are looking for solutions outside yourself—instead of looking the only place solutions can be found, namely in your own mind. You are simply not ready, and thus the teacher representing the only path cannot appear to you.

Anyway, at our 33-year anniversary in the Mystery School, we graduated to the highest program offered and started having direct contact with several ascended masters who helped us from their completely non-dualistic perspective. Our ascended instructors quickly realized that we could not truly go further until we had overcome the enigma that Lucifer and Satan represented to us. As a result, it was decided that Maitreya, Gautama, Jeshu and I would receive personal instructions from Sanat Kumara himself, something that had not been done before.

# 24

Before I explain how this took place, let me briefly describe another feature of the Mystery School. Some of the instructors had been trained to serve as messengers for the ascended masters. Every Sunday there would be a special service in the central hall (or in the summer on the central plaza) of the school complex. In the summertime, there could be up to 10,000 people there. We would follow a program of giving decrees for 7-8 hours in order to set an energetic forcefield and raise our own vibration.

One or several of the messengers would then go up on a stage so they could be seen by all. They would then take a dictation where an ascended master would speak through a messenger. This is a process that in today's world mistakenly (by design of the PCBs, of course) has been labeled "channeling," but the real form of supra-terrestrial communication is very different from what is popularly called channeling.

A messenger is not in a trance and the ascended master does not take over the messenger's body or four lower bodies. The ascended master cannot descend lower than the higher levels of the identity octave. The messenger must therefore raise his or her consciousness and tune in to the master at this level. This is fully possible but not something that is easy to do on a planet as dense as this one. Back then, it required special training and only a few people could do this. They were all venutians who had been trained in this ability before they took embodiment on earth. Needless to say, they had not experienced the kind of PCB programming to which Jeshu and I had been exposed.

When the messenger attuned to an ascended master, the master would speak through the messenger. The messenger would not hear a voice and repeat it. The master would blend with the identity mind of the messenger and the messenger would hear the words as they were being spoken. The messenger could stop the process any time, but as long as the messenger stayed in a neutral state of mind, his or her mind had little direct influence on the message. Of course, there was an indirect influence in terms of the messenger's background and how he or she used language. Yet there was very little interference from the messenger's mind so the message could come through in a very pure form.

Jeshu and I experienced this for the first time not long after we had entered the Mystery School, and it made a profound impression upon us.

We could both sense a stream of very high energy through the messenger and the message itself was also very profound. Over time, we developed the ability to tune in to the master who was speaking and receive our own inner instructions directly from the master. An ascended master does not have the kind of linear mind we have while in embodiment. A master's mind is spherical, meaning that if 10,000 people are listening to a dictation, the master can at the same time speak aloud through the messenger and speak to the heart of each person in the audience.

After many years, Jeshu came to a point where he could see the master appearing in his or her light body over the body of the messenger. I never saw that, although I often saw a light of various colors. Jeshu developed the ability to be so attuned with the master that he could speak the dictation with a low voice at the same time as the messenger was speaking. We would often sit in the back and I would be hearing the dictation is stereo, with Jeshu in one ear and the messenger in the other. We had no doubt that the process was real, as the vibration in the entire place shifted as soon as a dictation started. Of course, we also had a clearly heightened state of consciousness during a dictation, which could last from 20 minutes to over an hour.

As we worked our way up to higher levels of consciousness, and especially after we rose above the 96th level, we became aware that behind the outer mystery school was an inner school that had the purpose of helping people tune in to the ascended masters and experience them directly. This included training people to become messengers. For this purpose, there was a section of the temple complex where only the most advanced students were allowed to enter. Its central room had a special geometry, but it really was not the physical features that made it special. It was special because the instructors and high-level students maintained a very high energetic forcefield in the room. This meant that when you were in there, it was much easier to attune to the ascended masters.

\*\*\*

Maitreya and Gautama also had questions about the PCBs so the instructors decided that the four of us would form a group and attempt to do something that had not been done before. We went through a month-long program of purifying ourselves and creating a special forcefield in the inner chamber of the temple. We and our four instructors were the only ones allowed in during that time. During the program, we all attuned our consciousness to Sanat Kumara, and our entire focus was to attune to his vibration and mind.

After 33 days, we reached the critical point, and during one session, there was an unmistakable shift of energy. We all fell silent while looking at the center of the room. At first, there appeared a white light that grew in intensity until it was physically visible to all of us. Then, the light gradually turned pink and very slowly it started forming the outline of a person. Over several minutes, the person became more and more visible and finally we could all see Sanat Kumara as clearly as we had ever seen anything. Take note that I am not saying we saw him physically. At the time, I was not sure whether he had lowered his Presence to the level where we could see him with our physical eyes or whether we had raised our consciousness to where we could see something our physical eyes could not detect. Today, I know the latter was the case. Nevertheless, all eight of us saw this master appear out of nowhere and take on a form that we saw more clearly than we had ever seen anything.

Quite frankly, I had never experienced anything like it, and I still have rarely experienced anything like it in my two million years on this planet. On a natural planet, this is a normal part of the growth process, but on earth, the contrast between the density of this planet and the super-high vibration of an ascended master is simply mind-blowing. You could literally feel the intensity of his energy field with every chakra and every physical sense. I could feel all of my chakras spinning more rapidly than I had ever experienced. I could see Sanat Kumara more clearly than anything I had seen, I could smell something similar to roses, I could hear the constant humming of his energy field, I could taste something I had never tasted before and I could feel his energy field as a physical sensation all over my body. It was a total sensory and extra-sensory experience. We were all shaking and found it completely impossible to say anything. Yet over the next days we would gradually become more attuned to Sanat Kumara's vibration and be able to interact with him in a way that was not normal but supra-normal, although bearable.

Over the next seven days, we had sessions with Sanat Kumara where we could ask him questions and converse with him as we would do with our instructors. During this time, he answered all of our questions and revealed the full story of why the PCBs (and evil) had come to earth and why it was still here. I will tell that story in the next chapters by giving you highlights of the dialogue that took place. If you feel this book has until now gone far beyond your PIN, what will follow will go so far beyond that your PIN will be shattered beyond recognition. You might recall the old children's rhyme about Humpty Dumpty, especially the part about all the king's horses and all the king's men not being able to put Humpty together again. If you are still attached to your PIN, don't read on.

*** 

Sanat Kumara: "I am very grateful to the four of you for the fact that you have summoned my Presence. You have heard the saying that when the student is ready, the teacher must appear, and it is a great joy for the teacher to be welcomed by students who have made such an effort to be ready.

I understand that you are all reacting to the higher vibrations of my energy field and that it will take you some time to adjust. Therefore, I will begin by giving you some introductory remarks. The greatest challenge we of the ascended masters face when working with people on a dense-matter planet like earth is that people need to see us as being higher than themselves without idolizing or deifying us.

You need to see me as being higher than yourselves in the sense that I am beyond duality. You are all quite aware of the effect of the dualistic consciousness and that it forms a closed loop. You can reason your way *into* duality but you cannot reason your way *out of* it. You can escape only by directly experiencing something that is at a higher level of consciousness than your present level. This inspires you to say: 'I want to experience that,' and when you then rise, you can grasp an even higher level.

You have all been willing to work your way up through the levels of consciousness possible on earth, and you have all begun to glimpse the consciousness beyond duality. As you know, one has to reach a fairly high level before one can begin to have direct experiences of a level of consciousness that is beyond duality and consciously acknowledge what it means.

Yet because the core of your beings is the Conscious You and because it is beyond form, it is actually possible that any human being can have an experience of the ascended masters and our consciousness. It only requires that the person is willing to step outside of his or her normal perception filter. What you have done is to engage in a systematic, conscious process of purifying your perception filter so you can experience us with less and less of the preconceived opinions and beliefs programmed into people by what you call the PCBs. Because most people on earth are not aware of such a path, they will only step outside their normal perception filter in extreme situations. They will therefore have a brief glimpse of higher beings and they will instantly start projecting their preconceived opinions upon the experience and their interpretation of what it means.

That is why, throughout the ages, most of the people who have experienced the ascended masters have projected upon us that we are some kind of gods, or even a supreme god. If you look at all of the religions in your world today, you see that many of them started with one person having an extraordinary experience and then telling others about it. People then interpreted the experience, and they did so through their dualistic perception filter, of which they were unaware. They now turned us into gods or the ultimate god and they tended to build us up according to their own need to feel better than other people. They felt that because they had this high experience, it must be because they are somehow more worthy than other people and therefore the way they interpret the experience must be right or the only right one.

In reality, we are not gods and we are not truly above you. Obviously, we are "above" human beings in the sense that we have ascended beyond duality and therefore we have no fear-based energies in our beings. We have a much higher vibration than any human being in embodiment could ever have, and for most people the experience of the contrast between our vibration and their own is very shocking, often even generating fear or panic. This has been used by the PCBs to build the image of the angry god in the sky, an image that has nothing to do with how we look at human beings on earth.

We have ascended beyond duality, which means we have no value judgments. We do not see ourselves as being higher or more important than you. It is only *you* who can see it this way and project your own limited vision upon us, as you project it upon everything else you encounter, including yourselves. We see the oneness of all life and we see you as our unascended brothers and sisters. We do not judge you in any way, and our only response is how we can help you raise your consciousness to our level. This is the function we have chosen to take on, those of us who are working with unascended beings.

I know that most people would not be able to heed my words, but the four of you can surely do so as you have already raised your vibration much closer to mine. I therefore need you to make a shift and see me as your older brother on the path. I need you to shift so you see me as a being with whom you can interact as you have interacted with your instructors and with each other. If you cannot make this shift, there is not much I can do for you at this point, and you will need more training before we can meet again. So tell me about some of the questions you have."

I don't know how Maitreya was able to speak at this time, as Sanat Kumara's vibration almost paralyzed me, but he did. Maitreya: "We have all come to realize that in past lifetimes we have interacted with certain people that we feel are fundamentally different from ourselves. We have worked hard on experiencing the oneness of all life, and we do experience that oneness is a living reality at a higher level than earth. So we do not doubt that at a higher level all life is one. We can also feel a certain oneness with most people on earth.

Yet none of us can feel any oneness with these beings. We call them PCBs because of their quest for power and their aggressiveness. We feel that they so obviously feel no oneness with us or with any human being. Instead, they are willing to do the most horrendous things to violate others, and they seem to be doing this partly because they take pleasure in it and partly because they have some kind of agenda that we cannot make out. We know that when you harm others, your energies will be returned to you, but the PCBs seem to deny this and think they can get away with what they are doing.

We know that we should be getting to a point where we can feel oneness with all life, but because these people have violated us so severely in past lives, we cannot see how this can be done."

Jeshu: "We also don't understand where these beings have come from in the first place. We have talked about why they have come to earth. We know that the ascended masters must have allowed this to happen and there must be some reason for it, but we cannot make out what it is."

\*\*\*

Sanat Kumara: "These are very understandable questions, as are the many other questions I see in your auras. In order to begin answering them, I have to give you some background that you have not received so far in the Mystery School, for the reason that we reserve it for students who have reached your level.

You are aware that you are self-aware beings and that you have the ability to co-create with your minds. This ability is well-known on natural planets, but on dense-matter planets, most inhabitants are unaware that they are co-creators. You have been trained to more consciously co-create. Yet with what are you co-creating?

You are aware that in the world right now there are several civilizations who have different religions that all worship what they see as the superior deity. In the Mystery School we have not talked about a god, and the reason is that the concept of god found in the world is entirely created by the PCBs. We therefore do not want students to deal with this concept until they have reached your level.

As you have learned and experienced, you can create your own circumstances within certain limits. You know that you are on a dense-matter planet where the collective consciousness (and the density of matter, which is a product of the collective consciousness) sets certain limits for your creative unfoldment. Yet you are also all beginning to sense that you can, of our own selves, do nothing. You can create only by using energy that comes from a higher level, which you have so far seen as your own higher selves or I AM Presences. Of course, you also know that there are levels of vibration beyond the material spectrum on earth. The physical world is just one 'pocket' of vibrations and you know about the emotional, mental and identity levels and you know there is a higher realm beyond that. Yet even in this higher realm, there is a series of levels that reach towards an ultimate level of energy.

Where does your I AM presence receive the creative energy? It receives it from the ascended master (or pair of ascended masters) who created your Presence. Where do they get the energy they used to create you? They got it from ascended masters who are at a higher level than themselves. You now see that there is a stream of energy and consciousness that arrives at your level by being funneled through several higher levels, being stepped down to the level of vibration you can handle with your present level of consciousness. Where does it all begin, where does the first creative energy come from? It comes from the self-aware, creative Being who created the entire world of form in which we live. We can say that above you is a hierarchy of ascended masters that goes through several levels until it reaches the highest creative being. We cannot call this being an ascended master because it has not ascended, at least not within this world of form. I will therefore call it the 'Creator' in order to avoid the misused word 'god.'

There was a state (I am not saying 'time' because time had not yet come into being) where the Creator was aware of its existence and creative potential but had not yet formed the will to create or the vision of what to create. It then formed this will and vision and created its first world or sphere.

It is important for you to consider that there is a difference between creating and co-creating. When you are co-creating, you are receiving energy and you are creating within the framework of an already existing world. When you are creating, there is nothing there except you. You are creating by using your own being and consciousness, you are creating out of yourself.

The Creator started by defining a sphere inside which was only its own Being. This sphere was set apart from the larger reality, the Allness, but at this point I will not comment on this reality. The Creator defined a boundary around itself, and then it withdrew itself into the center of the sphere, into a single point so the sphere was now a void. From the center, the Creator radiated itself outwardly and created the first world or sphere inside the void.

The Creator then created structures in the first sphere. They were not like what you see today, but they can be compared to your galaxies, solar systems and planets. There was a structure based upon which what you call life could emerge. The Creator now created, out of its own consciousness, self-aware beings and sent them into the first sphere. The first sphere was created from energy, but it had a higher vibration than the energy used to make our sphere. Still, the first sphere had a certain density that made it possible to fashion forms that could be sustained. And these forms or structures made up the home of the first self-aware beings that descended into the bodies found on the first planets.

The Creator has a form of consciousness that is very different from what you have on earth, but also very different from what the first self-aware co-creators had. The Creator is everything within its own sphere and is everywhere within its own sphere. You cannot find a place where the Creator is not. The Creator has an omnipresent awareness and is, so to speak, "seeing" the entire world at once. Yet the Creator is seeing the world as an outside observer and is not seeing the world from the perspective of an observer that is inside the world. That is *our* job. We are the Creator seeing its own creation from the inside, but we are not just seeing because we are co-creating the world at the same time as we are experiencing it. The Creator sees the world from the outside through its normal state of awareness and sees the world from the inside through *our* awareness. Only, the Creator does not interpret what we see the way we do.

The first co-creators in the first sphere had certain creative powers and they had a completely free will as to how they would use them. These co-creators responded to the natural drive to expand and raise their consciousness and increase their creative powers. Over a long period of what you call time, they raised their sphere to a point where it could ascend to a higher level. Before this happened, their sphere had been impermanent, meaning no structure could be sustained indefinitely. After the sphere ascended, all structures and their co-creators became immortal, although they would still evolve. Immortality is not static in that immortal beings do not remain the same. We are also growing in consciousness, we are not angels who sit around on a pink cloud and play the harp for eternity.

The reason the first sphere ascended was that the self-aware beings in it retained their sense of oneness with their source and with each other. They had completely free will and could have gone into duality. They could have started seeing themselves as separate beings, separated from their source, their environment and each other. The Creator gave them the option to choose duality, but none of them did so. They had to have this option in order to have a completely free will, and they had to have completely free will in order to grow in consciousness and fulfil their reason for being. It was because they had the option to go into duality that the first sphere was not permanent. It only became permanent when the co-creators in the sphere had raised their consciousness to the level where duality becomes obsolete.

After the sphere ascended, the first co-creators became the first ascended masters. They now created a second sphere and used the co-creative abilities they had developed to create structures in that sphere. They then sent self-aware extensions of themselves into that sphere to begin the same process of expanding their co-creative abilities and self-awareness until they could raise the second sphere to immortality.

The second sphere also reached the ascension point and became raised to the level of immortality through the ascension process. Again, all co-creators had the option to go into duality but none of them chose to do so.

The newly ascended masters from the second sphere now created the third sphere and the process continued. Once again, the third sphere ascended and the new ascended masters created the fourth sphere. This is where a shift happened."

\*\*\*

Sanat Kumara: "The first sphere was created with a certain base vibration. As the co-creators in the sphere raised their consciousness, the actual vibration of the sphere was gradually raised. When it reached a certain level, the sphere could go through the ascension process, which is not a gradual change but a definitive jump or leap in vibration.

The second sphere was created with a more dense base vibration, meaning it was more challenging for the co-creators in that sphere to raise their consciousness. It required more work and more time to raise the second sphere to the ascension point. Again, the third sphere had an even denser base vibration and so did the fourth. In the fourth sphere, the base vibration was so dense that for the first time, some co-creators made the choice to immerse themselves in duality. In each of the previous spheres, some co-creators had experimented with duality in order to get an experience of what this consciousness really is. Yet none had gone into it on a long-term basis, they had not become immersed in it, identified with it. They had always come back to a non-dualistic state of consciousness without becoming stuck in duality.

In the fourth sphere, some co-creators did go into duality and became stuck there. What does it mean to become stuck in duality? As you are all aware, there is no ultimate argument in duality, one can argue for or against any viewpoint without finding a definitive answer. The reason is that there *are* no definitive answers in duality. Yet duality allows you to argue *for* any viewpoint, and that means you can also argue that one viewpoint is not relative but absolute. One takes a relative viewpoint and raises it to the status of being absolute, meaning it cannot or should not be questioned.

Once you have convinced yourself that a certain relative viewpoint is absolute, you are stuck, at least for as long as you refuse to question your "absolute" viewpoint. The reason is that the only absolute in an unascended sphere is free will. The only thing that can make your will unfree is that you make the decision that here is a viewpoint where you will no longer apply your free will, meaning you will not question it. When you refuse to question something, then your will has become unfree on that point, and it will remain so until you change your mind and become willing to question the unquestionable.

It is necessary for all co-creators to experiment with duality so that you know what it is and can consciously choose a higher approach to co-creating. How do you avoid becoming stuck? By always maintaining a frame of reference from outside duality. This frame of reference is your spiritual teacher, meaning the ascended master who is guiding you. As long as you see that nothing in duality is absolute and that there is an absolute frame of reference from outside duality, namely the higher vibration of the ascended masters, you cannot become stuck. You can go into duality as you go into a labyrinth, but you can always find your way out by following the higher vibration.

Once you elevate a relative viewpoint to the status of being absolute, you will at the same time deny that the only absolute is your experience of a higher vibration. You will now enter a frame of mind where the direct experience of a higher vibration has been reduced to something you can argue for or against, as you can argue for or against everything else— except what you have elevated to being absolute.

It is at this point that a momentous and decisive shift happens in your consciousness, namely that you lose the conscious contact with the ascended masters and therefore lose your frame of reference from outside duality. Instead of having a frame of reference from outside your mind, your mind becomes a self-referential system, a closed system. You have become immersed in the dualistic mind you have created, you have become identified with your own creation.

You have now lost your direct contact with your teachers, and therefore you cannot learn directly from us. How can you then learn? Only by seeing the matter of your sphere outpicture your state of consciousness. The world becomes your teacher and you learn by seeing how your self-referential mind co-creates circumstances that cause you suffering. Only when you have had enough of this suffering (which you may interpret differently in a variety of ways), can you again become open to a frame of reference from outside your mind.

We can also say that as long as you are experimenting with duality, you are still maintaining contact with the ascended masters. When you become stuck in duality, you will break this contact because you no longer want to face us. This is not because we are angry and judgmental. It is because we do not lower our vibration. So when you face our higher vibration, you will have a direct experience that there is a reality outside the relative belief system you have created in your mind. You can maintain your illusion that this belief system is based on an absolute truth only by avoiding a direct experience of our vibration.

As long as you do not have the direct experience, you can interpret the memory of past experiences in such a way that they validate your belief system. Therefore, you can maintain the illusion that there are certain things you do not need to question, which then supports the illusion that you do not need to shift your consciousness above duality. For example, some of the founders of religions have had a genuine experience of our vibration, but they have then interpreted it to validate their relative belief system and their belief that they are above other people because they had the experience."

***

Sanat Kumara: "In the fourth sphere, a small number of co-creators became stuck in duality and broke the contact with the ascended masters. As the sphere evolved, these co-creators became concentrated on a small number of planets. The vast majority of planets stayed in their natural state and the inhabitants there raised the vibration of their planets along with their own state of consciousness. When you are in duality, you are not raising your consciousness, on the contrary you must constantly lower it.

The reason for this is that all life is one. All self-aware beings are extensions of the mind of the Creator, and therefore all co-creators are connected in consciousness. When a majority of the co-creators embodying in a sphere are raising their consciousness, it creates a kind of magnetic pull on all other beings in that sphere. When a small number of co-creators go into duality, they are still pulled up by the much larger number of co-creators who are growing. They can maintain their dualistic states of mind only by going towards lower and lower states as the rest of the sphere is raised. They must resist growth harder and harder, and this inevitably becomes a struggle. They become more and more self-centered and more and more identified with their relative beliefs, becoming more convinced that they really are absolute. This is not a violation of their free will. It actually gives them what they say they want. When you go into duality, you go into a state of mind dominated by two polar opposites. Whenever you form an absolute viewpoint, it must have an opposite. It is absolutely true only by being in contrast to something that is absolutely false. When you go into duality, you are subconsciously saying that you want to experience what it is like to be outside oneness. How can you be outside oneness? Only by seeing yourself as a separate being, and a separate being must have something opposing it or it would not be separate. So the upward pull of all lifestreams who are not in duality becomes a force that the beings in duality experience as the opposition they want. Of course, if they shifted their consciousness, they would experience it as a liberating force."

*** 

Sanat Kumara: "On a natural planet, co-creators are co-creating, meaning they are not struggling against something that opposes their creative efforts. The matter element willingly takes on the forms that the co-creators are projecting upon it with their minds. Once you go into duality, you inevitably become susceptible to the illusion that there is something opposing your will. This is not because matter is opposing your creative efforts; matter is still willingly taking on the forms that you are projecting upon it. It is simply that when you are in duality, you are projecting forms that are not in alignment with the principle of oneness. Instead of co-creating something that raises all life, you are seeking to create something that benefits yourself while at the same time limiting others.

A natural co-creation maintains balance between you as an individual and all other co-creators. You co-create and let co-create. Once you go into duality, you see yourself and your belief system as more important than other co-creators. You see your subjective experience as being universal because it has some absolute authority. You are now seeking to force others into complying with your view, into accepting your subjective experience over their own. You are trying to make them believe that your subjective experience is not subjective but *universal* whereas their experience can only be subjective. You are using force against others, and this creates a fundamental imbalance between you and others. This inevitably leads to a struggle because you experience that there is something that is opposing your will. You become susceptible to the illusion that your will is not free but is being opposed by something.

In a sense, it is correct that your will is no longer free, but the lack of freedom exists only inside your own mind. It is the inconsistency and self-contradictions of your dualistic beliefs that restrict your will. You are refusing to question your "absolute" belief and therefore your will is no longer free but has to stay within the confines defined by your unquestionable "absolute." Of course, you are not seeing that your absolute is truly subjective because you have convinced yourself that it is absolute. Yet you experience that something is opposing the freedom of your will, and you identify it as being outside yourself.

When you go into duality, you must of necessity refuse to take complete responsibility for your state of mind. On a natural planet, you know that your physical circumstances are a product of what you and other co-creators have projected upon matter with your minds. You know that the world is what you make of it. When you go into duality, you deny this and you think the world is what some external force has made it, a force that seeks to restrict your freedom.

You now use the dualistic mindset to explain or justify why there is opposition to your free will from outside yourself. This can be done in numerous ways, but they all involve defining an external force (a deity, nature or other people) that is seeking to restrict your will and oppose your creative efforts. They all portray this as being not right, and this inevitably leads to the belief that the only way to get what you want is to use force to overcome the external force. Since the external force is using force against you, it is justified that you use force against others. You can now easily justify the use of force, even the destruction of other people.

Using force against other people is unthinkable on a natural planet because you experience that there is no need to use force. If you don't like what is currently manifest, you simply use your mind to manifest something else. You know that the only way to change your circumstances is to change your state of consciousness. In duality, you cannot do this because you are not willing to change yourself. Therefore, you think the only way to change your circumstances is to change something or someone outside yourself, and this only reinforces the struggle."

# 25

Sanat Kumara: "In the fourth sphere, some co-creators set themselves up as leaders on certain planets and they created very sophisticated civilizations. They were not unlike what you have seen on earth where there is one supreme leader at the top. Of course, in duality, there are always two extreme polarities and one cannot exist without the other. When you have a planet where one co-creator has chosen to raise one dualistic polarity to the status of being absolute, it is inevitable that this attracts another co-creator who has elevated the opposite dualistic polarity to being absolute. And these two leaders will inevitably clash.

As the fourth sphere was coming closer and closer to the ascension point, you saw a small number of planets where this was being outplayed. You had two civilizations with a supreme leader and they were fighting each other in what they saw as an epic battle. As a sphere comes closer to the ascension point, beings in duality will experience more of a pull on them, and this gives them a sense of urgency. They interpret this with the dualistic mindset to mean that it is becoming more urgent for them to defeat their opponent. They may even believe that it is vital for the cause of their deity or for the fate of the universe that they defeat their opponent.

As the fourth sphere came close to the ascension point, there were some planets where this struggle had been taken to extremes, leading to something similar to what you now call warfare. In a few cases, one civilization had managed to destroy the opposing civilization. This had caused the leaders of the victorious civilization to interpret events so that they were now the saviors of the universe or of god's plan.

According to the Law of Free Will, we of the ascended masters must leave people alone when they go into duality. On these unnatural planets, all of the people embodying on them had chosen to go into duality and believe the world view created by their leaders. We had no right to interfere with this unless asked, and people in duality rarely ask. Yet as the entire sphere came closer to the ascension point, the law mandates that we must confront the co-creators on unnatural planets with the need to change. A planet can ascend only through the free-will choices of its inhabitants so if they will not abandon duality, they cannot ascend with the rest of their sphere. Yet you cannot make truly free choices while you have experienced no alternative to duality.

As the ascended masters appeared on the few unnatural planets, it became impossible for the inhabitants and the leaders to ignore that there is a higher reality. This gave them the first truly free choice since going into duality. The majority of these co-creators chose to accept the offer to take them on a path that would lead them above duality. They received all the help they needed and were ready to ascend with the rest of the fourth sphere.

Yet some of the supreme leaders and some of their followers rejected the offer from the ascended masters. This meant that they could not ascend with the rest of the sphere, but the ascension of the sphere could not be delayed because of such a small number of co-creators.

In a sense this was not a problem and it was not unforeseen. The fourth sphere ascended, and the beings who refused to ascend were put in a temporary world while the fifth sphere was being created. When that sphere was ready for embodiment, the dualistic beings took embodiment in it and they were given planets created for their level of consciousness. We might say that these beings fell into the fifth sphere instead of voluntarily taking embodiment there.

They felt this was something forced upon them against their will, yet this was only their internal experience. In reality, their situation was a result of their own choices, but since they refused to see this, they had a direct experience of being forced to enter the fifth sphere. Thereby, they became even more convinced of the existence of an external force opposing their free will.

These beings fell into the fifth sphere because they refused to ascend with the fourth sphere. Therefore, I call them "fallen beings" in order to signify that they have fallen into their present environment instead of voluntarily taking embodiment as co-creators normally do.

In the fifth and sixth spheres, even more beings fell, and that is why your current sphere, the seventh and so far most dense, has from the beginning had a number of fallen beings. They were originally confined to a few planets created especially for them, but since then they have spread to other planets as the original inhabitants of those planets lowered the collective consciousness to the point where the fallen beings could embody on those planets.

This explains why there are beings on earth who have no respect for the original inhabitants of this planet. The fallen beings consider themselves far superior to all beings who originated in this sphere. In a sense, they *are* superior because they have so much more experience with using the duality consciousness to deceive, manipulate and force others. So when it comes to forcing others, the fallen beings really *are* more 'sophisticated.'

They are not here because they want to be here, even though they did choose to engage in a process that, by their self-created consequences, led them to be here. They rebel against being here and they have each constructed their own world view to explain why they are here, why it is unjust and why a deity has made a mistake in allowing this to happen. Some of them have created various scenarios where they are trying to prove that their self-created deity was wrong, and they are seeking to use human beings as tools in their quest to prove this. They even think it is their role to correct the mistake of their god, and they believe they are the only ones who truly know how the universe functions, which means they should be in charge of everything. Some of them believe god's mistake was to give all beings free will, and they think they should be allowed to force the will of all beings below them. Understanding this agenda is the key to understanding how the fallen beings think and why they have no sensitivity for life or respect for the free will of human beings.

I now see that you have many questions, so let us continue the discussion based on those."

***

Jeshu: "We have all experienced that there are some people we have met over many embodiments who are very different from us in that they have no respect for life. We have called them Power and Control Brokers because they are willing to use force in order to control others and they have no concern for the consequences this has for others. I now see that our understanding has been based on what we have observed here on earth, and your teaching about fallen beings gives us a far wider perspective. Can you tell us how you look at what we call PCBs in relation to the fallen beings?"

Sanat Kumara: "Not all PCBs are fallen beings and not all fallen beings are PCBs. There are some of the leaders you see today, and that you have encountered in past lives, who have not fallen from another sphere. All PCBs are stuck in the duality consciousness, or they would not be willing to force others. Yet some of them have entered that consciousness in this sphere, meaning they have taken it on temporarily and have a better potential for shifting out of it before this sphere ascends. There is a shift that happens when your first sphere ascends and you refuse to shift out of duality. As you fall into the next sphere, you forget the specifics of why you fell, but you retain the overall world view you had built before falling. Because you no longer remember how you developed this world view, or remember how it was challenged by the ascended masters, you are more identified with it. This does not mean you cannot awaken from duality, but it does mean it is much harder to do so. It requires more of a sense of humility, and most fallen beings have such pride in their sense of superiority and their sense of being right that it is very difficult for them to admit that they have been wrong in that their absolute beliefs were only relative.

I know it is difficult to distinguish between a fallen being and a PCB who has entered duality in this sphere, but the fallen beings are willing to go much further in proving their world view right. A PCB from this sphere is usually focused on gaining power for itself whereas a fallen being often has some agenda that reaches beyond personal power."

Jeshu: "Can you relate this to some of the beings we have personally encountered?"

Sanat Kumara: "Lucifer, Satan and Maleve are fallen beings. Lucifer and Satan fell in the fifth sphere and Maleve in the sixth. Lucifer and Satan are obviously fallen beings who are still acting as PCBs. Yet Maleve has started a path of moving out of the fallen consciousness, thanks in large part to her encounter with the two of you. She is no longer acting as a PCB in that she is not physically seeking to force others. This proves that fallen beings can awaken, partly by having had enough of the duality consciousness and the struggle it creates, and partly by encountering beings who are not in duality or not as deeply into duality as themselves.

Lucifer and Satan represent two polar opposites. As I explained, the Creator started the creation of this world of form. It did so by defining a boundary around itself and withdrawing itself into a single point in the center of the void. From there, it expanded outwards in creating the first sphere. There are two basic creative powers, an expansive, outgoing force and a contracting, ingoing force. Everything in the world of form is created by the balanced interplay of these two forces. If there was only expansion, no form could be maintained, as it would be blown apart. If there was only contraction, no form could be maintained, as it would collapse in upon itself.

The Creator represents the expansive or Father element and the matter world represents the contracting or Mother element. It is when the two are balanced that a form can be sustained over time. It is the ever-changing interplay of the two forces that makes growth possible. The Father element is always urging form to transcend itself. The Mother element has the function of upholding a form over time while also preventing any form from becoming permanent. If a form gets stuck, the Mother element will eventually cause it to collapse in upon itself. Of course, form is created by self-aware co-creators, and the Father element is urging them to continue to expand their creative abilities. The Mother element will eventually destroy the form that they refuse to let go of, but this is in order to liberate the creative being who has become trapped by its own creation. The function of the Mother element is to allow you to co-create an unbalanced form and to maintain it for some time, but not forever. The Mother will not allow you to be stuck in that form indefinitely.

The duality consciousness takes the two basic forces and perverts them. The perversion of the Father element is represented by Lucifer who has an agenda of proving something. You have experienced how his agenda varies from lifetime to lifetime, but that is because he is being controlled by another fallen being in the identity realm, the Dark Master. Some fallen beings have the agenda of proving god wrong. They are not actually seeking to prove the Creator wrong because a being in duality cannot even fathom the Creator. They are trying to prove wrong an unreal god of their own creation. This was an image of god that was created in the fourth sphere and reinforced in the sixth and seventh. Lucifer and other fallen beings have believed in the existence of this god for a very long time and are truly identified with it. What you see in Lucifer is always an agenda to prove something, and that is why he wants to deceive or manipulate you into supporting him. He has something to prove and therefore he must convince you, not simply force you to comply.

Satan represents a perversion of the Mother element. He is seeking to use the basic force of the Mother to create destruction and chaos. Yet he is not doing this in order to free your spirit but in order to enslave it by keeping it trapped in struggling against him and his efforts to destroy. In a sense, this is also an agenda because Satan is often controlled by fallen beings in the mental and emotional realms. They are not as "sophisticated" as the beings in the identity realm but they are still more intelligent in a linear, dualistic way than most people in embodiment. Yet whereas Lucifer always has a rationale, Satan often has no other rationale than the desire for destruction, which gives him a sense of being powerful. The more he can destroy, the more power he feels he has. And he has a desperate need for power because he has experienced that he cannot overpower Lucifer, and he has experienced that he cannot overpower the two of you."

Gautama: "You said that when our sphere was created, the fallen beings could only embody on planets created especially for them. Yet since then, they have spread to other planets because the inhabitants lowered the collective consciousness. Can you describe how this happened on earth? I assume earth was not created for the fallen beings?"

Sanat Kumara: "Earth was created as a natural planet. When it was created, a wave of co-creators took embodiment here, and it functioned in a similar way to what you have all experienced on other natural planets. The first life-wave, or root race, raised their consciousness and built on to the foundation they had been given. When they had raised their individual and collective consciousness to a certain level, they all ascended. After that, a second wave took embodiment, and they also ascended. The same for the third wave. When the fourth wave embodied, a shift occurred.

The fourth wave of co-creators were more determined to explore duality than the previous three waves. This did not mean that they went into the lower levels of duality. They did not use violence or force, and warfare was still unknown on the planet. Yet they developed highly sophisticated civilizations, far more sophisticated than what you have seen in your time on earth. There was nothing inherently negative about these civilizations, but the leaders of them had developed certain world views that they believed were absolute. Obviously, they were also static. Once you define something as absolute, how can you ever grow beyond it?

The Law of Free Will mandates that a group of co-creators can create any situation they desire on their planet. Obviously, they will experience what they co-create, and it is the hope that when they have experienced the same situation long enough, they will be saturated with it and will want more. This is because a co-creator is an extension of the Creator's mind and the Creator always strives to grow, strives for more. That is why the Creator decided to create. The drive for self-transcendence is the deepest, most fundamental drive in our beings.

By using the duality consciousness, the leaders of the fourth wave of co-creators had created a world view that said they did not need to grow, even that any change was dangerous. The result was that they had cut themselves off from direct encounters with the ascended masters. We could not challenge their world view. They also believed that it was their role to maintain their state of civilization indefinitely and that this was their highest calling. As I said, this was a very sophisticated civilization where all inhabitants had very comfortable, abundant and secure lives. From their perspective, it was a kind of paradise on earth.

Yet this was bought with a price. I have described how the beings in the fourth sphere used the polarities of duality to create a struggle against each other. Another aspect of the duality consciousness is that people can come to see opposites as dangerous. Earth did not have warfare as you see today, but it did have a time when there was a struggle between dualistic opposites. This was overcome because some leaders developed the philosophy that conflict was dangerous. This is, of course, not incorrect, but these leaders created a philosophy that had as its primary goal to remove all conflicts from society by making all people the same and by stopping any kind of invention and change, even change for the better. The status quo became their god.

This led to a civilization that had developed very elaborate measures for bringing up people in a certain way, even to the point of not allowing parents to bring up their own children. This was done in state-controlled institutions that literally brainwashed the children by destroying their individuality. The effect was that a society was created in which there were very few differences of opinion. This society was highly developed and it had an overall philosophy saying that the primary goal was maintaining status quo by preventing conflict. Yet this goal is contrary to the purpose of creation because none of the citizens of that civilization were growing. So the civilization could not be sustained over time, but it was impossible for the ascended masters to make people realize this. They had effectively shut themselves off from any view that challenged the official view because it was seen as dangerous and the source of conflict. The leaders of the civilization could easily dismiss the very ideas that could save it from self-destruction.

The ascended masters had no option but to leave the inhabitants on earth alone for a time, hoping they would eventually have had enough of the static state and want more. Obviously, a few individuals did have enough and the masters overseeing the earth at that time did work with them. Yet as time went on, it became clear that the civilization was not going to change on its own. This meant that the civilization started to activate the principle built into the Mother or Matter element, namely the contracting force.

You had a civilization that was very highly developed and in which all members felt their lives were secure and under control. Suddenly, things began to break down and people could not understand why. The ascended masters could have told them this, but they were not open to listening. Instead of adjusting to this by being willing to question their belief system, the civilization became even more identified with it. The leaders developed the myth of an external force seeking to destroy what they had created, and they encouraged resistance to this, meaning they got all people to cling to the existing beliefs.

Of course, in seeking to explain what was the outside force planning to destroy their civilization, the leaders developed the idea that certain groups of people were to blame because they were different. In fact, some groups of people had become willing to question the dominant world view, and they were now labeled as the cause of the trouble. The potential saviors became the enemy.

On natural planets, the inhabitants maintain the awareness that their physical circumstances are a result of their own state of consciousness. They also maintain a dedication to growth, and they know that growth always happens when there is an interplay between different people. Individuality, differences and diversity are therefore seen as a source of growth because they generate creative tension that leads to renewal.

Once this has been lost, as it always happens when people go into duality, there can be a shift where an entire planet now begins to see differences as the source of conflict rather than creative tension. People now begin to polarize into groups, and when some of them develop an epic mindset, it is seen that there is an ultimate cause and some people are working for it and others are working against it. Now, instead of using your creative powers to co-create a higher state on the planet, you are using your powers to restrict other people in order to maintain a status quo that is ultimately not maintainable because nothing in the world of form can stand still indefinitely.

It is precisely when the inhabitants of a planet lower their collective consciousness to this point that the planet becomes open to the embodiment of fallen beings. The ascended masters overseeing the earth at the time faced a delicate choice. They could easily predict that if they left the earth alone, the inhabitants would reinforce the downward spiral they had created. This would, within a relatively short period of time, lead to the total destruction of the planet through what has often been called natural disasters. The inhabitants of a planet do have the power to create a self-reinforcing downward spiral that causes the contracting force of the Mother to cause the planet to collapse in upon itself in cataclysmic events. Therefore, the masters could see that if left alone, the earth would be destroyed. Given that it is a considerable investment in attention and energy to create a planet, they decided to allow fallen beings to embody here in an attempt to awaken the inhabitants of the earth to the problem with the course they had taken."

Sanat Kumara paused and looked at us, and Maitreya said: "What was the reasoning behind allowing fallen beings to embody here?"

Sanat Kumara: "When a planet has gone so far into duality that its destruction is looming, the ascended masters have no easy choices. We cannot force the inhabitants to change, and it is possible that when they see the need to change, it is too late to save the planet. Now, this isn't necessarily a loss. It is a considerable investment to create a planet, but it is still just a thing that is created for the purpose of helping co-creators grow in consciousness. By seeing how they have contributed to destroying an entire planet, many co-creators have been awakened and have made decisions that set them on the path out of duality. We can therefore still see a positive effect even when a planet is destroyed. Yet we will make a last-ditch effort to prevent this, and one way to do it is to allow fallen beings to embody on a planet.

In the case of earth, the primary problem was the absolute belief in avoiding conflict. By allowing beings like Lucifer and Satan to embody on earth, this soon became impossible to uphold. The homogenous civilization that threatened to destroy the earth was soon replaced by several civilizations that were different and grew more different over time. This did have the effect that some co-creators realized that sameness destroys creativity, and this did cause a large number of co-creators to ascend over time.

Of course, it also had a cost, which is inevitable when you are dealing with beings in duality. The fallen beings soon introduced warfare on a large scale and there now followed a period where conflict and warfare became dominant on earth. Yet even this has had some beneficial effects. I am not thereby justifying warfare, I am only pointing out that anything that is done in duality will go towards extremes. The more extreme things become, the more there is an opportunity that people will have had enough and begin to ask for an alternative. This allows the ascended masters to step in and provide the alternative.

What you saw on earth was that some souls had experienced conflict. They had then experienced the creation of a society based on sameness. They now experienced even worse warfare created by the fallen beings. It is normal that when a planet goes to one extreme, the people tend to swing towards the opposite extreme. But since the earth had already done that, the extreme conflict created by the fallen beings made some people realize that neither dualistic extreme was viable so they asked for a higher way. And when people ask, we are allowed to give them that higher way, which is to rise above duality."

\*\*\*

Sanat Kumara: "When a planet has entered the stage of no growth and no conflict, it is harder for us to help the inhabitants than when there is diversity. Obviously, the fallen beings are good at creating diversity, but they are also good at using it to create conflict. Conflict can also destroy a planet. The choice we faced was that we could either watch the uniform civilization destroy the earth (which was at that time a certainty) or we could allow fallen beings to embody here and create conflict. This could also lead to the destruction of the earth, but it was not a certainty.

This does not mean that the ascended masters are cooperating with the fallen beings. They do not want to have anything to do with us and vehemently deny our existence. You will see that no religion on earth teaches about ascended masters for the simple reason that the fallen beings have attempted to write us out of existence for the people on earth.

Yet we are still the ones deciding which kinds of beings can embody on a given planet. Of course, by allowing fallen beings to embody on earth, we also made it possible that beings like yourselves could embody here. The beings who embodied on earth had a level of consciousness that fell within a certain range. The fallen beings who embodied here had a lower level of consciousness. The law states that when beings with a lower consciousness are allowed to embody on a planet, then beings with a correspondingly higher consciousness can also embody here in order to uphold the balance created by the original inhabitants.

This ensures that there is a limit to how far down the fallen beings can take a planet. Their efforts to pull it down will be balanced by the beings with a higher consciousness who are seeking to pull the planet up. By allowing beings with a lower and higher consciousness, the original inhabitants of a planet are also given a choice as to which beings they will follow: the avatars or the fallen beings.

# 26

By this time, I had adjusted to Sanat Kumara's vibration to the point where I was actually able to speak. I asked: "What you said about Satan and Lucifer, with Satan wanting to destroy and Lucifer having an agenda, helped me a lot in understanding my relationship with both of them. I quickly realized I could not reason with Satan and that he would do whatever he wanted no matter what I said. With Lucifer, I have in several embodiments had some deeper conversations and I have often tried to make him explain why he is doing what he is doing.

I have tried to understand how his mind works, but in the end I have never been able to fully grasp what it is that makes him do certain things. It is as if I can reason with him up to a point and then, when I have refuted all of his arguments, it is as if a veil goes over his mind and I can get no further. He then either shuts down completely and refuses to talk anymore or he comes up with what he considers a final argument and there is no more discussion. Can you help me understand what is happening?"

Sanat Kumara: "I want you to realize here that even though I am beyond duality, I have no final argument that can convince fallen beings. I am as powerless to persuade them as you have been. One reason is that in duality there are no final arguments, but there is also another reason. The fallen consciousness is based on a very subtle form of denial and the fallen beings have buried it so deeply in their subconscious minds that it is very difficult for them to free themselves from this denial.

You all recognize that I have a higher vibration than yourselves and therefore you acknowledge that my words come from a level beyond duality and therefore have authority. Yet a fallen being will not recognize ascended masters and it will help you to understand why.

As I said, there were situations in the previous spheres where certain beings had gone into duality and refused to transcend the dualistic selves they had created. They refused to let their dualistic selves die in order to be reborn into a non-dual self. You have all gone through the process of letting your former selves die without knowing what will replace it, and this is the process of self-transcendence. You must let a former self die before a new can emerge.

When these beings (who had not yet fallen) were confronted with ascended masters, they could not deny the experience. Those beings that fell decided to reject our offer of help, and they had to come up with some kind of reasoning that justified this rejection. Yet beyond that, they also made the decision that they never again wanted to experience being confronted with our reality. They had experienced our vibration in a way they could not deny, but they decided that they never again wanted to experience a reality they could not deny. This became the very deepest layer of their psyches after they fell into the next sphere. This denial where one decides that one never wants to experience a certain situation again is the essence of the dualistic mindset. The fallen mindset adds that a being never wants to experience the ascended masters in an undeniable manifestation.

The psychological mechanism is quite simple. A fallen being has the potential to turn around and start the path that leads to the ascension. Yet there is only one way to do this and it is, as it was for you, to encounter the vibration of an ascended master in order to gain a frame of reference from outside duality. If fallen beings were to acknowledge that ascended masters exist, they would also have to acknowledge that we have done what they have not done, meaning they have – as they would experience it – been wrong in an ultimate sense and have wasted all of the time and energy since they could have ascended. This is a very big and very difficult thing for them to do because it requires them to reverse all of the decisions they have made that denies their potential to walk the path to the ascension.

A fallen being could never experience what the four of you are experiencing right now because it would not be able to raise its consciousness to the point where it could perceive my Presence. You are all experiencing me with your physical senses but that is because you have raised your consciousness to a point where your physical senses can detect vibrations they cannot normally detect. You could not have done this if you had been in the same state of denial as the fallen beings. They simply cannot see us as having authority beyond themselves, they cannot experience our higher vibration. They literally think there is no higher authority than themselves or another fallen being that they see as their master.

Lucifer, for example, has a fallen being in the identity realm that he acknowledges as his master, but he thinks this being (who is obviously not ascended and thus not beyond duality) is the highest authority in the universe. This Dark Master fell in the fourth sphere and is therefore more sophisticated than Lucifer, but it is still trapped in duality.

A fallen being cannot recognize any authority beyond duality and thinks duality is ultimate reality. This denial is so deep that if the fallen being were to acknowledge it, it would begin to awaken from the fallen consciousness. This would mean that the person's fallen self would die in stages, and it will resist this. It is, obviously, a matter of life and death for the fallen self to uphold the denial.

We could also say that when you go into duality, the Conscious You refuses to take responsibility for its situation. Thus, a fallen self is created, and it lacks the fundamental ability of the Conscious You, namely the ability to go outside your current sense of self and life experience and experience something higher. The fallen self is like a mechanical device that can never go beyond its function. The fallen self can never recognize ascended masters and as long as the Conscious You will not take responsibility, the fallen being also cannot recognize us. Lucifer may think he is exercising his free will, but in reality he is allowing his fallen self to run every aspect of his life, and this fallen self is a slave of the Dark Master. Only by reawakening the Conscious You and experiencing a higher vibration, would Lucifer be able to make a truly free choice.

When you realize that a fallen being recognizes no authority beyond itself or beyond duality, you can see why you have no chance of persuading a being like Lucifer. Lucifer has an inner sense that he is a much older and more experienced lifestream than you are. This is true, in the sense that he fell in the fifth sphere and has fallen through the sixth also. So he has a lot more experience with matter and duality than you have. For that matter, Lucifer and his master are more experienced with using duality than I am as I ascended in this sphere. They consider themselves more sophisticated than any ascended master, and the reason is that they see us only as theoretical concepts. They cannot experience our vibration directly and therefore they can create any mental image of us they like, as they have done with their many false gods. They can create a mental image of us in such a way that they can justify ignoring us and ignoring the need to change their consciousness. They can ignore the fact that their consciousness is not the highest possible and thus they are not the highest authority.

A fallen being is constantly evaluating everyone it encounters based on a value judgment. It can vary a bit from one fallen being to the next, but it is always a matter of labelling and ranking people based on a criteria that makes the fallen being seem superior. When you meet Lucifer in any embodiment, he immediately ranks you as being lower than himself. Once you are classified as being lower than him, it follows that your arguments could never fully refute his own. You can never out-reason Lucifer—in his mind. You also have to take into consideration that Lucifer is not truly thinking independently. His mind is to a high degree controlled by his master in the identity octave. This Dark Master has no loyalty to Lucifer, as Lucifer has loyalty to him. He is simply using Lucifer to create change in the physical octave, and thus his primary goal with Lucifer is to prevent him from awakening. So when you reason with Lucifer and come close to refuting his arguments, the master will take over Lucifer's mind. One moment you are reasoning with Lucifer, the next you are reasoning with the master in the identity realm. This Dark Master sees itself as even more superior to you than Lucifer does, thus you have absolutely no possibility of out-reasoning or persuading this master. That is why you have felt that you have come to a point where Lucifer refused to talk anymore. Lucifer was simply gone and the Dark Master had taken over."

\*\*\*

Sanat Kumara: "It can be helpful for you to understand that when Lucifer was confronted with ascended masters in the fifth sphere, he experienced this as a great shock and humiliation. This was not something the ascended masters wanted, but it was inevitable.

Lucifer had a rationale for setting himself up as a superior leader on his planet in the fifth sphere. He had a long line of reasons for staying in duality and refusing to transcend himself as the sphere came closer to the ascension point. These reasons were all dualistic, meaning they all related to the fact that there was something outside of Lucifer that he needed to fight or resist. This is an inevitable part of the dualistic mind.

The natural mind is based on you being in the process of constantly transcending yourself. At any time you have a sense of self, and it may be sophisticated, but you never see it as ultimate. When you go into duality, you strive for an ultimate experience, including building an ultimate sense of self. Lucifer had done this by setting himself up as the all-powerful leader of an entire planet. He had therefore built a self that he considered the ultimate self. He literally thought there was no higher form of self than what he had built.

When he was confronted with the ascended masters, he could not deny that they had a form of self that was fundamentally higher than his own. So he was shocked out of his sense of having an ultimate self. How did he experience this? Well, you build an ultimate self in duality only by creating a value judgment that raises yourself up while putting all other people down. There is no other way to be above all others than by putting them down. Lucifer had created a value judgment in his own mind that he had so far applied only to other people. Yet when he was confronted with ascended masters, he had to acknowledge that he had not created the ultimate self. This did not mean that his dualistic self disappeared in a moment. It meant that he now started applying his own value judgment to himself for the first time. As he had used the separate self to set himself up to the highest possible position, the challenge of this self meant he now saw himself as having made the ultimate mistake and therefore suddenly being thrown to the lowest possible position.

This was such an unpleasant experience that he decided: "I never want to experience this again!" He decided that he never again wanted to experience being fundamentally wrong. The obvious way to avoid experiencing this again was to realize that it was a product of the dualistic self, which is simply a perception filter, like wearing colored glasses. This is what many other beings did, and it put them on the path to the ascension. Those who fell refused to do so. Lucifer therefore had to reinforce his dualistic self so that it would be based on this very deep denial. He never wants to experience being wrong so his outer self must deny any reality or authority beyond what he has created in his own mind. He is now put on a track of seeking to prevent himself from being proven wrong by preventing any outside influence from shattering his illusion of being right. This means he is on an endless track of seeking to control every being he meets so that they cannot challenge his sense of being right.

I am not saying it is *impossible* for a fallen being to be awakened, I am only saying that it is *unlikely* to happen as a result of anyone – be it you or an ascended master – reasoning with him. You cannot outreason a being who thinks it is always right. The ultimate absolute in Lucifer's mind is: "I can never be wrong." What argument from you could possibly override this?

Lucifer firmly denies that I exist and he firmly labels you as being lower than himself, meaning he can reject anything coming from both of us. The only thing that might awaken him is that he comes to a point of having had enough of always struggling and decides that there must be a higher experience in life. So far, this has not happened, but as an ascended master I do not use the past choices of any unascended being to predict the future choices of that being. I always hold the vision that a higher choice can be made at any time."

\*\*\*

At this point, I felt as if my entire being was shaking, and in a moment of total clarity I saw myself in my first embodiment. I said: "You said that the refusal to ever have a certain experience again is the essence of the dualistic mindset. This caused me to see what happened when I was tortured by Lucifer and Satan in my first embodiment. This was such a shocking experience that I decided that I never wanted to have that experience again. I see now that ever since then, everything I have been doing, including seeking to fight the fallen beings and destroy them, has been an attempt to prevent that I would ever have this experience again. Does this mean that when I had that experience, I actually went into the fallen mindset?"

Sanat Kumara: "As shocking as it may be to you, you are perfectly correct. The ultimate goal of the fallen beings (not necessarily Lucifer, but certainly the Dark Master) is to expose you to something so shocking that you decide you never want to experience it again. And in seeking to uphold that decision, you do go into the dualistic mindset. All four of you were in the dualistic mindset when you were trying to defeat the fallen beings. You could have stayed in that mindset until your sphere was ready to ascend, and then you might have fallen if you were not willing to undo your previous decision. This mindset is the same as the fallen mindset, but since you have not yet fallen, the denial is not as deep.

You have known fallen beings who are very aggressive, like Lucifer and Satan, but not all fallen beings are like that. There are fallen beings who may seem very benign, even very wise. They did not fall because of aggressiveness but because they did not want to look at the decision they had made that they never wanted to have a certain experience again.

This is a very important realization for all four of you because you cannot fully rise above the fallen mindset until you see the basic mechanics of this mindset and consciously undo it. Now, tell me, what is the mechanics of the fallen mindset, why does it become a closed system?"

Sanat Kumara was looking directly at me, and I felt such a love streaming from him that it took me a while before I was able to speak. Then, I had another moment of clarity and the words flowed effortlessly without any forethought: "Oh, I see what you mean. This is what I have been doing wrong all these many years. I have been thinking that in order to avoid ever having that experience again, I have had to control something outside myself. Obviously, I experienced that I lost the control over my inner situation that I had always had so far. And I experienced that it was Lucifer and Satan who caused me to lose this control. So I reasoned that in order to prevent myself from ever having that experience of total pain and shock again, I had to control Lucifer and Satan, or destroy them if I could not control them. Gosh, how dumb can one possibly be. So many years of wasted effort, so much energy and attention on a lost cause. What a waste of my life."

At this point, I felt such a beam of love energy from Sanat Kumara that I could no longer speak. He said: "My beloved, there is no greater joy for an ascended master than seeing his unascended student come to the realization you have just come to. There is, however, no reason to feel bad about this or about having wasted time. This has been part of your immersion experience on earth, and you had to immerse yourself before you could awaken. Only by doing this, could your awakening serve as an example that can help others. Now tell me what is the obvious alternative to the way you reacted to that first embodiment?"

Again, I had this moment of crystal clarity, and the words flowed effortlessly: "I see this so clearly now. In my first embodiment, I was so shocked by Lucifer's and Satan's behavior and intent because I had never experienced anything like it on a natural planet. So the contrast between what I expected and what actually happened was at its maximum and this is what caused the shock and trauma. Yet precisely because I had now experienced this, I could never again have had the same amount of contrast. Thus, I could never again have had the same experience, and it was therefore unnecessary to seek to control Lucifer and Satan. They could never again have hurt me as they did that first time because now my expectations of what can happen on earth had fundamentally shifted. So my decision was unnecessary and the effort to avoid having the same experience by controlling something outside myself was futile.

Of course, the real problem is that I experienced that it was something outside myself that caused me to lose control over my own mind. This is the real illusion, and I suppose it is the real goal of the fallen beings because I obviously gave them power over my mind. I now went into seeking to control my *outer* situation so it could never be the same again. The obvious alternative was to focus on controlling my *inner* situation so I could never again react the same way to anything the fallen beings could possibly do to me. I feel like an immense weight has fallen from my shoulders. It is like I am free from this original decision and I feel like I could fly."

I looked around, and I could see that my four brothers had had a similar experience of seeing their own individual decisions and also feeling free of them. We looked into each others eyes and congratulated each other on having achieved this momentous victory. We had almost forgotten about Sanat Kumara, but suddenly we all four looked at him, and we saw the most loving smile we had ever seen while feeling a joy streaming from him that was truly beyond anything we had experienced on earth.

Sanat Kumara: "My beloved students and brothers, my joy is full. This makes all of my effort with this planet worthwhile. Nothing gives an ascended master greater joy than seeing you go through an awakening experience like this. What sets you free from an unnatural planet is when you decide to focus on mastering your own mind instead of seeking to control your outer circumstances. What sets you free from the fallen beings is when you decide to focus on mastering your own mind instead of seeking to control them."

# 27

We later had other sessions where we had the opportunity to ask Sanat Kumara questions. Here are some excerpts of them.

Jeshu: "It sounds like there is a difference, or at least a nuance, between the duality consciousness and the fallen consciousness?"

Sanat Kumara: "Yes, that is a valid observation. The fallen beings are, of course, using the duality consciousness to create their world views and their value scales. What they add is the element of denial.

Duality is a state of consciousness that has the purpose of allowing a more experienced co-creator to define its own rules, or at least to get the experience that it is defining its own rules. You do this by going into duality and elevating a relative viewpoint to the status of being absolute, or at least beyond questioning. You then define a world view and a set of rules based on the view that there is an absolute that you do not question.

This is possible because there is no final argument in duality, meaning you can argue for any viewpoint and make it seem convincing—as long as you do not question the basic premise. Yet it is always possible that you can come to question this basic premise by hearing an argument that sounds convincing or by seeing matter outpicture the imbalances in your viewpoint. As you live, often for many lifetimes, based on never questioning a certain premise, you eventually can have enough of this experience, and then you become open to an argument that makes you question your premise. This can then lead you to create a new premise, but the process can eventually lead you to question why you always have to struggle or why there is nothing final. This can open your mind to the ascended masters. Duality itself is a tricky state of consciousness, but it is not a one-way street. Many co-creators have gone into duality, immersed themselves fully in it and have found the upward path and made their ascensions. You are all living proofs of this.

The fallen consciousness takes the basic element of duality, namely that there is a premise that you do not question, and adds an element of denial to it so that it becomes much more difficult to question the premise and therefore free yourself from it. You understand, I am sure, that as long as you will not question what you see as absolute (but which is truly relative), you cannot free yourself from duality. This can be outplayed in various ways, but it always involves a basic fear that terrible things will happen if you question the unquestionable. In Lucifer's case (and most other fallen beings) this is true in a sense that he would again experience being wrong.

We can say that in duality, there is a premise that you ignore and never question, but in the fallen consciousness you deny that it is possible or allowed to question the premise. Many fallen beings have created incredibly elaborate thought systems in order to justify why no one must ever question the basic premise. One obvious example is most of the religions found on earth, but you can go even deeper and look at the concept of god found on this planet."

Maitreya: "I really wanted to ask you about how the fallen beings have influenced the way most people look at god on this planet."

Sanat Kumara: "I have earlier explained the existence and role of the Creator. So there is a supreme Being in our world of form. Yet I hesitate to call this Being "god" because the concept of god on earth is so distorted by the fallen beings.

In reality, the Creator is of little relevance to beings in an unascended sphere because they have no way to interact with the Creator directly. You can interact with the ascended realm only through the representatives of the Creator, namely the ascended masters who have created your sphere and those who are working with the earth. The Creator does not directly involve itself in what is happening in an unascended sphere. It does so only indirectly through the ascended masters.

As I said, the fallen beings will not recognize the existence of ascended masters. To avoid this, they have created the concept of a god who is personally involved with the affairs of human beings, yet it is still a *remote* god. If you take a closer look (as most people are afraid to do because they think it is blasphemous), this god is a clearly based on a schizophrenic reasoning. The reason is that he is defined based on the duality consciousness where there will always be two polar opposites.

The fallen beings are saying that there is a superior or ultimate God who exists up there in a remote heaven. The purpose of this is twofold. One is to deny the existence of ascended masters who are much closer to you and ready to help you transcend your sense of self. Instead, there is nothing between you and god, at least nothing in the spiritual realm.

Such a god will seem remote, and also quite uninteresting to most people. Yet the fallen beings have added that this god is a personal god who, despite being far away, takes personal interest in the affairs of – *some* – human beings on this little, but somehow important, planet. God wants to save all people, but you must be a member of the right religion in order for god to help you. They also say that because this supreme god is so far away, only special people can interact with him directly. People need a representative to mediate between themselves and god, namely the priesthood of a particular religion. The true mediators between god and people on earth are the ascended masters, but the fallen beings have done everything possible to put themselves in our position—in people's minds, of course.

The entire purpose of this scheme is to make people believe that there is a supreme god who will either reward them or punish them. Whether you are rewarded or punished depends on whether you live up to a set of rules defined by the religion here on earth, which, of course, claims to have the rules and authority directly from god through its representatives or founder. In reality, the rules are defined by the fallen beings and they have only one purpose, namely to set themselves up as the undisputed rulers of earth. One way to do this is to make people think that the fallen beings are the only mediators between themselves and god, meaning that your reward or punishment depends on you obeying and blindly following the fallen beings here on earth. The number one rule is that your religion defines something you must never question, meaning people can never free themselves from the fallen beings."

Maitreya: "Are you then saying that all religion on earth is false?"

Sanat Kumara: "Well, if I were to be technical, then the concept of something being true or false is a dualistic term because you have two polar opposites that are defined in relation to each other. What we can say is that all religions currently seen on earth cannot deliver on the basic promise they are making, namely that by following the religion and its outer rules here on earth you will receive the ultimate reward of being saved by going to heaven. These promises are all unrealistic.

The only real form of 'salvation' or 'heaven' is to ascend. You ascend only by transcending your state of consciousness, your sense of self, until you transcend all dualistic selves. This will not be done for you by a remote god or any mediator he might appoint. It will happen in only one way, namely that you take total responsibility for your own state of consciousness and work with the ascended masters in order to transcend all aspects of the dualistic self.

Salvation cannot come to you from an *external* source, it can come only through an *internal* process. You need to be saved because you made the choice to go into duality. You can escape duality only by making new choices. You enter duality without being fully aware of what you are doing and what are the consequences. You exit duality only by becoming fully aware of your options and their consequences so you can make enlightened choices."

Me: "This makes me think about what you said about Lucifer who has a fallen being in the identity realm that he recognizes as his master. It seems to me that this Dark Master is Lucifer's god. Is it possible that the fallen beings in embodiment have modelled their concept of god on fallen beings, or one fallen being, in the identity octave? I guess what I am saying is: Is it possible that there actually is such a god, but that it is not the ultimate god but a being in the identity octave that is created or upheld by the fallen beings and by people who are tricked into feeding their energies to this fallen being by following a religion on earth?"

Sanat Kumara: "You have seen the basic mechanism of how co-creators can create even a god—that is, when they go into duality. In order to explain this, I would like to give you some background.

How do you co-create? You co-create by using the energy you receive from a higher source, but when you fashion that energy into a form, you endow it with some of your own consciousness. This does not mean that if you build a house, then the house has consciousness. It means that as you build the house, you create an image of it in the identity, mental and emotional realms. These three images are endowed with consciousness. As people live in the house, they can, over a period of time, build on to the identity, mental and emotional matrices of the house. This can give a house a certain atmosphere or even create the impression that the house is haunted. People who think a house is haunted are tuning in to the emotional, mental or identity matrices of the house.

A house is obviously a thing, but a thing is an expression of your state of consciousness. This means that before you can create a thing, you must first have created selves or internal spirits that exists in the identity, mental and emotional octaves. You use these selves to form a vision of what you want to create. When the creative energies descend from your I AM Presence, they are colored and shaped by the selves in the three higher levels of the mind.

When you are on a natural planet, you are also creating selves, but you do this consciously and therefore they do not take on a life of their own. You see them as part of your own being and thus they cannot become like separate entities living in your higher bodies.

On a natural planet nothing resists your creative efforts and therefore you have no sense of loss. You know that change is always a change for the better because you build on your previous creation and can create more. On an unnatural planet like earth, the density of matter does create resistance to your creative efforts. Therefore, you can indeed lose, which is reinforced by the short lifespan and the need to reincarnate. In duality, you are constantly seeking to build an ultimate state in a world where nothing is permanent. You might achieve riches or power in one embodiment, but then you die and you might be poor and powerless in your next lifetime.

What can you build on earth that has any kind of permanence when the material octave is so changeable? Well, the only thing you can build that has some endurance is your sense of self because you take your identity, mental, emotional and some of the physical selves with you from embodiment to embodiment. Many people have therefore become involved with building such a sophisticated outer or dualistic self that it can endure from lifetime to lifetime. It is an attempt to build something in duality that has permanence. In reality, this can never be done, but for a time you can have the illusion that it can be done. The hope is that by having this experience, you will have had enough and will want to go back to the path of self-transcendence where you are building a permanent self around your I AM Presence.

Take note of the underlying point. The selves you create in duality are created below the level of conscious awareness, meaning they are separate selves. Their function is to take over your reactions to certain situations so you do not have to consciously deal with and make decisions about those situations. You are essentially saying: 'I never want to experience this again,' and therefore you create a self to deal with such situations. This self is experiencing the situation so that you don't have to, but that also means you have no conscious awareness of the self once it is created. Because this self is separate and has a life of its own, it wants to perpetuate its own existence. It does so by seeking to gain more and more influence over you, and that is why most people on earth have their lives run almost entirely by such reactionary selves. Many people spend an entire lifetime without thinking a truly individual thought but having their lives controlled by these self-created selves. They are controlled by their own creation.

You have all been engaged in this process. It is what we call the immersion phase. You are building a self (or soul) that you think has permanence, and you do so by endowing it with your consciousness. The result is that as the self grows, you become more and more identified with it. You become immersed in it. The self also becomes more powerful in the sense that you have invested more and more energy and consciousness into it. This means the self gains more and more power to influence your conscious mind. The fear-based energies stored at the identity, mental and emotional levels (even in the cells of your physical body) can pull your conscious mind into repeating certain patterns.

Building such a self is a perfectly natural part of embodying on an unnatural planet. There is no reason to blame yourselves for this or to regret it. It is what you are meant to do on a planet like earth (in its current state). You have to come to a point of being fully identified with this non-permanent self, thinking this is you and this is all there is to you.

Of course, you are not meant to be immersed in this self forever because you are actually not growing while being immersed. You are growing only when you enter the awakening phase and start rising above the sense of identity defined by the non-permanent self. You let the outer self die bit by bit until you have reclaimed your true identity as a non-dual being. Precisely because you are a Conscious You that is pure awareness, it is very likely that you will one day have had enough of the experiences that the non-permanent self can offer. You will want more and this opens you to the path towards the ascension. At this moment, we can then step in and help you self-transcend by offering our vibration as a frame of reference."

\*\*\*

Sanat Kumara: "This is a long explanation, but it sets the stage for understanding the basic mechanism of co-creation and how a co-creator can become trapped in its own creation. As a co-creator, you can indeed create a self that becomes a being with a certain form of consciousness. This self does not have self-awareness as you do. It cannot step outside itself and see that it is limited and then want to transcend itself. Only the Conscious You can do this. What the outer self can do is to want to have more of what it is defined to want. A self that is defined to give you an experience of having power can (over several lifetimes) become so conscious that it wants to have more and more power.

As you (again over several lifetimes) feed energy into this self and endow it with consciousness, there can come a point where the self has enough awareness and energy to begin to influence your decisions. You have created a beast that wants to be fed, and it can be fed only when you give it attention and act upon its urges. The simplest way to explain this is an addiction to a physical substance, such as alcohol. A person can build a desire for escape through alcohol, and this creates a self that is fed only when the person drinks. Over several lifetimes, this self can become so powerful that it takes over the person's mind and gives him or her an uncontrollable urge to drink. The person might have a conscious reason for drinking, but the real purpose is to feed the alcoholic self. This self will get you nowhere, it mindlessly wants to grow bigger by getting you to drink. You have now become a slave of the self that you created, you have become imprisoned by your own creation.

The fallen beings are the ultimate examples of this process. When they fell, they created a self that they took with them. Lucifer and Satan may appear to have great personal power, but in reality they are total slaves of their own fallen selves. For example, Satan might get some sense of being powerful by destroying what others have built, but the real purpose of his efforts is to feed his destructive self. Satan, as a conscious being, is a slave of his fallen self.

Now, go back to the self that you have created. It was created by you and it can be fed only by you. An alcoholic self is fed only when you drink so it will (at regular intervals or all the time) urge you to drink. A warrior self will urge you to fight. A sex-based self will urge you to have sex and so on. However, and this is the crucial distinction, you are not a fallen being, which means that you are still receiving energy from your I AM Presence. It is this energy that feeds your non-permanent self when you express it through the activity that defines the self.

In contrast to this, when a being falls, it is cut off from receiving energy from its I AM Presence. It takes with it the energy it had gathered up until the point where it fell, but once it has entered the next sphere, it does not get new energy from a higher source. Lucifer, for example, had quite a lot of energy when he fell, and he used it to set himself up as a leader in the next sphere. Yet there came a point when this energy was used up, and from that point forward, Lucifer has been able to sustain his fallen self only by stealing energy from co-creators who are still receiving it from Above.

There is absolutely no way to understand what is happening on earth without understanding this mechanism. Virtually all activities that involve some people forcing others have the purpose of allowing some beings to steal energy. This is the central, underlying mechanism that directs every-thing that goes on in human affairs. Of course, the fallen beings know this, and that is why they will do anything in their power to deny this and to discredit anyone who promotes this knowledge. They know that if the population at large were to understand this one point, their power over humanity would be severely reduced. They will do anything in their power to prevent people from knowing this and from accepting it.

Another aspect of the equation is that it is not only fallen beings who need to steal energy from human beings. I have said that when you go into duality, you create an individual self that can take over your mind. Yet people will also create collective selves or entities that function the same way. An alcoholic has an individual alcoholic self. Yet all of the people who have been alcoholics on earth have created a collective entity. The individual alcoholic self is tied in to the collective entity and you can be influenced by the collective. This collective entity has more power than your individual self, and that is why some people can literally have their minds taken over by a collective entity that now controls their actions.

This can be most clearly seen in crowds. A crowd might start out as a collection of individuals assembled in a particular place for a particular purpose. Yet after some time, a shift can occur and now all of the people are acting as if with one mind. This might make them resort to violent acts that none of them would have taken as individuals, as seen in many riots.

It is the same mechanism that drives nations, empires, tribes or civilizations to go to war. Since the fallen beings introduced war on this planet, people have collectively created a very powerful war entity, sometimes even seen as a god of war. When a group is in conflict with another group, the citizens may have their individual aggressive selves, the selves that see violence as the only or the ultimate solution. Yet these are not enough to get the group to go to war. Only when the individual selves become portals that allow the collective war entity to take over people's individual minds and merge them into a collective mind, will a group go to war. The people of two groups might think they are fighting for a worthy cause, but in all cases, it is the same war entity that takes over the minds of both groups. No matter which group wins, the war entity is fed by the fear-based energy."

\*\*\*

Sanat Kumara: "I have now set the foundation so we can go back to your question about a god. There are two basic kinds of gods known to human beings on earth. One is the fallen beings who reside in one of the higher octaves. Another is the collective entities that have been created by humankind over a long period of time.

As you said, there is a very powerful and manipulative fallen being in the identity realm who has total control over Lucifer. He is Lucifer's personal god, but in past lifetimes, Lucifer had set himself up as supreme leader of various religions, thereby getting other people to worship this Dark Master as their god. It is also true that the general concept of god (the angry being in the sky who judges you and rewards you by heaven or punishes you by hell) is modelled on this fallen being, whose name has been translated into the Hebrew language as 'Yahweh.' This being has complete control over Lucifer's mind and the minds of other fallen beings in embodiment.

Over time, human beings who have worshipped this god have fed so much energy and consciousness into it that they have now created an entity that acts like this angry god. The entity itself is separate from the fallen being, and the fallen being has only limited control over it. There is, in fact, a certain warring between them as to who has ultimate control over this planet.

There are, of course, other fallen beings in the higher octaves and other collective entities created over time. This is the background for the concept found in several religions of a war in heaven or a war between gods. It is also the background for the fact that many groups of people have had competing gods. These are either fallen beings or collective entities that have used people in order to make themselves more powerful by stealing energy and thereby gaining greater influence on the planetary level.

As another example, there is a very powerful and destructive fallen being in the emotional octave who has control over Satan's mind. This being is in total rebellion against anything positive and wants to destroy everything that human beings build. This has also led to the creation of several destructive collective entities, and some of them have become very powerful. The concept found in several civilizations of a 'god of war' has its origin in this fallen being and the collective entities created through warfare. The same is the case for the many specific gods that take care of everyday life, such as a god of agriculture, hunting, love etcetera."

\*\*\*

Sanat Kumara: "Are there any real gods in the religions found on earth? Not if that god needs anything from human beings. Any god who needs to be worshipped, who needs sacrifices or who needs people to follow rules is a god who is not ascended. It needs people to engage in these activities in order to get energy from them. The reason is that it cannot get energy from a higher source but only from human beings.

I am not thereby saying that we of the ascended masters are the real gods for earth. We do not see ourselves as gods and have no desire to be seen as such by human beings. We have ascended, and this means we have risen to a fundamentally higher level of energy than your unascended sphere. We receive energy from a much higher source, and this means we need absolutely nothing from you. In reality, all of the energy you have used is coming from us and we have stepped a higher vibration down to the level you can deal with. Why would we need you to take this love-based energy, change it into fear-based energy and then give it back to us by worshipping us or killing other people in our name? Why would we need a lower energy when we have access to an unlimited supply of higher energy?

We are not interacting with human beings out of a need to get anything from you. You might say we have a need or desire to give something to you because we see you as our unascended brothers and sisters and we want you to have the opportunity to escape suffering as we have done. Thus, we offer you guidance on the same path that we have followed. As you can see from our interaction here, I am not receiving any energy from you. I am giving energy to you, but I have to step down my energy considerably in order for you to be able to receive it and bear being in my Presence."

Maitreya: "Are you saying that the Creator has no name or that the Creator's name cannot or has never been given on earth?"

Sanat Kumara: "The earth is a planet with a very low energy and this affects everything, including the languages used on this planet. There is a huge gap in vibration between earth and the most highly developed planet in this unascended sphere. There is a large gap between that planet and the ascended realm right above this sphere, meaning the sixth sphere. From there you have the other five spheres that have progressively higher vibrations, meaning that the gap in vibration between earth and the Creator is colossal.

The Creator doesn't actually have a name as names are seen on earth for why would it need one? Yet even if it had a name, there is simply no way it could be translated to the languages used on earth. The gap in vibration is so huge that the low-energetic languages and words, even the concepts, used on this planet cannot in any way express the reality of the Creator.

It is nothing but the pride of the fallen beings to think that the Creator has a name that can be expressed through the primitive languages on earth or that this name would give human beings on this low planet any access to or power over the Creator. This is the dream of the fallen beings and it has no reality to it whatsoever. Any claim that a word used on earth is the name of the highest god is a lie created by the fallen beings.

This does not mean that all names for god used on earth are completely false. The name 'Elohim' is the name of a specific group of ascended masters. These are beings who have attained the level of creative power that makes them capable of creating a planet. There were seven Elohim who created the earth in its natural state, and they are still overseeing this planet. Yet the Elohim do not want to be seen or worshipped as gods, and they do not want to be seen as the superior god."

*** 

After a long silence, Gautama spoke: "This is really a large mouthful for me (we all nodded and smiled), but it truly does explain so many of the questions I have had about conflict and warfare on this planet. I always knew it was not right, but I never could understand who benefitted from it. Now I see that the main purpose is to steal energy, which has nothing to do with the circumstances or arguments used to justify war.

This leads me to the question of how we can ever get the fallen beings off this planet? I mean, you have made it clear that the chance of awakening them is pretty slim, and the experiences we have all had with fallen beings certainly affirm that. So isn't it the goal of the ascended masters to free earth from the fallen beings so the original inhabitants can bring the planet to the ascension point? And if so, how can this be achieved, given that the fallen beings have influenced people's thinking in such profound and subtle ways?"

Sanat Kumara: "In its present state, our primary goal with earth is to use it as an educational institution and give as many beings as possible the opportunity to live out the extremes of the duality consciousness so they can hopefully have enough and start to awaken. In the long term, the main goal that the ascended masters have for earth is to bring the planet back to a natural state where it is following the upward spiral of the universe as a whole. It is correct that only the original inhabitants can do that, which means that the fallen beings are inconsequential for the ascended masters. Our main purpose for the earth is to awaken the original inhabitants.

It is a safety mechanism that fallen beings cannot destroy a planet, as the avatars cannot make a planet ascend. It is only the original inhabitants that can take a planet up or down. What the fallen beings *can* do is, of course, to manipulate and deceive the original inhabitants, as they have been doing. Yet there is a limit to how far this can go because the original inhabitants have not fallen, meaning they do not understand and agree with the agenda of the fallen beings. Many of them experience that the fallen beings are creating suffering, and when people have had enough of the suffering, they begin to rise up and protest against what the fallen beings are doing.

The only real way to get fallen beings off the planet is for there to be an awakening among the original inhabitants. Each fallen being attached to earth represents a certain state of consciousness. When a majority of the original inhabitants have had enough of that consciousness and shift out of it, then no fallen being with that level of consciousness can be associated with the earth in any of the four octaves.

There is a way to remove a particular fallen being. I know you have all heard fallen beings, such as Lucifer, claim that they are not reaping the energetic return (or karma) of their actions. This is both correct and incorrect. It is correct that when Lucifer manages to get a civilization to back him in going to war, then the karma of the outcome is shared by all of the people.

What Lucifer does not fully understand (because his master has hidden it from him) is that he is still responsible for what he does at a personal level. For each act where he forces another human being, he does reap karma and the effect of it is that he will shorten his lifespan. When a being falls, the attainment it had at the time determines how long of a lifespan it will have in the fallen state. We might compare this to having a certain amount of money. For each act, the being spends some of its capital and when the entire amount is spent, its time will be up."

Sanat Kumara paused, probably because he sensed we had questions. I was the first to speak: "During my first embodiment, I witnessed Lucifer violate Jeshu in the most horrendous way and later I was violated by him by being put into total pain. This was my first embodiment, so I was in a state of innocence when that happened. I mean, I had never done anything to Lucifer to warrant his aggression. So I guess my question is why Lucifer violating an innocent person does not spend so much of his capital that he has nothing left."

Sanat Kumara: "The Law of Free Will mandates that a being who falls will be given a very long time to turn around. A being can actually earn back some of its capital or time by performing genuine actions. So it is a very complex equation.

However, in the case of all of you, you need to consider what I have said about the immersion phase and the awakening phase. It is true that when you first come into embodiment, you are innocent, but you are also largely unaware of what kind of planet you are on and what kind of beings the fallen ones are. Contrary to what you think, you have actually done something to threaten Lucifer, namely to embody here. That in itself is enough to release the desire to destroy you because your mere presence is a threat to Lucifer and his master.

The really important point for you to understand is that your purpose for embodying here is to help awaken the original inhabitants. They have all become completely immersed in seeing themselves as human beings who are limited to planet earth. You do not awaken them by appearing here as some kind of superior being because they will not be able to relate to that. And the fallen beings will simply create a cult of idolatry around you and make you seem as gods that human beings can worship but not learn from and emulate.

The only way to help human beings is that you yourselves become immersed in life on this planet and then awaken yourself, thereby demonstrating that even those who have been immersed can find a path that leads to a higher state of consciousness. So you all had to become immersed. There is no reason for you to regret this or feel ashamed about it or feel like you made a mistake. This is a natural part of your mission on this planet.

This also explains why Lucifer, even though he did make some karma for violating you, did not make such a severe karma that he exhausted his capital. However, now that you have all entered the awakening phase, the situation has changed. If he violates any of you now, he will receive the full karmic return, and the closer you all come to being able to ascend, the more severe the return will be. If you have a person who can ascend in this lifetime and a fallen being violates that person, it becomes his judgment. The fallen being will either not be allowed to embody on earth again or the fallen being might have exhausted its opportunity and then goes through a ritual of what we call the final judgment.

This is a situation where the fallen being is confronted with all of its momentums and everything it has done in a way that it cannot so easily deny or explain away. This makes it clear for the being that it has fallen but also that it can return to an ascending path. It is offered help to walk the path, but it can, of course, refuse this help. If it does so, it will then be taken through what we call the 'second death' where the lifestream and all of its momentums is dissolved in the Court of Sacred Fire. The lifestream is dissolved and the Conscious You merges back into the I AM Presence. All energies are dissolved, even the memories of the actions.

So there are two ways that a particular fallen being can be removed from the earth. One is that a majority of the original inhabitants rise above the consciousness embodied by the fallen being. The other is that one being, usually an avatar, rises to the state of consciousness just before the ascension and then brings the judgment of that fallen being.

Take note that although the latter scenario will remove the fallen being and therefore bring a lightening of the load for the planet and the collective consciousness, this will not have the full impact until a majority of the original inhabitants transcend the consciousness. It is not enough to remove one fallen being because the consciousness remains. This can attract other fallen beings to the planet unless the people use the respite to raise their consciousness.

Now, you are all living at a rather dark period in earth's history, meaning that the collective consciousness is very low and there is a huge amount of fear-based energy in the four octaves (or bodies) of the planet. We have come from Venus in order to turn around the earth and get it out of the self-destructive spiral. This is our immediate goal and it is a huge task that can only be viewed from a long-term perspective. The fact that the four of you have responded to our coming and have raised your consciousness to this level is an important step. Of course, others have responded as well. However, you need to look at this as a long-term endeavour that has to go through several phases.

Right now, it simply isn't realistic to get Lucifer or Satan off the planet, because too many of the original inhabitants are still so identified with the consciousness they represent. We therefore need to take some measures that inspire people to rise above the Luciferian and satanic consciousness (if we name them by personalizing them). This is where the four of you can play a part if you so choose. You can also enter a path of seeking to win your individual ascensions as quickly as possible. This will bring you out of the planet much more quickly and require much less suffering. It will also help lighten the load of the planet because for each person ascending, there is a huge upward pull on the entire planet. However, there is no doubt that staying longer and working with us will have a greater impact on the planet so this is a decision that each of you needs to make."

Jeshu: "I have already made mine. I will stay as long as required and do whatever it takes to help raise this planet."

We all four spoke our agreements.

# 28

At one point during our session with Sanat Kumara, I spoke: "What I am sensing from what you have told us is that I might not have the full understanding of what brought me to this planet. I have so far been look-ing at myself in comparison to Lucifer and Satan in such a way that I have seen a very clear difference between them and myself. Of course, I know I am not a fallen being, but what I mean is that I have seen them as being trapped in duality, which is why they have no compunctions about violat-ing other people. I have seen myself as being unwilling to violate other people, and truly I could not do it the way Lucifer and Satan have been doing it. Yet I have killed many people in battle, and I have often justified this by thinking it was necessary in order to prevent Lucifer or Satan from committing an even greater atrocity.

I am now seeing that this really isn't so much better than what they are doing. They also have an agenda that makes them think their viola-tions of other people are justified. So the first thing I want to ask is this: I have in several embodiments fought or killed Satan or Lucifer, and I have always thought it helped prevent them from violating many more people and destroying entire civilizations. And maybe it did do that in the short run, but what you have given us is a long-term perspective, and I now sense that maybe what I was doing in fighting them did not actually help remove the fallen beings from the planet. I mean, I was only generating more fear-based energy by fighting them and I was certainly not setting an example for the inhabitants of earth that there is an alternative to their state of consciousness.

It is, of course, very hard for me to admit that I have been fooled by the duality consciousness and that I have also committed atrocities and contributed to the downward spiral of earth, but I really want to know the reality of the situation, so don't spare me."

Sanat Kumara again looked a me with the most loving expression and said: "My brother, it is a great joy for an ascended master to meet a student who is willing to look at everything, no matter how painful. However, before I answer your question, I want to reach back to what I said a long time ago. I said that in previous spheres, there came a point where it was necessary for the ascended masters to confront the beings who refused to ascend with the rest of the sphere. I also said that when these beings had to see what they had been doing, the biggest problem was that they tended to judge themselves as harshly as they had so far judged others. The reason being that they looked at their actions through the same perception filter that had allowed them to justify their actions—only now they could see that their actions were not justified.

The same now applies to you, with the difference that you are asking me to help you see reality. Yet I still need you – and all four of you – to make a conscious decision to shift out of the perception filter that caused you to do what you have done on this planet. I have no desire to see you judge yourselves through that filter. I will give you a moment to center in your hearts and to reconnect to the Conscious You as pure awareness, and then shift out of your perception filter."

*** 

Sanat Kumara: "Now, I will answer your question. The fallen beings are trapped in duality. One of their main goals is to pull all other beings into duality and keep them there. This is not really a conscious strategy on the part of the fallen beings. They are trapped in duality, but once you step into duality, you cannot see that you are in *du*-ality—you think you are in *re*-ality. In order for you to know that you are in duality, you have to have a frame of reference from outside duality because you must know that there is an alternative to duality. The effect of duality is to make you think you are absolutely right, and this causes you to lose the connection to the ascended masters. You have no frame of reference from outside duality and therefore you do not know you are in duality, meaning you cannot consciously want to pull all other people into duality. You simply unconsciously do what you do in order to get them into a state of consciousness where you know you can control them. The fallen beings want us to react to them because they think they are so important that no one should be able to ignore them.

Duality has two opposite polarities. This means that the primary unconscious strategy of the fallen beings is to force you in such a way that you will either submit to them or resist them. If you submit to them, you give them your energy and you take on much of the karma they generate. If you fight them, you also give them your energy and you make your own karma for fighting them. As you have correctly sensed, either way, you do not help lighten the load of the planet, you only help bring it further down. There is however, a third scenario. Duality has two polarities, but they form a scale. The polarities are at either end, and they are black and white. Yet the scale has a midpoint, and here everything is grey. There are many people on earth who have attempted to avoid submitting to or fighting the fallen beings by going into this grey zone. Some deny that there is such a thing as evil and think they can isolate themselves from the world and produce only love-based vibrations. Yet this cannot work on a planet like earth. You cannot be neutral, you cannot submit and you cannot fight.

You must find a different way to approach fallen beings and it can be done only by raising your consciousness to the point where you know what the fallen beings are and what they are about. You know what duality is and how it works, and you have consciously raised yourself above it. You have stopped being immersed in the consciousness of earth. You have raised yourself above it and you are *in* the world, but not *of* the world. This is a state of consciousness that we normally refer to by the universal name 'Christ,' meaning you must attain Christ consciousness. This is the consciousness where you have an inner connection to the ascended masters and this gives you a frame of reference for sensing the vibration of duality whereby you can expose it in all of its disguises. It is this state of consciousness that our system of initiation is designed to take you to, and you have all four made good progress.

It is in this way that you set the ultimate example for people on earth and it is in this way you can bring the judgment of the fallen beings. You can also use this consciousness to expose the plots of duality and bring forth new and higher teachings. However, even the Christ consciousness cannot bring forth an ultimate teaching on earth because the consciousness is too low. This will remain the case until earth once again becomes a natural planet."

\*\*\*

Sanat Kumara: "What happened to you before you came to earth? Perhaps the easiest way to explain this is to say that duality has stages. Every co-creator has to experiment with duality in order to make a conscious choice to abandon it and transcend it. So all have to go into it to some degree. The very first stage is where duality starts affecting your perception of life. It is like putting on a perception filter, comparable to (only more subtle) putting on a pair of colored glasses. You start seeing everything through this filter, and this means you start evaluating and labeling everything based on a scale with two polarities. At this point, it is still fairly easy for you to get out of duality. It is almost like a theater where you put on make-up and a costume and then go on stage to play a character that is not really you. When the play is over, you have no problem taking off the costume and make-up and going back to your normal self. At this stage, duality is like a game of pretending to be someone else while not forgetting who you really are.

The next stage is where your evaluation becomes more pronounced and you start to judge based on a value judgment. It is one thing to see dualistic polarities in a neutral way, such as black and white, it is another step deeper into duality when you start seeing the polarities as right or wrong, good or evil. This is when you start identifying yourself with the role you are playing in the theater, and it becomes difficult to take off the costume when the play is over because the play never seems to be over.

In your case, you had a long growth process on natural planets, and you experimented with every aspect of life, including the highest levels of government and natural spirituality. During this process, you naturally were quite focused on finding out what worked and what did not work in terms of helping the people you served live happy lives and grow in consciousness. When you had experienced everything there was to experience on your first planets, you started looking beyond single planets and developed more of a universal awareness. During this process, you also became aware that there are planets that are not natural.

This was a shock to you at first because you had never considered that an entire planet could descend into duality. You had, naturally, experimented with duality but you had no problem with going out of it again at the personal level. Now you became aware that there were many lifestreams who were trapped in duality and there were entire planets dominated by duality. You discovered to your shock that on some of these planets there was incredible amounts of suffering and even very shocking manifestations, such as war and torture. You had never considered that people could do this to each other, and you gradually became more and more focused on what could be done about such planets.

During this process, you were working with your ascended teachers, but you gradually started losing your willingness to listen. You started judging that what was happening on natural planets was wrong and that it should be stopped so people could be set free from suffering. You came to feel that since many of the people on such planets were forced by others against their will, this had to be a violation of the Law of Free Will and something had to be done to change conditions. You came to feel that your ascended teachers were not doing enough about this problem, and you started feeling that more direct measures had to be taken. This is why you were not willing to listen to your teachers when they tried to explain to you how unnatural planets work and what was actually being done from the ascended level. And that is why you feel that you came to this planet without truly understanding what you would be exposed to.

You can look at this process in two ways. You can look at it from inside your own experience, and you can feel now that you made a mistake by going into duality and by not listening to your teachers. You can also look at it the way I do, which is that it is part of the plan of the ascended masters to raise unnatural planets. One of the ways we do this is to have co-creators who have reached a higher level of awareness (but who have not yet ascended) embody on such planets.

Because you have not yet ascended, you can choose to embody on unnatural planets, which an ascended master cannot do. That is why I am not in embodiment on earth. Only those co-creators from Venus who had not yet ascended could take embodiment here and create this community. It is therefore an integral part of our plan for raising unnatural planets that some co-creators make the choice that the four of you have made. The question now becomes how you make that choice?

As ascended masters, we allow the free will of co-creators to work here. All co-creators who reach a higher level of consciousness will gain a more universal awareness. As part of it, you will look at unnatural planets. Some will have enough by studying them from a distance while others will become more focused on them. In your case, you may think that it was because you made a mistake that you ended up embodying here, but the reality is that if you had not done what you did, you simply could not take embodiment on a planet as low as earth. You have to go into the state of judging that something has gone wrong on earth, and that this something needs to be changed, in order to even embody on such a planet.

From my perspective, all four of you did exactly what you had to do in order to help raise the earth. Compare this to what I said earlier about the immersion and the awakening phase. You cannot help people on earth if you retain the higher consciousness you had before you came here. They simply will not be able to relate to you. So you had to become immersed in the consciousness of this planet, and it was inevitable that you would be exposed to Lucifer and Satan and that you would react the way you did by seeking to fight or restrict their abuse of others. Yet this is only a preparatory phase."

\*\*\*

Sanat Kumara: "Your real mission on earth begins when you go into the awakening phase. Here you will have to come to the conclusion that your efforts to fight the fallen beings did nothing to raise the planet—on the contrary. You do not defeat the fallen beings by becoming like them. Or rather, in order to defeat the fallen beings based on their dualistic state of consciousness, you have to become like them in the sense that you become willing to do what it takes to defeat them, be it with a sword, a gun or a ray weapon. You have to be as ruthless as them in terms of being willing to sacrifice the lives of others in order to defeat an opposing army.

Yet even though all four of you eventually became able to defeat Lucifer and Satan in all ways, you did not do anything to remove their consciousness from the earth. You *perpetuated* that consciousness. This can be a very difficult realization to come to, but it is a necessary one and you need to make a conscious effort not to judge yourself based on the judgmental state of consciousness. You need to not judge yourselves with the same state of consciousness you have used to judge the fallen beings, for if you do, you will have to condemn yourselves, and this will not help your growth. What you did was not the highest possible reaction, but it was what you did and as such it was necessary for your experience on this planet. You needed to immerse yourself in a certain state of consciousness and then awaken yourself from it, both for the sake of your own growth and for the sake of being able to help human beings.

Now that you are awakening from that state of consciousness, you need to truly awaken yourself by transcending the state fully and therefore not judging yourself through it. It was not a mistake that you fought Lucifer and Satan, it was simply what you did. It was a necessary part of your immersion experience on earth, and thus it can become an asset in your effort to help the people on earth also awaken from duality. You can learn something from this that you could never learn as an outside observer. You cannot learn about duality fully from a theoretical level. Those who really want to grasp duality, must immerse and then awaken. What you need to do now is to complete the awakening process so you become not only *physically* non-violent (in the sense that you would not use physical violence to defeat the fallen beings) but also *psychically* non-violent in the sense that you will not use psychic force to defeat them. You need to work with your ascended teachers to discover and fully integrate that there is a way to defeat the fallen beings that is not on their terms. When you look at your embodiments with Satan and Lucifer, you will see that in many cases you were able to defeat them, either on a battlefield or in a more political setting. Yet they were always the aggressors, meaning they were the ones who (through their actions) defined what it would take to defeat them. Again, they did not do this as a conscious strategy, but the simple fact is that *you cannot defeat the duality consciousness by using the duality consciousness.*

You need to transcend duality so you can avoid being pulled into a reactionary spiral with the fallen beings where their aggression defines the way you interact with them. You need to develop the Christ conscious-ness that allows you to interact with the fallen beings without letting them define your actions and state of consciousness. You define who you are and how you interact with the fallen beings—or whether you interact with them. You see that they have so far owned the privilege of defining the problem, and you now take onto yourselves the privilege of defining the solution."

*\*\*\**

Me: "I would like to hear more about the agenda of fallen beings. I know many people, including here in the Mystery School, who cannot understand the insensitivity of fallen beings. I have seen Lucifer and Satan make decisions that led to the killing of millions of people in one night. I have seen them both expose myself and others to horrendous forms of torture and humiliation. It is as if the lives of others and the feelings of others means nothing to them. Can you elaborate on that?"

Sanat Kumara: "It is very understandable that people cannot under-stand this. The reason is that you tend to think that because a fallen being is embodied in a human body, it should also think and feel like a human being, meaning yourself. This is because you do not have the knowledge that many different types of beings embody in human bodies, and you do not have this knowledge because the fallen beings have kept it from you in order to hide themselves.

One of the most common tendencies for beings is to project upon others their own state of consciousness. Because most people have empathy, they project that *all* should have empathy. When they meet someone who does not, they are confused. Yet look at how most people will swat a mosquito without thinking about it. The reason is that to them the mosquito has no feelings, no awareness. I understand that human beings do have feelings and awareness, but that is not how the fallen beings see it. They do not feel empathy for human beings because they do not feel the way human beings feel. Remember that fallen beings fell in a higher sphere. Their feelings were not the same as the feelings most people have on earth, and that is why fallen beings cannot empathise with human beings.

Fallen beings know that you have feelings and awareness, but to them your life experience is no more important than the experience of a mosquito. Everything is created from consciousness so even a mosquito has a certain form of consciousness. As a human being, you cannot (in your normal awareness) tune in to the consciousness of a mosquito and that is why it has no importance to you. I am not hereby saying you should start feeling guilty for killing a mosquito, I am simply illustrating through an example that the fallen beings place no importance whatsoever on your feelings.

In terms of their agenda, the ultimate agenda of the fallen beings is to prove that god was wrong for giving co-creators free will. Understanding this is tricky because however you describe it, it will seem contradictory. That is because in the duality consciousness, every argument or thought system is contradictory when you look at it neutrally. But let us look at one way to describe it.

When the beings in the fourth sphere were confronted with the ascended masters, they could not deny that what they had been doing was self-destructive. They, of course, saw it as a monumental mistake and judged themselves harshly. Yet a few of them refused to snap out of duality. Instead, they used duality to justify why what they did served a benign and necessary purpose.

They reasoned that the problem was free will and that god, as they could conceive of god, had made a mistake by giving co-creators free will. They used the fact that they had used their own free will to refuse to grow as a proof that free will would have disastrous consequences. I see from your auras that you are already confused and think this is contradictory, and I agree, but I am simply describing the process that happened to the first beings who fell. They decided that the very fact that they had gone against the rest of their sphere and refused to ascend was a clear proof that free will would in the end lead to a disaster. They then did what duality always does, namely project out that this was god's fault, not their own responsibility. They then reasoned that since god had made a mistake and since god would not listen to anyone, someone had to prove that god was wrong in an undeniable way. And, of course, they took upon themselves the task of proving god wrong. Take note that this was not the real Creator but a god they had created out of their dualistic state of consciousness. They refused to question their image of god, which, by the way, is the one mechanism that keeps most people on earth trapped.

Ever since then, they have been trying to prove god wrong, and they actually believe that one day they will succeed. They believe that there will come a point where they can prevent an entire sphere from ascending, and this will then prove the fallacy of free will. What they do not see is that even if this were to happen (which is highly unlikely even though each new sphere starts with a denser base energy than the previous one), it still would not change the fact that several spheres have indeed ascended with co-creators having free will. So free will has been abundantly proven to work, but not to those trapped in duality.

One might say the fallen beings are right that free will can have disastrous consequences because once co-creators go into duality, all the choices they make will lead to destructive consequences. Yet do beings in duality actually have free will? They think they do and that they freely choose one dualistic extreme over another, or freely choose the grey in the middle. Yet can you say that beings choose freely when they do not know there is an alternative to duality?

Yet it doesn't really matter how we reason about this because it doesn't change what is going on in the minds of the fallen beings. They are convinced that it is possible for them to prove god wrong. They can do this by getting as many co-creators as possible to go into duality and then keeping them there. Their overall strategy is to do anything possible to force co-creators into a reactionary pattern and to keep them there indefinitely. They do this in many ways, and the violations you have personally experienced is one of them. They expose you to such torture and abuse that it is virtually impossible not to react when you are newly embodied on this planet. Let us return to how they look at human beings on earth. To the fallen beings, humans are simply tools that they feel they can use in their ultimately benign quest to set right the mistakes made by god by giving co-creators free will. They think any amount of suffering and violation is acceptable for the fulfilment of this ultimately benign purpose. They firmly believe in the concept that the end justifies the means and that it is necessary to do evil that good may come. This is the very hallmark of the fallen beings, their signature. That is why you have felt such complete disregard for the lives and suffering of human beings.

Now, what I am telling you here does not apply to all fallen beings. Beings have fallen for different reasons and because they fall by going into duality, the fallen beings are not a homogenous group. They outplay all of the dualistic polarities and that is why there is a great rivalry and competition between them. For example, while one group of fallen beings want to prove god wrong, another group wants to defend god against all attacks, including the first group of fallen beings. They do this by creating a religion based on an absolutist claim and then seeking to destroy all other religions. Of course, as I have said, the fallen beings cannot even conceive of the Creator so any god they are talking about is a god of their own making.

The fallen beings can be said to have one overall agenda, namely: 'We cannot be wrong.' They are therefore engaged in a quest to prove themselves right and to never be proven wrong. Yet because they are in duality, they can never be absolutely sure that they are right and cannot be proven wrong. You can raise a relative viewpoint to the status of being absolute, but you cannot escape the ever-present opposite dualistic polarity. The certainty you attain in duality has doubt as its inescapable companion. So the fallen beings are locked in a quest that ultimately cannot be successful. Some of them eventually come to see this on their own. All will eventually come to see it, but it might take a very long time before this happens. The choice facing all people on a planet like earth is: 'How long do we want to follow the fallen beings on their impossible quest? How long do we want to allow our own state of consciousness to open the door for the fallen beings to embody on this planet?'"

# 29

We learned many other things from Sanat Kumara, but I will save them for later as I realize this is already a very difficult part of the book to read and comprehend, given that it is so far beyond the PIN of most people. Before I move closer to modern times, I do want to describe the fate of the Venusian Mystery School.

Jeshu and I stayed in the Mystery School until we were over 80 years old. For the latter part of our stay, Maitreya, Gautama and both of us worked on developing our ability to contact the ascended masters inside ourselves. We were trained to be messengers who could take dictations directly from the masters. The three others were quite successful at this while I had more trouble shutting off my own mind.

What the venutians had done was unprecedented on earth and therefore the fallen beings in the identity, mental and emotional realms had not foreseen it. Yet it did not take them long to realize that the school was in existence, and they immediately started to plot its destruction. Because the technology of the time was comparable to medieval Europe and because of the remote location of the school, it took decades before they had positioned their puppets in the physical octave in positions where they could mount an attack on the school. The fallen beings had sent spies to the school and later they sent people who tried to disrupt it, but they were not successful. They finally realized that only a physical attack by armies could destroy the school.

Lucifer, Satan and two other fallen beings created armies and led them towards the school. The four armies converged at the same time, and the community had no defence against such an assault, being completely non-violent. Obviously, the ascended masters knew exactly what was on its way so most of the inhabitants of the community were dispersed and moved to safe locations.

Only Maitreya, Gautama, Jeshu and myself stayed behind. We stood on the central square when the four armies rode into the temple complex from four directions. When the four fallen beings came to the square and saw us, they were incredibly angry. Yet none of them dared to kill us or have their henchmen kill us. After some deliberations, they decided to ignore us and then they ordered their armies to break down every building in the community. They four of us stood on the central square and watched them destroy everything built by the venutians.

This obviously took several days where we stood there with no food and drink. Afterwards, we watched one of the most insane spectacles I have ever seen. When the city was reduced to rubble, the four fallen leaders held a council. We could not hear what was said, but it soon became obvious that they were arguing. After some shouting, there was suddenly a great commotion as it turned out Satan had flown into a rage and killed one of the other leaders. This triggered the outbreak of a battle where the four armies fought each other.

The four of us literally stood in the central square and watched as these four armies, totalling over 20,000 men, hacked each other to pieces with swords, spears and axes. It is still one of the most bloody spectacles I have witnessed on this planet, and that says something. After a day of fighting, no one was left standing. Lucifer and Satan had both been killed and the armies were reduced to nothing. Some had run away from the insanity but most were dead and many wounded. The wounded were screaming in agony, but there was no one there to take care of them.

The four of us did what we could, but we had nothing to work with. Everything in the city had been destroyed, even the wells so there was not even water. We stayed there for some time while eating rations from dead soldiers, but eventually we had to resign ourselves to the fact that we could not save all of the wounded, most of whom had died by then anyway. We therefore made a very difficult decision to leave the battlefield and move on with our missions. Once again, we had witnessed the insanity of the fallen beings, but now with a deeper understanding of why this was happening.

***

One might think that with the destruction of the Mystery School, the Venusian mission on earth had failed. Yet the ongoing legacy was that many people (the venutians and the people from earth) had been trained to go out and start other mystery schools. Many have done so over the centuries and millennia. These small independent mystery schools have been there as an alternative to the major religions. The big religions have always been controlled and perverted by the fallen beings, that is how they got big. Yet the mystery schools have rarely been influenced by the fallen beings, except for the fake schools started by some fallen beings or the people they can control (as is the case for many such schools today).

One of the major mystery schools spawned from the Venusian school was founded by Gautama Buddha in his last embodiment. I know many Buddhists will object and say this was Gautama's only embodiment, but this is because Buddhism has come under the influence of the fallen beings. They have idolized the Buddha and made him so special that many Buddhists cannot see him as an example that they can follow. Obviously, a mainstream religion appeals to people who are still in the immersion phase and therefore cannot and will not take full responsibility for their state of consciousness. However, the original purpose for Gautama's Mystery School was indeed to work with those who were ready to take full responsibility and attain the main characteristic espoused by the Buddha, namely non-attachment to anything on earth, especially anything in duality.

I know this because Jeshu and I were students in Gautama's school and we followed him for his entire teaching life. We benefitted immensely from his greater experience and his insights into duality and how to escape it. Among many other things, he taught us that the only way to be truly free of the fallen beings is to seemingly let them win. Only by doing this, will you demonstrate complete non-attachment to them and only then will you be free.

However, the Buddha's approach to teaching was only one possible approach. Sanat Kumara talked about the two basic forces of creation, the expanding and the contracting forces or the Father and Mother. Gautama took the Father approach by establishing an ashram set aside from society and allowing students to come to him. Thereby, he did not directly challenge the fallen beings who were in control of the society of his time, and thus they left him alone. They considered him harmless, which of course was not true. Anyone who establishes the Buddhic consciousness helps pull the collective consciousness upwards tremendously. The fallen beings only realized his importance when it was too late to kill him, and then they tried to kill his example instead. The fallen beings did everything possible to pervert Buddhism, once it started attracting more followers. Their main strategy was to elevate the Buddha to an idol, not an example.

The Mother approach to teaching is that the teacher goes out into society and, so to speak, gets in the face of both the population and the fallen beings. This is in a way a much more challenging approach to the teacher because he or she cannot create a controlled situation. When you challenge the fallen beings directly, things are likely to get messy, and it is a great challenge to remain non-attached in the midst of chaos.


***


I am going to skip lightly over the next many embodiments that Jeshu and I had because I want to get closer to the modern era in order to talk about things with which most people are familiar. You might say this book is also an expression of the Mother approach and I want to get to the point where I can comment on the influence that the fallen beings have on today's society.

All I want to say at this point is that Jeshu and I went through a long phase where we did not challenge the fallen beings in a direct, physical way. We did not fight them with weapons or oppose them through political means. In fact, we started becoming less and less focused on the fallen beings.

We did have a number of embodiments where we encountered Lucifer or Satan. Although they did not have a conscious recollection of what happened in the Venusian community, both of them either sensed or were told by their masters that they could no longer violate or abuse us physically. Yet we did have a series of embodiments where they violated other people and where Jeshu and I had to demonstrate our non-attachment by not fighting Lucifer or Satan. These were, quite frankly, some of my most difficult embodiments because I knew I had the power to defeat both of them, both physically and through psychic means. Yet I also knew that this would only perpetuate my reactionary struggle with them and it would not ultimately contribute to having them removed from the earth.

I can assure you that both of these beings were extremely good at bringing us right to the edge of reacting. In a few cases, I was the one who helped Jeshu to avoid reacting, but in most cases, he was the one tempering me and he was holding a psycho-spiritual balance for me.

Eventually, we had demonstrated non-attachment to a point where we started embodying with Lucifer and Satan only rarely. We then had many embodiments where we focused on either starting a mystery school or being part of it. For example, we were with Plato in Athens when he established a mystery school there. We were with Pythagoras at Crotona, with Serapis in Egypt and with many mystery schools in the East and Middle-East.

Lucifer and Satan also went through a gradual change. Lucifer was not so much involved with politics and leadership of countries or armies but became more involved with the bigger religions. His master brought him to a point where he became one of the most capable deceivers ever to walk this planet. This, of course, is when we started encountering him again.

Even Satan became more tempered with time and became less destructive. He actually rose from being controlled by fallen beings in the emotional realm to beings in the mental realm, and eventually he became the student or chela of the Dark Master who also controlled Lucifer.

This happened because the mission of the venutians had the effect of setting the world on a track where knowledge became gradually more important than raw physical force. The fallen masters therefore became aware that it was necessary to have fallen beings in embodiment who could fight the battle for the minds rather than the bodies of humanity. And this brings me to what I want to go into next, namely the experience Jeshu and I had in what many people today call Israel.

# PART 6:

# PREPARATIONS FOR

# JESUS' MISSION

# 30

The preparations for Jeshu's final and most famous embodiment were elaborate and extremely complex. The ascended masters are here as advisors, not as all-powerful meddlers in human affairs. They are completely loyal to the Law of Free Will, which has, as its Mother polarity, the Law of Energetic Return (or karma). Jeshu's final embodiment required the bringing together of many different people who had different karmic circumstances. This became a very complex puzzle that even today's supercomputers could not have figured out. Yet the ascended masters managed to put together a process that, over several lifetimes, brought together all of the people who needed to be part of this drama. Of course, Jeshu, myself and all other players were unaware of this in our waking awareness.

Finally, came the point when Jeshu and I were born in a small town in Galilee, named Nazareth. It was not much of a town and it did not have a particularly good reputation. But the town itself was not spiritually significant, it was simply determined by the karmic circumstances of many of the people involved. It wasn't important where Jeshu was born, as long as it was in Galilee.

We were both born in the same year and we grew up knowing each other from before we could walk. Our parents lived close together, and they knew each other so we quickly formed an inseparable pair, making the neighborhood insecure. We were completely normal children. We were both brighter than average, but no so as to attract unwarranted attention. Jeshu's father, Joseph, and my father were both members of a mystery school whose name has not been preserved in the history books, and it is not important to name it here. Jeshu's mother, Mary, had been raised in the same mystery school.

I assume you are already seeing where I am going with this. You have realized that I am going to make the claim that the Jeshu I had known and embodied with for almost two million years was, in his final embodiment, the person we all know as Jesus. And that is exactly what I am going to do; only it is not a claim but reality.

I am aware that this will challenge the PIN about Jesus that has been so carefully and meticulously crafted by the fallen beings and that has been reinforced for 1700 years by that primary propaganda tool of the fallen beings, called the Catholic church. Yet if you had been attached to your

Programmed Illusion of Normality, you would not be reading this. I therefore assume you will want to see how I am going to challenge the official story about Jesus. So I might as well get on with it: All four of the gospels found in the New Testament were written under the direct influence of fallen beings in the identity and mental realms. They do all contain some facts, but they all distort them and put them in a context crafted by the fallen beings to destroy the example set by Jesus (as I might as well call him from now on). I am not thereby saying all four gospels are completely false. The Gospel of John does contain some genuine mystical teachings, but they have been distorted and dis-interpreted by official Christian theologians.

Ask yourself a simple question: Why didn't Jesus write down (or have someone else write down, if you believe the incorrect theory that he was illiterate) an official gospel or account of his life and teaching? As I will explain later, he had several reasons for this, but the important one in this context is that he knew that anything written would be distorted and disinterpreted by the fallen beings. He knew that if he wrote down something, the fallen beings would turn it into something static. The last thing he wanted was for his mission to result in the creation of another static religion controlled by the fallen beings. Since you are open to this book, you might be thinking: "But isn't that exactly what happened?" And my answer is that you are absolutely right. Therefore, the following chapters will be my account – as I personally witnessed it – of how Jesus intended his mission to be and how the fallen beings have done everything they could think of to destroy that mission, even to use it for their agenda of proving god wrong by preventing people from ascending.

\*\*\*

So let's begin with the beginning. The official PIN says that the birth of Jesus was an event of cosmic significance. One sign of this was that a star appeared over Bethlehem when he was born. This is complete brain-spin. If you think the heavens rearranges themselves because of something that is about to happen on this speck of dust we call earth, you have a grossly exaggerated sense of self-importance. What else could make you think this planet has some cosmic significance in a universe with billions of inhabited planets, 99,99 percent of which are natural planets that are beyond duality?

An exaggerated sense of self-importance is, of course, exactly what the fallen beings have. And that is one reason they have hi-jacked the story of Jesus and distorted it beyond recognition for one who was actually there. They want to use Jesus to make the earth seem significant in order to make themselves seem significant in a cosmic context. The reality is, of course, that no fallen being has ever been cosmically significant, and neither has the earth. So there was no star or any other visible celestial phenomenon.

Then, what about him being born in Bethlehem? First of all, Jesus was born in Nazareth, but the really important point is that it is not significant at all where he was born. Bethlehem was used only because the Dark Master attempted to tie Jesus into the myth that the Messiah expected by the Jews (an expectation crafted by the fallen beings) should come from the house of David. Therefore, he supposedly had to be born in David's city and this led to the myth about people having to be counted and Mary and Joseph traveling to Bethlehem.

Today, most scholars realize that there is no historical evidence of this counting of people and there is good evidence that it did not take place. So why insert this? Because one goal of the fallen beings influencing the gospels was to cast doubt upon Jesus being a historical figure. What better way to do this than to tie his birth to a historical event that would later be seen as not having taken place?

***

Another logical question at this point is: "But isn't it important that Jesus was from the lineage of David so the Jews could better accept him as their king and as the Messiah?" No, because the purpose of Jesus' mission had nothing to do with the Jews. He had no intention whatsoever of presenting himself as the king of the Jews or as their expected Messiah. The Jews themselves were insignificant to Jesus' mission because it was meant to be a mission for all people. It was meant to be a universal mission that presented the non-dualistic teachings that originated with Sanat Kumara and the Venusian Mystery School, namely the timeless teachings of the ascended masters.

Why then was Jesus born in that region of the world? For several reasons. One is that the people of the Middle East are some of the most closed-minded people on the planet and have been for millennia. This is partly due to the fact that they have been more easily influenced by the fallen beings than people in most other regions. This is something that goes back to other planets because many of the people in the Middle East (Arabs, Jews and others) are what one might call "laggard evolutions," meaning they are lagging behind other groups of souls on earth. They are not among the original inhabitants of the earth but came here after the fallen beings. Many of them did cause the destruction of their original planet, and they have been quite unwilling to learn from this and change their mindset. Even though most people on earth have now moved into an upward spiral, many people in the Middle East refuse to do so, which you can clearly see from a neutral evaluation of their mindset, their religion and their way of living.

It was determined that because of several factors, Jesus would not embody in the purest region of the world, but in one of the lowest in terms of the collective consciousness. I know that the official PIN refers to Israel as the "Holy Land" but this is another example of exaggerated self-importance on the part of both Jews and Arabs. I don't find it necessary to go into a discussion of whether the Jews or the Arabs have the most exaggerated sense of self-importance. Suffice it to say that one reason Jesus embodied in that region was precisely that so many of the people there have this sense of self-importance.

He was born in a Jewish setting because they had the concept of being god's chosen people. The reasoning behind this was that if he could help the Jews see beyond this need to elevate themselves above other people, then his mission would have a greater impact on people in the rest of the world. In other words, if Jesus could help people with the lowest consciousness on earth, he would be able to help anyone.

Let me briefly deal with the concept that a piece of land on earth can be considered holy. This is a creation of the fallen beings, and it is crafted in order to get people to fight over land, as you clearly see in the Middle East. Some Jews and Arabs are ready to release World War III because of a piece of rock called the Temple Mount. Incidentally, you will be hard pressed to find a location anywhere with a lower spiritual vibration than the Temple Mount.

In reality, no piece of land on earth is inherently holy. The vibration of a piece of land depends exclusively on the collective consciousness of the inhabitants. And because the collective consciousness in the Middle East is so low, it has some of the worst vibrations in the world. Why then do some Christians go to the places where Jesus was supposedly born or did certain things and feel a holy vibration? Because people have for 1700 years made pilgrimages to these places and over time they have created some very powerful collective spirits or entities that can overpower certain sensitive individuals and give them an experience out of the ordinary. These are not genuine spiritual experiences, but I realize it takes a higher degree of discernment to determine this. Many are fooled and will vehemently object to what I am saying.

The bottom line is this: There is absolutely nothing holy or otherwise special about the physical places where Jesus was born, lived or did certain things. Israel is not a holy land and the Jews are not god's chosen people. The Jews deserve exactly the same amount of respect as any other group of people, nothing more, nothing less. The entire idea that some people are more valuable or more important to god than others is simply dreamt up by the fallen beings to create conflict. It is, of course, also what they think of themselves. They actually think god has taken special steps to accommodate the fallen beings.

\*\*\*

What about the three wise men that appeared when Jesus was born? This has some bearing in reality. These were members of various mystery schools and they used their inner intuitive faculties (not an external star) to find Jesus. They came after he was born to pledge their support to Joseph and Mary and to help tutor Jesus when he was ready for it. The gifts they brought were not physical gifts but an offer to teach Jesus their own skills and wisdom.

What about Jesus being born at Christmas time? Most scholars today realize this is a creation of the Catholic church that took a popular pre-Christian holiday and made it Jesus' birth time. In reality, Jesus was born in the spring, but he does not want me to reveal the exact time or year (it wasn't the year 0) because it also has no cosmic significance and he does not want people to be focused on the specifics of his life (which is another reason he wrote nothing down).

Of course, no talk of Jesus' birth would be complete without addressing that most ingenious invention of the fallen beings, namely the virgin birth. This is a complete fabrication, designed to have the dual effect of either setting Jesus completely apart from all other people (doing even more to destroy him as an example to follow) or to make people reject the story of Jesus as being untrue. The fallen beings may not be able to predict everything, but they do understand how duality works. They know that if they make people accept one polarity (such as the virgin birth), it is only a matter of time before some people will begin to accept the opposite, namely that this is untrue and thus discredits the entire story of Jesus. By creating a story that involves something that is ordinarily impossible, they can make sure that some people will accept it and thereby accept the entire story blindly, while others will use the impossible as an excuse for rejecting the entire story. Anyone can see how well this works in the modern world.

The reality of the matter is that Mary was indeed brought up to enter a monastic order. Joseph was much older than her and did have several children with his first wife, who died in childbirth. Thus, their union in marriage was highly unlikely from a traditional perspective. One can say that their union came about as a result of Divine intervention, but only in the sense that they were both brought up to trust their intuitive faculties, which they had both developed to a high level. An angel did not physically appear to Mary, but she did have a genuine mystical experience where she felt a spiritual being approached her and showed her what she herself had volunteered to do as part of her Divine plan for that lifetime.

Joseph was also a practicing mystic and had several genuine experiences that led him to Mary. They both knew intuitively that they were supposed to bring forth a specific child, and they obeyed this inner prompting, despite the fact that it was very much unacceptable to their families and society.

So they got married and Jesus was conceived in a completely normal way. I know that none of us like to acknowledge the fact that we have been born because our parents had sex, and many Christians have transferred this to the parents of Jesus. Thus, they really want to believe in the virgin birth in order to avoid the image of Joseph and Mary doing what all other couples do.

And certainly, there was a Divine plan for bringing Jesus into embodiment. Yet even the plans of the ascended masters do not set aside natural laws when there is a perfectly natural alternative that will accomplish the goal to full satisfaction.

# 31

So back to what I actually experienced. As I said, Jesus and I were both fairly normal boys in the sense that we played and behaved within the normal range. None of us were aggressive or violent in any way, and this did lead both of us to be humiliated and even beaten up by some other boys. Yet we never responded with violence or anger, and in a surprisingly short period of time, the aggressive boys started leaving us alone.

There are some stories that have been crafted within the last couple of centuries, and even repeated by a modern author, namely that Jesus as a child had special abilities. It is claimed he could heal other children, bring dead people back to life or make clay figures and breathe life into them. As one who was with Jesus during his entire childhood, I can assure you this is complete brain-spin. It is inspired by the fallen beings in order to fool the people in the modern world who are open to a more mystical outlook on Jesus. The purpose is to once again make Jesus seem special and thereby make it seem impossible that we all have the potential to follow his example and attain Christ consciousness.

What about the flight to Egypt? Again, a nice story, crafted to tie Jesus in with the Jewish Exodus (another event that never took place as described in the Bible). It is not that this could not have happened. Herod was a fallen being in embodiment, and to kill all male babies born within certain years is by no means beyond what fallen beings might do. Yet it didn't happen, and Jesus and I lived our entire childhoods in Nazareth, rarely going far beyond the borders of the town.

\*\*\*

When I say that Jesus was a normal child, I should probably qualify it a bit. It is important for me to convey that he did not have supernatural abilities, but he did have a very strong intuition. This meant that he could not easily be swayed and it made him what many people in the community saw as headstrong and stubborn. Yet when you knew him, you knew he was not stubborn, he simply would not let any person or any outer circumstance or custom cause him to go against his inner knowing.

The Jews have a tendency to create customs and traditions that form such a tight cage around them that one can only wonder how they can stand living this way (If you have ever been in modern Israel during the Sabbath and tried to take an elevator, you will know what I mean). Although the traditions were somewhat different back then, they were still quite extensive, and Jesus had little patience for them. From the age of eight, he started refusing to participate in certain traditions that he found meaningless.

In the beginning, this led to some conflict in the home, and I witnessed a couple of situations. Mother Mary was an incredibly beautiful woman who was respected throughout the community, despite the fact that she had broken tradition by leaving a monastic order to marry an older man. Yet she was also quite young when she became a mother, and she did want Jesus to do what normal children did in the community. I think this was an expression of her protective instinct. She knew from before conception that Jesus was a special child, and she also sensed a need to protect him. The best way to protect him, she thought, was to prevent him from being noticed. She felt that if he did what normal children did, there was less chance of him being noticed by the wrong people.

I think she was right, but Jesus had little patience for this. At the age of eight, he refused to go to the equivalent of today's Sunday school. One day, I came to get Jesus so we could walk together to our class, and I found him dressed in his normal clothes, standing in the middle of the kitchen floor with his arms crossed. Mother Mary was standing in front of him with a raised index finger and a very determined expression I had never seen on her normally mild face. Jesus also had a very determined expression on his face, but that one I had seen many times before. Mother Mary said: "You are my child and I am telling you that you will go as every other child in this town!"

Jesus looked at her and calmly said: "Mother, I do not wish to disrespect you, but I will not go. What the teacher teaches makes no sense and I will not take it into my mind!"

Mother Mary became visibly upset and said with an almost angry voice: "Your mind cannot be damaged by knowing the beliefs and customs of the people we live amongst. And you will go because I am your mother and I am telling you to go!"

I could see that Jesus was upset too and he was about to say something. He was looking straight into Mother Mary's eyes, and I could almost see the tension between them. I was probably standing there with wide

open mouth, fearing some kind of explosion that would damage their relationship. Then, Jesus suddenly fell quiet and for a few seconds, it was as
if the entire situation was suspended in a vacuum. Suddenly, Jesus looked
down and said: "Mother I will go, but only because I love you and I do not
want to hurt your feelings." He then walked past me out the door, and as
I turned to follow him, I looked back and Mother Mary had an expression
of great relief on her face. She too had sensed the danger of the situation.

                                    ***

There were many other situations like that until Mother Mary learned
to allow Jesus to draw his own boundaries, which he was quite capable of
doing even at an early age. Where was Joseph, you might ask, but he was
older and had other children so he was more experienced than Mother
Mary. He knew that Jesus was able to handle himself and that it was best
to give him space.

However, it also played into the situation that although Joseph was at
a higher level of consciousness than most people, he was still lower than
Jesus and Mother Mary. Thus, he knew that he had to submit to their
greater authority. Mother Mary herself was almost as close to the 144th
level of consciousness as Jesus, and because she was the mother, she felt
that Jesus ought to obey her in certain matters. Yet because Jesus sensed
that he had as great spiritual attainment as his mother, he was not willing
to submit to her (or any other) authority. This is something that can happen to people as they come close to the 144th level, and in some cases it
can actually delay people's ascensions or limit their ability to carry out their
missions.

It is fine that when you have a higher level of consciousness, you do
not need to submit to any authority of a lower level. Yet, you still need to
be aware that your mission involves helping other people, and in order
to help them, you sometimes have to go along with them on the outer
without submitting on the inner. This can be a delicate balance that it is
difficult for many highly evolved people to find.

Later in life, Mother Mary would sometimes talk about how difficult
of a child she thought Jesus had been. And I understand that from *her*
viewpoint it did indeed seem so. Yet from *my* viewpoint, I admired Jesus
for not wanting to follow the meaningless customs and traditions that any

society finds it necessary to impose upon its children. I admired that he was not willing to conform whereas I rarely had the courage to rebel.

Jesus had a peculiar need to be alone, and this also created some conflict. Joseph had four children from his first marriage, and since he was a healthy man and Mother Mary a beautiful woman, they had two children after Jesus. With seven children in the household, there was enough work to do to keep everyone busy. Jesus had no problem doing his part of the work, and he was very capable and very fast. But when he felt he had done the chores assigned to him, he would often wander off to sit in the shade and look out over the hills and valley. I quickly learned not to approach him in such situations, simply because he would sit with closed eyes or an empty gaze, and he would not answer if spoken to. He could literally sit for hours without doing anything. I once asked what he had been thinking of, but he answered: "Does one have to be thinking? Is not thinking one of the greatest causes of misery the world has ever known." I didn't have much of an answer to that one at the age of ten.

Mother Mary was understandably overwhelmed by her work, and as Jesus grew older, she felt that when he had done his assigned chores, he could offer to help with other things, as there was always more to be done. There was a time when she tried to get Jesus to do this, but he could not understand why he was not allowed to finish his chores quickly and then be alone. He tried to explain his need to be alone, but Mother Mary could not understand it and called Joseph.

Joseph had a very calm manner about him, and he quietly listened to Mother Mary. Then, he asked Jesus to explain himself. Afterwards, he turned to Mother Mary, put his hand on her cheek and looked her in the eyes with the most tender expression. He then said: "My love, we both know that Jesus is not like the other children. I think it is best to let him be who he is because if you try to change him, it will only prevent you from being who you are, and that would be a loss to all of us." Mother Mary looked transformed by his love, and the topic was never spoken of again. It was truly a wonder to witness the love between Mary and Joseph. That is not saying there was anything wrong with the love of my own parents in that life, but there was an aura of mutual acceptance and appreciation around Joseph and Mary that is rarely seen among two people.

\*\*\*

What was unusual about Jesus and myself was that in previous embodiments we had both developed a strong interest in and knowledge of spirituality, mysticism and religion. Both of us started showing interest in this from an early age, and we studied this extensively. Joseph and my father often worked together in a workshop they shared (they were not only carpenters but able to do almost any kind of skilled work) and they would often tell us about their own mystical beliefs and about various religions, including the Jewish one. So instead of stories about adventures and heroes, we listened to stories about religion and mysticism.

As I said, both of us had reached a fairly high level of spiritual attainment during our past lives, with Jesus being close to the 144th level of consciousness. At this level, you can take with you much of the attainment from past lives, and you can start accessing it at a fairly early age. This is why Mozart could compose music at the age of five. So we both accessed our previous understanding of the spiritual side of life, and we had many discussions between us. My father had a brother named Joseph (known in the Bible as Joseph of Aramithea) and he was a merchant who traveled a lot. He was also in the mystery school of our fathers, and when he came home from his travels, he would tell us about the religions or spiritual teachings he had encountered. He would often bring someone home with him from far-away lands, and we would eagerly listen to and question them about their lands and the beliefs people had. Although we were not consciously aware of this yet, Jesus was educating himself to fulfil his mission.

***

The significant shift in our childhood came at the age of 12. Early childhood is a sort of grace-period where you (under normal circumstances) do not have to deal with most of your karma or your mission in that life. Yet at the age of 12, a main portion of people's karma descends, which explains much of the behavior of teenagers. This is also the age where the more advanced souls are capable of having an intuitive knowledge about their mission in this lifetime. It is one of the great lacks of modern society that children are brought up without a sense that they have a mission in life (or that life has any purpose in general) and therefore receive no help in recognizing their mission. Fortunately, both Mary and Joseph and my parents understood the importance of this and guided us to be ready to receive the vision of what we were in embodiment to do in that lifetime.

This intuitive recognition came in stages and not in one dramatic event. Yet one of the true events described in the scriptures is that we both were taken to the temple in Jerusalem by our parents at the age of 12. I would like to describe that event.

Today, many people (Christians and Jews alike) have a highly romanticized view of what the Jewish temple was like back then. This is often because they have visited Jerusalem and they think because it is such an old city, everything looked the same back then. And it is true that many of the buildings did look the same, but that is where the similarity ends.

When Jesus and I went to Jerusalem, we traveled several days in extremely hot weather. As we came to the city, we could both sense and see a cloud of black energy hanging over the town. We both had some ability to see energy fields, even though we had not started using it consciously at the time. Yet we both sensed the dark energy over the city, and as we came closer, we saw why.

Most people today do, of course, realize that back then, the center of the Jewish religion was that in order to enter heaven, you had to pay for all of your sins, and the primary way to do this was to perform animal sacrifices. Yet few people today bother to think about what that meant in practical terms. As we came closer to the city, we noticed flocks of animals being led towards the town. As we entered the walls, we could hear the sounds of animals over the din of the talking people and the shouting merchants. We could also sense the smell of the animals, the people and the excrements of both of them. Yet behind that we could sense a smell that we could not define. It was extremely unpleasant, but we had never smelled anything quite like it.

Quite frankly, coming to Jerusalem after having grown up in a small town was a shock to the senses and the mind. There were simply so many people, so many sights, so many sounds and so many smells that it overwhelmed not only our physical senses but our minds and emotions as well. There were people everywhere, and we had to fight our way through them towards the temple mount.

I am sure most Jews imagine that the temple must have been a spectacular sight, and it was, compared to the architecture found in that region at the time. It was not particularly large or impressive compared to many buildings found in the East at that time or many modern buildings. As we came closer to the Temple Mount, the smell we had sensed became stronger, and now we also noticed a distinct sound.

We had arrived on one of the days of the year when the Jewish priests performed the most animal sacrifices. Thousands of cows, sheep and goats were kept in enclosures on the Temple Mount. As the sacrifices started, the animals being sacrificed would scream, and when the other animals heard this and smelled the fresh blood, they would all start screaming, and this would continue for most of the day.

***

As we walked up the hill towards the Temple Mount, we saw streams of blood running down the stairs. Naturally, it pooled in places and quickly began to harden in the extremely hot sun. The combination of the smell of the drying blood, the excrement of the scared animals and the screams of those animals was simply so overwhelming and so abhorrent that any sense that this was a holy place was blown from your mind.

The process was very organized, I am tempted to use the modern word "industrialized," because this was animal slaughter on an industrial scale. There was a line of animals on one side of the sacrificial alter being dragged in and a line of corpses being pulled out on the other side. There was a line of people dragging the animals in, and then collecting the dead bodies as they came out. And this went on and on and on. The most scary thing was to watch the faces of the people who were there. They did not look at if they had experienced something holy, but they looked exactly like many soldiers I have seen on battlefields where they have been caught up in the act of killing. In reality, what happens is that the minds of soldiers is taken over by demons, and the people kill mindlessly. They always get a certain look, as if they are not quite present but still in an agitated or excited emotional state. They have a look of fanaticism in their eyes and they are clearly not thinking about what they were doing. This is the exact same look I saw on the faces of most people who had participated in the sacrifices.

Both Jesus and I could see this cloud of black energy hanging over the Temple Mount, and as we walked into it, it was almost paralyzing. We could barely walk and barely speak as we dragged ourselves up to the open square around the temple. Jesus turned towards me and said: "I sense no god living here, at least not a god I would ever want to have anything to do with." I said nothing because he had precisely expressed my own sentiment.

There was, of course, a god living in the temple, namely the false god that the Jews had collectively created, or rather built on to, as they took over the god created by the fallen beings and also merged into it several collective spirits created by various tribes in the area. Actually, the laggard evolutions who came to the Middle East from another planet had taken some of their collective spirits with them, and several of them had been merged into this god that it was claimed was the one and only, the supreme god of the universe.

As I stood there, facing the temple, I suddenly had a vision of this god, and I realized that it was this creature that had urged the Jews to put on this entire bloodbath. I knew with absolute certainty that a god requiring blood sacrifice could not possibly be the supreme god. I saw that thinking a god could be supreme and at the same time demand that its followers put on such a spectacle, was simply the most ridiculous thing I had ever encountered (in that lifetime). As this realization washed over me in waves, I literally threw up so violently that the others thought I was going to die.

When I regained some composure, I looked Jesus straight in the eye and without any forethought said: "Someone needs to liberate people from this kind of religion!" At that moment, Jesus looked like he had been struck by lightning, and he instantly fell to the ground where he lay for almost a minute while looking unconscious but shaking violently.

When he again became present and stood up, he looked at me and said: "And that is exactly why I am here!" We both knew the truth of it, and all four of our parents sensed it as well.

\*\*\*

After some time, we went to a part of the temple complex where some of the Rabbis were reading from the Torah and explaining the scriptures. It was an amazing experience to step into this room. The thick walls blocked most of the sounds from the slaughter and there was so much incense that even the smell was blocked out. It was as if your entire energy field started to relax, yet after some seconds I turned to Jesus and said: "These very same priests are the ones who have started this entire slaughter, and here they are, discoursing on some obscure points of the law less than a hundred meters away. Are they not aware of the contradictions in what they are doing?"

Jesus answered: "Some are not aware, but others are aware and do not care."

Our fathers had some business to attend to in Jerusalem and our mothers had some shopping to do. We were given the choice of whether to follow our mothers or stay in this hall. We decided to stay in order to listen to the discourse, and our parents said they would come to get us when they were done.

After our parents left, we moved closer to the center of the room so we could hear better. We did not know that the person leading the proceedings was the head of the supreme Jewish council, the Sanhedrin. We also did not know that this person was Lucifer in embodiment.

We both quickly sensed that this person was a master in talking to people, but we also sensed he was a master at confusing and manipulating them. He would read certain passages from the scriptures and then expound upon them in such a way that the listeners at first were brought into a state of complete confusion, not knowing what to think. Then, he gave his own interpretation and it was clear that most people accepted it without question.

After the main session, there was an open session where the listeners could ask questions or make comments. The first several people asked some questions that in no way challenged Lucifer and his interpretation of scripture. I could feel how Jesus became more and more excited, and finally he could not contain himself anymore. He stood up and with an extremely powerful voice said: "You say that the Jewish god requires sacrifices as a payment for sins, yet why does a supreme god need the spilling of blood in order to forgive sins?"

Lucifer looked completely taken aback, and I think it was more the vibration of Jesus' voice than the words. He took several seconds to find his composure, then said: "I think we have a future scholar in our midst," causing most of the people to laugh and look at Jesus with overbearing expressions. They clearly felt that this was not the place for a boy to speak. I think most people had expected Jesus to sit down, but he remained standing and looked Lucifer straight in the eye.

As it started to become obvious to Lucifer that Jesus was not backing down and that it was becoming embarrassing that he did not address the question, he said: "It is through the words revealed by god to the prophets that we have the command to perform animal sacrifices. It goes back to the command of an eye for an eye and a tooth for a tooth. The sins committed by spilling the blood of humans need to be compensated for by the spilling of blood, but instead of sacrificing humans, as was done in older times, we have been given the command to sacrifice only animals."

Jesus remained standing and said: "And how exactly can the spilling of the blood of innocent animals compensate for the sins committed by human beings when those human beings have not changed the consciousness that made them commit those acts of violence? Can you buy freedom from sin when you have not been willing to remove the beam from your own eye? Is your god a tradesman or does he want his people to grow beyond the violence and selfishness that clearly cannot give them entry into the heavenly realm?"

As Jesus was speaking, Lucifer looked like he had been struck by lightning and had been taken somewhere else. He was having a revelation of his own, being shown by the Dark Master that it was Lucifer's main mission in that life to destroy the mission of Jesus. After Jesus stopped speaking, Lucifer looked unwell and said he had some urgent temple business to attend to. He told one of his subordinates to take over the session, and then he withdrew. Several people now started making comments and asking questions that changed the subject without addressing what Jesus had said. Jesus and I then sat in the back until our parents came to get us.

*** 

As our parents arrived and we were about to leave, Lucifer and two other priests came up to us and Lucifer addressed Joseph: "I see you must be the father of the young man here, what is your name and his?"

After Joseph had answered, Lucifer said: "I immediately saw that young Jesus has a special awareness of the scriptures and a deeper understanding than most. We do have an apprenticeship program here at the temple, and after consulting with some of my subordinates, we would like to offer Jesus a position in our program. He will be taught in the law and can eventually enter the priesthood and even work his way to a position here in the temple, the highest religious authority in the world. He can even stay here today and begin the program immediately under my personal guidance." As he had been speaking, I noticed that Jesus looked as if he sensed an extreme danger, and I saw that Joseph and Mary clearly sensed it as well. At one point I saw Joseph look Jesus in the eye, and Jesus shook his head very slightly. Joseph then turned to Lucifer and said: "We are naturally honoured by such an offer, but it comes so suddenly that I feel we need some time to consider it more carefully. I am getting old, and it is time my sons begin to take over more of the business. I would like a few days to think about this and then let you know what I decide."

Lucifer looked greatly displeased by being gainsaid by a common craftsman. Yet as he looked Joseph directly in the eye, he realized he could not sway him, so he had to back down. He said: "Please let me know as soon as possible, as I feel it is urgent that we start his training as soon as possible."

Joseph mumbled what sounded like an agreement, and we left. As we went through the door, I looked back and saw Lucifer looking like the blackest thundercloud one could possibly imagine. I knew that this would not be the end of the matter, and it wasn't.

\*\*\*

After we had walked outside the city walls, Jesus suddenly collapsed and had to sit down. He was panting and said that he felt as if he had just escaped an extreme danger. I then said that we might not have escaped it yet because I had the sense that we were being followed. Joseph and Mary had sensed the same so we hurried on our way.

Fortunately, Joseph and my father knew a member of their mystical order who lived in a village not far from town. We stopped by his house and after having explained the situation, our host called several of his neighbors who were also members. They quickly organized some horses, and under the cover of darkness, we left with an armed escort of a dozen men.

Our fathers had decided that it was too dangerous for us to return to Nazareth because Lucifer knew where we lived. We therefore took a circuitous route in order to reach my father's brother, Joseph of Arimethea. It took us two days to reach him, and after a short council, it was determined that the safest course of action was to send Jesus with one of Joseph's caravans towards the East. Jesus was in full agreement because he had realized that his mission required him to gain first-hand experience with many different religions and spiritual teachings.

There was an emotional session where Joseph and Mary said farewell to Jesus, not knowing if they would ever see him again, which came true for Joseph, who died before we came back to Galilee. As this was coming to an end, I managed to get their attention and say: "You do all realize, do you not, that I am going with him. That is indeed part of *my* mission in this life."

They all looked at me and no one objected. Jesus looked at me and said: "I never thought of going without you, I just assumed you knew."

I said: "I did know, I just wanted my parents to know also."

We then took leave of our parents and set out into the unknown on an easterly course.

# 32

I mentioned that three mystics came to visit Joseph and Mary shortly after the birth of Jesus and that they each offered to tutor him in their knowledge and talents. After a strenuous but very exciting journey with a caravan, we did arrive at the mystery school of the first of the three wise men, situated in what is now Iraq. The names normally used for them are incorrect, and their real names are not truly significant so I will not mention them.

Our host had created a beautiful ashram with lavish gardens and he had a large group of students who made the entire place function as a self-sufficient community. He welcomed us with open arms and taught us many things. The most significant thing he taught us was how easily our senses are fooled. Today, most people are aware of what we call optical illusions and know how we can see, for example, the same image as both an old woman and a young girl. Our host taught us much of the same but went far deeper.

He taught us that our minds have been so accustomed to experiencing the world through our senses that we have grown up with a distorted view of how the world works. He had taken the teachings of the Greek atomist philosophers and had developed them into something that was quite sophisticated and not so far from what science has discovered today with sub-atomic particles, only described in a non-mathematical framework.

\*\*\*

Our host taught us that there are two aspects of the world. There is an objective world that functions the way it functions regardless of how we see it. Then there is a subjective world that exists only inside our own minds. If we can free our minds from the sensory view, the sensory perception filter, then we can experience the world as it really is. We can see beyond our subjective world and experience the objective world.

Our host took us through a rigorous process of using mind-exercises to question our perception and eventually free us from our sensory view. Jesus was very successful at doing this and soon learned to set aside his sensory perception and experience the workings of the world beyond the senses. I could do the same but only in brief glimpses. I experienced enough to know that our host's teaching was correct, I just couldn't do much with it.

Our host taught us that everything we perceive with our normal, sensory view is truly an illusion. Our senses and outer minds tell us that we live in a world made of objects that are separated from each other and separated from ourselves. In reality, every form we perceive with the senses is made up of smaller units, which our host called either atoms or vital particles. He did not have the concept of energy that we have today, but he did say that these particles were constantly vibrating, like the string of a musical instrument.

He taught us that our bodies are also made up of these vital particles. Our minds are not made up of the same kind of particles that bodies and things are made of. They are made up of what he called spirit particles, a higher form of particle. Spirit particles make up the vital particles. Therefore, our minds can learn to manipulate vital particles and thereby change the forms we perceive with our senses. Obviously, these spirit particles exist in the three higher octaves of the emotional, mental and identity realms that I have talked about before.

However, in order to be able to do this, we have to free our minds from the prison of the senses and the outer mind. Our host had spent his life working on this and had achieved some success. Actually, he had spent many lifetimes on this, as he was one of the Venusian instructors we had at Sanat Kumara's Mystery School. He had further developed the teachings we were taught back then. He reawakened in us much of what we had been taught so long ago and then helped us go further.

Our host taught us that our minds have the capacity to develop some mastery over matter, and he demonstrated this himself. He was able to move smaller objects by the power of his mind alone. For example, he could sit in meditation and with his mind move a small rock on a table in front of him.

As the first exercise, he had us go into deep meditation on the vital particles and the spirit particles behind them. We would then seek to extinguish a candle burning on a table in front of us. It took us months to free our minds from the captivity of the senses, but finally one day we were sitting in meditation when I heard Jesus exclaim: "It worked!" When I opened my eyes, I saw that the candle in front of him had been extinguished, and I know he had not moved a muscle. We were both ecstatic and rushed to tell our host, who shared our joy.

After this, Jesus made rapid progress and could soon move smaller things, such as feathers and pieces of wood. It is interesting that it took more effort to move a heavier object than a lighter one, but that is the way it is. While Jesus moved on to heavier objects, I was still working on the candle. One day, I thought it had worked because the candle did go out, but then I realized our host had opened the door and a draft had blown out the candle. Yet I continued to work on it, and one day it did actually happen to me. I had gone into meditation and in my mind I experienced the vital particles as clearly as I could have seen the candle with my eyes open.

I then experienced myself as spirit particles, visualized how the spirit particles made up the vital particles that made up the candle. Then, I visualized in my mind's eye the candle as being unlit. I affirmed this state as the only possible reality and projected the image of the unlit candle onto the lit candle I knew was standing in front of me. I sat there for some time holding the image of the unlit candle, and when I opened my eyes, I was not surprised at all to see the candle unlit. I then looked over at Jesus and saw one of the biggest smiles I ever saw on his face: "My brother, I greet you among the masters of mind over matter," he said with the mock solemn voice he often used, and we both burst into laughter. There was never a sense of rivalry or competition among us and we truly rejoiced in each others achievements.

# 33

We stayed with our first host for almost two years, and then Jesus felt it was time to move on. Our host had already corresponded with the second of the wise men who had an ashram in what is now Iran. He arranged our journey, and one day we arrived at our second host. He had specialized in healing, and his teachings were in close alignment with our first host, which was not strange since he was also one of the reincarnated Venusian teachers.

Our new host had focused on the body being made up of vital particles that were again made up of spirit particles. Yet he had gone further by reviving the Venusian teachings about the four lower bodies. He taught us that beyond our physical perception of the world is an emotional component, a mental component and our sense of identity. He taught that our physical bodies are created from the three higher bodies that combine to shape the physical body. Therefore, effective healing must involve cleansing and healing the three higher bodies.

He also taught that healing the physical body with the mind was a real possibility, and he had achieved some ability to do this himself. In fact, he would have many people who came to his ashram and they were taken through an extensive program that led many to be healed of all kinds of diseases. He would also have regular services where many people would invoke spiritual energy, as we had done in the Venusian school. This also caused many to be healed, especially when our host laid hands on them and used the mental healing techniques he had developed. Jesus became very fascinated by this and very determined to learn how to heal people with the mind.

***

Our host had a room in his ashram with a white wall. Opposite the wall was a small round window that had colored glass made in what we now call China. One day, he had us sit under the glass window and watch as the sun came around to shine through it. We saw how the glass pieces formed an intricate pattern on the wall. Our host then said: "I want you to look at the image on the wall and then answer me the question of whether the image is real. Is there really something there, something physical?"

Jesus answered: "There is nothing physical, it is only the light from the sun that projects the image onto the wall."

Our host then said: "Now look at your physical bodies and answer me the question of whether the body is real. Is there really something there, something physical?"

Jesus answered: "To my senses and outer mind, there is something there and it seems solid and physical. I assume you are hinting that the body is no more real than the image on the wall?"

Our host said: "Actually, the body is more solid or dense than the image on the wall, but it is no more real. What I want you to see is that the physical body is a projection, just as the image on the wall. Instead of the light of the sun shining through the glass, there is light from your higher selves that shines through the three higher bodies. Therefore, your physical body is merely a projection of the images found in those bodies. Change the content of your three higher bodies, and you can change the form of your physical body.

You can heal a disease at the physical level by changing the three higher bodies because a disease is not caused at the physical level. It starts in the three higher bodies and then filters down to the physical. Using a physical substance to deal with the symptoms at the physical level is not effective and will at best mask the symptoms or push them into the higher bodies. True healing addresses the higher bodies and then pushes the new image from those bodies into the physical."

Jesus then asked: "How come our bodies appear solid to our senses and outer minds?"

Our host answered: "Because we have all been deceived by the Prince of this World. He is the being created by the collective consciousness and he makes all people believe that the world really is as we perceive it through our physical senses. He also makes us believe that the world really is the way human beings have collectively interpreted it for a very long time, namely that it is separated from Spirit and that it is made up of actual objects that are separated from each other.

My dear brother taught you to see beyond your sensory perception and see the vital particles that make up all forms and then see the spirit particles that make up the vital particles. This is what we deemed as the first step on your journey. The deeper understanding that you are now ready for is that the vital particles have five different states or aspects. When you perceive a fire, your eyes can see the flame, your ears can hear the crackling of the wood, your noses can smell the smoke, your tongues can taste the smoke and your skin can feel the warmth. There is only one event, the fire, but you experience it in different ways through the five senses. This is because each of the physical senses is calibrated to detect a certain aspect of the vital particles that make up the event of the fire.

Yet your nose does not detect a fire. It detects a certain aspect of the vital particles [What science today would call a frequency]. So where does the concept of the fire come from? It comes from your minds at the physical level. To your conscious minds, it is too overwhelming to deal with the impressions from five different senses at once. Therefore, there is an aspect of the physical mind, and for most people it is subconscious, that puts together the sensory impressions to a whole that the conscious mind can deal with.

Besides this, you also have the practical aspect that human beings have a need to communicate and sometimes very quickly. Over time, this has developed into people inventing certain mental concepts and using them to refer to specific events. The word 'fire' is simply used to refer to a mental concept that gathers together the sensory impressions of an event and then labels it as a coherent whole.

There is nothing inherently dangerous about doing this, but it does have a potential danger. The word 'fire' refers to a distinct event and sets it apart from other events, such as 'rain.' So built into words is the tendency to label things as distinct and to set them apart from each other. Again, this is not in itself dangerous as long as people have a conscious awareness that they are spiritual beings and that words and concepts are only practical measures in order to communicate about physical events. The problem comes in when people start to lose their awareness that they are spiritual beings.

A long time ago, people on earth started forgetting where they came from, and then they started to believe that their mental concepts were not created by the mind but referred to real events. Instead of seeing a fire as an event made up of vital particles, they started seeing it based on the sensory perceptions and the coherent whole that their minds created based on them.

It is possible to describe a fire in an entirely different way, namely as an interplay of vital particles that is again projected by an interplay of spirit particles. When you no longer perceive the vital particles, you begin to think that a fire is an event that happens in a physical world that is separated from you. You then begin to think that your physical body is also something that exists in an objective, physical world. As the next step, you begin to identity with your physical body, and now you think the body and its limitations define you, even that you as a being might die when the body dies.

Because people have been doing this for a very long time, they have created a very powerful collective spirit, and this is what I call the Prince of this World. It was created out of the tendency to assign reality to the mental concepts created by the mind. Its primary function is to keep people trapped in the belief of the reality of this mentally created world and to prevent them from experiencing the objective world of vital particles and spirit particles.

Basically, when people started creating mental concepts, they were seen only as tools for communication. When people forgot who they are, their own creation now started defining them and their relationship to everything, including god, nature and each other. People have become trapped in their own mental creations, and the primary function of the Prince of this World is to prevent anyone from freeing himself or herself from this illusion. My primary function is to help you escape the Prince of this World."

I want to insert here that when we later returned to Israel, Jesus taught this concept of the Prince of This world, as you can even find examples of in the scriptures. However, because the Jews had developed the concept of an adversary of god and named it Satan, Jesus also used "Satan" as a name for the Prince of this World.

*** 

Our host now took us through a very intensive training in freeing our minds from words and mental concepts. This involved meditative exercises that challenged each of the five senses. We also had many discussions with him where he challenged our tendency to use words to label an event.

This was a very disturbing time for both of us because our host was relentless in challenging what had been programmed into us for many lifetimes. We also had to fight against the magnetic pull of the collective consciousness, reinforced by all human beings who have lived on earth for millions of years. The Prince of this World, created as a collective entity, has indeed become very strong.

We quickly came to a point where none of us truly knew what was real and not real. It was a state of mind that today would have been labeled as a psychosis, and it would have landed us in straitjackets or on heavy medication. Jesus and I had many discussions between ourselves, but they usually left us both feeling frustrated and not knowing what to believe. Our host was quite aware of what we were going through, but he also knew that he had to take a calculated risk. The only way to help us break through the programming was to drive us to the brink of insanity and then count on us getting through it without going permanently insane.

Some of the questions we were having to deal with were very similar to what quantum physicists have been dealing with (or not dealing with) over the past century. Our host was trying to help us see how much we are influenced by our perception and how our perception can become a closed system, a mental prison that keeps us trapped more firmly than any physical prison can. This is similar to the questions asked by many modern physicists, such as: "Is the world still there when no one is looking?" Or another question: "If a tree falls in the forest and no one is there, does it still make a sound?" In other words, we had to consider whether there is an objective world or whether our impression of an objective world is created entirely in our individual minds because we get overpowered by the collective mind. And if there *is* an objective world, will we ever be able to experience it while here on earth?

One day, Jesus and I had walked into the hills around the ashram, and we had a discussion that helped us start to break through. I started it: "The one thing that gives me the most trouble is my body. I can see my body, I can hear it when I snap my fingers, I can smell my body, I can lick my skin and taste it and I can feel my body. I also experience that I am inside my body and that I cannot leave it.

I know very well that I am more than the body, that I have a soul, a mind, a conscious self that is not the body. Yet right now, the body seems very real and it seems to have great power over the real me because I cannot leave it. I know the body is made up of a lower kind of substance than my soul, but it is very hard for me to believe that the body is not real at all. If it is not real, how can it have such power over me?"

Jesus: "I understand what you are saying. I have the same trouble. But what if we stepped back and asked ourselves what we mean when we say something is real?"

Me: "Like our host is talking about us using words to label everything. You mean the word 'reality' is another word that represents a mental concept. So you want us to question what we mean with reality?"

Jesus: "Exactly. Just think about how many times we use words without defining what they really mean. We just assume that we know what the word 'reality' means, but do we? So let us look at that."

I thought about this for a while and said: "If we take what our host is saying, he is saying that our senses can detect only a certain aspect of the vital particles and they cannot detect any aspect beyond a certain range. That would mean that because we human beings have forgotten that there is a world of particles behind our sensory impressions, we have limited our definition of reality to what we can detect with our senses."

Jesus: "Yes, and that means we become self-fulfilling prophecies who are using circular logic. We are looking for what is real, but we do not see that our definition of reality is based on what our senses can detect. As a result, we cannot free ourselves, or our perception, from the senses and that is why we cannot experience anything beyond the range of the senses. We have become trapped in the physical aspect of the world and cannot directly perceive anything beyond it. If we have glimpses of something beyond, we use our definition of reality to label it as unreal, as illusions, as hallucinations so we dismiss it instead of exploring it further."

Me: "Yes, but isn't that because we are afraid to look beyond the senses? I mean, we have grown up to find a certain security and stability in the world we perceive with the senses and that we think is real. I often find that the exercises we are doing are making me feel like I am losing my grip on 'reality' and I don't know if anything is real. It is like I am floating in some unknown space and I am afraid to let go because I simply don't know if there is anything real once I let go of the mental world I have so far thought was real. What can I trust, if not my senses? What is real, if not the world I grew up to see as real, the world that all other people also think is real?"

Jesus picked up a rock and said: "I feel the same, but let us try to step back again and look at it a different way. Our host is not saying that there isn't anything that is real. He is saying that the way we see it or label it is not the entire picture. It seems to me that we need to separate our sensory impressions from the words or labels that we have created based on those impressions."

He held up the rock and said: "What am I holding in my hand?"

I said: "A rock."

Jesus: "And you see: That is the problem. How do you know what I am holding in my hand?"

Me: "I can see it, of course."

Jesus: "Yes, but are you seeing a rock or are your eyes seeing something that has no label? I can feel this 'thing' with my hand, but what I am feeling is not a rock. I am feeling a sensation, and I can label it as something round and hard, but even 'round' and 'hard' are labels that I am putting on my sensory impressions. But let us just go with what we actually experience. I am feeling something round and hard, you are seeing something round and grey. If I throw you the rock [which he did], you are also feeling its hardness. But none of those feelings have anything in themselves to do with a rock. The concept of a rock is something we have put on our sensory impressions in our minds. We have created a mental experience out of sensory impressions.

So when you are saying you feel trapped in the body and the senses, it is not really the case. It is not so much the body and the senses that trap you but a part of your mind. It has created a mental concept of the senses, the body and the world outside the body."

Me: "Oh, that's a brilliant idea. So it's not the body and the senses I need to free myself from, but the aspect of the mind that upholds the concept of a body, senses and an external world?"

Jesus: "Exactly. I think that is what our host has been trying to tell us. Take what you just said, namely 'what is real if we let go of the senses?' It really isn't a matter of letting go of the senses. I mean, we are in physical bodies right now, and we are in a world of some sort. We are experiencing that material world through the senses, and there is really no reason to distrust what the senses are detecting. The eye simply sees what it sees.

Yet we are not experiencing the world only through the sensory impressions. We are really experiencing the world through the mental concepts that we have created in a certain part of our minds. And I think it is those mental concepts, this perception filter, we need to start questioning."

Me: "I can follow you completely. So let's set aside the question of what is real about sensory impressions. It really doesn't matter. What matters is how we label it. It seems less scary to me to question my mental labels than to question my sensory impressions. But I am wondering what we actually experience through the senses. I can see you are right that even saying a rock is round and hard is putting words on what the senses detect, so how do we get beyond that?"

Jesus: "If we take what our host has said about the four levels of the material world, I think we can get somewhere. It is really annoying to me that I know there is a deeper teaching about this, and I feel I have heard it before, but I cannot remember it."

(At the time, we did not have conscious recollection of everything we had learned in past lives, including the Venusian Mystery School.) Jesus continued: "Anyway, he says that what exists at the physical level is a projection of three images that exist at the emotional, mental and identity levels. Yet our physical senses are calibrated to detect only the physical level. So when I hold this rock, my physical senses detect something only at the physical level. I cannot see or feel the emotional, mental and identity components of the rock. Yet if they are there, it should be possible for our minds to experience them beyond the physical senses."

Me: "I agree. This makes perfect sense, but it is just so difficult to free the mind from the physical senses. Why is that?"

Jesus sat in silent thought for a long time (A habit he had, and which I had learned to respect by not saying anything). Then, he said: "Think back to when we were infants and had not learned to speak. At that time, we must have been experiencing the world without words, unless we had carried some awareness of words with us from past lives. But I think we must have experienced the world without putting words on it. So at that time, we experienced something that was beyond words, a pure sensory impression.

Then, we started being taught how to speak by our parents, and we quickly learned to attach words to our sensory impressions. As our host says, the words have a purely practical aspect in making it easier for us to communicate with other people. But more than that, we learned to attach certain labels to everything. I remember being very young and I tripped over a rock and scraped my leg so it was bleeding. That experience gave me an emotional label for a rock as something that was hard and sharp and could hurt me. I later came to understand that rocks are very hard to change. They have been here for a long time and it takes a lot of work to shape them. This caused me to create a mental label. Based on many other things I learned about the world, I eventually created a label at the identity level concerning what kind of world I live in and what my abilities are for shaping that world.

So what I am sensing here is that on top of the pure sensory impressions, we have built an emotional, mental and identity structure. You said it gives us a sense of stability and security, and I agree, but it also has a price. The price is that we are trapped in this structure because it defines who we think we are and how we can or cannot shape the world we live in. It becomes a prison for us because once we have defined a label, we don't think we can change the thing. We don't think we can change rocks or mountains or many circumstances in our own lives. So instead of seeing the world made of fluid particles that can always take on another form, we see it made of unchangeable things. We even think *we* are unchangeable beings.

So what if we could dismantle this entire structure? Perhaps we could then again experience our pure sensory impressions and perhaps we could also then see beyond the senses because we are not so attached to our labels? What do you think?"

Me: "I think you are absolutely right. My brother, you always have the ability to say things in such a way that I understand them. I know our host has been trying to help us see the same thing, but his words did not trigger the experience in me that your words have just done."

We then went back to our host and told him about our insights. He was very pleased and agreed that he had been trying to tell us the same thing in words that made sense to him. He knew it did not trigger the experience in us, but he was not sure how to find words that could trigger the experience. As he said, the existential problem for any mystical teacher is that he is trying to give the student an experience that is beyond words, but words are the primary means for triggering this experience.

Our host was very pleased that we had found it ourselves, and he used the occasion to teach us why there needs to be many different spiritual or religious teachings. The purpose of all true spirituality is to trigger a direct inner experience in the student. Yet the same words will not have the same effect upon all people, and that is why there needs to be more than one teaching so people can eventually find the one that unlocks the inner experience for them. That is why it is so devastating that the fallen beings have perverted our quest for understanding by claiming that there can be only one truth and therefore only one true religion.

# 34

Our host now took us through an extensive program of having us meditate on certain objects, such as a rose. He first wanted us to go beyond the physical sensory impressions of the rose and experience the emotional component behind it. He explained that any object in the physical world is created by an identity component, a mental component and an emotional component. They are like three panes of glass upon which are painted colored pictures. The light shining through them from the spiritual realm is what forms the projection that our senses experience and that our minds label as a solid, physical object.

Once we were at that level of understanding, it actually wasn't so difficult for us to experience the emotional aspect of a rose. What we realized was that the emotional aspect is really something created in consciousness, not something physical. It has no physical substance but exists in consciousness. We both learned to go into meditation, to mentally free our minds from the sensory impressions of the rose but to keep the mental image of the rose. After this, we could shift our perception and experience the emotional consciousness behind the physical flower. We could then learn to switch to a higher level and experience the mental consciousness and eventually the identity level consciousness behind the rose.

Our host then explained that because everything is created out of consciousness, nothing can be created without conscious beings. He explained (as the venutians had done) that the material world is created by the ascended masters at the Elohimic level. Yet the four levels of the material world is co-created by four types of conscious, but not self-aware, beings that he called elemental beings.

So there was an elemental being at the identity level which took on the matrix of a rose that was projected from the level of the Elohim. This elemental being literally became that thought matrix and took on the form of the matrix. Then, another elemental at the mental level took on the mental component and projected it into the emotional level. Here, a third elemental took on the matrix and projected it into the physical, where a fourth elemental took on the matrix and literally became the rose that we perceive with our senses.

What we were doing by experiencing the three higher levels of the rose was making conscious contact with the elemental beings at those levels.

We were experiencing consciously what those elemental beings were experiencing as they were creating and upholding the rose.

\*\*\*

Our host then taught us that there is a symbiotic relationship between human beings and elemental beings, which, of course, is something most humans are not aware of. The earth in its natural state was created by the Elohim and the elemental beings outpictured the forms projected from the Elohimic level. Yet once humans started embodying here, the elementals started taking on the forms that we have projected upon them. The elemental beings are, so to speak, our feed-back mechanism. By them outpicturing the images in the four levels of our minds, we get feedback on how we are using our co-creative abilities.

Of course, once humankind descended into duality, we started creating images that were based on fear. Once they were projected upon the elemental beings, the elementals had to take on the corresponding forms. The elementals do not have self-awareness and free will so they cannot refuse to take on a form that is based on fear. However, they can experience that this form is not natural and they feel a strain from having to take it on. It is this that can eventually develop their awareness so they can receive self-awareness and even incarnate as humans. There are people in embodiment who are evolved elementals, and they often have a very strong connection to the earth and an intuitive sense of how nature works.

Okay, I was going out on a sidetrack, but my point is that the symbiotic relationship between humans and elementals is what has created some very unbalanced states on earth and it has also made them seem permanent or unchangeable. As I have described, matter on a natural planet seems translucent so it is easy to see that it can be changed. It was the lowering of the collective consciousness of humans that caused the elementals to solidify matter so we cannot see that it is made from light. It is this that accounts for the condition where we think we live in a world that is beyond our powers to change. The irony being, of course, that we have collectively created this world, but we have now become so trapped by it that we think we cannot uncreate what we ourselves have created.

Our host taught us that this is why our physical bodies appear so dense. The density of matter is what causes so many diseases of the planetary body, namely what we call natural disasters. It is also what causes so many diseases of the human body. Or rather, it is the density of matter that makes it possible for the body to get sick by making us think the body has some continued existence. Therefore, we cannot change it quickly enough to avoid the build-up of energy in the three higher bodies that is the real cause of disease.

A disease begins at the identity level by you accepting some fear-based matrix about what kind of being you are. This could be the idea that you are only a human being and that you will die when your physical body dies. This filters to the mental level as the belief that you do not have the powers of your mind to change your physical body. It filters to the emotional level so that you live in constant fear that your body will get old and that you will have the diseases you see in other people, especially your family. Take note that even though science claims to have freed us from the superstition of religion, it has done nothing to remove this fear. It has actually reinforced it by making you think you are the product of your environment and your genes, two factors over which science claims you have no control.

When your thought matrix is formed in the identity body, the elemental being at that level takes on this form. And once it has taken on this form, it sees it as its job to uphold the form. The same holds true for the elementals at the mental, emotional and physical levels. So you now have a symbiotic relationship where you think you have to remain loyal to your belief system and the four elementals that make up your body think they have to remain loyal to the form of your body.

Yet once we step into fear, anything we create becomes subject to the contracting force of the mother. This force will slowly begin to break down the impure creation we have made, and this is not done to hurt us but to free us from a very limited state. This is actually the mechanism that modern science has discovered and called the second law of thermodynamics. It says that in any closed system, entropy (meaning disorder) will increase until the system reaches its lowest possible energy state and everything breaks down. What breaks down is every form that keeps your spirit trapped in a limited sense of self.

Take this idea of the closed system and ask yourself whether there really is any closed system? Science tells us that the physical universe is so huge that it is almost unlimited. It tells us that there are black holes that may be portals to other universes. Do you see that, in reality, there is no closed system because the universe is one interconnected energy system? For those who have eyes to see, modern science has already pointed to the existence of a realm of energy beyond what we call material energy, which is what mystics have been saying for a very long time.

Okay, I got side-tracked again. The point of all this is that there is no truly closed system. Yet because of free will, we are allowed to create what seems like a closed system. We are allowed to live in such a system for a long time, but not indefinitely. The hope is that we will eventually tire of the fear-based experiences offered by a closed system and decide to return to the natural state. Yet because a closed system can become a trap for our minds, there is a built-in mechanism that will eventually cause the structures we create to break down so as to show us the limitations of our fear-based approach to life.

Once we turn our four lower bodies into a closed system, both our own minds and the four elemental beings will cling to the matrices that define the four bodies. Therefore, we will seek to uphold those matrixes indefinitely, as you see people dreaming of achieving immortality of the physical body or upholding a state of wealth or power over time. The only way (within the Law of Free Will) to free us from this is to allow our closed system to break down.

Your physical body is created out of the matrices held in the three other bodies. A disease is caused by the imbalances you have at those levels. Yet once a disease manifests at the physical level, you will tend to focus blindly on the physical body and seeking physical means to remove the symptoms or destroy the disease, to kill the cancer. By doing this, you are actually reinforcing your own mind's tendency to uphold the matrices in the three higher bodies. And you are also telling the four elementals to maintain those images. How can this remove the cause of the disease? The disease is life's message to you that there is an imbalance in your four lower bodies. Yet you ignore the message and seek to solidify the imbalance, which can never remove the imbalance.

\*\*\*

As our host taught us this, Jesus became very excited and very eager to learn. He realized that in past lives he had already purified his own four bodies so very little fear-based energy was left. Yet he wanted to learn how to help other people be healed, as our host was able to do. Our host then gave us the following teaching.

He told us that after humankind descended into duality, we started creating all of these collective spirits that have become very powerful. This development was reinforced when the fallen beings started incarnating here. So today we have what he called the Prince of this World, which is a conglomerate made up of these many collectively created spirits. These spirits are so powerful that they can overpower the minds of individual people (if we allow them to enter our minds through our own choices) and they can also overpower the elemental beings.

He taught us that although these many spirits were created by human beings, they have now become so powerful that no human being can withstand or resist their magnetic pull by its own power. For each disease of the physical body, there is a corresponding spirit. Once such a spirit has gained influence over our minds and over the four elementals, we can overcome the disease only by freeing ourselves from the spirit. The real way to do this is to help people see why they invited the spirit in and then change the decisions in the three higher bodies. Yet many people are not able to make this leap and that is why our host attempted to give them relief from the physical disease and then seek to help them deal with the psychological component afterwards.

Jesus saw the logic of this and because of his great compassion, he wanted to learn how to heal people of the physical disease in order to set them free to pursue the spiritual path. Our host taught us that there was no way Jesus could do this of his own power. He needed the power of the ascended masters, the power of Spirit, what he called the Holy Spirit. Yet in order for him to open himself up to the flow of the Spirit, Jesus had to fundamentally change his sense of identity. Our host taught us that we could, of our own selves, do nothing but that only the power of Spirit within us could do the work.

Our host then said that we needed to overcome all human sense of identity, all sense that we were limited beings. He said that only the power of Spirit could overcome the gravitational pull of the Prince of this World, the collective spirits. Only the power of Spirit could free the mind of a human being and the four elementals making up his body from the lower spirit that manifested a certain disease. Only the Christ consciousness could override the forces trapping the elemental beings and set them free to outpicture the natural state of health.

How could we open ourselves to this power? Only by acknowledging and fully accepting who we really are, namely co-creators with Spirit. Back then, we were brought up in a tradition that did not talk about ascended masters or Spirit, but that used the word 'God.' Therefore, our host said that in order for us to become open to the power of God, we had to fully accept ourselves as Sons of God. We had to let our human identity die in order to flow with the Spirit.

We both became fascinated by this, and we knew this was the ultimate goal. Our host also told us that this was the most difficult challenge for any human being, namely to see ourselves as the Sons of God without thinking we had thereby become gods, as the fallen beings believed. He told us that this was something I might not be able to attain in that lifetime. Jesus could attain it, but it would be a long process for him to reach that level of fully identifying himself as a Son of God.

***

Our host took us through a program of learning to heal, and it had several layers. First, we needed to respect free will. Our host said that many people subconsciously do not want to be healed because the disease gives them an excuse for not taking command over their lives. We need to respect this by asking if the person wants to be healed. This can be combined with testing whether the person accepts that healing is possible. For example, we could ask: "Do you accept that I have the power to heal you?" If the answer was "No," then the person's mind was not open to healing. If the answer was "Yes," then the person could potentially be healed.

The next component was that we needed to be absolutely firm in our minds that no physical form could ever be permanent. The body and any disease is not something that exists over time. The body in its current condition is an image that is projected through the matrices of the three higher bodies. This image is being projected many times every second, it is simply that our senses and our outer minds cannot deal with the rapidity so our minds put it together as a continuous image (like a modern movie that is also still images projected in rapid succession). We needed to learn to see beyond this and see the body and the disease as an image that can be instantly changed at the physical level by changing the images at the three higher levels.

We then needed to recognize that the image at the three higher levels was instantly changeable, but only by shattering the hold that the collective spirit has over the person's mind and over the four body elementals. Only by shattering the fear-based images, would there be room for a love-based image of a wholesome body to filter through the four levels and become physically manifest.

In order to shatter this hold over a person's mind, we had to go against the entire collective momentum, and only the power of Spirit could do this. Yet when we fully accept ourselves as Sons or Daughters of God, this power can work through us. It can even begin to work through us in some measure before we have the full acceptance.

After having gone through some mental exercise for months, our host brought us to one of his healing services. We had already seen him heal people, but now we were allowed to try ourselves. In the beginning, we failed completely, but then our host would step in and heal the person. Instead of discouraging us, this spurred us on because the motto of the ascended masters has always been: "What one has done, all can do."

*** 

After some months of failing, we took another walk in the hills. We came to a very steep hillside and had to pass it on a very narrow goat trail. I slipped and fell down the steep hillside, and at the bottom I hit my leg against a sharp rock so the blood was pouring out. Jesus hurriedly climbed down to me and attempted to lift me up to a more comfortable position. Without any forethought, I put my hand on his shoulder to stop him. He looked at me confused and our eyes met. I held his eyes fast and spontaneously said: "I acknowledge you as the Son of God. Now heal me!"

Jesus looked like I had hit him in the face, but then quickly gathered himself. Suddenly, a completely different light shone in his eyes, an expression I would see many times over the coming years. He looked so completely focused and present that it was truly beyond the human level of awareness. He then put his hands on my leg and with a voice far stronger than his normal voice exclaimed: "I am indeed the Son of God, and I command you: Be thou made whole, NOW!"

I literally felt an energy surge come from his hands and enter my leg where it created intense heat. I was instantly at peace and felt this living silence pulsating within me. Jesus held his hands there for what seemed like a long time while he appeared to be in a trance. I finally pulled his hand away and I was absolutely sure there would be no wound. My leg looked completely whole, and I sat there for several seconds letting my eyes shift from my unbroken skin to the pool of blood on the soil beneath my leg. Here was direct, visible proof that my leg had bled and that the five centimeters long gash had vanished as if it was never there.

I then looked into Jesus' eyes, and we shared one of those moments that transcend time and space, a moment of total openness between two people and an awareness that we are not *two* people, for we are *one* in Spirit. Jesus then said: "My brother, I thank you once again for being there for me." I said nothing, but simply drank him in, as the truly magnificent being he was and is and ever will be.

*** 

After this, Jesus was in such a state of mind that he could heal most of the people who came to the services. He was very enthusiastic about this and because of his enormous compassion, he wanted to go out and heal everybody. He was sure that once people had been healed and had felt the power of God working in their bodies, they would be open to the spiritual path towards a higher state of consciousness.

It took some doing to persuade him that this was not the ultimate course of action for him. Our host told us that because we were only 16 at the time, certain faculties of our bodies (what we today call the brain and nervous system) would not be fully developed until we were over 21 years of age. Even though Jesus had opened the channels for the flow of the Spirit, he could actually burn out these delicate channels and do long-term harm to his body (as many people in the modern world do with drugs).

Our host also showed us some of the people he had healed in the past. Most of them had gone back to the same lifestyle they had before, and a substantial percentage of them had developed the same disease once again. Our host explained that whereas all people would like to be free from the symptoms of a disease, only a few are willing to change their consciousness in order to remove the cause of the disease. This was a realization that had a great impact on me, but it took some doing to make Jesus see that his ultimate mission was not to go around and heal people right and left.

One day, we again took a walk in the hills and we discussed the entire topic of healing and Jesus' mission. His compassion would sometimes make him blind to a broader perspective, and while I understood him, I had also come to see it as my role to keep my eyes focused on the broader mission, even though I could not yet see it clearly. I finally managed to make him see that although healing would be part of his mission, it was only a tool to get people's attention and to help some people get started on the spiritual path.

In the end, the argument that persuaded him was that I said: "But we are only 16 and surely we have more to learn. I feel it is time to move on and seek out our next teacher. Surely, you are not here to heal only the bodies of people, but their souls as well. And what do we truly know about the soul?"

Jesus sank into himself for a long time, and I patiently waited. I knew he needed space for his inner process, and after probably half an hour, he looked me straight in the eye and said: "My brother, who of us can see ourselves from the outside so who of us can do without those who will see us from the outside? I see that you are right. It is indeed time to move on and I have just seen what we need to learn from our next teacher. It is indeed lessons that are vital for my mission. So let's get going."

I could only admire the incredible one-pointedness that Jesus displayed once his mind was made up. He was truly a man on a mission. Yes, I did say he was a "man" not "god." Jesus never thought he was god, so why would I?

# 35

Our next host lived near the Himalayas in what is now the Kashmir Valley where he had an ashram near Dal Lake. When we first walked into the valley, it was right at sunup and the sky had a very intense pink glow. Jesus stopped, put his hand on my arm and said: "This place reminds me of something I knew long ago. This is one place where I could live for a long time." Well, you know what they say: "Be careful what you wish for." This is especially true as you come closer to the 144th level of consciousness.

Our third host was not concerned about healing the physical body but healing the three higher bodies, what many people would call the soul. Since Jesus and I had done a lot of this work in previous embodiments, our host merely took us through a refresher course that tied us back to what had happened at the Venusian Mystery School, and then he went beyond it. After we had healed the remaining traumas in our identity, mental and emotional bodies, our host started teaching us how to disconnect ourselves from all of the four lower bodies.

There has always among mystics been discussions about soul travel or astral travel. Even today, many spiritually interested people get taken in by gurus who advertise that they can teach people how to do this in a few easy steps. And one could say there is something to it, in the sense that for many people it is not that difficult to leave the physical body on a temporary basis. The problem is: Where are you going to go?

People who just want some temporary entertainment or an alternative experience often don't care where they go as long as they experience something different. These are the type of people who are sometimes taken in by the claim that some kind of drug can be a gateway to a spiritual experience. Here, we need to make a distinction. The human brain and nervous system are, as modern civilization is only now beginning to realize, extremely complex. We can basically compare the physical brain to a supercomputer, and as any computer, it is capable of building a virtual reality environment inside your head. In fact, 99 percent of all people live inside the virtual reality environment built by their brains and never see the light of reality.

What I am saying is that the brain can indeed produce all kinds of experiences, and since the brain is a physical device, it can indeed be affected by certain chemicals. This means the brain itself is quite capable of producing experiences that to the untrained person might seem like genuine spiritual experiences. So let me ask you to participate in a thought experiment.

Say you bought the biggest and best television set money can buy along with the best sound system. Or you buy the best virtual reality system. You sit down in a comfortable chair and you watch a movie about the Galapagos Islands. The movie may be so real that you forget where you are and you think you are actually on the Galapagos Islands. My question is: No matter how real this experience might seem to you, is your body going to get one centimeter closer to the Galapagos Islands?

You may take all kinds of drugs or perform all kinds of instant gratification "spiritual" exercises and this may give you experiences that seem very real. Yet no matter how real the experiences might seem, is it going to get you anywhere closer to real spiritual growth? No, it isn't, and here is why. Any experience that is produced by the physical brain can only tie you to the physical brain. Genuine spiritual growth is where you stop identifying with your physical body and with any of your four lower bodies. In other words, you shift your sense of identity away from seeing yourself as a *human* being towards seeing yourself as a *spiritual* being. The physical brain can never facilitate that shift because, as a computer, the brain can never go beyond its programming.

What I am saying is that many spiritually inclined people can fairly easily learn to have a part of them go outside the physical body. Yet if you have deep wounds in your emotional body, you will not be able to go beyond the emotional level of the collective consciousness. Now, roaming this emotional or astral realm can indeed give you many unusual experiences and they may be entertaining for a while. Yet as any drug user can tell you, there will come some bad trips because the astral realm is highly polluted by the toxic energies produced by humankind. The astral realm has many levels and some of them resemble the visions of hell that many people, such as Dante, have had throughout the ages. So the question is whether you want to experience this and whether you want to open yourself to the kind of demons that rule the astral realm?

How do you avoid being trapped in the astral realm? By healing the wounds in your emotional body before you attempt to leave the body behind. The same mechanism, of course, applies to the mental and identity bodies. The mental and identity realms have levels that may seem fascinating to many people, but they are also dead ends where you can roam indefinitely and feel very entertained while achieving very little genuine growth.

In this respect it is important to mention the paradox devised by the Greek philosopher Zeno. The question is whether a fast runner could actually run from one city to another. The paradox states that he cannot because he first has to cover half the distance between the two cities. Then he has to cover half of the remaining distance, and since you can continue indefinitely to divide the remaining distance into half, the runner would never arrive. This is comparable to attempting to gain spiritual growth by using the physical body and brain, and even using any of the four lower bodies. You can continue to explore more and more refined areas of the four lower realms indefinitely. True spiritual growth requires transcendence of the four lower bodies, which is what we today might call quantum leaps.

My point is that if you do not heal your three higher bodies, then attempting to leave the physical body is possible but risky. The reason being that you will be traveling with one or more of your three higher bodies and this will tie you to one of those levels. Your wounds will then open you up to being manipulated by the demons and fallen beings who exist in those three levels.

What Jesus and I did was a very different approach because we first did the hard work of healing all four of our bodies before we attempted to go outside the physical body. This meant we could leave behind any or all of the three higher bodies. And since we had no wounds, nothing could trap or tie us to any place or being in the emotional, mental or identity realms.

So what was it that travelled? It was not what most people call the soul because this is the three higher bodies. It was the Conscious You, which when it awakens to its natural state of pure awareness, is not tied to anything in the four realms of the material universe. Only when you have overcome identification with the four lower bodies, the soul vehicle, can you do out-of-body travel safely. This, by the way, was one lesson proven (although not necessarily learned) by the CIA experiments done in recent decades.

\*\*\*

Jesus and I quickly learned to leave our bodies and go anywhere in the four realms of the material universe, although Jesus was always quicker to learn than me. We first learned to go to various places in the physical universe, much like remote viewing practitioners attempt to do today.

The sessions we did all followed the same pattern. We would first invoke spiritual light from the ascended masters, including protection from Archangel Michael. We would then go through some simple meditative exercises aimed at calming all emotional and mental activity. We would then lie down on a comfortable bed and use one of several techniques for leaving the body. After some time (in the beginning only a few minutes and eventually up to half an hour) we would return to our waking consciousness.

Once day after a session, Jesus said: "By the way, your parents are doing well. They just had a baby girl. They will name her Sarah." I then learned to go to my parents and see for myself. However, unless you enjoy watching your parents have sex, you might want to exercise some discretion.

After another session, Jesus said: "My Mother sends her greetings to you and asks if there is anything you want to say to your parents?" He had learned to make contact with Mother Mary and since she was so sensitive, they could actually communicate with each other while she was sleeping. I eventually learned to do this myself and was able to give messages to my parents through Mother Mary to assure them I was doing well.

After exploring the physical octave, we started traveling into the emotional realm. As I said, this is highly risky unless you have no wounds in your emotional body. We travelled literally everywhere and saw everything there is to see. This was part of our initiations: You have to be able to look at anything in the four realms of matter without reacting to it. I can assure you that there are places in the astral realm that are worse than anything you could possibly imagine. Yet when you have seen a physical battlefield with 50,000 dead and mangled bodies spread around, how the hell can Hell scare you?

The greater challenge was the mental realm because it has some genuine beauty. There is not much that is attractive in the astral realm because it is generally more ugly than the physical octave. But the mental realm has beautiful places that can seem attractive compared to the physical. There are also some very clever fallen beings there who have set themselves up to appear as very sophisticated teachers. Many well-meaning spiritual or intellectual people have become seduced by this.

Jesus and I were not tempted to follow any of these teachers, but we did have to deal with the temptation to argue with them and prove them wrong. Jesus got quite engaged with one particular fallen teacher, and it took him some time to realize that this could go on indefinitely and that it was not what his mission on earth was all about. He was here to do something in the physical realm.

A more subtle challenge was the identity realm, which is even more beautiful. It is easy to think that this is actually the spiritual realm because there are fallen beings there who are very good at imitating ascended masters. We both had to independently pass the initiation of seeing through these fallen teachers and realizing they were not ascended masters. It helped us tremendously that we had been around Lucifer and Satan.

As I described, in my first embodiment, it was easy to see that Lucifer and Satan were fallen beings because of their insensitivity to life and their obviously selfish actions. Yet over time, they became much better at disguising themselves and we learned how to look for the subtle signs of their self-centeredness. This helped us a lot in our explorations of the identity realm, and we eventually came to the point where we could expose a false teacher merely by his vibration. This was when we started making contact with the genuine ascended masters.

In this respect, it was invaluable that we had purified our four lower bodies of all wounds. For example, the identity body is where your highest desires are located. These desires may seem genuine and unselfish, for example, many spiritual people today have a desire to help raise the planet and bring in a better age of peace and prosperity. It seems like a genuine desire, but it is often colored by a certain self-centeredness. For example, you see so many spiritual groups who all have the same basic idea of helping to raise the earth. Yet they have a sectarian approach to this, thinking that it will happen by all (or at least many) people coming to accept *their* guru or teaching. Many also have a desire to be seen as the ones that saved the earth. These are examples of how a genuine desire has been colored by self-centeredness, and it causes people to tie themselves to the false teachers in the mental or identity realms.

Our third host was very skilled in helping us purify our desires. This was especially a challenge for Jesus because he was the one who had an important public mission. He was not yet aware of what that mission entailed, but he was very conscious of having such a mission. Our host was very skilled at seeing through the coloring that Jesus had put upon his view of his mission and helping him purify his motives. This included some rather radical initiations.

***

During the phase where we were exploring the identity realm, our host would ask us to describe what we had experienced during our travels. On one of the first occasions, Jesus came back all excited about having made contact with a teacher and describing how sophisticated he seemed. Our host listened to the description and allowed Jesus to talk himself out. When Jesus finally stopped talking, our host looked at him with a stern look and said: "Now tell me why he is a false teacher." Jesus looked like you had thrown a bucket of cold water over him. Jesus could not see why this was a false teacher so we did several more session where both of us went to the same teacher in the identity realm. After the first two visits I also could not see anything false about this teacher who seemed very sophisticated and had a beautiful ashram set up in the identity realm with thousands of students.

After the third visit, our host again asked us, and I said: "I cannot see anything specific that is false about this teacher, but I am beginning to wonder why he has set himself up as being alone as the leader of his ashram? He seems to refer to himself as the uppermost authority, and it seems to me that a genuine ascended master would recognize a hierarchy of beings above itself. He would also have others at his own level that he cooperated with."

Our host said: "You are on the right track, but there is a subtlety. The fallen beings in embodiment usually have a guru in one of the higher realms. You can find a false hierarchy of fallen beings ranging from the physical through the emotional and mental realms to the identity realm. So you can find some fallen beings who refer to a higher authority. Yet in the identity realm you do not find this, as you have correctly sensed. The reason is that the fallen beings can exist only in the lower levels of the identity realm. There are 33 levels of the identity realm and fallen beings can exist in the first 11 levels. Beyond that, no fallen being exists because the vibration is too high for them. The being you have made contact with exists at the 11th level, meaning the highest level where fallen beings can exist. Since he cannot make contact with the ascended masters, he can recognize no authority above himself—except, of course, the false god created by the fallen beings.

This god also exists at the 11th level, but since it is not a self-aware being, the false teachers in the identity realm can refer to it in order to make it appear that they do recognize an authority above themselves. Since this teacher obviously does refer to this god, I am interested to know how you came to see that he truly recognizes no authority above himself?"

I thought about this and answered: "He always portrays god as a being who is remote, as being somewhere else. So he does not see himself as being one with this remote god, and that means there is a gap. It is in that gap that he can set himself up as the mediator between the remote god and his students."

Our host said: "A very good observation." He then turned to Jesus and said: "Do you see that this is a correct observation?"

Jesus looked very serious and said: "I completely see it and that makes me wonder why I did not see it before? I am not trying to sound superior, but usually I am the first to get the lesson. In this case I did not, and that leads me to conclude there was something in my psyche that blocked my vision. So what was it, because this kind of blindness can derail my entire mission?"

Our host looked very pleased and said: "Jesus, you have just passed an extremely important initiation of humility. Many students would have attempted to find excuses or explain away why your companion got the lesson and you did not. Because you have been humble in wanting to see your own shortcomings, we can now take the next step in your training. By the way, the short answer to your question is that you were blinded by your own sense of having an important mission, but you will see this more clearly later." As a side note, this being was the Dark Master.

\*\*\*

Our host now took us through an extensive program where he revived some of the teachings about the Christ consciousness that we had been taught in the Venusian Mystery School. I will repeat that the word "Christ" originally was a neutral word that referred to the level of consciousness where you begin to see beyond duality and thus can see the underlying oneness of all life. It is only after the fallen beings created official Christianity as an exsclusivist religion that the word took on a sectarian ring (I will later explain exactly how this happened).

Our host explained to us that the goal of following the mystical path is to attain or put on the Christ consciousness. This is a long process that has many stages and can only be completed shortly before you attain the 144th level of consciousness. This means that at different stages of the path, one will have different views of what the Christ consciousness is and what it means to attain it. He explained that what the fallen beings have done many times is to take a teaching that contains some truth about the path of Christhood and then turn it into a closed box by claiming that it is complete and therefore nothing else is needed, nothing is beyond it.

When you understand that Christhood is a process that leads through successive stages of perception, you see that no teaching can ever be ultimate. At a certain stage, you need a certain teaching to navigate that phase of the path. Yet once you go beyond that phase, you need a higher teaching in order to rise to the next level. If you think your current teaching is the ultimate teaching, then you will not be open to looking beyond it and thus you will get stuck at that stage of the path. This is, of course, exactly what the fallen beings want. They know that despite their efforts to eradicate or pervert all teachings about the Christ consciousness, they cannot destroy all of them. They cannot prevent that some people find a teaching that takes them up higher. So as the last-ditch effort, they try to get people stuck at whatever level they are at so they never reach the fullness of Christhood. People think they have to be loyal to the outer teaching rather than the inner process of transcendence. So we can never stop looking beyond our current level or teaching. Christhood is the never-ending quest.

Our host taught us that Jesus had reached the highest level of the path (not the same as the 144th level of consciousness) and I was on the level below it. I was not quite ready to take the final leap, but I could still benefit from watching Jesus go through the process, and I could help him do so. This I was, naturally, happy to do.

Our host said that Jesus had reached the stage where he had (in this and previous lifetimes) resolved the wounds and false beliefs in his four lower bodies and he had transformed the misqualified energies there. What remained was to shift his identity so he could fully accept himself as the Living Christ, the Christ incarnate (meaning you can accept yourself as the Christ even though you are still in a physical body). This required a series of very subtle and difficult shifts in his sense of identity.

Our host taught us that this is a very delicate process because you have to solve what will at first seem like an enigma, a riddle that cannot be solved. On the one hand, you have to give up your human sense of identity, but you still have to be able to function in a physical body and relate to other human beings. This is a highly schizophrenic process, and our host said he had seen several students go insane while struggling with the last initiations. It is therefore important that you have someone who can, so to speak, hold the balance for you and keep you tied to the material world and the human level.

*** 

We were taught that for us to complete this process, we first had to see that in order to function in our four lower bodies, we had created a series of spirits or selves that were tied to the four lower bodies. Although these selves originally had some kind of function (either to help us deal with difficult situations or express ourselves in the material world), they all become a hindrance on the higher stages of the path. Therefore, we had to go through a series of experiences where we came to see one of these selves and then consciously let it die. We had to die psychologically or spiritually in order to rise one step closer to Christhood. We had to die to the world in order to follow the Christ within ourselves. If we are not willing to let even one of these selves die, we cannot follow the Christ within ourselves.

We were now taken through a period where our host mercilessly exposed some of these remaining human selves. When I say 'mercilessly' I do not mean that our host enjoyed hurting us. I mean that he was completely objective about it. He had no sympathy for our human selves and exposed them in such a way that we could not explain away, make excuses for or hide these selves. This was a rather difficult and painful process because some of these selves are so ingrained in our sense of identity that we literally think we cannot live without them. When a self is being exposed, you think that if this self dies, then you will not know who you are anymore—and that is actually the point. Only when you come to see beyond your human identity, can you begin to glimpse the spiritual individuality that is anchored in your I AM Presence and is very different from what you have built in order to deal with the insane situations you encounter on a planet like earth. So the self has to die. The difficulty is that you will feel as if *you* are going to die, and you have to be willing to go through this phycological death over and over again. He who seeks to save his "life" shall lose it, but he who is willing to lose his life for Christ's sake shall find eternal life.

***

We had many sessions with our host where we did things similar to certain advanced forms of therapy known today. We also had sessions where we were taken to a deep basement under the ashram. Here was a room with such thick stone walls that they shut out all sound and light from the surrounding world. The room contained a stone box, similar to a sarcophagus. When we had seen a certain aspect of our human selves, we would be placed in the box and the heavy lid would be put on. We could not move this lid ourselves so you had the feeling of being trapped.

It was total sensory deprivation, and the trick was to come to a point where you could see the human self and then literally make the choice to let it die, to relinquish all tendency to cling to it. You had to completely surrender this self and know that it would die, and you had to trust that *you* would not die with it, that you would not be "nothing" (have no identity) when the self died.

Obviously, this wasn't something we were thrown into in the beginning, but we worked up to it over a long time. The first person to go through it was Jesus, and he was left in sensory deprivation for about two hours. When the lid was removed, he was lying with open eyes, staring into nothing, and at first I was scared he was dead or in a trance. When he became conscious, he seemed more shaken than I had ever seen him at that time (I would see him more shaken later), and it took quite some time before he was able to talk. He said it had been a very special experience, and he did not want to tell me about it because he wanted me to go through it without being influenced by his experience. At first, I thought he was teasing me (a habit he sometimes did not know when to turn off), but I realized he was serious and our host concurred.

So I was put in the box and the lid put in place. I was now in total darkness and total silence. Strangely enough, I wasn't scared, but I did feel a considerable excitement. I first made some sounds to break the silence, but I soon realized it was ridiculous so I focused on the task at hand. I knew what self I had to let die, and as I focused my attention on it, I quickly came to see it as a human-like figure that was begging me to let it live. It argued that since I had created it, I could not just let it die, just as we would not let our children die.

For some time, my mind was dealing with this argument, examining it from all sides. I then realized that precisely because I had created the self,

I also had the right to uncreate it. I had created it to help me deal with certain situations on earth, but since I had now reached a higher level of consciousness, I no longer needed the self. I had created it to help me, not to give it some separate existence that would come back and make demands on me or seek to control me.

I then saw myself as a figure of light standing next to the self, looking at it and feeling completely undivided in saying: "You have to go. I am letting you die." At that moment, the self literally fell to pieces and dissolved into something that looked like ashes. I then started hearing a very loud high-pitched sound, almost like what we today would call an electronic sound. It became louder and louder and it turned into a vibration that was shaking me out of my physical body.

In a flash, I felt like I was outside my physical body and in a tunnel. I was falling at great speed. Back then, I had naturally never experienced free fall, but due to modern technology I have now experienced it, and it was very similar to the experience of falling through this tunnel. The major difference was that when I was falling in the tunnel, I was falling in an upwards direction even though the feeling was the same as in a free fall. I was falling up.

I then started seeing a faint light ahead of me, and it quickly grew brighter. As it did, I could see that is had a very intense golden yellow tone, and before I knew it, I plunged through the end of the tunnel and was now literally one with the light. I *was* the light and the light *was* me and there was nothing but the light. This was extremely pleasant and far beyond what I had ever experienced on earth and even beyond what I had experienced on natural planets. I was totally in bliss for what seemed like a time beyond time, but then I became aware that there was a figure standing next to me and seeking to communicate with me. This was, of course, a non-verbal form of communication, but it took some time for me to receive the thought that was being sent to me.

What I experienced was an ascended master, and I had travelled in my Conscious You to one of the retreats kept by the masters in the higher levels of the identity realm. The figure was the Ascended Master Gautama Buddha, with whom I had developed a close connection during his last embodiment, a connection I had kept partially open during my later embodiments.

We took some moments to enjoy this more direct form of togetherness, and then he directed my attention to another ascended master. This was Maitreya, who had ascended after Gautama and with whom Jesus had a close connection. Maitreya explained that I had been given this experience because the council of masters overseeing the mission of Jesus had deemed it necessary. He then took me (I was simply a floating point of light) into another room with something resembling a giant television screen.

On the screen started playing what turned out to be various scenarios for how the rest of Jesus' mission might unfold. There was a high potential, a low potential and various scenarios in between. I was also shown how Jesus would face various initiations and how his reactions to these would determine which of the possible scenarios would play out. I was shown that although there was not only one way for him to complete his mission, there was a range of scenarios that would mean his mission would not be completed.

I was shown that I had the potential to hold the balance for him making the highest possible decisions by keeping a firm vision of his full potential and never letting any circumstance on earth make me accept anything less. I was also shown that I could do and say certain things to help him but that this was not set in stone and would be my initiations in the process. I was then told that because Christhood is not a predetermined process, I could not tell Jesus what I had seen. I could help him make the highest choices, but I could not tell him what the optimal choice was. I had to leave room for him to make the choice. Otherwise, he could not become the Living Christ and would fail his mission.

I was then surrounded by 12 ascended masters and I knew this was the council that oversaw the mission of Jesus. Among them were Sanat Kumara, and I was gratified to experience him again. These magnificent beings sent me a love that was beyond anything on earth. If I were to use a word, it could only be "unconditional" but even that is a degradation of the experience. It was simply beyond all description, but it is the love that the ascended masters have for each and every self-aware being (fallen or not fallen), and they are constantly radiating it to us. It is only the density of our consciousness that prevents us from experiencing it and accepting ourselves as worthy recipients of it.

Next, I experienced being back in the tunnel and this time I was falling downwards. I then became conscious of being back in my physical body, and after what seemed like a very long time, the lid was removed. I instantly opened my eyes, looked at Jesus with a stern face and said: "What took you so long, I've been awake for hours!" He laughed and helped me out of the box.

Naturally, we compared our experiences, and they were very similar. Only, whereas I had seen Jesus mission for that lifetime, he had seen mine. He had been told something very similar to what I had been told and had also been told not to tell me. After realizing this, we looked into each others eyes and Jesus said somberly: "So I guess we better be careful to listen to each other, don't we?"

I answered with mock seriousness: "How will you handle that, my know-it-all brother?"

He laughed and said: "Let me worry about that and you worry about your own initiations. I am sure they won't be easier for you than mine will be for me." And that was indeed perfectly correct.

\*\*\*

Although these were important experiences, they obviously were not the end of the process. We had to go through other sessions of surrendering aspects of the human self, and for Jesus this process continued until he was hanging on the cross. For me, it is still ongoing, as I am, in a spiritual sense, still hanging on the cross (representing our four lower bodies and the process of awakening from identification with them).

As we went through the process, we both refined our understanding of the Christ consciousness and what it means. Jesus, of course, was ahead of me so in many cases he would explain aspects to me that I could understand intellectually but that I could not yet grasp on an experiental basis. And this is, in a sense, the central dilemma for all spiritual teachers, and especially for the ascended masters. The problem wasn't quite as severe back then because people in general were not as absorbed in the intellect and analytical thinking. The problem has grown much bigger after the advent of the scientific age, and today it is a huge problem. So many people today approach the spiritual path based on analytical thinking and they think it is a matter of *understanding* something. They are constantly looking for a teacher who can give them this ultimate understanding that will – in one dramatic step – make them enlightened (or whatever they see as their goal).

In reality, understanding something is only a step on the path, and you do not truly shift your consciousness until you experience the reality of something. This can only be done – and I mean *only* – when you allow a particular human self to die, for it is precisely this human self that blocks the experience. There are many, many spiritual seekers today who have a great intellectual understanding of the path, but they have not actually risen higher on the scale of the 144 levels of consciousness. The reason is that they have not been willing to let the human selves die as their understanding has progressed.

Of course, the problem also existed back then, and Jesus and I would encounter it many times. We encountered it in the Brahmins of the Hindu religion, and when we returned to Palestine, we encountered it in the scribes and Pharisees. These were people who were so trapped in believing they could *think* their way into heaven that they would not recognize the Living Christ when he stood before them in the flesh. Today, people with this very same attitude are in control of every branch of Christianity and they likewise will not recognize the Living Christ if he – or she – appears before them (or in a book).

Jesus came to realize that Christhood is a state of consciousness, but it is not an absolute or final state. Back then, as today, many people thought that walking a spiritual path was a matter of reaching some ultimate state of consciousness, and then everything would be fine. Jesus began to realize that on an unnatural planet, the Christ consciousness is not final; it is an ongoing process. Jesus saw that the Christ consciousness will – on an unnatural planet – present a unique challenge.

Jesus explained to me how he had realized that one of the stages just before you attain the full Christ consciousness requires you to completely surrender the last aspect of human identity. He had a period where he was very focused on the concept that he could do nothing of his human power. Instead, he had to open himself to let the power of God, the Holy Spirit, flow through him so it was the Spirit that was the doer. He did many experiments with this and when he was able to set aside his human self, he became able to perform certain feats that seemed miraculous to a normal, human state of consciousness. I saw him do this so many times, but I never forget the first time he walked on water.

***

Before I describe this experience, I want to describe how Jesus came to realize that healing people or performing physical feats was not the most important part of his mission. The essential part of his mission was to learn to speak through the power of Spirit. During this phase, Jesus remembered how we had been taught, in the Venusian Mystery School, to serve as messengers for the ascended masters. He shared this with me, and I also remembered our training. Jesus realized that just as he of his own self could *do* nothing, he of his own self could *say* nothing, at least nothing that would liberate people from the Prince of this World. Instead, he saw that only when he was a messenger for the ascended masters and allowing a master to speak through him, would there be enough power to help people step outside of their normal state of awareness and see beyond the veil created by the collective consciousness.

Naturally, Jesus would practice this, and for a long time he would do so only in private. We took many walks in the hills where he would step back and allow an ascended master to speak through him. This was absolutely fascinating for me to experience, and it was amazing how profound were the teachings that were spoken through Jesus in those empty hills. I wish today that sound recorders had been invented, but then again, since Spirit is fully capable of speaking to us in today's world, there really is no loss. When Jesus was in the flow of the Spirit, his words would have the effect of lifting me out of my normal state of awareness. It was almost as if I was back in the Presence of the ascended masters I had seen in my out-of-body experience.

One day, we were walking by the lake and Jesus had just taken a dictation from Maitreya who was the primary ascended master training Jesus to take dictations. Maitreya explained that the most difficult aspect of the human self to overcome was the one tied to the body and the senses. It is very hard to stop labeling everything based on our human perception and our human concepts of what is possible and what is not.

Maitreya explained that in the description of how god created man, there was an error. In what Christians today call Genesis (2:19), it is explained that god gave Adam the power to name everything. This was an example of how the fallen beings had influenced the scriptures. It wasn't god who had given man the power to name everything, it was the fallen beings and this happened after we fell into duality. Duality causes us to see every thing as separate and set apart from other things. We now began to see everything based on differences that break up the one reality into separate things. This gave us the need to refer to these separate things with words because before we fell into duality, we could communicate by projecting thoughtforms into each others minds and words were unnecessary.

So it was the fall into duality that created the need for a spoken language (this is also depicted in symbolic form in the story about the Tower of Babel), and, once introduced, language itself reinforced the need to label all things by setting them apart from each other. The fallen beings had then taken advantage of this to make us forget who we really are, and this trapped us into believing that we are human beings who are limited by the powers of the physical body instead of having all four of the lower bodies being the chalice for the flow of the power of Spirit into matter, thereby giving us the power of mind over matter that was natural before the fall.

Maitreya explained that the challenge of the Christ consciousness is to free our minds from this human perception and the need to label everything based on separation. We can then start to see beyond the outer things and see that behind them was something else. He explained that everything was made of smaller particles, but today we can, with the concepts we now have, say that everything is an energy field and that things are interactions of energy fields, namely those of the four levels of matter. Maitreya explained very eloquently how it is possible to see that behind our sensory experience and the judgment of the outer mind is these infinitely small, vibrating particles that interact to form the most beautiful patterns.

Jesus was naturally completely absorbed in taking this message. I was walking beside him and looking at his face that, as was normal on these occasions, radiated a beautiful light. As I became totally focused on the words, I suddenly saw what they were talking about. It was as if my eyes were able to see something that is normally hidden from view because the mind filters out this type of sensory input.

I was walking in a daze as I was actually seeing Maitreya's words as vibrating energy that spread from Jesus in beautiful wave patterns. My normal analytical mind was neutralized, and I was not really hearing the words but picking them up as thoughtforms in my mind. Maitreya was saying that when we can see things this way, when we can see the unifying element behind all the separate things (that are not separate but only appear so to our minds), then we can also realize that what we today call the laws of nature are limitations that apply only to the human mind. When you see that all things are actually created out of this underlying sea of vibrations, you can see that any thing or condition in the physical is merely an expression of the finer energies in the three higher realms.

It is true that while we are in the human state of mind, our minds cannot change physical conditions. But when we go into the Christ mind, we have power over the three higher realms, and our minds can easily change the energetic pattern in the identity, mental and emotional realms. And once these are changed, the physical manifestation must follow—if only we can accept that this is possible and is a new reality. We must accept that the new vision, for example, of a healed body part is now the new reality and what we previously thought was real, namely the sick body part, is no longer in existence.

Maitreya explained that we can even come to see our entire bodies as manifestations of these vibratory patterns, and when we can (even temporarily) accept this as reality, then our bodies are no longer bound by the laws of nature. He explained that our bodies can then become pure light (what we today would call energy), and they can then go beyond even gravity. He said that when you see your body as made of pure light and the water of a lake as made of pure light, there is nothing to prevent your body from walking on water. I was so focused on Jesus' radiation and Maitreya's words that I had no doubt whatsoever that what he was saying is true. At that moment, Jesus stopped talking and there was total silence for a moment. Then, Jesus said: "And you now see this demonstrated by both of us."

I suddenly came back to an awareness of my body and surroundings, and as I looked down, I saw we were standing on the calm surface of the lake. I then looked around and saw that we had walked almost 50 meters out onto the lake. And truly, the first time you actually walk on water is, if you excuse the pun, a watershed experience. You can never quite look at the physical world the same way again.

It is, however, also a rather shocking experience, at least when you have not produced it but has been led into it by a person with more attainment than yourself. After a few seconds, my human mind was intruding and saying: "You are actually walking on water, but this is simply impossible. You cannot be seeing what you are seeing."

For just a split second I focused on this, and it broke the calmness of the state of mind I had been in. I instantly fell prey to gravity and sunk under the surface with an enormous splash. I can still remember the odd sensation of sinking into the deep water, hearing a bubbling sound as I almost went out of my body. It seemed like time stood still and I was suspended in the silence of the watery world. Then another natural law brought my body back to the surface, and I was spitting water while frantically trying to keep my head above the surface (I had not learned to swim).

After some moments, I realized I wasn't going to sink, and I looked up, seeing Jesus standing a couple of meters away, looking at me. As I caught his eye, he burst into laughter and he later explained that I had looked extremely comical as I was spitting water and trashing about like a dog. However, as Jesus laughed, he also lost his own inner focus, and now he fell through the surface with a huge splash. Again, it seemed like an eternity before he came to the surface, and I was just beginning to worry when his face appeared above the water, still grinning from ear to ear. I couldn't help laughing, and you really don't want to laugh hard when you are in the water and cannot swim. I swallowed some big mouthfuls and spent a couple of minutes coughing and spitting out water.

I finally regained some calm, turned to Jesus and said: "Perhaps we should have taken swimming lessons before we started walking on water. How do we get ashore?"

He swam close to me, took my hand, looked me in the eye and said: "The same way we got here; we walk."

I instantly felt his calm spreading into my body, and before I knew it, we were both walking up in the water as if on a staircase. When we reached the surface, we calmly walked to the shore, and then we sat down on a couple of rocks to process the experience. We said nothing because there was really nothing to be said.

***

As we kept letting our human selves die, Jesus became clearer about some of his deepest desires. He told me how he realized that when he had first encountered the fallen beings and been tortured by Lucifer, he had formed a deep desire to free the earth from these beings. He told me that this had caused him to think that in order to do so, he needed to understand them and know how they were thinking and why they were doing what they were doing. He explained that he had now realized that understanding the fallen beings is a necessary step, but in the end this cannot help you make a contribution to freeing the earth from them.

He explained how he had thought that there was one magical insight that would empower him to see through all fallen beings. He had now realized that this was a dream because different beings fell for different reasons. Because he had not seen this earlier, he had held on to the desire to find this magical insight, and it had given him a desire to find the ultimate teacher who could show him exactly what his mission was in this lifetime.

It was this desire for the ultimate teacher that had prevented him from seeing through the false teacher in the identity realm.

Jesus explained how he had been blind because he had such a strong sense of mission but did not know what it was. He thought there was a mission that was clearly defined for him in the spiritual realm, and defined in all detail. In other words, it was like what we today would call a movie script where the performance was described in minute detail right up to the happy ending. Jesus said that the most difficult initiation he had so far encountered was the realization that although there were certain parameters for his mission, it was not planned in every detail.

He explained that this had been very subtle for him to understand. When he had first realized he had a mission and that it was a mission he was the only one who could complete, he had thought that he already had the spiritual attainment necessary for completing the mission. (I will interject here that so many people today think Jesus was special from birth because he was already the Christ or the Son of God before he was born.) Jesus said he had realized that even though he did have attainment from past lives, this was not enough to complete the mission. His prior attainment was enough to get him to the point where he could begin the mission, but in order to complete it, he had to learn and to transcend himself to the very end. He did not have the attainment to complete his mission; it was something he had to acquire as he was performing his mission.

Jesus had also realized that many aspects of his mission had not been predefined because he had to make the decisions for how to complete them. It was up to him to define the mission as he went along. He explained that he had struggled with this realization for a very long time, and he had all along been hoping for that final insight that would reveal to him a predefined mission. It was this hope that prevented him from seeing through the false teacher. He wanted someone to decide for him. Now he had realized that it was truly part of his mission to decide for himself and that no one would tell him what to do. After explaining all this, he turned to me and said: "What do you think about this?"

I looked him in the eye and said: "What you have told me is in complete accord with what the ascended masters showed me, so I congratulate you for having arrived at this point."

# 36

We stayed with our third host for almost two years and at Jesus' 18th birthday, our host told us that he thought Jesus had learned everything he could learn from him and asked him to consider where he would go next. Jesus said that he had for some time felt that he needed to go out into the world and experience some of the things normal people experience so he could understand people better.

After some time, we took leave of our host and started walking. It was a joy for me to walk with Jesus so I wasn't paying much attention to where we were headed but allowed him to lead the way. However, after three days of walking, our food was running low and we were in a rather remote area with some low foothills. Jesus was happily walking and talking and seemingly paying no attention to the practical side of things. When we stopped for lunch, I pointed out that we had just eaten our last bread and had almost no food left. I also pointed out that there seemed to be no place to buy food, which wasn't so bad since we had no money either. I then made some remark that perhaps we should have thought about the practical aspects of our journey.

Jesus gave me one of his stern looks and said: "Well, if you could stop thinking with your stomach, you would realize I have already thought about the practical aspect. I am planning to learn how people live, not how one starves to death. Money will be provided for us, more than we will need."

I gave him an inquisitory look, but he refused to say more. We then walked on, but on the second day we were completely out of food and my stomach felt really empty. Jesus was hungry too, which I knew because he had stopped talking. At one point he turned to me and said: "Your constantly worrying about your next meal is disturbing my remembrance process. I have to ask you to walk 20 steps behind me so I can have some peace. I want you so far away that I cannot hear your stomach growling."

So we walked on with me some distance behind and Jesus walking with his eyes half-closed, as if he was in deep concentration. We had been following a goat trail in the foothills, but now Jesus turned up a narrow canyon that looked completely dry and desolate. Not even the goats had gone up there. I wanted to ask him how this would lead us to the promised land, but I knew I had better leave him alone. At first, he walked with a determined look, then he slowed down as the canyon split into several smaller canyons of very porous rock that seemed to have many caves. I thought: "I hope we are not going to become ascetics who live in a cave for years without food."

No sooner had I thought this than Jesus turned around and said: "Don't worry, we are not going to live in a cave."

He made a pause and continued: "For the time being."

I said: "So why are we here?"

Jesus replied: "To find the treasure, of course. Now will you give me some silence so I can work on remembering."

Jesus walked on, obviously having problems finding what he was looking for. Finally, he stopped, looked happy, and then walked with determination to the small opening of a cave. We crawled through into a slightly larger cavern, rounded a corner, and Jesus stood, pointing to the ground. He said: "This is where we need to dig, but I forgot to bring some tools. See if you can find a branch or a sharp rock."

I walked outside, found a couple of dead branches and brought them back inside. Jesus had dug with his hands, but had not made much progress. With the branches we made good progress, and about half a meter down, we hit what turned out to be a leather sack. As Jesus pulled it out, I could hear a jingling sound and it turned out the sack contained a fair amount of gold coins. Jesus looked at me and said: "I hid these in a past life and never got back to pick them up. So now we might as well put them to use in filling your stomach."

It took us one and a half days to find a town where we could buy food, but then my stomach did indeed get full. And Jesus' too, by the way.

***

For the next three years, we traveled around in what is now Kashmir, Pakistan, Iran and India. We spent a lot of time interacting with people, and it was amazing to watch how easily people opened up to Jesus. We were often invited to stay in people's homes or invited to family events, such as weddings or dinners. People were attracted to Jesus because of his spiritual light, but he could also be very open and joyful and had an ability to make people feel accepted and appreciated. This had to do with the fact that he did not judge or condemn anyone but acted the same towards the homeless person on the street as the richest man in town. We spent a lot of time in what we today would call taverns or bars, meaning places where people came to drink. Jesus would often drink wine in order to fit in with other people, but I never saw him the least bit drunk. When you reach that level of consciousness, alcohol, drugs or the faster working poisons have no effect on your body.

One time, as we left a tavern after spending all afternoon and evening there, we walked into the hills around the town. Jesus sat down under a tree next to a small lake. He was silent for a while and then started talking: "You know, sometimes I really don't know how to help people because they are so stuck in their minds that there seems to be no way out. Take a look at the people who were sitting in that tavern drinking all day, and who do this day after day. Their more immediate motivation is that they feel their lives are full of sorrow and suffering, and they are trying to forget by using the brain's ability to respond to a physical substance. But if you go behind what they feel consciously, you sense that there is a much deeper issue.

All human beings are really spiritual beings, and we were all created to be co-creators with God. Deep inside, we know this, and we know we have an ability to shape our life situations with the powers of our minds. Yet when we look at the physical world as it appears to us, we cannot see how we can use our minds to take control over our lives. And this is what makes people feel stuck, feel like they are wasting their lives, feel hopeless.

This entire situation, where our minds seemingly don't have power to change material conditions, is not natural. It is an artificial situation that has been created collectively by humankind over a very long period of time, but this has been directed and controlled by the fallen beings. So in one sense, the problem is created by the fallen beings, which means that people's inner pain is created by the fallen beings. I know we both know that the fallen beings don't have direct power over our minds, but indirectly, they have still created the situation by partly causing people to make the karma that comes back and limits them and then by spreading the false beliefs that make people feel these conditions are created by external forces and that they don't have the power in their minds to change them.

So the fallen beings have manipulated people into the current situation where they feel this inner pain. Then, the fallen beings have introduced drugs and alcohol as a way to get a temporary relief from the inner pain. In reality, the only real relief is to start co-creating so you are doing what you were created to do. But because the fallen beings are preventing people from even knowing who they are and what they were created to do, people can't do that. So instead they take what the fallen beings are offering and they dull the pain with alcohol. This gives them a temporary relief, but it also gives the demons behind alcohol access to their energy fields, and this sets them up for addiction. So what started out as a way to seek relief from their inner pain now becomes an additional problem that gives them even more pain and suffering.

The pattern I have come to see is that the fallen beings have created a problem, and they offer people what seems like a solution, but this only brings people further down in consciousness. Just look at what you and I have gone through in past lives. We were exposed to the horrendous abuses of the fallen beings, and we felt we had an obligation to try to stop the fallen beings from abusing people. We then fell prey to the subtle philosophies of the fallen beings, namely that it was justified to use violence to stop an even worse violence. So they had created a problem, and the 'solution' they offered was the dualistic struggle, promising that by winning some decisive victory, we could solve the problem. As we both experienced, this was a complete lie and it only tied us further to the fallen beings and created karma for ourselves that limited us and caused personal suffering. We eventually saw this and then spent many lifetimes freeing ourselves from the consciousness that tied us to the fallen beings. I mean, just look at how much effort over so many lifetimes that you and I have put into being where we are now, where we have no personal ties to the fallen beings.

Now look at the people we were drinking with today. Look at the gap between their state of consciousness and ours. I know exactly what is the problem in their lives. I know exactly what it would take for them to free themselves from those problems and start the same path that you and I have followed. Yet despite the fact that I have all this knowledge, I simply cannot communicate this to them because the gap between my consciousness and theirs is so big that they will not be able to grasp what I am telling them. Their view of life is so subtly influenced by the lies of the fallen beings that they would reject the truth that I could give them, the truth that would set them free. It would not only be too far from what they now believe about life, it would also require them to change their lives in ways they either cannot even conceive of or would not be willing to act upon.

So here I am, I have followed this long and hard path to free myself from the influence of the fallen beings, yet I am no closer – or so it seems to me right now – to being able to help other people become free. I know

I have the solution, but the problem is how to communicate this to people. And If I cannot communicate it to people, then how can I fulfil my mission? My mission is not to free myself and ascend, my mission is to give humankind something so that during the next spiritual cycle people will have a way to free themselves from the influence of the fallen beings. Yet it sometimes seems to me that the fallen beings have created so many lies, so many layers of deception, that I don't even know where to begin to set people free. I literally sometimes feel that changing this planet is a hopeless task, and certainly far too big for my abilities."

At this point, Jesus turned to me and looked me in the eye. His eyes were watering with tears of compassion and they radiated a deep, inner pain that I would come to know all-too-well in the years ahead. I could only look back and radiate my deepest love to him, for I naturally had no answers to the dilemma he had so eloquently outlined.

*** 

After almost three years of interacting with people, Jesus one day said that he felt this phase of his process was complete. We then started working our way towards the Himalaya mountains where we eventually ended up in a Buddhist monastery. It was situated in the foothills of the mountains and Jesus had chosen it because it had a special tradition. The monastery itself had the usual training programs for monks, but it also had a special program. Around the monastery were a great number of caves, and in many of these, monks lived in complete isolation, often not seeing or speaking to other people for years. The monastery would bring food to the caves so the monks could stay alive, but otherwise people in this program would decide on their own when to come out of this great silence.

Jesus explained to me that he wanted to enter this program, and he said that he hoped I would not feel left by him, but this was something he needed to do. I answered that I was only there to support him and that I would be happy to stay in the monastery and bring him his food. So everything was arranged, and one day I followed Jesus to the opening of his personal cave, watching him disappear and not knowing when I would see him again.

Over the next years, I would bring him food every other day, but I did not see him or even receive any signs of life, other than the food would usually be gone next time I came up. There were, however, times when he did not eat for up to three weeks, and at those times it was kind of difficult not to worry about whether he was still alive. I learned, however, to silence my mind and tune in to him, even to the point where I would not bring him food when he did not need it.

\*\*\*

During this time, I was not standing still in my own growth. I entered a teacher-student (or guru-chela, as it was called) relationship with one of the monks at the monastery. I first noticed him one day in the dining hall because he had some unusual wounds on his arms and legs. Just a few days later, they were gone, and it had been far too short of a time for them to heal naturally. I asked him to tell me about his process, and after giving me a penetrating stare, he agreed.

My mentor had grown up in India and from an early age, he had been fascinated by Hindu Holy men and gurus. He had run away from home at the age of ten and had sought out various gurus, trying all kinds of spiritual techniques. Eventually, he came to study under a guru who had specialized in taking complete command over the physical body. This is what most people today know as fakirs who sleep on nails or stick knives through their bodies. However, this master had gone far beyond and could control even his heart rate, breathing, pulse and blood pressure.

My mentor had studied under this guru for many years, but when his guru made his transition (died, as most people would say), he had gone on a journey and had ended up at this monastery. He said he had not known why he had to be at this particular monastery, but seeing me, he had realized the reason: It was because I needed to learn to control my physical body and especially to control my reaction to pain. As he said this, I instantly saw this was true, although I did not see how this would later help me assist Jesus in the final stages of his mission.

\*\*\*

So while Jesus was alone in his cave, I was working with my mentor to learn all about the physical body and how to control it. This was a gradual program, and in the beginning it was difficult for me because I had to go through a great change in my view of the human body. I realized that since my first embodiment on earth I had developed a rather negative view of the human body as a limited device. This was partly based on my remembrance of the bodies I had on natural planets and partly based on the incredible pain inflicted on my body by Lucifer in my first embodiment (and many later ones).

My mentor showed me that I had to completely let go of such feelings and come to fully accept the human body in its current form. He showed me that spiritual people can go one of two ways in dealing with the body. One is that you seek to disidentify from the body so you free the Conscious You from all attachment to the body. This is a viable process, and it has been taken by most spiritual people. He explained that in the end, we do, of course, leave the physical body behind so there is nothing wrong with freeing ourselves from it. However, for my mission in that life, this approach would not work because it inevitably causes people to look down upon the body. And one cannot look down upon the body and at the same time master the bodily processes. It simply cannot be done, and since mastering my physical body was essential to my mission, I could not take this approach. Thus, I had to instead take the approach of fully accepting the body and learn to work with it in its present state.

This took me over a year, but then I could finally accept my body and begin to work with it instead of seeking to force it. My mentor took me through a gradual program that started out fairly moderately but eventually became extremely extreme. This involved building up the ability to handle literally any kind of pain inflicted upon the body, even the total pain inflicted by Lucifer in that first embodiment. I started out by learning how to deal with the body's reaction to cold, an easy condition to experience in the Himalayan winter. Yet over the years, I had to inflict pain upon myself, and my mentor several times exposed me to total pain by whipping me like Lucifer had done.

I had to relive my experience with Lucifer to the point where I could imagine going through it and not reacting emotionally, mentally or at the identity level to the pain. I many times had to endure the most extreme physical pain while remaining completely calm and centered, being able to speak normally. This involved being able to calmly recite Buddhist sutras while being tortured by my mentor. It even involved having a normal, day-to-day conversation with him while he was torturing me. I know this seems rather extreme, but as they say: "I really had nothing better to do," and it did prove very useful when Jesus and I had our final encounter with Lucifer.

\*\*\*

One spring day, I was sitting in meditation when I felt the presence of Jesus. I immediately got up and walked to the cave where I saw him sitting outside. Or rather, I saw a man sitting outside who had such long hair, beard and nails that I barely recognized him.

As I walked closer, I mockingly held my nose, preparing to make some joke about the deplorable state of personal hygiene in Himalayan caves, but to my surprise, Jesus exuded a smell of blooming roses. I sat down next to him and remarked: "My brother, I hope you have learned more during these years than how to produce the scents of flowers."

Jesus said: "And I am happy to see you, too."

We both laughed for a long time and then embraced for even longer. While Jesus had his arms around me, he projected into my mind a series of images and thoughtforms that gave me a very concentrated view into the amazing process he had gone through during the past five years. I saw how he had seen every one of his embodiments on earth and he had seen the entire history of the fallen beings on earth, even the entire history of Lucifer in previous spheres. After this, there was really no point in asking any questions, and we silently walked to the monastery where I gave Jesus a manicure, a shave and a haircut—in that order.

# 37

In the following time, Jesus told me more about his experiences during his five years of silence. By the way, his father, Joseph, had died during that time, which we had both realized through our contact with Mother Mary. Jesus had been told by her that it was acceptable to her that he did not come home for the funeral, which would not have been possible anyway due to the deplorable absence of jet airplanes.

Jesus told me how he was now ready to go into a more active phase and preach some of the universal principles and insights he had received during his silence. He said he needed to practice this before we could go back to Palestine where he would begin the final and fatal stage of his mission. I wasn't sure what to think about the "fatal" comment, but I had learned that he often said things jokingly while being fully serious. And I knew that once we were back there, Jesus would become an instant target of Lucifer and his companions in the Jewish leadership.

We now started a phase in which we would wander around over a large area and Jesus would preach in the towns and also heal some people. When possible, he would speak in a religious setting, such as a Hindu or Buddhist temple, but many times he would stand up in an open square and start speaking. Sometimes nobody would listen to him, but in many cases, he quickly gathered a crowd and could keep them spellbound for hours. Most of what he said was, of course, dictations from ascended masters.

In some cases, we would encounter opposition from the local religious authorities. In a couple of places, it went so far that we had to get out of town very quickly in order to avoid violence or imprisonment. This was due to the fact that Jesus gave a message that was universal, but he also challenged whatever religious dogmas were believed by the people.

Jesus had one simple goal, and that was to set people's minds free. He had realized during his silence that back in those days, the major factors imprisoning people's minds were all kinds of superstitions and then religious beliefs. The religious landscape back then was very simple. Whatever religion was dominant in an area, an elite of priests (or other leaders) had formed, and they kept the people locked in false and limiting beliefs and practices.

The priesthood always claimed that the people would be saved from the misery on earth by following the dogmas and practices of the outer religion. Jesus knew this to be a false claim, as no outer religion could ever save people. The only form of real salvation is to ascend from earth, and that simply cannot happen by any external force (be it priests on earth or a saviour from heaven) doing anything to or for you. It can happen only by you doing something to raise your consciousness. This, naturally, begins with your willingness to question your existing beliefs about god and the spiritual path, so you can gradually acquire Christ discernment and know truth from within yourself rather than from an outer source.

Obviously, this was a message that was not popular with the religious authorities who did not want to lose their comfortable lives or their power over the people. For that matter, it was not a message that was popular with most people, as it quickly became clear that most people simply were not ready to take responsibility for their own salvation. They actually wanted an outer religion that allowed them to live their daily lives as they wanted but with the assurance that by following a few, easy practices, they would be guaranteed a place in heaven after life on earth. They weren't really ready to make radical changes in their lives in order to follow a spiritual path towards a higher state of consciousness.

\*\*\*

During our travels, Jesus would often talk to me about what he saw as the essential dilemma of his mission. He had realized that since the fallen beings started embodying on earth, they had taken the general population so far down into a state of feeling powerless that it was almost impossible to get people to reconnect to their true, inner power. People had come to feel so powerless that they simply could not believe that they could be saved only through their inner power, meaning a spiritual power working through themselves. Instead, they had become prey for the false claims of the fallen beings, namely that they could be saved only by a power external to themselves.

This was the quintessential example of how the fallen beings had created a problem and then set themselves up as the only ones who could solve the problem. The fallen beings had managed to make people forget about their inner power, and now they claimed that people could be saved only by following the fallen religious leaders. Jesus' essential question was how it would be possible to break this deadlock.

Jesus explained how he had realized that when we go into duality, we, meaning the Conscious You, create a self that is mortal or carnal. Today, many spiritual teachers call it the ego. He said that the Conscious You still is who it was created to be, but in the here and now, the Conscious You is who it sees itself as being. We act based on how we identify ourselves.

In its pure form, the Conscious You knows it is a spiritual being and that it has access to the energies of the emotional, mental and identity realms as well as the spiritual energies from the ascended realm. When we go into duality, we lose this conscious awareness and now we begin to see ourselves based on the limited perspective of the ego. The ego was born out of the lower energies and the limited perspective of the duality consciousness so it cannot see itself as a spiritual being Therefore, it cannot see that every condition we encounter on earth is made from the energies of the four octaves, identity, mental, emotional and physical. The only way to truly change any condition is to raise the energies that make up the condition, and this can happen only by opening ourselves to receiving a stream of energy from our I AM Presences and the ascended masters. *Only* these energies will accelerate the conditions that limit us on earth.

The problem is that when we have come to identify ourselves as separate beings, as human beings, we cannot access these energies from within ourselves (except in rare instances). Jesus explained that once the majority of humankind had descended to this low level of identity, people were, for all practical purposes, cut off from the spiritual realm. This meant that the people now could no longer save themselves. Therefore, the claim made by the fallen beings that people cannot save themselves by their own power is actually correct.

What the fallen religious leaders always fail to mention is that the condition of people being cut off from their spiritual power is not natural. It is an artificial condition created by the very fallen beings who now claim we have no other way out than to blindly follow them. Of course, the fallen beings have no access to spiritual power, so they can never deliver on their claim that they can save us. The more advanced fallen beings have no problem with this, as they are not trying to save us. They want to prevent us from ascending in order to prove that free will is a mistake that will cause us to abort our salvation.

Jesus said that the more clever fallen leaders did not claim that they had the power to save us, but that some kind of Messiah or savior would one day come from heaven to save people. The fallen leaders were simply there to help people make themselves ready for this savior whenever he would arrive in a distant future. Of course, the fallen beings knew the savior would never arrive, and they used the myth of a savior only to keep the people following them indefinitely.

\*\*\*

Jesus explained to me, many times, how the essential problem he saw was how to awaken people to the acceptance that while they do not have personal power to save themselves, they do have the option to open themselves up to receiving spiritual power directly from Above. And it was only when they opened themselves up to receiving this power from within themselves that their four lower bodies could be accelerated to the point where the Conscious You could go through the ascension process.

The problem is that once people have forgotten that they have inner power and come to identity themselves as separate beings, they cannot believe that any human being has access to this power. They now see it as supernatural, even though it is perfectly natural. Jesus had realized that it simply was not enough to talk about this inner power. Given the state of the collective consciousness (which, even though it may be hard to believe, was even denser than today), he simply had to demonstrate that a human being could have this power.

The quintessential problem was how to demonstrate that he had power without people taking the fallen concept of an external savior and transferring it to him, Jesus. He once said: "You know me and have known me for a very long time. You have walked the same, gradual, slow spiritual path that I have walked. You have experienced from within yourself that the path works, and therefore you know that I was not born or created with my current powers. You know I have worked long and hard, over many lifetimes, to get to my current level where I can be an open door for the power of Spirit to flow through me and create what seems like miracles to people in the dualistic state of consciousness. You know I actually have no power of my own.

You know that my goal is to set people free by demonstrating to them that when you follow the universal, mystical path that is open to all people, you can eventually acquire the kind of powers I can demonstrate. You also know that there is a huge gap between our state of consciousness and the state of consciousness of most people. So when I begin demonstrating the power of Spirit through me, most people will not see me as an example to follow. They will refuse to believe that they can acquire such powers by following the same path I have followed. Instead, they will take the image of the external savior created by the fallen beings and they will project that I, Jesus, am the savior they have been waiting for. They will elevate me to an idol to worship rather than an example to follow.

Do you see how clever the fallen beings are? The cleverest ones of them know that they are losing ground. They know that we are approaching a time when many people are ready to demonstrate spiritual powers. Their way to try to counteract this is to create the myth of some external savior that will be sent from heaven. This is found in most religious cultures, and you know the version in the Jewish mindset.

Once I start demonstrating unusual powers, some will believe I am the promised Messiah. So we will now have two groups of people. Some will reject that I am the Messiah and they will continue indefinitely waiting for an external savior. Some will believe that the Messiah is me, meaning they will accept that the external savior has already come, and now they just need to follow the religion that claims to represent him. Yet both of them will miss the whole point of my mission, namely to demonstrate the path that all people can follow and through which they can open up to the power of Spirit working through and in themselves. How do I break this deadlock, how do I break the spell cast by the fallen beings? If I cannot break this, then my mission will fail. The fallen beings will simply misdirect people's attention so they, as they have done for millions of years, look outside themselves for the solution that can only be found within."

***

During our travels, I started having more vivid experiences during sleep that I was visiting the retreats of ascended masters in the identity realm. The masters keep such retreats for various purposes, one of which is to educate people who have raised their consciousness to the point where they can leave the physical body at night and travel to these retreats. Most spiritually aware people are spiritually aware because they travel to these retreats at night. Most of the time, we are not consciously aware of this or think it is just dreams, but I started becoming more conscious of what I learned. This tied me in to the experience I had of being shown by the ascended masters the low and high potential for Jesus' mission. I therefore started to see that it was part of my mission to help Jesus go through what was clearly a very difficult phase where he often felt hopeless about his mission.

One day we were sitting in the hills outside a small town where Jesus had been preaching, and he again started to talk about the dilemma. Without any forethought, I exclaimed with unusual force: "Why are you so focused on the possibility that your mission could fail? Why have you allowed yourself to believe that the success or failure of your mission has anything to do with the fallen beings?"

Jesus looked shocked, then fell silent and said: "I sense this is one of those instances where I need to listen to you. Please explain."

I said: "What have you been preaching? You have been telling people that we all have access to the power of Spirit from within ourselves and that no external force can prevent us from contacting Spirit within ourselves. You have been telling people not to let any power on earth stand between themselves and their inner connection to Spirit. 'Let no man take thy crown,' as you said the other day. So why don't you take that and apply it to your own mission."

Jesus looked perplexed so I said: "Do you see the fallen beings as being external to yourself?"

Jesus answered: "Of course."

"Then, are you not talking as if you think that a power external to yourself can cause your mission to fail? As I see it, your real mission is to demonstrate personal Christhood, meaning that a human being can raise his or her consciousness to the point of overcoming duality and becoming one with Spirit whereby we are no longer human beings although still in a human body. This is an entirely internal process, and the success or failure of it depends on nothing outside yourself—according to what you preach to others. So apply this to yourself and realize that if you do manifest and demonstrate the fullness of your Christhood, your mission is a success.

You seem to have tied the success of your mission to people's reaction to it, but that is not Christhood. As the Living Christ you must respect people's free will. Thus, you can only give them a choice but you cannot control, or even be concerned about, what they choose. Right now, people know nothing about the path to Christhood and they have never met a person who has walked the path and reached the higher levels. Right now, people can only choose among the disempowering options created by the fallen beings.

By you demonstrating that it is possible to reach Christhood, you give people an option they do not have right now. But why should you be concerned about whether people select that option or not? Is it not the fallen beings who want to control people's choices by limiting their options? You do not want to control people's choices, but you are right now allowing people's choices to control you by thinking people's choices can make your mission fail. Yet nothing can make your mission fail except your thinking that it will fail. So be true to what you actually preach and apply it to yourself. Physician, heal thyself."

I probably looked pretty surprised at this point, as this was clearly the power of Spirit speaking through me, which didn't happen often, but Jesus didn't notice. He first looked what I can only describe as embarrassed, but then he fell silent, and suddenly his entire aura started changing. The light came back into his eyes. He looked me directly in the eyes with such power that it almost knocked me to the ground. Then he walked over to me and embraced me, saying: "My brother, truly none of us can walk this path without teachers and the teacher can appear in many forms. Wise are those who follow the teacher even if he appears as an ant."

He let go and I said: "So, you think I'm an ant now?" We both laughed, and then we started running up a steep hill, not stopping until we reached the top. As we stood there, looking over the vast landscape, we suddenly realized a change in the energy field. As we looked around, we became aware of an increasing white light appearing a few meters from us. As we watched spellbound, the light grew denser until faint outlines of figures started appearing. Gradually, the light became denser until we saw three ascended masters appearing in a visible manifestation next to us.

One of the masters we could easily identify as Sanat Kumara, the others were Maitreya and Gautama Buddha. Sanat Kumara stepped forward and made a sign for us to kneel. He then took a staff and touched Jesus on the forehead where the third eye chakra is located. Jesus' body became completely rigid and then he slowly fell over while shaking violently, almost as a person with an epileptic seizure. After a few minutes, he came back to normal awareness and again knelt. Sanat Kumara then said, with a very powerful voice that made the words visible as cups of light being sent into Jesus' aura: "You are my beloved Son, and this day I am well pleased with you having taken this leap beyond the most subtle poison of all: doubt. Go forth and doubt no more in the worth and value of your mission."

Then the three masters slowly faded away, and we were left staring into each others eyes without saying anything. Once again, no words could possibly do justice to such an experience.

\*\*\*

As I said, we walked around and Jesus would preach in many of the towns we passed through. He always gave a universal message about raising your consciousness by following a systematic path. This was a *universal* message, meaning he never said that people had to give up practicing their religion. He did not say they had to start following a new religion started by him. Instead, he adapted his message to the local religion and described the path by using the terminology and the concepts of the local religion. Naturally, this did challenge some of the doctrines and the priestly interpretations of that religion.

Jesus described the path as an inner, personal path. This meant that people did not need an elite of priests as an intermediary between themselves and whatever god or spiritual realm the local religion talked about. And it was this element of Jesus' message that often got him in conflict with the local power elite of priests or Brahmins. As soon as Jesus started attracting a crowd and becoming popular with the people, the elite would come down upon him and try to get us to leave or even try to imprison or kill us.

This was a pattern that happened virtually everywhere, as there was always a power elite that did not want to lose their grip on the people. And Jesus' message was indeed a threat to any kind of power elite seeking to control the people because every religion at the time said that people needed a class of priests as mediators between themselves and the spiritual world. It was this belief that Jesus challenged, and the path he offered would make people completely independent of any power on earth. If you know you have direct access to the spiritual realm through the Christ consciousness within yourself, why would you be subject to any power on earth? I will talk more about this later, but I am mentioning it because I want to describe a few instances. In one small town in what is now Iran, Jesus had attracted quite a following when the local elite sent a group of henchmen after us. This happened in the evening, and Jesus was intuitively aware that this was coming. He told me we were leaving and we immediately got up and started walking out of town. We walked into the hills around the town, but we were followed by a group of ten armed men, and they were closing in on us.

We moved into a narrow canyon, but it soon became clear that it was a dead end. We could hear the people behind us closing in fast when Jesus pulled me aside and told me to be silent. He closed his eyes and I could tell he was concentrating deeply. Within seconds, the people came walking by us in the canyon and although the closest one was three meters away, none of them saw us. They simply walked right by us, and when they reached the end of the canyon, they had a loud discussion about where we could have gone. They soon started walking back out of the canyon and again passed us within a short distance. When they had gone, Jesus turned to me and said: "So this is how the Cloak of Invisibility works."

He then explained that because we were able to raise our vibration to that of Divine love, the people had not been able to see us. Their vibration was so fear-based that they could not perceive us. Or rather, their eyes could see our higher vibration, but their brains could not accept what they were seeing and therefore, they had not detected us as human shapes.

*** 

In another instance in India, we were also being pursued by a gang of armed men led by a Hindu Brahmin. Again, we fled into the hills and came upon some rather treacherous terrain with lots of loose rocks. I was getting nervous, and as a result of me going into a fear-based vibration, I slipped and hurt my leg.

I was lying on the ground, looking up at Jesus and saying: "You must heal me, or they will catch up to us and kill us." I still remember the shock when Jesus looked me straight in the eye and said: "No, it is time that you heal yourself. The power of Spirit can works as well through you as it can through me."

I was stunned but as I heard the people behind us, I started arguing with Jesus, saying how I was not able to do this and that he needed to do it. I finally exclaimed: "If you don't do this, they will catch up to us and kill us and you can't let me have that on my conscience!" Jesus calmly looked back and said: "If you don't want my death on your conscience, I suggest you open yourself to let the power of Spirit heal your leg so we can move on. Be at peace and let the Spirit flow through your heart chakra."

I suddenly realized that Jesus was serious and that he would let himself be killed rather than healing my leg. Instead of panicking, I suddenly felt a deep inner peace and I surrendered myself entirely into the hands of Spirit. I was completely resigned that I could of my own power do nothing in this situation and I was in complete acceptance that if Spirit did not do the work, I would be captured and killed. I felt a total acceptance of the situation, and then I felt the most powerful flow of spiritual energy coming through my heart chakra and like liquid light flowing into my leg. After a few seconds, I knew my leg was healed and I got up, looked at Jesus and said: "Let's run." He smiled a sort of wry smile and then turned around and ran.

After running a short distance, it suddenly hit me that what I was doing was ridiculous. I exclaimed: "Stop" and Jesus stopped, turning to face me.

I said: "Why are we running? I just saw the power of Spirit heal my leg in a very physical way. Why should I doubt that this same power can get us out of this situation without us having to run as if we were afraid that the power of Spirit cannot help us?"

Jesus grinned and said: "I have been waiting for you to reach this conclusion. I am getting tired of running out of every town, but you seemed so convinced that running was the only option."

In a flash I realized that he had indeed been trying to question my sense that we had to run, but I had not been ready to listen to him. I simply could not change my view of the situation that when there are men with swords and knives coming at you, you either fight or run, and if you do not want to fight, your only option is to run. I looked at Jesus and said: "I am now ready to follow the way of Spirit, come what may."

We turned around and faced our pursuers who were now quite close. As they saw us, they paused as if they did not know what to do with people who were not running. You could see the doubt working in their minds, but eventually the biggest and most brutal looking man stepped forward and raised his huge sword. Yet as he was ready to strike, he looked into Jesus' eyes and then he literally froze. Jesus stood still and I could physically see the stream of radiant love coming from his heart chakra towards the man. I could see how it entered the man's heart chakra and then spread to his solar plexus chakra, which had been greatly agitated as it always is when people are about to engage in violence. His solar plexus chakra quickly calmed down, and the man seemed to shrink before our eyes. He fell to his knees and quietly started sobbing.

When this happened, the Brahmin became greatly agitated and started yelling to the others to kill us. I could see how this priest was a fallen being who was able to direct a very dark energy into the auras of several of the other people. Three of the men became to blinded by rage that they rushed towards us with raised swords. Jesus then seemed to become larger and yelled: "STOP. Whatever you attempt to do to me shall immediately be returned to yourselves. Do not say I have not warned you."

The men seemed unable to decide what to do, but the Brahmin again started yelling and he quickly took control over their minds. The three men rushed forward and struck with their swords. I was at this point once again in complete inner peace and acceptance of whatever would come. I watched almost in slow motion how the swords were being swung towards us and hitting like a white cloud of energy, from which they bounced back and hit the aggressors. The three men instantly fell to the ground with severe wounds from their own swords.

This seemed to shatter the priest's black magic and the rest of the men immediately ran away. Jesus then stepped towards one of the wounded men, touched his wound and healed him. He then stepped towards the second man while gesturing for me to heal the third man. When all three men were healed, Jesus turned to the Brahmin, who stood there as if transfixed. Jesus walked up to him and said: "I now give you a choice. Will you renounce your black magic and from now on follow the path to Christhood, or will you have me pronounce the judgment of the Living Christ upon you?"

The man looked stunned, and I could see how there was a small flicker of light in his heart chakra. It almost looked at if it was going to spread, but then a red-hot light, like molten lava, poured out of his solar plexus chakra. His face was contorted, as he screamed at Jesus: "I hate you. I HATE YOU! Get away from me, you Living Christ, I will have nothing to do with you. I HATE YOU and all that is of the light."

Jesus stepped back while the man was still screaming, and then he calmly said: "I hereby pronounce the Judgment of the Living Christ upon you, Abaddon, priest of Satan. It is done!" No sooner had the words left Jesus' mouth than the man fell silent, and then his body literally burst into flames before my eyes. I am not sure I have ever, in two million years on this planet, seen anything more decisive and irreversible. Within seconds, his entire body was turned into melting flesh. He did not even have time to utter a single sound, but the flesh of his body seethed as it literally melted from the bones. The bones cracked as they exploded under the intense heat. It took only a few minutes, and the man's body was reduced to a pile of black lumps and ashes.

Jesus turned to me with a shocked expression on his face (probably matching mine) and said: "I had not imagined that a person could contain that much hatred against the light. And although I had just seen what happened to the three other men, I did not think this man would be so utterly destroyed by the return of what he sent out. Imagine what he would have done to us, if his hatred had not been returned to him?"

\*\*\*

After the incident with the melting Brahmin, we became more cautious about letting people attack us. We started slipping away earlier so as to avoid a direct confrontation. However, in one town in what is now Pakistan, we were pursued by an angry mob of ordinary villagers armed with stones. This was a Hindu area, and the people believed in the concept of karma.

When the crowd came towards us, Jesus stopped and I naturally stayed with him. We faced the mob, and when they raised their hands to throw stones, Jesus raised his right hand. The crowd froze, and Jesus said with a very powerful voice: "Let the person who thinks it is possible to escape the karmic law throw the first stone." It was amazing to watch how the people's facial expressions went through a step-by-step transformation from anger, to shock, to doubt, to internal argument to awakening and resolution. They all reached the state of resolution at the same time, threw down their rocks and walked away. Jesus turned to me and said: "I thought that went well."

# PART 7:

# THE CONCLUSION OF

# JESUS' MISSION

# 38

One day, Jesus said he felt it was time to start working our way back to Palestine. We both knew exactly what that meant, namely that we would both have to confront Lucifer and that Jesus would most likely be killed. Jesus obviously wasn't looking forward to this, and I also had a sense of foreboding. I knew this would be a series of difficult initiations for Jesus and I also sensed that I would have to face difficult initiations myself.

On our long journey back, Jesus did not preach and he generally said very little. He was so internally focused that he could barely get any words out and I left him alone because I sensed he needed to have plenty of space. However, once in a while, Jesus would speak, and a couple of incidents stand out.

After a long day of walking through the desert, we went aside from the caravan we were following and sat on a hill overlooking the endless sand dunes. Jesus suddenly started speaking: "I have been wondering why I chose to incarnate in Palestine for my last embodiment, and I have reconnected to the fact that it is because the people there are more stuck in the duality consciousness than almost all other people on the planet. To the Jews, Israel is a holy land, but I see that it is actually one of the darkest areas on earth. The reason being that the Jews are so firmly in the grips of the fallen beings that they don't even see how completely self-centered they have become.

When you think about the ascended masters, you realize they are completely selfless beings. Or perhaps we could say they are selfish in a higher way because they see that all life is one and that the best thing they can do for themselves is to seek to raise the All. It is a matter of whether you define selfishness in relation to the One Self or to the separate selves. When you look at people on earth, you see that all people are stuck in self-centeredness to varying degrees, and the Jews are some of the most stuck people you can find. Just look at how we were brought up to believe that the Jewish god is the highest god there is, yet if you look at it objectively, he is one of the worst tyrants you could ever find. At the same time, the Jews are so sure that this supposedly highest god is intimately concerned with them and every aspect of their lives.

I mean, I know the duality consciousness enables people to distort everything, but isn't it outright unbelievable that an entire group of people can accept such a distorted view of god? How could a truly almighty, all-knowing god behave like the god of the Jewish scriptures? We know, of course, that this god is a composite of many tribal gods that have been lumped into one and given the name Yahweh, but the Jews don't even seem to notice the glaring inconsistencies. They are so duped by the fallen beings that they simply switch off any critical thinking when it comes to the scriptures and their own history. They don't see that the genocide they committed when they moved into Israel simply could not have been ordered or justified by the highest god of the universe. They think they can get away with this because it was ordered by god, and they completely refuse to see that the Law of Karma will make sure they will reap what they have sown. When that day comes, they will likely refuse to accept it as the return current but will claim to be victims because they are the chosen people and all others envy and persecute them.

I am facing a very unpleasant dilemma. I know that part of my mission is to preach to the Jews because the ascended masters determined that if we could make the most self-centered people on earth grasp the path to Christhood, we could awaken just about anyone else. Yet I cannot preach to the Jews without mentioning their history and their scriptures because if I do they will not listen to me. Yet the God that I know, meaning the ascended masters, is so fundamentally different from the Jewish god that I don't see how I can bridge the gap.

I also know that the main part of my mission is to bring forth a teaching and set an example that is universal and that can appeal to all people around the world, regardless of their religion or lack of it. Yet I am concerned that if my teachings ever gain a following, people will think that because I appeared in Israel and referred to the Jewish scriptures, those scriptures should be incorporated in the total teachings I gave. And this will put any movement based on my teachings in a very difficult situation. Partly because any association with the Jewish tradition will make it sectarian and therefore make people think they have to abandon any other religion in order to follow my teachings. Partly because dragging along this mishmash of Jewish scriptures can only create confusion, especially because the image of God I will give, will be fundamentally different from the Jewish god.

I know you will say that I don't need to worry about this because the ascended masters will speak through me and say what needs to be said. And that is true, but the masters can speak only in the actual situation and will adapt themselves to the people hearing it. What I am concerned about

is what happens later when people look back at my words and start thinking they should stand for all time. I don't want to start a movement that
becomes like the Jewish tradition and so many other religions where they
look back to what was said by a dead founder and have no renewal directly
from Spirit for their time. I want to start a living movement that is guided
by the ascended masters and therefore cannot become stuck in looking to
the past and interpreting what was said in the past.

My worst nightmare is that someone is going to write down a small
portion of what I will say, and then someone is going to turn this into a
set of official scriptures that are considered the Word of God. Then, all
future generations will have to try to understand my message based on
this fragment while not having direct access to constant guidance from the
ascended masters. Imagine that people 2000 years from now will have a
fixed set of scriptures and that they will use the mindset people will have
then, which will no doubt be very different from what the Jews have today,
to interpret the words that were spoken based on the current mindset. I
mean, how can anyone grasp my true message based on such a starting
point?

My vision is to start a different kind of movement that will not become
stifled by scriptures and the need to interpret what was said in the past. I
want a movement that remains open to direct input from Spirit, from the
ascended masters, and myself as an ascended master, so that it cannot be
taken over by the fallen beings. They will set themselves up as an elite of
priests and claim that they alone can interpret the scriptures from the past.
They will claim that there is no new revelation from Spirit, for the simply
reason that they cannot receive such revelation and they do not want anyone else to receive it because they cannot control the ascended masters.

I know this has never been achieved before on this planet, and I know
it is pretty naive to think I can accomplish this. But I still want to try. Will
you help me?"

I was taken aback by the question, and stammered: "Of course, I will,
in any way I can."

Jesus then looked me straight in the eye and said: "You know that you
have already qualified to ascend after this lifetime. Will you vow to stay in
embodiment for the next 2000 years and help make sure my true message
will not be completely lost? I know this is asking you to make a huge sacrifice, but if you will promise me to do this, I will feel more at peace and feel
like we may have a chance to preserve my true message."

Without even considering this, I promised that I would do this. Given what I have seen the fallen beings do over these past 2000 years, I have often wondered about my tendency to make quick promises that take a long time to fulfill. But let me not get ahead of myself. At least I did what I could to support Jesus in one of his difficult moments. I know many Christians believe Jesus was so superior that he never had any difficult moments, but that can only be because they have not closely read the fragmentary scriptures about him. Or they may have read them with the official overlay that denies the humanity of Jesus and thereby destroys the most important aspect of his entire mission, namely that he demonstrated the path to Christhood that we all have the potential to follow. By denying the humanity of Jesus, you kill him as an example.

*** 

Another time, Jesus and I were resting under some trees near Damascus when he spoke: "You know that when we get to Palestine, everything will become very hectic. There will soon be so many people around us that you and I will rarely be alone and have time to talk. I am concerned that you will feel left out by me or feel that I no longer care about you."

I answered: "Don't worry. I have seen the importance of your mission, and I know that it is a great privilege to be able to be a part of it. I wouldn't miss this opportunity for anything in the world, and I am happy to stay in the background and support you however I can. I don't want you to ever be distracted by worrying about me."

Jesus went on: "I knew you would say that, but I still want you to come to me and tell me what you sense I need to hear. Let us not forget our vows to listen to each other."

I nodded. He paused, and then continued: "My other great concern about my mission is what Lucifer will do to me. I know that he will most likely kill me, and he will want to do it publicly. This will mean letting the Romans be the henchmen, and that will likely mean crucifixion like a common thief. I know that will be painful, but I don't think it will be a problem. What I am concerned about is what he might do to me before then. You know yourself that when he exposed you to total pain in your first embodiment, there was no way to endure this without withdrawing, and that left you open to the programming of your three higher bodies that it has taken you over a million year to rise above. I can't have him do this to me again since I have to ascend after this lifetime. I can't quite see a way to deal with this dilemma?"

I answered: "My brother, as you say, several scenarios are possible, so it is difficult to say exactly what to do until we know what will actually happen. But even if Lucifer will expose you to total pain, I have a way to deal with this situation, I can assure you. He will not be allowed to abort your mission or your ascension, of that I can assure you, so you can be at peace about this and not worry about it."

Jesus looked doubtful and said: "But how can you possibly assure this?"

I answered: "I will not tell you now because knowing it will only distract you. It is important for you that you focus completely on your public mission and do not worry about the ending of that mission until we are there. Then I will tell you, and I can assure you that whatever Lucifer does, there is an answer that will neutralize his destructive intent. I spent the five years you were in the cave training for the worst-case scenario, and I can assure you that it will work. Will you trust me on this and not worry?"

Jesus said: "You know that at our level of spiritual attainment, we never trust what anyone says but always want our own confirmation, but this time I will make an exception because I sense you are right. So I will put this out of my mind until the time comes. Just remember, you have only vowed to stay in embodiment for the next 2000 years, not any longer."

# 39

There came a day when we walked into what was then considered Israel, walking north around the Sea of Galilee. As we crossed the unmarked border, Jesus fell behind, and I suddenly heard a crashing sound. As I turned, I saw that Jesus had fallen to his knees and his skin looked ashen, his face contorted. As I asked him what was the matter, he said: "I just felt the weight of the entire planetary force of anti-christ descend upon me. I had never realized just how powerful is the force we are up against. I now feel how they will do anything to stop me from manifesting and demonstrating Christhood. There is nothing they consider a greater threat to their reign on this planet. I don't know if I can do anything with this weight of energy upon me. I need to get it off."

I suggested that we use some of the techniques we had learned at the Venusian Mystery School to invoke the light of the ascended masters, especially the protection of Archangel Michael. We went aside and started making these decrees. After some time, Jesus felt better. I then said: "My brother, I will take it upon me as my personal task to invoke the light on your behalf during your mission. That way, you can focus on doing what you need to do."

Jesus: "Are you sure you can do this by yourself, given the weight of what they are directing at us?"

Me: "No, but as we go along, I am sure I will find people to help me."

This proved to be the case. During the entirety of Jesus' public mission I spent several hours every day invoking light from the masters in order to neutralize the fear-based identity, mental and emotional energies directed by the entirety of the dark forces associated with this planet in all four levels. I quickly found other people to help me with this, including Mother Mary, and towards the end, we were 12 people doing this for hours every day. Of course, invoking the light of the ascended masters cannot interfere with people's free will. It can give them a freer choice, but in the end there is no telling what people will do. This explains why Jesus did end up on that cross.

\*\*\*

Finally, one day, we rounded the last bend in the road and could see the town of Nazareth. We immediately saw two women standing at the entry to the town, and it was our mothers. Mother Mary had naturally sensed we were coming, and she had told my mother so they were both there to greet us.

As Jesus embraced Mother Mary, she let out a sharp cry and stood as if in a stupor for so long that the three of us were getting worried. She looked very pale, and eventually stammered: "My son ... how can you possibly deal with this opposition to your mission ... how can I help you?"

We assured her that there was a way to help Jesus, and from that day on, she helped me invoke light on behalf of Jesus, never failing to do her share. Jesus and I soon realized that Mother Mary had gone through a tremendous growth process while we were going through ours. She was, as I said, a member of a mystical order and while she did not have the kind of teachers we had, she had used its teachings and tools to raise her consciousness to a very high level. She radiated a greater inner peace than both of us, for in our youth, we were still too focused on doing outer things in this world to attain this inner peace. This was, of course, natural for us, given Jesus' mission and my vow to support him, but we both received much comfort and support from Mother Mary. She could, of course, also be quite direct when the situation called for it.

***

For some time, Jesus was holding a low profile and never did or said anything too obvious in a public setting. In the beginning, he was clearly needing to get used to the energies in Galilee, which were much more intense than what we had been used to. Yet after some time, it became clear to Mother Mary and I that he was reluctant to take that final step beyond the point of no return. Not long after that, some of Joseph's relatives had a wedding to which we were all invited. It was in what is now known as Cana.

I might interject here that we had naturally met many people since we returned, and everywhere we went, people were very interested in what had happened to us. Most people sensed that there was something special about Jesus and they were very eager to hear about our experiences in foreign lands. It is hard for people in today's information age to imagine how people back then knew very little about the world outside their immediate area and how starved for news people were. Yet, the only source of news was when they met people who had travelled to other areas.

At the wedding, Jesus quickly became the center of attention and was telling stories about our exploits. He was quite selective and avoided anything about his mission, and he was attempting to entertain people. I should interject here that when you reach the level of consciousness that Jesus had reached, you cannot really hide your spiritual attainment or your light. Not everyone can sense it, but many people can. As Jesus was telling his story, he came into the flow of the Spirit, and he had the crowd completely spellbound, everyone sensing the energy radiating from him.

At one point, he took a break and then Mother Mary pulled him aside. I saw how she looked Jesus directly in the eye and said with a very stern tone of voice: "Jesus, the hosts have no more wine left. I do not want them to be embarrassed because they are poor and do not have enough wine for their daughters' wedding. You know what you must do."

I also caught Jesus' look as he physically pulled back from her and with a distorted voice said: "Woman, why are you chastising me? Can I not take the time I think I need?"

Mother Mary looked back with one of those looks that no one, not even Jesus, can refute and said, in a tone of voice no one can ignore: "Your life was never your own and neither is your time. And the cosmic time-table cannot wait any longer."

Then, she turned to some of the others, who had been looking at them in astonishment, and said: "Do what he tells you to do." And then, she walked away. I could tell she was shaking all over from the power of Spirit that had been flowing through her.

Jesus then instructed the people to bring whatever pots they had and fill them with water. He then raised his hands and exclaimed with a voice as powerful as that of Mother Mary, but very quiet: "Father, not for the glory of man, but for your glory, I command that this water be transformed into a drink worthy of thy glorification as the only source of sustenance for us all."

Jesus then walked away, also shaking from the power that had come through him. I had, naturally, seen with my inner sight how light of multiple colors flowed from Jesus' I AM Presence through his hands and into the water. I had no doubt that it was turned into wine, but the other people were looking on dumbfounded and obviously did not know what to do. So I said: "Well, taste the wine and see for yourselves." They hesitantly did and were astonished to find that what they knew had been water was now the best wine they had ever tasted. This, naturally caused quite a stir and the story soon spread far and wide.

You will notice that at this point, contrary to what it says in John, Jesus had not gathered any disciples. After the wedding, he started his public mission, and the first step was to walk around Galilee where he would preach in public places and also select his disciples, or rather, let them select him.

***

Jesus was constantly aware that he had only a very short period of time to get his mission underway. I once (in this lifetime) heard a Christian minister claim that Jesus' disciples had at least a year to get their affairs in order before they followed him. What nonsense. Jesus' mission lasted a total of three years so how could he give his disciples time to prepare?

Imagine you are a fisherman cleaning your nets at the banks of the Sea of Galilee. You have lived a very protected life and rarely traveled more than a few kilometers away from your birthplace. Suddenly, you look up and see a stranger approaching you. He has long hair and beard and a very intense look on his face. He walks right up to you, looks you directly in the eye and says with a very intense voice: "Leave your nets and follow me, and I will make you fisher's of men." Then, without another word, he turns away from you and continues walking without looking back.

This is literally how Jesus called several of his disciples. If they immediately dropped everything and followed him, they would become his disciples. If they were not willing to leave everything behind, they had lost the opportunity. However, this only applied to some of his disciples, namely those who were the most trapped in the fallen consciousness. Such people had *one* opportunity to follow Jesus, and if they did not take it without hesitation, they were left behind. Jesus did make sure that when he approached them, he was so in the flow of the Spirit that they clearly sensed the energies of the Spirit flowing through Jesus.

Jesus had the clear intent of starting a movement that could grow and eventually spread far and wide. Thus, he called many more than 12 disciples. The number 12 was chosen by the gospel writers to tie it in with the 12 tribes of Israel. In reality, Jesus called hundreds of people who became his direct disciples. Most of these did not follow him around all the time but met him when he came near where they lived, which he did with regular intervals as he literally moved around in Israel for the three years available to him.

Many of his disciples were incarnated venutians. They had been there at the Mystery School, and they had volunteered to embody in Israel at the time in order to support Jesus' mission. That is why it had been such a complicated puzzle for the ascended masters to bring all of these people into embodiment at the same place at the same time, given that they all had their individual karma. Yet, there were approximately 10,000 people who had incarnated at the time in order to support Jesus' mission, and he managed to make contact with the majority of them. The rest were then contacted by others after his crucifixion.

Many of the 10,000 had been working on their personal Christhood ever since the Venusian Mystery School, and many of them had reached the point where they could instantly recognize Jesus as the Living Christ. Seeing Jesus and listening to him preach was enough to awaken their inner memory of who they were and what the path to Christhood is all about. To imagine that Christianity got started by a mere 12 people is quite frankly unrealistic. It took many more people who were willing to speak out about the universal path that is an alternative to all official religions. The incarnation of these many people is the only reason Jesus' teachings could spread in a world with such poor communication.

# 40

Jesus was very clear that the last thing he wanted to do was to start a movement that would become as the official religions we had encountered on our journey, such as Hinduism and the Jewish religion. All official religions are created or distorted by the fallen beings, and they have only one purpose, namely to bind the people to a physical and spiritual slavery under the fallen beings. You can expose such religions very simply by seeing whether they have inserted an institution and a class of priests between the people and the spiritual realm. This is the fallen beings attempting to set themselves up as the intermediaries between people and god, a position they can never fill in reality.

In contrast to this is the true path brought here by the venutians, but found here in various forms even before they came. This path places all power and all responsibility on *you* by stating that there is no external authority or savior who can or will bring you to heaven. The path is an inner process whereby you gradually raise your consciousness until you no longer see any distance between you and heaven. Thus, you are *in* heaven while also being in embodiment on earth.

If you have grown up with official Christian doctrines, you might say that Jesus never preached this path. However, this is because official Christianity blatantly ignores the few signs that are found in the scriptures. To those who can read between the lines, these signs are unmistakable.

The Jewish religion at the time was a typical example of a fallen religion. One aspect of this was that it promised salvation after this earthly lifetime, meaning salvation was somewhere else, sometime else. You definitely could not attain it *now*. It is almost impossible for modern Christians to understand just how provocative it was for many Jews when Jesus went around and everywhere preached that: "The kingdom of God is at hand!" This was such a blatant contradiction of the claims made by the Jewish priesthood that they became highly provoked by it. You might say that official Christianity also preaches that salvation comes after this lifetime, and you are completely right. The explanation being that official Christianity is also a fallen religion, and I will later explain exactly how it was perverted by the fallen beings.

Another example of how Jesus preached the inner path is that he said: "The kingdom of God is within you." You can read a whole world into that seemingly simple statement, especially when you take it in context. Before making this statement, Jesus had said to the Pharisees that the kingdom does not come with observation. Hereby, he attacked another claim made by the fallen religions, namely that by following the outer prescripts of your religion, you will automatically qualify for salvation. The promise made by the fallen beings is that if you obey them without question here on earth, they will guarantee your entry into heaven.

In his real preaching, Jesus made it abundantly clear that the claim made by the Jewish religion was false, even that it was satanic. I need to interject here that the Hebrew word that has been translated into the English word "Satan" does not refer specifically to the being I have called Satan. It is actually a construct of the fallen beings with the purpose of disguising the reality that the Creator has no opposite. The dream of the fallen beings has been to create a force so powerful that it can oppose and distort the Creator's purpose for the universe. I have explained that this is a futile dream because nothing can oppose the Creator. Yet as the fallen beings have created a false god, they have also created a false adversary that supposedly opposes god. However, the adversary does not oppose the real God but only the false god created by the fallen beings. This false god is created out of the dualistic consciousness, and as everything in duality, it must have an opposite polarity. Thus, you have the rather widespread concept that there is an adversary that opposes god and seeks to prevent people from attaining salvation. It is true that there is a force that seeks to prevent people from attaining salvation, namely the fallen beings, but this force does not oppose the Creator.

Okay, I digressed. The point was that in the Jewish culture, Satan was a common name for the adversary of god, so by calling the Jewish priesthood satanic, Jesus delivered the ultimate provocation. He explained that Satan is a state of consciousness that seeks to create an idea here on earth and then seeks to make everything and everyone conform to this idea. That is why those trapped in this consciousness believe they can define a series of doctrines and rules, and if people follow them, they are guaranteed to enter heaven. Jesus explained very clearly that this is a completely false claim and that no amount of observation of earthly rules will qualify you to enter heaven. The only thing that will qualify you to enter heaven is that you raise your consciousness beyond duality and attain the Christ consciousness. There is no cheating when it comes to entering the kingdom. This is also explained in several of his parables, including the one where a man had entered the wedding feast without a wedding garment (the Christ consciousness) and was thrown into outer darkness (by remaining in the duality consciousness).

It is difficult to understand today, but Jesus was very direct in talking about fallen beings, only he did not use those exact words. Again, there are hints in the scriptures, such as the situation where he says to the scribes and Pharisees: "Ye are of your father the devil, and the lusts of your father ye will do. He was a murderer from the beginning, and abode not in the truth, because there is no truth in him. When he speaketh a lie, he speaketh of his own: for he is a liar, and the father of it." Is this not a clear description of what I have called fallen beings and their motives and methods? Jesus, of course, gave a much more detailed teaching about this than what is recorded in the scriptures. However, he did not give this advanced teaching in public but only to his direct disciples.

Jesus also made it clear that the only way to attain the Christ consciousness was to literally let your old sense of self die gradually until your identity had been completely reborn and you had become a new being in Christ. You will see that Paul had understood this whereas Peter never got it. Jesus said many times that those who were not willing to lose their lives in order to follow him (attain the Christ consciousness) were not worthy to be his disciples. This did not mean you had to die physically (although you had to *be willing* to die if necessary), but that you could not be attached to anything in your worldly life. You had to put attaining the Christ consciousness before anything in this world. You didn't necessarily have to give up everything and become a recluse. You had to *be willing* to give up everything. Many of Jesus' original disciples continued to live active lives in society while expressing and demonstrating their Christhood. It was never Jesus' intention that his disciples should withdraw from society but that they should demonstrate to their peers that there is a different approach to life.

***

As I have mentioned before, Jesus could easily have had people write down what he preached. Yet Jesus expressly forbade his disciples from writing down anything he said or did. Why? There are two main reasons.

One is that he knew that once something was written down, it would become fixated in time. Every official religion claims to have a scripture with some ultimate authority. This scripture was given sometime in the past and it cannot be renewed. It must therefore be interpreted by the class of priests who are now the ones who have been given the authority of the original founder although they do not have the ability to receive a teaching from beyond the material world. In many cases, a religion has been founded by a person who had contact with the ascended masters and who therefore received a genuine revelation. Yet those who control the religion later have no such ability and thus make a virtue out of interpreting while claiming they have the authority to do this.

Jesus did not want his movement to repeat this pattern and that is why he did not want anything written down. He wanted to create a movement that had a clear tradition of continually receiving revelation from the ascended masters through the flow of the Spirit. He did not want his disciples to write down what Spirit said through him because he was training his disciples to themselves be messengers for receiving direct revelation from Spirit. Jesus wanted to create a movement with a constant stream of revelation directly from him as an ascended master so that the fallen beings could not disinterpret the revelation given in the past. This would also ensure a movement that could raise itself as times changed, rather than becoming stuck in trying to fit everything into the scriptures of the past. Just look at how much the collective consciousness has changed in 2000 years and then see how ridiculous it is that official Christianity is trying to fit modern life into an interpretation of scriptures that are 2000 years old (and that were not pure to begin with). No wonder more and more people are giving up on Christianity.

The second reason Jesus did not want anything written down was that he was very determined to avoid creating a movement focused on him. The last thing Jesus wanted was to be seen as an *exception*. He wanted to be seen as an *example*. He wanted people to see him as a person who had followed the universal path to Christhood, thereby demonstrating the path that is open to all. As I said, the motto of the ascended masters is: "What one has done, all can do." Thus, Jesus felt that what he did or said was unimportant. It was far more important that many other people became able to speak the Living Word of Spirit so that the movement would remain focused on bringing forth new revelation, constantly seeking to raise up those who had sufficient Christhood to be messengers of the ascended masters. The last thing Jesus wanted was that he was turned into an idol and seen as the only one who could do what he did. You might say: "But isn't that exactly how official Christianity has portrayed Jesus since the Nicene Creed portrayed him as: 'one Lord Jesus Christ, the Son of God, begotten of the Father [the only-begotten; that is, of the essence of the Father, God of God,] Light of Light, very God of very God, begotten, not made, being of one substance with the Father?"' And you are right, of course. I did mention, did I not, that official Christianity has from its inception been a fallen religion?

***

The real problem for today's Christians is, of course, that they never heard Jesus preach. Yet there are (surprisingly) some hints in the official scriptures that are really not so hard to read.

Let me begin with the statement that if everything Jesus did or said should be written down, then the world itself could not contain the books that should be written. Now, if I had grown up in a Christian religion (as I did in many lifetimes over the past 2000 years), I would have read this and thought: "But I would like to know some of the things he said that are not in the scriptures. Maybe something really important was left out? Maybe these missing teachings could explain some of the many questions that official doctrines cannot explain?" Yet even today most Christians don't seem to think that way. They sit in their churches like cows chewing the cud, being satisfied with the scriptures presented to them by the fallen beings and with the (more and more artificial) interpretations by the priest who (unwittingly for most of them) represent the fallen beings and perpetuate their control over the minds of the people.

Another example is the statement that Jesus taught the multitudes in parables, yet when they were alone together, he expounded all things to his disciples. Now, if I had grown up in a Christian culture, I would have thought: "But I want to know what Jesus told his disciples. In fact, I want to be one of his disciples. But then I obviously have to look outside the scriptures." I would also have realized that I would have to look outside the closed system created by the priesthood.

After all, how many people have asked a question of their priest that could not be explained by official doctrine, only to receive the highly condescending answer: "It's a mystery, my child."

What nonsense! Here we have, in the official scriptures, the clear demonstration that Jesus had a vast teaching that is not in the scriptures. One would assume that a priesthood that has the audacity to claim that they represent Christ on earth would have made an effort to become disciples of Christ and thus have some idea of this hidden, inner teaching. The very fact that the priests do not have some of these inner answers demonstrates more clearly than anything how utterly false is their claim that they represent Christ. And if they do not represent Christ, whom do they represent?

\*\*\*

Back to my statement that the problem is that Christians have never heard Jesus speak. Well, first of all, if Christianity had become the kind of movement Jesus intended, modern Christians *would* have heard Jesus speak. Ideally, every priest should be able to serve as a messenger who could be an open door for the Living Word of the Spirit. This means that every Sunday, people should be able to go to their Christian church and hear the priest deliver a dictation from the ascended masters. And which master do you think would like to speak directly to all Christians, if only he had mouthpieces who could deliver such a release and people with ears willing to hear?

There is absolutely no element of deception in the Christian church worse than the fact that this church (beginning with the Catholic church but upheld by the vast majority of churches to this day) has written the Ascended Master Jesus out of Christianity. According to the church, Jesus came to earth 2000 years ago, gave a teaching, and then he went back to heaven from where he has done nothing to help us ever since. Instead, Jesus is supposedly trusting that his representatives in the official church will do everything that is necessary to bring us to the kingdom. How anyone can believe in such utter nonsense is beyond me.

Who is Jesus today? He is an ascended master. Jesus is fully capable of and willing to deliver the Living Word to us today, as he has been for the past 2000 years. He trained his original disciples to receive this Living Word directly from Spirit, and the purpose was that he himself could continue to speak to his followers after his ascension. Jesus was very much looking towards the future, and he was intent on creating a living movement that would never lose his guidance. That is why he promised to send another comforter once he had gone to his father. That comforter is in the broadest sense all ascended masters, but also himself in his ascended state.

The greatest travesty of Christianity is that this Living Word was systematically suppressed, squashed and rooted out by the fallen beings who took over the movement and created what became the religion of Christianity. They did this, of course, because *they* could not receive the Living Word and they could not control it when others received it. Just imagine that this tradition had been upheld and Jesus could have continually given messages over these past 2000 years. Imagine that the priests did not have to interpret the scriptures of the past but had the Living Word flowing constantly. Do you not think Jesus could have steered Christianity away from some of the insane events that took place during that time? Do you not think Jesus could have answered all of people's questions, and continued to do so as times changed and people received new knowledge? Do you think Jesus has no answers to the claims of materialism? Do you really think Jesus is incapable of giving us a teaching that is relevant to people in the modern age and can help us meet the challenges of our age?

***

I mean, if you look at the official picture of Jesus, you must conclude that he was a very strange being. As the first example, look at the undeniable historical fact that official Christianity has perpetrated a long string of atrocities, such as the massacre of the Cathars, the crusades, the witch hunts and the Inquisition. I have literally experienced how leaders of the inquisition spent a whole day in the torture chambers, inflicting the most cruel torture upon people. Then, after the day's work, they went into the church, knelt in front of the crucified Christ and were absolutely convinced that Jesus looked down upon them with approval. After all, they were torturing people's bodies in order to save their souls from hell. I have seen Christian crusaders ride into a Muslim village with drawn swords and hack to pieces men, women and children, while feeling Jesus (the same Jesus who told us to turn the other cheek) was approving their actions.

So, you can't deny that this actually took place. Your only option is to say that either Jesus approved of the behavior of the Catholic church or the church was completely out of touch with Christ. If you choose the first option, you must have a very strange image of Jesus, for how could you reconcile the approval of torture with the man who preached to turn the other cheek, do unto others and love thy enemies? Do you really think

Jesus preached or would have condoned mass torture as a means to save people's souls? Do you really think Jesus does not know that all torture is instituted by the fallen beings and that it has only one purpose, namely to destroy people's souls so that the demons of hell can continue to steal people's energy over many lifetimes? Certainly, if this is your image of Jesus, it has nothing whatsoever to do with the being that I have personally known for two million years and still experience today as a living, ascended master.

Then, look at the fact that Christian doctrines and the priesthood that claims to represent Jesus cannot answer so many of the questions people have in the modern age. You have to ask yourself whether God or Jesus does not have answers to all questions we could possibly ask? You have to ask why there is always an element of hiding something in official religion? Do you really think that God or Jesus has something to hide from us? Or could it be the fallen beings who have something to hide and therefore want us to stop asking questions? Did not Jesus say that the truth shall make us free and did he not expound all things to his disciples?

Now, you may ask why he then taught the multitudes in parables and did not openly say everything? This is a very valid question that I would like to comment on.

# 41

I have explained that the fallen beings came to earth a very long time ago and that ever since then, they have attempted to distort what people know. I have also explained that the fallen beings were allowed to come here because people had created closed societies in which they were not growing. Why are people not growing? It is because they are not taking responsibility for themselves. Instead of using the ability to know truth from within, they are seeking to let other people do their thinking for them by following an external authority.

The ascended masters could see that if a majority of the people on earth kept following their relatively benign leaders, then the planet would eventually self-destruct. The masters knew that by introducing the fallen beings, people would soon start following them. The masters also knew that the fallen beings would create such bizarre consequences that it would be difficult for people to continue to blindly follow these leaders. People would simply have to acknowledge that blindly following the fallen beings would lead to such outrageous consequences that they would have to wake up and take responsibility for themselves and their societies. This hope has to a large degree been fulfilled, as you see in the democratic societies of the modern world. What remains is simply the last step of people becoming aware of the existence and influence of the fallen beings so we can get them off this planet for good. But I am again getting ahead of myself.

When Jesus started his mission, it was clear to the ascended masters that most members of the general population were not ready to follow the path to Christhood directly. That is why it was decided that Jesus would teach at two levels. One level was for the general population, and for this he gave his parables and other outer teachings (many more than recorded in the scriptures). The other level was for those who were ready for the path, and to them he gave a much more advanced teaching about the path to Christhood. This teaching could not be written down because the fallen beings would then have perverted it. And it was not necessary to write it down as long as the tradition of the Living Word was maintained.

Jesus therefore intended to create a movement that had two levels. It had an outer teaching that gave people certain rules and teachings that could help them live their daily lives in a more aware manner. The purpose was to get people on a gradual path that would eventually lead them to the point where they were ready to engage in the path to Christhood directly. When people had become ready for this, they would then have a structure of more mature people who had already walked the path. They could guide the newcomers as Jesus guided his disciples. The newcomers would then receive much of the teaching that Jesus gave to his disciples, but in a constantly updated form, adapted to the times.

One of the main purposes behind Jesus training his many disciples was that they would form a movement where there was made available to the people this inner, mystical path. His disciples would be following this path so that they could serve to help others, as people became ready for it by following the outer teaching. Had this been maintained, your local priest (in order to receive ordination) would himself – or *herself* – have followed the mystical path and reached a certain level. He or she would therefore have found inner answers to the deeper questions of life and would have had more to offer you than the claim that there are no answers to your questions and that there is something wrong with you for asking questions that the church (meaning the fallen beings) cannot answer.

\*\*\*

The last thing I want to mention here is that if you look at the official picture of Jesus, you must reason that he was very cruel in first coming here to stir things up and then leaving us alone with a promise that he will return sometime in the undetermined future. As I have explained, Jesus fully intended to keep his promise: "I am with you always, even onto the end of the world." He intended to do this as an ascended master through the tradition of the Living Word. You simply cannot understand why this promise has not been fulfilled unless you know what I have told you about the fallen beings.

To the fallen beings, the ultimate threat is that a person becomes the open door for a flow of the Living Word from the ascended masters. The fallen beings know that they can never qualify to have this flow, and although they can imitate this (as many modern channelers do), they can never reach the real thing. Secondly, they cannot pervert the Living Word. They can never gain control over it because it comes directly from the ascended masters—there is no interpretation or mediation needed. The fallen beings want scriptures that are written down because then they can interpret them, and through duality they can distort anything. The Living Word cannot be interpreted while it is flowing. It can be interpreted afterwards if it is written down, but if there is an ongoing tradition for having the Living Word, then new messages can correct and challenge such interpretations. Therefore, what Jesus attempted to do, by creating a movement with the flow of the Spirit, was seen as the ultimate threat by the fallen beings, meaning they have done everything they could think of to destroy it.

Why have they been successful? Because a majority of the people have gone along with them in denying the Living Word. The reason is simple, namely that people are not willing to take full responsibility for their salvation and state of mind. The Living Word is highly disturbing to people, as demonstrated by Jesus himself.

***

You cannot understand Jesus without knowing that he saw himself only as a mouthpiece for Spirit, for the ascended masters. It is a mockery when the fallen beings have made Jesus into the only Son of God who has all power to do anything he wants. Jesus himself was very direct and very stern in refuting any and all attempts to idolize him.

I still remember one situation. Jesus often had sessions where people could ask him questions. Often, he would get the answers as a form of dictation from the ascended masters, but other times he answered them from his own Being. Well, during such a session, a man approached Jesus and he clearly had this attitude that Jesus was someone special. I could immediately sense how Jesus reacted to the man's servile attitude, and then the man spoke: "Good master . . ."

He didn't get any further before Jesus interrupted him: "Why are you calling me good? There is none good but God." This was said with such force that the man literally fell backwards and was shaking from the power of the Spirit flowing through Jesus. The man was so shaken by this that he did some soul-searching and eventually became one of Jesus' disciples.

Of course, you also have the fragments from the scriptures where Jesus said that he could of his own self do nothing and that it was the father (meaning the ascended masters and his I AM Presence) who was doing the works through him. Anyway, my point here was that Jesus never saw himself as the originator of the power flowing through him. He knew it was the power of Spirit and that he could not own or control it.

Back to my starting point, which was that the power of Spirit was highly disturbing to many people. As soon as Jesus started speaking, many people would be unable to sit still. Many would latch on to one thing he said that went beyond or contradicted what they already believed, and they would use this as an excuse for rejecting Jesus and walking away from him. The reality was that the power of Spirit was so disturbing that people subconsciously knew that if they stayed in Jesus' Presence, they would have to let go of their existing beliefs. Since they were not willing to do that, they had to walk away from him, and the outer claim that he was giving a false teaching was just an excuse. This was a pattern often seen in the scribes and Pharisees and those who followed them. Basically, the higher people were up in the Jewish hierarchy, the more likely they were to find an excuse for rejecting Jesus.

Yet many among the people also rejected him, and the reason was simple. In the religions created by the fallen beings, people are set free from taking responsibility for themselves. They are told that if only they follow the outer rules, they are guaranteed to be saved after this lifetime. Since a fallen religion rarely (except by accident) allows the Living Word of the Spirit, people have nothing to challenge the official claim. The mechanism is simple. The priests have no power of Spirit so it is easy for people to believe that they themselves can be saved by being in the same state of consciousness as the priests. After all, the people have never experienced the power of the Spirit that would challenge the reign of the priests.

This illusion is challenged when people meet a person who is the open door for the power of Spirit. People cannot deny the experience that this person has something they themselves do not have. They subconsciously know that this person has attained this by reaching a higher state of consciousness. This threatens to awaken the inner memory (that all people have encoded in their identity bodies) that we all have to attain a higher state of consciousness in order to be saved. We all have an inner knowing that we cannot enter heaven with the duality consciousness, we cannot enter heaven while still being selfish and self-centered.

This experience can be very disturbing to people, depending on how attached they are to remaining in the unaware state of mind and rejecting responsibility. The encounter with Spirit threatens to awaken them so they are faced with the necessity to take responsibility for themselves and change their comfortable lifestyles. If they are not willing to do that, they have to find a way to avoid being awakened, and the most common method is to find fault with the person who has the flow of the Spirit and use some outer thing to reject it. Many people did this with Jesus, using anything from his birthplace ("Can anything good come out of Nazareth?") to his personal appearance or his way of talking. However, the primary means was to take some of his words out of context, compare them to official scriptures or interpretations and then reject him as a false teacher.

The fallen beings are very good at appealing to loyalty. Their reasoning is so simple. In this case it was that since the Jewish religion was obviously true, if Jesus was a genuine teacher or even the Messiah, he would not say anything to contradict Jewish teaching. Incidentally, the majority of Christians today would reject the Living Word of Jesus if it contradicted official doctrines (as many Christians will no doubt use the same reasoning to reject this book).

The problem here is, of course, that if the official doctrines (as is always the case) are created by the fallen beings, then Spirit can set people free only by saying something that contradicts the doctrines. So if people use this as an excuse for rejecting what can set them free from the fallen beings, then they must remain as the blind followers of the fallen beings for one or several lifetimes.

Anyway, my point being that many people rejected the teachings of Jesus and especially the disturbing flow of the Spirit. This is part of the explanation why the tradition of the Living Word could not be maintained. As an official Christianity started to emerge, many people preferred this more comfortable religion to the much more difficult and challenging path of discipleship under Jesus. Another part of the explanation is, of course, the influence of the fallen beings, as I will talk more about later.

# 42

There is, however, another reason many Jews rejected Jesus. You cannot understand this without knowing the political climate found in Israel at the time, something not remotely described in the scriptures.

There are certain situations in the scriptures where Jesus seems to refer to himself in such a way that it can be interpreted to mean he saw himself as the Messiah prophesied in Jewish tradition. This is a construct of the gospel writers, who (for the synoptic gospels) had an agenda of describing Jesus in a way that would make him acceptable to specific groups of people. This is out of touch with how Jesus saw himself and described himself.

The Jewish concept of a Messiah is very much a product of the fallen beings. The Messiah is seen as an exception who has godlike powers and therefore will come to save the people by using those powers. Again, the people do not have to do anything, except, of course, follow the Jewish priesthood of the fallen beings. Jesus did everything he could to avoid presenting himself in a way that could make people see him as the Messiah. He directly and openly refuted any attempt to tie him in with the myth of the Messiah.

Now, you might ask why the fallen beings had created the myth of the Messiah. There are several reasons for this. One is that it propagates the illusion that salvation will come in the future. Yet another is that the fallen beings had foreseen that Jesus would take embodiment in Israel. They had therefore attempted to create a myth that would be so different from how Jesus actually portrayed himself that it would prevent the Jews from accepting Jesus.

Again, there is a subtlety here. Jesus was very clear, in his own mind and in his teaching, that his mission was universal, meaning it was meant for all people and not specifically for the Jews. You can see this from the fact of how he associated himself with many people who were outcasts in Jewish society. You can see it from the parable of the good Samaritan and other parables.

Jewish society was extremely elitist and hierarchical, another hallmark of the fallen beings. Any society that allows the division of the people into separate classes, some having privileges and status far beyond others, is a society influenced by the fallen beings. Elitism is their calling card. Jesus always reached out to the groups of people that were looked down upon by the Jewish elite. He also made sure his teaching was not too tied in with the Jewish religion by always speaking in a universal language, using many concepts that went far beyond the Jewish religion and culture.

However, Jesus also knew that part of his mission was to give the Jewish people something that could take them beyond being so controlled by the fallen beings. I have said that Jesus embodied in Israel because it was one of the darkest places on earth. What made it dark was that so many people were so controlled by the fallen beings. The primary means that the fallen beings used for controlling the Jews was the myth that the Jews were god's chosen people. In a sense this was true. The Jews *were* the chosen people of the false god created by the fallen beings, but the real God of the Creator has no chosen people, as all are extensions of its own consciousness. The myth of a coming Messiah, naturally tied in with this idea of the Jews being so special that they merited special treatment from god.

When you consider this, you realize that it was an extremely hard blow for the Jews that god's chosen people could be conquered and ruled by the Romans. By the way, this is a typical example of how one group of fallen beings will defeat another group of fallen beings. Anyway, to the fallen beings ruling Jewish society, it was a major problem that another group of fallen beings had conquered Israel. Part of the problem was to explain how this could happen when god was supposedly on the side of the Jews. However, they could always refer to the past where the Jews had suffered so many humiliations, despite being the chosen people of the most powerful god (like in the story of Job, the exile and so on).

Nevertheless, what had happened at the time was that the myth of the Messiah and the myth of the chosen people had been merged in popular culture. Many people believed that in the near future, a Messiah would come who would act as a warrior king and lead the Jews in a violent uprising that would defeat the Roman Empire. You will see from a purely pragmatic viewpoint that it was utterly impossible for a nation with such a limited population to defeat the might of the entire Roman Empire. Yet if you had grown up in a culture with the myth of how David slew Goliath, you might believe that with god's help, it was possible for the Jews to throw the Romans out of Israel.

\*\*\*

After the fist couple of years, Jesus had done so many unusual things that he had received a reputation of being able to perform supernatural feats. There was a powerful underground resistance movement at the time and they were training and organizing for a violent revolt against the Romans. Naturally, this was not officially sanctioned by the Jewish religious leaders, but in reality Lucifer was the instigator of this movement, although he was not its leader. There came a point where Lucifer had become aware of Jesus, and he sent the leaders of the resistance movement to him in order to ask Jesus to lead their uprising against the Romans.

Based on everything I have explained about our involvement with Lucifer and Satan and how we had eventually transcended all desire to use violence against them, it should be obvious that Jesus never had any intention of participating in a violent uprising of any kind. As Jesus said: "Render unto Caesar that which is Caesar's and unto God that which is God's." The real meaning is that Jesus did not consider the Roman occupation of Israel as having any relevance for his mission. Instead, he had come to show the Jews the one thing that could take them beyond being controlled by the fallen beings, namely an entirely non-violent approach to life. Naturally, getting involved with any kind of violent movement would go against Jesus' purpose.

Lucifer knew that Jesus would not lead the resistance movement, but the purpose of sending its leaders was not to persuade Jesus. The real purpose was to get all of the people who supported the resistance movement to reject Jesus. Naturally, this worked and as word spread, a majority of the people rejected Jesus and his teaching based on the fact that he had refused to lead the violent revolt against the Romans, thereby proving in their eyes that he was not the promised Messiah. And if Jesus was not the promised Messiah, why should the right-thinking Jews pay any attention to him?

This is the real reason behind the situation where Pontius Pilate gave the crowd the choice between releasing Jesus or Barabbas. Because Jesus had refused to fill the role as Messiah, as warrior king, most Jews would rather see a murderer than the Living Christ released.

By the way, the myth about the Messiah as a super being has worked so well that the Jews to this day reject the teachings of Jesus. Thus, the Jews are as stuck under the yoke of the fallen beings today as they ever were. The story of Moses leading them out of the slavery of Egypt is truly the story of how the representatives of the ascended masters can lead the people out of the slavery under the fallen beings. The Jews accepted Moses, but rejected Jesus, and they will not get free from the fallen beings until they acknowledge this mistake and accept Jesus (not official Christianity) as the next step in their spiritual evolution. The fallen beings will no doubt be removed from this planet in the near future, and the brutal fact is that in their present state of mind, most Jews will have to follow them to wherever they go.

The point being that when Jesus entered the third year of his mission, a majority of the Jews had already rejected him. Yet he still managed to gather greater and greater crowds. Many people came because of the healings he performed, but they still encountered the power of the Spirit and they still heard the teaching given by the ascended masters through Jesus.

***

You might be wondering why official Christianity does not contain the concept of ascended masters. There are several reasons for this. One is, of course, that language develops over time. The exact words "ascended masters" were not used back then, and the reason for this is subtle, but important. It is very difficult for most people to imagine how the collective consciousness has evolved over time. We often look back at Jesus' time and think people back then knew almost as much as we did. In reality, we know this is not the case, but we tend to forget this. Even more importantly, we do not understand that people back then had a very different view of the world. We know that they did not see the earth as a round sphere and they did not understand the concept of the solar system that we take for granted. Yet we fail to understand how limited people's ability was to think in ways we take for granted.

As a simple example, take numbers. It is said in the scriptures that Jesus once spent 40 days fasting in the wilderness. This has caused some people to think that if they also fast for 40 days, they will receive some special spiritual experience or be healed of a disease. Yet, it is life-threatening to fast for that long and Jesus never did so. He did several times go away to be alone for some time, but never for 40 days. So where does the number 40 come from? It came from a Hebrew word that was used to refer to numbers larger than 12. Most people of the time rarely had to count higher than 12, and many people were unable to do so. They could not conceive of an amount larger than 12. Thus, they had a word that referred to numbers larger than 12, and it could be anything from 13 and up. This word was later translated into the exact number 40. Yet at Jesus' time it was not an exact number. Over time, people's ability to mentally deal with numbers has increased, and that is why we want everything to be in exact numbers.

Another example is how people today think of the solar system as existing in a three-dimensional space. Back then, most people could not think in three dimensions when it came to anything beyond the visible landscape. They could not conceive of a round planet floating around in a vast, three-dimensional space.

Because of people's limited ability to think, it was determined that Jesus would not speak publicly about ascended masters but refer to them only to his disciples. Of course, he used other words, such as the heavenly host.

It was not that Jesus deliberately lied or hid something from the public. It was simply that people were not able to grasp what he said. Jesus (or the ascended masters) through him would often give certain hints that would be overlooked by most but picked up by those who were ready for the path of Christhood.

***

Is there a hidden clue about ascended masters even in the official scriptures? Well, surprisingly, in Matthew 17, there is: "1. And after six days Jesus taketh Peter, James, and John his brother, and bringeth them up into an high mountain apart. 2. And was transfigured before them: and his face did shine as the sun, and his raiment was white as the light. 3. And, behold, there appeared unto them Moses and Elias talking with him."

Moses and Elijah were historical figures who had died centuries before Jesus. How could they appear to Jesus? Well, the simple explanation is that the ascended masters can, in certain cases, appear to people. In many cases, this happens (as with us when we saw Sanat Kumara in the Mystery School) when people have raised their consciousness. And with Jesus, this happened on a regular basis. Only one instance his recorded in the scriptures, but there were many more. In fact, let me describe a typical "day at the office" for Jesus.

# 43

It should by no means be construed that the following describes a unique day. On the contrary, days like these became more common towards the end of Jesus' mission. This was partly because Jesus raised his consciousness and grew in Christhood and partly because he attracted more people who had reached a certain level of Christhood. Back then, the collective consciousness was so low that it took a great number of people to create an opening for the ascended masters to appear.

In this case, we had been in the area north of the Sea of Galilee. We had been there for almost three weeks. Jesus had walked around to the different villages and preached in public places, also performing healings. This was the public aspect of his mission and it was open to anyone. Jesus' doings would typically last an entire day in the same place. Naturally, there would come a time when many people would have had their fill and would go home. Those who remained were told that on a particular Sunday, there would be a special event in a particular place, and they were welcome to attend.

After such a day was over, we would then walk to the next village if it was close. If the distance was greater, we would take part of the next day to travel. It was amazing to watch how Jesus was able to sustain such a rigorous schedule, but he was clearly strengthened by the power of the Spirit. The rest of us found it hard to keep up with him.

***

When the day for the special event came, we had gathered the day before so we were all well-rested. Those of us who invoked light on behalf of Jesus got up before dawn, as was our custom. On this day, Jesus joined us, which he usually did only when he was burdened by energy from the people he had ministered onto during the weeks prior. After we had invoked light for a couple of hours, Jesus looked full of energy. The sun had now risen, and after breakfast, we went to the place for the event.

Jesus had, as was normal, chosen a place where the hills formed a natural amphitheater. This would allow him to stand in the level space between the hills and the people could sit on all sides. People could therefore easily see him, and they could also hear him better as the sound was reflected from the hills.

Some people had already started coming, and we soon had them giving invocations. These were more simple invocations than the ones we gave in the group, but they were still very powerful. The entire purpose of the day was to create an energetic platform so we would create a higher vibration in the area than normal. The purpose was two-fold. One was to make it easier for the people to raise their consciousness and attune to the ascended masters. The other was to make it possible for the masters to lower their vibration so that some people could see them directly. You might say it was an interactive effort between the ascended masters and the people attending, and the purpose was to give the people a direct experience of the masters.

*** 

By mid-morning, several hundred people had arrived. We now had a session where some of the people who had been trained by Jesus would give teachings about the path to Christhood. These were far more direct and detailed teachings than the ones given at the public meetings. The purpose was that people who were new could gain a deeper understanding of the path offered to them by the people working under Jesus. The people who gave these presentations were usually from the local area so they could serve as the teachers for those who were willing to engage in the path.

This session lasted until mid-day. We then gave people the opportunity to eat food they had brought with them. We would have the people who wanted to eat move back up the hills. Others would move closer and we would have them invoke light. People would then rotate until all had eaten.

After this, Jesus entered the central place. On this particular day, he looked very bright, as his energy field was shining so powerfully that even his physical countenance seemed to radiate a subtle glow. He started by asking who needed healing before they could focus on his teaching. Naturally, some of the people had received healings during the previous weeks, but some had not. As these people came forward, Jesus would do something he did not do during the public sessions. Instead of laying hands on people and praying for them, be would now read people's auras. He would then explain what changes the person needed to make in his or her mind in order to be healed.

If the person was able to shift his or her perception, then the healing would occur. Other people in the audience with the same problem could also be healed as they shifted their perception. For each disease, Jesus had a relatively simple explanation of the corresponding illusion that needed to be overcome. Jesus would explain the illusion in a very direct manner. If people had their eyes opened and gave up the illusion, they would be healed. Some people rejected the exposure and felt offended by Jesus' directness. They could not be healed, and most of them left in anger. In some cases, other people in the audience, unwilling to give up the same illusion, also left.

The purpose of this was twofold. One was, obviously, to heal those who could be healed so they were free from worrying about the disease and could participate fully in the rest of the event. The other purpose was to filter out those who were not willing to raise their consciousness. These people would be a dead weight that would drag down the rest of the group. If there were too many of them, the group might not be able to raise its consciousness sufficiently for the ascended masters to appear.

*** 

After the healings, we would again invoke spiritual light for a time. This would last until Jesus determined that the energetic forcefield had been raised sufficiently. Because I could see auras of the people and of the group as a whole, I could see when the shift happened and all fear-based energies had been pushed away or transformed. The people were now free from the gravitational pull of the mass consciousness and were open to a higher teaching.

Jesus would then stand up and start talking. He would often tell stories about his previous lifetimes and how he had faced various challenges on his own path. It never failed that the examples told by Jesus were relevant to a large part of the audience, and I could see how people's auras shifted as they listened to Jesus. I could often see how a specific person had an energetic knot in his aura that was limiting the flow of energy from the I AM Presence. As the person was listening to Jesus, the knot would begin to loosen, and at a certain point, it would literally fall away and the person's aura would start to pulsate more brightly than before. During this process, many people would start crying or even shake violently. As the release happened, they would fall still and their eyes would be shining brightly.

This session could last several hours until Jesus had helped every person in the group resolve some knot in their three higher bodies. It is obvious that by Jesus telling so openly and honestly about his personal challenges, every one in the audience could relate to him as an older brother who had simply walked further on the path than themselves. None of the people who attended these sessions ever saw Jesus as anything but an example. None saw him as an idol, let alone as the only son of god.

\*\*\*

When the audience had been cleared sufficiently, Jesus would start talking more intensely, soon coming under the flow of the Spirt. This was something that also happened at public sessions, but in this case it was even more intense. This was still Jesus speaking, although with a power that clearly was beyond his own. It is not really so important what was said here, as it was a message tailored to the particular audience and aimed at raising their consciousness further.

After some time of this, Jesus would fall silent. He would then explain more clearly about ascended masters and explain that nothing he did or had ever done was by himself or his own power. He directly acknowledged that he was working under the lineage of the ascended masters and that they were the ones directing his mission. He also explained that a step up from speaking by the power of the Spirit was to take a direct dictation where a master would speak through him.

On this day, he explained that Archangel Michael would address the people. Jesus then closed his eyes to focused within, and after a few seconds, he opened his mouth and said: "I AM Archangel Michael, the protector of all of God's people . . ." Jesus was not in a trance but was fully conscious of what was being said. Yet he had been trained to set aside his mind so it would not interfere with what was said. Jesus could break off the dictation, but his mind did not limit the master speaking through him. In this case, the dictation lasted almost an hour and it gave profound teachings about the history of the fallen beings on earth. I will not give it verbatim here as it was completely in line with what Sanat Kumara had told us at the Mystery School.

It was amazing to sense the difference in vibration between Jesus speaking, Jesus speaking under the power of the Spirit and Jesus taking a direct dictation. Each time it was a distinct step up in vibration. Naturally, I could see the ethereal figure of Archangel Michael over Jesus, and some people among the audience could see this as well. Yet he majority of the audience could not directly see the master.

After the dictation was over, the audience repeated a mantra that was given to us by Archangel Michael. It is not easy to translate directly into English, but it was very similar to this:

Archangel Michael, banish all fear-based energies in this place.

We are set apart from the world, being *in* the world, but not *of* the world.

We are of one accord in one place.

We are the Body of God on earth.

We acknowledge the heavenly host as the Body of God in heaven.

We use the authority of Christ within us to call forth a thinning of the veil between heaven and earth.

We acknowledge Jesus as the open door between heaven and earth.

We acknowledge our oneness with the heavenly host.

We form the Body of God, as Above so below.

After the crowd had repeated this mantra many, many times, most people could physically hear a very high-pitched, pulsating, vibrating sound. They could then see a white light appearing around Jesus in the center. By this time, Jesus was standing with his eyes closed, his face turned upwards and the palm of his hands turned upwards. After some time of continuing the chant, there appeared three cylinders of the most intense white light you can possibly imagine. Each cylinder seemed like a portal for looking into what we today would call another dimension.

At this point, some of the people in the audience could no longer handle the higher vibrations. They would start crying and some would fall to the ground, shaking violently.

Very slowly, there now appeared within each cylinder the outline of a figure. This outline seemed to be gradually filled with light, and eventually most people in the audience could see an ascended master. This was a truly amazing sight, although its clarity varied from person to person. Some could see only a faint outline while others saw the master with such clarity of detail that it was more clear than anything they had ever seen. In today's concepts, it would be the equivalent of seeing a photo on an old-fashioned computer screen and seeing it on a high-resolution or retina display.

On this day, the appearance of the masters lasted for some time and one of the masters spoke with Jesus, giving him instructions for the last part of his mission, including his going to Jerusalem. Only a few people could hear this, some of it could be heard by Jesus only.

As was the case with every such event, the masters remained visible for as long as a certain percentage of the group could keep up the chanting. The light of the masters was so intense that more and more people could not handle it, and they either fainted or sat quietly. As the number of people chanting decreased, the masters started to fade. On this day, the entire apparition lasted for almost an hour, which was more than usual.

\*\*\*

After this apparition, there was not much anyone could say. Jesus allowed people a long time to sit with closed eyes and process the experience individually. Finally, most people had opened their eyes, and there was a shift in awareness as we all realized we had gone into the evening and we were all starving.

Most people had not brought enough food, but as was the custom, Jesus asked that all people bring their food forward and place it on the ground before him. When it was done, he raised his arms and said with a very powerful voice: "We acknowledge our oneness with the masters of

Spirit and we are grateful beyond measure for this visible proof of your existence and your unfailing guidance. We know we are truly spiritual beings in human bodies, not human beings in animal bodies. We acknowledge that our spiritual needs are far superior to our bodily needs. Yet as we have spent the entire day being focused on our spiritual needs, we also acknowledge that we have bodily needs. We therefore ask you, our masters in Spirit, to multiply this food we have brought forward so that there will be enough for the sustenance of our bodies that we may go out and spread the message of the true path to God. We accept it done this instant in all four levels of matter. Amen."

The entire audience repeated the "Amen," and instantly the food was multiplied manifold. It literally shifted in an instant from the previous amount to the new amount. People came forward and we took some time to fill our bodies. Interestingly, a few people had not brought some food forward, instead preferring to keep it for themselves, and the food they had kept had instantly disappeared when the other food was multiplied. To him that gives, more shall be given. To he that seeks to keep, even what he has shall be taken away.

***

When all had eaten, it was evening time, and people had to get home or to their sleeping places before dark. Despite having been going since before dawn, Jesus stood at a place near the exit so that all who wanted to could walk by him. He greeted each person individually, often giving them some personal instruction, and this lasted until after dark.

Then, it was time for all of us to rest, and many of us slept in the hills under the open sky, not truly wanting to leave the energetic forcefield that was still very intense. Jesus walked up into the hills hand in hand with Mary Magdalen, who had been his faithful companion since the second year of his mission.

# 44

Naturally, my remark that Jesus went off into the hills with Mary Magdalen raises the topic that most Christians are extremely reluctant to talk about, let alone think about, namely sex. Even more taboo is the topic of sex in relation to Jesus. I mean "Did Jesus have a sex life?" could be considered one of the most forbidden questions of Christianity. And that's precisely why I will comment on it.

The first thing we need to understand is that the topic of sex was viewed quite differently at Jesus' time. This is primarily due to the fact that people had not been exposed to that singularly sinister idea of original sin, channeled by that fallen being in embodiment, Augustine, from his fallen master in the identity realm. For almost 1700 years, the Christian world has been programmed with this highly artificial concept of sex that has completely distorted people's view of the topic.

At Jesus' time, people had a more relaxed view of sex, although it varied widely from place to place. Back then, there was no mass media so there was no public debate about anything. No one could write a book or article that could then be read by thousands of people. Talk about any topic was between people in the local area, and it varied widely how people talked about sex (or didn't). But in general, people were far more relaxed than many mainstream Christians are today.

That is not to say that there was no stigma related to sex at the time. You cannot even begin to have an aware conversation about sex without understanding how the fallen beings work. You can find a hint of this in the story of Adam and Eve. Before they ate the forbidden fruit, they were naked but didn't think anything of it. After they had eaten the fruit, they suddenly saw their nakedness as something shameful and had to cover their bodies.

If you are willing to look at this based on its symbolic value, the forbidden fruit represents the duality consciousness. Before you enter duality, you see it as perfectly natural that you are naked. What is the need to cover the way you were created? However, even on natural planets people generally wear clothes, partly because of shifting temperatures and partly because they like decorating their bodies. On a natural planet everyone has a beautiful body and thus has nothing to hide, but there is still enjoyment in using beautiful clothing. The way you dress is simply one way to express your creativity.

As soon as people enter duality, they fall into performing value judgments. This does not automatically mean they judge it as shameful to be naked, but this idea can so easily be introduced by the fallen beings. The serpent in the Garden of Eden is a symbol for the fallen beings, even for the duality consciousness in a broad sense.

Naturally, once the fallen beings have introduced the sense of shame about being naked, people will want to be naked only in private. Since most people are naked while having sex, then sex also becomes a private matter and then the sense of shame relating to sex is easily introduced by the fallen beings.

Take care to see the broader picture. On a natural planet, people do not have sex. There is a process whereby people of what we call opposite sexes can come together and achieve a sense of oneness, but it is not based on having sexual organs. This sense of oneness is very difficult to achieve on an unnatural planet because of the density of the physical bodies.

On an unnatural planet, bodies must develop sexual organs, as that becomes the only way to propagate. It now becomes possible that sexual intercourse can give a man and a woman a deeper sense of oneness than they can achieve otherwise. This becomes even more important on an unnatural planet because the development of distinctly male and female bodies creates an unavoidable imbalance.

On a natural planet, all beings are balanced within themselves and do not actually need any other being to find balance. On an unnatural planet, it is very difficult to find balance within oneself. It can be achieved, but only when one reaches the upper levels of the 144 levels of consciousness. All people at lower levels (meaning 99 percent of the people on earth) find it very difficult to achieve balance within themselves. Thus, it is natural on an unnatural planet that men and women have sexual intercourse in order to balance each other. Therefore, one must say that on an unnatural planet, sex is very natural and beneficial. It is, of course, also necessary in order to produce offspring.

Can you sense how sinister is the fallen beings' plot to make sex shameful? Sex is necessary for propagation so all physical bodies have programmed into their subconscious computers the desire to have sex. Besides that, all people have an imbalance in their four lower bodies between the masculine and feminine energies, meaning all people have a desire for achieving balance and subconsciously know sex is one way to do this. So people *need* to have sex and they *want* to have sex. How extremely sinister to take this tendency and use it to cause conflict in the individual and conflict between men and women.

How incredibly deceptive to make people at war with their physical bodies and with those of the opposite sex (or the same sex). How futile to give spiritual people the impression that the only way to be truly spiritual is to suppress the sex drive. How many spiritual people have, over the millennia, spent their energy and attention on suppressing the sex drive while making no spiritual progress as a result? Render onto Caesar (the body) that which is Caesar's and onto God (your spiritual growth) that which is God's. In other words, as long as sex does not distract you from your spiritual pursuits, there is nothing wrong or anti-spiritual about it. In fact, for most people, sex practiced with a certain awareness can be beneficial to their spiritual growth.

***

Naturally, Jesus was quit aware of this. I earlier described how Jesus for some years went out among the people to experience how they lived and thought, including drinking with people in bars. Did you really think Jesus did not explore sex during that time?

Jesus did indeed have sex and with many different women. Now, this does not mean Jesus was acting like many young people do today. Jesus was quite conscious that he had more spiritual light than most people. People would not consciously know what was different about him, but they would sense it subconsciously. This meant Jesus could make just about any woman fall in love with him because she would fall in love with the light. Jesus was quite aware that this was not what he wanted so he was very careful about not giving women an opportunity to fall in love with him, as he had no intention of settling down anywhere.

Yet Jesus also had a desire to explore sexuality, even though he had obviously done so in previous embodiments. As a result, Jesus only had sex with women who were not likely to fall in love with him, which primarily meant prostitutes and women who were sexually promiscuous without making a living from it.

After some time, Jesus began to be dissatisfied with this, but he still felt he had not transcended the desire for sex. His goal was, of course, to transcend all bodily desires so he had no attachments. He once told me that the only bodily activity he had trouble giving up was sex. However, after reflecting on this, he realized that his reluctance to give it up was related to the desire to have balance between masculine and feminine energies.

\*\*\*

Soon after, Jesus felt he was led to find a special monastery in the Himalayas that admitted both men and women. This monastery was dedicated to helping spiritual seekers deal with their sexual desires in a variety of ways. They had a special herbal product that prevented women from becoming pregnant so they could freely have sex. They also had various ways to prevent sexually transmitted disease.

At the lowest level of the monastery, you would find people who had developed an unbalanced desire for sex in previous embodiments. They would attend a special program with several elements. One element was that the people were told about the emotional octave, or the astral plane that is the lower part of the emotional octave. This is where you find a lot of lower beings, often called demons or addictive entities. These are collective spirits that human beings have created over time, and they have become so powerful that they can overpower people who have a certain weakness in their psychology.

These mass entities are behind every addiction known to humans. They are extremely ugly beings, and if you could see how they have inserted hooks into your aura, it would increase your motivation to get rid of them. The people in the monastery were taught about this and even shown drawings made by some clairvoyant monks. They were told how the entities were using the addiction to sex to drain people of their energy. They were shown that the entities had created an artificial desire for sex, a desire that was impossible to fill. No matter how much sex people have, the entities will always want more because their need goes beyond what they can get from one individual. You are literally like a cow that is tied up and milked for your energy, your spiritual light.

In today's world, partly through the availability of pornography and the free talk about sex, most young people have literally become addicted to sex, and the addiction often lasts for a lifetime. These people are milked for their creative energies, and the energies go into a black hole. People who are sex addicted will make no spiritual progress for that lifetime. This, of course, is the real purpose of any kind of addiction.

The people in the monastery were taught this and they were asked to consider if they truly wanted to overcome this sex addiction. Only those who made a vow to do this, were allowed to stay. These people were then given spiritual techniques for invoking the light of the ascended masters. There are certain ascended masters, such as Archangel Michael (but also the other six archangels) who will protect you from the influence of the astral plane (not against your free will, naturally). There are other masters, such as Shiva and Elohim Astrea, who can cut you free from any ties to the astral plane.

Once you have isolated yourself from the astral plane, you can begin to look at the fact that what made you vulnerable to a sex addiction was that you had developed an unbalanced desire for sex in past lives. You can then realize that the only way to truly overcome this desire is to have so much sex that you have enough of it. You are saturated with the experience.

Many young people today have the subconscious sense that they have a need to have a certain amount of sex. It is a legitimate sense because they do need to overcome the unbalanced desire for sex. But because they have not been taught about the astral plane, their legitimate desire for sex becomes an addiction. An addiction becomes a black whole that can never be filled, meaning many people never reach the saturation point. Instead of coming to a point where they feel they have had enough sex and can move on with their spiritual growth, people become stuck in an unfulfillable desire.

The people at the monastery were given help to saturate themselves with sex without becoming stuck in an addiction. Most of them could relatively quickly move on to a higher level. Incidentally, Jesus and I did not enter this program, as we had already overcome any addiction to sex (or anything else).

*** 

The next step up was to teach people about the masculine and feminine forces and the fact that our physical bodies have an imbalance between the two energies or elements. People would be given teachings on this, and they were also given the opportunity to practice sex that had a higher purpose than satisfying the bodily needs. The purpose was that a man and a woman would practice sex in order to help both of them achieve balance between masculine and feminine energies.

Jesus wanted to enter this program and encouraged me to do the same. I had no particular desire for it, as sex really never had that much of an interest for me. But since I had taken advantage of every other opportunity for growth I had come across, I entered the program and was assigned a partner. She was a truly beautiful being and we were very successful in achieving balance.

After some time working on balance, we went on to the highest level of the program, which was to use our newfound balance to practice sex for the purpose of achieving a spiritual union or oneness. The fallen beings wanted to pervert people's view of sex partly to prevent people from attaining balance, but they especially wanted to prevent men and women from achieving oneness. This horizontal oneness can be developed into a vertical oneness where the partners help each other develop oneness with their I AM Presences. The fallen beings will do anything to prevent this. Naturally, they had no influence within this hidden monastery.

I want to mention that using sex to achieve spiritual union is not the same as what many people today see as Tantric sex, at least not the most popular forms of tantric sex. In its lower form, Tantra is aimed at raising certain energies that in Hinduism are called the Kundalini. This is a practice that should only be performed by students who have been trained by and are under the supervision of an experienced teacher. For the unguided, raising the Kundalini can be dangerous and can lead to severe imbalances, even insanity. Many modern spiritual students have ended up in mental institutions as a result of seeking to force the Kundalini in an unbalanced desire for spiritual experiences. The problem, again, is that many people engage in Tantric sex without having cut their ties to the addictive entities in the astral plane. This is a recipe for disaster.

In the monastery, the forms of sex practiced at the higher level did not have the goal of raising the Kundalini. It had the goal of creating genuine union between a man and a woman, and this cannot be forced. It can be achieved only through genuine love, meaning a non-possessive love. The pairs engaging in this level knew they would be partners only for a time so they did not develop any attachments to each other. Yet they also developed a genuine love that meant there were no barriers between them. Both partners only wanted to achieve this spiritual union. Some pairs did end up forming life-long partnerships after the program, but many also went their separate ways to pursue their spiritual growth individually, now that they had transcended any pull from sex. I am not thereby saying all spiritual people have to transcend all sexual activity. The higher union can be pursued by a man and a woman dedicated to this without allowing themselves to develop the obsessive-compulsive patterns that are normally called a love relationship in the modern world.

It took Jesus almost a year before he felt he was done with this program, and that is when we moved on to the monastery where Jesus entered the cave. Jesus had to overcome the last remnants of any desire for sex, he had to balance his masculine and feminine energies and he had to achieve the higher union with a woman that led him to a higher union with his I AM Presence. *Then,* he was ready to spend years alone in a cave.

***

Let me go back to the plot of the fallen beings, which goes even deeper. I have explained (a long time ago) that the material world was created from two basic forces, the expanding force and the contracting force. On an unnatural planet, it is obvious to associate the expanding force with the male or father element and the contracting force with the female or mother element. The physical body of a man has an imbalance where the masculine element is stronger than the female. The physical body of a woman has the opposite imbalance. This is due to the density of matter and so far has nothing to do with the fallen beings.

Yet the fallen beings quickly realized that the existence of male and female bodies gave them the potential to create a fundamental division between men and women. It can therefore be stated with unequivocal clarity that any and all conflicts between men and women on earth originated with the fallen beings. They have ruthlessly used the differences between our bodies to create a state of animosity, even sometimes war, between the two sexes. This is all done in order to increase the tension and chaos on earth. The greater purpose is to get us to destroy ourselves so we will (in the eyes of the fallen beings) have proven the fallacy of the Creator giving us free will. Men and women have simply become pawns in the utterly pointless power game of the fallen beings.

\*\*\*

Jesus was, naturally, well aware of this. He was therefore determined to create a spiritual movement like no other on earth. In the official scriptures, it is described that Jesus called only male disciples. This is a complete distortion of reality. Jesus had as many female disciples as he had male disciples. It is a blatant distortion of the fallen beings to deny this.

Jesus also made it very clear that in the movement he initiated, there would be no discrimination of woman. He wanted a clear break with the persecution of women and with the entire mentality that portrays men as superior to women. This, of course, is another tool used by the fallen beings to increase conflict between the sexes.

Do you see how sinister this is? The fallen beings have an overall goal of creating as much conflict as possible. This is most easily done between groups of people who have clear differences, such as race, ethnicity, nationality and so on. Yet this conflict between groups takes place at an overall level, the level of society. The fallen beings were not content with this, but wanted to take their conflict into the basic unit of society, namely the home. You will notice that in most cultures, the leaders of society have limited authority to interfere physically with what takes place within the home. Yet they don't need to interfere physically when they have already created a conflict between men and women that (both back then and today) can often turn the home into a war zone.

The war between men and women was, naturally, developed because the fallen beings want to create war between various groups. Since men's bodies are generally stronger physically, they were more suited for primitive warfare requiring hand-to-hand combat. It was therefore easy to develop the concept that men are created by god to be superior. The other aspect of this is that men are more easily manipulated into going to war, and the reason is that they have an imbalance of the masculine, expansive element. In its most unbalanced form, this gives the desire to conquer territories or even spread one idea as the dominant one on earth. So men were physically more suited for war and psychologically more prone to be manipulated. That is the only reason the fallen beings pronounced men superior to women.

Jesus wanted a movement that was based on an understanding of the natural roles of men and women. Women are in no way shape or form created inferior to men. Co-creators in female bodies are fully as capable of attaining spiritual growth as men. Therefore, Jesus wanted a movement where women could hold any position and participate in any activity. He wanted a movement where it was not a person's sex that determined what it could achieve, but only its willingness to walk the path and achieve genuine progress. As a result of this, Jesus also taught the truth about the myth of the Garden of Eden, as I have relayed it here. It is another plot of the fallen beings that the Christian scriptures came to incorporate the Old Testament and the creation myth in its original, primitive form.

Take note also that I have given a slightly distorted view of the incarnations of Jesus and myself by only describing male incarnations. We both had female incarnations as well. This is the case for most people. When you embody as a male for several lifetimes, you tend to get imbalanced in the masculine energies. If you cannot change this consciously, you must incarnate as a female is several embodiments until you have restored some kind of balance. If you are balanced, you can choose in which sex you want to embody.

Naturally, Jesus and I had many embodiments where we were fighting the fallen beings, and that meant we tended to embody in male bodies. Yet when we got too unbalanced, we would have to embody in female bodies for a time. Incidentally, if you have embodied in female bodies for a time and then shift to a male body, your three higher bodies cannot shift so easily and carry with them more of the female energies. This explains why some people cannot identify with the sex of their physical bodies, be it homosexually or transgender issues. Naturally, the same goes for people who have embodied in male bodies for a time and shift to female bodies. Usually, after another couple of embodiments, people will adjust and now accept the sex of their physical bodies.

\*\*\*

Back to Mary Magdalen and Jesus. I mentioned a long time ago that Jeshu had met a woman who was an avatar and had taken embodiment on earth specifically to help him ascend. This creates a bond between two life-streams that in many spiritual teachings is seen as a "twin flame" relationship. Jesus and Magda embodied together in many embodiments and often had a love relationship. I have not written much about this so far, as it really didn't have an impact on the main story.

Yet once people have formed such a strong bond, they will often gravitate together and find each other despite being born in different places. Whom do you think was Jesus' partner in the monastery where he practiced sexual union? It was, naturally, Magda. After Jesus had completed that cycle, they parted, but naturally they kept in telepathic contact. So after we returned to Galilee, Magda traveled there and found us during the first year of Jesus' mission.

I know there are many stories about Jesus and Mary Magdalen being married, but they are untrue. There are two reasons for this. Magda (as I will call her from now on) had actually been married before entering the monastery. She had been forced by her parents to marry an older man who already had several wives. She knew this was contrary to her Divine plan and had used the same herbal remedy as used in the monastery to avoid becoming pregnant. Her husband had been abusive and had become increasingly more so as she was not giving him children (all he cared about from her). She finally decided to run away (no easy task for a woman back then) and eventually found her way to the monastery and Jesus. By the way, she was not from Magdala, but Magdalena was her middle name, and it became used to distinguish her from the several other Marys associated with Jesus (it was a common name at the time).

Back then, there were no passports, marriage certificates or computer records. Since Magda had not been married in Galilee but in what is now Iran, once she was in Galilee, no one knew she was married. So theoretically, she and Jesus could have married. However, if Jesus had married her, he was sure Lucifer would have found out and then Magda would have become a target for Lucifer. Jesus was hoping that by keeping a low profile, Magda would slide under Lucifer's radar, but that hope was only partially fulfilled, as we will see later.

I need to mention also that Magda naturally was not a prostitute. This was something added by the fallen beings in order to discredit her and the idea that Jesus had female disciples. Also, Magda was not the woman out of whom Jesus cast seven devils. This was actually Maleve who had deserved the opportunity to have her seven chakras cleared in order to put herself on the path to Christhood.

What I wanted to mention here was that Jesus and Magda did have what we today would call a sexual relationship. However, it was not sexual in the way we see this in the modern world. Yes, they did have sex, but it was for achieving the higher union and the balance between male and female energies, as they were taught in the monastery. This is beyond what is today seen as a sexual relationship. This was something only a few of Jesus' closer associates knew about, and although it is true, as it says in the Gospel of Philip, that Jesus would occasionally "kiss her on the mouth" when the disciples were present, this never happened in a public setting.

\*\*\*

The really important thing about Magda is that she became the most advanced of all of Jesus' disciples. This was not because Jesus showed her any special favours but because in previous lifetimes, Magda had already developed a very high level of consciousness. She was therefore very quick to respond to Jesus' teachings.

Why was she quicker than the other disciples? Because the disciples were chosen to represent the entire range of human consciousness, from the lowest to the higher levels on the scale of the 144 levels. Now, there obviously were few people at the highest levels to choose from so Magda had the highest level of consciousness of all of the disciples. There were many to choose from among the lowest levels, but most of them refused to follow Jesus.

The disciple with the lowest level of consciousness was Peter. He represented the levels right below the 48th level. I have explained that a new lifestream originally descended to earth at the 48th level. Going below that means going into duality. This is not done out of any selfish intent, but actually because one becomes deceived into thinking that one is doing this for some benign purpose The trick is that one believes one knows and can define what is benign. In other words, you think you know better than those with a higher state of consciousness, and thus you think you can tell them what they should do. This is the stage where you fall in love with an idea and begin to think the universe should function according to your idea.

Peter represented this state of consciousness. Naturally, it was the hope that under Jesus' guidance, he would rise above it and lock in to the path to Christhood. Unfortunately, Peter was not willing to do this, as was the case with the vast majority of people at the time. As we will see, this had a major impact on Christianity, making it so very easy for the fallen beings to turn the movement started by Jesus into such an efficient mind-control machine. But I am again getting ahead of myself.

# 45

Contrary to what it says in the scriptures, Peter was not a fisherman. He had been born into a family of fishermen, but he was not satisfied with this trade because he had a compulsory desire to be an important person. He had therefore left his family and gone to Jerusalem to seek a higher status. He had eventually come in the service of Lucifer who had him do various jobs, some of which required the use of sharp weapons and were of questionable morality. He was a sort of religious enforcer. Peter had become very impressed with Lucifer and held him in high regard. When Jesus came back to Galilee, Lucifer was told this by his master in the identity realm. However, there was no immediate cause to kill him so Lucifer sent Peter to keep an eye on Jesus.

Jesus was naturally aware of this but allowed it because the ascended masters tutoring Jesus evaluated Peter as having the potential to be turned around by Jesus. So Jesus knew that Peter was not on the same level as the other disciples, but he was hoping Peter would lock in to the true path. Peter did have an ability to recognize something special in Jesus, and Peter did have some mystical experiences as a result of following Jesus.

Peter had quite a temper and he could become violent. He also had an acute sense of status and a desire to set up a pecking order among the people following Jesus—with himself on top, naturally. This became a constant frustration for Peter, as Jesus never responded to his attempts to set up a formal rank among the disciples. To Jesus, there was only one way to evaluate people, namely based on their willingness to transcend their current level of consciousness and then the level to which they had currently risen. Peter simply could not get this, and, to be fair, he was not the only one, as this sense of rank was very important in the Jewish culture back then. Of course, rank is important in any culture dominated by the fallen beings because they always want to create a hierarchy with themselves as the undisputed leaders.

\*\*\*

Peter's desire to be more important than the other disciples led to many bizarre situations. I will relay just one. For a time, a boy at the age of 10 was following us. Jesus allowed this and the boy began doing various small services for anyone in the group needing it. Peter took advantage of this and almost made him his personal servant. The boy had followed us because he sensed Jesus' light, but he was not mature enough to realize that not everyone following Jesus had the same level of consciousness as Jesus. Thus, he assumed (as did many adult people) that all of Jesus' close disciples had a high level of Christhood. A common problem in all religious and spiritual movements: elevation by association.

One day, the boy had done a job for Peter and Peter was not satisfied with the execution of it. I came by when Peter was in the process of giving the boy a chastisement. Because I could see the red anger in Peter's energy field, I stayed and watched. Peter worked himself up to quite a state and at one point grabbed a stick and was clearly going to beat the boy, something entirely alien to Jesus' teachings. I quickly stepped between them and said gently: "Peter, I think he has understood your point and there is no need for violence."

Peter looked at me, and at first he was amazed. I must interject here that I had no special status amongst the people following Jesus. They knew I had known Jesus since childhood, but neither Jesus nor I talked about our journey together and I was always in the background. I was not one of the disciples and did not participate when Jesus taught them. Instead, I was invoking light or performing other tasks to help Jesus. I was therefore not looked at as being anyone special and most of the disciples considered me an unimportant person.

Peter was, naturally, one of them, and when he saw it was me who had interfered with what he saw as his legitimate business, his surprise quickly turned to disdain. It was clear that in Peter's mind, he was *somebody* and I was a *nobody* so I had no right to tell him what to do. His disdain quickly turned to anger, and he stepped closer to me, saying: "And just who are you to tell me what to do. I don't recall asking for your advice, and if I want to give this boy a beating, I will do so, unless you want to take it instead."

At this point, I focused my attention in my heart chakra and became completely neutral. There was uncompromising peace inside of me, and I looked Peter directly in the eye with no aggression but also with no submission. He was obviously confused by this, as he had expected me to either cower and withdraw or to fight back. Our eyes locked for what became one of these moments where time stood still. Peter was the one who blinked first, and he turned away from me, taking a couple of steps. Then, he quickly turned and swung the stick at me. I knew this was coming, so I was completely at peace, in my mind forming a perfect mirror, as I had learned from Jesus. This meant that as Peter was striking me, the four levels of my mind did not react to his aggression. I was not afraid and I had no desire to strike back or punish.

The result was that all of the aggressive energy Peter directed at me was reflected back to him instantly, literally knocking him to the ground before the stick hit me. Peter was shaking and lay senseless for some time. I calmly turned to the boy and asked him to help me do some menial task. Peter never referred to the incident, but from that time on, he kept a wide distance to me, and we actually never spoke again (which we had hardly done before).

***

I know many Christians (especially Catholics) want to keep Peter on the pedestal upon which he has been put by the Catholic church. However, this cannot be done when one is telling the real story of Jesus' life and mission. I know some will say: "Well, what about the passage in Matthew 16 where Jesus says that Peter is the rock upon which he will build his church?" My answer is that the official interpretation of this is completely out of touch with what actually happened and what was Jesus' intent. However, explaining this requires us to go into some subtleties that illustrate the deeper purpose of Jesus.

First of all, Jesus never, *ever* did or said anything that was relevant only to a specific situation or person. Everything he did or said had some wider, more universal purpose. As I said, each of the disciples represented a certain level of consciousness. Peter represented the lowest level of consciousness that was capable of responding to Jesus. Peter himself thought Jesus cared about him personally, but Jesus was completely impersonal in his dealings with people. Everything Jesus did or said relating to Peter truly was directed at all people with that level of consciousness. Jesus was well aware that his mission was not to save specific people but to give a universal teaching that could help all people qualify for salvation by transcending all lower levels of consciousness. Now, here is a question that few people bother to ask: "What did it take to be one of the early followers of Jesus?"

I have met many Christians who assume that if they had been around at Jesus' time, they would naturally have recognized him and followed him. They usually become angry when I suggest that they most likely would have rejected Jesus because their minds are as closed as were the minds of the scribes, the Pharisees and the many other people who rejected Jesus. The minds of modern Christians are closed precisely because official Christianity is exactly the same kind of religion as the Jewish religion of the time. A religion led by the fallen beings will never recognize the Living Christ.

In order to follow Jesus, one had to be willing to look outside the official doctrines. What would make a person capable of recognizing that Jesus had something special? Jesus did perform many so-called miracles where people could physically see a change, such as a lame man being able to walk again or water turned into wine. Yet even amongst people who physically experienced such miracles, only a few actually followed Jesus. What was the difference between those who recognized Jesus and those who did not? It can be summed up in one modern word: "Intuition."

\*\*\*

I have said that all of humankind has descended into and become blinded by duality. I have said that the duality consciousness becomes a self-fulfilling prophecy because we cannot see beyond it. And it is correct that we cannot see beyond it with the outer mind, the analytical mind. There is no analytical reasoning that does not have an opposite viewpoint, meaning you can never find a final argument. It simply is not possible to come up with a final rational argument for Jesus' teachings, which is why modern Christians have such trouble with materialism.

I realize many religious, political and materialistic theories claim to have a final argument, but that is because the fallen beings are so good at elevating one relative viewpoint to the status of seeming absolute. How do they do this? By defining that there are certain basic conditions that one should not or cannot doubt, either because they supposedly are self-evident or have some absolute authority (based on a religious scripture, a political necessity or the laws of nature). While this gives the appearance of being a final truth, it also will be unable to explain many questions. You will not find answers to these questions until you go beyond the "final" truth.

So the people who recognized Jesus did not do so based on analytical thinking. They did so because they followed their intuition, they followed their hearts. It is true that duality blinds us, but we have been given a safety mechanism that means we can never be completely blinded by duality. That safety mechanism is the ability to read the energetic vibration of anything. What we today call intuition is (in its basic form) the ability to read energies and therefore sense that some energies are higher than others. Anyone reading this book will have continued to read to this point only because the book stirred an intuitive sense that there is something worthwhile. Anyone can center their attention on the heart center (in the center of the chest) and feel whether a certain situation or idea creates a sinking feeling or an uplifting feeling. This is intuition in its simplest form, and all people have it. We all have the potential to read vibration and therefore sense the validity of an idea in a way that is beyond rational argument and analytical thinking.

You can never lose this ability, but you can deny it and cover it over. The ultimate example of people who have done this are the fallen beings. Lucifer had completely and utterly denied his intuition. It was the only way he could have fallen in the first place and the only way he could continue to be in the fallen consciousness. His intuition clearly told him that refusing to self-transcend in his original sphere was not the highest choice. His intuition could have told him this here on earth, but he had buried it so deeply that he never noticed it.

Because the fallen beings do not have conscious intuition, they cannot read a vibration that is beyond duality. Thus, they cannot sense that something is valid, even if there is no rational argument for it (or even if there is a rational argument against it). Therefore, they have done everything possible to make all people on earth distrust, deny and bury their intuitive faculties. The last thing the fallen beings want is for people to use their intuitive faculties because the fallen beings know that if you have good intuition, you will not be fooled by any of their clearly dualistic arguments or thought systems. You may not be able to come up with a rational explanation for why you reject this fancy idea, you simply *know* that it does not "vibrate right." Just look at how those who represent the fallen consciousness in today's world (found in both materialism and official Christianity) will mock this statement.

The deeper reality is that in the design of your being is incorporated the ability for the Conscious You to step (at least partially) outside your four lower bodies and thereby sense a vibration or impulse coming from your I AM Presence or the ascended masters. When you have this frame of reference, your heart chakra can compare it to the vibration of any idea on earth. You will then experience whether the idea vibrates at a lower level than the impulse from your I AM Presence. If it does, you know "there is something rotten in Denmark."

One goal of the fallen beings is to make all people distrust their inner guidance so they only follow some kind of external authority, or at least their rational, analytical, linear mind. The fallen beings know they can never control your intuitive prompting, and they know they are in control of all of the external authorities found on earth—every single one of them, regardless of the claims they make officially. They also know they can run circles around your rational mind.

*** 

Okay, I digressed again. The point was that all of those who recognized Jesus did so because they were using their intuition to some capacity. This goes for Peter as well. Peter did not respond only to the outer miracles, he also had some intuitive prompting, although not as clear as those of the other disciples. So now take a look at this passage from Matthew 16:

15 He saith unto them, But whom say ye that I am?
16 And Simon Peter answered and said, Thou art the Christ, the Son of the living God.
17 And Jesus answered and said unto him, Blessed art thou, Simon Barjona: for flesh and blood hath not revealed it unto thee, but my Father which is in heaven.

The key words are: "for flesh and blood hath not revealed it unto thee, but my Father which is in heaven." This is a clear reference to intuition. "Flesh and blood" refers to the analytical, outer mind and the "Father" refers to the I AM Presence. So what Jesus was really saying was that Peter had some intuition and that is why he could recognize Jesus as the Living Christ. Now look at the next verse:

18 And I say also unto thee, That thou art Peter, and upon this rock I will build my church; and the gates of hell shall not prevail against it.

Again, Jesus was not here specifically talking about or to Peter. He was talking about the intuitive faculties that all people have. It is this intuitive faculty that is the rock because it gives us a firm place to stand in the turmoil of the opposing, relative claims of duality. It is also this intuition Jesus talked about in the parable about building a house on sand (the duality consciousness) and rocky ground (the Christ consciousness).

The real meaning that Jesus had in mind was that as long as his followers continued to use their intuition and get direction from the ascended realm (through himself as an ascended master), then the gates of hell (meaning the fallen beings and the duality consciousness) should not prevail against his movement (Jesus never used the word "church," this is a deliberate addition of the fallen beings). Jesus knew full well that if his followers ever stopped using their intuition, then his movement would quickly be perverted by the fallen consciousness. Jesus also knew that those who were most likely to instigate this perversion would be the people who were at the same level of consciousness as Peter. They had enough intuition to recognize Jesus, but it was not clear enough so that they were willing to follow Jesus on the ongoing, never-ending path to Christhood.

*** 

The problem with the consciousness that Peter represented can be understood by looking at the next passage in Matthew 16:

> 21 From that time forth began Jesus to shew unto his disciples, how that he must go unto Jerusalem, and suffer many things of the elders and chief priests and scribes, and be killed, and be raised again the third day.
> 22 Then Peter took him, and began to rebuke him, saying, Be it far from thee, Lord: this shall not be unto thee.
> 23 But he turned, and said unto Peter, Get thee behind me, Satan: thou art an offence unto me: for thou savourest not the things that be of God, but those that be of men.

I find it peculiar that Catholics always refer to the previous verses in order to justify that the Catholic church is built on Peter and thus represents Jesus while at the same time completely ignoring that Jesus called

Peter "Satan." The deeper reality here is that the Catholic church is based on the consciousness of Peter, but the real problem is that this church has not transcended this consciousness, even after 1700 years.

\*\*\*

Was Jesus schizophrenic? How could he at one time call Peter the rock upon which he would build his church and then later call him Satan? The deeper reality is that Jesus used "Satan" as a general reference to a specific state of consciousness. Peter did have a genuine intuitive impulse that Jesus had a higher vibration. What he ideally could have done (and which some of the other disciples did do) was to reason that if Jesus has a higher vibration, it is because he has a higher state of consciousness. Jesus says that I too can achieve this higher consciousness, and it rings true to me. Yet how can I achieve the same consciousness as Jesus? Only by allowing Jesus to take me on a journey whereby I transcend my present state of consciousness.

If Peter had recognized this, he would have understood the main element in Jesus' teachings, namely that in order to let go of one state of consciousness, one has to allow the self based on that state to die. Just look at the following verses in Matthew 16:

24 Then said Jesus unto his disciples, If any man will come after me, let him deny himself, and take up his cross, and follow me.
25 For whosoever will save his life shall lose it: and whosoever will lose his life for my sake shall find it.

With "coming after" Jesus means attaining the state of consciousness that Jesus demonstrated, namely the Christ consciousness. Jesus was a mystical teacher. His goal was *not* to give his students outer, intellectual knowledge that they could mindlessly repeat at an exam and get a diploma. His goal was to fundamentally transform their consciousness. The measure of Jesus' success as a teacher is *not* to have a bunch of theologians who can present cleaver intellectual discourses on Christian doctrine. The measure of his success as a teacher is to what extent he can duplicate himself by taking students to the same level of Christhood. So how do you think

Jesus himself rates his current success as a teacher based on the behavior of most Christians?

What does it take to follow Jesus? You have to take up your cross. This is a symbol for engaging in the path to Christhood whereby you realize that you are bearing a cross with four arms, meaning your four lower bodies. In each body there are dualistic elements, and your task is to systematically purify all four levels of your mind from the illusions of the fallen beings (remove the beam from your own eye). This requires you to deny yourself, meaning that you realize that you have a certain sense of self that is based on the illusions you currently have. This self cannot be perfected; it cannot become worthy to enter the kingdom no matter what you do in terms of observing an outer religion. This is the grand lie of the fallen beings.

The reality is that walking the path to Christhood means rising up through the spiral staircase of the 144 levels of consciousness. For each level, there is a self that must die. If you seek to save your life, meaning saving any of these lower selves, you will lose your spiritual life because you will not be able to join Jesus in the eternal life of the Christ consciousness. If you are willing to give up all of these lower selves in order to follow the example of Jesus, then you will indeed find the eternal life that is the Christ consciousness. The "only begotten Son of the Father" is not Jesus as an individual being but the Christ consciousness. No one comes into the kingdom of heaven (the ascended state) without putting on the wedding garment of the Christ consciousness. The Christ is, in its broadest sense, what allows us to come back to our original innocence after we have descended into duality and become lost.

Most of Jesus' disciples had grasped the basic idea of letting the present self die in order to follow Jesus. Peter simply never got this point. You will see from the previous quote that Peter had a clear mental image of what should and should not happen to Jesus. When Jesus said he would suffer many humiliations from the authorities in Jerusalem, this did not fit in with Peter's image. Ideally, Peter should have used this discrepancy to realize there was something wrong with his image and then begin to question it, eventually letting it die and rising to the next level of consciousness. Instead, Peter sought to save his "life" and even attempted to project his image upon Jesus, wanting Jesus to conform to his mental image. This was further demonstrated later by how Peter three times refused to identify himself as a follower of Jesus.

The consciousness that demands that the Living Christ should live up to its mental image is indeed the consciousness that Jesus called "Satan."

It is the hallmark of the fallen beings. They believe they own planet earth. They believe that the Living Christ has no right to be born here. If the Living Christ manages to be born anyway, then the fallen beings feel it is their right to demand that the Living Christ should live up to their mental image and not challenge it. The Living Christ should conform to the current conditions on earth, including the density of matter.

So much of what Jesus did or said, including the miracles, was aimed at challenging the collective mental image that matter is so dense that there are certain limitations we cannot escape. Jesus wanted to set people free from this illusion and help them see that the current density of matter is a product of the collective consciousness. By raising the collective consciousness, we will make matter less dense. Thus, with men (with the current level of consciousness) many things are indeed impossible. But with God (with the Christ consciousness) all things are possible.

\*\*\*

Take note of a subtle distinction. If you look at official Christian churches today, what is the main thing they are telling their followers? It is to *believe*, to have faith. Look at how Christian churches are telling people to have faith despite the challenges of materialism and rationality. Yet Jesus never, *ever* used the words faith and belief. I know you can find examples in the scriptures that say differently, such as when Jesus asked a man if he believed Jesus had the power to heal him or told people that it was their faith that made them whole. Yet these are deliberate distortions by the fallen beings.

Jesus never told anyone to follow him out of faith. He wanted his disciples to *know* based on their intuitive confirmations. He did not ask people: "Do you *believe* I have the power to heal you?" Instead, he asked: "Do you *know* I have the power to heal you?" If they merely *believed*, they would not be healed. If they had used intuition and *knew* (based on a recognition of the light in Jesus), they would indeed be healed.

Belief is wishful thinking. It is having a mental image of how you want the universe to work and then hoping that God or Jesus will force the universe to work according to your image. This will never, *ever* happen. God has given us free will, and we have used it to get ourselves into duality. God has then given us the Christ consciousness to help us get out of duality. If we reject this and refuse to let our dualistic selves die in order to follow Christ, then there is nothing more God or Jesus can do. We must continue in the School of Hard Knocks until we have had enough of the outer knocks and become open to inner direction.

It is the fallen beings who want you to *believe* in what they say and have faith that they can take you to heaven. The ascended masters want you to use your intuitive faculties to *know* from within through a direct experience.

***

I need to add here an extremely important distinction. If you look at the disciples of Jesus, you will see that they all had some intuitive insight (which later led to conflict between them). If you look at today's Christians, you will see many who claim they have had inner experiences that confirmed the validity of the Bible as the Word of God or Jesus as the only road to salvation. You can also find all kinds of spiritual people who say they have had intuitive confirmation that heir guru or their teachings is the only true one or the key to a golden age on earth. Each of these people is equally sure that their intuitive experience was valid and therefore showed them an absolute truth. Obviously, since their outer claims are contradictory, they cannot all be right, and this has given a free ride for sceptics and materialists to deny the value of intuition. So what gives?

The simple key to resolving this enigma and the conflicts it creates is to realize that each person is, at any given time, at a specific level on the scale of the 144 levels of consciousness possible on earth. At any given level, you are capable of having an intuitive experience. However – and this is the key – this experience can only show you the *next level of consciousness up* from where you are. It will *not* show you some ultimate truth.

In order to correctly use your intuitive faculties, you have to understand what I will call the "Peter Conundrum." The fallen beings are very clever, and they know that they cannot prevent all people from having intuitive insights. Instead, they seek to make sure that your *first* intuitive experience becomes your *last*. They do this by spreading the subtle attitude that your intuitive insights should be interpreted within your current belief system. For example, if you are a Christian, an intuitive experience should be interpreted within the Christian system, meaning your experience will seemingly validate your system. There are many atheists who have had genuine intuitive insights and have interpreted them as proof that all religion is false (all religions on earth *are* false, but that doesn't mean there is no spiritual reality beyond the material universe).

The mechanism here is simple. You are having an intuitive experience that is one step above your current level of consciousness. Because of this, the experience seems very real to you. It is the contact with a higher level of consciousness that gives you this sense of reality—not any kind of interpretation that the four levels of your mind project upon the experience. The challenge of having an intuitive experience is to avoid doing what Peter did to Jesus, namely to take the sense of reality and transfer it to your outer beliefs. When you do this, you solidify your current level of consciousness.

The intuitive experience is given in order to give you a frame of reference that allows you to realize that your current level of consciousness is not the highest possible and that your current self must die so you can go higher. When you misuse the sense of reality of the experience, you refuse to follow Christ and therefore you become even more trapped in your current self. This is exactly what happened to Peter, as we will see. The bottom line is that an intuitive experience *never* gives you an absolute truth. It only gives you a lifeline that you can use to pull yourself up to the next level where you can see an even higher insight. Do not let the lifeline become the rope with which you hang yourself.

# 46

I am now facing the same conundrum as the gospel writer, namely that if all the things that Jesus did or said should be written down, then the world itself could not contain the books that should be written. On the other hand, I am far more free than that gospel writer because I don't have an agenda of portraying Jesus in a political light and therefore being forced to leave many things out. I can tell the story as I witnessed it happen, leaving out only what I think is unnecessary in terms of giving an impression of Jesus' real mission and teachings. So I will now skip the middle part of Jesus' mission where he walked around in ancient Israel but stayed away from Jerusalem. I will skip to the final stage where Jesus did enter Jerusalem.

Before this happened, Jesus one day came to me and asked me to walk with him. We walked up into the hills, and Jesus started to explain that he had realized his mission was going into the final stage where he would be killed by Lucifer. You might wonder where Lucifer had been in all of this, and the explanation is that so far Jesus had stayed away from Jerusalem and Lucifer had stayed away from Jesus. The center of power was obviously Jerusalem and Lucifer felt he had good control over it. As long as Jesus preached only in the countryside, he was not a direct threat to Lucifer, and Lucifer felt he could take a waiting position to see how the people responded to Jesus. As long as he did not gather too many followers, he was a threat that Lucifer could live with.

You might ask why Lucifer would accept having to live with Jesus instead of just getting rid of him. The explanation is that because Jesus had reached such a high level of Christhood, killing him was not a straightforward thing. The Dark Master who controlled Lucifer knew that by having Lucifer kill the Living Christ, Lucifer would receive the Judgment of Christ and for sure be taken out of embodiment, perhaps going through the second death. That is why the Dark Master told Lucifer to take a waiting position, hoping that the people would not respond to Jesus in great numbers. The Dark Master thought he had such control over the people on earth that they would not be able to respond to Jesus, or that he could destroy the movement from within by having the followers of Jesus fight amongst themselves. He was hoping that the Jesus problem would go away gradually without requiring any action with drastic consequences.

***

As we were walking, Jesus explained to me that he had started feeling a stronger and stronger pull to go to Jerusalem and challenge the Jewish leaders directly. He again expressed the concern that Lucifer would torture him and how he could go through this and still make his ascension. After Jesus had expressed his concerns, we both felt the vibration changing. A white light started appearing next to us, and gradually Sanat Kumara. Maitreya and Gautama Buddha appeared in their light bodies.

Sanat Kumara confirmed that it was necessary for Jesus to go to Jerusalem in order to force Lucifer and his master to react to Jesus. He explained that it was not a given that they would torture or kill Jesus. It was indeed possible that they could respond without killing him. However, given their history, it was likely that Jesus would be captured, tortured and killed, most likely by crucifixion.

Jesus asked how he could go through this and still ascend, and Sanat Kumara turned to me and asked me to explain. I turned to Jesus and said: "I told you that while you were in the cave, I had been trained by a guru to endure any kind of pain inflicted upon the physical body. Now put this together with how one of our teachers taught us to go out of the body, and what do you get?"

Jesus at first looked slightly annoyed that I was giving him a riddle instead of a straightforward answer, but then he saw the potential and said: "Are you suggesting we switch bodies? But we have never tried that."

I answered: "Well, they say there is a first time for everything, so let us do a dry run."

Sanat Kumara then gave us some instructions and the three masters left. Since it was the first time of trying it, we first went through some of the preparatory exercises we had done before leaving our bodies during our stay at the ashram. We then faced each other and embraced so all of our chakras were aligned. We then centered in our hearts, kissed each other on the mouth and within a few seconds, we both felt how we left our bodies and entered into the other body.

We then walked a few steps back and looked each other in the eye. There was no doubt to me that I was looking into the eyes of Jesus, but I was also looking at my own physical body. This wasn't quite as dramatic an experience as it would have been today because we did not have the proliferation of mirrors found in today's world. Yet we did, of course, know what we looked like so it was very strange to see Jesus' eyes shining from my own body.

Jesus also looked quite astonished and finally said: "This is positively one of the strangest experiences I have had on this planet." As usual, there wasn't much to be said after that.

We then walked down from the hills and joined the others. For the next two days, we stayed in each others bodies and I played the role of Jesus. Fortunately, there were no major events taking place so not much was required of me. I would like to mention that I did not take advantage of the situation in regard to Magda. But I did take the opportunity to tease some of the other disciples in a good-natured way.

After a couple of days, we again went aside and once again embraced, switching back to our own bodies. We did try it several more times, until we were sure we could do it without much preparation. After some time, Jesus felt confident that it could work, and from then on he was more at peace with going to Jerusalem although he obviously didn't look forward to it.

***

Now, in saying that Lucifer had a "If you leave me alone, I'll leave you alone" policy concerning Jesus, this needs to be explained. Lucifer had not taken any action to directly kill Jesus. However, he had not restrained and had somewhat encouraged that the representatives of the Jewish religion challenged Jesus. The scriptures are correct in portraying that the scribes and Pharisees often challenged Jesus and even sought to lay traps for him so they could accuse him of blasphemy.

Where the scriptures fail is that they do not accurately portray Jesus' motivation for interacting with them. If you just read the scriptures, what is the impression you get? Well, most Christians have not thought about it, but you might get the impression that either Jesus liked sparring with the intellectuals or he was attempting to convince them. Neither was the case.

Jesus had no illusions whatsoever that he could convert the scribes and Pharisees. He knew they were firmly in the fanatical mindset, meaning that their minds were taken over by fallen beings in the mental and identity realms. He knew that whatever argument he could come up with, they would use the duality consciousness to come up with a counter-argument that in their minds was more convincing than anything Jesus could say. For the same reason, he obviously did not enjoy interacting with these people.

Let me just make this a bit more direct. In today's world, you can find quite a few people who are absolutely sure about their beliefs and whose minds therefore are completely closed to anything else. You do find them in a religious setting, but you can also find them among scientific materialists and adherents of political systems or factions. As an example, just look at the United States and you will see the same closed-mindedness among fundamentalist Christians, materialistic college professors (the so-called militant atheists) and very conservative republicans.

You can reason with such people until you are blue in the face, but you can never come up with an argument that will convince them. The problem here is that you think you are talking with normal human beings who will respond to an argument better than their own. This is not the case. You are not reasoning with normal human beings. Some of these people are fallen beings in embodiment, but even those who are not fallen beings are not having minds that are open to arguments. Their minds are completely taken over by fallen beings in the mental or identity realm. You are not arguing with a real person; you are arguing with a fallen being who is in a higher realm and thus completely convinced that anything you (a mere *human* being in embodiment) could come up with is per definition invalid. You have no chance of convincing such people of anything. Believe me, if Jesus could not convince such people, nobody can.

Jesus had two motives for engaging with these people. One was that they always attacked him in public because they were seeking to discredit him in the eyes of the people. This gave Jesus an opportunity to reach some people in the audience. In reality, Jesus had far more run-ins with the scribes and Pharisees than recorded in the scriptures. Yet even if you read the scriptures, you can see that Jesus did not generally argue with them in a linear or intellectual way. He always attempted to make short, concise statements that challenged their way of looking at things. This is a technique used by Socrates and later developed by the Zen Buddhists. Many of Jesus' statements were like what we today call Zen koans.

As an example, take the situation where Jesus is asked when the kingdom of god will come. He first says it will not come with observation, and then he says that the kingdom of god is inside yourself. This was a highly confounding statement to people locked in the worldview of the time. They saw the kingdom of god as an external, actual place that existed in heaven. Yet their idea of heaven was different from how most people today conceive of heaven. They thought of it as an actual place that they saw as being somewhere else on earth. They also thought that in the future they would be led to it, as the Jews had been led to the promised land by Moses. They thought that only those who strictly observed the rules of the Jewish religion, would be able to enter. So to say that following the outer religion would not get you there because the kingdom is an inner place (or state of consciousness, as we can say today) was so beyond how people saw life that they simply did not know what to do with it. Unfortunately, those statements are also so beyond how most Christians see life today that they also don't know what to do with them. This, however is by design of those who perverted Jesus' teachings on how to enter the kingdom.

The point is that Jesus did not make such statements because he thought they would have an impact on the scribes and Pharisees. He did it because he (or the ascended master speaking through him) knew they would have an impact on some people in the audience. It was amazing to hear how many people would start following Jesus and explain that it was because one of these confounding statements had made them reconnect to what they knew to be true in their hearts.

The second reason for Jesus challenging the scribes and Pharisees was that he knew that it would bring the judgment of Christ upon them. The Law of Free Will mandates that people are allowed to enter the duality consciousness and thereby turn their minds into closed systems. People are even allowed to forget that there is anything outside the "reality" they have defined in their own minds, or rather by letting their individual minds be taken over by a collective entity.

Yet the law does not prohibit that a person with the Christ consciousness can confront people. In other words, they have a right to make themselves blind, but they do not have the right to remain in this state forever. There comes a point where a person has been in that state for so long that it is time to move on (for the person's own sake). This does not mean that the person must of necessity be confronted with a person who has the Christ consciousness. But if such a person is available, then the person has no right to avoid the confrontation. And if the person has a confrontation with the Living Christ (and thereby experiences that there is an alternative to duality) and then rejects that encounter, then the person will bring a judgment upon itself. This often means that the person will not be allowed to reembody on earth after this lifetime. Instead, the person may go to another planet or to the astral plane, but the person goes to a place where it becomes more difficult to uphold the dualistic illusion. In practical terms, this means the new place is denser than earth, meaning the suffering is more intense and thus forces the person to reconsider its approach to life.

Jesus knew very well that if the earth was to move forward (meaning the collective consciousness is raised) in the two thousand-year period that he was meant to inaugurate, certain people would have to be taken off the planet. This would remove their pull on the collective consciousness. It would also reduce the influence of the fallen beings in the identity and mental octaves because they would not have as many people to work through. The majority of the intellectuals who challenged Jesus did receive this judgment of Christ and they have not been allowed to take embodiment over the past 2000 years. This has been a large factor in raising the collective consciousness during this past era, the Age of Pisces.

***

I want to explain something that is not relevant to the story line, but relevant to how people see Jesus today. A fundamentalist Christian, of course, believes the Bible is the Word of God and should be interpreted literally. Naturally, this is a contradiction in terms. You are either literal or you are interpreting, but I will let that one go. The point is that many Christians think Jesus' words should be taken literally, and in doing so they actually enter the same mindset as that of the scribes and Pharisees. You will see that they often used a literal interpretation of the Jewish scriptures in trying to catch Jesus saying something they could use against him.

Christhood is a state of consciousness in which we begin to see beyond duality, but coming to fully see beyond is a process that takes time. Jesus was not meant only to demonstrate Christhood but also to be an example for others to follow, meaning he demonstrated a progression towards higher states of consciousness. When we entered Israel, Jesus had reached a fairly high level of Christhood, but he still progressed during the next three years. This is difficult to see in the scriptures because they do not follow a linear time line, but it can be reconstructed if you read between the lines and know what I have told you in this book.

As Jesus progressed in Christhood, his statements became affected by this. In the beginning, he was reluctant to say anything about himself, meaning he rarely made an "I AM" statement during the first two years. In the last year, he did say certain sentences beginning with the words "I am," but *he* did not say them and they were not said about himself. The lower stages of Christhood is where you have the ability to discern between a dualistic illusion and a non-dual reality. You can read the vibration of statements and discern their validity based on this. As I said, millions of people all over the world have reached this stage. At higher levels, you become an open door for your I AM Presence and later the ascended masters. At even higher levels, you come into oneness with the Christ mind, and the Christ mind is one, undivided mind. You can talk about individual Christhood in the sense that an unascended person on a planet like earth can attain a higher level of consciousness than the rest of the people on earth. Yet the higher you go in Christhood, the more you overcome the illusion that you are a separate being (the primary illusion of the fallen beings) and you begin to see yourself as one with the universal Christ mind. This is a somewhat schizophrenic phase because you are balancing the fact that you are still in embodiment on an unnatural planet with the fact that you are beginning to experience oneness as the underlying reality. The denser the planet, the more difficult it is to balance these extremes, and it was not an easy phase for Jesus.

The point I am getting to is that when you begin to experience oneness with the universal Christ mind, you can now make statements that are not made by you or about you. It can be an ascended master speaking through you or you can make statements from this state of oneness with the Christ mind. As an example, take one of the statements most misconstrued by Christians: "I am the way, the truth and the life, no one comes to the Father but by me." Most Christians interpret this to mean that unless you are a member of a Christian religion (being baptized at least), you will not be saved. Just look at how many believe that only Christians will be saved. Yet the stark reality is that there are no Christians in heaven. Neither are there any Muslims, Hindus or Buddhists in heaven.

The Christ mind is universal, meaning it is based on oneness. The labels constructed on earth have the purpose of dividing, of setting apart. "Christian" is a word used to set some people apart from others. Such a divisive term can only come from the duality consciousness. It is *always* defined by the fallen beings for the purpose of creating conflict between people.

How will you enter heaven? Only by overcoming all of the divisions created from the duality consciousness and the illusion of separation. You enter oneness by overcoming the illusion of separation. How do you overcome the illusion of separation? By entering a state of oneness, and the absolutely only way to do this is to become one with the universal Christ mind that is defined in order to ensure oneness between our Creator and its creation.

I know that in today's world, "Christ" is not seen as a universal concept, but that is because it has been hijacked by the fallen beings and used to create division. In reality the term "Christ" refers to the one, undivided, indivisible, universal mind that can give you oneness with your Source and with all life. This mind is the only source of oneness.

So when Jesus uttered the words above, it was not Jesus as an individual, separate being who was speaking. Jesus was so one with the universal Christ mind that it was this mind speaking through him. Thus, the words truly mean that it is the universal Christ mind that is the way, truth and life. No one comes to the father without becoming one with the universal Christ mind. It has nothing whatsoever to do with Jesus as a historical person. It has nothing to do with being a member of a particular outer church.

Being a member of an outer church (that is based on duality instead of Christhood) is no guarantee that you will enter heaven. In fact, for most people it is a guarantee that they will *not* enter heaven but will have to reincarnate. Why do you think there are so many people in today's world who either do not believe in Christianity and seek spiritual knowledge elsewhere or who are very angry with Christianity? Take a look at many atheists, such as the militant atheists that have emerged over the past couple of decades. Ask yourself why they are so angry and so anxious to prove Christianity wrong. The explanation is that in past lives, these people embodied in a Christian culture and they bought the claim that if they were good Christians, they would enter heaven after that lifetime. They then died and found out they had not qualified for their ascension but had to reembody. This made them so angry that they came back with a desire to prove Christianity wrong. The sad fact being, of course, that these people have not taken responsibility for themselves and the raising of their consciousness.

Anyway, take another statement: "Before Abraham was, I am." Now, based on what I have told you in this book, the statement could have been made by Jesus based on the fact that he had been in embodiment since long before the time of Abraham. Yet the statement was again made by and about the universal Christ mind. It demonstrates that this mind is independent of time. In fact, time as most people see it is a product of the duality consciousness that again divides life into past, present and future. It is only through the Christ mind that you can overcome the illusion of time. Finally, take the statement where Jesus tells his disciples to go into all the world and make all people his disciples. Again, this has been misconstrued by Christians to mean that Jesus wanted his followers to make all people members of the Christian religion—always seen as "their" particular Christian church. In reality, this was again the universal Christ mind telling us to be walking the path towards oneness with this mind and then helping other people do the same. Being a member of an outer religion does not guarantee your oneness with the Christ mind, in fact, it usually closes you to the universality of this mind. How can you be one with the mind that unites all people when you judge those who are not members of your religion?

Now, there is a twist to the statement that no one comes to the Father but by me. Today, Jesus is an ascended master who holds a particular spiritual office as the Planetary Christ. This means that no one can enter the ascended state without going through this spiritual office. So in a certain way, you can say that no one can ascend from earth without going through Jesus. However, this is Jesus as an ascended master. While he was still unascended, he did not hold this office and thus could not have made that statement about himself.

***

We now come to the point where Jesus enters Jerusalem. The scriptures are correct in describing that he was received as a king, but they do not explain why. I have earlier described that there was a large underground movement seeking to overthrow the Romans, many of them waiting for the Messiah as a warrior king. I said that Jesus refused to be the leader of their movement, but some of them still thought he was the warrior they had been waiting for, and their belief was only strengthened as Jesus became more famous. They thought Jesus simply had not "come out of the closet" and that he eventually would. They thought that his entry into Jerusalem signalled this change, and that is why they arranged for their followers to receive Jesus as the king. Obviously, some other people were caught up in the fray and it became a relatively big event.

In the days following, it became clear to the leaders of this underground movement that Jesus would not fill the role they had defined for him because he had an entirely different agenda. That is why they rejected Jesus at his public trial and wanted a murderer to be released instead of

Jesus. But I am getting ahead of myself. When Jesus saw the size of his reception, he thought Lucifer would immediately have him arrested, and he wanted me by his side constantly so we could switch bodies with a moment's notice. However, nothing happened, and even when Jesus started to preach and heal publicly, no action was taken. By the third day, Jesus was getting impatient and that is when he went to the Temple Mount. Here, he did overturn the tables of the money-changers because they symbolized how the fallen beings have set themselves up in privileged positions in so many ways. They get the people to pay their hard-earned money to them and they really do nothing in return, aside from the fact that their self-created system requires them to do it this way. What is the modern equivalent of the money-changers? The entire financial industry that collects interest, commissions and fees for nothing more than giving you access to the system. By the mere fact that they have their positions, you have to pay them.

While he was at the Temple Mount, Jesus did call out with a loud, powerful voice and called forth the judgment of Christ upon the Jewish religion and its leadership and the fallen beings behind them. I was there, and Jesus' voice was so loud that you could hardly believe it was a human voice. In today's age, it could easily be imitated with loudspeakers, but not with the human voice alone. It was literally so powerful that the air seemed to vibrate, and many people fell to the ground, shaking from the power of the Spirit. Within minutes, the darkest thunderclouds I had ever seen appeared out of nowhere, and there was a lightning storm that lasted for several minutes and had the brightest light and the loudest thunderclaps anyone had ever experienced.

Even after this, it was as if Lucifer hesitated, and the main reason was that he had trouble talking Pontius Pilate into arresting Jesus. Pontius was not stupid and he knew Lucifer was attempting to use him for some purpose. Although he didn't know the purpose, he sensed it could not be good. It was only when Lucifer threatened to organize an uprising that Pontius relented, reasoning that Jesus was likely to cause unrest either way and since his main task was to ensure order, he might as well deal with Jesus now rather than later. So Pontius was not a fallen being and acted purely on rational grounds, not any hidden agenda.

Finally, came the moment in the Garden of Gethsemane as depicted in the scriptures. However, Jesus was not distraught or "sweating drops of blood." He obviously knew he would die within a few days, so he wasn't making merry either. When we saw the soldiers approaching, Jesus and I embraced and switched bodies. I am not here going to say much about Judas, other than that he was a representative of the underground resistance movement. They actually thought that by getting Jesus arrested, Jesus would be forced to show his power and that this would be the beginning of the uprising. They had armed men all over Jerusalem and outside, ready to attack the Romans by any sign that Jesus was ready to lead them. So Judas acted on a set of rational intentions (I am not saying I agree with them). He was not a fallen being and did not make a severe karma for his actions. He is today an ascended master, but he is not working with earth due to the condemnation still directed at him by Christians.

***

One significant incidence was that when the soldiers came to arrest Jesus, Peter did draw a sword and wounded one of the soldiers. I can assure you that this event was perceived as being very shocking to Jesus and the other people present. Jesus had from the start preached complete non-violence, as anyone reading the scriptures can see. None of the other disciples could even conceive of carrying a weapon and there had never been any weapons or body guards at any event held by Jesus.

When Peter pulled out the sword he had been carrying hidden under his clothing, everyone was in total shock, even the soldiers. Peter didn't cut off the soldier's ear, but wounded his arm very severely. There was again one of these moments that seemed frozen in time. My mind was raising with the dilemma. I knew that I did not have the power to heal the soldier's wound, but I knew Jesus wanted it healed, partly for purely humanitarian reasons, partly to avoid that Peter and potentially other disciples would be killed by the other soldiers. Yet Jesus obviously couldn't step forward to heal the soldier in my body, and for a split second, my mind seemed paralyzed.

I then caught Jesus' eye and I received a telepathic image. I instantly stepped forward, put my hands on the soldier's wounds and said with the loudest possible voice: "In the name of the Living Christ, I command ye, be thou made whole!" Jesus then healed the man from a distance and the wound simply vanished. The remaining soldiers were so astonished at this that they did not use their weapons against Peter or the other disciples. Instead, their leader commanded Jesus (meaning me in Jesus' body) to follow them and he/I did. As they took me away, I looked back and caught Jesus looking at me with a worried look, as if he wasn't sure I could pull this off. I gave him a quick smile before I lost sight of him. I will never forget the image of him standing there among the trees. From the eyes I could tell it was Jesus, but he was in *my* body. Again, one of the stranger moments I have experienced on this planet.

# 47

The soldiers did not take me to the Roman headquarters, as one would have expected. Instead, I was taken to the basement of an unmarked building near the Temple Mount. I was put in a small cell in what seemed to be the lowest level of the building. I was there for several hours, and while there I went into a meditative state and suddenly had a total recall of the situation where Lucifer had tortured me during my first embodiment. I was lying on a wooden platform and shaking violently as I relived the entire event. It was, to put it mildly, a shocking experience and I did not even sense the coldness in the cell.

During the experience, a strange sensation started growing in me. It was a sense that there was something I had missed in the original situation. I sensed that I had missed an opportunity and failed an initiation, but I could not bring to my conscious mind what it was about. I was thinking very intensely about this and seeking to solve the enigma, but the harder I speculated, the more the solution seemed to evade me.

Suddenly, my thinking was interrupted by four temple servants who took me to a larger underground room. I was stripped naked and my arms were tied to two metal rings on the wall so I was facing outwards with my arms spread to the sides. On a small table was a whip similar to what is today called a cat-o'-nine-tails. The situation was, naturally, very similar to what I had just relived in my cell. The difference between the original situation and this one was that I knew exactly what was coming and I had achieved the mastery of mind over body that was designed to help me deal with it in a different way.

After an hour, Lucifer entered the room, dressed entirely in black and with an ominous look on his face that was no doubt intended to scare me. Instead, I had a hard time not laughing, but I restrained myself because I was curious to see how he would go about this. He first looked at me and seemed surprised when I looked him straight in the eye. After just a couple of seconds, he averted my eyes and instead started talking: "So, you are the Jesus that I saw in the temple so many years ago. I have been waiting for you to show up again, and I must say you have gone through quite a development since I last saw you. Quite the man now, are you not. But let us see how Jesus, the man, can withstand my cat."

He picked up the whip as he was saying the last sentence. He gave me an ominous look, and I again met his eyes, which shocked him. He immediately looked aside and continued talking: "I see you do not scare easily. You might think you can withstand the pain of a whipping, but I can assure you that no human has ever withstood the total pain I can inflict with this simple instrument."

He paused, as if waiting for me to speak, but I said nothing and continued to look directly at him. He continued to avoid looking me in the eyes, and after a few seconds he felt like he had to say something since I remained silent: "I hear wild stories of how this Jesus is preaching to the people, teaching them all kinds of blasphemies. Do you have nothing to say to me? I was expecting you to try to convert me to be one of your followers? Have you nothing to say to me?"

I answered, and the words were flowing directly from my I AM Presence: "I have nothing to say to you because there is nothing that I personally want to say and there is nothing the ascended masters want to say to you. It is too late for talk and by taking actions against me, your days on this planet will be done."

Both I and Lucifer were shocked at the intensity in my words, and Lucifer gave me a surprised look. I caught his eyes for a split second and then said: "Oh, I see that your Dark Master has not informed you of the real consequences of the actions you are about to take, whereas my masters of light have shown me exactly what will happen. Has he not told you that by killing a person with my level of consciousness, you will receive the Judgment of Christ and will be taken out of embodiment soon after? Has he really led you to believe that you can do this and avoid the karmic consequences? I had no idea you were that naive."

As I spoke, Lucifer turned bright red and looked as furious as I had ever seen him. Yet, I felt completely calm inside, and a strange sensation started to grow in my heart. At first, I was confused and could not understand it, but I then had to admit that what I felt was an unconditional love for Lucifer. This shocked me at first because I suddenly realized that since that first embodiment where he had killed all those innocent people, I had never been able (or rather, willing) to feel love for Lucifer. I had been able to feel love for many other people who had done terrible things, but never Lucifer. In a flash, I saw that what I had been missing during all this time was that in order to be free of Lucifer, I had to love him unconditionally. Only when my love for him was truly without conditions, would there be no conditions in my mind that would tie me to the fallen consciousness and give Lucifer an inroad into my mind.

In the meantime, Lucifer had picked up the whip and in complete rage, he started whipping me all over my body, starting with the genital area. This was not the methodical whipping he had given me the first time, but an uncontrolled rage. This meant it didn't actually hurt as much, but at that level of pain, the difference between "much" and "not so much" is purely academic. However, my guru had trained me well, and I was in complete control over my four lower bodies.

After some time, Lucifer seemed to sense that I was not reacting as he expected, and he took a break to catch his breath. I said, in a completely calm tone of voice: "Lucifer, I love you unconditionally, as God and all ascended masters love you unconditionally."

Naturally, Lucifer's name in that embodiment was not Lucifer, but I used the name "Lucifer" and he instantly recognized it. The effect was astonishing. He literally looked like I had hit him between the eyes with a two-pound hammer. He looked at me in complete shock and I caught his eyes. He could not avert his eyes and looked into mine for what seemed like another interval beyond time. During this time, I saw mental images of key points in his life, going back to the first sphere in which he had fallen. I felt his feelings and knew exactly how he had reacted to every situation. I did not realize this at the time, but he was seeing key points of my life and my reactions, including my reactions to him. He also saw how I would have reacted to all of the situations he had faced, including his original fall. Apparently, this was the first time he had ever seen that there was a different way to react than the one he had chosen.

Lucifer then lowered his eyes and stood for a long time in complete silence. Finally, he dropped the whip, turned away without a word and left the room. I stood there for a very long time, and then soldiers came. They took me to the palace of Pontius Pilate where I had the public trial described in the scriptures.

\*\*\*

While the trial wasn't exactly as described in the scriptures, I have little comment on the situation. I will mention the situation where Pilate asks me if I am a king and I answer that I came into the world to bear witness onto the truth. This obviously was an ascended master speaking through me, but the interesting thing is Pilate's answer: "What is truth?"

Many Christians look down upon this answer, but it is actually a very honest answer. Contrary to popular belief, Pilate was an advanced soul (and is now an ascended master). He had not consciously found the path of Christhood, but he was in the preliminary stages. One of these stages is where you begin to realize that what you have been told growing up is not the truth. In fact, you begin to realize that most of it was a lie. This is when you begin to have some Christ discernment and can sense that the lies of the fallen beings are indeed lies. You can read their vibration.

We all need to go through this phase of radical doubt where we even come to doubt that there is such a thing as truth in this world. I have already explained that no absolute truth could ever be expressed in words. Absolute truth can only be experienced and only through the Christ consciousness. For all of us, we will have one or more embodiments in which we have reached the radical doubt, and as a result we do not dare to trust our own intuition. We therefore doubt everything, but it is only a short step to begin to lock in to the value of intuition that can help us rise above doubt. And once we do so, we can quickly make progress towards Christhood. Pilate was not yet there, but he reached that stage in his next embodiment.

Naturally, Pilate was charged by his superiors to keep the peace in Israel and he knew full well that a rebellion was brewing and could be triggered by various events. He saw that the arrest of Jesus, which had not happened by his initiative, could be such a trigger event. This is why he made the trial public and why he left it up to the people to decide Jesus' fate. By the people choosing to release Barrabbas and thereby condemning Jesus to death, they could not use Jesus' arrest and death as an excuse for the rebellion. Pilate therefore bought some time.

\*\*\*

Naturally, Jesus (in my body) had not been able to get near enough to me to switch bodies during the trial. The opportunity did not come until I was carrying the cross through the narrow and overcrowded streets of Jerusalem. By the way, contrary to the standard picture, I was not carrying the full cross but only the crossbar. Crucifixion was such a common punishment that there were trees or vertical posts that were always in the same place. This way, you only needed to nail a person's arms to the cross-bar, hoist the bar up with a rope and then nail the person's feet to the vertical post. This also made it much quicker to take down the crucified person and be ready for the next execution. You have to give the Romans credit for efficiency.

So there came the point where I saw Jesus in my body approach me in the crowd. I pretended to drop the beam, stood up and Jesus quickly embraced me. I managed to catch his eye and say: "Careful, this might sting a bit," and then we switched bodies. As he entered his own battered body, Jesus let out a cry of agony, as he had not been prepared for the pain from the open wounds. Yet he quickly gathered himself, picked up the beam and walked on. I walked with him at some distance, needing a few moments to orient myself in my own body and get used to not having to constantly compensate for the pain from the wounds.

***

Then came that moment where the Roman soldiers laid the crossbar on the ground, forced Jesus to lie down with his hands on it and nailed his hands to the beam. They had obviously done this many times before, and they quickly hoisted the crossbar up on the vertical post. One soldier held Jesus' feet together and another hammered the nail through them. It was surprising how little blood came from the wounds in his hands and feet, the soldiers having hit the exact spot where no major blood vessels were cut (meaning the person would live and suffer longer on the cross).

I will never forget standing there with Mother Mary and some of the other disciples, looking up at Jesus as he was hanging on the cross. At first, he took some time to get used to the pain and the constant agony of hav-ing to keep his body raised so his lungs would not collapse and suffocate him. After some time, he found a new balance and was calmer. As I was standing there, I was focused on holding a spiritual balance for him, but instead I received telepathic images of what was going on in his mind.

I now realized that in his mind, Jesus had a certain expectation that he had to go through the crucifixion but that he would not have to die on the cross. He had some hope that the ascended masters would send angels to rescue him from the cross and that this would then be such a miraculous event that it would lead to a new phase of his ministry where even more people would accept him.

I saw how he at first held firmly to this image, but after some time, another impulse started to come to his conscious awareness. I saw how he at first resisted this, but then finally he decided to look at it. He instantly saw that he would indeed have to die on the cross and that there was no way around it. This is when he cried out: "My Master, my Master, why have you forsaken me?"

This was a truly decisive moment, and even at this point, Jesus could have failed the initiation and missed his ascension. As is even recorded in the scriptures, Jesus had the power to command angels to set him free. Because of the Law of Free Will, Jesus could have used his attainment to command the angels to set him free, and the angels would have had to obey him. However, this would also have meant that the judgment of Lucifer and the Dark Master would not have been complete, the people who rejected Jesus would not have been judged and the example of Christhood would not have been set. Therefore, the planet really would not have taken a decisive step forward and Jesus would have had to reincarnate in order to fulfil his mission.

I saw this all in my mind and looked up at Jesus, for the first time being really concerned about what he would choose. I saw how crucial was his choice and how everything was hanging in the balance in those split seconds. It was as if our section of the universe was holding its breath.

I then saw how a calmness came upon Jesus and he accepted the situation fully. He had seen that for the example to be fully given, he had to show that the Law of Free Will even gives people on an unnatural planet the right to kill the Living Christ. He also saw that only by letting his physical body die, could he ascend and thereby demonstrate that when you reach Christhood, the physical body can no longer limit you. You are free of what is truly the most cruel prison on an unnatural planet, namely the cycle of death and rebirth.

I saw how Jesus made this decision and how he immediately saw the heavens open up to him. I saw a brief glimpse of clouds parting and a staircase of white light leading up into another dimension. I saw how Jesus also saw this and how he decided that he was completely and utterly done with earth. I saw how he had a glimpse of his entire sojourn on this planet, including his last embodiment and his hopes for creating a spiritual movement that could withstand the onslaught of the fallen beings. I also saw how he fully and finally let go of any and all desire to change anything on earth. He let go of all desires for the Christian movement and fully accepted that it would be entirely up to the free will of the people left in embodiment. He then "gave up the ghost," meaning he consciously let go of the last remnant of the separate self that tied him to his body and everything it represented. (Consciously leaving the body is, by the way, a major sign of attainment.). Jesus then left the physical body, and he even left his emotional, mental and identity bodies. I saw in a split second how he, now a point of brilliant white light, rose out of the body and disappeared into a light that was so high in vibration that I could not see inside it.

It is correct that at this point there was a darkening and a fierce thunder and lightning storm, as even the nature spirits reacted to the departure of the Living Christ from the four octaves of earth. The difference between Jesus being in embodiment and leaving was so intense that the elemental beings could not handle it without reacting, and it shook the four octaves. I have later seen how the departure of Jesus created energetic waves that moved like shock waves through the four realms. It literally was an event that had a planetary impact and that all people felt at some level or another. Most of them were not aware what it was, but all felt some disturbance in those moments.

***

I was completely caught up in my visions, but I suddenly realized someone was squeezing my arm so hard that it hurt. It was Mother Mary, and as I turned to her, she embraced me and cried out in the deepest agony I have ever felt from a human. At this point, I could no longer hold back my own feelings and I cried also. We cried for so long that it was a question of who was supporting whom. I was actually aware that this was not my personal sorrow, for I knew full well that Jesus would not die and that I would see him again. Yet I realized that both Mother Mary and most of his disciples and followers thought Jesus' death on the cross was the final end to his ministry and that he would leave them behind as he had felt left by God on the cross. So I let the tears flow, as I realized it would ease the collective burden.

Finally, I stopped, and as Mother Mary felt this, she also stopped and looked up at me. I looked her in the eye, and I knew that she telepathically saw my mental images of how Jesus would come again in an ascended body. I could feel her surprise, and I then focused on my images of why Jesus had to die. As Mother Mary saw this, she accepted it, and then she felt the inner peace of knowing that everything was as it should be and that Jesus' death on the cross was a momentous spiritual victory. She looked in my eyes once more and sent me the impulse: "Thank you." No words were necessary as we walked away arm in arm with big smiles on our faces (to the surprise and consternation of the people who were still there).

# 48

In the coming chapters, I will talk about what happened to Jesus, what happened to the Christian movement and what happened to Lucifer. I will begin with Jesus and the movement, since their fates are intertwined.

The Conscious You of Jesus completely disidentified itself from his physical, emotional, mental and identity bodies. It rose to one of the higher levels of the identity octave where it started getting used to its new identity as a being outside embodiment. This obviously takes some time when you have been in embodiment for over two million years on a planet as dense as earth. During the first three days (of earth time), Jesus was fully occupied with this. Then followed a brief period where he appeared to Mary Magdalen, Mother Mary and other key followers in order to get the Christian movement underway. After this, Jesus entered the ascension spiral, which lasted 33 days. During this time, he did not appear to or communicate with anybody. This was an initiation for all of his followers to see what they could do on their own by getting directions from within themselves.

\*\*\*

As far as Jesus' physical body, it is correct that Joseph of Aramithea used his connections to get the body from the Roman authorities. It was taken to Joseph's family grave, but this was meant to be only a temporary hold. I was helping Joseph with transferring the body as were several of the women, including Mother Mary and Magda. At night, the women went home and Joseph and I stayed to keep watch. We had heard rumors that one of the militant groups wanted to steal Jesus' body and attempt to use it to stir people to action. I know this sounds illogical given that they had rejected Jesus, but if you want logical thinking, you have embodied on the wrong planet.

We had set a watchman, and in the middle of the night, he reported that a group of people were approaching, and they were obviously searching. We hurriedly took Jesus' body out of the grave and fled in the opposite direction. We had no time to roll back the stone, but also did not want to, as it made the grave look unused. We transported the body outside of town to a location in the hills. We had no time to contact anyone.

The next morning, Mother Mary, Magda and a third woman came to the grave to bring us food. They naturally found it deserted and empty with the stone rolled aside. By the way, anyone reading the official gospels will see that they each tell a different story of what happened at the grave. This in itself should be enough to show anyone that the official scriptures do not give a complete description of the actual events. They were not written based on one source of Divine inspiration, which one would assume could get the story straight. They were written by four different human beings who each had different source material and a different agenda.

It is correct that Jesus appeared to the three women in a body made of higher energies than his physical body. That is why he did not want Mary Magdalen to embrace him: "Don't touch me, for I have not yet gone through the ascension spiral." In the following days, he also appeared to several other of his followers.

Soon after the women had arrived at the tomb, I came back and told them what we had to do. They were then sent to gather certain select followers and take them to a location in the hills outside Jerusalem by the next day. I took the food from the women. Joseph, myself and our helpers transported Jesus' body to the location where we would meet the others.

The next day when the others had arrived, Joseph explained what had happened and that we had received instructions from Jesus to cremate his body. This was not an easy task in a land with little wood, but we had managed to gather the wood necessary. All of those who were there (Peter was not) had no objections and we proceeded to burn the body without much ceremony.

As I sat there and watched this physical body burn, I knew this was the end of my physical sojourn with this beautiful lifestream and I felt a deep inner emptiness. It had been absolutely wonderful to be in the Presence of this Being. I was almost tempted to go into self-pity, when I suddenly felt a shift in vibration and I had a vision of Jesus sitting next to me. He projected the thought into my mind: "What makes you think you will not be in my Presence from now on?" I couldn't stop myself from laughing out loud. The others naturally all turned to me with question marks in their eyes, and I said: "I just had a vision of Jesus assuring me that he will always be with us. Just focus in your hearts and he will appear to you also." They all did what I said and within a minute they all broke out in smiles and laughter. It is the only cremation I have attended where all of those present were laughing.

\*\*\*

I earlier said that Jesus' disciples and other followers represented a certain range of consciousness, meaning they were at different levels of the 144 levels of consciousness possible on earth. Most of them were in the range from the 36th level to the 96th level. Naturally, they reacted to the news of Jesus' death on the cross according to their level of consciousness. Yet they all faced the same basic initiation, namely the question of whether the fact that Jesus had been killed meant that his mission had been a failure.

All of Jesus' followers had to deal with this question. I was the only one who did not because I had followed Jesus for so long that I had learned not to have any expectations. How can you have expectations of what should or should not happen on a planet where there are fallen beings and where free will reigns supreme?

At all levels of consciousness, some people reasoned that Jesus' death did indeed mean his mission had been a failure, which meant Jesus had been a fraud from the very beginning. They reasoned they had been fooled, but since they were not willing to take responsibility for themselves, they turned things around so that Jesus had been responsible for fooling them and they had been innocent victims. You see the same thing today when people become disgruntled with their religion or guru. So these people simply left the movement and wanted to have nothing more to do with Jesus. At the lower levels of consciousness there were more people reacting this way, and the percentage dropped at you came closer to the 96th level.

Those who reasoned that Jesus had not been a fraud now faced the initiation of how they could explain what happened. None of them had expected that Jesus would be executed as a common criminal or that he would allow this to happen without using some of the powers that they had seen him demonstrate. So they all faced the challenge of somehow explaining this in a way that made sense to them at their level of consciousness.

The most interesting and fateful reaction were from those who were below the 48th level or right above it, such as Peter. Peter refused to consider Jesus a failure for the simple reason that this would mean that he, Peter, would have been a fool for following Jesus. Peter's pride prevented him from even thinking about this, which meant that he accepted that he had been right in following Jesus. This also meant that Peter had to find an argument that would make Jesus seem right, even though he had been killed. This was no difficulty for people in the Peter consciousness because they had a momentum of projecting their own views upon Jesus.

You might recall that I earlier said that the satanic consciousness is the one that uses its own limited vision to form a mental image of how the world *should* function and then it demands that the world should function according to its image. People at this level of consciousness can recognize the Living Christ, but instead of letting their separate selves die in order to follow the Christ, they use those selves to project upon the Christ how he should be.

Peter and other people like him now came up with the idea that Jesus had allowed himself to be killed because he wanted his followers to take over and run the movement he had started. This was, of course, not incorrect as that was indeed what Jesus wanted. However, he did not want those in the satanic consciousness to run the movement, he wanted those who had started to attain Christhood to run the movement.

Peter, naturally, could not see this, and he became convinced that he was meant to play a leading role in the movement. Do you see the psychological mechanism that comes into play here? Peter's main concern was that he would not be proven wrong. Jesus' death was at first a great challenge that threatened to shatter Peter's fragile sense of infallibility. After he decided on his explanation for why Jesus had died, this now became tied to his fear of being proven wrong. In other words, Peter became locked on the explanation for Jesus' death that he had come up with in his outer mind. From then on, it was a matter of life or death for Peter that his view of Jesus' mission would not be proven wrong.

This meant two things. First of all, the followers at higher levels of consciousness mostly used their intuition to go within and get a direction from their I AM Presences or the ascended masters as to the real purpose of Jesus' mission. All who asked with open hearts received such direction according to their level of consciousness. The higher you went in consciousness, the deeper was the understanding people could receive. And the deeper was their respect for the fact that other people might have a different understanding. Peter did not use his intuition but decided with his outer mind. This meant he had no sense that other people might have an understanding that was more profound than his own. Instead, he saw diverging views as a threat and he attempted to suppress them.

The obvious effect of this was that Peter, and the people near his level of consciousness, became unable and unwilling to cooperate with anyone who had a different view of Jesus. Within a surprisingly short period of time, this formed two main groups among Jesus' followers. There was the group centered around Peter and then a larger group of people who had diverging visions but also tolerance for each other. These latter people were willing to try to cooperate with the Peter group, but Peter's group would have none of this. They wanted to be in charge and they saw any-one who had a different view as an enemy to be suppressed with force, although not violence.

I have said that we were left alone by Jesus during the 33 days where he went through the ascension spiral. And during that relatively short period of time, it became clear that the movement started by Jesus was already fragmenting into one large block around Peter and a larger group consist-ing of different views with no clear leader. There were two devastating effects of this.

***

The first effect was relating to women. Ever since we had been in the Venusian Mystery School, we had been aware that the conflict between men and women was engineered by the fallen beings. Jesus had been very clear that he wanted to start a spiritual movement that would not discrimi-nate against women. He wanted a movement where women could hold any position and where it was not their sex that decided their position but their level of consciousness. In other words, the people with the highest level of consciousness on the scale of the 144 levels should be in charge. This was something all of Jesus' closer followers had heard him say, including Peter.

During those first 33 days, several gatherings happened spontaneously, and one in particular stood out. There were several hundred people present in the hills, and there were representatives for every level of consciousness. The discussion had gone back and forth with various people speaking out about their vision of what was the essence of Jesus' mission, how it could be spread and how a movement could be organized. It gradually became clear that there were two main groupings. People around Peter wanted a centralized movement with a hierarchical structure with one person at the top. They argued that this is how it had been when Jesus was present and he had been the undisputed leader. They recognized that no one was like Jesus, so they wanted a small group of people to be the leaders of the movement. In contrast to this was a group of people with a higher level of consciousness. They thought there was no need for a strong centralized organization as they were sure we would all be led by Jesus through our intuitive contact with them.

One of the people speaking for this form of movement was Magda. She claimed that when Jesus had appeared to her outside the empty tomb, he had shown her an image of a movement led by the Spirit through those who were able to have direct contact with him in his ascended state. She had barely finished describing her vision when Peter stood up and challenged her, saying that there is no way Jesus would have given this vision to a woman. To my surprise, there was widespread acceptance of this view and I estimated that a majority of the people present also doubted that Jesus would have wanted Magda to have a prominent position in the movement even though they knew Jesus had a personal relationship with her.

I then stood up for the first and only time. I knew it was not my role to have any leadership position in the Christian movement, but I felt moved by the Spirit to speak. I said: "Peter, let us assume that we did create the kind of centralized movement you describe, who should then be members of the leading council? You have heard, as we all have, Jesus talk about the true role of women and how they are spiritually equal to men. It seems clear to me that if we created such a movement, the governing board should have the same number of women as it has men, and it seems obvious to me that Magda should be a member of that board."

I barely got the last sentence out before Peter interrupted me: "Look around you and see what kind of world we are living in. It is a patriarchal world and everywhere men have the dominant positions. Jesus has charged us to go out into all the world and make all people his disciples. How can we possibly carry out this task if we start a movement led by women? People will simply laugh us to scorn and see us as being controlled by women, something no one will be prepared to accept. By allowing women to be leaders, we make it impossible for us to spread the message of Jesus. We kill the movement before it is even born. As for Mary Magdalen, she may have had a personal relationship with Jesus, but he is no longer here and we need those who can lead and get our movement going. And as for you, who are you to tell me what is right. You have always been the silent man in the background and I do not see Jesus ever giving you any authority. Me, on the other hand, many of you here remember how Jesus called me the rock upon which he would build his movement."

Peter looked around, and without any forethought I said: "Peter, I have heard from three different sources how you denied being one of Jesus' followers after his arrest. To me, this is a clear sign that you are not willing to go all the way with Jesus, being one with him and being crucified with him if necessary. How can you claim to represent Jesus when you three times denied your oneness with him? How can anyone here believe that Peter adequately represents Jesus? And why do we need to decide on a leadership structure now when it is just a matter of time before Jesus will give us direct instructions through the power of Spirit. Do not forget he promised to have the ascended masters send us another comforter, namely himself as an ascended master. Why are we in such a hurry to decide right now who is to lead, why can't we wait for Jesus to direct us?"

Peter looked stunned, and I could tell there was an inner conflict in him. Part of him recognized that what I said made sense, but another part of him thought that if I managed to win the argument, Peter would have been proven wrong. Since his dominant psychological mechanism was that he could not be wrong, he was not willing to agree with me. I could see how he was searching for something to refute my argument, and I could see how his aura opened itself up.

I could see how an impulse came to him directly from the Dark Master of Lucifer in the identity realm. Peter's demeanor shifted from confusion to certainty and he said with a loud voice: "And where were you after Jesus was arrested? Where were any of you here? Did you (looking at me) get arrested and crucified with Jesus? Did any of you (looking at the others)? Nay, indeed none of us were able to go with Jesus all the way and this only proves that none of us are worthy to represent him. Therefore, we should admit in all humility that we are not worthy to fully represent Jesus. Yet we all know something about his mission so we are worthy to represent him to some degree. Thus, we should do what we can, given who we are. I for one intend to use my last breath to spread the message of Jesus as I have been given to understand it, and I encourage all those who are willing to join me. And I definitely do not intend to let women hinder me in my efforts so I will organize a movement led by men and dedicated to spreading the message of Jesus as we have been given to understand it. Those who will not join me, can go your separate ways and spread the message as you understand it."

Peter then fell silent as if he had run out of words, but the reality was that he could not maintain the connection to his source in the identity realm. At this point my outer mind was tempted to refute Peter's argument, but I used my intuition and got a very strong feeling that this was not the right course of action. I remained silent and looked around. It became obvious that a majority of the people present were in agreement with Peter, especially because they also did not want a movement in which women had leadership roles. For most of these, it was a purely practical matter of realizing that a patriarchal culture would indeed look negatively on a movement led by women.

At this point, I centered in my heart and suddenly received a vision of how the Christian movement had been locked on a track by the division centered around Peter. I saw how Peter had just started a tradition of letting man-made views rather than direct communication with Jesus determine the course of the movement. I saw how this would lead to the fragmentation of the movement into many factions, some of them indeed dedicated to maintaining direct communication with Jesus. I saw how this would gradually lead to the emergence of a centralized church based on Peter's denial of his ability to be one with Jesus. I saw how this would lead to the formation of one centralized church, eventually becoming the Catholic church. I saw why this church would see Peter as its founder, claiming he was the first pope, something there is absolutely no basis for in the official scriptures or the actual words of Jesus.

I saw that this was an inevitable development based on the level of the collective consciousness, the presence of fallen beings in all four octaves and the fact that those who will not listen for inner direction must be allowed to outplay their consciousness in order to experience the physical consequences. Given the level of consciousness at the time, there simply were not enough people who were open to Jesus' mystical message that a true mystical tradition could be formed. I also saw that despite this, it was vital that a mystical side of Christianity would survive or be recreated. I saw how this would be especially vital towards the end of the two thousand-year period in which Jesus, as an ascended master, would be the leading spiritual figure. Thus, I realized that it was not my role to interfere with the Peter consciousness but to focus on helping those who were open to direct communication from Jesus.

This fragmentation created by Peter was a watershed event in the early Christian movement. If Jesus' intent had been carried out, it would have become a movement in which women could hold any position, including becoming messengers who could take dictations from the Ascended Master Jesus. Such a movement would have encountered opposition, but it could still have grown and it would have reached much higher than the movement that eventually became the Catholic church. This would have altered the history of the Western world in a very dramatic way with many of the wars and other atrocities we have seen over the past 2000 years being avoided. Our society would have been very different today if it had been based on a two thousand-year tradition of equality between men and women in all levels of society.

When you look at Peter's argumentation, it is exactly the same consciousness that Jesus rebuked when he said: "Get thee behind me, Satan." Jesus clearly wanted to challenge the patriarchal society by creating a movement with equality for women. Peter argued that because we had a patriarchal society, we should not challenge that society. This is exactly the consciousness of Satan that wants the Christ to conform to current conditions instead of challenging them.

***

There was one more event that had an impact on early Christianity. It was the event that in the scriptures was described as the day of Pentecost. In reality, this happened 36 days after Jesus' death when he had completed the 33-day ascension spiral that began three days after his death.

The scriptures make a key remark, namely that the disciples were "of one accord in one place." This meant that those present were all united in their desire to hear from the ascended Jesus. All were open to his direction. This also meant that Peter and those around him were not present, despite what many Christians believe. Why were they not there? Because the event was called by Jesus and he could, naturally, call only those who had some attunement with him. You will recall that Peter was called the rock upon which Jesus would build his church. This meant that Peter had the ability to recognize the Living Christ when he appeared in a physical form. This is the foundation upon which Jesus would build his church; the ability all people have to sense a higher vibration. So one can claim that

Peter is a symbol for the foundation and therefore the Catholic church has some validity.

Yet would you consider a building complete if it only consisted of a foundation and had no walls or roof? Obviously, Jesus did not mean to stop at Peter's ability to recognize him in a physical form. He intended to build on this foundation by helping people develop their intuitive abilities to recognize the Christ in a non-physical form. Those of Jesus' followers who had developed their intuitive abilities were all able to attune to him and receive the call to come together in one place at a certain time.

Now, Jesus did go quite far in calling people to this event. There were some people who were at lower levels of consciousness and who did not yet have the trust in their inner visions. To such people, Jesus did appear in a more tangible form, as depicted in the story of Thomas who wanted to put his hands in Jesus' wounds. Jesus even appeared to Peter in such a form, but Peter was not able to get the message of where and when the event was to take place. He instead interpreted it as a sign that Jesus had been resurrected bodily, a concept Jesus never spoke about, as he knew one has no need for the physical body in the ascended state.

So the day arrived, and there were about 500 people gathered. At first, there was some confusion since Jesus was not there, no one was in charge and no one had any clear idea of what should happen. Yet Magda took the initiative to organize a session where we invoked the light of the ascended masters, as Jesus had taught us. We spent several hours doing this and we could feel how an energetic forcefield was gradually built around us.

Suddenly, a silence fell upon us and it lasted for several minutes. Then, Magda stood up and started speaking with a loud voice. She was taking a dictation from Jesus and he spoke through her for about ten minutes. Then, Magda sat down and another disciple stood up, also taking a dictation from Jesus. This continued for almost two hours and in the end 12 people had taken direct dictations from the Ascended Master Jesus. It was quite an event, and everyone was in awe.

I want to interject here that there is an interesting reference in the scriptures that claims the people present had heard the disciples speak in their native tongues. This has been interpreted to mean that when the disciples spoke under the power of Spirit, they either spoke in a foreign language or people could hear them in several languages. This, however, is a crude interpretation made by those who were not there but heard about it later and interpreted it through a lower level of consciousness. The reality is that the people present all heard Jesus speak directly to their level of consciousness and their outer background, such as sex, race, ethnicity and religion.

The real significance of this was that all those who were there fully realized the universality of the mission of Christ. They saw that Jesus did not come to start a movement like any of the religions known at the time (or later). He did not want to start a movement that set itself apart from or in competition with other religions. Instead, he wanted to start a movement dedicated to showing people a systematic path for raising their consciousness towards the highest level possible on earth. This path can be pursued by anyone, regardless of their outer background. So the dictations given by Jesus did not speak to each person in their physical language. It spoke to each person's universality in spirit. Thus, people heard the message in a way that was familiar to them and that they could grasp with their level of consciousness.

The universal Christ consciousness is the one mind that is meant to give all co-creators a way to attain oneness with their Creator and with each other. The Christ mind recognizes that people have fallen into duality and cannot raise their consciousness beyond it. That is why the universal Christ mind decides to send representatives of itself into the world in order to reach people at the level they are at. As I have said before, the goal is *not* to give an ultimate teaching but to give people a teaching they can grasp with their current level of consciousness and that can take them higher. When they take advantage of the teaching and raise their consciousness, they can then receive a higher teaching that can take them further towards the 144th level of consciousness where you transcend all divisions on earth.

The approach taken by Peter is based on a complete misunderstanding of this purpose. Peter repeatedly denied this approach of seeking oneness with the Christ mind. Peter did this to the very end of that lifetime, even to the point of wanting to be crucified upside down, so as to demonstrate his unworthiness to be one with Jesus. Peter acknowledged that he was not worthy to represent Jesus but still claimed that he was the leader of the Christian movement. This was the consciousness adopted by the Catholic church and this explains why it had to elevate Jesus to being superior to any human being. Only by elevating Jesus to superhuman status, could the church elevate itself to having superior status among humans. Only by elevating Jesus to being above any individual, could the fallen beings elevate the institution to be above the individual human being.

All religions who deny the path towards oneness with the universal Christ mind are based on a denial of Christ. And where does the denial of Christ come from? It starts with the fallen beings, of course. Thus, any religion that denies or ignores the universal path towards higher states of consciousness is a religion controlled by the fallen beings. This applies equally to the religion of scientific materialism that claims we are nothing more than evolved apes and that we have no capabilities beyond the physical body.

***

After the session of dictations had ended, we all sat in silence. In the center of the crowd was an open space, and we suddenly started to see the air vibrating there. This became more intense and the area became filled with a white light. Gradually, the outline of a human form appeared, and it became denser until it formed the exact image of how Jesus' physical body had appeared on the cross. I mean, he was not on the cross but standing before us, but his body had the wounds of the cross so we could see it was him. We, of course, all knew his physical body had been cremated so we knew it was not that body that had been resurrected. Jesus simply wanted to make sure we could all identify him.

After a few minutes, Jesus' body started vibrating and the wounds disappeared. His body became even more symmetrical and harmonious, taking on a beauty that is beyond this world. He then started speaking with a voice that sounded like no human voice but vibrated in a way that I can only describe as totally alive. It was a sound I can never forget. He said: "I greet you, you who are my real followers, having followed me in the only place one can follow Christ, namely in the heart. For these past days, I have gone through the initiation of the ascension spiral, and with the help of the ascended masters, I have passed these initiations and I am ready to go through the ritual of the physical ascension, which you will witness today."

"I know it has been difficult for you to be left alone for these days, but this has been your initiation to see whether you had internalized enough of my teachings that you could keep your inner connection with me. Your presence here proves that you have indeed passed this initiation, and I congratulate you. Whatever you do after this, make maintaining this direct connection to me your first priority and we shall go far together in transforming this planet."

"It has been determined by the ascended masters that it is important to create a record that a person, who has embodied in a human body, can physically ascend from earth. This has, naturally, happened in past ages, but it has not happened for a very long time. The ascended masters want this record created so that people, during the next spiritual age, can tune in to it and know in their hearts that the ascension is a real possibility for all who follow the path of Christhood, becoming one with the universal Christ mind. People from any spiritual tradition or background will be able to tune in to this record if they are willing. Therefore, they can know that the message you preach is indeed real. They can know that one person has gone through the physical ascension, and they can then come to recognize that what one has done, all can do."

"I have nothing more to say to you now, for I will indeed speak to and through many of you for as long as you can maintain the connection to me. I am indeed with you onto the end, not of the world, but of the Age of Pisces, even beyond if I determine that this serves a purpose."

Jesus stopped speaking and closed his eyes, obviously focusing within. After a minute, his "body" started visibly vibrating at a higher frequency, and it gradually rose into the air in front of us. A cylinder of intense white light (so bright one could hardly look at it) was lowered around him. His body became less visible and started rising into the cylinder.

Jesus' body became more and more faded as he rose higher. At one point many of us saw how the clouds around the cylinder parted. We could see into what we today would call another dimension, but which most people saw as heaven. We saw millions of angels in grand formations. We saw hundreds of ascended masters waiting to greet Jesus as he rose through the cylinder. The last thing I saw was Jesus stepping out of the white cylinder and being greeted by an ascended master I recognized as Sanat Kumara. At that point, the clouds again closed and there was nothing more we could see with our physical eyes. Yet many of us centered in our hearts and received inner visions of the ceremony whereby Jesus was recognized as an ascended master. It was truly beautiful and I shall refrain from describing it, as words would only detract from its purity.

Naturally, there was not much anyone could say after such an experience. I am describing it because it is important for people to know that there is an energetic record of Jesus' physical ascension. Anyone who is able to use intuition, will be able to tune in to it and thus receive an inner knowledge of the reality of the ascension process and the path to Christhood that leads you towards it.

***

I also want to point out that one effect of the event was that all of those present realized that the message of Jesus is truly universal. We realized it can be expressed in many different ways, partly to different cultures but also to different levels of consciousness. We realized that there was no need to start another exclusivist religion because the message of Christhood could be preached and practiced by people from every religion. Following the path did not require people to abandon their religion. Higher consciousness can be pursued within any religion or no formal religion.

We also realized that there was nothing we could do to stop people, such as Peter, from attempting to turn Christianity into a centralized religion. But we did not have to do anything about this because it seemed very unlikely, given the poor communication at the time, that such a central religion would be able to spread and take over the Christian movement. We realized that our primary task was to focus on spreading the message of Christ as we were given to do so directly from Spirit without worrying about how other people did it, let alone competing with or fighting them. So the people present each went away with an impetus to spread the message as they were led to do so directly from within.

This doesn't mean that the ascended masters could not foresee the emergence of a centralized Christian religion. It does mean that they had us take the most practical approach, and as long as many different groups maintained a direct link to Jesus as an ascended master, the Christian movement would remain alive. Of course, the ascended masters respect the Law of Free Will. They knew well the central challenge they faced. They knew that the fallen beings would at first hope that the movement never became big enough to pose a threat to them. The masters knew that if the movement ever grew in popularity, the fallen beings would attempt to actively suppress it. If they could not do that, they would attempt to distort it.

The masters realized that the fallen beings would pervert Christianity by creating one centralized church. They would make sure this church was perverted so that the original message of the path to Christhood was left out. They would then claim that this was the only true church and they would use whatever power they had to actively destroy all competing views. The masters also knew that they had no way to prevent this. The only effective way to prevent the emergence of a centralized church created by the fallen beings was to create a centralized church led by the masters. However, given how free will works, such a church was likely to also be taken over and perverted by the fallen beings, as had happened in past ages. The reason being that while the ascended masters have absolute respect for the free will of human beings, the fallen beings have absolutely no respect.

So the masters knew that there was nothing they could do that could not be perverted and they made the choice that seemed most productive for the time. And for several hundred years, the path to Christhood was kept alive by many small and often unconnected traditions or mystery schools, producing enough people with Christhood that it could raise the collective consciousness. Of course, this process was eventually stopped by the fallen beings when they managed to create a centralized Christian church with the military power to suppress all dissent. But I am again getting ahead of myself.

# 49

You might be wondering why Jesus' public mission lasted only three years. Why didn't he take more time to train his disciples so they could have come more into unity and created a more whole movement that could allow women to hold leadership positions? There are several reasons for this and the ascended masters are always working with a set of very complex equations to determine the timetables for important events. One of these factors was how well people responded to Jesus' message, and although there was a response it was not as large as the masters had hoped for. The determining factor here was not the number of disciples Jesus attracted but the response from the general public. The greater the response from the public, the more quickly it is possible to shift the collective consciousness. The lower this response, the longer it will take. Thus, there was less incentive to keep Jesus in embodiment when it was a huge advantage for the earth that he ascended.

However, one of the many factors behind keeping Jesus' mission so short had to do with Lucifer and his Dark Master in the identity realm. This master was working very actively to create a violent rebellion against the Romans in Israel. The purpose was to create such chaos that very few people could respond to Jesus' message. Obviously, Jesus' message was completely non-violent and in a war-torn country where the temple had been destroyed by the Romans (as did eventually happen), who will listen to someone preaching non-violence?

By letting himself be killed at that time, Jesus prevented this from happening, and the later war was not as devastating as it could have been. However, the most important aspect of the death of Jesus was that it brought the judgment of Christ upon Lucifer and the Dark Master. The importance of this can hardly be overstated, even though it has, naturally, become lost in official Christian doctrines.

\*\*\*

The more visible effect was that Lucifer was taken out of embodiment. This happened three days after Jesus' death on the cross, and it is not recorded anywhere. Thus, the event deserves to be described. Obviously, I was not an eye-witness to the event, but I have seen it later in the Akashic records.

Lucifer lived in the temple complex upon Temple Mount. At the third day after Jesus had died on the cross, Lucifer was having a meeting with a group of temple leaders. Suddenly, and with no prior warning, Jesus appeared out of thin air in front of the group. He appeared in a light body, but it had taken on such density that it could be seen and felt by people.

Jesus was facing Lucifer and at first said nothing. Lucifer (and the others) looked upon him with disbelief and fear for almost a minute. Lucifer finally found speech and stammered: "But, you are dead. I saw you die on the cross . . . This is impossible. I refuse to believe this apparition."

He then started to give some incantations designed to ward off lower spirits (something black magicians are good at and have a frequent need for). Naturally, the incantations had no effect on Jesus. After several minutes, Lucifer realized the futility of this and fell silent. Jesus approached him and said: "I am not dead. Feel my body."

And he reached out and took Lucifer's hand. Lucifer started to turn grey and threw Jesus' hand as if it had been burning hot. Lucifer then turned to a table and took up a sacrificial knife. He attempted to run it through Jesus, but the knife and Lucifer went right through Jesus' body. Lucifer dropped the knife, and Jesus again approached Lucifer and took his hand, saying: "My physical body you could kill, but my Light body is not subject to the laws of the physical world. You cannot kill it and you cannot escape it in any other way."

Lucifer stammered: "Why . . . are you here?"

Jesus said with a thundering voice that made the air tremble: "I am here to take you to the Court of Sacred Fire where you will face the final judgment."

At this point, Lucifer fell to the ground from the power of Spirit, as did all those in the room. After a few seconds, the other people got up and ran in great panic. Lucifer also got up, but he started running towards the Temple while shouting: "You cannot withstand the power of Yahweh. You cannot follow me into the Holy of Holies."

He then ran across the Temple Square and into the Temple itself, running behind the curtain to the Holy of Holies where the Ark of the Covenant was kept. Naturally, Jesus followed him and had no problem withstanding the forcefield, even though it was indeed very intense in the Holy of Holies. The intensity was created by a combination of the people of Israel worshipping the false god for so long and also by the power of many fallen beings. At the time, the Holy of Holies of the Jewish Temple was the most intense focus of the fallen beings on earth (in the physical octave).

Lucifer took refuge by the Ark of the Covenant. It is said that no man could approach it, but a black magician of Lucifer's status could indeed walk right up to it. Naturally, Jesus had no problem with the forcefield of the black magician and walked right up to Lucifer who at this point realized he had nowhere else to go. Jesus again spoke with a thunderous voice: "I hereby pronounce the judgment of Christ upon you, Lucifer, and your Dark Master in the identity realm, the false god Yahweh!"

No sooner were the words out of his mouth than Lucifer started screaming as I have never heard a human being scream. He then literally burst into flames. I would not call it spontaneous human combustion as it was definitely brought about by the judgment of Christ activating all of Lucifer's momentums of darkness. In other words, it was Lucifer's own momentums of darkness that was now turned towards his physical body. This became such an intense energy that it burned his body. It took several minutes for Lucifer's body to be burned, but then all that was left was a surprisingly small pile of black ashes.

Jesus then turned to the Ark of the Covenant and again pronounced the judgment of Christ, demanding that it be withdrawn from the physical octave. The gold-covered chest gradually dissolved, leaving no physical trace behind. The ashes of Lucifer's body were also gone. The Holy of Holies was literally empty.

Naturally, the Jewish leadership never revealed this to the people, as it would have caused a crisis of faith and doubt in their leadership. They managed to keep up the illusion until the Temple was destroyed by the Romans, which gave them an excuse for not explaining how the Ark (If it was given my the most high god, how could it be destroyed?) could disappear. Instead, they created the seeds of what has now become the source of conspiracy theories about the Ark still being there somewhere, or being found by the Knights Templar, Indiana Jones or what have you. All of them are, of course, nonsense as the Ark is gone from the physical octave.

***

There is no question that Lucifer had reached such a momentum of black magic that it was a great relief for the planet that he was taken out of embodiment. Had he stayed in embodiment, he would have created far more havoc than what we have seen over the past 2000 years. I know this may seem hard to believe, but I have indeed seen Lucifer's capacity for destruction, and Stalin and Mao are schoolboys in comparison.

However, the really important outcome of Jesus' death on the cross was that it brought the judgment of Lucifer's master. It might be tempting to call him Yahweh, but this was just one way he has deceived people on earth. His original name has no meaning on earth, so I have referred to him as the "Dark Master." The Dark Master is an extremely powerful fallen being, not so much in raw, physical power but in his ability to deceive all those who do not have a fairly high level of Christ discernment. He was also the serpent in the Garden of Eden story. You might recall that in the Book of Revelation (Chapter 20) there is the following passage:

1 And I saw an angel come down from heaven, having the key of the bottomless pit and a great chain in his hand.

2 And he laid hold on the dragon, that old serpent, which is the Devil, and Satan, and bound him a thousand years,

3 And cast him into the bottomless pit, and shut him up, and set a seal upon him, that he should deceive the nations no more, till the thousand years should be fulfilled: and after that he must be loosed a little season.

Now, the Book of Revelation is actually the closest to a direct dictation from the ascended masters that you find in the official scriptures. However, it must be noted that it was given for an audience in a certain culture and with a certain level of consciousness. That is why it seems so ominous to us today. Also, the person who was a messenger for receiving it was not able to get it accurately so it cannot be taken literally, considered universally valid or particularly relevant today. It does not prophesy about events in our time, except as I will explain later. The words "Devil" and "Satan" were not the actual name of the Dark Master, they were names that the audience could relate to. However, when you look beyond that, the passage does refer to the fact that after the judgment of Christ, the Dark Master was bound and locked up. It was not for a thousand years but for the entire spiritual age for which the Ascended Master Jesus has been the spiritual overseer, namely the past 2000 years, the Age of Pisces. This has been very significant in the sense that had the Dark Master still been able to influence earth, the planet would have entered such a spiral of darkness that it would almost certainly have been impossible to stop it. The downward spiral would have become self-reinforcing and virtually irreversible. So the fact that this has not happened is largely attributable to the absence of the Dark Master.

***

Having described what happened to his master, let me describe what happened to Lucifer. As soon as his body was burned, Archangel Michael and a number of his angels took Lucifer's soul to a place called the Court of Sacred Fire. It is located in the central sun of our galaxy and presided over by the highest ascended masters in our galaxy, namely Alpha and Omega.

I have said that there is a hierarchy of ascended masters ranking from the masters working with earth through progressively higher levels and going all the way to just below the Creator. Our sun is a focus of the ascended masters working with earth. It is part of an even larger unit, and you can keep going to higher levels until you reach the central sun of our galaxy. Naturally, our galaxy is part of an even larger unit, and there is a central sun for the entire physical universe. There are also succeeding levels in the spiritual realm, meaning the first six spheres that ascended. It is difficult to fathom this with the linear, human mind, but once you have seen glimpses of it, you can never go back to the limited perspective on life with which we have been brought up by our so-called sophisticated civilization.

The central sun of our galaxy is a truly magnificent place. I am, naturally, not talking about a physical place, as the ascended masters are focused in the identity octave. It is designed like a city, but far beyond anything ever seen or dreamt of on earth. There are buildings, but because they are not subject to the density found on earth, their design is so different that an architect on earth could not even imagine it.

The most magnificent building is the central hall, which is on a scale beyond any building on earth. Is is shaped like an upside-down funnel with a spire that reaches so high that it actually touches the spiritual realm and acts as a direct funnel for spiritual energy. This energy flows down through the roof structure of the building and is spread out to the entire galaxy.

Inside is an immense room where the roof seems to disappear into a mist. Along the edges are columns that are incredibly tall yet seem so light they are almost floating. When you are used to seeing buildings on earth, these columns seem to be made from light, not a physical substance. They bear some resemblance to tubes made of white glass with a light shining inside them.

The interior of the hall is shaped like an amphitheater, and the walkways all lead down to a central area. On one side of it is a platform, and on it sits two thrones. These are the thrones upon which sit Alpha and Omega when they are conducting one of the many sessions that take place in the room. I have only seen Alpha and Omega as two clouds of white energy that have very bright eyes. This is because my consciousness is not high enough to see their actual shape. Jesus has told me that he can see their actual forms and that they are magnificent beyond all description.

Between the thrones of Alpha and Omega is a white cube of a material unknown on earth. It is brilliant and pulsating, and it literally forms the heartbeat of our galaxy. A slight change in it's vibration would affect the entire galaxy. If you are standing before the thrones of Alpha and Omega, you can see a flow of energy between them. It forms a horizontal figure-eight and its nexus is right above the white cube. If you focus on the nexus and let go of all other emotional, mental and identity activity, you can see through the nexus and experience the Creator itself. You cannot "see" the Creator because it has no form, and thus cannot be called a "he" or a "she." But you can sense that this formless Being is your source as a being with form. You can sense that the Creator knows you personally and loves you with a love that is purely and utterly unconditional. These are, of course, only words because no words can accurately describe the feeling. Once you have experienced the feeling, you will never be the same, and that is why having this experience can only happen when you are ready to surrender your identification with your four lower bodies and anything in the material universe. It truly can happen only in your last embodiment when you know you are not coming back to this planet.

Anyway, I got caught up in describing the most life-changing experience I have ever had, so back to Lucifer. In the Central Sun is another building, namely the Court of Sacred Fire. Every Central Sun has such a facility and it serves various purposes. One of them is that it is the only place that a Conscious You can be dissolved. As I have described, the Conscious You is sent down by an I AM Presence and is meant to have many experiences until it voluntarily chooses to reunite with the I AM

Presence in the ritual of the ascension. If a Conscious You, as did Lucifer, refuses to ascend, it will be given a very long time to experience the state of separation in the hope that it will eventually have enough of it. However, if it continues to refuse to ascend, there will come a point when its opportunity has been used up and it will be dissolved in the Court of Sacred Fire. Lucifer's opportunity had been close to running out, but it had been shortened by the fact that he killed the Living Christ.

So Lucifer's soul was taken there by Archangel Michael whose angels had also bound a large number of demons in the emotional, mental and identity realms that were created by Lucifer and the Dark Master. These were all taken to the central room in the Court of Sacred Fire. This is a very large space and the room has twelve sides, the roof being shaped like an intricate diamond. In the center of the room is a platform of very intricate design and upon it burns a flame that is unfed, meaning it receives no fuel from this unascended sphere. It is driven entirely by spiritual energy. It appears more like an electrical flame than a physical flame.

***

Lucifer's final judgment was a very complex event. When I say "judgment," this is using the language from the Book of Revelation. It really should be called Lucifer's final opportunity to choose to walk the path towards the ascension. The reason it was complex was that in order to give Lucifer the best possible opportunity to make a different choice, he was to be confronted with all lifestreams he had ever violated. This would happen through a special procedure.

On one side of the Court hall was a holding area where all of the demons had been bound. They were so paralyzed by the higher energies in the court that they were unable to move or utter the bizarre sounds that demons exude. On another side was a platform where Lucifer was held. Opposite him was a huge screen. Behind Lucifer were seats that could hold a large number of participants.

When proceedings began, Omega stepped towards Lucifer and said: "This session in the Court of Sacred Fire is hereby opened. Our purpose is to assist this lifestream in seeing all of its actions and the consequences they have had for others, thereby giving the lifestream a final opportunity to leave behind its separate identity and accept that all life is one, and then walking the path towards oneness with its I AM Presence." Omega now turned to Lucifer and said: "Ever since you stepped into the dualistic consciousness, you have built a separate self. This self has been like a filter that has distorted the way you experience everything. The effect has been that everything you have perceived has – seemingly – reinforced the view that you are a separate self. You have even come to believe that as a separate self you have become so powerful that no force in the universe can do anything to you. You have been allowed to build this illusion because the Law of Free Will allows you to go as far as you can conceive of going into separation.

As you have now experienced, your separate self was not invulnerable and it has now been bound. In order to give you an opportunity to experience life without this separate self, all of the energies that make up this self will now be transmuted by the Sacred Fire."

Omega then stretched out her hands and it looked as if she lifted part of Lucifer's aura away from him. This appeared like a cloud of black, grey and red energy. It was amazing to see that after this was lifted from him, Lucifer appeared like a tiny dot of light inside a faint human form. Omega then moved her arms and Lucifer's energies were moved into the Sacred Fire in the center of the court. As soon as it entered the flame, the flame started burning very brightly and there was an incredibly loud hissing sound. The flame kept pulsating for several minutes until all of the energy was consumed. It was incredible to see how the very dense energy gathered by Lucifer over such a long period of time could be burned in just a few minutes. It left you with a sense of how awe-inspiring of a power is held by the ascended masters and how nothing the fallen beings have generated can withstand this power. One also got a deep respect for the fact that the ascended masters have such power yet restrict it in order to allow free will to outplay itself.

Take note that what was consumed were the energies that were misqualified through Lucifer's separate self, it was not the self that was consumed. Lucifer had created this self by making choices, and he could uncreate it only by making more aware choices. The difficulty being, of course, that as long as the energies of the self colored his vision, he could not make those new choices. By taking the energy, there was a drastic reduction in the magnetic pull that the separate self had on the Conscious You. By being shown his actions and their consequences from a different perspective, Lucifer then had a better opportunity to come to see the limitations of his separate self and then start to make more aware choices.

Also, take note that what was taken were only the energies making up the separate self, not all of the energies in Lucifer's aura. One might say that what was taken was the energies that affected his view of himself, not the energies misqualified through his actions.

Omega now turned to Lucifer again and said: "You will now be given an opportunity to see on this screen all events where you have violated specific lifestreams that you had personal contact with. These lifestreams will step forward one at a time. The recording from the Akashic records will then be played on the screen. After this, all of us here will make calls for the Akashic records to be finally dissolved. All of these lifestreams have ascended and thus raised themselves above these records. Because you have not ascended, the records remained as to give you this final opportunity. After you have seen the record, the record will be permanently dissolved and the lifestream will be completely free of you."

The first ascended master now stepped forward, and the screen was filled with scenes from Lucifer's life in the fourth sphere. Lucifer now experienced a situation without the perception filter he had at the time, the perception filter that made him feel justified in violating the other lifestream. He also experienced how the other lifestream had experienced the situation at the time. When the scene had been played, the beings in the Court all made some short calls, and the record was dissolved in the Sacred Fire.

Given that Lucifer was such an old lifestream, this scenario obviously continued for a very long time. I will leave it for now, as there were important events taking place on earth in the meantime. I will later return to give you the final chapter in the existence of the being I have called Lucifer.

# 50

The 33 days during which Jesus was going through the preparations for his ascension was also a testing period for all of his followers. The crucial issue was whether they were able to carry on, in his absence, what he had trained them to do. Were they willing to form the kind of spiritual movement that Jesus had trained them to form, including allowing women to hold any position in the movement. During this time, it became clear that the majority of Jesus' followers were still so trapped in the patriarchal mindset that they were unwilling to create the kind of movement outlined by Jesus.

The best case scenario would have been that Jesus' followers would have been willing to carry out the vision given to them by Jesus. This would have allowed Jesus to sponsor this movement in a very direct way, including that he could have appeared in his ascended "body" on a regular basis. Because the majority of the followers were not willing to carry out this vision, primarily because of their view on women, they activated the Law of Free Will, and this prevented Jesus from having the most direct influence on the new movement. This left Jesus to decide what to do instead of his original scenario. Take note that although I have portrayed Peter as a leader in the rejection of women, he was by no means the only one. As you can see even in today's age, the programming of the fallen beings towards woman can be very difficult to transcend.

***

Jesus had planned to keep his promise to be with us always in a very physical way, in the sense that he would have used his ascended "body" to appear in many situations. This would only have required a leader who was able to serve as a messenger for Jesus and a crowd of people willing to set an energetic forcefield. I described one of the events where Jesus was a messenger and where the ascended masters appeared visibly to people. This was to be the archetypal event for the Christian movement, with Jesus being the ascended master appearing whenever a gathering had raised their consciousness sufficiently.

Since this could not be done on a broad basis (it did happen on some occasions), Jesus decided on a different course of action. Jesus had council sessions with the ascended masters supporting him, and they decided that Jesus would be given a dispensation to materialize another physical body and live for a time on earth. He could not do this in Israel and he chose Kashmir as his location. Here, he would create a mystery school that could continue the tradition of the venutians and teach those of his followers who were ready for higher initiations. By doing this, it was the hope that gradually more and more people could be trained to receive direct dictations so that over time, the movement envisioned by Jesus could be built.

It was decided that Magda, myself and a few other of his followers would accompany him. This was to some degree done for the protection of Magda, partly from the fallen beings in Jewish leadership and partly from Peter and his followers. We therefore departed Israel in secrecy, even going to the extent of having Joseph of Arimathea set up the decoy mission of claiming Magda had been taken to Southern France. To this day, some people believe in this, having given rise to the many myths about Mary Magdalen in France, even carrying Jesus' child and starting a royal bloodline. Amazing that modern people can believe that a device as primitive as the human gene can carry the characteristics of Christhood. The entire purpose of Christhood is to demonstrate that you can rise above physical limitations. It is nonsensical to think that you need a certain genetic combination in order to manifest Christhood. This is truly the fallen beings and their dream of a mechanical salvation. They would love to have Christhood reduced to something encoded in genes or other physical things so that they could gain control over it. It cannot be done.

\*\*\*

After we arrived in Kashmir, we took some years to build the mystery school and then we started receiving students. Magda, myself and several other people had been trained to teach the students and bring them to a level where they were ready to receive instructions from Jesus. Jesus did live in a body that seemed quite normal. Only if you saw him over a long period of time, would you know that his body did not age. As my hair started to turn grey, Jesus still looked like he was in his mid-thirties. Of course, Jesus was active as an ascended master at the same time because his ascended consciousness could span the two different worlds.

Jesus and Magda did have children, but there is no special significance to them as heirs to a dynasty or whatever people might come up with. They were actually souls with which Magda had karma from past lives or who deserved the opportunity to be close to Jesus. Jesus took the opportunity to help Magda pay off as much karmic debt as possible. It is far easier to pay off your karmic debts while still being in a physical body.

You might wonder how anyone knew about the mystery school and how we recruited students. The answer is that when a person was ready, Jesus would sense this and he would then appear to that person and direct them to come to the school. They would then remain there for as long as they needed, until they had been put in contact with their Divine plan and could go out into the world and carry it out. Paul is one example of how Jesus appeared to a student who was ready at inner levels, even though his outer mind was not ready. Paul did attend the mystery school in Kashmir, but naturally he was not allowed to tell this to anyone and thus there is no record of it. By the way, many of the negative remarks about women attributed to Paul were not actually made by him. They were inserted in the scriptures by the fallen beings. It must be stated, though, that Paul is an example of a person who could not free himself from the patriarchal heritage. That is indeed why he became accepted by the various congregations that had sprung up. So Paul's influence on Christianity did not live up to its highest potential, but he did bring the movement forward. Paul is today an ascended master.

\*\*\*

Being in the Mystery School of Jesus was a wonderful experience for me. I can only say that on this planet, the best times I have ever had were in the Venusian Mystery School and in the "Jesuvian" school. It was a daily inspiration to see Jesus interact with the students. He had a unique way to shake people out of their perception filters, partly because he could do just about anything he wanted with his physical body.

It should be said that he used his abilities only with students who had reached a certain level because he was very careful not to encourage idolatry. The last thing he wanted was for the students to feel he was so far above them that they could never reach anywhere near his level. That is why he took on a physical body and appeared to be like the rest of us.

As all things on an unnatural planet, the Mystery School of Jesus also came to an end. This was partly determined by the response of the students, partly by the process of judging Lucifer. I have said that Lucifer's "show and tell" session lasted a very long time. In the Central Sun, time is very different, but in earth time it lasted 48 years. Thus, in the year where Jesus would have turned 81, the session was over. At the same time, Magda's physical body had reached the end of its lifespan, and Jesus determined to close the mystery school and prepare for his spiritual ascension. Jesus stayed in embodiment long enough to cremate Magda and I stayed in embodiment until Jesus ascended. Even though his body appeared to be physical, it did not die and did not need to be cremated. Jesus had manifested the body and he simply withdrew it, or rather, raised the energies. After that, I also took my leave of the body and before I came into my next embodiment, I was fortunate enough to witness both the final judgment of Lucifer and the ascension of Jesus.

# 51

I have described how Lucifer had to face many of the lifestreams he had hurt since his entrance into duality. As I described about my first embodiment, Lucifer had often been instrumental in the killing of millions of people. He did not have to encounter all of these people, but only the ones with whom he had direct, personal interaction. When it came to mass killings, he would be given a general view of the situation.

Towards the end, Jesus and I were invited to be part of the process. Jesus went first and I was allowed to witness this. It was truly invaluable for me to see the situations that took place before I came into embodiment and how Jesus had been drawn into a reactionary pattern by Lucifer. I naturally saw Jesus as being a more advanced or experienced lifestream than myself, and it was a relief to see that he had been forced into a reactionary pattern in much the same way as I had. I could therefore overcome my own last little bit of idolatry for him by realizing that when it comes to the fallen beings, it doesn't matter how advanced you are. Once you take embodiment on an unnatural planet, it is impossible to avoid going into a reactionary pattern. The atrocities committed by the fallen beings are simply so shocking and intense that only a fallen being could avoid reacting to them. You can only avoid reacting when you see others as separate beings. When you have a sense of oneness with life, you will feel compassion for the people violated by the fallen beings, and this means you must react.

I also saw how Jesus had started to come out of his reactionary spiral much earlier than me, and I saw what it was that had triggered this for him. Even though Jesus had many embodiments where he was fighting the fallen beings, he came to see that for each act of violence, he added another thread to the rope that tied him to them. This made him see the futility of fighting, and he started looking for a different way to respond. This culminated in the embodiment where Jesus and I fought each other on the battlefield and we decided to look for an alternative to violence. This helped me let go of the last remnants of my desire to find a force-based solution to the problem of the fallen beings. It was beautiful to see how Jesus in the end completely forgave Lucifer. I was allowed to see how this severed the last energetic tie that Jesus had to Lucifer. Jesus was now completely free of the fallen consciousness.

\*\*\*

When it came to be my turn, I was watching (this time from the outside instead of from the inside) the entire situation where Lucifer had exposed me to total pain. This was invaluable to me because I now got to see every bit of programming that Lucifer had put into my mind while I had been withdrawn from the body. I therefore learned that Lucifer had put a very clever piece of programming into my mind. It had several layers. First, he had used my own shock over his actions to program into me that there was nothing worse in the entire universe than a fallen being. He then programmed into me that the worst thing that could possibly happen to me was that I discovered that I was a fallen being. Lastly, he programmed into me that before I came to earth, I had indeed been a fallen being and had committed far worse atrocities than Lucifer had ever done.

When I witnessed this, I realized that ever since that experience, there had been something in my own being that I had been afraid to look at. I now saw that when I was exposed to the original trauma, I had decided that I never wanted to experience pain like that again. This was a natural enough desire, but here is how it became turned into a chain that had kept me enslaved for nearly two million years.

I never wanted to experience pain like that again (or worse pain). At the same time, I now had a program in my mind that made me believe that the worst imaginable pain would be to discover that I was a fallen being. I also had a program saying that I *was* a fallen being and that I had committed terrible atrocities in the past. The effect was that the desire to avoid the worst possible pain prevented me from looking at the programs Lucifer had inserted. The mere suspicion that I might be a fallen being was so painful that I had never been willing to look at it. You think you will die if you look. And of course, there is only one way to overcome such programming, namely to look at it and experience that you didn't die. You can never be free from something until you have looked at it. It really doesn't matter whether it is true or not. By looking at it, you can go through it and then you will discover that you are more than whatever the programming says you are.

After this session with Lucifer, I went aside and found a quiet place. I went within and got in touch with the fear of even considering that I might be a fallen being. The pain was extremely intense, but I decided to walk right into it instead of seeking to avoid it, as I had always done before. There is an interesting mechanics involved. When you seek to avoid something, you actually create a different kind of pain, and it is a pain that you will carry with you as long as you are in avoidance mode. However, you get used to it and therefore it seems bearable compared to the pain you fear.

I had known the value of going into the pain for some time and often used it for other issues in my psychology, including the other programming inserted by Lucifer. I now decided to apply it to this issue and went right into the pain caused by the fear that I might be a fallen being. As always, once I went into the pain, it wasn't as bad as I thought. In fact, there really is no such thing as an unbearable pain (I am talking about emotional, mental and identity pain, not physical). There is a mechanism in the mind that labels a past experience as having given you unbearable pain. Your mind is then creating a mental image and it is only according to this image that the pain is unbearable. This creates a resistance in you towards ever experiencing such pain again, and it is your own resistance that can make a situation unbearable. It is perfectly true that there are many situations on a planet like earth that give us immense pain. Yet it is only when we resist having the experience that the pain seems impossible to bear.

Once you decide to experience a painful situation without internal resistance, but with total surrender, you immediately realize that the pain is bearable. It might be very intense, but it is bearable. So as I went into the pain caused by the fear that I was a fallen being, I found that the pain was bearable. I then decided to go right into the core of the pain, to experience it with no restrictions. I openly considered: "So, if I really were a fallen being, then what would happen?" I then realized that regardless of who I had been in the past, I had proven my commitment to the path of self-transcendence and thus I was not a fallen being now. I then quickly went through the pain and found a state of inner peace.

I was now able to look at the claim that I might be a fallen being, and I was given a vision of my entire lifespan, showing clearly that I had not fallen before I came to earth and that I had never committed any of the atrocities that lucifer had committed. The reason being that I had never developed the total insensitivity to life that Lucifer had developed.

This was another lesson I learned from watching the replay of some of Lucifer's reactions. I saw that his insensitivity to life was complete. This was something my mind simply could not wrap itself around, and I see this reaction in many other people. I have no doubt that many of the people who read this book will doubt that the fallen beings really can be so bad.

This is because such people have sensitivity to life, and we simply cannot imagine that a being could be completely devoid of such sensitivity. That is why we think it must be possible to reason with the fallen beings, and that is why we get involved with them, as you see from my example. Some people have even developed "sympathy for the devil" and this has led to them putting themselves in a mental prison from which it is extremely difficult to escape. This is especially true for those who have the pride of not wanting to admit that they were wrong.

\*\*\*

After I realized that I am not a fallen being, I had faced the worst possible fear, and nothing could ever be as bad again. This was a great liberation. A parallel to this can be when people are close to death and realize nothing could ever be as terrifying again. The fallen beings gain control over us by making us afraid to look at something in our own psychology. As long as the fear of looking at it is greater than the pain caused by not looking at it, we can be well and truly stuck. It is only a raised awareness that can cause us to break the deadlock and move on.

Given that I had now overcome my worst fear, it was possible for me to take a look at my second-worst fear. I quickly realized what it was. During my two million years on earth, I had maintained the desire to understand Lucifer and to either help him or do something to help the earth be free of him. I had struggled and suffered a lot during those two million years, and I wanted it to mean something. I wanted it to have caused some kind of progress so it had not been a waste of time. I wanted it to have been worth it.

Can you see what was my second-biggest fear? It was my personal variation of one of the most common fears on this planet, namely the fear of being wrong. I was afraid that I could have been completely wrong about the fallen beings. I was afraid that my interactions with Lucifer had not had any impact on him whatsoever. I was afraid that all of my suffering had been a complete waste of time, that I had wasted two million years on an impossible quest.

Naturally, I went right into the pain, and I was helped by watching the final chapter of Lucifer's trial.

\*\*\*

After Lucifer had encountered all of the people he had hurt and experienced their reaction to him, Omega and several other ascended masters approached him. They wanted to hear his reaction. They were looking to see if this experience had caused Lucifer to be willing to leave behind the fallen consciousness and instead start the upward path towards Christhood, including transmuting all of the energy he had misqualified in this and past spheres. Apparently, this "life review" often reawakens the compassion of a fallen being and jolts it out of its state of denial. By experiencing the reactions of others, the fallen being is often awakened to the fact that it still has a spark of light within itself and thus a tie to the oneness of all life. It quickly became clear that this had not happened to Lucifer, as he started arguing with the masters.

At first, Lucifer argued that what they were doing to him was a violation of his free will. He argued that for free will to be absolute, he should be allowed to do whatever he wanted for all eternity, if that was what he wanted. Therefore, the fact that he had been forced to watch this was a violation of his free will. The masters reasoned with him, explaining that free will would not exist if choices did not have consequences. And the choice to go into denial about the fact that choices have consequences for other beings or oneself must eventually lead to a lifestream in denial being faced with consequences it cannot ignore or deny. In other words, the masters were not forcing Lucifer's free will. Lucifer himself had forced his free will. What he was experiencing was not caused by the masters but was the ultimate consequence of his own choices.

To me, this was fully convincing, and I sensed that Lucifer realized he could not refute it. As all people in denial, he refused to admit this consciously and instead sought to divert attention by going into another line of reasoning. This time, he argued that he had only done what someone had to do. Given that beings had been given free will, it was inevitable that some of them would go into duality. Since duality had two polarities, someone had to play the role of the adversary. Therefore, it was an inevitable consequence of god's choice to give people free will that there had to be someone who would act the part of the devil, opposing everything that god did. Someone had to be bad so that people could have something to avoid and make themselves feel good.

The masters explained that all of this was perfectly true. Once beings with free will had stepped into duality, the evolution of two polarities was inevitable. Yet both the people who embodied the *good* dualistic polarity and those who embodied the *evil* dualistic polarity would face the consequences of their choices. This was, again, what Lucifer was facing. The fact that the appearance of dualistic polarities was inevitable did not neutralize choice. First of all, people had to choose to step into duality. They then had to choose which polarity to embody, and they also chose how to outplay that polarity. Again, if choices had no consequences, there could be no choice so the ultimate consequence of what Lucifer had done was that his opportunity to choose duality must come to an end.

Lucifer again had no rebuttal and went into arguing that by giving beings free will, god had effectively given the earth to the fallen beings. It was their domain and they had a right to do with it whatever they wanted. Thus, the ascended masters had no right to interfere with earth or to seek to free humankind from the fallen beings. It was the choices of the people on earth that had invited the fallen beings here, and it was only the choices of the people of earth that could remove them. Thus, the ascended masters were interfering with the law by seeking to free humanity from the fallen beings.

The masters explained that the fallen beings had actually taken away the choices of people on earth because people cannot choose an option that they cannot see. Thus, the masters do have the right to show us that there is something beyond duality, which is exactly what the Buddha, Jesus and all other true spiritual teachers are about. The masters also explained that as long as a critical mass of the people on earth did not rise above the fallen consciousness, the fallen beings could not be completely removed. Yet beyond this, there is also the life of an individual being, and Lucifer had simply reached the end of his personal opportunity. He had already been close, but the killing of Jesus had hastened the end of time for him.

Lucifer then went into trying to argue that this all proved that free will is a sham and that it is not truly free. This became rather repetitive, as he was simply regurgitating his previous arguments with new words. It became clear to me that he simply did not get the rather basic truth that being able to do anything you want without facing any consequences is not free will.

\*\*\*

Finally, Lucifer argued that the free will given to us by god is a sham. It is not truly free because god wants us to act a certain way and this is proven by the fact that we must face the consequences of our actions. It was only by rebelling against god and everything he stood for that Lucifer had gained a will that was truly free. The masters explained something I had never thought about, but which I saw was very profound. They explained, again, that a choice that led to no consequence was not actually a choice.

The essence of free will is that the material universe (actually all four octaves) form something similar to what we today call a virtual reality environment or a biofeedback device. We are exercising our free will in an environment that responds to us. What we project out with our four lower bodies, will be reflected back to us as physical circumstances. The entire purpose of this is that we see a feedback of our choices so that we can refine those choices. This is how we grow.

We start out with a point-like sense of self. We form impulses based on our sense of self and project them out. As we experience the reaction from the feed-back device, we use this to expand our sense of self. We can now formulate a broader impulse and as we see the result of it, we again expand our sense of self.

When we go into duality, we deny this process. We refuse to expand our sense of self. Instead, we come to believe in the illusion that the physical circumstances we encounter are not the result of our own projections but are created by some remote god or some impersonal laws of nature. We have now denied the most basic purpose of life, namely the transcendence of our sense of self. Instead, we are now limiting our sense of self.

As I have explained, from this point forward, we have closed ourselves to direct input from the ascended masters. As we densify our consciousness, we densify our material environment, and this inevitably limits our powers and causes suffering. This limits our choices even more, and we can eventually come to a point where we have basically taken away our freedom of choice. This can be reinforced by the fallen beings and the entire purpose for this is really only to bring us to the point where we realize that duality does not work, that denial does not work. Thus, we again become willing to look at what our physical circumstances say about our state of consciousness and then change our state of consciousness, transcending the elements that limit us.

In other words, nothing in duality matters. There is no outcome that needs to happen in the physical world. It is not a matter of finding the ultimate religion or political system and establishing it as having dominance on earth. All such epic ideas are created by the fallen beings to keep us trapped in duality. Duality is necessary in order to make free will complete. However, the only purpose of everything that happens in duality is to bring us to a point where we have had enough of pain, limitations and suffering. We can then realize that this is all caused by denial (of oneness). When we consciously decide to abandon denial, we can once again engage in the upward path of expanding our sense of self.

Lucifer again tried to argue that we only have truly free will when we can do anything we want, meaning our past choices do not limit our future choices. The masters explained that the material universe is a feed-back device that returns to us what we project out. However, in order to project out a certain impulse, we have to first create a matrix in our identity, mental and emotional bodies. Lucifer had created this matrix in order to play the adversary. There is nothing wrong with this, and as long as we are conscious that we are more than the matrix, we can easily get out of it again.

As Lucifer had taken on the matrix of being the adversary, he had projected out impulses and he could not escape facing the consequences. Even though he had often managed to make other people bear part of the karma for his actions (for example, by deceiving a nation into supporting his war), he still faced the fact that someone was opposing his attempts to take unlimited power (exemplified by Satan and even by Jesus and myself in some embodiments).

Here comes the crucial point. We are actually allowed to play any role in the theater of earth. There was nothing inherently wrong with doing many of the things Lucifer had done, given that this is an unnatural planet, designed to let people outplay the duality consciousness until they have had enough of it. However, once you go into denial about the fact that the consequences you face are a product of what you have projected out (and thus, the only way to change what is coming back is to change what you project out by transcending the consciousness you used to project the impulse), you can no longer see that you are simply playing a role. Instead, you now become identified with the role, meaning you begin to think this is who you are.

You then use this role to project other impulses, and when they come back, you again deny that this is your doing. The effect of this is that by rebelling against what Lucifer saw as god, he did not gain an entirely free will. Instead, he limited his will to being entirely reactionary. He simply failed to see that he was not rebelling against the real God, but against a dualistic god created in his own mind. Thus, while Lucifer was thinking he was working to prove god wrong, he was in reality reacting against his own identity, mental and emotional matrices. Lucifer thought he was at war with god, but he was truly only at war with himself. Lucifer had not himself created the matrix of this dualistic god, as it was created by the Dark Master. So he did not see that it was not the real god he was fighting, but actually the Dark Master, who was claiming that he was helping Lucifer become truly free.

The masters explained that the mechanism is simple. We go into a state of consciousness, a sense of self, and we use it to project out an impulse. When we experience a return current from the cosmic mirror that we don't like, we have the opportunity to change the matrix in our minds. If we refuse to do this and go into denial, we actually give up our free will because we now think that we are not responsible for what is coming back, meaning we cannot change it. We give away our power to change our situation. We may think this is freedom (because we deny that our choices have consequences), but it is actually condemning ourselves to reacting to circumstances over which we think we have no control.

The effect is that we now identify ourselves with the role we have taken on (as an actor who refuses to take off the costume and make-up when the play is over, but continues to think he really is Hamlet). Of course, we cannot then avoid sending out new impulses through that matrix. As they come back, we now think that the universe is affirming that there really is some objective world out there that is forcing us. Thus, we begin to believe that the only way to change our situation is to change the external world.

Yet this is another layer of denial, and as long as we uphold it, we are in what philosophers call an infinite regress. Our consciousness sends out an impulse. When the reaction from the cosmic mirror comes back, we go into denial. We then reinforce our dualistic self and send out a more powerful impulse. When it comes back, we must reinforce our denial, and this can go on as long as we can gather the energy to continue the process.

When I heard this, the proverbial light bulb went off in my head, and I truly saw how free will works and how wisely the universe is designed in order to help us grow. Unfortunately, there was no light bulb in Lucifer's head.

\*\*\*

It became clear to me that Lucifer simply did not get the reality of free will and how his own denial was what had taken away his freedom of choice. I realized this was because he was not willing to abandon his denial, and the reason was that he had such arrogance that he would not even consider that he could have been wrong. Lucifer was absolutely convinced that he was right and that god was wrong in an absolute sense. So if Lucifer had to admit that his reasoning had been wrong, it would mean that Lucifer had been wrong in the worst possible way.

I then thought that I had better not be as unwilling as Lucifer to consider whether I had been wrong, and I took another look at my journey on earth. I saw very clearly that my thinking that I could somehow persuade Lucifer had been a complete and utter mistake on my part. I had just experienced that ascended masters could not persuade Lucifer so I realized it was arrogant of me to think that I could do so. I then completely surrendered any desire to change Lucifer or any other fallen being. I felt how something broke inside me, and I felt a freedom I had not known since being on natural planets.

I then realized that everything I had done to fight the fallen beings was also a mistake, despite the fact that in my mind it was all done to set the people or earth free from the tyranny of the fallen beings. I realized that I had spent over a million years in this mode of seeking to destroy evil. Think about how many embodiments you can have in a million years, especially when many of them are cut short because you die in war. Think about all the trouble of being born as a drivelling baby, having to deal with dirty diapers and learning not to smear oatmeal all over your face. You go through all that trouble to grow up, and then you enthusiastically join the fight for good, seeking to defeat evil, only to be taken out of embodiment and having to start all over again. And it was all for nothing. It did absolutely no good. It never brought the planet one step closer to being free of the fallen beings. In fact, it only misqualified energy that delayed the freedom of humanity.

I went into the pain associated with admitting that this had been a mistake and then I went through it. As I came out on the other side, I did completely and fully admit that this had not been an enlightened choice. I also saw that the pain of admitting this had been caused by a simple mechanism. When we go into duality, we go into a state of mind with two opposites, namely right and wrong. There is now a sense of elation associated with being right and a sense of shame or embarrassment associated with being wrong. This is why we start believing that if we do the right thing, then we will always feel right. It is those people who oppose us that are wrong. In other words, if we were proven wrong, we would have to be as judgmental towards ourselves as we have been towards those bad people. Because this would be unbearable, we refuse to even consider it. The very consciousness that causes us to fight others also prevents us from admitting that this is senseless.

Once I went through the pain of judging myself based on my old, dualistic state of consciousness, I realized that I am more than my dualistic self. I had simply taken on a role, and by admitting this, I also gained the freedom to take off that role. By acknowledging this, I no longer needed to judge my actions through the dualistic self, through the filter of the role I had been playing. I then realized that there was no denying that my one million years of fighting evil had done no good. On the other hand, I needed to have that experience in order to come to the realization that I wanted more than duality. And if that was the time it took for me, then that was perfectly okay from a cosmic perspective. It was perfectly within the time limit given to me by my own choices, and really it wasn't such a long time seen in a larger perspective.

The effect was that I took full and final responsibility for having made the choices I made. By doing this, I saw that these choices were made because I was looking at life through an unreal self. When I saw this self, I dis-identified myself from it, and then I reconnected to my formless self. This meant I could take responsibility for my former choices, learn and integrate the lesson from them and then totally forgive myself, thereby dissolving the self that caused me to make those choices. I was now free from my past, *completely and utterly free.*

\*\*\*

Lucifer was not free of his past and consistently refused to do the one thing that could set him free. At one point, I had the thought that while I had been trying to understand Lucifer from a distance in order to change him, there was one thing I had never done. It was to project myself into Lucifer's mind in order to experience life as he experienced it. This at first seemed scary to me, but then I realized that given my new state of freedom, I had no need to be afraid. There was nothing in Lucifer's mind that could deceive me anymore. So at one point I was sitting there watching

Lucifer as he tried to refute something a master had said, and I then centered in my heart and projected my Conscious You into Lucifer's mind.

The effect was the most shocking experience I have ever had. From an outside perspective, Lucifer seemed to be completely sure that he was right, and it had seemed to me that he must be feeling he had great power. Thus, I had assumed that, given all his apparent arrogance, he must be feeling pretty good about himself. Yet once I was inside his mind, I realized that he was the absolutely most miserable being I had ever come across.

I had been feeling pretty bad about myself when I recognized that I had wasted a million years fighting the fallen beings. Yet Lucifer had spent a much, much longer time span in his mind. I thought he had used that time to build an impenetrable self-assuredness, but instead the tension of his constant strain to uphold his denial had taken him into a bottomless abyss of feeling so miserable that it was infinitely worse than anything I had felt. It was truly unbearable to me, and I had to very quickly project myself out of his aura in order to avoid being overwhelmed by the feeling of self-loathing and misery.

Interestingly, Lucifer had sensed it immediately when I projected myself into his aura. He fell silent and turned to face me. When I projected myself back out, he was still looking at me with a stunned expression, as if he had never experienced anything like it either. I now looked at him, and for the first time, I saw past the facade that he had projected with such incredible skill that it had fooled me up until that very moment. I finally saw that Lucifer was not a powerful being, but a being exactly like myself. However, contrary to myself, he was still trapped in this self-reinforcing state of misery where every new denial forced him to spend more energy coming up with another layer of denial.

Lucifer now looked at me with an extremely angry expression, and he was about to say something, when I interrupted: "STOP! I will now do what you have been afraid to do since you first entered duality, namely go right into your fear of being proven wrong. You truly cannot be a powerful being when you are afraid to go into the feelings that are ruling your entire life experience."

I then once again projected my Conscious You into Lucifer's mind. Once there, I focused on the downward spiral of energy that dominated his energy field. Instead of resisting it, as I had done the first time, I now went right into it. At first, it felt like I was being sucked downwards at incredible speed. Gradually, the movement slowed down, and I now received impressions that were worse than the images of hell seen by Dante and others.

I was seeing the misery that Lucifer had created since his fall, something he still carried with him in his energy field. Truly, it was not so much the impulses coming to him from without that required him to be in denial. The denial was needed in order to avoid that he would look at the fact that for every selfish deed, he carried an energetic record in his own aura.

I kept moving downwards and finally came to the moment when Lucifer decided to rebel against self-transcendence. All of the subsequent denials only had the purpose of preventing him from looking at that original decision. I had somehow expected that, given the consequences of Lucifer's denial, this would be a decision of epic importance. Instead, it was a shockingly petty decision. He simply did not want to give up the sense of superiority he had built and have to start over on a blank slate. Rather than seeing it as an opportunity for growth, he saw it as a loss and he refused to give up what he had. If he had been willing to grow, he would have risen much higher than where he was. So he was literally like a beggar who refused to give up one Dollar in order to get a million Dollars.

As I went through this very core of Lucifer's separate self, I now experienced Lucifer's real self. I had barely been able to contemplate that Lucifer must have an I AM Presence, but now I saw it in all of its beauty. I saw that nothing Lucifer had done had affected his I AM Presence negatively. Instead, it had learned from his experiences and increased its spiritual maturity. I also saw that the Presence loved Lucifer unconditionally and only wanted him to be free of denial so he could return to oneness with itself. And I saw that regardless of how impossible the task seemed to me, it was entirely possible for Lucifer to gradually throw off all layers of the outer self and return to the state of pure awareness with which his Conscious You first descended. I literally experienced how there is nothing we can do with free will that we cannot overcome through free will. Any choice can be transcended by learning from it and making a more aware choice. *That* is why free will is truly free. Of course, we cannot learn from a choice if we will not look at it. So it is the refusal to look that keeps us trapped by our past choices.

After having experienced this, I was back to Lucifer's mind, then out of it and into my own mind again. Lucifer still looked at me, as if he was unable to move. I looked him straight in the eyes and said: "Lucifer, I thought you were such a powerful being, but you are the most powerless being I have ever met, for you are afraid to look into your own mind

You truly had fooled me into thinking you were feeling very good about yourself and your ability to refute any argument, but I have now experienced just how miserable you are. How anyone can want to continue in this misery is beyond me, but this has got to be the height of stupidity. I thought you were so smart and sophisticated, but I now see you are beyond comparison the dumbest being I have ever met.

Yet I have also seen past all of your separate selves and seen the beauty of who you really are. I have seen that you can actually come back to your original purity and truly feel good about yourself. Why you would not want this is beyond me. Can you please explain that to me?"

I fell silent while still keeping eye-contact with Lucifer, literally forcing him to not break the contact. I felt in my right to demand an answer from Lucifer, and I was completely immovable in forcing him to face me. I was aware that this was something that an ascended master was not allowed to do, but because I had been in embodiment with Lucifer and had not yet ascended, I had the right to force him to face me.

Lucifer looked completely transfixed. I could sense a great conflict inside him and how he was trying to pull himself away from me, yet he simply did not have the power. I felt how my mind power had become greater than his, and thus I could block all of his momentums of denial, forcing him to keep facing me. After what seemed like an eternity, there was a noticeable shift, and suddenly Lucifer broke down. He was not in a physical body, so he could no physically cry, but his higher bodies literally wept, and he continued for a very long time. He finally fell silent, and looked around with a clarity I had never seen in him before. For the first time, I felt that inside Lucifer was a being with whom I could relate. He said with a quiet voice: "What can I do?"

*** 

At that point, the ascended masters stepped forward and very lovingly offered Lucifer all of the help necessary to get himself on the upward path of transcending every separate self until nothing was left than the Conscious You in its state of pure awareness. Truly, a path was laid out for Lucifer that he could follow all the way to his ascension. It was even shown that because of his many experiences, he would become a very sophisticated ascended master. This process took quite some time, and I can only say that everything was being done to help Lucifer begin the path to the ascension.

Yet after a long time of deliberations, Lucifer decided that he did not want to walk that path. His only reason was that he simply did not want to face the many choices of denial he had made. It was not that he denied that the path was possible and that he could follow it. Yet he also realized that he could fail the initiations and again go into duality. He did not want to take the risk that he could again inflict suffering upon others or himself. In the end, he decided that he simply did not want to go through it all again. Thus, he asked that his Conscious You would be dissolved in the Sacred Fire.

A council of 12 masters then held a meeting in the Court, and they decided that the only course of action was to respect Lucifer's choice and commit him to the second death. Hereby, Lucifer's lifestream (the Conscious You, all dualistic selves and the entire momentum of misqualified energy) would be dissolved in the Sacred Fire. However, one final thing was needed, namely the agreement of the I AM Presence that had sent Lucifer's Conscious You into embodiment. This agreement was given, as the I AM Presence decided to respect the choice of the Conscious You.

This does not mean that Lucifer's life had been wasted. The I AM Presence experiences everything we experience but not through our limited sense of self. Thus, the I AM Presence can turn any situation into a positive life lesson that expands the identity of the I AM Presence. Obviously, the I AM Presence quickly learns that a certain action does not work, and when we repeat it countless times, the I AM Presence gains no new learning from this. Yet the I AM Presence of Lucifer had learned many positive lessons from Lucifer's choices and had therefore expanded its sense of self immensely. It would have preferred to have the Conscious You of Lucifer experience this, but an I AM Presence knows the risk of sending part of itself into an unascended sphere, and it respects free will.

\*\*\*

Anyway, the approval was made to commit Lucifer to the Sacred Fire, and this was carried out by Archangel Michael. The process was quite complicated, but it really was just a matter of pushing all of Lucifer's energies and selves into the flame. As this happened, the flame again burned very brightly with a big "swoosh" that lasted some time. But then, suddenly, the flame fell back to normal as if nothing had happened.

For me, it seemed like an anti-climax. After all, the immense drama created by the fallen beings makes you think they actually have reached some state and that it must take some effort to consume it. You think that what they have taken so long to build, will take some time to dissolve. Yet the final end of Lucifer was quite undramatic.

I will say though, that despite the lack of drama, I have never experienced anything with such a sense of finality to it. I got a very strong sense of just how immense is the power of Spirit and just how insignificant is any power gathered by the fallen beings. Despite all of his posturing, Lucifer's lifestream was erased so effortlessly and with such finality that I realized just how temporary is this unascended world. Gosh, how naive to think we have any power on earth compared to the power of those who created the entire universe and could erase it in a split second if they wanted. As Jesus put it: "There, but for the Grace of God, go I."

# 52

I then got to witness the spiritual ascension of Jesus, and it was a much happier occasion. However, in some respects it was similar to the process gone through by Lucifer. Jesus also faced many of the beings with whom he had interacted since he first was sent forth as a Conscious You in the beginning of our unascended sphere. The review of his embodiments on natural planets took place in the Court of Sacred Fire in the Central Sun. Some of the beings he met had ascended and appeared in their ascended master "bodies." Those who had not ascended were taken there in their finer bodies.

These sessions were very joyful as there was no karma involved. It was in many ways like a reunion where the beings and Jesus reinforced the positive lessons they had learned together. However, the process was guided by a group of ascended masters who helped Jesus and the others learn even deeper lessons.

When it came to the beings with whom Jesus had interacted on earth, only a few of those had ascended. A being from an unnatural planet usually cannot travel to the Central Sun, so we now moved to the identity realm over earth. Here, the souls of the people were taken, and Jesus met them one by one. The purpose here was for Jesus to ask for the people's forgiveness and to forgive them. It was a very humbling experience for me to see how Jesus, despite all his attainment, was completely frank in reviewing a situation with a person and then admitting how he had been wrong. He would be totally humble and sincere in asking for the person's forgiveness.

Some people forgave Jesus, and this meant that they were also set free from the past, speeding up their spiritual growth. Some people refused to forgive Jesus or accept his forgiveness of them, and this reinforced their non-constructive momentums. However, by so openly asking for forgiveness and forgiving others, Jesus was set free from the situation regardless of the reaction of the other people. This process took quite some time, but for each person he encountered, Jesus seemed lighter and more free.

\*\*\*

Finally, came the most difficult part of the process, and it took place in the Court of Sacred Fire. Here, Jesus had to face what was the greatest challenge to his ascension, namely the one thing that more than anything tied him to earth. This challenge was his mission in his last embodiment and his attempt to create a spiritual movement that would set people free from the fallen beings.

Jesus had put all of his attainment into designing the Christian movement and giving it the best possible start. He naturally wanted to see it succeed, and he was keenly aware that the future of the movement was by no means secure. Only a few people had attained a high enough state of consciousness that they could serve as messengers for him, and there was no guarantee what would happen after they had to take their leave from earth.

Again, the ascended masters are dealing with extremely complex calculations when it comes to what they are allowed to do in the physical octave. Jesus had been given a dispensation in order to take on another body and start the mystery school. Due to the karmic circumstances and the reaction of the people, this dispensation could not be extended. Jesus therefore faced a choice. He could choose to take embodiment again (without karma) in order to continue to work with the Christian movement. However, this would mean that he would not ascend and thus could not work with earth as an ascended master. Other masters could fill that role, but Jesus could not both ascend and take embodiment again.

By choosing to take embodiment and not ascending, Jesus would also have to abandon the greater plan that called for him to take up the spiritual office as the main overseer or hierarch for the earth during the coming 2000 years of the Age of Pisces. Another master could fill this position, but it was truly Jesus' position to fill, and he was uniquely suited to the task by having so recently ascended from earth.

It was amazing to see that even though there was clearly an overall plan for Jesus to ascend and fill this position, the respect for the individual's free will was such that Jesus could have freely chosen to return to embodiment. How could Jesus make the choice in this situation? Well, in order to be truly free to choose, he had to first overcome all attachment to the Christian movement.

At one point, Jesus and I had a chance to be alone, and he explained to me how difficult it was for him to leave behind the movement for which he held such hope. He showed me on a screen the potential consequences of each choice, both the best-case and the worst-case scenarios. It was clear that given how free will works, once Jesus had ascended, he no longer had any direct influence on the Christian movement. And the worst-case scenario was pretty grim (I will later explain what actually came to pass). Yet by going back into embodiment, his influence would also be limited. He could do more for Christianity by taking embodiment, but he could clearly do more for the earth by ascending.

Jesus was very open in admitting that he really did not know what to do. I finally said that he first had to make sure he was completely free to choose either option, and that meant he had to make sure he had no attachments to the Christian movement. He should be able to choose freely by being willing to let free will outplay itself, even if that meant seeing the Christian movement be taken over by the fallen beings and used to enslave people even more rather than setting them free. Jesus admitted that this was true and decided to take some time alone to work on his attachments.

\*\*\*

While Jesus was in solitude, Magda approached me. She had vowed to stay in embodiment during these coming 2000 years, as I had done. She asked me if Jesus had told me about his difficulties in choosing, and I explained what I had advised him to do. She said she had given him the exact same advice. We then realized that our minds were working in parallel and that we might not be the only ones. We now started contacting other souls that had been involved with Jesus' mission and also many of the venutians who had not yet ascended.

We received great help from a group of ascended masters, and we soon managed to contact 10,000 souls who were all willing to make the same vow that we had made. They were willing to stay in embodiment for the next 2000 years and dedicate themselves to preserving and preaching the true message of Christ.

After some time, Jesus came out of his solitude, and Magda and I could both see that he still had not decided. We then invited him to a meeting in an etheric retreat located over Saudi Arabia. Here we had gathered the 10,000 souls in their identity bodies, and we all made our vows in front of Jesus. He was deeply moved by this, and I saw how he made up his mind to ascend.

\*\*\*

The last part of Jesus' ascension process took place in the Court of Sacred Fire. Jesus was prepared by the ascended masters for some time, and then the final ceremony took place. During this ceremony, Omega took the last remnant of a separate self from Jesus. This was not anywhere near the complex structure of Lucifer. It was a very simple self and in the end, it had served only to keep Jesus in a physical body. Yet Jesus had to surrender it, and it was then put into the Sacred Fire where it was instantly dissolved.

There was nothing left of the separate self, and I suddenly realized I felt a certain emptiness. I had known Jesus for so long, and although I had clearly seen both his higher self and his separate self, I had come to love both. Jesus had gone through an elaborate ascension process in order to fully disidentify from his lower self, but I obviously had not gone through this process. The dissolution of Jesus' separate self was as final as the dissolution of Lucifer, and I suddenly realized I missed that part of Jesus. I spontaneously turned to Magda, and I could see she felt exactly the same.

After the dissolution of the separate self, there was a magnificent transformation in the sense that Jesus gradually grew into taking on a light body, similar to that of other ascended masters but with his own individual characteristics. This was a truly beautiful process, and it cannot possibly be described in words. I can only say that Jesus stood forth as a truly magnificent ascended being, and I felt such a joy from seeing him that it goes beyond anything I have ever experienced on earth. He has, naturally, only become more beautiful over the past 2000 years where he has gone through a growth process that we can scarcely imagine from the unascended state.

\*\*\*

Before I went back to earth for my next embodiment, I got to witness another ascension, namely that of Mother Mary. You will notice that while the Catholic church allows people to worship Mary, it is said that only Jesus ascended whereas Mary was only "assumed" into heaven (try to make a Catholic priest explain the difference between ascension and assumption). This is, again, the attempt to create an idol out of Jesus so that no one could ever be like him. After all, who could be like the *only* Son of God. Mary might be a daughter of God, but in a patriarchal culture, you know what daughters are considered to be worth. So naturally, she had to have a lower entry into heaven than Jesus in order to uphold the fallacy of the fallen beings.

In reality, Mother Mary ascended, and the process was as magnificent as the ascension of Jesus. Mother Mary became an ascended master like Jesus, and she has ever since held several spiritual offices. She is currently holding the Office of the Divine Mother for planet earth. This means she represents the Divine Feminine to all people on earth—not in any way limited to Catholics or Christians. This is one of the other great lies of Catholicism, namely that a spiritual office is only working for people of the "only true church." The saints claimed by the Catholic church are mostly a creation of the church and have no spiritual reality (Including John Paul II). Some of the saints claimed by the church are ascended masters, but they minister to all people. For example, Paul is today and ascended master, but he ascended before the Catholic church was formed so did not ascend because of the church. On the other hand, Peter has not yet ascended. Any spiritual office is universal and can never be limited to a particular institution or group of people on earth. Any claim to the contrary can come only from the fallen beings.

# PART 8:

# HOW THEY CREATED

# CHRISTIANITY

# TO DESTROY

# JESUS' MISSION

# 53

During the first couple of centuries after Jesus' death, I had two embodiments and in each one I lived a long and non-violent life. When you come into embodiment, you lose the specific memory of your previous lives. However, once you reach the higher levels of consciousness, you come in with a strong sense that you are here to do something and find something. So in each of my embodiments, I found and became involved with one of the many Christian mystery schools that had sprung up during that time. In each lifetime, I quickly reconnected to Jesus as an ascended master and became able to take direct dictations from him. I was therefore instrumental in helping the two mystery schools flourish, and I helped many students raise their consciousness.

When modern people look back at that time, it is almost impossible for them to imagine just how limited life, and especially communication, was back then. We tend to look at the past through the filter of the much more global awareness we have today. For example, we have grown up with the awareness that there is a worldwide Christian movement so we tend to think this is the way it always was. In reality, people at the time had such a local awareness that there was no one who had any sense that there was a world-wide Christian movement, or even that Christianity was as significant as we see it today.

Naturally, there were local congregations that grew during the time, and they gradually developed a more coherent sense of being a movement, but it was by no means a unified movement. I was involved with the mystical aspects of Christianity, and by its very nature, mysticism cannot be institutionalized, at least not on a large scale. The schools I was involved with were set apart from society and only received the students who found us by word of mouth. They found us because they followed one of the other groups and then came to understand that Jesus' true message was mystical in nature. This led them to the mystery schools. We were focused on helping individuals attain the Christ consciousness, not on creating a coherent Christian movement with creeds, doctrines and rituals. That, however, was the focus of another group of people.

In the beginning, Christianity was a very diversified movement. There was room for many different preachers who preached the message of Jesus according to their level of consciousness and their cultural background.

This was very much in alignment with what Jesus had started, although he, naturally, would have preferred that all groups had someone who could serve as a direct link to him as an ascended master. For all practical purposes, he knew this to be impossible.

Over the first couple of centuries, two tendencies emerged. One was the mystical side, which was not trying to spread its message to all Christian groups. The other was a group that wanted to create a unified movement that had a clearly defined identity and beliefs. Many people today will look back at this and think it is obvious that the Christian movement should be unified and should have a clearly defined set of doctrines and beliefs. Yet why do so many people think this is the obvious, even the *only*, way for Christianity to function?

***

In order to understand this, we have to realize that Jesus' mission and ascension was an almost incalculable setback for the fallen beings. It threatened to overthrow the religious institutions that they had so carefully built over thousands of years, thereby taking away their control over the majority of the population. This was in large part due to the fact that Jesus actually won his ascension and ascended both physically and spiritually. By walking the path of Christhood in such a public way, Jesus set an example that threatened to overthrow the disempowering approach to religion that the fallen beings had so carefully crafted.

What is that approach? It is that we human beings are inherently limited. Although there are many limitations, the main point is that an individual cannot serve as an open door for Spirit to act directly in this world. As I have said, the real significance of Jesus' mission is that he demonstrated the potential we all have, namely to serve as open doors for the ascended masters. This is the highest human potential. It is a potential that scares the fallen beings more than anything because they know they have no direct power to block this. How could they control that an individual, such as Jesus, walked an inner path and developed the Christ consciousness and then suddenly went public? How could they control or stop this if 10,000 individuals did this at the same time? So what can the fallen beings do? They cannot stop you from developing your Christ potential—unless they can get you to deny that you have it and thereby limit yourself!

You can look at everything that has ever happened on this planet, you can look at every idea that has ever been presented and gained some influence, and you will see that either the idea was created by the fallen beings or they attempted to influence it and use it for their ends. All this was done for one purpose, and one purpose only, namely to get all of us to deny that we have the potential to become open doors for Spirit, thereby giving humankind a frame of reference that is beyond the duality consciousness and cannot be manipulated and controlled by the fallen beings. As I have tried to explain earlier, the fallen beings can control us only through duality, in which everything is relative and thus everything can be twisted in infinite ways. What comes from Spirit is much harder for the fallen beings to twist, although it is not impossible, as we shall see. So their most important line of defense against a global awakening is to get as many individuals as possible to deny their Christ potential. They want to make sure that people do not have a frame of reference from beyond the relativity of the duality consciousness.

After they were shocked by the fact that Jesus did fulfil his mission, the fallen beings were frantically scrambling to counter-act his mission. In this they were severally limited by the fact that Lucifer was no longer in embodiment and that the Dark Master had been bound and thus taken out of the equation. It took them over three hundred years to fully overcome this shock and "get their act back together." You simply cannot understand the early history of the Christian movement and the emergence of a dominant church without realizing that the fallen beings were doing everything they could to gain control over the Christian movement.

*** 

When one understands the intent of the fallen beings, one can gain a new approach to world history. One can begin to see the hidden influence of the fallen beings in ways most people would never suspect because they seem so benign. The brutal fact is that the fallen beings are very clever, and because they have no respect for free will, there is nothing they won't do if they think it serves their purpose. As even the scriptures say, the children of this world (the fallen beings) are in their generation wiser than the children of the light. This means that the fallen beings in the identity realm, such as the Dark Master, are very clever and they are constantly seeking to bring ideas into this world that can help them in the long term. These fallen beings have a historical perspective that goes far beyond that of the average person even today.

On the one side, you have the ascended masters who are constantly looking for individuals who can serve as open doors for ideas that can help bring humanity forward. On the other side, you have the fallen beings who are looking for individuals who can be the open doors for ideas that can be used to limit humanity or counter-act the ideas brought forth by the ascended masters. If you do not understand this dynamic, you will *never* be able to understand what has been happening on this planet. You will never be able to correctly evaluate the validity of ideas.

In order to understand how cleverly the fallen beings had tried to antic-ipate the impact of Jesus, we need to go back to Aristotle. This ancient Greek philosopher had the Christ-like example of Socrates, who was an open door for the ascended masters, although not mentioning them by name. He also had the example of Plato who, according to the knowledge of his time, described a universe where visible phenomena had hidden, unseen causes (as just one example, take the allegory of Plato's cave). Yet because he had an ambition to be the greatest philosopher, Aristotle (who had a Christ potential) came under the influence of the fallen beings, espe-cially the Dark Master.

This is not to say that everything Aristotle brought forth came from the fallen beings or was false. But he did bring forth the idea that every-thing should have a natural cause, a visible, measurable cause. And then, as the master-stroke of the Dark Master, he brought forth what is today called Aristotelian logic. This form of logic says that a statement must be either untrue or true, for it cannot be both at the same time. Do you have any idea how much this one idea has influenced our civilization and how it has been abused by the fallen beings?

You might say that it is obvious that a statement must be true or untrue, but that is because you are the victim of over 2,500 years of programming. If you take what I have said about the duality consciousness, can you begin to see the problem with Aristotelian logic? What has it done? It has limited the number of options we consider to just two: true or untrue.

What is the essence of duality? It is a state of consciousness that sees only two options, two opposite polarities, such as true and untrue. Yet none of those two options are the ultimate understanding of an issue because they can exist only in relation to each other. Good is defined as the opposite of evil and evil as the opposite of good. The real problem here is that we have now limited our minds to considering only two options, and if the fallen beings can control both options, they can have total control over our minds. They simply define one idea and then they define an opposite that is obviously false, claiming this means the first idea must be true. This is what they have done for a very long time on this planet, much longer than recorded history.

What is the deeper reality? It is that the human potential is to walk a systematic path that raises our consciousness. There are currently 144 levels of consciousness we can attain on this planet. The higher we go, the more our vision is expanded, meaning we gain a broader perspective and can see many more options. The principle is simple. In reality, it is never so that a complex question can be reduced to only two options, of which one must be true and one must be untrue. When we have such a scenario, you can be almost completely sure that both options are defined by the fallen beings because they have captured the "privilege of defining the problem." The more aware approach is to say that beyond the two options is a deeper understanding, and only when we reach for that, will we find the optimal way to deal with the problem. With that deeper understanding, we might see that both of the opposites are untrue, or at least limited.

I have mentioned that before humanity sank into duality, new lifestreams would come into embodiment at the 48th level of consciousness. Most would go *up* from there, but some would go *down* and become gradually more selfish. Back then, no one would be affected by the duality consciousness unless they went below the 48th level. Today, duality has become so pervasive that you need to rise above the 96th level of consciousness before you can truly free yourself from duality. This means that people's way of thinking is now much more influenced by duality than it was when the earth was pure.

Duality can also be seen as black-and-white or either-or thinking, meaning people see only two options. This is what appeals to people below the 48th level because they have no frame of reference from the ascended realm. As you go higher in consciousness, you see that there is a deeper understanding and that many of the more complex questions of life cannot be reduced to two options that are either completely true or completely false. As you go above the 96th level, you realize that what you have right now is only a temporary understanding. As you continue to climb, you know you will gain a deeper understanding so you never allow yourself to think you have the ultimate understanding of an issue. You are always open to a higher understanding coming from the ascended masters.

Black-and-white thinking causes people to accept a very simplistic definition of "truth" as the ultimate understanding, and then they close their minds to anything coming from the ascended masters. Instead, their minds inevitably come under the control of the fallen beings.

\*\*\*

When you go below the 48th level, you become gradually more selfish. How can you do this, how can you justify doing what you want regardless of the consequences it has for other people? You can do so by using the relativity of the duality consciousness so you raise up one idea as being absolute and therefore something you don't need to question.

Lucifer was at the absolute lowest level of consciousness possible on earth, meaning he had the highest degree of selfishness allowed here. His mind was dominated by dualistic thinking in which there were only two options. Lucifer had a superior cause, and anything that he could do in order to further that cause was fully justified. He never needed to question his actions or their consequences for others. As a result of this, Lucifer had reached the ultimate state of insensitivity to life. If not, he could never have done what he did.

Take more recent examples of people who were also near the bottom of the barrel in terms of consciousness. If he had not had near absolute insensitivity to life, how could Hitler have implemented the "Final Solution" to exterminate all Jews? If he had any sensitivity to life, how could Comrade Stalin have killed 21 million people in the Soviet Union? If he had not had an unquestioned belief in the validity of his cause, how could Mao have instituted the killing of 70 million Chinese? No one with a normal sensitivity to life could do such things because they would be shocked by the consequences. Only total denial can lead to such atrocities, and total denial can come only from a total emergence in the duality consciousness.

What is the essence of the duality consciousness? It is that there are only two options. I am absolutely right and anyone who disagrees with me is absolutely wrong, meaning I am justified in doing whatever it takes to silence them. Another outcome is that a person in this state of denial can do anything it wants in order to steal energy from people. Lucifer and Satan saw nothing wrong about creating wars in which millions of people died so that they, and the demons and fallen beings in the other octaves, could steal their energy. Lucifer was a pedophile, and in some embodiments, I was repeatedly raped by him as a child. In other embodiments, I saw him do this to other children. Given the devastating psychological effects of this, modern pedophiles can only do what they do because they have no sensitivity to life. They are convinced that raping a child is justified so that they can steal the life-energy they need in order to continue staying in embodiment. They may not realize this consciously (although some of them do), but the need to steal energy is the driving force behind such actions.

\*\*\*

I got side-tracked again. What I am saying here is that Aristotelian logic is a creation of the fallen beings because it is what you need at the ultimate level of insensitivity to life in order to justify what you are doing. The more insensitive your actions become, the more absolute of an argument you need in order to justify those actions (in your own mind and to the world). Does this mean Aristotelian logic is completely wrong? Well, that depends on from which level of consciousness you consider the question.

The truly devastating effect of Aristotelian logic is that it limits the number of options we are willing to consider to just two. We think that all questions in life can and should be reduced to a problem that has two opposite polarities and thus can be expressed in a yes-and-no question. Once we have done this, we need to accept the one polarity and reject the other. The problem here is that it prevents us from seeing more nuances, and that is essentially why our civilization is facing more and more situations that defy these simplistic solutions. We cannot solve problems because we fail to see the nuances of the situation and it is in these nuances that the key to progress is hidden.

The real trick of the fallen beings is to try to reduce every problem to having just two possible options, a true one and a false one, a good one or an evil one. Once this is defined, we simply accept the true or good one and, supposedly, paradise will be manifest on earth. It is obvious that if the fallen beings can define what is good and evil, they can cause us to always do what they define as good (or do the opposite of what they define as evil). Unfortunately for us, what the fallen beings define as good is what is good for them or their cause to prove god wrong. In other words, the fallen beings may claim to be working for truth, but they have no dedication to truth whatsoever. They only use the concept because it is an efficient way to manipulate most people.

For over a thousand years, the Catholic church used this form of logic to define solutions to our problems, but they could not solve our problems. For several hundred years, the popes of scientific materialism have used the same kind of logic to define solutions to our problems, but what they have given us is more powerful ways to kill large numbers of people.

The Christ perspective on the matter is that any issue we face can be looked at in many different ways, depending on your level of consciousness. As you raise your level of consciousness, there will come a point where you begin to see beyond the simplistic, dualistic definitions of problems. You see that it simply cannot be true that all of Germany's problems are caused by the Jews, and thus exterminating all Jews will not automatically solve all of Germany's problems. You can then begin to look for a deeper understanding of the issue, and this opens up for a more empowering approach where you can pursue multiple causes of action towards improving your situation.

The fallen beings are trying to reduce every situation to a problem with an easy, black-and-white solution (usually to use force against another group of people). They claim there must be only one truth and once you know it, you know how to deal with every similar situation. The Christ perspective is that there is not simply one solution to all problems but that each situation is unique. Jesus did not act the same way in similar situations but acted (through the power of Spirit) based on what was most likely to awaken the person in the actual situation.

*** 

I know many will say that Aristotelian logic must have some validity. For example, take the question of whether the earth is round or flat. It is obvious that the earth must be either round or flat; it cannot be both at the same time. However, are round or flat the only options when it comes to describing the shape of the earth? We know today that the earth is not round, meaning it is not a perfect circle but a more complex shape. Yet if we think the earth must be round, how would we ever discover a deeper understanding? It seems obvious to most people today that the medieval church was simplistic in describing the earth as the center of the universe. Yet, ironically, scientific materialism also presents simplistic solutions based on Aristotelian logic.

Naturally, there are many questions for which Aristotelian logic can be applied for practical purposes. I am either sitting here writing this book or I am not sitting here (although we can discuss what we mean with "I" and "here"). Yet, the problem with Aristotelian logic is not practical, physical situations but that this form of logic has been applied to everything! This includes the deepest questions of life, including the question of whether god exists or moral issues. For such complex questions, seeking to reduce them to a true-untrue statement leads to incredibly simplistic thinking.

As an example, take the Old Testament. Moses was an example of a person who could serve as a messenger for the ascended masters, and he did receive the Ten Commandments as genuine revelation (although they were adapted to the people's low state of consciousness). One of the commandments says: "Thou shallt not kill." Do you see any room for interpretation in that statement? Does it define any conditions whereby killing becomes acceptable or justified? Then how come the Jews, after having received this commandment, went into what they thought was the promised land and committed genocide against the people who already lived there? How do you explain that the Jews felt that killing all of these people was justified by the very same god who had given them the Ten Commandments?

The explanation is that the Jews had made the unqualified commandment relative. They had used the dualistic mind to create an Aristotelian sentence (even though this kind of logic had not yet been formalized by Aristotle), saying: "The Jews are god's chosen people." This statement was either true or untrue, and to the Jews it was true and beyond questioning. The consequence was that god's chosen people deserved to have the land that god had chosen for them, and that meant it was justified to exterminate the people already living there. The Jews did not need to question the statement that they were god's chosen people and thus did not see that it led to actions that were a direct violation of the Ten Commandments that they normally thought had come from god. They didn't need to question how god's chosen people could commit actions that were not approved by god and still remain the chosen ones.

Take note that I am not saying the Jews were evil or stupid people. They were simply blinded by the dualistic consciousness and thus did not see what should be obvious today. Neither did they see the even deeper reality that the material universe serves as the cosmic mirror that reflects back to you what you send out. The effect of the fallen logic is that people feel justified in doing whatever they want and think they have no responsibility and will produce no consequences (karma).

*** 

As I have said, the universe *is* a feed-back machine defined to give you the exact conditions that you tell the universe you want to experience. You may say: "Well, how exactly did the Jews tell the universe that they wanted to experience the Holocaust?" They did so the same way that all people below the 48th level talk to the universe: through their actions against others. What you do to other people is a message to the universe that you want to live in a world where such actions are possible and can be justified. Jesus was perfectly aware of this, and he was also aware that people at the time could not grasp how profound this is. Yet consider the deeper layers of meaning behind Jesus' statement to do unto others what you want them to do to you. A similar statement can be found in most religions on earth, and the explanation is that it comes from the ascended masters. It is meant to illustrate that what you do to others tells the cosmic mirror what kind of world you want to live in. A mirror can only reflect back what you project into it.

Take note of the real significance of this. When you send an impulse into the cosmic mirror that is based on the duality consciousness, you send an impulse saying that you want to live in a world dominated by two polarities. This is done by people below the 48th level, meaning they cannot receive direct teachings from the ascended masters. How can they then become free of this consciousness? Only by coming to the point where they have had enough of duality, meaning they have had enough of both polarities.

Naturally, when you do something to others that violates them, you consciously want to always be the one in power. Yet in order to become free from duality, you cannot experience just one polarity. You must experience both, meaning you must experience that others do to you what you have (most likely in a past lifetime) done to others. When you make other people the victims of your actions, you condemn yourself to becoming a victim sometime in the future—unless you change your consciousness in the meantime. When the Jews went into the promised land and committed genocide against the people there (killing men, women and children *is* genocide), they said to the cosmic mirror that they wanted to live in a world where it was possible to feel justified in committing such actions. Because of the cosmic delay factor built into the universe, the Jews did not experience the karmic return of this for a long time. This is a grace period so that people have the opportunity to raise their consciousness before the return current comes back.

Because the Jews did not raise themselves above the dualistic consciousness (by giving up the desire to be god's chosen people), they did receive a return current from the cosmic mirror. It took the form of another group of people who had also become blinded by the idea that they were god's chosen people and that they had the right to exterminate all who stood in their way. Thus, the Jews had another opportunity to raise themselves above the consciousness of thinking they are god's chosen people and accepting that they are like all other people and have no special status or privileges.

I know this will be insulting to many Jews, but that is because they are not willing to take responsibility for the fact that it is not god who is deciding their fate but their own state of consciousness. I know some will immediately label me as anti-semitic, but how is it anti-anything to want to free the spiritual being that lives inside of all human beings and is trapped by identification with external characteristics?

By the way, because of how the Law of Karma works, anyone committing dualistic actions must experience the opposite. Thus, many souls that were incarnated as Jews during World War II are now incarnated in Germany. Many of the souls who were Nazis are now incarnated in Israel. That is why you will see that some of the more militant Israeli leaders are acting as the Nazis they were just one lifetime ago.

# 54

Okay, I got side-tracked once more. What I wanted to get to is that people who are below or close to the 48th level of consciousness are very susceptible to Aristotelian logic and the simplistic, black-and-white thinking that follows. The early Christian movement was no exception. Over the first couple of centuries, a movement started to emerge that applied Aristotelian logic to Christianity.

In order to understand this, you need to see the incredible diversity that existed back then. This was to some degree veiled by the lack of communication, but if you had seen it with today's means of communication, you would have said that the early Christian movement was – from a linear perspective – quite chaotic. There were some groups who took the outer teachings given by Jesus and interpreted them from below the 48th level of consciousness. Some of these used various scriptures, many more than were eventually included in the official canon (we know many of these scriptures today). There were also some groups who had maintained the direct connection and were receiving dictations from Jesus or other ascended masters. Yet even these messages were adapted to people's level of consciousness and cultural background so they did vary somewhat even though they came from the same source.

Then, there were some groups that were not able to have a connection to the ascended masters, but they were connected to fallen beings in the mental and identity realms. The fallen beings created what we might call impostors of Jesus and other ascended masters. This meant that there were some groups who claimed to be receiving messages from Jesus or from ascended masters, even though they were receiving them from the false hierarchy impostors. This is the case for many of the so-called Gnostic gospels, of which only a small fraction have been preserved. Naturally, the messages brought forth by the fallen beings contained some truth but also some deliberate errors that contradicted what was said through the groups with a genuine connection. Or they contradicted the interpretations given by other groups. One example is the idea that the world is created by a demiurge that is the inevitable opposite of god because even god is part of a dualistic system.

If you want a comparable image of what it was like in the first couple of centuries, you can look at what is today called the New Age movement and the phenomenon of channeling. It is also quite chaotic with many channellers claiming to get messages from some genuine spiritual being, but the messages are often contradictory. The natural response of many people is to look at all this chaos and reject everything. This, of course, is exactly what the fallen beings want people to do. They have deliberately created the chaos on one side in order to herd people into the other extreme, which they have also created.

As many people today refuse to look at the chaotic state of alternative spirituality, many people did the same in the first two centuries. This is actually a refusal to exercise our potential to develop Christ discernment so we can read the vibration of something and thereby discern its validity. The fallen beings are scared stiff of our discernment and want us to use the linear, analytical mind instead. This mind can argue for or against any issue in seemingly convincing ways. This will cause some people to believe in the definitions of the fallen beings, and it will cause others to be so scared of the chaos and the many counter-claims that they stick to one interpretation that seems to have authority. This is also what the linear mind is good at, namely creating the impression that there can be only one true teaching or church.

This led to the emergence of a movement within Christianity that claimed that all of the diversity was dangerous and that an official, unified church ought to be formed. The people leading this movement were the ones who were building on the branch of Christianity founded by Peter. In fact, the lifestream of Peter was also in embodiment during that time and was instrumental in forming the movement. Gradually, this movement grew stronger and it started defining a set of Christian scriptures and doctrines, all of them based on the interpretation of Jesus' teachings that is possible for people below the 48th level of consciousness. That is why the members of this "Peter movement" were susceptible to Aristotelian logic, and as we will see, that is why they created such devastating consequences while thinking it was all justified by Christ.

*** 

The goal of the Peter movement was to create an official religion, but this does not mean that it was particularly unified. This was due to the fact that most of its leaders were fallen beings, and getting them to agree on anything is like herding cats. I have portrayed Lucifer and Satan as being completely controlled by the Dark Master. However, many of the fallen beings with lower "attainment" are not fully controlled by fallen beings in the higher realms. This is because they are so selfish that they will not let anyone control them. Their vision is not nearly as broad at that of Lucifer, and they are generally focused on their personal interests, meaning they always do what is best for themselves. Many of them have a desire for power, and that is why they gravitate to where power can be had.

Because of their lower "attainment," they often cannot come to power in established institutions so they often seek power in new institutions that are beginning to emerge. For example, the higher-ranking fallen beings had taken up the positions of power in the Roman empire so some of the lower-ranking fallen beings became attracted to the Peter movement once it started to gain some influence.

The brutal fact is that those who were not trapped in duality gravitated to the mystical branches of the Christian movement. Those trapped in duality plus the fallen beings were attracted to the Peter movement. This can be seen no more clearly than in the so-called Arian controversy, a series of theological disputes between Arius and Athanasius who were theologians from Alexandria, Egypt. This led to a confrontation that involved physical violence, the burning of churches and even killing, a process that in its methods bears an uncanny resemblance to fights between Mafia families or drug cartels. It eventually led to a split between the Catholic church and the Eastern Orthodox church. But I am getting ahead of myself.

The point is that the efforts to create a unified Christianity ran into a mechanism that is the only reason the fallen beings do not have total control over this planet. The equation is simple. Who is it that has an ambition to create a unified whole that can grow to attain total control over human affairs? Only fallen beings have this ambition and would start such an endeavour. Yet because fallen beings are trapped in duality, they will always be divided. Some will take one dualistic polarity and others will take the opposite polarity. This makes it very difficult for them to create any unified movement. In fact, it can only be done through forceful control where one group manages to subdue all other groups.

If you study the history of the early Christian movement, you will see the emergence of many different churches or congregations, many of which thought they were the only true Christian church. Yet despite their disagreements, this still created a more publicly visible movement. This caused the fallen beings leading the Roman Empire to start seeing

Christians as a threat to the order and unity of their empire. There is nothing the fallen beings hate more than when they think they have complete
control over a powerful empire and then something comes up that seems
to threaten that control. Thus, we enter the age of the persecution of
Christians by the Romans.

***

The Age of the Martyrs was basically a blind alley in the evolution of
the Christian movement. It was based on a fatal misinterpretation of Jesus'
teachings by people below the 48th level of consciousness. In order to
understand this, we need to look at reincarnation again.

Basically all of the mystical branches of the Christian movement taught
reincarnation. This was partly based on them preserving the historical fact
that Jesus taught reincarnation to his disciples and also on the fact that
when you walk the mystical path, you will come to a level of consciousness where you begin to have an intuitive sense that you have lived before.
Reincarnation explains so many of the baffling questions of life (such as
why one child is born gifted and another with devastating handicaps) that
you come to see it as self-evident. If you want historical evidence that
reincarnation was openly talked about in the early Christian movement, it
is not difficult to find out that many early theologians and writers wrote
about the topic. Examples are: Origen, St. Augustine, Clement of Alexandria, St. Gregory of Nyssa, Justin Martyr, St. Jerome. I am not saying they
all agreed on the topic, simply that it was debated openly.

The non-mystical branches of the Christian movement did not teach
reincarnation and some denied it openly. This was the case for the congregations or churches led by fallen beings or people below the 48th level
of consciousness. People below the 48th level often find it difficult to
accept reincarnation because they are unable to take full responsibility for
themselves. Thus, they do not like the idea that they can be held accountable in a future lifetime for actions committed in this lifetime. They also
don't like the idea that they have to work to attain salvation and that this
requires them to change their state of consciousness. They are much
more interested in an external form of salvation where being a member of
the right church and following its outer rules (something they like doing
because doing everything "right" makes them feel superior) will give them

an automatic or guaranteed salvation. They especially like the idea that by being a member of the right church, they will be guaranteed to be saved after this lifetime.

For the sake of completeness, there are billions of people in eastern religions who accept reincarnation. I am not saying that all of these people are above the 48th level of consciousness. The fallen beings seeking to pervert those religions have developed a very fatalistic view of reincarnation that is very far from reality. Thus, this form of reincarnation does appeal to people below the 48th level because it makes it seem like you cannot take responsibility for your life because everything is determined by past karma. You are not responsible because everything in the now is determined by your past choices, conveniently ignoring that at some point you must have made choices that were not determined by previous choices.

Inspired by the fallen beings, some of the early congregations developed the idea that Jesus was the ultimate form of saviour sent by god. They started believing that instead of being an example for all to follow, Jesus had special abilities, meaning he would save us. In order to qualify for this salvation, it was not a matter of developing the Christ consciousness, as Jesus actually taught. It was a matter of being a member of the right church and following a set of outer rules. This was the beginning of a tradition (upheld by many Christian churches to this day) that salvation is basically a product that you buy by living up to conditions defined here on earth. The fallen beings made such people believe that entry into heaven can be guaranteed or blocked by conditions defined in this world. As I have described before, this is the satanic consciousness.

\*\*\*

This movement inevitably led its members to develop their own variant of the consciousness that caused the Jews to think they were god's chosen people. This is a consciousness in which the fallen beings are firmly trapped because they do believe they are inherently superior to all human beings. Yet despite the fact that the fallen beings are trapped in this state, they are nevertheless very successful in using it to control people. Thus, many early Christian churches and congregations started to believe that because they were followers of the only true saviour, they were superior to other people.

They also started to forget that Jesus told us to render onto Caesar that which is Caesar's and onto God that which is God's. In other words, don't fight the Romans but focus on developing the Christ consciousness that will give the ascended masters the authority to deal with the Romans. Many of these Christians now began to believe that instead of following the laws of the empire, they should follow the laws of god, as they (or rather the fallen beings) had defined them (people, of course, thought Jesus had defined these laws, another testament to the propaganda skills of the fallen beings). This now led these people to take a more confrontational approach to the Roman authorities, and this is what led to these authorities starting to persecute Christians.

The fallen beings now completed their ruse by combining the belief in an automatic salvation with the idea that Jesus had been a martyr. The fallen beings made people believe that Jesus had ascended to heaven because he had made the ultimate sacrifice to die for his beliefs, meaning that if people did the same, they too would be guaranteed to be saved. In other words, the slow way to qualify for salvation was to live according to your beliefs, and the fastest way was to die for those beliefs.

This created the kind of spiral that the fallen beings are so good at creating (sometimes without realizing what they are doing). It leads to a self-reinforcing confrontation, and the more the Christians acted as if they saw spiritual laws as being more important than the laws of the empire, the more the authorities felt threatened. The more these authorities persecuted the Christians, the more the Christians believed in the importance of martyrdom, and before anyone realized what had happened, far too many people had been killed. Once the killing started, no one knew how to stop it because neither side would back down. This is so typical of the conflicts created by the fallen beings.

***

I have said that by letting himself be killed on the cross, Jesus brought forth the judgment of Lucifer and the binding of the Dark Master. You may therefore think that by other people letting themselves be killed, it should also bring the judgment of fallen beings and thus help improve the situation on earth. However, in Jesus' case, it worked only because Jesus had reached the 143rd level of consciousness (he achieved the 144th level while hanging on the cross and "giving up the ghost.") The rule is that a Christed Being must have reached the same level of consciousness as the fallen being had reached before it fell. Therefore, by people under the 48th level of consciousness letting themselves be killed, it has no effect in terms of bringing forth the judgment of specific fallen beings. Obviously, when fallen beings kill people, they always incur karma for it, and this will shorten the time such fallen beings have left. However, this is not the same as the judgment of Christ.

In terms of the effect it had for the Christians who were killed, it was actually negative. These people had come to believe in an illusion created by the fallen beings. They were firmly convinced that by going to their death for the sake of their Christian beliefs, they were guaranteed to go to heaven. After they left their bodies, they found out that because they had not attained the Christ consciousness, they could not ascend but had to go back into embodiment. This made some of them angry and they sank deeper below the 48th level. Exactly what the fallen beings wanted.

The pattern was that one group of fallen beings (the Roman leaders) provided the outer circumstances for martyrdom. Another group of fallen beings (those among the Christian leadership but also those in the mental and identity realms) provided the inner circumstances by making people believe in an illusion. The net effect was that even though the Christians thought they were helping the cause of Christ, they were actually helping the cause of the fallen beings. One group of fallen beings provide the problem, another group of fallen beings provide the "solution," and the net effect is that it lowers the collective consciousness.

Naturally, this mechanism is exactly the same as you see in modern-day terrorism. When a young Muslim man blows himself up or joins ISIS, he also thinks that by dying for the cause of Allah, he will be rewarded with 70 virgins in heaven. Yet he will also be sent back with a package of karma to balance, and it is likely to make the soul angry. In a couple of generations, Muslim countries will see a number of people who come into embodiment with a great anger against Islam. Not that it will be much help at the present time. Again, you see that a group of fallen beings have (almost from its inception) managed to pervert Islam and set the stage for much fighting in the name of Allah. Of course, Islam was originally meant to bring peace to the warring tribes of the Arab people. They were warring because of fallen beings in leadership positions.

Mohammed had the potential to set forth the same example as Jesus, only in a different cultural setting. He failed the initiation because he resorted to violence in order to defend his physical life. Had he allowed himself to be killed, Islam would have had the same non-violent foundation as Christianity. Because Mohammed failed this initiation, the later revelations did not come from the ascended masters but from the fallen beings in the identity realm. That is why you find the concept of Jihad in the Koran. Of course, even if Islam had been given a non-violent foundation, it could still have been perverted by the fallen beings.

# 56

Back to the Christian movement. The basic dynamic on earth is that the ascended masters are constantly seeking to bring forth ideas that can set people free from the control of the fallen beings. Because these ideas come from beyond duality, the fallen beings cannot predict the exact event or the ideas themselves. However, because they are aware of what the ascended masters are doing in general, they try to set themselves up so they can minimize the impact of a new idea as soon as it is released.

The fallen beings were taken aback by Jesus' mission. In the beginning, they were hoping it would not catch on. However, they were still working to pervert the Christian movement, and this effort increased as the movement grew larger. The motto of the fallen beings has always been: "If you can't beat 'em; join 'em." As the Christian movement grew, the fallen beings in the identity realm sent fallen beings in embodiment into the movement to take up leadership positions.

The ultimate dream of the fallen beings is to create a centralized institution that has almighty (or at lest unquestionable) power on earth. As I have said, this is an impossible dream because the fallen beings will always polarize into dualistic factions. Yet this does not stop them from pursuing the dream, and world history has seen many variations of the attempt to gain world domination. So when the fallen beings joined the Christian movement, they naturally started arguing for the creation of a centralized movement with firm doctrines.

This was partly because this is simply what fallen beings do. However, the more clever fallen beings in the identity realm did this specifically to create a Christian movement that could suppress the mystical branches of Christianity. They knew that through the fallen beings in embodiment, they could control the centralized movement. They also knew that they would never be able to control the mystical branches. They knew that a centralized movement under their control was not likely to produce many beings with Christhood whereas the mystical branches might indeed produce Christed beings. What better way to suppress Christian mystics than by creating a centralized Christian movement to do it?

Very gradually, the fallen beings moved the Christian movement towards becoming more centralized, and in this they were helped by the fallen beings in Roman leadership. By persecuting Christians, the Roman authorities helped define Christianity and give it a public face. Essentially, the Roman authorities defined Christianity as that which they were persecuting. Hardly anyone from the mystical branches were ever persecuted by the Romans, as they never challenged Roman authority or law. So that which was persecuted became the official Christianity, and the Christian groups actually relished in this because it increased their sense of self-righteousness.

***

This all set the stage for the coup-de-grace of the fallen beings, namely the "elevation" of Christianity to the official state religion of the Roman Empire. For this, they needed only a fallen being in embodiment, and this is where our old acquaintance, Satan, enters the picture. Satan was embodied as Constantine, and by studying his life, you can clearly see the hallmark of a fallen being with a big momentum on misusing power.

Constantine was facing a delicate situation because the Roman Empire had, as all structures created by the fallen beings, become divided. Constantine was opposed by another fallen being who claimed to be the rightful Emperor of Rome. Constantine also knew that the empire was deteriorating from within, and one reason was that the belief in the old Roman gods was slipping away. The Roman gods were much like the god of the Jews, namely deities that required some kind of sacrifice, which then obligated them to do something in the daily lives of the people who worshiped them. This was simply one version of the idea that salvation or godly favors is a piece of merchandize that you can buy. It is inevitable that, over time, people will realize that the gods they worship this way simply cannot deliver.

The only true way to attain mastery over your life is to raise your consciousness to the level of the Christ consciousness, as demonstrated by Jesus in his mastery of mind over matter. Jesus gave us an image of God that is radically different from the Old Testament god. He also set the example that what people thought god was supposed to do for us, we can do for ourselves through the Christ consciousness. The fact that Jesus did not use his power to save himself from the cross is because he had a higher agenda, as I have explained.

Anyone who cares to analyze this with a neutral frame of mind, will see that you cannot reconcile the Old Testament god with the loving God portrayed by Jesus. I have explained why Jesus did not write down his teachings and why he wanted a movement that did not have fixed scriptures. It was the fallen beings who inspired the writing of many Christian scriptures and then other fallen beings started compiling a set of official scriptures. In doing this, these fallen beings also decided that the old Jewish scriptures should be incorporated in the Christian scriptures. This was not what Jesus wanted because once it became clear that the Jews would largely reject him, he wanted to set the Christian movement free from any Jewish heritage. He wanted it to be universal.

The fallen beings in embodiment did not fully understand what they were doing by incorporating the Jewish scriptures. Yet the fallen beings in the identity realm did have a clear agenda. Part of it was to drag the false god they had created (the wish-fulfilling god, Yahweh, who can be bought with sacrifices) into the Christian religion. A more long-term perspective is to sow the seed of conflict that can lead to war.

Had it not been for the incorporation of the Jewish scriptures, there would not have been such a focus on Israel as the Holy Land. This focus has so far led to the Crusades, and it has created a situation in the modern world where it is possible that another war will start over Israel. This is in large part because so many Christians in the United States feel obligated to defend the so-called Holy Land against a Muslim invasion. Many Christians (and Jews and Arabs, of course) are willing to fight World War III over this, and they think Jesus would approve. In reality, there is nothing Jesus wants less than a large-scale war over an insignificant peace of real estate in the insignificant city of Jerusalem.

*** 

The fact that the faith in the Roman gods was waning did not mean that most Romans had started rising above the consciousness of wanting a wish-fulfilling god. They had simply started to think that the Roman gods were no longer powerful enough to fill their wishes so they were open to a more powerful god. Constantine could provide such a god because the Old Testament portrays the Jewish god as the ultimate god, the highest god, the almighty god. At the same time, by turning Jesus into god's son (nay, his *only* son), it could be shown that this god really cared about human beings. Constantine himself was not aware of how ingenious this was, but the fallen beings who controlled him were aware. They saw that by turning the Jewish god into the ultimate god and by turning Jesus into his only son, they could provide the Romans with a deity that seemed far more powerful, yet also more present, than the remote old gods.

Take note that the Christian god is a god who cannot as easily be disproved as the Roman gods. If you want a god to do something concrete for you and it does not happen (despite your sacrifice), you may lose faith in that god. Yet the Christian god is supposed to take you to paradise, which does not happen until after the end of this life. Thus, this god cannot be proven wrong in this lifetime, meaning you will remain under the control of the fallen beings for the rest of this lifetime. Naturally, once you die and discover that you will have to reincarnate, you may lose faith and this explains why today's world has so many people who have lost faith in Christianity or are angry with Christianity. They have experienced the fallacy of the Christian promise so many times that they come into embodiment with a deep mistrust of the official churches.

***

The real stroke of genius of the fallen beings was to marry the Roman state with the religion they had just created. This created an institution that had both the power over people's minds provided by the church and the power over their bodies provided by the state. The fallen beings in the identity realm could hardly contain their excitement over having pulled this off. It seemed that they had created an institution that could last for a long time, and it was indeed their hope that it would last for the entire period for which Jesus was to be the spiritual hierarch for earth. They were sure that if their institution could last for the entire period, they could prevent the "second coming of Christ" by preventing significant numbers of people from following the example of Jesus and attaining the Christ consciousness. Did I forget to mention that the second coming was never meant to be Jesus coming again? It was meant to be thousands of people attaining the Christ consciousness and thus raising the collective consciousness to an entirely new level.

The Roman image of a wish-fulfilling deity was transferred to the god of the Old Testament (which wasn't hard, as this god was also created by the fallen beings). Then, Jesus was elevated to being the only begotten son of this god, making him virtually unreachable as an example to follow. You might remember that the Jews thought salvation would come in the future and that Jesus provoked them by claiming the kingdom of God was at hand. He meant that the Christ consciousness can be attained in the present time here on earth, not in some future in heaven (as the fallen beings want us to believe in order to prevent us from challenging them here on earth). By the creation of the Roman Catholic church, the fallen beings again pushed salvation into the future. They destroyed Jesus as an example and as a teacher who is always with us. They turned him into an unreachable deity that we cannot reach on our own (as he wanted), but a deity that we can reach only through the earthly hierarchy of the only true church.

Is it really so hard to see the irony here? Jesus came to set people free from a religion dominated by the fallen beings. The Jewish religion was exactly that kind of religion, and that is why its leaders had Jesus killed. It took the fallen beings only a little over 300 years to turn the Christian movement into the exact same kind of religion. And once they had a religion with the military might of the Roman Empire behind it, they started persecuting all of the mystical branches of Christianity, systematically wiping out all who attempted to do what Jesus wanted people to do, namely reach for direct, inner contact with him, the kind of contact that cannot be controlled by the fallen beings. They labelled it as heresy to do what Jesus wanted us to do, and they made people believe all heretics would burn in hell. Later, when the threat of hell didn't seem enough, the Catholic church started burning heretics at the stake or torturing them in order to steal their light.

*** 

Let me just be clear here. I have explained that the consciousness of Satan is the one that demands that any representative of Spirit, meaning the Living Christ, must conform to conditions on earth. The Catholic church has, from its very inception, been based on the consciousness that Jesus rebuked when he said to Peter: "Get thee behind me, Satan." That is exactly why this church claims to be based on the authority of Peter as the first pope. Well, Jesus never appointed Peter as pope or gave him any other authority. The consciousness of Peter was simply too low for him to have any kind of spiritual authority, and the same goes for the Catholic church. Yet because this church had such total control over the minds of the people for over a thousand years, it has been able to rewrite history in its own favour. That is why you have never heard about the mystical branches of Christianity that flourished until they were brutally squashed by the very church that claims to represent Christ on earth. This church has been the instrument for such a sophisticated propaganda apparatus that it almost dwarfs anything else the fallen beings have created (I said: "almost").

As just one example, take the fact that the Catholic church has portrayed itself as a religion. In a sense, this is correct because the fallen beings have defined religion as something that is an intermediary between god and humans. As I have explained, Jesus and all true teachers have come to give us the truth that we need no intermediary between us and Spirit. The only true intermediary is the Christ consciousness, and it must be achieved on an individual basis; it can never be institutionalized.

The brutal fact is that the Catholic church truly is not a religion. It has from its inception been an apparatus for controlling the people. It is an entirely political institution, and a neutral study of the church's history will prove this to anyone.

Another brutal fact is that from a cosmic perspective the Catholic church does in no way represent Jesus Christ or the universal Christ consciousness. It represents the opposite of this consciousness. The Christ consciousness wants to set people free from the fallen consciousness. The Catholic church is designed from the ground up to keep people trapped in the consciousness of anti-christ, making people the slaves of the fallen beings.

If Jesus was to appear today, the Catholic church would be the first to condemn him as an impostor, as an apparition of the devil. If Jesus did appear, or if anyone attained the Christ consciousness and became an open door for Jesus, the Catholic church would say that unless Jesus' words conformed to Catholic doctrine, they would be false. In other words, if Jesus came to set us free from the Catholic church, he could not be genuine.

This is turning the real teaching of Jesus completely on its head. It is perverting these teachings and turning them into instruments for the consciousness of anti-christ. To me, this means that the Catholic church, and much of modern Christianity, deserves to be seen as Satanism in disguise. And no marvel; for Satan himself is transformed into [appearing as] an angel of light.

# 57

As I have explained, Jesus was well aware of the existence and methods of the fallen beings. He did not use this expression because at the time, people had no foundation for understanding it. So he called them "sons of the devil," as in this quote: "Ye are of your father the devil, and the lusts of your father ye will do. He was a murderer from the beginning, and abode not in the truth, because there is no truth in him. When he speaketh a lie, he speaketh of his own: for he is a liar, and the father of it."

Jesus gave his disciples many teachings about the fallen beings and their methods, but only fragments were ever put into the official scriptures. One was his advice for how to recognize the fallen beings: "On their fruits ye shall know them." This refers not only to the actions but also to the ideas of the fallen beings. But let us start with actions.

I know that some fallen beings would say that I am presenting an entirely black-and-white picture of the Catholic church and that, surely, there must be more nuances. After all, the church has done much good and there are many well-meaning Christians who have been inspired to do good for their fellow man. And while this is perfectly correct, it does not hide or excuse the fact that the leaders of the Catholic church have consistently acted as only fallen beings can do.

I know some fallen beings will say that I am presenting my own version of Aristotelian logic by making it seem like the church is satanic and that this must be accepted as true or untrue. However, let us not confuse Aristotelian logic with fact. You see, logic is applied to conditions that cannot be proven through factual means. Yet I don't need logic in order to prove that the Catholic church has been led by fallen beings. I just need historical facts.

I know, of course, that many Catholics (and other Christians) are in complete denial about the past of the Catholic church. Yet anyone who is not in complete denial, will have to acknowledge that the undeniable actions of the Catholic church present an inescapable dilemma. As I have said, Jesus' teachings were entirely non-violent, proven by the fact that he did not resist his crucifixion. So how can a church claim to represent Christ, even to be his *only* representative on earth, and commit so many acts of violence? I know many sincere Christians have considered this without finding an explanation. I am now offering such an explanation, namely the influence of the fallen beings. Let us look at a few historical facts.

\*\*\*

Very little is known about what happened in the first couple of centuries after the formation of the Catholic church. That is because the church has rewritten history to make itself seem to have always been right. What really happened was a brutal and ruthless suppression of all those who refused to accept the authority of the Catholic church. Much focus has been given to the persecution of the early Christians by the Romans. This is partly done to disguise the fact that the persecution of all non-catholic Christians by the Catholic church was even more ruthless. Grant you, the methods were not quite as violent as those of the Roman authorities, but they were more effective.

Within a couple of centuries, all of the mystical branches had either disappeared or been forced to exist only in secrecy. The writings of the Greek philosophers had been banned and most of their books had been burned. All theologians who differed from official doctrines were suppressed and their writings banned as heresy. It can be difficult to imagine today exactly how much influence the early Catholic church had over people's minds. This was due to the fact that the Roman Empire was a fear-based empire, which most people who have grown up in the West cannot imagine. People who grew up in the Soviet Union have a better frame of reference, although the collective mindset was much more fear-based back then.

The effect of the fear-based mindset was that most people at the time reacted with almost complete submission to the authorities. When the Catholic church banned an idea as heresy and threatened that anyone believing in or promoting the idea would be anathema (meaning he would be cursed by the church and damned to an eternity of torment in hell), most people accepted this without question. Thus, you can find historical records proving that in the year 553 the concept of reincarnation was officially banned at a church council in Constantinople. This was in specific response to the writings of the theologian Origen who wrote extensively about reincarnation. From that moment onwards, the concept of reincarnation was officially removed from Christianity, and strangely enough no modern church has gone back and acknowledged that this happened for entirely political reasons.

Part of the political reasons was that the emperor Justinian had a wife, Theodora, who did not like the idea that she could be held responsible in a future lifetime for what she had done in this lifetime. She also did not like to think that she might reincarnate as a common woman. So she used her influence over the emperor who used his influence over the church to move towards banning the idea. Yet another part of the reason is that the church itself did not like the idea. This was in large part because the fallen beings don't like the idea of reincarnation given that it prevents them from having complete control over the people.

What the fallen beings had created with the Catholic church was a one-shot form of salvation. If you followed the dictates of the church, you were guaranteed to be saved after this lifetime. Naturally, this in itself contradicted the idea of reincarnation. People who believed in reincarnation were less likely to submit to church authority. After all, if you could have more than this lifetime to secure your salvation, why submit fully to the church in this lifetime? If your salvation depended on your state of consciousness, why would you blindly believe in what the church told you to believe or act as it told you to act?

During several centuries, the Catholic church came to be the largest single land-owner in Europe. Considering that Jesus never owned any land, can you see the irony? How did this happen? Well, it happened in large part because people gave land to the church. Why did they do this? Imagine a rich landowner who has lived the good life but is now nearing death. He calls in the Catholic priest to make a last confession. He can clearly see that it doesn't look too good for him, but the priest can offer a solution. If he will donate part of his land to the church, then the church will take away his sins so he can be saved.

\*\*\*

Now, let us jump forward to another undeniable fact. In the year 1209, Pope Innocent III started a crusade against a Christian sect in Southern France, called the Cathars. They were an example of groups that had sprung up and who held beliefs that went beyond and in some cases contradicted official church doctrines. Virtually all of their literature has been destroyed, but the Cathars taught an individual path to salvation and they taught reincarnation. They also had some dualistic ideas so I am not saying the Cathars were completely in alignment with the real teachings of Jesus.

The pope entered an alignment with the King of France, and the result was a major crusade that lasted 20 years. The net result was to wipe out the Cathars. The church got what *it* wanted, and it brought the entire region under the influence of the French king, which was what *he* wanted. Estimates say that between 200,000 and one million Cathars were killed. The real number is 350,000. Most of those killed were women and children who were brutally slaughtered as they sought refuge in churches and did not resist. Experts say that this crusade introduced genocide in the Western world and linked divine salvation to mass murder, making slaughter as loving an act as Jesus' sacrifice on the cross. So I ask you: "How did a church that claims to be based on the non-violent teachings of Christ ever come to the point that it could institute such a slaughter and at the same time feel this was approved by Christ?"

Can you explain this to me based on the official Christian doctrines or materialistic science? Can you think of any other explanation than the influence of the fallen beings with their total insensitivity to life? Can you see how they turned the teachings of Jesus completely upside-down in order to make people believe that slaughtering other people was an act based on the love of Christ? Is this not similar to the Jews and their genocide in the promised land? Does this not prove that such acts are not human and are not tied to any particular group of people? They are decidedly non-human and can come only from beings who are not human, namely the fallen beings.

***

Naturally, we can go on talking about the crusades against he Muslims, the Inquisition, the witch hunts and the persecution of the early scientists. Yet do we really need more examples of the fact that the fallen beings have perverted the teachings of Jesus to an ultimate degree? Does not the fact that Christians were able to kill and think they were doing it in the name of Jesus prove that his teachings were perverted in an extreme manner? And who could have done this except the fallen beings, lifestreams who have an absolute dedication to proving god wrong by destroying anything positive? Is there any other explanation? What I want to get to here is that these historical facts present us with several questions. One of the big questions is why it was necessary to go to such extremes in order to defend the Catholic church? What I am saying here is simple. The official line was, of course, that this was all done for some benign purpose, such as freeing the Holy Land from Muslim domination or saving the souls of those who would otherwise go to hell. Yet this is all camouflage. When you strip all of the fake rhetoric away, you see that the purpose of these truly extreme acts of violence was to defend the unquestionable authority of the Catholic church. Why did the church need defending?

The official claim was, of course, that the church of Christ was under attack by the forces of Satan, and thus it needed to defend itself. Yet if you take what I have said in this book about the real mission of Christ, you see that if a church was truly based on the teachings of Christ, it could never think it needed to defend itself with violence. Instead, it would follow the example of Jesus and thereby bring forth the judgment of Christ upon the forces of Satan. So, a church that truly represented Christ would never need to use violence, meaning that a church that *does* use violence cannot be based on the true teachings of Christ. It is based on the dualistic ideas of the fallen beings, and that is why a church created by one group of fallen beings has to defend itself against the threat of another group of fallen beings. On their fruits ye shall know them. Their primary fruit is death.

\*\*\*

Let us take this one step further by considering what I have said about duality. When you are in alignment with Christ, you realize that you are presently at a certain level among the 144 levels of consciousness. Therefore, you see what you see and you cannot allow yourself to think this is the ultimate understanding. You therefore make no absolutist claims to have the truth or the only truth. You are dedicated to constantly raising your consciousness, and you know that as you do this, you will gain a higher understanding and see things you cannot see now. You are on a path of constant self-transcendence. You are therefore not threatened by other people having a different view than you have. You know that their beliefs are a product of their state of consciousness, and you focus on raising your own consciousness, thereby pulling up the collective consciousness to free

others as well. When you are in alignment with anti-christ, you cannot see
life as a path that does not end in this world. Instead, you seek security in
this world, meaning you want to belong to an institution that has an absolutist claim to authority. Once you claim to have the only truth, it inevitably
follows that you are being threatened by any idea that differs from your
"only" truth. You cannot see the raising of the collective consciousness
as a solution. You see only control as a solution, meaning you engage in
a constant battle to defend your only "truth" and to destroy all diverging
"truths" or the people who promote them.

When you are in alignment with Christ, you see that no idea is worth
killing for. When you are in alignment with anti-christ, you think that your
only truth is indeed worth killing for and that doing so is fully justified by
the epic importance of upholding your only truth.

Again, only the fallen beings can act as if the defense of an idea justifies mass murder. But why is it so epically important for them to defend
their only truth? What are they afraid of? They are simply afraid that the
population at large will stop believing in the only truth and thereby free
themselves from the control of the fallen beings.

For almost a thousand years, the fallen beings had near total control
over the people in Europe through the Catholic church and its various
political alliances. For a certain group of fallen beings, this was as near
to heaven on earth as they have ever come. What overthrew this control? Partly that the real teachings of Jesus were discovered and applied by
enough people that it raised the collective consciousness. And partly that
another group of fallen beings worked very hard to overthrow the dominance of the first group of fallen beings, from which they felt excluded.

***

Let us now go even further and consider why a dualistic "truth" needs
to be defended? From what does it need to be defended?

First of all, we have the illusion created by the fallen beings that an
absolute truth can be expressed in words. This is an illusion, especially on
a planet where matter is as dense as it is on earth. Again, why didn't Jesus
want his teachings to be written down? Because he wanted his followers
to have a direct, inner experience of him as an ascended master. It is this
direct, mystical experience that is the only absolute frame of reference

possible on a dense-matter planet. No words could ever give us an absolute frame of reference.

So the claim that one has the only truth is based on a flawed foundation. Why do the fallen beings make this claim? Because their ultimate desire is to have absolute power, and how do you get that unless you have a claim to absolute authority, based on an absolute truth?

We now come to the fact that duality always has to polarities, thus any dualistic line of reasoning has a contradiction. As soon as the fallen beings formulate a doctrine that they claim is an absolute truth, there is a built-in contradiction, or rather many contradictions. Thus, the very moment you formulate an absolute truth, you will at the same time create multiple contradictions. This means that you put yourself in a position where you constantly have to defend your truth.

Of course, when you make the claim to have absolute truth, you are also saying that you are the ultimate authority when it comes to defining truth. You are claiming to be infallible. This puts you in a position where you cannot afford that anything you say is proven wrong. If even a minor detail is proven wrong, your entire claim to infallibility is threatened. This is exactly the position that the Catholic church was in, and this is why it was so epically important to forcefully suppress anyone who could bring their infallibility into question.

The lower-ranking fallen beings do not understand what I have just explained. They are very frustrated by the fact that their absolute truth is under threat and constantly needs defending. Yet some of the higher-ranking fallen beings in the identity realm do understand that any statement made with words will have an inescapable contradiction. They obviously cannot do anything about this because they cannot see beyond duality. Yet they are not actually concerned about creating an absolute truth. They are concerned about creating as much chaos as possible, and getting someone to claim they have an absolute truth ensures that there will be chaos on earth. In fact, no single factor has ever created more chaos on this planet than the claim that a relative truth is absolute.

This explains why the Catholic church has from its inception been engaged in an effort to explain away the basic contradictions in its approach to religion, and it is still engaged in this process today. It also explains why the Catholic church can never win this battle. It has defeated itself from the very beginning. For a time, it can forcefully suppress opposition to itself, but it cannot do this forever.

\*\*\*

On their fruits ye shall know them. One fruit of the fallen beings is that they create an absolute truth. In doing so, they elevate one relative statement to being the only truth, and at the same time they create contradictions that are difficult to explain. In order to try to explain these, their argumentation become increasingly complex and artificial.

One example is the attempt to elevate Jesus to having some ultimate status that sets him far above the rest of us. They first came out with the idea that Jesus was god's son, then god's *only* son and then that he was of the same substance as the father, that he was never created but was the "only begotten son of the father." This is what set the stage for the Arian controversy because Arius pointed out that if Jesus was the son, then the very concept of a son means someone who is born. And if Jesus had a beginning, there was a time when he was not, meaning he could not be of the same substance as the father. So one group of fallen beings came up with the artificial idea that the son was of the same substance as the father, and another group of fallen beings came up with the idea that the son had a beginning. They now started splitting hairs over these arguments, including the interpretation of a Greek word, "homooúsios," which means that Jesus was of the same being as the father.

This gradually led to the concept of the trinity, namely that god is one god expressed as three beings. If you can get anyone to explain this to you in a way that makes sense, you can do something I can't do. The reality is, of course, that the Creator is one, undivided Being but that it has given a spark of its own consciousness to all self-aware extensions of itself. Jesus is only one such extension, meaning he had a beginning as an individual being. There was a time when Jesus was not.

You can say that the universal Christ consciousness is the first begotten of the father because the Creator created this universal consciousness before it created any individual extensions. The purpose of the universal Christ consciousness is to make sure that an individual co-creator can experiment with free will, including duality, and always have the option to come back to oneness with its Source. There is no illusion we could create in duality that we cannot overcome through the Christ consciousness.

Now, the real question here is why the fallen beings are so concerned about defending the artificial ideas they have defined? Why does defending an idea seem like a matter of life and death? It is, again, because the fallen beings really think they will lose their aura of infallibility if a contradiction is proven. The aspiring power elite is often seeking to prove inconsistencies in the doctrines that the ruling power elite have created in order to gain power.

In this battle between two groups of fallen beings, the arguments often become increasingly complex and increasingly artificial. Yet they all end up in the same place, namely that people need to deny the contradiction. The fallen beings will first try to explain or explain away the contradiction, but if they cannot, they will try to get people to deny it. If that doesn't work, the next step is some kind of force, which quickly leads to violence, such as the crusades, the Inquisition and so forth. Do you think science has liberated us from this pattern? Well, think again.

# PART 9:

# THE FALLEN BEINGS IN

# THE MODERN ERA

# 58

We human beings, naturally, have many needs. An American psychologist, Abraham Maslow, defined a hierarchy of human needs, shaped like a pyramid. The idea is that there are some basic needs that are very important as long as they are not filled, but then fade into the background, giving room in our attention for higher needs. The most basic needs are biological and physiological, meaning food, water and shelter. The second level are safety needs. Then comes love and belonging needs. Next is esteem needs and the need to accomplish something. Finally comes our needs for self-actualization.

When you combine this idea of a hierarchy of needs with the 144 levels of consciousness and reincarnation, you see that a soul goes through a progression from lower to higher needs over many lifetimes. At the lower levels of consciousness, people are focused on physiological end security needs. For example, people living as hunter-gatherers focus mostly on food and shelter. People like Hitler, Stalin and Mao were focused on safety needs and in their paranoia created elaborate security forces to protect them against any threat, even the ones existing only in their minds.

As you go beyond the 48th level of consciousness, the higher needs begin to take prominence. First, is the need to belong to some group, be it a personal relationship, family or larger group. Once you have this need somewhat fulfilled, you begin to focus on accomplishing something to either boost your self-esteem or gain recognition from others. When these needs are met (over many lifetimes), you begin to feel an inner emptiness, and you realize that life must have some kind of meaning beyond mere material existence. You then begin to feel what Maslow called the needs for self-actualization. These needs can be divided into three general categories.

We have a need to understand how life works, who we are, where we came from and how the universe functions. We also have a need to feel that life has meaning, a purpose that reaches beyond the material world and beyond our personal lives. We also have a need to feel that there is a goal in life and that we are moving towards that goal. These are the needs that can be fulfilled only by following what I have called the spiritual or mystical path, namely the path that leads you towards the 144th level of consciousness and the ascension.

The fallen beings have denied these self-actualization needs in themselves. Or one might say that they have perverted the needs so that they seek a goal in this world. It may be absolute power or to prove god wrong, but it is a goal that cannot ultimately give them fulfilment. If they actually achieved their goals, the fallen beings would still feel empty and unfulfilled. However, the real issue is that the fallen beings are scared of these higher needs because they know that once people recognize their higher needs, it is very difficult to prevent them from pursuing the spiritual path. And once people find the true path, it is very difficult to stop their progress. If enough people discover and follow this path, then they will inevitably raise the collective consciousness to the point where the fallen beings cannot remain on this planet. Thus, the fallen beings will do anything in their power to prevent an awakening so that a critical mass of people become aware that the only real way to change the earth is to raise consciousness on an individual level until it has a collective effect. If you do not understand this dynamic, you cannot truly understand the underlying motive behind world events.

\*\*\*

Before we move on to the modern era, let us just look at the society that the fallen beings had managed to create in Europe during the Middle Ages. It was pretty close to their dream society because the majority of the people were the virtual slaves of a small power elite of fallen beings.

I have said that because the fallen beings are trapped in duality, they tend to form at least two opposing groups. In many societies you have seen one group of fallen beings form the religious elite and another group form a secular elite as the rulers of society. Naturally, you also had this during the Middle Ages, in the form of the Catholic clergy and the kings and noblemen. Yet during the Middle Ages, the dynamic was a little different because the kings and the noble class were put in power by the Catholic church, and they knew it, at least for a time.

This development started when Christianity became the state religion of the Roman Empire. This unified the religious and secular powers, although there was still an uneasy sharing of power between the popes and the emperors. Nevertheless, it was clear to both sides that they needed each other. As the Roman Empire dissolved, things became much more chaotic for a while. There was a potential that Europe could descend into anarchy and chaos, with lots of small kings fighting each other. What prevented this was the Catholic church, which remained a source of continuity in a chaotic world.

There was a potential that the Catholic church could morph into a new kind of power with both religious and secular control (for a time, the church did own large areas of land in Italy, had its own army and fought its own wars). Yet neither the church nor Europe were unified enough for this to happen. Instead, what emerged was a new type of secular ruler, starting with Charlemagne, who had the backing of the Catholic church and in return swore loyalty to the church. This led to the emergence of many secular rulers that were loyal to the church. These kings and emperors ruled the common people through a class of noblemen who kept the people living as their slaves, doing the work on the land owned by the landlords.

Take note of the real reason I am bringing this up. The feudal system could never have been put in place had it not been for the debilitating fear that the Catholic church had instilled in the minds of most people in Europe. After centuries of programming, most people were so mortally afraid of burning in hell for all eternity that they did not even dare to consider going against the church. So when the church made it clear that going against the secular rulers backed by the church was the same as going against the church, which was the same as going against god, then most people accepted this.

This was in large part helped by another lie of the fallen beings, namely that life in this world really didn't matter. Life was so short, and what really mattered was to secure your place in heaven for all eternity. Thus, it was a small sacrifice to submit to the church while here on earth. It simply didn't seem to matter that the church or a secular ruler controlled you here on earth as long as you would be rewarded with an eternity in heaven. Of course, the promise that by submitting to the fallen beings here on earth will secure your place in heaven is a complete mockery of the real teachings of Jesus.

\*\*\*

The feudal system was not by any means a completely unified system. There was much infighting, and one of the major motives behind the crusades was to get the warring kings and noblemen to fight a common enemy outside the borders of Europe instead of fighting each other. However, the feudal system was an ideal system for the fallen beings because it kept the majority of the population under the tight control of a very small power elite, most of whom were fallen beings in embodiment. The noblemen literally owned the peasants who were born on their land and the people had very little choice as to what they would do with their lives.

The reason for bringing this up is that it relates to my talk about the hierarchy of needs. It has always been a conscious goal for the fallen beings in the identity realm to keep the majority of the population trapped in pursuing the lower levels of needs. Their goal is to prevent the small percentage who are ready to pursue self-actualization needs from doing so. They want to keep these people trapped in a situation where they are either focused on the lower needs or are prevented from recognizing and pursuing their higher needs. They do not want these people to attain any degree of personal Christhood.

For almost a thousand years, the fallen beings kept the people in Europe locked in the feudal societies in which hardly anyone had the opportunity to pursue self-actualization needs. Most people were so poor that the physiological needs were dominant. And there was still the constant threat of violence and wars that kept people focused on security needs. A few managed to reach the level of belonging needs, but that was as far as it went for the population. Some members of the noble classes (not all of whom were fallen beings) could focus on esteem needs, but very few made it to self-actualization needs. You might say that some people became monks and nuns so they supposedly had time to focus on self-actualization needs, but this happened under the auspices of the Catholic church.

As I have explained, the doctrines and practices of this church were carefully designed to give people the impression that they were working on their salvation while keeping them from following the path of Christhood. So even though some monks and nuns were ready to pursue self-actualization, the church was very efficient in keeping them from reaching a level of Christhood that was a threat to the fallen beings. Surely, you can mention a few Catholic mystics that were exceptions to this, but they were too few to overthrow the dominance of the fallen beings.

Once you understand that the goal of the fallen beings is to prevent people from pursuing their self-actualization needs, you can gain a new perspective on what is happening in the modern era. You can especially gain a new perspective on what has been called the war between religion and science.

# 59

The feudal society was the dream society of the fallen beings. It lasted for a long time, but why did it not simply go on indefinitely? There are three primary reasons. I have already said that the earth is one among billions of planets with self-aware life forms. Most of those planets are natural planets that are in an ascending spiral. Because everything is connected through consciousness, this creates a magnetic pull that pulls on the four lower bodies of all beings in the universe, including people on earth. This upward pull means that the fallen beings cannot keep people trapped indefinitely because some people will respond and raise their consciousness. I said that the feudal system was put in place because people feared torment in hell. Yet the upward pull of the entire universe did (although it took some time) pull the collective consciousness to a point where more and more people started doubting the reality of this threat. A particular fear can enable the fallen beings to control the people, but only for a limited time. You cannot scare all of the people all of the time.

Another factor in overthrowing the feudal system was what I have earlier described as the second law of thermodynamics. The feudal system was a closed system, and all such systems will, because of their built-in contradictions, start to break down from within. When all leaders are fallen beings, they all want to have more and more power. This can only lead to conflict, and there is really no way to avoid it, even though the church managed to keep a lid on it for a while. As I said, it became necessary to start the crusades as a diversionary tactic to keep the noblemen and clergy-men from fighting each other. Better to get the warriors to go somewhere else and fight an external enemy. The crusades, I have to say, were an example of how good the fallen beings are at deceiving even each other.

The third factor in the equation is that the ascended masters are con-stantly seeking to bring forth ideas that can set the people free from the fallen beings and help them discover the path of self-actualization. The masters brought forth many ideas during the Middle Ages, but the most important of all of them was science. Science was from the very beginning designed by the ascended masters in order to set people's minds free from the tyranny of the fallen beings. I have said that the core of the satanic mindset is that you create a mental idea and then project it upon the world, wanting the world to conform to your idea. This was what the Catholic church had done with most of its doctrines. Science was meant to free people from this by establishing a procedure whereby theories of how the world *should* work could be compared to how the world *does* work.

***

The tyranny of the fallen beings was based on the perversion of Jesus' teachings, but the core of it was that the fallen beings had created a system that seemed impossible to challenge. Jesus was the only road to salvation and the Catholic church was the only true representative of Jesus on earth. You could not be saved without being a member of the church, meaning that anyone who was excommunicated was doomed to eternity in hell. Naturally, in order to establish its authority, the church had to claim infallibility. The doctrines of the church and the word of the pope were infallible. The fastest way to be excommunicated from the church was to challenge the claim to infallibility. If one little detail in the church's system was proven to be fallible, then it would threaten the entire claim to infallibility.

The net effect of this was that the pope and the clergy could say just about anything they wanted because no one dared to challenge them. This led to the doctrine that the earth was the center of the universe, which was a direct effect of the fallen beings and their desire to seem very important to god. The ascended masters were keenly aware that as long as this state of affairs was in place, the people could not free themselves from the fallen beings. Thus, the masters decided to bring forth a method (already found on natural planets) whereby direct observations of the material universe could be compared to theory, or rather doctrine.

Of course, the ascended masters had also inspired some people to create telescopes. The masters knew that by using these telescopes (as primitive as they were) to make direct observations of the heavens, it would be possible to disprove the Catholic church's claim that the earth was the center of the universe. They also knew that by disproving something as central as the basic image of the universe, it would raise doubt about many other aspects of Catholic doctrine.

The masters had also brought forth new technology that would make it possible for people to spread information. The Feudal society was established on fear, but fear always springs from ignorance. If you know enough, your fear simply fades away. During the Feudal era, the fallen beings (mainly through the church) had a monopoly on information. Take note that the fallen beings always seek to keep people from having information because they know that knowledge is power. They know that it has always been a lack of knowledge (or false knowledge) that has enabled them to rule, and it has always been an increase of knowledge that has taken away their power over the people. Once people really know why they have been ruled by an elite, they will no longer submit to that elite.

We take so many things for granted in the modern world. Have you ever considered how difficult it was to challenge the doctrines of the church in a society where most people could not read and where the only way to distribute information was word of mouth or books copied by hand? For a thousand years, the Catholic church had a monopoly on distributing information. Most people could not even read the Bible, partly because they couldn't read and partly because it wasn't available in any other language than Latin. The Catholic priests would read from the Bible and then interpret it for the congregation. Truly, the fallen beings did not give people any room to challenge their doctrines.

The most important single factor in bringing about the modern age is a relatively simple technological invention, namely the printing press. Without the ability to distribute information, the feudal system might still be in place and the Catholic church might still have a monopoly on information. Naturally, Gutenberg was an example of a person who was able to attune his consciousness to the ascended masters and receive the idea for the printing press. Yet many other people played a part in this by ensuring that literacy spread to a greater and greater part of the population. Books don't really do a lot of good if no one can read them.

\*\*\*

Contrary to popular opinion today, the early scientists were highly *spiritual* people. They were not *religious* people, and they had overcome their fear of Catholic threats. They were what I have called mystics, and they all had an ability to tune in and receive ideas from the ascended masters. Roger Bacon and Francis Bacon were two incarnations of the same lifestream, and they both received some of the fundamental ideas for developing the scientific method. Galileo received many of his most important ideas as inner revelation from the ascended masters. He had learned to attune to the masters over several lifetimes. The same is true for many of the early scientists (such as Newton and later Einstein) and many scientists and inventors today. Many of these people are not consciously aware of where their ideas are coming from, but the ascended masters are not concerned about being credited for their ideas. They are concerned about setting people free from false ideas.

What I am getting to here is that the claim that there is a war between science and religion is not a universal truth. It all depends on whether you look at it from the perspective of the fallen beings or from the perspective of the ascended masters. What I have tried to explain in this book is that the way our modern societies look at religion is not the only way to look at religion. Our image of religion is created by the fallen beings. The fallen beings have created what we see as religion, but it is really a political institution for controlling the people. The Catholic church is the perfect example.

True religion, which we today need to call spirituality or mysticism, is an expression of our self-actualization needs. When we reach a certain level of consciousness, we naturally become open to the need to find meaning and to understand how life actually works. While we are still focused on the lower needs, we do not want to *know* how the world actually works. We want to *define* how the world *should* work, and this is an attempt to deal with our lower needs, first of all the need for security.

The Catholic church was not entirely forced upon people. The fallen beings who defined Catholic doctrines very cleverly appealed to people below the 48th level of consciousness where security needs are a big concern. The fallen beings themselves had created the violence and warfare found in the world. They now offered people a way out of this, namely that by being a member of the Catholic church, you would soon escape the chaos of this world and find eternal rest in heaven. This was a clever way to appeal to people's security needs. One group of fallen beings drove people into the arms of another group of fallen beings. It works every time—until people become aware of what is happening.

I got side-tracked. True spirituality has nothing to do with defining how the world *should* work. Most religions have doctrines that attempt to define how people (or the fallen beings) would like the world to work, including what god will do for them if they obey the outer religion on earth. "God, I do this for your church, and then you have to do this for me." True spirituality is a process where you realize that what you understand about the universe right now is a product of your level of consciousness. You therefore engage in a systematic effort to raise your consciousness and then you will gain a wider perspective. As you approach the 144th level of consciousness, you will discover how the world truly works, not how the fallen beings would like it to work.

Why does this scare the fallen beings more than anything? Because they know they can't go to the higher levels of consciousness. They will always know less than those who reach the higher levels, meaning that those who attain Christhood can always expose the shortcomings of the fallen beings, as Jesus did with the scribes and Pharisees. Since the fallen beings know that their power over the people depends on keeping the people ignorant, they know that one person with some Christ consciousness (Galileo) can ruin what a thousand fallen beings have taken centuries to create (Catholic doctrine).

***

True spirituality is an open-ended process of gradually raising our consciousness so we can discover how the universe really works. And true science is exactly the same process.

A long time ago, I talked about the two basic forces of creation, the expanding and contracting, the Father and Mother. The only way to truly know how the world works is to use both forces. Using your intuitive faculties to reach for ideas from the ascended masters is the Father aspect of our abilities. The Mother aspect is to conduct physical experiments and observe how the material universe responds to our actions. This is what I have called co-creation.

The ascended masters saw that the Catholic church had made it very difficult for people to use their intuitive faculties to reach for new ideas. Yet the church had not fully shut down people's ability to make observations and conduct experiments. This was something that had been done by the alchemists, but they had (mostly) managed to slide under the radar of the church. Thus, by building upon this tradition for experimentation, the masters inspired the early scientists.

Naturally, the masters were practical realists and they saw that given the situation, it was more feasible to get people to use the Mother element than the Father element. Yet it was never the intention of the masters that science should be disconnected from the Father element so that scientists would deny their intuitive faculties or deny the existence of a realm beyond the material world. The masters knew that science can reach its full potential only when scientists see that their current ability to understand the universe depends on their level of consciousness. Thus, a scientist is walking the path of Christhood because he or she knows that this is the only way to fulfil the highest potential of science.

True spirituality and true science are both expressions of our desire to know how the world really works. As I have said, you need to reach a certain level of consciousness before you overcome the desire to define how the world *should* work. Thus, true spiritual persons and true scientists see themselves as walking the path towards higher states of consciousness. They see how naive it is to expect that we can uncover the highest secrets of the universe while being in a lower state of consciousness.

***

Is there a war between religion and science? Well, there is always an established power elite and an aspiring power elite, and these two groups of fallen beings will use anything available to wage war. The established power elite had a firm grip on the Catholic church so when the ascended masters brought forth the ideas that formed the basis for science, the aspiring power elite saw an opportunity to use science to take power from the fallen beings controlling the church. They saw that by twisting science, they could use it to discredit the Catholic church (and all religion) and thus leave a power vacuum just waiting for someone to fill it. Beyond that, the fallen beings in the identity realm saw that they could use science as they had used Catholic doctrine.

The Catholic church was defined by the fallen beings who had also defined religion. The aspiring power elite managed to pervert science by creating the materialist belief system. So if you define religion based on the Catholic church and define science based on materialism, then there is indeed a war between science and religion. If you define religion and science as expressions of our need for self-actualization (for knowing how the world actually works rather than defining how it *should* work), then there is no war between science and religion. They are two complementary ways (and none of them can give us complete results without the other) for discovering who we are and how the world works. So let's take a look at materialism, this ingenious creation of the fallen beings.

\*\*\*

You can't understand materialism fully without realizing that some fallen beings have it as their highest goal to prove god wrong. As a natural result of this, they are always seeking for ways to destroy people's faith in god and religion. You might say: "But aren't you saying that the fallen beings have defined religion?" Of course they have, but they have done so in a way that is designed to give them power over the people by giving people a false image of god.

The fallen beings know that they cannot keep the people blindly following a particular religion indefinitely. Any false image of god will eventually be challenged by the upward progression of the universe. So the fallen beings in the identity realm define a false image of god, and when people start losing faith in that image, they seek to undermine people's faith in god as a general concept. The false image of god that the fallen beings gave people through the Catholic church was perfectly suited for undermining people's faith in any form of religion and in god as a general concept. This, of course, is a perfect example of black-and-white thinking. Either a particular religion must be infallible, and if it is not, then no religion is any good and we need to abandon all religion. This, naturally, obscures the possibility that by raising our consciousness, we can discover a new approach to spirituality that can give us a higher understanding of God and ourselves.

As I have said before, there are fallen beings in the physical octave who are firmly believing in the cause for which they are fighting. Most popes through history have been fallen beings but they have firmly believed in the Catholic church and its image of god, even that the church was a force for good in the world. Yet these fallen beings were largely controlled by fallen beings in the identity realm, and they have no allegiance to any organization or belief system on earth. For them, anything is a tool to be used as long as it works and then abandoned for another one. They are always playing both sides of the fence, seeking to set groups of people up against each other. These fallen beings immediately saw how science could be used to shoot down the false image of god they themselves had foisted upon the people through the Catholic church. Thus, they immediately started creating scientific materialism. And just see how marvelously it has worked. You now have a classical fallen being confrontation between two groups of people. On one side, the religious people (primarily Christians) who are fanatically seeking to hold on to their faith in Christian doctrines. On the other side you have the scientific materialists who are equally fanatical in promoting their belief system and proving religion wrong. The net result is that these two groups simply cannot communicate in any meaningful way. They are both so focused on defending the doctrines of the fallen beings that they cannot make a heart-to-heart connection and realize the basic reality that we humans are more than our beliefs. We are universal spiritual beings who are able to communicate as such and therefore discover our true, inner oneness. The divide-and-conquer strategy was invented and perfected by the fallen beings over a long period of time, and the goal is always to make people focus on outer differences so they forget their inner humanity, or rather spirituality.

# 60

I am not here going to go into looking at the specific claims made by scientific materialism. The reason is that if you are reading this, you are not a hard-core materialist. You therefore already know that materialism cannot answer your deeper questions about life. If you had been satisfied with the materialistic explanations, you would not have been reading this book.

But think about it this way: Why can't materialism answer your questions about life? Materialism is a thought system that is very similar to the system created by the Catholic church. They both claim infallibility and they both claim to have the only true image of how the world works. Like Catholicism, materialism also has a priesthood of people who claim to be the only ones who can tell the people what to believe. And they are as reluctant to consider any challenges to their claim to infallibility as the popes of the Middle Ages, seeking to inflict retribution upon those who dare challenge them. I admit that their methods are not as violent so their main weapon is public ridicule. Anyone daring to question materialism is immediately labeled as a religious fanatic or simply a kook (just look at what they will say about this book). Any scientist who dares to propose a theory beyond materialism, will be ridiculed by the materialist thought police, might be frozen out of a job or find it difficult to get research grants. Surely, the methods are not as openly violent as the rack, but they are just as aggressive in seeking to neutralize any challenging ideas and the people who promote them.

Like the Catholic thought system, materialism defines an area where we can seek knowledge and then says that anything outside this area is forbidden. The Catholic church defined a set of scriptures and doctrines where it was permitted to seek knowledge, but anything outside was forbidden. Materialism defines the material universe as the area in which it is allowed to search for knowledge whereas it is most strictly forbidden to seek knowledge outside the physical octave. Given that I have explained how the world has four octaves and that anything in the physical is an effect of causes in the emotional, mental and identity octaves, you can see how this can only limit our ability to understand the world and ourselves.

Materialists make the same claim that all fallen beings make, namely that *they* can give us all the knowledge we need and thus we should be satisfied with that. This is what worked for the Catholic clergy for a thousand years, but it only worked because of the violent suppression of alternative sources of knowledge. The Catholic church claimed that all answers to our questions about life could be found within its doctrines. That is why the church has, for its entire existence, been engaged in this effort to explain everything within doctrine, giving rise to some very complex and artificial lines of reasoning. They truly were a form of superstition, and they were rightly criticized by the early scientists.

What has been "overlooked" by most materialists is that materialism has created equally complex and artificial doctrines in its attempt to explain our basic questions about where the universe came from and how it works. However, when it comes to explaining the deeper questions, such as the meaning of life, materialism has taken a new approach. Instead of defining this within its doctrines, materialism has defined these questions as meaningless.

If you live in a universe that is essentially created out of random events that have been shaped by a process of natural selection, then how can life have any general meaning? If your thought process, and your desire to find meaning, is simply a product of more or less random processes in your brain that will stop when your brain dies, then how can your personal life have any meaning? Your quest for meaning is simply a mistake by nature that will eventually be selected out, and humanity will be purified of such nonsense so all that is left is people who ruthlessly seek to further their self-interest. Brave new world.

This is a new approach compared to earlier thought systems that were usually religious in nature. In other words, in previous ages, the fallen beings did not seek to ignore our questions about meaning and god. They attempted to make use of them and give us a false image of god that required us to submit to their control here on earth. With materialism, a group of fallen beings took this to another level by flat-out denying the existence of any world beyond the material.

They did this for two main reasons. One is that the aspiring power elite had to set themselves apart from the Catholic church. Since it seemed impossible for them to create another church that would give them power, they attempted to deny anything the church stands for. So they were caught in defining their doctrines as a denial of the church's doctrines. However, the more important reason is that some fallen beings in the identity realm have reached a state of blindness where they are so arrogant that they think they can actually get a majority of the people to deny the existence of god and deny their deeper questions about life. One has to say it is a bold experiment, and it remains to be seen how well it will work and for how long people will accept the claim that their questions about life's meaning are meaningless.

*\*\*\**

I said I won't go into detail with materialist claims, but I will give some examples of how materialism has led to inescapable contradictions. However, first I want to make a distinction between science and materialism. I am in no way against or critical towards science. It is a valid and valuable process, and in its essence it is open-ended. It seeks ever-deeper explanations and never accepts any limits to knowledge, therefore accepting no absolute or final "truth." In contrast, materialism (as Catholicism) is by nature closed-ended. It seeks to define a particular viewpoint as the absolute and final truth beyond which nothing could be found. It may be that such a viewpoint actually has some validity, but the fact that something is valid at the present level of the collective consciousness does not mean it is the highest understanding we could ever discover. Thus, materialism is as debilitating for scientific inquiry as Catholicism is for spiritual inquiry.

As an example of a valid viewpoint that is not the final understanding, take the laws that Isaac Newton received from the ascended masters. They were exactly what humankind needed (and what they were able to grasp) at the time. Newtonian physics allowed the development of technology that took society forwards and thus set the stage for an even deeper understanding. This came when Einstein received the ideas for the theory of relativity from the ascended masters. Just before Einstein, many materialistic scientists thought they were close to being able to explain how the universe worked, having only some details to fill in. Einsteinian physics did not invalidate Newtonian physics, but it went far beyond and uncovered a deeper layer of explanation. And quantum physics has gone beyond what even Einstein was able to accept. It is simply arrogant and ignorant to claim that materialism has the final truth about how the universe works.

This becomes clear when we compare thermodynamics and Big Bang theory. As I have said, physicists have discovered a law of nature that they consider to be universally valid, meaning it applies to all systems. It is called the second law of thermodynamics, and it states that any closed system will (as long as it receives no outside influence) go towards its lowest possible energy state. The example is a steam engine that receives no fuel or water. It will eventually stop producing anything and reach a state of thermal equilibrium.

Now, you can formulate the second law in a different way by saying that a closed system cannot produce any work without receiving anything from outside itself. You can construct a steam engine so that the physical machinery is there. Yet if you do not add coal and water from outside the engine, then the engine cannot get started.

Now take what materialists say about the entire universe. They say it is an entirely closed system because there is absolutely nothing outside it. They say the entire universe (with all of its billions of galaxies and with the incredibly complex structures, such as the human brain) started when all of the energy in the universe was compressed into a singularity. Then, all of this energy exploded outwards in a random explosion, but out of this randomness started (spontaneously and randomly) all of the complex structures we see today. Do you see that this process is in direct contradiction to the second law of thermodynamics?

This law says that in any closed system, evolution can go in only one direction. If the system is closed, there is only a certain amount of energy available to drive any work that produces something new. As this energy is used up, the system cannot produce more and more complex structures. Instead, the structures that are there will gradually break down until nothing is left. So how did the closed universe even get started on producing increasingly complex structures?

According to the second law of thermodynamics, the energy being hurled out by the Big Bang should have simply continued to expand until it ran out of steam. Then, the universe should have started contracting until it had again reached the state it was in before the Big Bang. In other words, if the material universe is a closed system, then the second law states that it can only produce a series of expansions and contractions. It cannot – as a matter of principle – produce an evolutionary process that leads to increasingly complex structures that seemingly are not running out of steam. Scientists have now discovered that the billions of galaxies in the observable universe are not only moving away from each other, they are moving at an accelerating rate. This expansion requires energy, but where can this energy come from in a closed system?

I know the fallen beings can and will argue with every point I am making here, but the bottom line is that either the second law of thermodynamics is incomplete or the theory of the Big Bang is incomplete.

The alternative is, of course, to realize that the universe is not a closed system. The material universe is evolving because the evolutionary process is driven by a constant stream of energy that comes from the emotional, mental and identity octaves and eventually from the ascended realm. Without this influx of energy, evolution simply would have no energy source, and as Einstein proved, matter is simply another form of energy.

***

Just one more example, namely that favorite brainchild of the fallen beings: evolution as a random, unconscious process. Charles Darwin was not a fallen being but had entirely good intentions and was very intelligent and observant. Unfortunately, he was a child of his time, meaning he only knew religion in the Catholic/Anglican variety. He did not know an alternative, namely the kind of spiritual process (evolutionary spirituality) I have presented in this book. Had he known this, he might have been able to attune his mind to the ascended masters and receive the real theory of evolution. Instead, the fact that he saw the shortcomings of official Christianity while seeing no mystical alternative caused him to attune to fallen beings in the mental realm, and he received their version of evolution.

Naturally, the world was not created instantly in six days, as it says in Genesis. There is indeed a gradual, evolutionary process. In fact, the entire purpose for the existence of the world is that we, who are self-aware beings, start out with a localized, linear sense of self and gradually evolve an omnipresent, spherical sense of self. However, what Darwin received was the brainchild of the fallen beings behind materialism, namely that evolution is not directed by any conscious mind and that it is the result of a random process.

What did I say was the concept that Jesus called Satan? It was that Spirit must conform to conditions in matter. Well, Darwin's theory of evolution (and the elaborate structure that materialists have built upon it) essentially says that everything is shaped by conditions in matter, including us human beings. Everything must adapt to and is shaped by current conditions in matter. However, now take this process and push the rewind button.

We are obviously very complex life forms. We are supposedly the latest step in a very long process that goes back through billions of years. As we go back, we find more and more simple life forms, until we end up with single-celled organisms. It is deceptively appealing to say that all of the complex life forms evolved from the first single-celled organism because this organism had to adapt to changing physical conditions. Okay, but where did the first single-celled organism come from?

Or rather, how did the first life-form arise as an adaptation to physical conditions? How can something that does not exist, suddenly come into being as an adaptation to something that it does not know exists? You begin to see the problem? Even materialists are not comfortable talking about this. In our use of language, it is easy to say that the first single-celled organism was created, but this sounds too much like religion so materialists talk about the "origin" of life. However, they cannot explain how life originated. And the reason is that they have limited our inquiry to a process of evolution as adaptation.

If evolution is an adaptive process, an adaptive process cannot bring forth something radically different from what already exists. Before the first single-celled organism "originated," there was no organic life. There were only inorganic compounds. According to evolutionary theory, these compounds had evolved from the Big Bang through a very complicated process. The Big Bang supposedly started a process where a few initial particles reacted with each other and through adaptation created new particles that gradually formed atoms that gradually formed everything else. Yet organic life is radically different from inorganic matter so how can matter adapting to matter create something so radically different?

Let me try to make this more concrete. Most of us have been told in school that life originated in the oceans. When fish had evolved, some of them started evolving legs and lungs and eventually went on land. Yet how could this happen as an adaptive process? The principle is that an organism can gradually adapt to an environment, but only if it can survive and reproduce in that environment. If you look at the ocean, you see that it has zones with a lower content of oxygen. You can see organisms that have evolved so they can live in zones with very little oxygen, but you see no organisms that can adapt to areas where there is no oxygen.

Well, for a fish in the sea, there is no oxygen on land. Naturally, we know that there is oxygen in the air, but a fish cannot know that. Evolution has no consciousness that allows it to discover that there is oxygen in the air and that there might be an evolutionary advantage to a fish developing legs and lungs that would allow it to live on land. Evolution can only *passively* adapt, it cannot *actively* anticipate. A fish that is thrown on land or is left in a tide pond simply dies if the water disappears. So please explain to me how a fish could – by an unconscious process of adaptation – evolve organs that give it no survival advantage under water? How can a fish adapt to surviving on land when the fish that is left on dry land simply dies and cannot reproduce. This fish cannot adapt to an environment in which it cannot survive long enough to reproduce. Thus, an unconscious process of adaptation cannot explain how life went from sea to land (or back again).

*** 

Again, evolution is a perfect example of how the fallen beings are trapped in the limitations of dualistic logic. The aspiring power elite who developed materialism were eager to deny the claims of the established power elite and their religion. The established elite claimed that everything in the universe was created by god and was thus god's will. Thus, the aspiring elite denied the existence of god and in so doing had to deny that there was any kind of consciousness that could influence the process of evolution. In other words, there was no consciousness that could see that there was oxygen in the air and that it could be an advantage for fish to develop organs for surviving on dry land. In order to deny this directed evolution, they were forced into stating that what drives evolution is a completely random process.

Here they make use of the main feature of dualistic logic, namely that everything must have an opposite. For thousands of years, we have observed that everything is an effect of a cause and we have been engaged in a quest to discover the cause behind all phenomena. Yet according to dualistic logic, the concept of a cause must have an opposite, and the opposite of cause-and effect must be complete randomness.

Materialists have conveniently ignored that if evolution is entirely random, then science has with one stroke become meaningless. Science is basically an attempt to discover laws or principles behind visible phenomena so we can use those to produce certain effects and avoid others. If the universe is the result of a random process, what sense does it make to discover natural laws? In randomness, there can be no such laws. And since materialists present evolution as a natural law, then it cannot be entirely random or it is a contradiction in terms. Of course, materialists will say it is not entirely random because it is directed by natural selection, however, this is not logically consistent. Again, we can take what we observe today and go back to previous states. If we go back to the Big Bang (by the way, this theory was developed by a Catholic priest in order to reconcile the church's doctrines of instant creation with the discoveries of science), it says that all matter and energy was compressed into a single point, called a singularity. No one, of course, can explain what this singularity was and how all matter and energy could be compressed into an infinitely small point. Yet they say that all energy and matter was hurled out from this point in a completely random explosion. Yet within a few milliseconds of time, this random explosion spontaneously and randomly started to form organized structures.

Just pause for a minute and consider how this could happen. How can a completely random process produce organized structures? How can random events build upon each other and combine to form a complex structure that seemingly has a purpose? Why didn't the Big Bang simply continue as a random explosion? The answer is very simple. Since we can observe that the Big Bang (or whatever the process was) did produce complex, organized structures, we must conclude that it could not have been completely random. If it had been a random process, we wouldn't be here to argue about it.

The real problem with randomness is how single random events formed structures where new random events built on previous random events. Do you see the dilemma faced by the fallen beings here? We can all observe that we live in a universe with many complex structures that work together. The human body has trillions of single cells, but they are all organized into a whole that functions as one body. According to materialists, the only process that can account for the existence of the body is found inside each cell, namely the DNA. Yet when it comes to DNA, each cell is a self-contained unit and the only mechanism for change is a random mutation in the cell's DNA. How do you then explain that random mutations caused trillions of cells to form the structure of the human body that can act as one, coherent unit? How did the first single-celled organism randomly mutate into a dual-cell organism? There is no materialistic mechanism that can explain the combination of single cells into a coherent whole, but I have a very simple explanation: consciousness.

Materialists face the same dilemma as the Catholic theologians. They are trying to create an absolutist explanation for life, but a neutral observation of life contradicts the theory. Anyone with a telescope could observe that the Catholic claim that the earth is the center of the universe does not conform to observation. You can also observe that the materialist claim that life was formed by a random process does not conform to observation—and you don't even need a telescope for that.

\*\*\*

If you don't believe me, then do what scientists always do, namely conduct an experiment. Get out the dice and start rolling them. Let us say you have six pieces, and your goal is to have six ones. Mathematicians have calculated the odds that you will get six ones, and while it is indeed possible, it could take a very long time. In fact, if the dice are truly random, it is possible that it would never happen. But now imagine that you roll the dice and get a one. You then put it aside and roll the remaining pieces. When you again get a one, you put it aside and continue until you have six pieces showing a one. Suddenly, this becomes much more likely.

What you see from this experiment is the difference between an entirely random process of evolution and one that is directed by a form of consciousness. I know some say that if evolution was random, there hasn't been enough time since the Big Bang to produce the complexity we see. Yet I am talking about more than time, namely that even an infinite number of random events cannot produce organized structures where many individual acts work towards a goal. Anyone can observe that evolution is a goal-oriented process that produces increasingly more complex structures and life forms. A goal-directed process simply cannot be produced by a truly random series of events because events that are random cannot form a series.

It was not just one mutation in one cell that caused the first fish to develop lungs, legs and a skin that doesn't dry out in air. It took many mutations, and how did those mutations ever come to work towards the goal that a fish could survive and reproduce on dry land? Truly random mutations could never have done this, as they could have gone on forever producing random genetic changes that didn't turn the fish into a creature that could live in an environment where the fish cannot live. In fact, a random process could never have formed the fish in the first place.

If you still don't see the point here, just keep rolling the dice. What you are doing is exactly what materialists say led to the spontaneous formation of organized structures. So just keep rolling the dice until you see them form an organized pattern. Or alternatively, ask yourself how long you will have to do this before you begin doubting that the universe is random.

This is an example of how the fallen beings end up in logical blind alleys and have to force the rest of us to not think about the topic. Materialists are trying very hard to prevent us from thinking logically about evolution. The reason is that they are in the same blind alley as Catholic clergy. They claim infallibility so if one element of their theory is proven wrong, then the whole claim falls apart. In order to prevent anyone from questioning evolution as an infallible theory, they are ready to stop scientific inquiry and discussion. This is not science; it is as alien to true science and Catholic doctrine is to true spirituality. The open-ended process of science has been hijacked and turned into a closed system. The footprints of the fallen beings are all over it. This prevents people from opening their minds to the new ideas from the ascended masters that could bring science forward and take us to a much higher level of civilization. Instead, we get denial and taboos that set limits for our minds. Well, I for one accept neither the Catholic nor the materialist doctrines as limits for my mind.

***

A creation story that is an alternative to both religion and materialism is presented by the ascended masters. They say that consciousness always comes before material manifestation. The material universe is made from energy that has been organized into structures. This energy enters the material octave from the emotional octave, but before that it comes from the mental octave and the identity octave. Before that, the energy comes from the ascended realm, which has layers. Ultimately, all energy comes from the Creator and is then stepped down in vibration. This process happens through the minds of self-aware, conscious beings who are co-creators with the Creator. The ascended masters (who serve at the level right above our universe) step down the vibration of the energy to the identity level and even to some degree all the way to the physical. However, we humans (as the dominant life form on earth) also step down some of the energy from the identity to the physical level. The ascended masters first created the earth and started the evolutionary process. They stepped in at certain key moments to take the process to a higher level, such as creating organic life, creating dual-celled organisms, creating mammals, primates and so on. Yet since we unascended beings started taking embodiment on earth, we have collectively influenced the material conditions found here. And ever since we fell into duality, we have actually devolved what the ascended masters had evolved before that time.

When an ascended master steps down the energy, it happens from a level that is beyond fear, beyond duality. We humans often step the energy down to the lower level of vibration characterized by fear in its many forms. Thus, we are not passive victims of god's will or random acts of nature. We are to a very large degree (a larger degree than most people can deal with) the co-creators of our current material circumstances. I know this can sound harsh, but it is ultimately liberating.

Catholic religion was pacifying to an almost unbelievable degree. We were created by god as sinners and sent into a universe with all kinds of suffering. There was nothing we could do about this, except hope for a better situation after this world. Yet in order to achieve this salvation from suffering, we had to submit ourselves to a power elite here on earth, which greatly increased our suffering. Yet if only we suffered enough here on earth, we would eventually be free from our sin (that we had not chosen) and escape suffering.

What many people have overlooked is that the materialist religion is equally pacifying. We are the outcome of an entirely random process that has no consciousness and thus no compassion whatsoever. Nature is "red in tooth and claw," having no consideration for the suffering that it inflicts upon us. Neither does it care that its unconscious process has produced us with a consciousness that allows us to be aware that we suffer—and therefore suffer more than unconscious creatures. At any moment, you could discover that you have an incurable disease as a result of your genetic heritage or a random mutation in your own cells. And there is nothing to do about it, except submit yourself to the power elite that runs materialistic establishments and then hope they can ease your pain. Why worry about the meaning of all this since there cannot be any meaning in a universe produced by random and unconscious processes.

The bottom line is that both Catholicism and materialism are pacifying belief systems, and this is precisely the main characteristic of all belief systems created by the fallen beings. The ascended masters present us with a view of life that is ultimately empowering. If every material condition has its origin in consciousness, and if all of us have the potential to raise our consciousness to higher levels, then there is something that we (individually and collectively) can do about any condition that makes us suffer. The way out of any kind of suffering is to raise your consciousness above the level of consciousness that produced the material condition that causes the suffering. When enough people do this, then that condition will disappear from the earth and the planet will be raised another step closer to being a natural planet where there is no suffering. This is ultimate equality because we all have equal opportunity to transcend our current level of consciousness.

In contrast, the beliefs systems presented by the fallen beings have a fundamental inequality built into them. The purpose of these systems is to disempower us so we will submit ourselves to the elite of fallen beings. They always present us as having some kind of flaw whereas there is a small elite who are created or evolved to be superior. Therefore, we should follow them and allow them to have special privileges, making ourselves the slaves who produce those privileges if necessary.

Yet what is it that is really behind the belief systems created by the fallen beings? It is the attempt to deny our true potential for transcending our current level of consciousness and attain Christ consciousness. It is all about getting us to voluntarily abandon the potential that no force outside ourselves can ever take away from us.

As a side note, you may say that what I have presented here is both confusing and contradictory. Yet the fallen beings are deliberately seeking to cause confusion and they do this by inspiring people to bring forth contradictory claims about any topic. One reason they do this is that by getting people to feel really confused, some people will submit to the authority of the fallen beings and never again question them. Another reason is that the fallen beings are seeking to prove god wrong or prove that there is no god. To this end, the more confusion the better.

By the way, I am quite aware what materialists would say to this book. They would say that it is a product of an entirely subjective experience and as such has no validity. I agree with the first half of that sentence but not the last half. You might recall that in the very beginning, I made it clear that this would be an entirely subjective account. But notice the inconsistency in the claim made my materialists. They say that if you accept that there is a spiritual reality beyond the material world, this is an entirely subjective experience that is produced by the machinery in your brain. However, when the say materialism gives the real truth about the world, this is an objective reality based on a higher truth.

So please explain to me how the claims made by a materialist is *not* a subjective experience produced in his or her brain? I mean, according to materialism, there is nothing more to the mind than material processes in the brain. Yet somehow most materialists make themselves exceptions to this. A spiritual world view is subjective whereas the materialistic world view is objective and describes how the world really works. If materialism is correct, it gives no meaning to talk about a higher truth as we are unable to recognize it with our subjective brains. Thus, if materialism were true, it would render itself worthless.

Aside from being a comical contradiction, this type of double standard is also one of the hallmarks of the fallen beings and their mindset. They always make claims about the limitations of human beings but manage to make themselves exceptions. *We* shouldn't have power but it is okay for *them*. *We* can only be subjective and can never rise above subjectivity. Only *they* can be objective. I have no problem saying that my current world view is a subjective experience. I recognize that my world view will be subjective as long as I am in a physical body. I also recognize that I have the potential to raise my consciousness beyond the *subjective* experience and have an *individual* experience. The materialists won't recognize this potential, and they won't recognize that their denial is engineered by the fallen beings because it is the one thing that scares them the most. I don't think that is very smart. But then again, I respect their right to have the subjective experience they need until they have had enough of it.

# 61

Saying that a thought system is created by the fallen beings does not mean I am saying that all of the people who promote that system are fallen beings or are evil or bad people. Most Christians are very well-meaning people who honestly think they are working for a good cause. Likewise, most materialists are well-meaning people who think they are working for a good cause. Both groups are unaware that they have been deceived by the fallen beings so that their efforts will never lead to the result they envision. In fact, their efforts will never produce any good but will only increase the conflict that is the ultimate goal of the fallen beings in the identity realm. Ignorance is the perennial tool of the fallen beings, and there is no greater ignorance than thinking you have the ultimate truth. When they can get people to believe this, then the fallen beings really feel they have achieved something.

Many of these fallen beings know there is no ultimate truth because they have for so long come up with dualistic arguments that they know any claim has a counterclaim. They don't care about truth; they only care about using people's quest to find truth. They know that most people below the 48th level have a need for ultimate security, and therefore they are looking for an ultimate truth to give them a sense that they will be saved or that they know how the universe works. Even the "knowledge" that the universe is random and has no meaning can make people feel they are superior to those who do not know this "objective, scientific truth."

Yet what is really behind both Catholicism and materialism? It is the quest of the fallen beings for preventing us from discovering and claiming the potential for raising our consciousness. Catholicism presents an external salvation where it is Jesus who saves you. Your membership of the church and your compliance with its doctrines and rules play a part, but these are a matter of changing your actions. There is nothing about raising your consciousness to the same level demonstrated by Jesus.

What is the central aspect of materialism (as far as the fallen beings go)? It is that it claims our consciousness is a phenomenon that is entirely produced by the materialistic processes in our physical brains. The reality is that consciousness comes before the physical manifestation, but materialism says that material manifestation comes before consciousness. There are two purposes for this doctrine.

The first one is to prevent scientists from truly researching consciousness. The fallen beings knew that if scientists applied the method of science to consciousness, then they would eventually discover the higher potential for human consciousness. Thus, they created materialism as a system for denying that consciousness is a topic for scientific inquiry. Materialism says that anything that happens in consciousness is entirely subjective, and since the goal of science is to discover objective truth (meaning it is not affected by consciousness), there is no point in using science to research what can only be subjective. Of course, the second reason is to prevent humanity from discovering our potential for raising consciousness and thereby recreating the material conditions without the fallen beings.

***

Take note of the incredible deception attempted here. The fallen beings are saying that the incorrect doctrines of the medieval church and the differences between religions proves that anything related to religion is a matter of belief, and belief is entirely subjective. Thus, the goal of science is to discover an objective truth, meaning that the scientist conducts experiments in such a way that they are not influenced by his or her consciousness and can be repeated by others. They say it is possible to conduct experiments that produce objective results because the scientist is merely a neutral observer who does not influence the outcome of the experiment.

It is somewhat understandable that this claim had appeal before the discoveries of quantum physics. This science deals with the realm of subatomic particles, which is considered the most fundamental level of matter. In fact, scientists still have not resolved the so-called wave-particle duality, which means that a subatomic entity can behave as both a matter particle and an energy wave. The really stunning discovery of quantum physics is that at the level of subatomic entities, there is no such thing as a neutral, objective observer. It has been proven over and over again that when scientists conduct an experiment with subatomic entities, the outcome of the experiment is a product of the interaction of the subatomic entity, the instrument used (a particle accelerator) and the consciousness of the scientist. The scientist is not merely *observing* a phenomenon but is *co-creating* the phenomenon. This has baffled scientists and it has largely been ignored because materialists do not want to lose the grip they have on science.

The explanation is, however, very simple. The atom is the smallest unit of matter in the physical octave. Once you go to the subatomic entities, you are right on or beyond the borderline between the physical octave and the three higher octaves. This explains the baffling phenomenon that a sub-atomic particle can suddenly appear out of "nowhere," divide itself into several particles that then meet and disappear back into nowhere. What happens here is that energy from the emotional octave crosses the line to the physical, appears as a particle we can observe with current (rather crude) instruments and then goes back into the emotional octave. There is no magic here, simply a higher understanding.

I have explained how energy flows from the ascended realm into the four octaves of our universe. This process is influenced by our conscious-ness, and this is the simple explanation of why quantum physicists are not neutral observers but are co-creating the phenomenon they are observing. This also proves the potential of our consciousness. Since our minds can influence the most fundamental level of matter, it is logical that we can indeed recreate the physical conditions we see on this planet. It is also logi-cal that we have collectively created some of these conditions.

***

There is no such thing as a neutral observer. No matter what we do – individually and collectively – our minds do influence physical matter. The fallen beings will do anything to prevent us from acknowledging this because they know that when we see reality, they can no longer control us. Take note of how they have controlled us so far. They have first deceived us into creating current conditions in matter by going into duality. They have managed to make us forget that we have done this. Now, they are telling us that our minds are the product of current conditions in matter, meaning we have no way of re-creating what we have co-created in the first place. They are saying we cannot get out of our current situation by using our free will.

This works because most people do not see that we got into our cur-rent situation by using our free will. Thus, people are not aware of the fundamental principle of free will, namely that we can never make a choice that traps us permanently. Any choice we make will have a consequence that we experience, but we can transcend that consequence by rising above the consciousness that caused us to make our previous choices. In other words, we could never make a choice that cannot be undone by making a higher choice. There is no such thing as inescapable consequences that trap us forever and ever in hell. What the fallen beings really do not want us to know is that although we have submitted ourselves to their control, we can (individually and collectively) walk away from this control any minute.

Why do the fallen beings so desperately want to keep scientific inquiry trapped in the boundaries imposed by materialism? Because they know that if scientists truly investigate consciousness, they will discover our true potential. Science has a great potential for liberating us from psychological limitations, the limitations so carefully engineered by the fallen beings, the limitations that is the only way they have of controlling us. Naturally, they don't want this control to slip away from them—*but it will.*

\*\*\*

One more thing about objectivity. At the so-called macroscopic level, meaning the level of everyday things, it seems as if a scientist can make an experiment and get a certain result. Anyone else duplicating the experiment, will get the same result. Thus, it seems the result is objective. If we throw a stone into the air, it will fall down every time, no matter what we believe about it. As I said when I talked about Aristotelian logic, there are certain physical events about which we can make objective observations. The problem is that materialists are not content to make only observations, they also want to *interpret* these observations.

Take the materialist claim that there is no god and nothing beyond the material universe. This claim is not based on an objective observation. It has not been observed by science that there is no god. A god has not been observed by science. You cannot observe that something does not exist, you can only say that you have not discovered it with the methods used so far. If materialists were truly neutral and objective, they would have to say that science cannot say anything about the existence of god. The reason is simple. Materialists have defined science as a method for observing only the material universe. Objectivity is based on observations. If god is beyond the material universe, it follows that science could never make observations about god, and thus it cannot claim to have an objective basis for evaluating god's existence.

The goal of materialism has been to find *natural* explanations for the existence of the universe. The goal is to find a natural process that can explain how matter and life originated. That is why Darwin became such an idol for materialists because his theory of evolution could be interpreted as providing an alternative to the biblical creation story. Suddenly, god wasn't necessary and was reduced to existing in the gaps that science cannot yet explain as a result of natural processes.

This entire process is not a matter of objectivity. It is a matter of interpreting scientific findings in order to attain a specific goal, namely to prove that the universe could have come into existence without the god of the Bible. Yet such an interpretation aimed at a specific goal is not and can never be objective.

Thus, we have the age-old dynamic that a group of fallen beings have set themselves up as an elite who have a monopoly on defining truth. Only *they* are worthy to interpret scientific findings. The real irony here is that the priests of materialism use every opportunity to scorn the priests of Christianity. However, in their claim to infallibility, they display the exact same arrogance as the medieval Catholics. And is it any wonder since this boundless arrogance is the main characteristic of the fallen beings? They literally believe they can define how the universe *should* work. Did Catholic doctrines alter the basic function of the universe? No! Do materialist doctrines alter the basic function of the universe? No! It is the classical claim of the fallen beings. *They* are objective, *we*, the people, can only be subjective so we need to follow them blindly.

***

Now put this together with what I have said about duality. As you go deeper into duality, you go deeper into the sense of being separated from god, nature and other people. The fallen beings with the lowest level of consciousness allowed on earth see themselves as completely separate beings, and that is why they have no sensitivity whatsoever to other human beings. What have I said is the only way to know God? It is to have a mystical experience where you experience oneness with God. What is the only way to truly know any material phenomenon? Every material phenomenon is an expression of a certain matrix in consciousness, at the three higher levels. If you want to truly know a tree, you need to have a direct experience of the consciousness that manifested the tree. You can get that only through a mystical experience of the three higher matrices that manifested the tree. Albert Einstein saw the theory of relativity in such an experience, and then it took him years to translate his vision into a theory expressed in the language of science.

So the real basis for knowing something is to experience oneness with the matrix in the three higher octaves. You can only do this as you go towards the 144th level of consciousness. At lower levels of consciousness, you cannot experience oneness with the three higher levels so you must create a theory that describes the phenomenon. You are then relating to the material phenomenon through a thought matrix created in your own mind—as opposed to experiencing a thought matrix existing outside your mind. You know the phenomenon at a distance.

The basis for our entire approach to knowledge is this process of creating a theory in the mind and then projecting it upon the external phenomenon. This process goes back to when fallen beings first embodied here, but in our civilization it truly started with Aristotle and his dualistic logic. Our entire approach to knowledge has been and still largely is dominated by the logic of the fallen beings. It appeals to us because so many people are still below the 48th level of consciousness. They cannot have an experience of oneness with a higher level of consciousness but because they still have a need to understand the world in which they live, they are susceptible to the claim that we can know things though a theory. The closer you go to the lowest level of consciousness, the more people become open to the concept that we human beings on this low planet can create an absolute theory that gives us the infallible truth about how the universe works.

It was the hope of the ascended masters that science could help us grow out of this approach to knowledge by helping us compare the absolutist claims of the Catholic church to how nature actually works. Naturally, the masters knew well the limitations of science. Investigating current material phenomenon will not enable us to realize that these phenomena are affected by our collective state of consciousness.

The fallen beings have so far managed to pervert science and what I am pointing out is that materialism is based on the exact same mindset as the Catholic church. It is the claim of the fallen beings that they are able to define how the universe *should* work. This claim seems credible to people at lower levels of consciousness. However, due to all of the factors I have talked about, more and more people are beginning to rise above the 48th level of consciousness. Therefore, it takes only a slight, conscious switch in the mind before one sees the fallacy of the materialist and religious approaches to knowledge. When that shift happens to a critical mass of people, the fallen beings will very quickly lose control over this planet.

Their arrogance will suddenly become so obvious that people will no longer believe in their claims to infallibility. When will a critical mass of people have had enough of the arrogance of the fallen beings? When will people look at the emperors of duality and exclaim: "But the emperor has nothing on!"

# 62

One of the greatest triumphs of the fallen beings was to take the entirely non-violent teachings and example of Jesus and turn them into a religion that condoned large-scale violence, even outright war. By creating materialism as a way to discredit the Christian religion, the fallen beings backed themselves into a corner because it is difficult to make science justify violence and warfare. Of course, it has not been difficult to get scientists to produce the weapons for violence and warfare, even the weapons of mass destruction available today.

But in order to take their new materialist philosophy and turn it into a real tool for creating violent conflict, the fallen beings had to create another classical polarity between two systems. This became the confrontation between communism and capitalism that the world still has not fully overcome.

If you have grown up in the West, you may think this confrontation was created by communism and that communism came first because capitalism is just a natural state of the economy. But which came first, the chicken or the egg? The reality is that in a dualistic polarity, both opposites appear at the same time because one cannot be defined without the other. Capitalism did not naturally occur and then communism was formulated as the opposite system. Nay, the fallen beings in the identity realm conceived of both simultaneously, it simply took some time to bring both into the physical octave and to set up a confrontation between them.

\*\*\*

Despite the fact that both capitalism and communism were conceived by fallen beings in the identity realm, the fallen beings in the lower levels did not understand this. They are always blinded by their lower level of consciousness and that is why they are inherently divided into an established and an aspiring power elite.

It is often said that the principal philosopher behind the capitalist system is Adam Smith who talked about a free market economy. The idea is that there are certain market forces that will automatically regulate the economy in a way that works best for society. Thus, there is little need for the government to intervene in the economy. Now, one might think that what Adam Smith did was to simply put to a theory the way the economy had been working in more primitive societies. But just give me one example of an organized society with a free market economy.

Sure, you can go back to the stone age or bronze age and you can see an economy that was not controlled by anyone. Yet in any of the more organized societies the world has seen, you see the same pattern. A centralized authority begins to emerge and it regulates the economy by giving special privileges to small groups of people. This is the age-old pattern of the fallen beings seeking to set themselves up in a privileged position.

So at Adam Smith's time, you did not have a free market economy. Throughout the Middle Ages and beyond, you had a highly regulated economy. In the feudal societies, the noblemen had a complete monopoly on land and on agriculture. Beyond that, certain tradesmen had privileges for trading and certain craftsmen had privileges to do, for example, building work. This was a highly regulated system where small groups of people had special privileges, and on top of the pyramid were a small group of fallen beings who could reap the rewards of the people's labor.

As science provided the foundation for industry and shipping over long distances, a new type of industrialists and tradespeople emerged. They wanted to get rid of the privileges of the established elite—not to free the people, but so that they themselves could grab privileged positions.

So again, every situation created out of the duality consciousness has an opposite. What is the opposite to the situation where the economy is completely regulated to the advantage of a small elite? It is to claim that there is such a thing as a free market economy where unseen market forces are able to regulate the economy so the government needs to do nothing. This was, naturally, tied in with the emergence of democracies. As democracy became a realistic possibility, many people looked to get away from the tight control of past societies and it was appealing that the same could happen in the economy. Why not let the economy be free and trust that some natural forces would regulate everything? Obviously, this was simply an aspiring power elite seeking to overthrow the established elite.

Is there such a thing as a free market economy that requires no government intervention? If not, why has this idea been so appealing to so many people? Well, the reality is that a free market does exist—but only on natural planets. When everyone is above the 48th level so they are not seeing themselves as separate beings and acting based on their interests as separate beings, then it is possible to have a free market economy where the ascended masters and the flow of the Spirit will regulate the economy for the betterment of the whole. Yet on an unnatural planet, there is no such thing as a free market economy. When fallen beings are present, then the attempt to establish a free market economy simply leads to another form of disaster than the openly elitist economy. In fact, on earth, a free market economy leads to the same kind of total control by an elite as we saw during the Middle Ages.

\*\*\*

After spreading the ideas about a self-regulating free market, the fallen beings were quick to develop them further, and this led to the emergence of ideas about capitalism as an economic system. Many people today, especially in the United States, believe that a capitalist economy is the same as a free market economy. In a sense, this is true when you realize that a free market cannot be free as long as fallen beings are part of the equation. Capitalism is simply an attempt to legitimize that one power elite takes control over the economy.

We can always debate whether capitalism was defined by Karl Marx or already existed before he defined the confrontation between capitalism and communism. It is certainly the case that Marx created the conflict between the two systems that is so characteristic of the fallen beings and their dualistic thinking. What was communism? Well, the Middle Ages had an established elite, and it lost power over the economy when the aspiring elite created capitalism. So the old elite created communism as an attempt to create a system where the state is again in control. It was the old elite's attempt to take back power from the new elite.

Of course, the fallen beings in the identity realm knew that neither capitalism nor communism was based on ultimate truth. They saw the confrontation between them as a way to create conflict, but some of them also had a deeper agenda. They had never quite been at ease with controlling people through religion because their ultimate goal is to prove god wrong. One aspect of this is that they are seeking to create a planet where life can seemingly function without god. Thus, they wanted to create a situation where a society was not controlled by religion but through entirely materialistic philosophies. For this purpose, they used fallen beings in the mental realm to spread new ideologies through people in embodiment. What I am pointing out here is that the fallen beings are always divided. In the identity realm, you find two main groupings. Some fallen beings are conscious of the goal to prove god wrong. Members of the other group are not as conscious of this but are focused on creating as much conflict and destruction as possible because it gives them a sense of power. These two groups in a sense work against each other, but in another sense they are both furthering the agenda of proving god wrong by creating as much chaos as possible, thus "proving" that free will was a mistake.

The fallen beings in the identity realm use fallen beings in the mental realm to spread new ideas. The ideological fallen beings are always seeking to bring out one thought system that can attain complete dominance. Yet each time they bring out one system, the power-hungry fallen beings define a dualistic opposite and seek to create conflict between the two systems. When the first group defines a religion that supposedly has the absolute truth about god, the other group defines another religion and they seek to set them at war with each other. Of course, both groups use fallen beings in the mental realm to bring these ideas into the physical octave, and these fallen beings actually believe in the ideas they are promoting. Some of them believe, for example, that the Catholic church is the only true church and others believe that communism is the ultimate economic system.

Again, the overall point is that neither capitalism nor communism is an ultimate truth or an ultimate economic system. They are simply two ways of achieving a situation where the economy is controlled by a small elite and where the people have become the slaves of that elite. What is the essence of communism? It is that the economy is controlled by a centralized authority, namely the state. The claim is that this is for the good of the workers, but in reality those who control the state control the people.

What is capitalism? Simply a more subtle way to achieve the same goal. In a Capitalist system, the government is supposed to step back and let the free market forces regulate the economy. The practical outcome of this is that in the long run, there will be the emergence of a few businesses who become so big that they can begin to destroy new, upcoming businesses or small independent businesses. Thus, an unregulated capitalist system will lead to the emergence of corporations that become bigger and bigger until they start swallowing up each other. The ultimate outcome is that one corporation controls the entire economy, and when that happens, then that corporation will also have de facto control over the state. The exact same centralized system as in a communist economy, but achieved in a slower and more deceptive way because many people believe the economy is free.

In reality, the power elite running the capitalist system does not have the patience to wait for the so-called free market forces to concentrate power. They have, at least since Rockefeller and Morgan in the late 1800s, attempted to use the democratic government to speed up the process. They did this by making use of the fact that a capitalist economy will go through phases with great chaos, such as bank failures. They used this chaos to argue that the government had to step in and provide stability. In reality, this gave special privileges to the already established businesses and sped up the process of them becoming bigger. What the fallen beings didn't realize is that because people are not stupid, it wasn't so easy to use a democratic government to further the interests of monopoly capitalism, so the development has not been as quick as they hoped. However, the so-called free world is still inexorably moving towards a state where a small elite of the super-rich own or control almost all assets in society. Just look at how most Americans believe they live in the most free country in the world, yet the top two percent of the population control 90 percent of the wealth. How is that a free economy?

\*\*\*

In this respect, let me refer to something that is one of the pillars of communism. What is the enemy of a communist state and of the workers? According to Marx, it is the bourgeoisie, or what we today call the middle class. If you take what I have been saying all along, you see that while the fallen beings have great control over society, they do not have total control. There are forces that are constantly raising people above the control of the fallen beings. These forces led to the emergence of industrialism and democracy. What was the main effect of this? It was that it overthrew the dream society of the fallen beings, namely a society with three classes of people.

In the feudal society, for example, you have the power elite on the top, consisting of the king, a few noblemen and some clergy. Below them you have a group of people who are, for all practical purposes, the henchmen of the elite who keep the population in line. Then, you have the general population who are virtually the slaves of the elite. As the Middle Ages ended, you saw the emergence of a fourth class of people, namely people who had a greater degree of independence from the elite. They could read and write so they could educate themselves about many things, and thus they started to form a force that could not be ignored yet was not easy to control.

The people in the middle class are simply too well-informed to be controlled through ignorance, and since society made it difficult to control them through brute force, the fallen beings had a real conundrum. Communism was one attempt to solve this problem by defining the middle class as the enemies of the workers and therefore of the state. This justified that all communist countries have brutally destroyed the middle class by killing them and seizing their assets.

What needs to be added to this is that the middle class are the people who drive positive growth in society. This is because they are educated and they have free time. The power elite might be educated, but because they are always concerned about maintaining their privileges, they can easily be controlled by the fallen beings. An educated middle class with time and attention left over to pursue a higher state of consciousness is the principal enemy of the fallen beings.

In a capitalist system, especially one with democratic governments, eliminating the middle class is extremely difficult, but not impossible. This is due to the worst setback that the fallen beings have suffered over thousands of year, namely the concept that all people have rights that are not defined by the state and cannot be violated by the state. The fallen beings hate the idea that all people have rights, but they can accept it as long as they can define those rights. They absolutely hate the concept of inalienable rights that are defined by an authority that is beyond the material realm.

Yet the fallen beings never give up. If you look at what has been happening in the capitalist countries, you can see a long-term development that is directed by the fallen beings. This is most clear in the United States. What is happening is that there was a period where a relatively free economy spread the wealth so that more and more people attained a higher standard of living. Yet over several decades the trend has been to concentrate wealth in the hands of fewer and fewer people whereas the real income of the middle class has declined. In the United States, the top 10 percent own over 90 percent of the wealth and the top two percent control the majority of that wealth. This has been achieved because the fallen beings realized that they could not engineer a communist take-over of the entire world (partly because a communist economy cannot sustain itself). Instead, they have attempted to eliminate the middle class by expanding the power elite. In other words, they are allowing the top of the middle class to step into the top class, primarily through ownership of stock and other financial instruments. At the same time, they are decreasing the wealth of the bottom part of the middle class so they slowly sink into the lower class, meaning people who only make money through their labor, not through the labor-less means conceived by the fallen beings.

Again, you see that since the emergence of a capitalist economy, the fallen beings have attempted to use their economic freedom to create all of these financial instruments for accumulating wealth without performing any labor that provides a service or a product. They have attempted to create an artificial economy that gives themselves special privileges without them having to contribute to the economy. They are simply leeches that suck the wealth of the people who do perform actual labor.

\*\*\*

The bottom-line economic principle was described by Jesus in his parable about the three servants who were given 2, 5 and 10 talents by their master before he went away. When the master came back, two servants had multiplied the talents and one had not. The two were rewarded and from the last was taken the talents he had. The principle described by Jesus is that when you do something that helps the growth of the whole, then you have multiplied the talents, meaning energy, you have received. This energy will then be multiplied by the ascended masters and given back to you so that you can do even more. This is how the economy has grown.

You will see that during the feudal age, the overall economy grew very little. The reason was that there was no opening whereby the majority of the people could do something to improve the whole. The power elite did nothing to improve the living conditions of the people because they only wanted to maintain their privileges. With the emergence of a more free economy, more and more people have been able to do something to improve their own lives, and this has improved the whole. Thus, the entire economy has grown and the fallen beings have not been able to stop it. They have, however, been trying to take advantage of it by concentrating more and more wealth in their own hands, thus working towards a society where they again control the majority of the wealth. If they managed to achieve this, the economy would again start to contract and the system would collapse. This is the reason communism collapsed because there simply was not the mechanism that allowed people to multiply their talents.

To prevent that the economy again becomes entirely controlled by the fallen beings, it is necessary for a democratic government to limit people's ability to concentrate wealth in the hands of a small elite (of individuals and corporations). I know many Americans will immediately cry socialism, but it has nothing to do with socialism. It is simply a matter of knowing how the economy works and knowing the methods of the fallen beings, then realizing that it is the principal role of a democratic government to prevent the fallen beings from turning its citizens into their slaves. This can only be done through an enlightened regulation of the economy aimed at preventing the fallen beings from controlling it. In practical terms, this means that you simply cannot allow people to make money out of money itself. People must be allowed to make money only by producing products or providing a service that actually helps the growth of the whole. This is the only way to prevent the economy from being turned into a closed system by the fallen beings. I trust I have explained adequately what happens to all closed systems.

\*\*\*

Speaking of systems, the dream of the fallen beings is to create the ultimate system that will be an alternative to the process created by God. Did you catch the hint? The fallen beings create *systems;* the real God has created a *process.* All systems are closed because they are seeking to attain and then preserve an ultimate state in the material world. God's process is open because it is constantly transcending itself, eventually leading to the entire material universe ascending and becoming part of the spiritual realm.

Does this mean I am saying that all of the religious, philosophical and political systems created by man are out of touch with reality? Yes, that is exactly what I am saying. The proof is that although some have lasted for a long time (if you call a thousand years a long time), they have all been replaced by another system. This is because the fallen beings have created a process described by the philosopher Hegel. When the fallen beings create a system, it becomes a thesis. Because it is created from duality, it will inevitably have an anti-thesis and this creates a struggle between the two. Eventually, the struggle will lead to a synthesis between the two. However, this synthesis will then become a new thesis that has its own anti-thesis so the struggle continues.

This process can go on for a long time, although it cannot go on forever. Furthermore, it cannot lead to an upward direction but only into a downward spiral because the process is a closed system that will self-destruct. You may say that the process created by the fallen beings on earth has existed for a long time, but that is because it has not been allowed to go into self-destruction. This is caused by the many beings who have incarnated here in order to pull the earth up. They have counter-acted the self-destructive spiral of the fallen beings, and thus they have in a bizarre way given it longevity beyond its own power. Yet this does not mean it can last forever, as it will inevitably be pulled up by the magnetic pull of the rest of the universe.

Yet the real lesson is that we can never create an ultimate system. You can create a thought system that has much truth. If applied correctly, the system will enable people to come up higher in consciousness and thereby raise the collective consciousness. Yet once a new level is reached, there will be a need for a new system that can take us higher. The fallen beings are becoming increasingly desperate in their attempts to create systems that seem to be absolute. It is their futile attempt to stop the progression of the planet into a new age where they are no longer part of the equation. They are not really seeking the survival of their systems but the survival of themselves and their reign on earth.

# PART 10:

# THE ARMAGEDDON OF

# THE 20TH CENTURY

# 63

There are Christian groups, mainly in the United States, who seriously expect that anywhere from next week to next decade, the Battle of Armageddon will take place. This will be the final confrontation between good and evil where good will eradicate evil and Jesus will come back to reward the faithful, mainly the (sometimes just a few hundred) members of their church. All the rest of humanity will be condemned to an eternity of suffering in hell, but that's just the price you pay for not following the right pastor who has the most literal interpretation of the Bible.

I fail to see how anyone can look at the history of the 20th century without realizing that the Battle of Armageddon has already started and is ongoing. From two world wars, the cold war, numerous more localized wars, terrorism, ISIS and machine-gun-powered tribal warfare in Africa, how is this not the Battle of Armageddon? When you put this together with this quote from the Book of Revelation, Chapter 12, you see the cause:

> 7 And there was war in heaven: Michael and his angels fought against the dragon; and the dragon fought and his angels,
> 8 And prevailed not; neither was their place found any more in heaven.
> 9 And the great dragon was cast out, that old serpent, called the Devil, and Satan, which deceiveth the whole world: he was cast out into the earth, and his angels were cast out with him.
> 10 And I heard a loud voice saying in heaven, Now is come salvation, and strength, and the kingdom of our God, and the power of his Christ: for the accuser of our brethren is cast down, which accused them before our God day and night.
> 11 And they overcame him by the blood of the Lamb, and by the word of their testimony; and they loved not their lives unto the death.
> 12 Therefore rejoice, ye heavens, and ye that dwell in them. Woe to the inhabiters of the earth and of the sea! For the devil is come down unto you, having great wrath, because he knoweth that he hath but a short time.

Naturally, this quote is not entirely accurate because I have already explained that there cannot be war in "heaven." Archangel Michael does not fight the fallen beings, but simply remains immovable to their dualistic consciousness. Because no dualistic force can stand against this, the fallen beings cast themselves out. Incidentally, this is not "heaven" as many Christians see it but merely the lower levels of the identity realm. So who is this great dragon, old serpent, Devil and Satan? Well, it is the Dark Master that I talked about earlier when I said:

"Now, the Book of Revelation is actually the closest to a direct dictation from the ascended masters that you find in the official scriptures. However, it must be noted that it was given for an audience in a certain culture and with a certain level of consciousness. That is why it seems so ominous to us today. Also, the person who was a messenger for receiving it was not able to get it accurately so it cannot be taken literally, considered universally valid or entirely relevant today. The words "Devil" and "Satan" were not the actual name of the Dark Master, they were names that the audience could relate to. However, when you look beyond that, the passage does refer to the fact that after the judgment of Christ, the Dark Master was bound and locked up. It was not for a thousand years but for the entire spiritual age for which the Ascended Master Jesus has been the spiritual overseer, namely the past 2000 years, the Age of Pisces.
This has been very significant in the sense that had the Dark Master still been able to influence earth, the planet would have entered such a spiral of darkness that it would almost certainly have been impossible to stop it. The downward spiral would have become self-reinforcing and virtually irreversible. So the fact that this has not happened is largely attributable to the absence of the Dark Master."

Given how the Law of Free Will works, it was the choices made by the original inhabitants of the earth that made it possible for this Dark Master to come here in the first place. Therefore, he cannot be permanently taken until a majority of the original inhabitants have forsaken the state of consciousness that he represents. For the past 2000 years, the dominant spiritual influence on this planet has been the teachings given by Jesus. In their original form, these teachings were completely and entirely non-violent. They were especially designed to counteract the primary lie of the Dark Master, namely that the epic importance of giving one idea dominance over the earth can justify the killing of one person or one million persons. I have talked about a human life being a unique opportunity and that a non-physical idea cannot ever justify physical killing.

It was the hope of the ascended masters that people would use this break from the influence of the Dark Master to raise themselves and the collective consciousness above this state of consciousness. If this had indeed happened, then the Dark Master would still have had to be let loose for a season. But if very few people had responded to him, then he could fairly quickly have been taken from the earth again. Because not enough people did raise themselves above this consciousness (in large part because Jesus' teachings were perverted into a philosophy that actually justified killing people for the sake of an idea), then the Dark Master was let loose in the late 1800s and he has not yet been bound again.

The result of this can be clearly seen upon world events. Just look at the atrocities that have been committed over this past century, all driven by the belief that an idea is more important than the lives of millions of people. Isn't Nazism the textbook example of people thinking they have a superior idea of how the universe works and being willing to kill 50 million people to establish the dominance of their idea? And isn't communism another radical example? Stalin killing 21 million people within the borders of the Soviet Union is an example of how far people controlled by the Dark Master will go to uphold the illusion of their superior idea. The idea cannot be allowed to fail, and no amount of killing is too much, as proven by Mao ordering the killing of 70 million of his own people. But then look what ISIS is doing today. And look at what that self-proclaimed bastion of freedom and democracy did in Iraq, supposedly to spread freedom and democracy (an idea) to a totalitarian nation.

Is it really so hard to see that this is a direct effect of entire nations coming under the spell of the Dark Master, thereby believing that their idea is so epically important that it justifies the killing of any number of people? Is it really so hard to see that unless a critical mass of people finally see this idea for the lie that it is and consciously raise themselves above it (purifying their four lower bodies of all traces of it), then the atrocities will have to become gradually more extreme until they finally become so bizarre that people see the absurdity of them. However, take note that seeing the absurdity of, for example, the Holocaust without seeing the cause behind it is not enough to truly raise yourself above the consciousness that caused the Holocaust.

Jesus made a great effort to give the people of this planet an opportunity to raise themselves above this consciousness. He has worked very hard these past 2000 years to make this happen and to counteract the onslaught of the fallen beings who are still working on earth. He is indeed very close because there are millions of people on this planet who have overcome the lie in their three higher bodies. All that remains is that these people have the conscious breakthrough of seeing the lie for what it is and making the fully conscious choice to say: "We will no longer allow this lie to affect our planet!" When that happens to a critical degree, the Dark Master will be permanently removed from the earth and this planet can finally enter the Golden Age that the Ascended Master Saint Germain has planned for the next 2000 years.

\*\*\*

Several books could be written about how the fallen beings have so obviously influenced world events during the 20th century. There have been so many fallen beings in prominent positions that anyone who has the key should be able to see it. And the key is simply the knowledge that fallen beings exist and that they have an agenda and a state of mind that has never been exposed in any public teaching, be it religious, scientific or philosophical. Neither their agenda nor their state of mind can be explained by any mainstream belief system. As I have said, the agenda of the fallen beings runs contrary to common sense and any rational thought.

Naturally, during the years where the Dark Master was bound, there were other fallen beings seeking to control people from the identity, mental and emotional realms. And there were many fallen beings in embodiment. Some of these did bring forth a variety of false ideas and ideologies, but they simply did not have the deceptive power to create the havoc that we have seen since the Dark Master was released. Again, a book could be written about how the fallen beings have brought forth ideas that were aimed at either controlling people or creating as much confusion and chaos as possible. Several revered theologians, philosophers and scientists were either fallen beings or had their minds controlled by fallen beings. What happened after the Dark Master was released was that he brought many

of these ideas together and attempted to set up the ultimate clash between
ideas and ideologies. He wanted to create the final battle, the epic battle,
between groups of people who all believed that upholding their idea justified the killing of other human beings. To accomplish this, he has worked
with every single opportunity created by other fallen beings or by human
beings who were trapped in the belief that there is only one truth and that
it has epic importance to spread or defend this superior idea.

Naturally, he has worked with religion but found it somewhat difficult
to accomplish what he wanted this way. Due to the murder and mayhem
unleashed by the Catholic church during the crusades and the inquisition,
most Christians have made some progress towards being unwilling to kill
in the name of Christ. Naturally, he has had some success, for example the
war between Protestants and Catholics in Northern Ireland and in later
years the Muslim extremists of various varieties.

Yet his real success was to use scientific materialism and its offshoots,
such as the idea of survival of the fittest. As I said, Charles Darwin was
not a fallen being, but he was open to the fallen version of evolution. This
made it very easy for the fallen beings to work with certain people, such as
the philosophers Herbert Spencer and Nietzsche to bring forth teachings
of a superior race that had a natural right to assert itself, even an obligation to root out the weaker races for the sake of raising humanity to an
edenic state. This became the philosophical underpinnings of Nazism. At
the same time, the fallen beings worked with the teachings of Marx and
Engels to bring forth the basis for communism and an inevitable dualistic
struggle between classes. This set the stage for the attempt to make communism take over the world, and it also set the stage for a battle between
the Soviet Union and Nazi Germany.

Take note that the Dark Master had no particular loyalty to any of
these movements or ideologies. He would have been fine if Nazism had
defeated communism and eradicated the Soviet Union. His aim was only
to polarize people into groups and create as much war and havoc between
them as possible. When Nazism was defeated, he immediately started
working on setting up a conflict between the Soviet Union and the so-
called capitalist world. And he probably would have succeeded in unleash-
ing World War III, had it not been for the atom bomb that caused some
people to see the madness of a nuclear war. They started seeing (although
most of them could not have put words on it) that there wasn't much point
in establishing your idea as the superior one if the cost was that there was
no one around to worship your idea.

You can see how the Dark Master works by looking at the aftermath of the first world war. In this war, ideology was not the primary driving force, it was mainly a power struggle for whether England, Germany or France should dominate Europe, something those countries had attempted to accomplish for centuries. Yet take note of the aftermath, and you will see the footprints of the Dark Master in the Treaty of Versailles that dealt a heavy blow to the Germans. This was the very factor that set the stage for the emergence of Adolf Hitler, and it was one of his primary motivators. Again, you see how, after the second world war, Europe was (at the Yalta conference) divided into an eastern and a western block. This was accomplished because three fallen beings in embodiment, Stalin, Churchill and Roosevelt, had their minds taken over by the Dark Master and set the stage for the next confrontation. Another textbook example of the workings of the Dark Master is the environmentalist issue. He has created the classical dualistic polarity between human beings and nature. Nature was supposedly in an edenic and balanced state before we human beings (apparently by accident) arrived on the scene and started disturbing the balance of nature. Humans are alien creatures in nature (even though we were supposedly brought forth by a perfectly natural process) and we can only destroy. Anything we do will disturb the balance of nature and that is why we should be forced (by ourselves) to do as little as possible, living in cities that are separated from nature. Take note that the existence of an edenic state with perfect balance of nature is highly illogical when compared to Darwin's survival of the fittest and "nature red in tooth and claw." Yet people overlook this because it ties in to the soul memories of both avatars and the original inhabitants, namely that the earth was in an edenic state sometime in the past.

The problem is, of course, that we will never get back to such an edenic state as long as we are trapped in duality, and environmentalism is designed to keep us there. The real way to take care of the environment is to raise ourselves beyond duality so we can fulfill our intended role as co-creators on this planet. One of the main goals behind environmentalism is to trap people in a form of self-denial that will make it acceptable to them that active measures are taken to limit the size of the human population. The fallen beings have always been afraid of the population becoming too large because it makes it very difficult for them to set themselves up as a privileged elite with the general population as their slaves. It is the quest of the fallen beings for a privileged position that is the real cause of most environmental problems because they are the ones driven by an insatiable desire for profit and they are the ones who have no sensitivity to anything on this planet. So once again, they have created a problem, and now they are trying to set themselves up as the saviors who can solve the problem.

In reality, this planet was designed by the Elohim to sustain 10 billion people in a state of material affluence that we can scarcely imagine today. How is this possible, you might say? Well, by returning nature to its original state, it will be able to produce abundant food for all. However, we first need to get rid of the power elite of fallen beings because the planet cannot feed 10 billion people with the current very unequal distribution of resources.

Human beings are not alien creatures and it's a lie that we can only do harm to nature. It is true that after the collective consciousness was lowered, the densification of matter has led to many problems that also affect nature. However, it is possible to raise the collective consciousness and then we can become co-creators who are actually the key to maintaining a true balance of nature. We are not alien creatures on this planet; we are the very reason for being of this planet.

As I said, an entire book could be written about the manipulation of the fallen beings, but let me get away from this impersonal perspective and describe my personal confrontation with one of the primary actors in the stage play, namely our old friend Satan. This is a being we need to dispense with before the story can reach its conclusion.

# 64

In my last lifetime before this one, I was born into a family in Copenhagen, Denmark. My father was a Jew and my mother was of German descent but was born and raised in Denmark. She was the typical Aryan with blond hair and blue eyes. My father was not immediately recognizable as a Jew, but did have black hair and brown eyes. My younger sister and I had blond hair and blue eyes so I looked exactly as the pictures on a poster for Hitler Jugend.

I have been a little hard on the Jews and their belief in being the chosen people, but in Denmark the Jews had transcended this. My father did not in any way stand out in Danish society and did not see himself as a Jew living in Denmark. He saw himself as a Dane who was of Jewish descent and therefore paid a reasonable (but not obsessive) respect to his culture and religion. Most other Danish Jews felt the same way, which is why there was no significant anti-Semitic sentiment in Denmark. In my growing-up years I never had anyone call me or any member of my family "Jew!" We were never singled out, and this is one reason the Danish Jews were largely left alone even after Nazi Germany invaded and occupied Denmark on April 9, 1940. The Germans in charge of the occupying forces had a silent agreement with the Danish government that as long as they didn't call attention to themselves, the Jews would be left alone. It only lasted until 1943, but even then most Jews escaped to Sweden with the help of non-Jewish Danes.

I was born in 1932 so I was 8 years old when the occupation happened. Naturally, I had some awareness of Hitler and the outbreak of war, and we had heard stories of what happened to Jews in Germany. But the occupation itself was not much of a shock to me, and life continued virtually as normal, at least for us children. This was in large part because our parents did everything they could to protect us, and they never told us what my father was doing when he didn't come home at night.

\*\*\*

My father had a position as a clerk in the Danish government, and this gave him access to some information about German activities in the country. Partly because he felt patriotic as a Dane and partly because of what he knew happened to the Jews in Germany and other countries, he decided to join the Danish resistance movement. This was an underground movement that attempted to conduct sabotage against Germain installations and plans in Denmark. It was quite large at times and received considerable support from England, mainly in the form of weapons drops. Many Danish resistance fighters were captured by the Nazis and either executed or sent to concentration camps. Some were even kept in a makeshift prison at the top floor of the Gestapo headquarters in Copenhagen in the hope that this would discourage the Brits from bombing the building. Interesting that the Nazis thought the Brits would be more humane than themselves, as the Nazis would have had no compunctions about bombing their own if the objective was important enough. The RAF did bomb the building in 1945 and in the process hit a school and killed 86 children.

As I said, the Danish Jews lived relatively normal lives during the first years of the Nazi occupation. Then, in October of 1943, the Nazis started rounding up Danish Jews and sending them to German concentration camps. However, the commander of the Nazi forces in Denmark had warned the Danish government in advance that he had been ordered to take action against the Jews. He more than hinted that if the Danish Jews were to escape beforehand, things would only be so much easier for him. As a result, the Nazis captured only 500 Danish Jews whereas the other 95 percent escaped to Sweden (which had bought its freedom from invasion by promising to supply the Nazis with Swedish iron ore).

My father and mother decided not to flee to Sweden. They felt that the Nazis would never arrest my mother and that my father's position in the government would protect him. I was 11 years old by then and, naturally, I understood something about what was happening, yet my parents still did everything they could to protect us children from feeling disturbed.

I was also still happily unaware of my father's involvement in the resistance movement. This lasted until one night in early 1944 when there was loud knocking on the door of our apartment. I still remember walking out in the hallway to see my father, in night dress, open the door. Four Gestapo officers walked in, and I can only say that their black uniforms with the silver skulls on the hats seemed to me to radiate pure evil. The leader told my father he was under arrest and that my parents had 10 minutes to get all of us dressed and pack two small suitcases. They then proceeded to search the entire apartment.

My mother attempted to protest in her fluent German. I understood German and I remember the Gestapo commandant telling her that she could either come along or her husband would be shot on the spot. She then gave in and told us to get dressed, whereupon she started packing. Allowing us to pack suitcases was naturally a complete scam, designed to give us the impression that there would be some normal life, even life, where we were going.

***

When we were done getting dressed, we were taken down to the street and loaded into the back of a small truck. We were driven to the Gestapo headquarters, which was known as the Shell House. Before the war it had been the corporate headquarters of the Shell oil company in Denmark. It was confiscated after the occupation. Sort of fitting that one totalitarian force takes over the building of another totalitarian force.

My mother and us children were put into a cell with no further comment. My mother attempted to comfort us and reassure us that everything would be okay, but she soon ran out of words. My sister did not run out of tears and sobbed the entire night. I, being a typical Danish boy, could not cry as, at that time, big boys didn't cry. It was a very long night even though it was past 4 o'clock when we were put in the cell.

My father was taken somewhere else to be interrogated and tortured. The Gestapo expected they could get some information out of him that would give up his fellow resistance fighters, but he never said anything, even when they threatened to kill his family. At one point he looked the Gestapo commandant in the eye and said: "If you are prepared to kill a German woman in your obsessive quest for world domination, then there is nothing I can do to stop you. Are you willing to sink to that level of inhumanity?" I am not sure whether the Gestapo "machines" would actually have killed my mother (or us children), but this remark may have saved our lives by convincing them that they could not make my father talk this way. Instead, they tortured my father in their usual brutal fashion, but even this did not make him talk. This torture lasted for three weeks.

My mother and us children remained in our cell for two full days without anyone talking to us. We got some food but otherwise had no contact with the outside world. It was rather humiliating to have to use the toilet in front of your mother and sister, even though they were looking the other way. I had no idea how quickly I would be forced to lose the luxury of this kind of normal sensitivity. In fact, I would lose all sense of normalcy.

After the two days, we were taken out of the building during the night and loaded into the back of a larger truck. In it were a number of (other) Danish Jews, but my father was not there. My mother tried to get some information out of the German guards but they did not even acknowledge her. These were lower-ranking Gestapo officers, and they were not burning with fanaticism. Thus, they had to shut down all humanity in order to carry out their orders (and avoid getting shot). They had taken on the look of being completely closed to human sensitivity, a look I would learn to know all too well in the coming year.

We drove for what seemed like an eternity with only short bathroom breaks. At one point we were taken onto a ferry between Denmark and Germany. Once in Germany, we were loaded into railroad cars that were literally converted cattle cars with a hole in one corner for going to the bathroom. The cars were not as full as the ones I would encounter later, but they filled up before we reached our destination. We found ourselves among desperate people who feared the worst and had given up all hope of escape. I think the hardest thing for me was to see this look of silent resignation, the acceptance that they had no control over their destiny. Even at that age, I was not about to give up and I intuitively knew we are not powerless, even in such severe circumstances.

We finally arrived at what was the Nazi concentration camp of Theresienstadt, which was located in what was then occupied Czechoslovakia (now the Czech Republic). This was the luxury version of Nazi concentration camps because it was not a death camp. However, there was not much hint of this when we got out of the cattle cars on a very dark and grey morning. Compared to the beautiful buildings in Copenhagen, this seemed like a very dreary place. I remember thinking that nothing good could possible come out of being in a place like this. Yet I was also thinking about my father and wishing he had been there with us.

After we were inspected by the personnel, I was separated from my mother and sister. They were taken to the women's section and were at least allowed to be together. I was taken to the men's section and for the first time in that lifetime found myself alone in the world, surrounded by strangers who seemed to have lost their capacity for compassion. I was shown a bunk and crawled in there, pulled the blanket over me, curled up in a foetal position and prepared to withdraw myself from the world. However, rather than crying, I felt as if I left my body and rose up into a higher dimension. I was again falling upwards and soon started seeing a golden light at the end of a long tunnel. After some time of falling upwards, I plunged into this light, and it felt warm and wonderful. To my surprise I found myself surrounded by beings that radiated a soft, warm light that made all earthly concerns seem completely and utterly irrelevant. Naturally, these were the ascended masters that I had worked with before planning this embodiment, and I was given this experience because it was time for me to reconnect to who I really was.

As I have said before, when you come into a new embodiment, you forget who you are and forget your spiritual attainment. This usually lasts until you are 12 years old. From that time, you are ideally supposed to reawaken and reconnect to the Divine plan you made before coming into embodiment. It is another engineering success of the fallen beings that so many teenagers in the modern world have no sense of purpose and direction and therefore spend their teenage years partying, effectively blocking their re-connection to their Divine plans with drugs, sex and Rock and Roll, not to mention alcohol (the potentially most damaging invention of the fallen beings).

During this experience, I was shown my Divine plan and what I had to accomplish. When I came back into my body, I forgot most of this, but I did take with me the sense of inner peace that I had attained over the past many embodiments. I also had a strong sense of purpose, trusting that whatever would come, it served a larger purpose that I had volunteered to carry out. This was an invaluable help for me to meet the challenges that lay ahead. It was a grace that I did not have conscious awareness of what these challenges would be, as it simply would have been too overwhelming for my mind to deal with.

\*\*\*

In today's age, the memory of the Holocaust is quickly fading from the consciousness of most people. The most bizarre development of all is the Holocaust deniers that you can find on the Internet. These are actually

540 My Lives with Lucifer, Satan, Hitler and Jesus

reincarnated Nazi death camp guards and officers who have refused to take responsibility for what they did. Thus, they cannot move on and are instead forced to attempt to deny that it ever happened. They somehow think that if they can get the whole world to agree with them, then they will not have to face the demons in their own subconscious minds.

My point here is that it is impossible for modern people to have a frame of reference that allows them to understand how the entire concentration camp system was based on an utter and total dehumanization of people. Not only were the inmates dehumanized, but the people who were in charge of the system had to dehumanize themselves in order to do what they were doing. This form of dehumanization is actually – and bizarrely – an aspect of a survival mechanism. When we are faced with circumstances so extreme that we cannot deal with them emotionally and mentally, we can create impenetrable walls in our minds. We can compartmentalize our minds so that we can, for example, act as a concentration camp guard during the day and party with friends at night. The most extreme example of this was the commandant of Auschwitz, Rudolf Höss, who lived at the camp with his family. During the day, he would oversee this massive camp, including the gassing of thousands of children. Yet after a day's work, he would go home to his family and play with his own children like a normal, devoted father.

This form of extreme dehumanization is the final triumph of the fallen beings. Nothing pleases the Dark Master more than watching people go into this dehumanized state and treat each other in completely inhumane ways while being firmly convinced they are furthering the supreme idea that for them seems all-important but to the Dark Master is simply a tool for waging wholesale destruction. The fallen beings are experts in setting up situations that are so extreme that people feel they have no other option but to dehumanize themselves. For the fallen beings, it is a kind of sport to see how far they can get people to go, once they have been forced into this dehumanized state. Naturally, only people below the 48th level of consciousness can be manipulated into becoming completely insensitive. People with some level of Christhood will rather let themselves be killed than violate their own sense of humanity or violate the humanity of others.

Okay, I got lost here, but what I wanted to get to is that there were no human considerations in the Theresienstadt concentration camp. I was given no information about my mother and sister and they knew nothing about me. Neither of us knew anything about my father. Actually, the deportation of about 500 Danish Jews to the camp did have some effect, in the sense that it made the Danish government, including the Danish King, take an interest in how their own citizens were treated (never mind the Jews from other countries). This led to some Red Cross inspections, but the Nazis turned this into a sham. The inspectors were given a glorified tour, including seeing barracks that were built especially for the purpose and never occupied by inmates. The Nazis even made a propaganda movie in the camp, and it is interesting that while they were carrying out this wholesale destruction of humanity, they were still concerned about maintaining an appearance to the rest of the world. This is another example of the compartmentalization, making the Nazis think they could actually do something like this and still maintain the appearance of being a civilized, even a superior, nation. The propaganda was clearly aimed more at themselves than the world.

However, the interest from the Danish government probably kept conditions in the camp from deteriorating and secured the survival of many inmates. This included my mother and sister who both survived the camp physically. Unfortunately, my mother never recovered psychologically from the experience, and my sister was condemned to spending the rest of her life taking care of a psychologically crippled individual. At that time, PTSD was not a recognized psychological condition. And how would society have healed that many people with PTSD anyway?

\*\*\*

After three months in this alien environment (where I knew nothing about the fate of my family), I was woken up one morning and without any explanation taken to the railroad tracks. I was hurriedly pushed into a cattle car that was already so filled with people that it was standing room only. In fact, it was so full that you had to stand up and go to the bathroom. I was jammed in among adult men, and as I was small for my age, my nose was rather close to the outlets of their bodies. It was even worse when I myself had to go, as I tried to hold it for as long as I could and then finally had to let go, defecating all over myself, feeling it run down my legs. You might have thought that nothing could be worse than the daily life of a concentration camp, but this was definitely worse.

We drove for what seemed like an eternity, and at one point I even think I managed to doze off, leaning on the bodies around me. Then, the rumbling of the wheels gradually slowed and finally there was the shrieking of breaks. The doors were pulled aside with this scraping sound that ended in a metallic clang. The bright sunshine burst into the car and completely blinded us as we were leaving. I could see nothing but golden sunlight, and for a split second I thought I might have arrived at a better place. How wrong I was, as this was indeed Auschwitz, the darkest place on earth at the time (and the energetic records still haven't been cleaned up).

***

As I stood there on the platform, I gradually regained my ability to see clearly. However, as that was happening, I also regained my ability to smell normally. Instead of being dulled by the smell of urine and feces, my nose started registering a new and unknown smell. It was the smell of burning human bodies that hung over Auschwitz as an invisible but ever-present cloud. You may visit the camp today, and if you are sensitive to energies, you can still feel the energetic cloud hanging over the place. But you will never be able to fathom the stench of burning flesh. Of course, after a mere days, you had become desensitized even to that. As I looked around, I saw that on my platform were hundreds of people in concentration camp uniforms, as they had been transferred to this final destination from other camps. Yet on the next platform were people in normal clothes and they were carrying suitcases. It suddenly hit me that there was a clear distinction between the facial expressions and the auras of the two groups of people. In my group, all people had the dehumanized expression, while the other group still had some normalcy and hope. Incidentally, they were Hungarian Jews, sold out by their own government, and they still had not fathomed what was awaiting them. Of course, one cannot blame them as it is not possible to fathom this within the normal register of human understanding and emotion.

The guards (all with the dehumanized expression) made us go slowly in one direction. As we started to move, the crowd thinned out, and suddenly I heard my name called out: "Hans, Hans, my boy, my boy!"

I turned around, and a man came running towards me with open arms. For a split second, I thought this man had gone mad from the strain, something I had seen on several occasions. Yet then I recognized that it was indeed my father. He had been shaved bald and his beard was gone, but the reason I did not recognize him was that he had lost the spark in his eyes that I had always loved so much. As he knelt down and hugged me, I not only saw but felt that I was standing before a broken man, a human being who had been exposed to such inhumanity that he had given up all desire to be human.

After crying frantically for some time, he finally looked at me (the tears making clean lines on his dirty cheeks) and started asking about my mother and sister. Before I could answer him, I heard the loud: "Los, los!" of a guard and my father was brutally struck on the cheek with the butt of a rifle. He fell flat on his face, and as I bent down to help him, I was struck also and pushed away from him. I had to move forward, but managed to look back and saw my father get on his feet and start moving as in a daze. Several guards had moved in, as if they sensed something threatening (and I suppose a father reuniting with his son was threatening to their ability to block out all human concerns for the prisoners).

We were forced towards some buildings that were half underground and told we were to take showers. We were told to take off our clothes and people slowly did so, as if they resisted this final humiliation of standing naked out in the open with hundreds of other people. A young Nazi guard was standing at the entrance, calling people to go in, saying with a half insane grin: "Snell, snell, you don't want the water to get cold, do you?"

I suddenly noticed my father was at the front of the line by another building, and as he was about to enter, he looked over and caught my eyes. I could perfectly well read the question marks in his eyes and spontaneously shouted: "They are both alive, in Theresienstadt."

I was then brutally hit with the butt of a gun, but I managed to catch how my words ignited a faint glimmer in my father's eyes. Not that it did him much good, as he only had minutes before he turned blue and cold from the Cyclon-B gas. I have always wondered why it seemed necessary to the Nazis to go through this charade of disguising a gas chamber as a shower. I have found no answer because I know too well that the fallen mind is neither rational nor logical. It wasn't just a matter of getting people to go in without being forced, as is the official explanation. It was something deeper, an element of the perverse "logic" of the fallen mind.

Just before I was ready to go into another of the gas chambers, a woman and two male guards appeared. The woman pointed to me with a fake smile that I would get to know all too well. The guards grabbed me and led me to another part of the camp where I would be given special and unneeded medical treatment by a doctor named Josef Mengele.

Naturally, I didn't know that my father had died in a gas chamber instead of being given a shower so I kept hoping to find him again in the camp. It took months before I learned what really happened in those low buildings.

After I had arrived at the medical facility, the nurse (whose name was Ilse) asked me if there was anything I wanted and I innocently said: "I would really like to get that shower you took me away from."

She laughed so hard I thought she was going to get ill, and then she took me to a shower room and actually watched me as I showered. She helped me dry myself, and in the process managed to put her hands all over my body. Then, she gave me clean clothes, showed me a bed and I quickly fell asleep.

# 65

There now followed a period of several months where I lived in a part of Auschwitz occupied mainly by children who were subjected to medical experiments performed by Doctor Mengele. This was in one sense the most bizarre area of Auschwitz because the children lived under far better conditions and were far better fed than normal inmates. However, despite the fact that their living conditions provided for survival, their average lifespan was much shorter than normal inmates. This was, of course, due to the medical experiments performed by Doctor Mengele and his staff.

In the beginning, I, of course, had no idea what was going on. I only observed that the children were well taken care of, but that most of them had bandages or had other obvious physical ailments. I assumed this was a kind of hospital where sick children were given medical treatment, and it seemed quite humane compared to the rest of the camp and what I had seen in Theresienstadt.

Doctor Mengele would visit the children almost daily and he seemed to take personal interest in several of the children, even knowing details about their lives before they came to Auschwitz. He seemed very eager to treat the children with kindness and foster trust in his benevolence. It seemed important to him that the children looked at him as someone who was not out to hurt them but only had a benign purpose for everything he did. And in reality, he *did* have a benign purpose at heart—as he defined it based on the Nazi thought system. More on this later.

One of my first days in the area, he sat down next to me and seemed happy that I could speak almost fluent German. He asked me several questions about where I came from, and when he heard my mother and sister were in Theresienstadt he said that he might be able to get them to Auschwitz so our family could be reunited. Fortunately for them, he was prevented from carrying out that promise. He seemed very interested in the fact that I had a Jewish father and a German (or as he said: "Aryan") mother. He mentioned something about a mixture of genes and how the genes of my mother must have overridden the genes of my father to give me blond hair and blue eyes. Since I had no clue what a gene was, I could not understand his point. In the coming time, he would conduct a number of experiments on me, many of which included introducing (through injection or by cutting my body open) foreign genetic material into my body to see how it would react to it.

***

I had no idea what was coming so one morning, a few days after my arrival in the medical facility, I was woken up by the nurse who had gotten me outside the "shower" rooms. Ilse smiled the same fake smile I had seen when she saved me from the gas chamber. I soon learned to realize that when I saw that smile, things were only going to get worse. You might ask yourself what could be worse than the gas chamber, and the answer is: "Medical experiments by Doctor Mengele."

Ilse took me to a room that was entirely white, except for an operating table and several smaller tables and cabinets in stainless steel. Ilse handed me to the medical personnel in the room and then left. There were several people there and they were all wearing face masks so I did not recognize any of them. They seemed completely impersonal, or what we in today's world call "professional." Without any explanation or small talk, I was lifted onto the operating table and strapped in so tightly that I could barely move a muscle. I could move my left little finger and wrinkle my nose, but that was about it.

A doctor (it was Doctor Mengele, but he didn't identify himself) then started taking what seemed like an endless number of samples from almost every part of my body. This included extracting tissue and blood samples with hypodermic needles and scraping off skin with a sharp knife. As he cut out a skin sample, the pain was so intense that it reawakened in me my old momentum of controlling my body functions and being able to endure pain. I had grunted in pain earlier, but now I focused my mind inwardly and relaxed my body, spreading the pain all over my aura so the intensity became bearable.

Naturally, Doctor Mengele noticed that my body relaxed, and he first remarked to one of the other doctors that I must have fainted. Upon examining me, including shining a bright light into my eyes and pricking me with a needle, he realized I was still awake but in a different state of mind. This surprised all of them and they had a lengthy discussion about it. After some time, Doctor Mengele called them to order and it seemed like they got back to their planned program. Next, he stuck a hypodermic needle into my left eye in order to inject some substance, apparently to see if he could change my eye color from blue to brown (he had an elaborate theory about how eye color was inherited, and apparently my Jewish father should have given me brown eyes and he could not understand why this had not happened).

Finally, he cut open my leg and performed a lengthy procedure of implanting some material (nerve material from another person). Naturally, this was even more painful, but I remained completely relaxed and he commented on how he had never seen anything like it. He talked about the need to study this phenomenon for the purpose of finding out how I controlled pain since it could be useful for wounded soldiers, allowing them to keep on fighting until the enemy was defeated.

I was then taken out of the operating room and placed in a recovery room, still strapped to the movable operating table. Here, I soon fell asleep and awoke to find Ilse with her hands on my genitals. She quickly removed her hands with an almost embarrassed look, the only time I ever saw her look human. Otherwise, she was always in complete control over her feelings and facial expression.

Ilse called for Doctor Mengele who soon entered and started a virtual cross-examination in order to determine how I had managed to control the pain of his procedures. It turned out to be disappointing to him because although I had recovered the ability to control pain, I had not recovered the memory of how I acquired this ability. So rather than giving him a magic bullet, I could only tell him that I just knew how to do this. He seemed disappointed, but then seemingly decided that he could not expect an 11-year old boy to provide extensive, scientific explanations. His eyes then took on a very determined look, as if he had decided to find a scientific explanation for this riddle.

\*\*\*

Doctor Mengele's sense of astonishment only deepened in the coming months. He was surprised about two main factors. The subjects (his term) upon whom he performed experiments were afterwards put in a bed and given good food. If they did not recover within two weeks, they were unceremoniously sent to the gas chambers. I, however, recovered far faster than others and over time, I reacquired my ability to heal my body, sometimes almost instantly or within a few hours. Doctor Mengele was greatly astonished at this and seemed determined to find out what secret my body could hold that could facilitate such rapid healing. He openly talked about the potential of healing soldiers right on the battlefield so they could keep fighting. Naturally, being a complete materialist, he could not even imagine that this was an ability of the mind. He could see only that somewhere in my body's machinery was a hitherto-fore undiscovered secret.

Another "element of surprise" for Mengele was that no matter what genetic material he introduced into my body, it had no effect. Apparently, he even tried introducing material that should have killed my body, but I survived as the first person he had encountered. Again, he could only assume that my body machine had some undiscovered ability that allowed it to destroy any foreign genetic material. He was convinced that if he could identify this gene, he could transfer it to other people. He talked about how this could potentially be used to purify the entire human race, and one time he remarked to one of his subordinates: "Helmuth, imagine that we could purify the Jews of their destructive genetic material so we could clean up the human race without the gas chambers. We could make them all Aryans with a mere injection!"

Because of these factors, I got to spend a lot of time with Doctor Mengele, and occasionally he would let down his guard and talk more freely, partly because he thought a young boy would not understand anyway. And granted, most of the time he was sticking needles into my body or cutting into it with a knife so a lot of my concentration was on dispersing the pain, but I still heard every word he said. And this gave me a very different view of this man than what has become the official picture of the sadistic Nazi doctor. So let me take this opportunity to comment on one of the enigmas of Nazism and how the Dark Master manages to hypnotize people into thinking an idea is more important than the lives of human beings.

✳✳✳

Hitler, Himmler and Göring were fallen angels, as were many of the other top Nazi commanders. However, what has generally not been acknowledged is that these fallen beings could not in themselves have generated the success that Germany had in the first years of the war. The reason was that they simply did not have the necessary psychic energy do drive the thrust that literally rolled over most of the countries in Europe. When two nations go to war, the outcome is not primarily determined by their physical, military strength but to a far greater degree by the identity, mental and emotional energy available to the two nations. This is not simply a matter of the number of people in each nation, even though that does have some impact. However, it is primarily a matter of which nation has the largest number of people with a higher level of consciousness, meaning they have risen higher on the ladder of the 144 levels of consciousness. It is also a matter of how many of these people are wholeheartedly supporting their country's war effort.

It is generally assumed that Hitler was evil and that he was surrounded by evil people. This ladder is not entirely correct. Hitler had managed to attract a large number of people who had some level of Christhood. He had even attracted quite a number of the incarnated venutians. The question naturally arises: "How could people with some degree of Christhood ever be attracted to Hitler and the Nazi ideology?" The answer is that there is a point on the path towards higher consciousness where you have developed the ability to recognize certain higher ideas, but you have not developed the full Christ discernment. You can recognize an idea as having some truth, but you cannot discern the vibration of the people promoting the idea. This makes it possible that you can be fooled by an idea that contains some truth but is used as a tool by the fallen beings.

It is often said that Hitler had great charisma and could hypnotize people. And it is true that he did hypnotize many Germans with a lower level of consciousness who were simply overpowered by the psychic energy streaming from, or rather through, Hitler. This is what you see in the mass rallies where people fanatically screamed "Sig Heil!" or "Heil Hitler!" But beyond that, some people with this lower level of Christ discernment felt a power from Hitler and recognized some validity in the ideas he was promoting. Because they could not discern the vibration of his intent, they were convinced Hitler would lead them and the world towards a better place. Incidentally, Jesus also spoke with great power and many people followed him for the same reason as people followed Hitler: They recognized the power and the validity of the ideas. It takes a higher level of Christ discernment to see the difference between a fallen being with dark power and a Christed being with the power of light. The Dark Master is an expert in creating situations that fool people with lower levels of Christhood, thereby causing them to release some of their spiritual light. He can then use this light to further a cause that is not as benevolent as promised in the idea or ideology. There were quite a number of relatively mature people in Germany who were fooled by some of the key ideas behind Nazism. This includes some of the reincarnated venutians, and it is easy to see why.

The beings who live on Venus have a more ethereal appearance than human beings on earth. When the venutians first incarnated here, their bodies had very pale skin, they had blue eyes and very light, blond or golden hair. Many of them have maintained this until today. Obviously, the venutians came to earth on a rescue mission in order to purify this planet and create a better, even an ideal society. This, of course, also applies to many others avatars. It is easy to see how Nazism triggered the inner memories of many venutians, especially those who felt somewhat superior to the original inhabitants of the earth. Thus, many of them were fooled into supporting Nazism because they thought this was a good cause that would bring some dramatic and much needed changes to the earth. They were generally tired of embodying on a dense planet like this and were looking for some dramatic way to have a positive impact.

Nazism offered that when you didn't know more than the German people knew at the time. It is easy to look in retrospect and say that people should have known better, but they didn't know better and thus (as is always the case on a dense-matter planet) had to make decisions based on what they knew in their outer minds and their level of spiritual attainment and Christ discernment. Their Christ discernment enabled them to recognize certain key ideas behind Nazism as having some validity, but their attainment wasn't good enough to sense the vibration and intent behind Nazism.

I am describing this in detail because it is a key factor in understanding how the fallen beings can create some of the atrocities we see over and over again. We have the saying that the road to hell is paved with good intentions. In reality, it is paved with good intentions and partial Christ discernment. This explains why so many people over time have been fooled into supporting causes that are engineered by the fallen beings. The fallen beings always incorporate some ideas that are valid and seem to lead towards an improved or even ideal society. Then, they give them a twist that in the end takes society in a downward direction or gives them more control.

This explains why so many people in the West were fooled by Marxism, thereby energetically feeding the Soviet Union and keeping it alive much longer than necessary. It also explains why so many people with a higher consciousness support the environmentalism that has been engineered by the fallen beings. It explains why so many Americans supported George Bush and the Neo-conservative invasion in Iraq, which had very little to do with spreading freedom and democracy.

I am not saying this in order to criticize anyone. I am only pointing out the mechanism so that those who are willing can step up to a higher level of Christ discernment and admit that they have been fooled by the fallen beings. Only by seeing and admitting this consciously, can you free yourself from the influence of the fallen beings and thereby contribute to getting the Dark Master off this planet. There is no shame in having been fooled by the fallen beings—we have all been fooled. It is, however, not constructive to have been fooled and not being willing to see it, thus remaining fooled. You are then doubly fooled, first by the fallen beings and then by your own ego that never wants to admit is has been wrong. Such people are beyond the help of anyone and must go through the School of (very) Hard Knocks.

***

Back to Doctor Mengele. He was not a venutian but still had a fairly high level of consciousness. He had grown up in a European society where there was no true spirituality available. He had the traditional Christian influence, but he was mainly attracted to scientific materialism. As I have said, scientific materialism is just one more ideology created by the fallen beings, and Mengele bought it fully. He was absolutely convinced that there is no spiritual world beyond the material and that everything that happens in the minds of human beings and in society has a material cause. The body is a mere machine, and it is simply a matter of finding out how the machine works and you can cure any ailment.

He was also completely convinced by the Darwinian idea that the natural order has selected some races and nationalities because they are more fit. To him, it was only natural that these naturally selected races used their nature-given ability to give nature a helping hand in furthering the selection process that would purify the human race of its obvious flaws and thus bring forth an ideal society. He got many of these beliefs, as did many Nazis, from the philosopher Herbert Spencer who actually coined the term "survival of the fittest" and developed Social Darwinism. He said that normal compassion for other people should be overcome when it applied to those people whom nature was in the process of selecting out anyway. We should not prevent the natural selection process but should let these people, from individuals to entire races and populations, go the same way as the dinosaurs.

When this was combined with Francis Galton's ideas of eugenics, we have a deadly cocktail that is so typical of the fallen beings. Eugenics means "well-born" and the idea is that just as you can improve the characteristics of plants and livestock through selective breeding, the same can be done on the human population. This, naturally, leads to the creation of a standard (one hallmark of the fallen beings) for judging human beings. Those who do not meet the standard, should not be allowed to breed. It is only a short step to the view that those who are not fit to breed are not fit to live and that it is the responsibility of those who *are* fit, to give nature a hand in actively selecting out those who are unfit. It is from there only a hair's breadth to the gas chambers.

I don't want to go too much into the ideological underpinnings of Nazism because the details are not important in understanding why Mengele fell for the deception. It was his good intentions and his ability to recognize some genuine ideas (I am talking about the creation of an ideal society, not Eugenics) combined with his inability to read vibration and intent. Yet had it not been for his materialistic world view, he would not have been so completely sucked into the ideological jungle of Nazism. Had he been taught the value of intuition and helped to develop it a little further, he would have been able to intuitively sense that we cannot look at human beings from an entirely materialistic view.

When you incorporate the knowledge I have given in this book, it is obvious why these ideas fall short. Outer characteristics, such as race, may have some connection to consciousness, but you can never set up a materialistic criteria, such as race, and judge all members of that race as being the same in consciousness. That is why the claim that all Jews behaved such and thought such is completely false. There were and are many mature lifestreams in the Jewish group as there are in any other groupings you might create based on our physical bodies.

It is completely naive to think that you can improve the human race by working only at the level of the body. You can improve humanity only by raising consciousness but that can never be done through force, only by starting with yourself and thereby inspiring others.

Anyway, my goal here is to show how Doctor Mengele had been convinced by this mix of ideas that people who did not belong to the German or Aryan race were only material beings and could therefore be treated in an entirely mechanical way. Doctor Mengele found it logical that the superior race of the Aryans would give nature a helping hand in removing these unfit people from Europe in order to create a future Utopia. When he interacted with the children in person, he did feel a certain compassion, and that is why he attempted to make the children see him as a benevolent uncle. Yet once he stepped into his official role, he became completely insensitive to them as individuals, even as humans. They were simply mechanical bodies, and it was his role to experiment with the mechanical processes of the body in order to expose the workings of the body machine and thus engineer improvements and cures. Sure, they suffered, but their thoughts and feelings were only products of the body machinery and as such could be ignored in order to further a cause.

What I am simply saying here is that despite the sadistic image that has been projected on Doctor Mengele, he was not very different in world view and attitude from most of the doctors who practice medicine today or most people with a materialistic world view. I grant that his methods would not have been accepted today, but still materialistic medicine is forcing so many toxic and painful procedures upon people that it will be seen as incredibly primitive in just a few decades. As just one example, it is the materialistic hold on medicine that has prevented a real cure for cancer, causing doctors to inject some of the same chemicals found in mustard gas in order to supposedly cure cancer. Yet chemotherapy is simply a matter of either killing the cancer or killing the patient, in any case removing the immediate problem. Curing cancer is not a matter of killing the cancer or anything else. It is a matter of exposing how the physical symptom of the body's cells self-destructing is caused in the three higher bodies and then working with that cause.

Modern doctors and researchers are regularly experimenting on animals, but are they not also experimenting on humans? Is not the entire foray into materialistic medicine one big human experimentation process that has its origin in the deadly ideologies of the fallen beings? Materialism is simply an expression of the satanic mindset, which says there is nothing beyond the material world and thus we can evaluate, judge and treat people based on them being entirely materialistic beings. People – who are really spiritual beings – should therefore conform to current conditions in the material world. Okay, I got sidetracked again, back to Doctor Mengele.

***

The last thing I want to point out is that Mengele escaped after the war and successfully hid in South America for decades. The reason for this was that he was never willing to admit that he had been wrong about swallowing the Nazi camel. Other prominent Nazis either died in the end of the war or shortly afterwards. This is because when a lifestream has made such a monumental mistakes and sees this, it is better for the lifestream to leave embodiment quickly so that it can receive help from the ascended masters to process the experience and focus on learning a positive lesson from its mistakes.

As I have said, the ascended masters never judge or condemn anyone. They are willing to work with all people who are open to their help. It doesn't matter that someone has made a momentous mistake. The masters will seek to help that lifestream move on, but it requires that the person admits that it made a mistake and is willing to learn why it did so and how it can avoid it in the future. This would apply even to Hitler—not that he was likely to admit making a mistake.

Because Doctor Mengele would not admit his mistakes, he was allowed to stay in embodiment in order to give him more of an opportunity to have an awakening. As long as a person is in the same embodiment, it is easier for it to see its mistakes because it has to live with them. It has to constantly struggle to uphold the denial of its mistakes, and this strain can eventually cause it to give up and admit what it has done. It can then leave embodiment and start healing and learning. Unfortunately, Mengele never came to that point and his soul has reincarnated with a very heavy burden of guilt and denial.

# 66

One final thing Doctor Mengele did for me was to put me in the company of the main person of the time. In January of 1945, Mengele had to flee Auschwitz because of the advancing Soviet troops. Although there are claims to his whereabouts, he made an excursion to Berlin that has never been recorded.

I experienced this as follows. One day, again with no prior information, I was woken up by Ilse and taken to Doctor Mengele. He told me that we had to go to meet a very important person that I could help. I was then taken into his car along with Ilse and another person I did not know. We drove for some hours on small roads and even a short stretch on an Autobahn. As we drove into Berlin, Doctor Mengele gave me an injection and I fell asleep. Hours later, I slowly woke up and opened my eyes. Above me I saw a very rough concrete ceiling of a kind I had seen when we practiced air raids in Denmark. I realized I was underground in a concrete bunker.

I turned my head and looked around. I was in a small room, lying on a metal table that was raised unusually high above the floor. As I looked down, I saw another table upon which was lying a man. I then noticed that a needle had been inserted into my left arm and a tube was going from my arm to a needle in the man's arm. I was in complete amazement when I realized that my blood was flowing directly into the man's veins.

At first, I had trouble focusing my eyes on the man's face, but as I managed to do so, I had one of the most startling moments in my two million years on this planet. In a flash, I realized that my blood was flowing into the veins of Adolf Hitler.

\*\*\*

I was so startled by this that I sat up. The man had his head in the opposite direction, and he also sat up, meaning we were now facing each other, me looking down upon the Führer. As we looked into each others eyes, I had a total recall of who I am and my entire history on this planet. I instantly recognized that the lifestream who had embodied as Adolf Hitler was indeed the one I have called Satan. I know he also had a total recall and realized he was much more than Adolf Hitler, recognizing our history together. It was another interval where time stood still, as it seemed even the mighty Führer was lost for words.

During this time, I noticed how ill Hitler looked, and it is now common knowledge that Hitler was ailing towards the end of the war. His normal doctors had been pumping him full of amphetamines and other drugs, but his body could no longer sustain itself. The real reason for this was that Satan's opportunity was finally running out and this was to be his last embodiment before he was taken to the Court of Sacred Fire. When he was born, he had a natural lifespan, but when you do what Hitler did and generate such suffering, you will shorten this lifespan. The more suffering you inflict upon others, the more it will be reflected back to you and your body will break down.

Doctor Mengele had heard about Hitler's health crisis from a friend, and he reasoned that my extraordinary ability to heal must mean that my blood contained some undiscovered ingredient that could be transferred to another person. When he found out I had the same blood type as Hitler, the thought a transfer of my blood could sustain him for some time, perhaps even heal him. He had used his connections to get a message to the Führer's main physician and out of sheer desperation, the experiment had been allowed to take place. It was their intention to transfer as much blood as possible without me dying and then keep me alive so they could continue milking me as a cow. (Naturally, Mengele had hidden my Jewish descent.)

It seemed like Hitler was about ready to say something, but at that moment, Doctor Mengele came into the room. Hitler turned to him and with a gruff voice exclaimed: "What do you want; why are you disturbing us?"

Mengele asnwered: "Mein Führer, I must disconnect the tube or he will lose too much blood and potentially die. Do you feel any different, mein Führer?"

"Yes, I feel better than I have for weeks. Now do your work and leave us alone; I want to have a conversation with this being."

Mengele looked astonished and apparently wanted to ask a question, but thought better of it and bit his tongue. Hitler sensed this and said: "You have brought me what is not just a boy, but a being I have interacted with for many lifetimes. He has many times gotten the better of me, but I am happy to have him in my total power so he can witness my final triumph!"

At this point, I could see Mengele felt Hitler was talking about the triumph of winning the war, and he thought this was completely unrealistic. However, Hitler was referring to something entirely different, as I soon learned. When Mengele had done his work, Hitler exclaimed: "Now, leave us. And don't disturb us unless Stalin, Churchill and Roosevelt are standing outside, ready to surrender."

There now followed the most bizarre conversation (mostly monologue with a listener) I have had on this insane planet.

# 67

Hitler: "Mengele is such a dummkopf. So naive and easily deceived by his own quest for superiority, like most of the others. He thinks I was talking about winning the war, and he knows this is now completely unrealistic so he thought I am losing my mind, just like some of the others, including that dummkopf, von Stauffenberg, who tried to blow me to pieces. It is the most deplorable aspect of life on this shitty planet that there is no one who can appreciate who I really am and what I am trying to accomplish here.

They think I am the answer to the longings of so many Germans and that I came to restore Germany to its full glory and bring them the world domination that they think they deserve. They thought I would give them power over millions of people after we had won the war. Such dummköpfe, how would they ever rule the world if they were given that kind of power? They would only make a mess of it, as they have made a mess of the war, letting those subhumans from the East run over them just because they could not stomach the cold. Gosh, I remember how Napoleon's soldiers were whining during the Russian winter, and now the Germans are no better.

But the Russians—do they complain? Nay, they simply don't have enough humanity to complain. And look at their commanders. They have no compunctions about sacrificing ten Russians to kill one German, and that is the only reason they are winning. I would gladly sacrifice 20 Germans to kill one Russian if that could win the war, but I simply don't have that many Germans to sacrifice. Damn it, just because of the deplorable breeding rate of the German population, later generations will think Stalin is more ruthless than myself. Gosh, Stalin is such an amateur compared to me. He is so driven by his own psychological wounds and his quest for recognition and pride, whereas I have raised myself to the stage of being truly impersonal. I do not let my personal feelings get in the way of my higher mission here. I go beyond all personal concerns and sacrifices in order to pursue my eternal mission, a mission no one will understand.

But what does it really matter? It is laughable to think how self-infatuated intellectuals will look back at my life and seriously think it was my goal to win the war and establish world domination. Such dummköpfe. They simply don't understand that world domination can never be achieved, partly because any force attempting it will always generate an opposite counter-force and partly because this planet is just a little bit too big. Damn those Elohim who created the planet that way, but you have to give them that they knew what they were doing.

Even more laughable is how these self-appointed experts will analyze every aspect of my childhood and life in order to find an explanation for why I turned out to be so evil. They will no doubt make a big deal of my attempts as a painter and reason that if only I had been recognized, the world might have been spared the war and the concentration camps. Ha-hah, such completely self-deceived dummköpfe. What do I care about dots of paint on a canvas? I am indeed an artist, but of an entirely different kind than what the world has ever seen.

What is my art, you might ask [looking at me and not noticing that I had not asked]? Well, I'll tell you. My art form is the ultimate art form, namely destruction. I paint not with paint but with the blood of humanity. I do not tell stories with images but with the real suffering of millions of people who will carry those scars in their souls for lifetimes upon lifetimes, maybe never overcoming them. My canvas is not a piece of cloth but the energetic bodies of the planet and four bodies of humanity. I paint there in order to leave a mark that can never be erased.

Ha-hah, they talk about the "mark of the beast," but I want to leave the "Mark of Satan" and it shall never be erased from the energetic bodies of this planet. How can it, when hardly anyone recognizes the existence of these energetic bodies, having so tamely conformed to the Dark Master's deception of materialism? How will they ever understand what is happening in the physical octave when they don't know about the moving causes in the three higher octaves? How will they ever understand how my armies rolled over Europe and Russia in the early days, riding the waves of energy in the three higher bodies? How will they ever understand our defeat when they do not see that we simply ran out of psychic energy? They will not, and that is why they will never get us off this planet. We will indefinitely be able to deceive dummköpfe like Mengele into supporting our causes, giving us the energy to keep going.

What will it benefit us, you might ask? Well, the Dark Master, for all his sophistication, has a goal of proving god wrong, but only I have seen the fallacy of this. I know that there is no ultimate purpose or meaning, and that is why I have dedicated my entire being to destruction. Not to achieve any goal but simply to express the art form of destroying all that those damned masters and those idiotic humans have built. What do I get out of it, you might say? Well, I have nothing to get out of it; I am aiming for no goal. I get out of it the experience of being in the middle of Ragnarok and seeing things fall apart that others have built. It is in experiencing how destruction breaks down everything built with good intentions that I get my satisfaction.

Such dummköpfe to think it is my goal to win the war and accomplish something for Germany. I have no loyalty to Germany. I would gladly have chosen another nation, if there had been one with the exact right characteristics. Japan was close, but they were lacking in humanity and thus had this tendency for blind fanaticism that I cannot use fully, although it does lead to spectacular individual efforts, such as the Kamikazes. Why not Russia, you might say, but the Russian people simply do not have the level of humanity needed for them to fully support a cause.

Just look at how they failed to respond to the ideology of Marxism and how Lenin and later Stalin had to force communism upon the Russians with Red Terror. Only the threat of death makes the Russians react whereas they simply don't have the humanity to respond to a truly noble idea. But in Germany, you had the almost perfect combination with so many highly evolved people that still lacked discernment and could so easily be pulled into working for a "gooood" cause.

What dummköpfe to think I ever cared about Nazism. It was simply a tool used to deceive the German people. I never thought up Nazism. I simply got up there in front of all of those people screaming "Heil Hitler" and I channeled what the Dark Master gave me while absorbing the light the people sent at me with their misguided devotion. What a thrill to stand there in the nexus between the Dark Master and the deceived people. You might think this can compare to what you have experienced with the ascended masters, but it can't because the masters don't steal people's energy so you don't have as much energy flowing through you. Ha-hah, you are on the wrong team, my boy, you should know the power of the Dark Master and you wouldn't give a damn about those ascended masters.

I never cared about Nazism, I never cared about Germany and I never cared about the Germans. I simply used them to set up my ultimate art work, the total war that I am hoping will go on indefinitely. Yes, Germany might be defeated, but did not the first world war set the stage for this war? So why would not this war set the stage for the third world war and so on, ad infinitum? Just wait and see how Stalin will be able to create a division in Europe that will be even deeper than the one between Nazism and the self-proclaimed and self-deceived free world. And this is all *my* doing because had I not created the aggressive force of Nazism and attacked both East and West, how would the two ever have seen the need to form a temporary alliance that the Dark Master will surely turn into the next big conflict. Perhaps I can even continue my work, either in this lifetime or the next.

Of course, I never cared about the Jews either. They were simply the available scapegoat, partly because they always seek to stand out and never want to integrate with German society and partly because of their ridiculous belief that they are god's chosen people. Ha-hah, as if god ever had any chosen people on a planet like earth. Of course, if the German Jews had integrated like the Jews in Denmark, I couldn't have used them, but then I would have found someone else.

People will also think that I cared about the Aryan race and purifying humanity. But do I look like an Aryan? This was just another way to appeal to the Germans by using a common characteristic, namely blond hair and blue eyes. And then the Dark Master wanted to use it to fool the venutians and prevent them from ascending or manifesting Christhood. Oh, what a deception it has been. Such a thrill to see so many people fanatically worshipping an idea and completely setting aside the sanctity of human life, including their own. Is there any greater fun that watching young men who are ready to sacrifice their lives for a cause that you know is a complete sham? Is there any greater sense of power than to deceive those who have spiritual light into giving it to the dark cause? I think not."

\*\*\*

Me: "You say you want to leave a mark on history, but don't you think most people will see you as a madman, as the embodiment of evil, and never understand what you are really doing?"

Hitler: "Of course they will, but that is part of my art work. Your problem is that because you are an avatar, you have come to this planet in order to accomplish a goal, namely to turn it back to a natural planet. You have come to think that in order to accomplish this, you have to remove evil, meaning you have to remove me and all other fallen beings. And you also think that in order to do this, you need to *understand* me, you need to understand why I am doing what I am doing, what makes me tick. But you will never understand me.

You see, you already look confused. You are thinking that I am imply-ing that you are not smart enough to understand me, but that is not what I am saying at all. You will never understand why I do what I do because there is nothing to understand. There is no logical, rational sense-based explanation for most of my actions. The real explanation is that they are spontaneous expressions of my art, just like an expressionistic painter has no logical reason for putting a particular spot of paint in a particular place. It just flows spontaneously as the process of painting the picture unfolds.

You dummkopf, you still don't understand what we are really about, do you? Even after two million years, you are still confused. You think you can reduce our actions to a set of rational criteria and you even have the arrogance to think that if you understand our rational motives, you will be able to reason with us and change us. *You are so naive!*

What the Dark Master has accomplished on this planet is to create total confusion. He knows there are many avatars that the ascended mas-ters have allowed to embody here in order to pull humanity up. He knows you all have this compulsive desire to understand. He has then diverted this by using modern science to create the belief that it should be possible to understand everything rationally. And so many of you avatars have been fooled by this, always seeking to understand every aspect of spirituality and life.

But you see, we are not rational. Himmler gets off on having a woman submitting himself totally and dominating her with a whip. Göring gets off on having a prostitute dress up in black leather and dominate him with a horsewhip. Why the difference? Well, there is no rational, logical expla-nation. Why does one person like apples and another likes oranges? No reason at all.

The worst dummköpfe of all are the materialists. They have defined the boundaries of the universe as ending at the border between the physi-cal octave and the emotional realm, saying there is nothing beyond the material. They will look at me and be unable to understand why I did what I did because they cannot find a material cause.

They actually think that by reducing a human being to its basic mate-rial components and understanding those components, they will be able to explain every aspect of human behavior. Ha-hah, what folly. How can you even begin to understand my physical actions unless you know my emotions, my thoughts and my sense of identity? Yet even if you know my three higher bodies, you still will not be able to explain why I decided to invade Poland. You will look for some rationale, but there was none. I decided to invade Poland in order to see how this act of destruction would unfold. I simply enjoy destroying countries and people—it has nothing to do with rationality.

They will use my own words to say that I invaded Russia because I wanted lebensraum for the German people, but that was just an excuse. Nay, what I really wanted was to put the German armed forces up against the ultimate challenge. I know what happened to Napoleon, but I also know how much the technology of the time had to do with his defeat. I simply wanted to see if the outcome would be different with modern technology; if tanks could accomplish what horses could not. Now, we know the outcome and does it really matter whether Russia or Germany was defeated? It would have been better if both sides had destroyed each other, as almost happened in Stalingrad. Had it not been for my own general using his rational mind to reason that surrender was better than total destruction. How can surrender be better than anything and *how can anything be better than total destruction?*

The Dark Master has managed to convince most of the world that they need to seek a rational understanding of everything and that such an understanding can be found within the material universe. This is such a stroke of genius because the world will never understand my physical actions without understanding the existence of the higher realms and fallen beings. And how can you give a materialistic explanation for fallen beings? It can't be done, and this ensures that we will be able to influence the earth without being seen for as long as materialism rules society.

So much of what I have done was inspired by the Dark Master in order to simply create confusion. He projects that people should be able to find a rational explanation, and then I do something that defies rational explanation, keeping people either in a state of confusion that causes their minds to shut down, or keeping them indefinitely seeking for the theory of everything.

And you, my boy, have been fooled by this right up to this moment, always thinking you should be able to understand us and that it was a shortcoming on your part that prevented you from understanding us. Hahah, what a dummkopf you are. This could go on forever. Imagine how scientists will look for these subatomic particles and attempt to find an explanation for the actions of Adolf Hitler. It is like looking only at the sea in order to discover the cause of the tide."

\*\*\*

Me: "Actually, I gave up the desire to change fallen beings as I watched Lucifer go through his final judgment in the Court of Sacred Fire. In the end, he saw that his entire existence since he fell had been based on an illusion. Yet instead of facing all of his decisions and undoing them, he chose to have his entire being dissolved."

Hitler (looking shocked): "You are lying. Lucifer is simply on another planet where I have lost contact with him, being so focused on destroying this one. One planet at a time, as I always say."

Me: "Lucifer's problem was that he had not been told everything by the Dark Master, and I can see the same is the case for you. Lucifer had not been told that killing Jesus would cause him to be taken out of embodiment and taken for his final judgment."

Hitler: "Well, I have no intention of killing you. But I also don't have to, as I can use you to keep this miserable body alive until I can finish my ultimate artwork of destruction that will put an indelible mark on the history of this little, ugly planet. And when I don't kill you, those masters you love so much won't have the authority to take me out of embodiment."

Me: "Again, you have been deceived by your master. Lucifer was taken out of embodiment because he killed Jesus, but he was taken for the final judgment because his time was up. His lifestream was dissolved in the second death. He is no more, and that is why you cannot tune in to him. You will go to the same place after this lifetime, and I suspect you will also refuse to redeem yourself. So you will soon be no more and the earth and the entire universe will be free of you. You may still have left a mark on this little planet, but you will not be around to enjoy it."

Hitler (now looking greatly upset): "Again, you are lying. There is no final judgment and there is no dissolution of those of us who have reached this stage. You think the ascended masters are the only ones who have achieved immortality, but you fail to understand that every new sphere that is created starts out being more dense than the previous one. That means more lifestreams will become trapped in duality, and that is why we fallen beings are as needed as the ascended masters. We need to act out duality to the extremes that new lifestreams dare not do so that new lifestreams can have a chance of ascending with their sphere. We are an integral part of creation, and beings like Lucifer, myself and the Dark Master have also achieved immortality. I am so much older than you, having fallen through more than one sphere. How dare you even think you can know better than me when my time will be up."

Me: "You are sounding like you have a cause and are not simply the artist at work. Or rather, you sound like there is a cause that you actually believe in. And I thought you had transcended such folly and realized the universe is meaningless?

I do not claim that I know on my own when your time will be up. I simply observed what happened to Lucifer and I have been told by Jesus that your time is also up and that you will be taken for the final judgment after you go out of embodiment. I also know that I was put together with you in order to make sure you will go out of embodiment as soon as possible."

Hitler: "And how do you propose to do that? Surely, you can't be stupid enough to try and kill me. You wouldn't want to make that kind of karma again."

Me: "I don't have to kill you. You have already killed yourself by killing so many people."

Hitler: "Fortunately, you are in the body of a 12-year old, and I can do with it whatever I want. I can already feel how your blood is strengthening me so by keeping you alive, I might be able to keep my body alive for years and continue the total war that is my ultimate artwork. And despite all your attainment, you do not have the power to stop me. I hear from Mengele, that naive idiot, that you have been resisting all his attempts to kill you so I am sure we will be able to keep you alive. How does it feel for a person with your level of Christ consciousness to be used as a tool to keep Satan alive and killing?"

Me: "Mengele does not understand why I resisted his experiments and stayed alive, but it was indeed in order to meet you face to face and allow you to violate me, whereby you have brought the judgment of Christ upon yourself."

Hitler: "But I have not killed you, so how have I violated you?"

Me: "Killing the body is just a means to extract spiritual light. You have done that by forcing me to give you some of my blood and thereby some of the life force that you have no right to take from me because you have the option to get it from the source. This will take you out of embodiment."

Hitler: "You are forgetting the mechanics of the material octave. As long as I can keep this body alive, I will not be taken, and as long as I have your body, I can keep this one alive. So you are at an impasse and I can assure you that we will prevent you from killing yourself, if that is what you have in mind."

I looked him straight in the eye and said: "No, *this* is what I have in mind." I then closed my eyes and activated my past attainment to deliberately and consciously withdraw myself from my physical body. I did not do anything to kill the body; I simply withdrew my three higher bodies and my Conscious You, and this turned off all life-force keeping the body alive. It was as instant as when you turn off the power to your television.

Hitler, or Satan, was in total amazement for several seconds. Then, he cursed loudly and called out: "Mengele, Mengele, er ist tot, er ist tot!" (He is dead.) Mengele and Hitler's main physician came rushing into the room and were astonished to find my body lifeless. They tried to revive it, but nothing worked. Not even the best emergency room available today could have revived that body.

Hitler's death was not instantaneous, as enough blood had been transferred from me that it kept his body alive for several weeks. Yet, he did fade and die. As his last act, he himself killed Eva von Braun (with a Cyanide pill), who was actually Maleve. She had made progress on the path and had chosen to reincarnate with Hitler/Satan in order to overcome her fascination with fallen beings more powerful than herself. By seeing how pitiful of a human being Hitler really was, Maleve had already overcome most of her attachment to fallen beings. The fact that he killed her was the final act that set her free. She has since moved on and there is a real potential that she will qualify for her ascension before too long.

The claim that Hitler committed suicide is both true and untrue. He did indeed shoot himself, but he was so near to death that his body had only a few hours left. Him shooting himself was another act of defiance that meant absolutely nothing—except in his own mind. He felt that by shortening his life those few hours, he was demonstrating that he had the power to defy god one more time. I am not saying this makes any sense, but how much of what Hitler did made any sense—from a normal perspective.

# 68

By referencing my last conversation with Hitler, alias Satan, I have already explained that the fallen beings have no rational reason for many of their actions. Yet since the Holocaust became public knowledge, many experts have attempted to explain Hitler—as he predicted. How could one person become so evil? How can such evil even exist? Where does such evil come from? As always, we do, of course, have two opposite polarities attempting an explanation within their thought system, namely Christianity and materialistic science. Let us look at what they have to offer.

Christianity is in a bind when it comes to evil. This has several causes. One is that Christianity has taken over the false god Yahweh, engineered by the fallen beings. Christianity cannot question the image of god they have taken over from the Jewish religion, and thus it is bound to defend god as being both almighty and benevolent. This raises a simple question. If god is almighty, he must have the *power* to eradicate evil. If god is benevolent, he must have the *desire* to eradicate evil. Since we can clearly see that evil has not been eradicated, we must ask why god has not done so. If god *cannot* eradicate evil, it means he is not almighty. If god *will not* eradicate evil, it means he is not good. Either way, the Christian god is seriously in doubt. Since Christians cannot resolve this dilemma, their only remaining option is the one that has worked so well in the past, but is loosing its power over people: denial.

Denial explains nothing, and in our time, more and more people feel there must be an explanation. There *is,* of course, but it cannot be found within the confines of Christian dogma. Speaking of dogma, since the Christian god is the creator of everything and cannot make mistakes, did god create evil? Did god create Hitler exactly as he was? Or does the presence of evil mean that god made a mistake? Again, the "perfect" god is in doubt and more denial is the standard option.

Now take scientific materialism. It claims, of course, that we human beings are the products of materialistic processes. This means a person's personality and psyche is shaped by his genes and by his upbringing. The problem is that you can search Hitler's family tree without finding anyone who even remotely approaches his level of evil. You can look at his upbringing and see that many people have grown up under far worse conditions without becoming anywhere near as evil as Hitler. Did just one single mutation in his parents' genetic material create a person so monstrously worse than them? And what about evil people in general? Since they are obviously destructive for the survival of the entire human race, why hasn't natural selection selected them out in order to secure the survival of the rest of us? Or is the human race destined to reach a stage where only completely evil and selfish people survive simply because they are the most fit? If so, what can explain that good people, freedom and democracy still survive? What can explain that we seem to be making some progress in overcoming evil? The standard *materialistic* doctrines seem as inadequate at explaining Hitler (and evil in general) as the standard *Christian* doctrines. Again, materialists have nothing left but denial. It is as massive as the Christian denial.

Can we find other explanations? Yes, but only by looking outside the two dominant thought systems of our time and outside all other thought systems engineered by the fallen beings. These systems all have one underlying purpose, namely to hide from the rest of us the existence, mindset and methods of the fallen beings. Of course, this is not limited to official thought systems. The fallen beings always prefer to keep the population in ignorance, as for example during the Middle Ages and the Soviet era. The ascended masters released modern communications technology in order to make it possible to spread the knowledge that can set people free from the fallen beings. They were not able to stop this, but as always, they seek to take advantage of what they cannot stop. Thus, the fallen beings have created many ideas that are spread over the internet, and their superficial purpose is to create confusion so that most people will not know what to think and keep endlessly seeking for the rational explanation that can never be found. However, the deeper purpose is to make it possible for the fallen beings to discredit any information that exposes their existence and methods.

One of their most successful efforts is the entire area of conspiracy theories. In fact, it was fallen beings who came up with the term when it became obvious to them that they could no longer hide the fact that various groups of fallen beings have, throughout history, formed various conspiracies. However, their real goal was to hide the ultimate conspiracy, namely the existence of themselves. To this end, they have either taken over the minds of people in embodiment or they have paid people to fabricate one theory more outrageous than the next. The purpose is to create a sentiment in the population so that once an idea or book is labeled as a conspiracy theory, most people will reject it without even taking a look.

Obviously, this book can easily be labeled as just another cooky conspiracy theory. This effort is not so much aimed at the general population, but more at the people who have some level of Christhood but have not developed the full discernment of being able to read vibration and intent. They are the ones the fallen beings are most concerned about fooling. They know that those with a higher level of Christhood will be able to read the vibration and intent behind this book, and the fallen beings can do nothing about it.

The last thing the fallen beings want is for the general population, but especially the people who are beginning to awaken, to realize that the only real explanation for the monstrous evil we can observe throughout history is the existence of a class of beings who are not like the rest of us because they have no empathy with human beings and they have a hidden agenda that makes no sense whatsoever to normal beings. The real explanation for the origin of evil can be found only in the teachings of the ascended masters. By the way, the thought systems of the fallen beings have as their second-most important goal to hide the existence of the ascended masters or discredit their teachings (often by seeking to discredit those who are messengers for the masters). Much of the New Age movement, especially the phenomenon of channeling, has as its purpose to spread so many outrageous ideas that it either confuses people are predisposes them to reject anyone who is a genuine messenger for the ascended masters. Only by getting us to deny both their own existence and the existence of the masters, can the fallen beings keep us completely trapped in duality, having no frame of reference from outside this mindset.

Take note of the subtle outcome of these two fallen belief systems. Christianity gives a bad rap to god, meaning that god must have created evil or allows it to continue to exist. Materialism gives a bad rap to humankind, implying that since one person could become as evil as Hitler, all of us have the seeds of evil in our minds. In reality, god is not responsible for the worst forms of evil and neither is humankind. The kind of evil you saw in Hitler is not a potential for all human beings. The vast majority of human beings could never, ever approach the evil of Hitler. Only fallen beings can manifest that level of evil and no amount of changes in our genetic material or psychological make-up could make us as evil as fallen beings. This, of course, does not mean we do not have responsibility for the continued presence of evil on this planet. We have the potential to surrender to evil by dehumanizing ourselves and each other, as described earlier.

\*\*\*

So how do we explain the existence of evil? We first need to dispense with the Christian image of an all-powerful and benevolent personal god who takes special interest in this little planet. The real Creator is both almighty and benevolent, but it has given free will to all the beings it has created out of its own Being. This means the Creator has suspended its almighty powers when it comes to planet earth, or rather this entire unascended sphere. Who is it that *has* almighty power on earth? It is the original inhabitants of this planet. Who is it that *wants* almighty power on earth? It is the fallen beings in all four octaves.

We might say that the existence of evil is made possible by free will. This will instantly be used by the fallen beings to argue that the chaos and atrocities on earth proves that the Creator made a mistake by giving humankind free will. However, the chaos on earth is first of all created by the fallen beings misusing *their* free will. Yet they never say god made a mistake by giving *them* free will. It is giving free will to humanity that was the mistake, and that is why the fallen beings are trying to make us give up exercising *our* free will and follow them blindly.

Until we ascend and become immortal beings, our free will is exercised in an unascended sphere where nothing is permanent. This means we have the option to go into the consciousness of separation and start using our free will as if we were separate beings. Thereby, it seems that I can hurt you without affecting myself—a complete illusion made possible only by the density of matter.

Those of us who have chosen to go into duality are given an environment where we (originally through mutual consent although most people have forgotten this) can help each other discover how it plays out when separate beings are doing whatever they want. The purpose is to allow us to play this out until we have had enough of it and attain the awareness (based on experience, not theory) that all life is one and thus we cannot harm others without affecting ourselves. When we consciously choose to align our free will with the facts of life (oneness), we become immortal beings, ascended masters.

Anything we do in an unascended sphere can never become permanent, meaning any mistake made can be completely and utterly erased and undone. So even what we see as the monstrous evil of the Holocaust is only energetic records, and the energy can be completely purified and requalified so that none of these records remain. What remains is the positive lessons learned by people in their causal bodies, which includes lessons about what does not work.

In summary, evil exists not because the Creator has created it or allows it. It exists because beings with free will have created evil. The worst forms of evil were created by the fallen beings, but it was the original inhabitants of the earth who made the choices that allowed fallen beings to start embodying here. Thus, it is the choices made (or not made) by the original inhabitants that can keep evil on this planet.

Eventually, as more and more people raise their consciousness and tune in to the minds of the ascended masters, all fallen beings will be removed from the four octaves of this planet. Eventually, the collective consciousness will be raised so that duality will be transcended, matter will become less dense and the earth will once again be a natural planet. This, however, will most likely take a long time. Thus, the more immediate goal to reach is that a critical mass of people fully and finally see through the lie that an abstract idea can justify the killing of concrete human beings. This will lead to the removal of the Dark Master and then the earth will finally have passed the initiations it was meant to pass during the Age of Pisces, with Jesus as the main spiritual overseer.

The earth can then move fully into the next cycle, the Age of Aquarius where the Ascended Master Saint Germain will be the overseer. He has plans for manifesting a Golden Age that will lead to tremendous progress, although it will not (in the next 2000 years) be possible to fully return the earth to the status of being a natural planet. It will simply take longer to raise the vibration of physical matter to the level of a natural planet, as seeking to force this process would create cataclysmic earth changes.

\*\*\*

As for Hitler, or Satan, after he left embodiment, he was allowed to stay in the emotional octave for a time. From there, he attacked several people in embodiment, and he finally attacked one with sufficient Christ attainment to be taken to the final judgment.

I witnessed this, but played no role in it. Satan was unwilling to see the mistake he had made by falling, and he kept screaming profanities at anyone he encountered, including the ascended masters. He also rambled on about his own greatness, as you see in my dialogue with Hitler. This continued until he was committed to the Sacred Fire, convinced to the last that he could not be erased but was indeed immortal. He went into the fire screaming: "I am immortal. You cannot erase m . . ." Obviously, once he had been erased, there was nothing left to see that he had been wrong. So in the end, there was no redeeming Satan because he had no redeeming qualities.

# EPILOG

I know some will say this is a disappointing ending because there is no grand finale. Others will wonder why I don't go all the way and expose the fallen beings in today's society. The reason for the latter is simple, namely that it is not my intention to start some kind of witch hunt process. We do need to get the fallen beings off the planet, but we actually do not have to identify them as individuals in order to accomplish this.

Let's say that a nation decided that it wanted to identity all fallen beings in that society and then imprison them or at least prevent them from holding positions of power. In order to do this, that nation would have to go into the exact same state of consciousness that the fallen beings are in, namely duality. As I have described, I spent a good million years seeking to fight the fallen beings with force, and it was a very hard awakening when I finally realized that all of my efforts had only helped keep the fallen beings on the planet. It is not my intention with this book to get anyone else to repeat my mistakes.

The one and only key to getting the fallen beings off the planet is that we raise our consciousness on an individual level, which then eventually raises the collective consciousness. Naturally, a society can do something to facilitate this, and a society can also do much to identify the ideas and the manipulation coming from by fallen beings. Yet this does not mean a society has to identify individuals as fallen beings and then seek to neutralize them. Naturally, a society has a right to use its own laws to keep anyone responsible for actions that violate the laws. Yet there is no need to go back to the methods used in some societies for eradicating unwanted people.

The real key to removing the fallen beings is increased awareness. It is obvious that because the fallen beings have so far managed to keep their existence and methods hidden from the general population, they have had an unfair advantage. The knowledge in this book could change that equation. Once people understand that fallen beings exist and that they have no empathy with human beings, it becomes much easier to free ourselves from their manipulation. Once you understand that they have a hidden agenda, you can avoid being pulled into supporting their false ideas.

I know that some people will interpret this book from a black-and-white perspective and want to wage a war against the fallen beings. Yet this book is not written to encourage this reaction. This book is written in total respect for free will. It was the choices of the original inhabitants of the earth that allowed fallen beings to come here, and it is only the choices of these same people that can get them off the planet. The question is whether these original inhabitants are ready to rise above the state of consciousness that invited the fallen beings here? Are they ready to take full responsibility for their own growth and for the future of this planet, or do they want more time being the followers of the fallen beings? I cannot answer that question, and I have no desire to force anyone to react a certain way to this book.

I know that I have done what I can do on this planet by first immersing myself into duality and then climbing the long way back out of it. I know millions of other lifestreams have done the same and are very close to breaking through to a conscious awareness of who they are and why they are here. I know that writing this book was part of my personal process for freeing myself from the immersion phase on this planet. I am setting the book free with no hopes, desires or expectations as to what reception it will get or not get. I have done what I need to do in order to qualify for my ascension, and I am putting in for a transfer to the ascended realm.

Every human being is having an entirely subjective experience. All struggles between people is the result of the fallen beings presenting their subjective experiences as universal and seeking to force them upon others.

www.ingramcontent.com/pod-product-compliance
Lightning Source LLC
Chambersburg PA
CBHW022233020726
47496CB00004B/878